CRITICAL ACCLAIM FOR TIMOTHY RIZZI'S
THE PHALANX DRAGON

"Rizzi's credible scenario and action-filled pace once again carry the day!"

—*Publishers Weekly*

"Rizzi is at his best....A high-speed chase that pits complex U.S. military technology against the Iranians....Great techno-speak and top-gun action!"

—*Kirkus Reviews*

"A tense military thriller...an exciting story full of enough action to keep the keenest fans on the edges of their seats!"

—*Booklist*

"Loaded with action....Rizzi...knows how to combine action and technology into a whale of a story!"

—*Abilene Reporter-News*

THE PHALANX DRAGON

TIMOTHY RIZZI

LEISURE BOOKS **NEW YORK CITY**

For my children:
Kirk, Jason, Lindsey, Dixie

A LEISURE BOOK®

December 1995

Published by special arrangement with Donald I. Fine, Inc.

Dorchester Publishing Co., Inc.
276 Fifth Avenue
New York, NY 10001

For further information, contact: Donald I. Fine, Inc., 19 West 21st Street, New York, NY 10010

The name "Leisure Books" and the stylized "L" with design are trademarks of Dorchester Publishing Co., Inc.

Printed in the United States of America.

ACKNOWLEDGMENTS

Special thanks to Major Jim Clark, U.S. Air Force (Ret.), for taking the time to answer my questions on weapons systems, planning and development. Any mistakes are mine alone.

This wouldn't be possible without the Cowboy who was just a phone call away. May your Eagle *always* reign supreme in its domain.

To the public relations department at Microelectronics and Computer Technology Corporation for access to their three-dimensional Laser-generated storage devices.

Thanks to Jason Poston, Don Fine and the entire team at DIF, also to my agent Roberta Pryor, for all their help and support throughout the process.

As always I owe everything to Diana. This work is as much hers as it is mine.

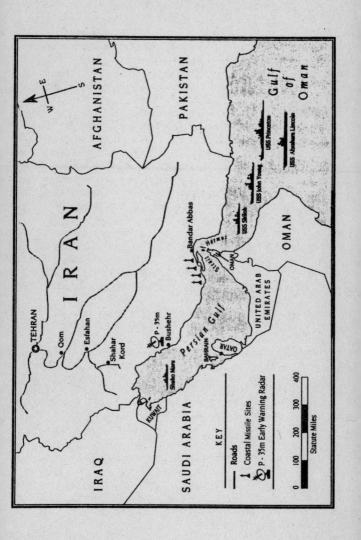

GLOSSARY

ACM	Advanced Cruise Missile.
AMRAAM	Advanced Medium-Range Air-to-Air Missile.
AWACS	Air Borne Warning and Control System.
DARPA	Defense Advanced Research Projects Agency.
DCI	Director Central Intelligence.
ECM	Electronic Counter Measures. Systems designed to obscure and interrupt enemy radar equipment.
EVS	Electro-optical Viewing system. Allows B-52 air crews to see the terrain they are flying over at night.
EWO	Electronics Warfare Officer.
ELINT	Electronic Intelligence. This is information gathered through monitoring enemy electronic transmissions. It can be done by aircraft, ship or satellite.
FLIR	Forward Looking Infrared. A heat sensing system fitted to an aircraft that scans its flight path detecting objects which radiate heat.
HARM	AGM-88A, B or C model. Highspeed Anti-Radiation Missile. Designed to home in on and attack enemy radar antennas.
HUD	Head-Up Display. A rectangular piece of clear glass located in front of the pilot and behind the windscreen of an aircraft. Essential flight data is projected on the display allowing the pilot to fly the aircraft without looking down into the cockpit.
IFF	Identification Friend or Foe. A coded electronic pulse emitted by an aircraft which allows an attacking force to identify it as friendly on a radar screen.
KC-10A	Converted DC-10 jetliner used for refueling military aircraft.
KDP	Kurdish Democratic Party.
KH-12	Code Name "Key Hole". A CIA controlled spy satellite used to gather photo and infrared real time data.

KH-14 Same as KH-12 only it is also equipped with a Synthetic Aperture Radar capable of seeing through clouds and at night.

LANTIRN Low-Altitude Navigation and Targeting Infra-red for Night. This system allows a fighter crew to fly low level at night avoiding, over any terrain, find and lock onto their target with a laser. On an F-15E the infrared picture is projected on the HUD.

NPIC National Photographic Interpretation Center is located in Federal Building 213 eight blocks from the Capital on New Jersey Avenue. Using a massive array of computers the NPIC is responsible for analyzing billions of bits of satellite information into usable intelligence.

NVGs Night Vision Goggles.

Rials Iranian currency.

SAVAK The former Shah of Iran's secret police.

SAVAMA Iranian Intelligence Service.

SEAD Suppression of Air Defenses. These fighters carry a mix of HARMs and it is their mission to fly just ahead of a strike package locating and destroying enemy SAM and Anti-Aircraft Artillery before they can threaten other aircraft in the group.

RWR Radar Warning Receiver. An antenna mounted to an aircraft that warns the pilot when he's being scanned by an enemy radar.

SATCOM Satellite Communications.

SAM Surface to Air Missile.

TACTS Tactical Air Combat Training System. Pods are mounted on aircraft missile stations that relay the aircraft's behavior to ground based receivers. The data is then transmitted to a computer storage system for display and review.

TEL Transport-Erector-Launchers. Used to hoist a missile into firing position.

VVI Vertical Velocity Indicator.

THE PHALANX DRAGON

Chapter One

For the crew of the Spooky Zero Seven flight, the opening hours of the Gulf War resembled a routine training mission, very long and tedious. Each checkpoint and tanker rendezvous had been reached on time and without any problems. That in itself was amazing, considering the big strategic bomber had flown halfway around the world nonstop.

Major Troy Rossili, Jr., the aircraft commander, nudged the throttles back slightly and watched the B-52G's glowing, lime-green airspeed indicator fall a few knots. The bomber's eight turbo-jet Pratt & Whitney engines filled the flight deck with a low rumble as they pushed the half-million pounds of dull gray aluminum and steel through the cold night air. While maintaining radio silence, he forced the yoke forward, dropping the big bomber's nose away from an Extender's refueling boom. The major searched beyond the windscreen, trying to pierce the dark desert sky to catch a glimpse of the tanker above him, but the KC-10A had faded into the blackness.

The thirty-four-year-old bomber pilot, a 1979 Air Force Academy graduate, knew this mission was going to be a bitch before he climbed into the cockpit. A small, dark-skinned, full-blooded Italian, Rossili had believed that Saddam Hussein would back

13

down before it came to this. Looking back, he felt foolish assuring his wife she wouldn't have to worry about him flying into combat. The United States would never go to war over a meaningless Middle Eastern country. He had told her the President would probably send a squadron or two of F-15s to Saudi Arabia, then turn the matter over to the UN. That was five and a half months ago. Now the memory of their parting, her eyes wet and face puffy, was difficult to get out of his mind.

Rossili double-checked his altitude one more time before banking to the east away from the tanker cell. Six other Stratofortresses, all from the 596th BWS/2nd Bomb Wing based at Barksdale AFB, Louisiana, were cruising to the south six hours behind him. They would launch their standard AGM-86C air-launched cruise missiles on SAM sites approximately forty-five minutes earlier, and were now being escorted by F-15Cs. Unlike the other B-52Gs, his bomber, Grim Reaper II, would not be flying in a standard three-ship B-52 formation. Their classified mission would take them into Iraqi airspace, where they would launch their load of advanced cruise missiles against high-priority targets. During the opening minutes of the war.

Rossili's compass showed a heading of 002 degrees, north. His global positioning system plotted them precisely 274 miles south of the Iraq border.

"How you holding up, boss?" copilot Captain Bobby Gibson asked to break the monotony. The six-man crew had taken off from Barksdale AFB seventeen hours earlier, and it would be at least another seventeen before they were back on the ground.

"I'll make it. Just keep an eye on those space racers. Don't know if they can stay awake when they're not flying by the seat of their pants." It gave the major little comfort to know two F-15Cs were above him flying MiG CAP (Combat Air Patrol), and a Wild Weasel team consisting of an F-16C and F-4G was 500 yards off his left wing. As far as he was concerned, fighter pilots were nothing more than glorified race car drivers with unharnessed discipline and huge egos.

Rossili's bloodshot eyes drifted to the instrument panel looking for red idiot lights, warning indicators, which were placed all over the cockpit—a design flaw of the G model. The soft, green backlit dials and gauges showed everything was operating normally. The Reaper was thirty-two years old and had flown more than eighty combat missions over North Vietnam during Linebacker operations. On a lengthy flight, it would be unrealistic to expect everything to operate at a hundred percent.

Rossili keyed the internal radio mike. "Butler . . . give me an update."

"Right on schedule, sir," First Lieutenant Charles "Buck" Butler, the freckle-faced navigator seated on the lower deck, reported. "We have a four-minute launch window, and I have that sucker nailed."

"Roger. Keep me posted." Rossili smiled under his oxygen mask. Butler, the youngest member of the crew, was damned good at guiding the Grim Reaper from way-point to way-point, and he didn't have any problems letting everyone know it. The major wouldn't have it any other way; he wanted his men confident and ready.

If everything went as planned, Grim Reaper II would be in position to launch her weapons after the first wave of F-117As hit the highest-priority targets in and around Baghdad. Air Force planners had given him an option on the weapons' launch leg of their mission: they could come in at high level or take their chances hugging the deck, flying nap of the Earth. Rossili knew the same planners had developed an attrition scenario before the B-52s began the mission. During the opening hours of the attack, Iraqi defenses would be strongest and the older, slow-moving B-52 wasn't expected to fare well. It wasn't very encouraging, but the bombers were the only planes capable of carrying the advanced cruise missiles.

The Iraqis operated a complex network that used overlapping surveillance radars, each site fiberoptically connected to an integrated computer system. The data collected by each site were fed to a number of command and control centers throughout the country using a high-speed data-link relay system. Having the sixth-largest air force in the world, the Iraqis operated an impressive mix of weapons, including 750 combat aircraft, 17,000 surface-to-air missiles and over 10,000 antiaircraft artillery pieces.

Rossili could come in under their long-range surveillance radars using his terrain-following radar to maneuver the lumbering B-52 at 300 feet above the rolling hills of the desert. This way they could avoid most of the SAMs unless they passed directly over one of the sites. However, they would still be defenseless against the primary killer of aircraft: antiaircraft fire. CIA controlled electronic detection, and ferreting satellites had detected several hundred self-propelled ZSU-23-4 and towed S-60 57 mm antiaircraft guns scattered around and between the SAM sights along the route to his launch point.

At 30,000 feet, the Iraqi SAM operators could take their time looking at the Grim Reaper on their radar scopes before launching their missiles. Rossili was counting on surprise, the black night and a simple plan to keep him and his crew safe. Cross the border, launch the missiles and get the hell out of the area. In his words: one pass and haul ass.

"Two hundred ten miles out," Butler radioed. "AWACS reports mission is go and skies are clean."

"Roger," Rossili answered, feeling his heart quicken. "All right, gentlemen, batten down the hatches. Here we go."

The pilot tightened his shoulder harnesses and glanced over at his copilot for the familiar nod that he was ready. Cutting the throttles, Rossili pushed the paint-chipped yoke forward and felt the strain of 1.5 negative Gs come across his body. The B-52 nosed over for the ground.

TALLIL EARLY WARNING STATION, IRAQ

The Tallil operations center controlled the Iraqi air force's air defenses in south-central Iraq. Located 214 miles north of the Saudi border, the concrete-reinforced underground bunker housed the central command authority responsible for 483 SAM sites armed with low- to medium-altitude SA-6s, SA-2s and high-altitude SA-5s. Along with the surface-to-air missiles, the site also commanded 235 antiaircraft guns strung along Iraqi's southern border. Most of the SAMs and triple-A guns had been moved into the area only thirty days prior, and many had become operational within the last forty-eight hours in an effort to confuse U.S. surveillance satellites.

"Stay alert," Major General Mulla al-Hammadi, a Republican Guard air force two-star, barked as he paced between the four rows of electronics and radar equipment. The unlit bunker was crude compared to the lavish ones his superiors were operating outside Baghdad. It was hardly large enough to hold twenty men and their equipment, and the ventilation system was poor, making the room unbearably stuffy and humid.

The twelve radar scopes received real-time data from seven early warning and long-range surveillance radars scanning the

Saudi border to the south. The PRV-11 and PRV-9 radars, strategically located, methodically swept the sky for hostile targets. Over the last six months, General al-Hammadi and his team of technicians had fine-tuned each radar system to guarantee enemy aircraft would never make it across the border undetected.

. The general's penetrating eyes were set above a long, pointed nose. He wore a short, cropped mustache reminiscent of Hitler. The UN's imposed deadline for the withdrawal of Iraq's troops from Kuwait had passed, and he expected that the United States would attack at any time. The only aircraft in the air presently were the usual AWACS flying their circular patrol pattern, the same ones they had been monitoring for the last fourteen days.

General al-Hammadi filled his lungs with stale air, releasing it slowly.

"Status report," he demanded, making his way to the front of the room.

"Sector one clear."

"Sector two clear."

"Sector three and four . . . clear."

The general checked his watch. 0235.

Rossili watched the airspeed indicator flutter at 460 knots for a moment before dropping back to 430. He kept steady back pressure on the yoke, bringing his B-52 out of its dive. The Gs bled off as he leveled the bomber at 2,000 feet. Inching the throttles forward, he nursed every ounce of power from the engines.

"Engage EVS now," Rossili ordered.

The radar navigator turned the bomber's electro-optical viewing system to active. The two ventral scanner turret faring housings, located under the nose, rotated 180 degrees, exposing the low-light television on the port side and the infrared scanner on the starboard side. The two sensors displayed IR and real-time images on the cockpit consoles in front of both pilots and the two navigators. The pilots' consoles also had terrain avoidance track and steering command symbols superimposed on them, along with critical data such as airspeed, radio altimeter reading and the time-to-go for weapons release. Rossili studied the EVS heads-down display until he was satisfied the information was accurate and the system was functioning properly. Only then did he cautiously nose his bomber down to scream over the desert sand at 300 feet, continuing north.

Grim Reaper II was the first B-52 bomber of Operation Desert Storm to cross the border, the only bomber that had been secretly modified and equipped with ACMs, advanced cruise missiles or AGM-129s. Officially, the faster, harder-hitting AGMs wouldn't be operational until the late '90s, but the rocket scientists back at Barksdale had decided this would be a perfect opportunity to test the stealthy, follow-on version of the standard AGM-86Cs that the other bombers were carrying.

Inside Reaper's bomb bays, the coarse, dark-gray graphite skin of the AGM-129s waited to absorb full spectrum radar signals. Each eight-foot missile, being only twenty-four inches in diameter, was more compact than the previous models. With a shovel-shaped nose angled back forty-five degrees, stubby V tail and fuselage of triangular configuration, each looked as if it belonged in the water instead of the air. Two air intakes, one on each side of the fuselage, had jagged edges to reduce the head-on radar cross section. Due to their great speed, just over Mach 1, they didn't need the lifting wings used by standard cruise missiles.

"I'm showing an E-band . . . a Side Net 300 miles north," the electronic warfare officer radioed from his workstation.

Rossili didn't respond. A Side Net is the NATO code name for a PRV-11 long-range surveillance radar. Operating on E-band between 2.56 and 2.71 GHz, the radar would only be a threat once they were within 110 miles of it. Ironically, the major felt reassured knowing the Side Net was out there. Air Force Intelligence and the CIA had both reported the Iraqis were operating SA-5s in the area. The Side Net functioned in association with SA-5s, implying the intel was accurate.

Readjusting his grip on the yoke, Rossili guided the bomber up and over a large sand hill. The FLIR, forward-looking infrared, screen presented the lime images of rock outcroppings and one-lane dirt roads snaking through the desert. The time-to-go display showed they were twelve minutes from the border and eighteen minutes until weapons launch.

Rossili glanced at the mission clock. It was 0302 local, H-hour. The war had started.

"General al-Hammadi, sir . . . I just lost contact with central command in Baghdad." The young Iraqi communications officer spoke unsurely as he pressed the left side of his headphones, hoping to pick up the signal that had abruptly stopped.

General al-Hammadi bolted from the opposite side of the bunker. He looked over the man's shoulder, inspecting the receiver's frequency.

"I was updating them on our current situation when my headset was filled with loud static. Now I hear nothing. No response, and all radio signals have stopped."

"General, I am looking at a possible target approaching from the south," a sergeant reported from another station. Just then a red triangle appeared at the bottom of his scope. The sergeant's heart pounded with each strike of his fingers on the keyboard.

"Confirmed . . . target bearing 189." The radar return was large. The unknown aircraft was flying low-level at a high rate of speed.

On the upper edge of the cockpit, a rectangular warning light flashed yellow. The electronics threat panel indicated a weak E-band sweeping out of the north.

"Threat to the north." Captain Gibson spoke grimly from behind his sweaty oxygen mask.

"Yeah, I see it," Rossili said. The time-to-go display read 8:14. Still eight minutes from weapons release.

The major kept his eyes on the terrain avoidance track and steering command symbols. He instinctively kept the Grim Reaper at 300 feet, following the contour of the desert terrain.

"I'm taking her up to 500 feet. We'll need room to maneuver," Rossili thought aloud as he edged the B-52 up. "Get ready with the chaff and flare dispensers. Come on, baby, just seven more minutes . . ."

"Major, I'm showing a new threat. A Thin Skin B sweeping to the northwest. They're looking at us." The well-trained electronic warfare officer sounded calm.

The cockpit threat panel lit up, showing a new enemy radar operating at 7.56 GHz.

"Copy. Two bad guys watchin' us." Captain Gibson looked over at Rossili. He could see the flickering cockpit lights reflected in the pilot's eyes.

Thirteen miles north of Grim Reaper II, on a high, windswept desert ridge, an SA-6 Gainful launch battery sat quietly with its target acquisition radar turned to standby. The battery had been set up in typical SA-6 combat square formation twelve hours earlier. Four TELs, transport erector launchers, were spaced roughly 250 meters apart on each corner. Each TEL contained three SA-6 SAMs pointed at a thirty-degree angle to the horizon. In the center, a single Straight Flush target engagement radar, its antenna pointed south, was parked next to the Ural 375 command and control vehicle. The radar operator inside wouldn't activate the system until ordered to by General al-Hammadi.

Butler, the B-52's navigator, concentrated on the AN/ASQ-151 EVS on the instrument panel. Two screens allowed him to see everything the pilots were viewing in the cockpit above him. Butler also had been supplied with a series of computer-enhanced strategic intelligence maps, courtesy of the CIA. Resting next to his computer keyboard were a dozen stereo-enhanced topography reconstructed KH-12 satellite photos, along with prearranged flight plans. In theory, the plans would allow the Reaper's crew to avoid most, if not all, of the SAM sites, but the reconnaissance photos were twenty-four hours old and a lot could happen in a day.

The computer-generated image of their B-52 crossed the Iraqi border on the screen. They were now in enemy airspace. Butler keyed his mike.

"Major, satellite nav shows a narrow line of hills ten miles to the east. Take a new heading of 023. After we clear those, there's no place to hide; the terrain's as flat as my first girlfriend."

"Roger nav. Zero two three," Rossili responded.

General al-Hammadi was puzzled. *Why weren't Iraqi planes patrolling the skies? It wasn't as if this was unexpected.* He watched the sergeant manipulate the computer keyboard. The amber-colored screen focused on the southern half of Iraqi territory. Black lines, superimposed borders, cut across the radar scope.

"There, General. Heading 023. Altitude 150 meters, speed 439 knots. Two more targets picked up." The sergeant pointed to the red triangles, representing the unknown aircraft, inching along the lower half of his scope.

"Where's the nearest SAM sites?" al-Hammadi asked rapidly.

"Here . . . and here." The sergeant moved his finger above the smooth glass, north of the targets' positions. "Two SA-6 batteries were moved early this morning."

General al-Hammadi studied the area on the scope. SA-6s were capable of engaging targets at medium to low altitude. If the targets stayed on their current heading, they would pass to the west of the SA-6 sites, well within their range.

"Contact those SAM sites," he ordered, calculating the time it would take for the targets to come into range. "Instruct them to prepare to activate their radars, on my order only."

Rossili's attention shifted from the FLIR to the low-light television and then back to the FLIR. He was guiding his bomber along the series of stone-covered ridges that were strung out a half mile to the right side of his aircraft. He allowed his bomber to drift back down to 300 feet, using the terrain to hide and break up her radar signature. The threat panel showed only the E-band as it continued to paint the Reaper.

"Five minutes to weapons release," Gibson called out.

"Weapons check," Rossili radioed to the offensive systems operator on the lower deck.

"Eight up and ready."

General al-Hammadi watched the lead aircraft proceed toward the first SA-6 site. He double-checked that the IFF receiver was still showing a negative reading. "Time to launch?"

"Thirty seconds . . . twenty-five seconds," the sergeant counted down, feeling exhilarated. The first aircraft was within striking distance, but for the SAMs to get a clean kill the general would wait until the exact moment.

"Ten seconds . . . five." The sergeant held his breath, then spoke rapidly. "Now. They're all in range."

"Bring up those radars and give the order to fire when ready." General al-Hammadi clasped his hands behind his back and grinned slightly.

Rossili continued to concentrate on the EVS. He thought briefly of the surprise attack on Baghdad and hoped it had caused enough confusion that the Iraqi command and control structure would overlook his flight. He eased the bomber over a series of winding hills, then suddenly they broke into a long, shallow valley. The threat panel lit up like the Fourth of July.

"Shit! Spike . . . right two o'clock near . . . bearing 078," Gibson shouted.

Rossili instinctively pulled back on the yoke, gaining several hundred feet of altitude. "What's looking at us?" he radioed his electronics warfare officer.

"It's an H-band, sir, sweeping four miles northeast. Looks like a Straight Flush in acquisition mode."

"Jam that son of a bitch!"

"Roger. Starting music now." The electronics officer deftly worked his controls, then called out, "I-band, Major. The prick's trying to lock up on us."

"I show a launch. Two o'clock," Gibson announced.

Rossili keyed his mike. "Hey, you Magnum guys. I need some help. *Now!*" Magnum was the launch code for the Wild Weasel team flying escort.

"Copy, Grim Reaper. Don't worry. We got 'em."

Rossili caught sight of the distant, fiery plumes of two SAMs rocketing into the air. The brilliant flames pushed the missiles straight up before they nosed over and streaked to the south, away from them. Ten degrees off the nose, three more missiles shot up from the ground, this time heading toward Rossili's aircraft.

"*Magnum . . . Magnum.*" Rossili's heart skipped a beat as he heard the code for the launch of two AGM-88A HARM missiles. He saw two high-speed antiradiation missiles stream off the wing rails of the F-4G streaking past his bomber. The missiles accelerated quickly, locking onto and following the powerful H-band radar beam tracking the Grim Reaper. A dazzling fireball a mile in front told Rossili the HARMs had impacted the SA-6s' radar antennas.

"Lights out, fuckers!" Gibson shouted.

An instant later, the remaining airborne SAMs twisted right and left, unable to lock onto their target.

"New threat. Launch. I'm showing . . . one . . . two. Right, one o'clock near. They're heading this way!" Gibson jerked his head up from the console and pointed out the right side of the cockpit, as the threat panel lit up again.

"I'm taking her up to a thousand feet. *Damn it!*" Rossili cursed, as his assurance in the CIA's satellite maps waned. He banked the Reaper to the west, and she glided through the air away from where the missiles had launched.

Two miles northeast, the desert night flashed in a white blazing light as two more SA-6s lifted off their transport vehicle. It only took a few seconds for the bomber's ALQ-117 deception jammers, facing sideways out of the bomber's nose, to receive and analyze the enemy I-band frequency. The ECM, electronic counter measurers, computer instructed its antenna to broadcast an identical 7.85 GHz frequency. The strong bursts of radio waves flooded back to the SA-6s' main antennas.

Rossili kept watch on the nearest SAM. It snaked back and forth across the night sky, weaving a trail. A moment later it lunged straight down. The major closed his eyes a split second before the bright fireball could affect his night vision.

"Where's that other SAM and where the fuck are those weasels!" Rossili turned his head right and left, straining to see out the cockpit windows.

"Behind us . . . four o'clock. It's tracking," Gibson called out, looking over his shoulder.

"Tell me when." Rossili tightened his grip along with every muscle in his body. The vast bomber was laboring over the desert at 539 knots, and there was no way in hell she could outturn a speeding SAM. He and Gibson had practiced maneuvers over the Gulf of Mexico a hundred times. The pilot could bank his bomber into the SAM's path, changing his radar return, then lay out a thick corridor of chaff so the missile would lose its target. Rossili's mind was clear as he thought out the procedure and prayed the SAM had learned its part in the maneuver.

"Hold tight, Major," Gibson warned, keeping his eyes fixed on the white fleck of light from the SAM's rocket boosters. "Two thousand yards."

"Start the chaff," Rossili ordered.

"Three . . . two . . . one." Gibson braced himself. "Break *now*." Rossili pushed firmly on the yoke, urging the Reaper to bank to the east. "Come on, baby."

The force of the turn slammed the crew back into their seats as the massive bomber shuddered in protest.

"Where is it?" Rossili grunted above the subsiding noise from the engines as he leveled the bomber.

"I don't know." Gibson searched the skies desperately for the SAM that had streaked in behind their aircraft.

Their silence seemed to be an eerie prelude to an imminent explosion.

General Mulla al-Hammadi watched the SAMs and the targets on the radar scope. The targets were still in the air, pressing their way north.

"Get more missiles in the air. I want those aircraft brought down!" al-Hammadi shouted.

"The sites are reporting heavy ECM. Negative contact from site three." The general could demand all he wanted, but it wouldn't change the fact that the American's powerful ECM equipment had shut down the SAM sites.

"*Magnum!*" The call crackled through their headsets.

"Shit . . . it's about time." After thirty seconds, what seemed an eternity, the launch call told both pilots the tactic had worked. It had given the Wild Weasels time to target and launch on the nearest site. The last SA-6 had been confused by the chaff and jamming, losing its lock on the reflecting radar signals.

Rossili banked the Reaper to a new heading of 015 degrees, dropping back down to 300 feet. The H-band acquisition radar was fading behind them, and the threat panel displayed only the E-band in the distance.

"That was too damned close," Gibson breathed heavily, unhinging his oxygen mask. It was the first time they had ever dodged live SAMs.

Rossili didn't reply, his mind working ahead on higher priorities. His hands were still tightly wrapped around the yoke. He automatically looked at the time-to-go data displayed on the EVS. They were one minute, thirty seconds until weapons release.

"All right, Gibson, it's time." Rossili keyed the internal mike. "I'm taking her up to 4,000. Ready weapons launch."

He pitched the nose up fifteen degrees and watched the VVI, vertical velocity indicator, as the B-52 climbed 6,000 feet a minute. The eight advanced cruise missiles attached to a rotary missile launcher waited, ready to destroy Iraqi command and control bunkers scattered throughout central Iraq.

"Open weapons bay," Rossili ordered.

"Weapons bay open," the offensive weapons operator replied. The Grim Reaper leveled at 3,970 feet. Rossili throttled back, dropping the bomber's airspeed below 350 knots. The aircraft yawed right and left when the bay opened. Using the rudders, he compensated for the added drag.

"Fire when ready," Rossili commanded, checking over his instruments.

The OWO flipped the red launch switch to "go," and the first ACM dropped out from under the bomber.

The cruise missile fell only fifty feet before its 600-pound thrust motor kicked in, propelling it to a top speed of 380 knots within a minute. With the motor operating at 100 percent efficiency, the terrain contour mapping, TERCOM, computer software came to life. This, combined with a digital scene-matching area correlator, directed the missile's small control surfaces to create a stealthy projectile.

"Two away, sir," the operator informed Rossili.

The major watched the mission clock as the OWO announced the release of the ACMs every eight seconds.

"Eight birds away and they're all sierra hotel."

"That's it, Major. We're outta here." Gibson's voice relayed everyone's relief.

"All right, men, the steaks are on me at Bubba 'n' Bucks." Rossili jammed the throttles forward, banking forty-five degrees to the west. He forced the nose of the bomber down quickly, picking up airspeed.

Twelve miles to the northeast, the seventh ACM's navigational computer shut down prematurely. During the drop, a section of copper tubing, used to carry liquid hydrogen coolant to the high-speed gallium arsenide chips, had been jarred loose. As a result, the computer heated to a point where it no longer functioned. The missile arched up, twenty degrees nose high, before coming level at 3,500 feet. It continued its northerly course for a few minutes before making a low, sweeping turn to the east. The AGM-129 ACM was off-course and heading toward Iranian airspace.

Chapter Two

Horagh navigated his old dented Chevrolet pickup truck along the narrow dirt road southeast of Haft Gel, Iran. He pumped the clutch, maneuvering it between the rock-filled ruts spiraling at the base of the Zagros Mountains. To the east, the morning sun was hidden by the high ridges, casting long shadows across the massive sand dunes.

Horagh cursed himself for not getting an earlier start, as he had lost the cover of darkness that hid his presence. He made this trip only once a week, traveling the road up the mountain to the secluded cave where his wine-making still and jars of Western-made grape juice and sacks of sugar were stashed.

He shifted the truck into second gear and was jostled about by a ditch in the road. Horagh had purchased the pickup new in 1975, when the Shah was still in power. It was quite amazing that the vehicle was still operable, considering its appearance. Only splotches of the original green exterior paint showed between the powdery white primer mixed with rust. The vinyl seats and dashboard were worn and cracked from the hot sun and blistering heat.

Many of the engine parts, as well as the tires, had been replaced several times; either he had purchased them on the black market or his sons had stolen them from other vehicles. That was life in Iran: survive the best you could, even if it meant stealing. His

26

children knew they couldn't get caught or the Horagh clan would disown them for breaking the laws of Iran.

Horagh himself had been through as much as the dilapidated truck. Both had survived the revolution and the Iran-Iraq War. Life had not been good to Horagh and his family since the days of the Shah. A former lower-ranking officer in SAVAK, the Shah's brutal secret police, he was one of the fortunate few who had not been murdered during the opening days of the revolution.

However, because of this tainted past Horagh could never hold another job within the revolutionary government. Now in his late fifties, he made his living selling homemade wine to the men traveling into and out of Haft Gel on business trips. Officially, alcohol of any type was strictly forbidden by the laws of Islam, although the farther from Tehran, the more government officials tended to slacken up on the laws. If they arrested everyone who drank alcohol privately, the jails would be packed with otherwise law-abiding people.

Horagh checked his watch as he rounded the last sharp turn, geared down and headed into a long valley. The low morning sun, reflecting off the amber sand, made it difficult to see. He shielded his eyes and saw something unusual in the distance. Resting on the edge of a dune fifty meters in front of him was a long, dark gray object. At first he thought it was a large piece of wood or cast-iron pipe. He studied it for a second or two, not sure. It looked like nothing he had seen before: smooth, with angular lines running in several directions, and on one end were several protruding objects.

Do not concern yourself, Horagh thought. *A strange object in the sand will get you in trouble. There will be many questions.* His first instinct was to just drive by it and let someone else inform the authorities. *But* it quickly occurred to him, *if someone else finds it and it turns out to be very important, they may also find my still.* If Horagh told the police, he could steer suspicion away from his place of operation. He could tell the authorities he was up here hunting, hunting fox and rabbit for their furs. They would believe him, the mountains were full of animals.

Stopping the truck, Horagh made his way across the fine desert sand toward the object. As he neared it, he could see the nose wasn't pointed, as he had expected; rather, it was wedge-shaped and stubby like a shovel. The object was cracked but not broken, and Horagh could see several jagged-edged panels. The object rested on its side, and what looked to be a small air intake was dented and broken from the impact.

"It is a missile," Horagh spoke under his breath in amazement. A thin layer of frost covered the side shaded from the sun. He knelt down and touched the object's coarse gray skin. It was cold and hard like dense plastic, yet when Horagh pushed with his thumbnail he left a small indentation. A moment later the dent disappeared, the skin returning to its original shape. Around the panels meeting the main part of the missile body, he noticed where a gray puttylike material had been used to fill in a couple of cracks. He tugged at the putty, trying to pull some off for his own use; it was waxy but hard.

Horagh's eyes swept the rear half of the missile, stopping at the vertical fin. Peering under the fin, his breath was taken away by the faint image of an American flag. Under the flag were a series of numbers, light gray and hard to read.

It is American. Of course, the war had started, he reminded himself. He had heard the screams of several jets streaking through the sky from the west during the night. In a straight line, directly behind the missile, was a shallow ditch. Horagh looked to the west and could see where the missile had impacted the sand a hundred meters or so away. It looked as if the missile had hit the ground at a low speed, the sand cushioning its impact.

Horagh's mind raced; this was his chance. *This could bring me back into favor with the revolutionary guards. They could trust me again because of what I will bring to them. Possibly I could even get a good job again, my family could be proud of me.*

Horagh ran back to his truck and turned it around. He was no longer bothered by the cold or his own filth.

Chapter Three

Sheik Ali Bin Bakhtiar's driver braked the 300SE Mercedes Benz to a full stop. A late-model black Volvo station wagon pulled up behind the Mercedes, and two armed security guards exited. The guards, wearing black berets and neatly pressed khaki uniforms, rushed toward the Mercedes. They swept their AK-47s left and right, searching the entire area. The wood-stocked assault rifles held single curved thirty-round magazines and were alternately loaded with armor-piercing and tracer bullets. The weapons' fire-power could easily cut down anyone threatening the Iranian defense minister.

A third man, also dressed in a khaki uniform but only packing a side arm, climbed out from the front of the Mercedes.

"You men stand there and there," Hassan Zadeh, the minister's personal bodyguard and private aide, shouted, pointing for the guards to take up positions on either end of the car so no one could approach unnoticed. At six and a half feet tall, Zadeh towered over everyone. Bronze-skinned, with a thick beard and swelled muscular chest, Zadeh flashed his dark eyes quickly as he stood for a few seconds examining the street and buildings for anything out of the ordinary. Only a few merchants preparing to open shop and several street people sleeping on the sidewalks were visible. When everything seemed to be safe, he pulled a

29

back door of the Mercedes open and motioned for the minister to come out. Taking him by the arm, Zadeh helped him onto the sidewalk.

"I do not need your help. Move out of the way . . . out of the way." The sheik spoke irritably, jerking his arm loose from Zadeh. The minister knew it was for his own safety that his aide behaved overly cautiously, but it stifled him just the same.

Zadeh obediently dropped his grip, but undaunted by the harshness stayed close to the sheik.

"I am not an old man yet. Allah has given me a few more years," Bakhtiar grunted. "And if one of Iran's militants or some other Middle East leader wished to kill me, you and two banal guards would be of little help." The seventy-three-year-old minister mumbled on as he strode into the building trying to get ahead of Zadeh.

The sheik caught a glimpse of his aged and weathered hands, then clenched them at the thought of being led around and protected like a helpless child. While other men of distinction lived with it gracefully, Bakhtiar felt true leaders of men needed only faith in Allah and the conviction bestowed in the words from the holy Koran. He believed it was this lack of faith that caused the Arab world to follow like sheep being led to water in the desert.

Zadeh reached the entrance of Iran's central government building and motioned for one of the guards inside to hold the door open. Located on the corner of Val-Ye-Aer and Imam Khomeini Avenue, the beige and brown three-story structure also housed the office of the prime minister. Zadeh led the way through the heavy steel door, past three security posts and down the hall, with a guard in front of and behind Bakhtiar. Each guard systematically checked the doorways and connecting halls.

The discolored gray corridor walls leading to the minister of defense's office matched the faded, worn and scratched tile floor. A row of 60-watt lightbulbs barely allowed one to see the standard display of pictures of Khomeini and Iran's other religious leaders. Several military photos were hung on the walls, also— glossies of Iranian F-5E fighter aircraft in tight formation over Tehran, T-72 main battle tanks speeding through the desert in western Iran, even Kaman-class missile patrol boats cruising through the Straights of Hormuz armed with Harpoon missiles.

The minister disliked the military pictures after his country's defeat in the war with Iraq. But he knew they boosted the morale of the leaders under his command. Something his people needed.

This morning, as with most mornings, the defense minister liked to pray alone in his office before the building filled with government staff people and his daily routine began. The fact that he had been up most of the night praying for Allah's guidance at this possible turning point for his country would not make this day any different. The members of the Supreme Defense Counsel, Iran's secret, powerful branch of the government, would be praying soon in order to decide the future of the Iranian revolution. And he was determined the revolution would continue.

"Minister Bakhtiar . . . Minister Bakhtiar." One of the minister's deputies dashed up behind him just outside his office. "Captain Jaleh of army intelligence is here to see you. He has been here for three hours. I have asked him of his business, but he will not tell me."

"Then his business must not concern you," Bakhtiar replied flatly, not looking the man in the face and walking around him.

Zadeh pressed himself between the two men, opening the door for the defense minister. He then closed it swiftly, shutting the young deputy out.

Hassan Zadeh walked over and took up a watchful position behind the defense minister's desk. He folded his huge arms and stared straight ahead.

Bakhtiar took notice of the officer who stood at attention when they entered. Captain Oskar Jaleh was dressed in unkempt civilian clothes, olive drab pants, no belt, tennis shoes and a stained, short-sleeve plaid shirt. From his stubble and uncombed hair, Bakhtiar guessed he had not shaved or showered for several days. The man's narrow, bloodshot eyes told the story of his lack of sleep. The minister let the man continue to stand while removing his cloak and sighing, knowing he would not get to start his day the way he had planned.

Jaleh was one of only a dozen elite officers Bakhtiar assigned to special missions. They had been handpicked by him from various branches of Iran's military special forces. Each officer was a religious idealist, a Shi'ite, totally committed to Islam and Iran's ambitions of exporting the revolution. They called themselves the *JundAllah*, or soldiers of Allah. None of the men were married, and Bakhtiar preferred orphans, believing this would ensure complete attention and loyalty for the protection of Iran.

"Did you bring it?" Bakhtiar finally asked.

"Yes . . . yes, sir," Army Captain Jaleh answered nervously. He motioned to the TV and VCR on the wall to his left. "I have already placed the tape in."

"Then sit down, I am ready." The minister spoke curtly and sat in the chair behind his desk.

The captain hit the play button. A moment later, Bakhtiar could see by the darkened sky and red horizon that the recording had been filmed in late evening. The cameraman was standing on a balcony above a crowd filling a large area. It was a section of the city of Tabriz that Bakhtiar knew well, a two-kilometer-square courtyard used as an open market, bordered by shops, stalls and vegetable stands.

The Iranian defense minister estimated the crowd to be at least 250,000. Mostly men, angry and afraid. They were rioting, burning the Iranian and Iraqi flags. They held signs that denounced the government and chanted *"Death to Hanifnezhad and food for our children."* He could see several of the shops were on fire, flames and smoke billowing from the rooftops behind the protesters.

It should have never come to this, Bakhtiar thought. *We have waited too long. These are Kurdish revolutionaries controlled by the Americans.*

Bakhtiar shook his head, feeling his face turn warm with growing anger. The Ayatollah Abdol-Rasul Hanifnezhad had been Iran's Islamic leader for the past six years. Bakhtiar considered him an honest, religious man. But it took more than religion to lead a country. A lengthy illness had taken its toll on Ayatollah Hanifnezhad's determination. He had spent most of the past six months in bed, and privately the Iranian doctors admitted the colon cancer was consuming his body and they didn't expect him to live another six months. The frightening part, the part that tore at Bakhtiar's insides, was that these people were not only turning against their country, but they were turning against their holy religious leader as well. Bakhtiar could feel his body starting to shake with rage. A surge of anger caused his mind to blur. The people of Iran were being influenced by the evils of the West. There wasn't any question that Iran was losing its revolutionary battle. The West and the United States were slowly swallowing the morals of his country like a great and hideous monster.

"How long ago did this take place?" Bakhtiar snapped tight-lipped through his thick gray and white beard.

"Yesterday evening," replied the army captain, looking at his wristwatch. "Seven hours ago. It started about noon when the market ran out of goat's milk, meat and bread. The city has not had fresh vegetables or fruit for three weeks."

"I'm well aware of the situation." Bakhtiar glared at the captain, then looked back at the screen. "I do not need you to remind me."

"The crowd grew by the late afternoon and the rioting began just before dark."

"I can see when it started. Just tell me . . . were there any Western reporters on the scene taking pictures or talking with the people?"

"No. My men made sure of it."

"You are certain?"

"Yes." Jaleh answered the challenge without hesitation.

The defense minister stared at the television screen, watching the massive crowd chanting and raising fists, denouncing Iran and Iraq. He watched until he could stand it no longer.

"Why wasn't this brought to me sooner?" Bakhtiar shouted, turning away from the video. "I need to know when this is happening, not after the fact."

"Minister Bakhtiar, your orders were clear. I shot the videotape myself and brought it here to you. No one else has seen it. And I can assure you no one outside this office knows of its existence or followed me, just as you instructed."

Bakhtiar sighed, knowing the captain had done his job correctly. His anger was misplaced and he knew it. In the past thirty days similar riots had taken place in Kermanshah and Hamahan, large cities south of Tabriz. Other members of the *JundAllah* had brought him comparable reports from Iran's northwestern provinces. Because of the uprisings, he had ordered loyal Revolutionary Guard ground troops into the area as a show of force. The ploy seemed to work. A strong message was sent to the people that the leaders in Tehran would not tolerate their disloyalty to the revolution. The riots were subsiding, but he now wondered for how long. The food shortages were still a problem and Iran's harvest for the fall was expected to be well below last year's. It was going to be a long winter.

"I want you and your men to return to Tabriz at once. Find out who is organizing these riots and turning the people against us. Have one of your men uncover their base of operations, then infiltrate the group. I want you to be personally responsible for getting the information to me.'' Bakhtiar stood from his chair and stared into the captain's eyes. ''I swear we will destroy this Satan.''

''Yes, Minister.''

''Go now. We do not have time to waste.''

The captain saluted and left the room, closing the door behind him.

Iranian Prime Minister Mehdi Mahmoudi sat alone at his desk sipping his midmorning tea, a mixture of herbs and spices imported from Turkey. Yellow streaks of morning sunlight cut through his smoke-filled third-floor office, dust and dirt gleaming as it floated in the air. A chain smoker, Mahmoudi crushed out his fourth cigarette, exhaling the smoke out the side of his mouth. He reached for another one, his fingertips soiled yellow from the nicotine of four packs a day.

For a man in his early seventies, Mahmoudi looked surprisingly fit. Most Western news agencies reported his age as ten years younger than he actually was. His neatly trimmed gray beard was offset by his peppered hair and dark, bright eyes. His face had aged slowly, with only a few wrinkles, but his teeth were a telltale sign—they were brown and rotting from many years' lack of care.

Mahmoudi drew in a lungful of smoke and sat back in his chair. He had come to his position of power much like the other leaders of Iran, through purges and falsified election results. However, Mahmoudi considered himself an outsider in the strange world of Iranian politics. He wasn't a religious radical looking to convert the world to Islam and he wasn't constantly involved in corruption and scandal to justify throwing his enemies in jail. He was born in Khorasan in 1931, in the small landowning region of Sabzevar. His father was a powerful cleric; the people of the region had known him as *ostad*, or teacher. Mahmoudi followed in his father's footsteps, studying at the Center for the Propagation of Islamic Truth and aligning himself with Khomeini before the Shah was overthrown. In 1975 Mahmoudi was exiled to Iraq, only to return after the revolution was a year old. It was that year his father died, and Mahmoudi was no longer overshadowed by his reputation. Two years ago he was handpicked by Iran's holy man, Abdol-Rasul Hanifnezhad, to become Iran's prime minister, and the Revolutionary Guard saw to it the election reflected Hanifnezhad's wishes. Mahmoudi accepted the post, secretly hoping he could bring the Iranian people into the mainstream economic world. Even with small children and women starving on the streets, the job was proving to be much larger than he had anticipated.

Using a handheld remote control, he turned up the volume of the BBC World Service. This morning, he was interested in how the world was changing . . . again. The Israelis had decided to give up even more territory than expected in the next step to furnish the Palestinians with a homeland. This was not something that would help reunite the Arabs. It would only force them to become more fractured and divided. The United States would no doubt have even more influence over the region and Iran would become more isolated. This was not good news for Iran, the revolution, and most of all the hungry people in the streets. It would harden Iran's religious leaders against the West and the winds of change. Mahmoudi feared the Supreme Defense Council would look upon this as another reason for Iran to become more militant and hostile. *Our country is falling apart and these fools wish to isolate us further.* A direct confrontation with the West was something Mahmoudi had tried to steer his nation away from. He knew they could never win.

He heard a quick knock at the doorway and turned his head to beckon the visitor in. Mahmoudi gave a scarce nod to Akhbar al-Yawm, Iran's interior and security minister. Al-Yawm came in quietly and sat in an empty chair next to the desk. They listened to the broadcast. He was the only other member of the Supreme Defense Council who agreed that Iran must change, open its borders and join the rest of the world in trade and culture. Nearly bald, he boasted a full black beard that covered much of his face. Thick wire-framed glasses gave his eyes the appearance of twice their normal size.

Mahmoudi had chosen al-Yawm for his chief assistant on internal affairs not only because the man was bright and respected by the religious right, but also because he was open-minded. They often talked privately of Iran's future, agreeing that if they were ever going to feed her people again, they should make peace with the West.

"You are aware of the new riots in Tabriz. They have spread to the surrounding area." Al-Yawm spoke worriedly during a break in the news. "One hundred twenty people are dead this time, and the riots have not stopped. I fear the Kurds may be ready to send in ground troops to take advantage of the turmoil."

Mahmoudi nodded calmly. "Yes, I am aware of the rioting."

Al-Yawm stood solemnly and walked over to the window. He gazed straight ahead. "It is out of control this time. We cannot send in any more troops to maintain peace. The rest of the nation will not tolerate it."

"Yes, I know. It would only provoke more rioting," Mahmoudi answered, still watching the pictures on the television.

"What are we going to do?" Al-Yawm turned to the prime minister, his voice agitated.

"We have only one solution." Mahmoudi flicked his cigarette into the nearly full ashtray. "We must feed our people, Akhbar. It is the only way to stop the riots."

Al-Yawm moved in front of Mahmoudi's desk before speaking. He knew the prime minister must have devised a plan by his resigned manner. "Of course that is the solution. But how do you intend to do it? We must first rebuild our country."

"I plan to travel to Syria . . . secretly, in a few days. It is time we open a dialogue with the West." Mahmoudi reached for another cigarette, then thought better of it. Instead, he looked back at his interior assistant, waiting for a reaction. Seeing only a blank stare on the man's face, he continued. "I will meet with a British envoy and start the process. Iran has been isolated too long. We must begin to rebuild our economy soon or risk being ripped apart by our very own people."

"What will you propose?"

"A simple trade. I will promise that Iran will no longer support terrorism if the West agrees to purchase more Iranian oil and open their markets to Iranian goods. I will also suggest a timetable to open full diplomatic relations. First with Great Britain, then later with the United States."

Al-Yawm's emotions were mixed. Exporting more oil was just the beginning of driving their economy upward. Iran needed access to high technology, computers and medicines. The Sudan was presently their only ally, and it couldn't supply any of these needs. The fact that Syria had made peace with Israel and now traded openly with the West was not only proof but seemed to be the brass ring for the reaching. However, the Islamic Jihad and the *HizvAllah*, radical Shi'ites, wouldn't approve of any dealings with the West, even if it was in the best interest of their country.

Though he knew Mahmoudi was correct, an overwhelming fear rose in al-Yawm. The risks of such a plan were plentiful enough for the both of them.

Mahmoudi got up from his chair and walked over to the window. He cracked open the blinds, letting more sunlight fill the room. "I want you to come with me, Akhbar. I will need your assistance."

Al-Yawm's face flushed and his heartbeat quickened from the prospect of the danger it would put him and his family in. "Tell me the truth, Mahmoudi. Are you meeting with the Americans?"

"No. Not this time. I plan to discuss this plan with the British and Syrians only." He paused before his next words came out in the hushed room. "I am not a fool. I know if I move too swiftly I will be killed."

"Defense Minister Bakhtiar is here to see you," Mahmoudi's personal assistant interrupted. He had rapped on the door twice before entering.

Mahmoudi's eyes went to the digital clock on the edge of his desk. He wasn't scheduled to meet Bakhtiar for another hour.

"I will speak with you again before the day is over, Akhbar." Their eyes met before al-Yawm turned wordlessly and walked out the door.

"Send him in," Mahmoudi grunted, turning off the television. He lifted his teacup to his lips, then set it down upon finding it cold.

The prime minister watched Bakhtiar move across the room and stop in front of his desk. As usual, the short defense minister's intense gray eyes seemed to be examining him before he spoke. Bakhtiar's stare always managed to send a chill down the prime minister's spine. He couldn't remember if he had every seen the somber man smile or relax, even for a moment.

"Do we have a scheduling problem?" Mahmoudi asked, lighting a cigarette and blowing the blue smoke out his nose. "My defense briefing is not for another hour."

"This cannot wait for your briefing. I am here to see you on an urgent matter that needs to be addressed." Bakhtiar walked around the chair and sat on the edge of the seat, his back rigid.

"If you are here to tell me about the riots, you are too late. I already know about them," Mahmoudi reasoned, trying to disarm the hotheaded defense minister.

"The riots are only the result of a much bigger problem."

"Yes, and that problem being . . . ?" Mahmoudi asked.

"The revolution. *That* is the problem. It is in grave danger. The Supreme Defense Council has waited too long to correct the situation. They should have listened to me. They should have allowed me to react to the riots months ago. And we should act *now* to bring our country back together. It may already be too late!" Bakhtiar's voice had risen, though his face was set as if in stone.

Mahmoudi took a long drag from his cigarette. He looked at Bakhtiar through the haze. The prime minister knew better than to verbally spar with Bakhtiar without thinking things through first. Mahmoudi held a great deal of respect for his defense minister, although he didn't necessarily trust or like him. Sheik Bakhtiar was a true patriot and religious leader. He had taken his position not because he craved power or desired the destruction of his personal enemies, but to keep the fires of the Iranian revolution burning and spread it throughout the world. It was such men that kept Iran isolated, its people ignorant and hungry.

The defense minister, annoyed with Mahmoudi's silence, rose from his chair and walked over to the television equipment. He turned it on. Neither man said a word for the next ten minutes as they watched and kept their own thoughts.

Mahmoudi, letting out a long sigh, was the first to speak. "I am aware of what is happening and you are correct to be concerned."

"Then why will the Supreme Defense Council not—"

"Stop, Bakhtiar." Mahmoudi raised his hand for the man's patience. "I can assure you each member of the Supreme Defense Council shares your hatred of the Kurdish rebels. They are just as aware of what is happening. But what are our options? More ground troops? Airpower? Do you wish to kill hundreds of innocent women and children? There is a limit to our military strength when it comes to the will of our people." His gaze went back to the screen and his brow furrowed. Iran's military field commanders would not order their troops to attack unarmed citizens. Bakhtiar was not foolish—he neither wanted that nor believed that it would happen.

Bakhtiar leaned forward on the prime minister's desk. "It is time we unite our people and stop being so cautious. My military has the resources to correct a situation such as this. It is time I give the order for the Phalanx Dragon to be used."

Mahmoudi sat up, glaring directly at the defense minister. This was definitely unexpected news. "All the tests have been completed?"

"I have one final test that I wish to perform, but . . ." Bakhtiar hesitated, satisfied to have the prime minister's attention. "Yes, the Phalanx Dragon is operational. You just have to give me the order to deploy it."

"How many of these missiles have your engineers constructed?"

"I now have 148. If given the command, we can manufacture 100 per month." Bakhtiar's enthusiasm was genuine; he believed every word he said. "We have the means to become the most powerful country in the Gulf. But only if the Supreme Defense Council has the courage to proceed."

"The courage, Bakhtiar?"

"Allah is on our side."

Mahmoudi lowered his head into his hands. His earlier conversation with al-Yawm was upsetting, but had much more promise than what the defense minister was suggesting. Gaining the people's loyalty and reuniting them using some military ploy was not encouraging, and could possibly prove disastrous.

The prime minister raised his head. "Perhaps you should complete your final test before we speak any further on this matter." He decided to appease Bakhtiar at the moment so he could get on to productive issues. "It could be that the project is far from completion and we are discussing this prematurely."

"Of course. You are right." The defense minister, taken aback, felt impudent. "I should not have come to you until it was completed." Perturbed by his own rashness, he rose from the chair and excused himself. "*Salam aleikom.*" Mahmoudi nodded his head and repeated the courtesy.

Bakhtiar strode to his pinewood desk. The top of it was covered with stacks of papers and files. On the left side were three black telephones, linking him with the Revolutionary Guard commanders for the navy, army and air force.

He stared at the bulky, oval rug in the center of the office. It brought a brief memory of his wife, who had purchased it in Turkey two years ago, before her death.

Bakhtiar rubbed his forehead. He had warned the Supreme Defense Council that revolution was once again in the air and this time the government might not be able to regain control. Perhaps now they would listen to him. A quarter of a million rioters could not be ignored.

Bakhtiar contemplated the changes of the last few years. The assassination of Saddam Hussein, cut down by a sniper's bullet while he visited a neighborhood school in central Baghdad, had thrown Iraq into a bloody civil war. Kurdish rebels in northern Iraq were now warring with troops loyal to Iraq's Baath party and the new dictator, General Ali Razargani, Saddam Hussein's half-brother. That turmoil had spilled over into northern Iran, and the Kurdish Democratic Party (KDP) was calling for independence from both Iran and Iraq. It was demanding an autonomous, UN-recognized nation, one that would cut Iran and Iraq in half. This demand was the greatest threat to the revolution since the war with Iraq. Yet Bakhtiar knew there was more to these revolts than calls for independence and a new Kurdish state. The men in the streets were demonstrating not for freedom or over religious ideology but because they didn't have the basic needs of human beings. They didn't have jobs and their families were going without food. A three-year drought had crippled entire regions. Iran's crumbling infrastructure had dropped its oil production to 1.5 million barrels a day. All this coincided with a five-year low in world oil prices. Iran's controlled economy was on the verge of collapse, and its leaders were placing their hopes and dreams in their faith. Faith in Allah was a great thing, but it did not feed or clothe hungry and desperate families. There was no peace of the soul as long as there was no peace of the body.

Bakhtiar paced the floor, the weight of his heavy clerical robes feeling unusually burdensome. As a student, Iran's minister of defense had been active in quite a few political organizations. After completing two years of military service, Bakhtiar returned to the university to teach economics. Soon after he began lecturing on religion and the dangers of the secular West. In the mid-seventies, Bakhtiar was arrested by the Shah's SAVAK henchmen and spent three years behind bars, where he was tortured repeatedly.

When he was released, Bakhtiar bore the scars of SAVAK's interrogations not only on his back and arms, but within his heart as well. He worked diligently to overthrow the Shah, joining in Khomeini's revolution. His strong conviction and outspoken personality helped him climb in rank and stature until he became an adviser to the Revolutionary Council. After Khomeini's death and the war with Iraq ended, he was then asked to join the secret Supreme Defense Council and was given the title minister of defense. The knowledge he acquired during his brief military career was just what Abdol-Rasul Hanifnezhad wanted. The Revolutionary Guard still feared a secular military. They saw a structured army, air force and navy as the greatest threat to the revolution. Bakhtiar's mission was rudimentary: transform Iran's fractured military into a force that would protect it from external and internal threats. Nothing must threaten the revolution. And now there was a threat and it didn't appear to be coming from the outside, as most of the leaders of the Supreme Defense Council had feared. The uprising was from within.

"Zadeh, have someone bring me hot tea with lemon."

He stroked the worn cover of the Koran, which was always placed in the center of his desk. Opening it, he glanced over the words without reading them. Ten years ago, the Kurds would have been killed for being the counterrevolutionaries behind the riots. That was not acceptable today.

As minister of defense, he had the moral responsibility to keep the flames of the revolution alive and well among the people. Bakhtiar held the book lightly as if the answers he needed would jump out at him. He had for a long time advocated that the revolution must be renewed and that there were only three things that would bring the people of Iran back together again: armed struggle, more armed struggle and yet more intense armed struggle. The people must be reminded that no amount of social enticement, whether high-paying jobs, social prestige or the false happiness of luxury items, would ever replace the need for armed struggle.

Zadeh entered the room quietly. The tray with the elegant silver tea set looked out of place in his huge hands.

"I can fix my own drink." His hand flew in a shooing gesture at Zadeh, who had placed the minister's heart medicine on the tray. The doctors had warned that if he did not follow their instructions, the next heart attack would be fatal.

"Zadeh, make sure no one enters," Bakhtiar ordered, after swallowing the pill with a burning gulp of tea.

"Yes, Minister." Zadeh left the room and stood directly in front of the door.

Bakhtiar opened a cabinet door behind him and removed a pile of books and papers to reveal a small steel safe. He twisted the lock of the safe until he heard the final click, then swung open the thick door. A thin, dog-eared file was inside. Leaving the safe open, he sat with the file before him, staring at the bold black lettering he had written himself across the front—PHALANX DRAGON.

It was the code name Bakhtiar had chosen for one of Iran's secret weapon programs. He examined the contents, surveying the black-and-white photographs of the American cruise missile as it was first found in the desert in February 1991. A military helicopter had transferred the missile to a top-secret weapons research center near Esfahan air base in central Iran. Then he saw the CNN coverage of Tomahawk cruise missiles streaking above downtown Baghdad, following the streets to their targets. It was then he realized that Iran could learn much from a weapon such as this. The Supreme Defense Council gave Bakhtiar permission to pull several of Iran's best engineers from other projects in hopes of learning the secrets of the missile. They began taking the cruise missile apart piece by piece. Slowly, methodically, the technicians had learned every detail of the missile, and under Bakhtiar's guidance Phalanx Dragon had emerged as Iran's greatest technological breakthrough.

Bakhtiar reflected on the last few years. The sheik prudently had not built large, sprawling weapon compounds that the Americans could easily learn about, then target and attack. He had kept the manufacturing complex modest and limited to the minimum number of people. He wanted it in a place where it could be saturated with defensive weapons and still not draw much attention. Bakhtiar shrewdly decided to build the complex inside one of Iran's maximum-security prisons, outside the Esfahan air force base. The entire structure took only two one-room buildings that had been buried underground and hardened against attack.

After years of testing and experimentation, Iranian engineers had ascertained it was the missile's outer skin, a mixture of high-strength graphite, that absorbed the full spectrum of radar waves. It was difficult to detect until a few seconds before impact. With more arduous work they determined how to manufacture this skin.

Bakhtiar closed the file and returned it to its secure place. He then walked to the center of the room and knelt slowly to the east. Bending from the waist, he began chanting his prayers.

Chapter Four

"There she is, General. The toughest bad-ass B-1B bomber in the fleet. The ground crew refers to her as Screamin' Sue," Major Pete Hodges said, leading the way to the parked aircraft inside the brightly lit hangar. The sun had set several hours earlier, leaving the dark desert sky filled with white flickering stars. "The maintenance team is fine-tuning her avionics right now. They'll load the HARMs before we take off in the morning."

Major General Richard "Duke" James was quiet as he followed several feet behind the smaller test pilot. He watched Hodges stop and look up at the cockpit windows of the aircraft. James had known Major Hodges for only two weeks but had discovered he was a confident pilot and a demon for details. The major possessed a degree in aerodynamic engineering and had worked side by side with USAF engineers to modify the B-1B's engines for supersonic flight.

Sitting in the center of the immense hangar, the dark green and gray B-1B didn't look any different from any other B-1B. Several of its exterior access panels were open, and two red-and-yellow ventilation hoses were feeding the interior of the aircraft with cool air. Painted on the side of the fuselage, below the pilot's window and in light gray paint, was a wild horse, his head down as if in a dead run. An Indian was riding the horse bareback, a bolt of

43

lightning held high in one hand and a tight grip of mane in the other.

"I thought you meant Sue as in female, but I see you meant Sioux as in Indian, Major." Duke smiled, and for an instant his thoughts flashed back to Ellsworth AFB in Rapid City. Back in the days when there was an SAC and they kept its pilots on alert and the tough, ready attitude was portrayed through those simple symbols painted on the sides of aircraft. He never thought he'd miss those days, but right now, seeing these aircraft up close again, he missed being on the fight line full time.

"As a matter of fact, General, she does remind me of this girl I once knew. Fast and hot. But she was no comparison to this baby here. Only one beefed up to go Mach 1 at low level. I had her out at Nellis two months ago. A group of F-15s tried to take me out . . . ha! No way, man, no way. With these new engines they couldn't catch me, much less lock on long enough to get a shot off." Hodges showed off a boyish grin. "At 200 feet she's faster than a forty-five-caliber bullet."

Duke folded his arms across his chest as he examined every inch of the aircraft. "So, the fighter pukes couldn't catch you."

"Hell no, they couldn't. Several of them got a fix on my position, but by the time they turned to intercept me, I was done gone."

"I'll bet that bugged the shit out of them." Duke laughed heartily at the thought of frustrated fighter pilots. Particularly the F-15 pilots. He walked past the nose gear and under the aircraft. He could see a weapons rack containing six white-and-black AGM-88C HARM missiles being readied to load into the B-1B's number one weapons bay. As part of Duke's current assignment, special assistant to the chairman of the Joint Chiefs, he had scheduled himself to pilot the B-1B on test flight for tomorrow morning. He felt it was his duty to check out the latest machinery and weapons himself. Something he believed all people in higher positions should do—know what's going on from the ground up.

"Think you can handle her, General?"

"Are you worried about me and my flying proficiency?" Duke asked with a cocked eyebrow. "Or about your bird coming back in one piece?"

Hodges, not in the least bit rattled by the question coming from his superior, merely answered, "Just want to make sure you're ready, that's all."

Duke nodded. "I'll be ready, Major." He looked at his watch.

It was ten minutes to eleven. He would get less than six hours of sleep. "Oh five hundred is going to be here before we know it. Let's head back and get some shut eye."

"Yes, sir." Hodges turned to lead the way out.

"And, Major . . ."

"Yes, sir?"

"I'll fly her as if my own children were on board." Duke and Hodges took one last glance back at the B-1B. Her sleek features gleamed in the light of the hangar, and it seemed as if she was going Mach 1 just sitting on the ground.

ESFAHAN, IRAN

The fragrance of frying goat's lard and simmering spiced tea filled Perijan Reza's small bedroom. She bowed her head and smiled, knowing her father had been up before dawn preparing the day's meals. That meant her father was feeling better. The warm, pleasant smell filled Perijan's mind with memories of her childhood. She recalled the happier times when she would rise in the early morning with her mother. They would cook and clean for her father and three older brothers until they returned filled with stories of their work. It was a time when they were a close family, full of dreams and hopes. She remembered their late evenings of long talks, sharing their own individual desires and futures. Her smile faded as she thought of her plans to marry and start a family of her own. The disturbing memories followed no matter how she tried to block them out.

The war with Iraq swept through her country like black death. Her two eldest brothers were the first to leave for the front, as Iraq pushed deep into Iran. The devastating news that they were killed a day apart during the Wal-Fajr offensive near Dezful in October 1983 was only the beginning. A week later her third brother was called to service. During an Iraqi Scud-B missile attack, while defending the town of Dezful, he was also killed. In 1983, 180,000 Iranian soldiers were killed, with five times that amount wounded. Despair touched almost every part of the country. The deaths, though agonizing, were a part of life Perijan could accept. But to see the life drained from her parents was more than she could bear. Six months after her last brother's death, Perijan's mother died in her sleep. A young teen at the time, she recollected how the slight smile upon her mother's face convinced her the woman she loved so dearly had found some dream world she chose not to wake from.

After the funeral, her father would lie in bed, unable to get up in the mornings. He repeatedly apologized to Perijan and promised to work the next day. But the days passed and he didn't go, and soon he lost his job at the local bakery. He would occasionally clean businesses and public restrooms so they would have some money to buy food.

Perijan sighed, forcing the thoughts out of her mind. *What is done is done,* she told herself. *I can only change the future.*

"Perijan, are you up? Are you ready? The guards will be here shortly and you still must eat something." Her father appeared from behind the heavy cloth drapes that separated Perijan's room from the rest of the house. He held a spoon in his hand as he fretted over his only living child. "Now, hurry or you will be late."

"Yes, Father. I am hurrying," Perijan answered, watching the gray-haired man shuffle away while she sat on the edge of her unmade bed. She loved her father more today than when life was good. His helplessness brought out her nurturing instincts, and even if his emotions appeared to be numb and intimate moments were few, she knew he felt the same.

"The guards will not be on time, Father. You know they are always late," she called out, and leaned over to finish tying her shoelaces.

Perijan and her father had continued to live in the mountain village of Esfahan. People they had known all their lives had changed. Friendliness and caring were simple pleasures of the past.

After the Ayatollah Khomeini and his band of followers had stripped the Shah of all power, the people and leaders rejoiced, knowing that life would be better without him and his brutal security forces. Soon after, however, men carrying rifles and pistols calling themselves Revolutionary Guards arrived in Esfahan. They closed the military base, killing many of the leaders stationed there. Taking control, they promised the people Iran could now return to the values of Islam; the scourge of the Shah was over. The men took everyone who had been loyal to the Peacock Empire from their homes, and in the months and years that followed, the disappearances and killings of leaders and followers of the former government continued. As with most promises that had been made to Perijan in her youth, it became evident that life in Esfahan would not get better. The revolution evolved into a backward step for Iran. Iran became a self-serving country ruled by a handful of religious zealots. Perijan and her father were poorer now than ever before.

Taking a seat in front of her mirror, Perijan ran a brush through the long, thick black hair surrounding her oval face. Large dark eyes stared at the image of a still youthful-looking woman with a fair olive complexion. Thin arms gave no hint of hard manual labor, and neither did the willowy hand and fingers clutching the brush handle. A tiny dark birthmark above her right eyebrow was befitting of Perijan's mysterious beauty.

As a child, these distinctive looks only added to Perijan's other mystifying qualities. It was soon discovered she had the capability to recall details and bits of information she read or saw. Whether or not this was what enabled her to read and comprehend material several grades ahead of others her age was something the teachers could only guess at. This gave her a high status in school and garnered the attention of government officials.

She was now employed as an engineer. She knew the income was modest by Western standards, but it kept Perijan and her father from living among the desperate poor in the center of the village. She had managed to make enough so it was no longer necessary for her father to try and work.

Perijan was tucking her hair inside a hejab, the Islamic traditional cloth she and the other women wore to cover their hair in public, when her father's voice startled her.

"They are here, they are here." His voice sounded fearful, yet it was laced with contempt. Perijan heard the front door open without a knock. The soldiers' rudeness never ceased to amaze her. *My home is not government property,* she thought.

Perijan emerged from her room into the main living quarters. Standing at the open door was an armed soldier wearing a dark green Iranian special forces uniform. Half his face was covered with a beard, and although it was clear by his unwavering stare he found her intriguing looks attractive, Perijan made sure she didn't look at him directly.

"Everything is all right, Father," Perijan said soothingly and stroked his shoulder reassuringly. "The soldiers do not bother me." She did not want her father to know how angry she was at having to return to work for a second shift.

Her father reached up and patted her smooth hand. The drapes were drawn and the room was dark. Perijan turned the knob of the kerosene lantern and the room brightened with a warm glow. She had heard her father coughing during the night. His drawn face looked no different than any other day, but the circles beneath his eyes appeared to be darker.

"I love you. Now, I want you to rest today and I'll be home as soon as I can." Perijan ignored the guard's unwanted presence, and her full lips pressed on her father's cheek in a kiss. She picked up a small leather backpack containing her work clothes.

"But you did not eat," her father insisted, still annoyed at the guard. "You will get sick, you are so thin."

"I will not get sick," Perijan said, trying to smile. "I promise I will eat something today. Good-bye."

Perijan stood by the door waiting for the soldier to go first, then followed him out into the cool morning air.

FALLON NAS, NEVADA

The gray-and-brown lunar landscape of the Nevada desert flashed below the B-1B in a blur. Racing north 200 feet above the rocks and sand at 580 knots, the Avenger, call sign for the Arapaho 127, hugged the ground, trying to mask its presence from the simulated enemy radar sweeping the sky to the northwest of her current position. The nose of the strategic bomber pitched up a few degrees as the terrain-following radar guided the swing-wing jet up and over a chain of rolling hills and back down the other side. Banking two degrees left, the B-1B leveled again, cutting through the rapidly warming morning air.

The pilot, Duke James, swept the deep blue sky looking for any "unfriendly" fighters in front of and above him—a flashing of reflected sunlight or the dark gray flick of an attacking navy or air force jet fighter.

The DoD had come to Duke with several positions, knowing he wouldn't settle for anything less than being in the cockpit of a jet from time to time. Duke didn't want to be like some of the generals who gave lip service to their men. He wanted to be just as good a general as he was a pilot—know every aspect and angle and stay on top of the mechanics of the military for the best possible decisions at any given time.

He keyed the internal mike. "Talk to me, Hooter. What's happening out there?"

"I show a spike bearing three zero niner. Looks like an SA-5," First Lieutenant Michael "Hooter" Rawlings, the bomber's defensive systems operator, called from his console located behind Duke and his copilot, Major Pete Hodges. The defensive electronic scope showed a radar sweeping the airspace ahead of the B-1B. "He's in a search mode . . . doesn't know we're out here."

"They know we're out here, Hooter. They just don't know where we're at this second. I'm more worried about the fighters," Duke observed, continuing to examine the airspace in front of him.

"I'm not picking up any fighter radar emissions. They must be flying with electronics off."

"Copy," Duke replied, returning his attention to the instruments.

The flight test had taken off from Edwards an hour earlier, intercepting a KC-135 tanker over Bakersfield before continuing north at 24,000 feet. After topping off fuel tanks, they skirted the eastern edge of Yosemite National Park, giving the crew time to check and recheck the bomber's offensive and defensive systems. They then dropped down to 12,000 feet, crossed into Nevada, and finally flew into airspace controlled by Fallon Naval Air Station.

Duke and his crew were set to test the launching of two live HARMs at a radar site located deep inside the northern part of Fallon's Echo Whiskey test range—Echo Whiskey stood for electronic warfare. The HARM was designed to destroy the enemy search radars that prevented attacking aircraft from penetrating enemy airspace. Unlike the standard HARM launch, which was line-of-site—meaning the missile's seeker head had to pick up the threat before it could be targeted—the HARMs Duke was about to launch would be prompted from a strategic intelligence satellite in geosynchronous orbit above the western United States. The space-based sensors would detect and locate an electronics threat long before the B-1B's onboard sensors. Air Force F-16Cs and Navy EA-6Bs had proven the concept worked; however, this was the first time a B-1B had tested the system in a simulated combat arena. Duke and his crew not only had to worry about getting the HARMs' launch inside the target window, but they had to look out for enemy fighters, F/A-18s and F-16Cs, and simulated ground threats such as SAMs and triple A. The idea of testing was to make it sufficiently realistic for reliable results. Consequently, that made it unforgivingly deadly.

"Way-point Romeo in fifteen seconds, sir," Major Hodges reported.

"Roger. Okay, here we go. It's time to play ball." Duke wrapped his fingers around the center control stick and disengaged the terrain-following radar. He sucked in a deep breath of cool oxygen, letting his adrenaline surge with the speed of the aircraft. The bomber drifted up 300 feet before leveling at 512 feet above the desert, speed 576 knots. Her nose pitched up and down a few degrees in rapid succession for a second or two. Duke's stomach rolled over as he let out an uncontrollable "Shit!"

I should have had a few more check rides, he told himself, steadying the bomber. Pete Hodges glanced over at him without a word or smirk that would have been justified. The fact that Hodges had over 2,000 hours in the left seat of the B-1B, including 600 hours of flight test, was reassuring only to the men on the ground. Technically, if the aircraft got into trouble, the major would take over, but up in the air they both understood that when a man sat in the left seat, everything was his call.

Flying a high-performance jet aircraft in combat, simulated or otherwise, wasn't like riding a bicycle. A pilot had to practice to keep up his efficiency; Duke knew that as well as any competent pilot. He had flown this particular B-1B a half dozen times over the test ranges here and at Edwards in the last two weeks, but still a pilot flying full time would always be the best. It seemed to Duke that it was only yesterday he had been one of the first pilots to fly operational B-1Bs out of Ellsworth AFB in South Dakota. He was a top dog then, without a doubt possessing superior piloting ability. But the realization that years had passed and his new position no longer allowed him to be with the cream made him feel less confident. He wisely shook the feeling, knowing that if he made one small screwup, he and the rest of the four-man crew would be a burning ball of steel in the desert. *Besides,* he reminded himself, *I may be older, but I know a lot more tricks than most of these greenhorn flyboys.*

"Your men picked the right name for her, Major. Screamin' Sioux. She's going to give me a ride, all right."

Duke used his fingertips to gently work the hair-trigger control stick of Arapaho 127. As special assistant to the Joint Chiefs chairman and the secretary of defense, Duke's official job was to coordinate the testing and evolution of aircraft and new weapons systems that could be used for both Navy and Air Force operations, or composite air wing missions, as the brass in the Pentagon now liked to refer to them. This included joint weapons operations, such as the AGM-137 tri-service standoff attack missiles, or TSSAM, and the JDAM, joint direct attack munitions. On paper, this concept made a lot of sense. Shrinking defense budgets made it impossible for both services to research and develop a relevant quantity and quality of aircraft and weapons systems separately. Everything the Air Force needed or wanted would have to be designed for Army, Navy and Marine use, and vice versa.

The position of special assistant was one that had been created specifically for Duke. He left NASA eighteen months after the *Atlantis* shuttle he was commanding went down in northern Chad. He and his crew had been taken prisoners but, fortunately, were rescued by a composite military team. Duke was not only intrigued by this new way of command but had decided he preferred to be armed when going into the unknown. His wife, Katie, had finally conceded to his desire to go back to their military lifestyle, knowing if he wasn't happy she wasn't going to be, either. All the notoriety of Duke's being the only living commander of a failed shuttle mission was taking its toll on their personal lives, too. It wasn't easy being married to a man as competitively ambitious and energetic as Duke James.

"Two minutes to hostile territory," Hodges warned. He snapped his oxygen mask into place.

Duke, feeling quite secure with the aircraft now, didn't respond but continued his routine checks. He was savoring each and every moment, wanting to fill the gap he knew he'd be left with after the flight was over. He envied the major for flying the B-1B just about every day and getting to know her better than anyone in the Air Force.

"One minute and counting."

"Okay, let's run through the checklist one more time," Duke commanded. "Satcom uplink?"

"Satellite communications on line and functioning," Hooter Rawlings reported, verifying that the B-1B's ASC-19C transponder and receiver were operating.

"Air data recorders on?"

"Electronics up and running."
HARMs?"
"Antiradiation missile hot and ready, sir,"
Duke checked the instruments one more time before keying his
mike. "Nav . . . position."
"On time. We'll be over the range in ten seconds," the offen-
sive systems operator radioed back, checking the SKN-2440 INS
(internal navigation system).
"Roger, contact Falcon. Let them know we're ready and on
schedule."

ESFAHAN, IRAN

A shiver went down Perijan's spine despite the heavy cloth of
her chador. She watched her frosty breath float off into the dark
evening sky. The western horizon was glowing pink with the hint
of a colorful sunset. She wished she could see at least part of it,
but knew memorable sunrises and sunsets were something she
had learned to live without. Working underground all day, and
many times during the night, only allowed her to see the blue sky
on Fridays, her one day off.
At the end of the short walkway, a five-passenger Iranian air
force mini-bus was waiting, its engine running. Greasy blue fumes
pouring out of the vehicle's exhaust pipe burned Perijan's eyes
as she approached. It was the same routine six days a week; she
climbed in, making her way to the back, and sat down, not saying
a word. She would be the only passenger.
Perijan knew that, because of who she was, the men responsible
for getting her to the complex were generally curious and apprehensive. The daily trips were always silent. An Iranian woman
traveling alone would never speak to a strange man, much less a
soldier. They treated her respectfully yet were annoyed with their
duty of escorting her. Only the one soldier whom she caught
staring at her seemed at ease. She wondered at times if he could
read her mind.
The bus pulled away from the curb, heading down a single-
lane gravel road. A hundred yards later it turned onto the main
avenue that ran across the north side of the city. They would stay
on the road until reaching the outskirts of Esfahan air base, ten
miles to the northeast.
Perijan gazed out the window, staring at the rows of weathered

and rundown apartment buildings as they passed by. A few lights shone through makeshift cloths hanging over windows. Esfahan was a dirty mountain city where people lived packed together in the three- and four-story buildings. They lined both sides of the streets and were filled with more people than they should house.

The only time she had been away from the city and her father was two years ago, when she had been given an opportunity to study advanced mathematics and computer technology in Britain and the United States.

She was afraid to leave her father, but after having a restless dream of a beautiful land without so many restrictions, she felt a yearning that had to be filled. She knew it would also benefit her father to accept the offer of an education in return for doing government work. They would not have to worry about food or a place to live again.

Perijan was readily accepted into the Massachusetts Institute of Technology for two semesters. Her roommate, a woman in her early thirties named Patty Thompson, said she was there to freshen up on some courses. They were a perfect match: Patty, older and more experienced, Perijan, still naive. Besides sharing a room, they also shared many of the same interests. Patty was born and raised in Iowa, the daughter of a corn farmer, and had that small-town friendliness that Perijan remembered from her early childhood. Before long they were inseparable.

Late at night, when the lights were out, Perijan revealed her innermost secrets to Patty: her silent hatred of Iran's revolutionary government (this was the first time she had admitted it to anyone other than her family), how her three brothers were killed in the war and the fact she was convinced her mother had died of heartbreak. It was such a time as Perijan had never known. She learned so much more than the curriculum and blossomed, feeling alive again.

Two weeks before the end of the last semester, Patty and Perijan were once again in their room having one of their now familiar conversations. It was hard to think of returning home. Her life in Iran weighed even more heavily on Perijan after having experienced such freedom and wonders. Patty suddenly grew grave and told Perijan that she had something she wished to share, but it was of vital importance that it never be repeated.

Patty slowly revealed that she worked for the United States government and that they were looking for young Iranians who would want to make a difference in their country. An informant of sorts. They were needed to report on Iran's internal economic conditions and other pertinent information but were never expected to put themselves in any danger.

At first, Perijan refused, feeling betrayed. It seemed that the things she had been taught about the evil West were true. Working for the U.S. government was just a nice way of saying the CIA; Perijan was smart enough to know that. She broke off the friendship, not speaking to Patty for the remainder of the two weeks.

In the short time she had been in America, Perijan wondered if everything the Iranian government had told her about the country was a lie. America didn't seem to be the land of Satan. It wasn't filled with drunken, sex-crazed people without regard for law and the ways of Allah. Why would her government allow her to travel to such a place? There were too many pieces that didn't fit together.

Perijan's search brought her back to Patty. It was understood she could quit at any time, but if she ever exposed her contact in Iran, the consequences would more than likely be fatal.

Twenty minutes later, the van pulled to a dead stop in front of a cinderblock guardhouse several feet inside a heavy wire gate. A weathered sign hanging on the side of the guardhouse read ES-FAHAN MAXIMUM SECURITY PRISON. The large powerful flood-lights suspended from metal poles were already flickering on.

"Identification," a stern-faced guard demanded roughly, although Perijan was sure by now he knew everyone inside the van. The driver handed over all their photo ID cards. He took them and disappeared into the guardhouse, where he checked the IDs against an updated computer readout listing personnel with clearance into the compound.

The driver gave a slight wave to one of the other guards standing on the left side of the gate. Another man on the right paid no attention to the van and its occupants, as he was struggling to restrain two vicious German shepherds. The animals barked loudly at the parked vehicle while pulling against their leather leashes.

This was the only entance to the prison complex and it was well guarded. Iranian engineers had built the compound in the shape of a large square, a half-mile long on each side, with fifty-foot towers at every corner. Each tower contained two guards armed with fully automatic machine guns and grenade launchers. The prison was also ringed by two electrified steel wire fences topped with ten-foot-diameter rolls of barbed razor wire. In the center of the compound was the main building, a two-story concrete structure housing 153 of Iran's most dangerous political prisoners. A third barbed wire fence enclosed the structure, allowing only enough room for one person to pass through a gate, which of course was also guarded. The space between this fence and the building was for a favored prisoner who was allowed to come out into the fresh air from time to time. Near the back of the prison complex, away from the main building, were two more concrete structures roughly the size of double-wide trailer houses. These contained the cooling and ventilation system for Iran's latest top-secret, advanced underground weapons manufacturing complex.

"You may proceed." The guard's eyes searched the interior of the bus one last time as he handed the IDs back.

The gate was rolled open and the driver put the bus in gear. They turned left, taking a dirt road to the farthest building.

Perijan exited the bus, following one of the guards, and made her way to the underground laboratory deep beneath the desert.

FALCON AIR FORCE BASE, COLORADO SPRINGS

On the edge of Petersen AFB, east of Colorado Springs, the USAF Space Command center buzzed with activity. The men and women working there were responsible for some of the most secretive and advanced early warning, tracking and weapons systems in the world.

In a windowless ten-foot-square room off the main command center in building number 1, Lieutenant General Nick Gladstone stood behind the computer monitoring equipment. Gladstone headed the air force's 73rd Space Surveillance Group and this morning he took special interest in the flight test over Fallon Range. A short, stout man with thick gray hair, heavy eyebrows and sideburns, the general was known as "Ironsides." Everything was going as planned with the flight test, but he was still growing impatient. He folded his arms while studying the control panel, giving him an even more rigid look.

"They're twenty miles out and inbound, General," Bobby Garcia, a retired Navy Lieutenant Commander, said from behind his large forty-eight-inch computer monitor. His round, sausagelike finger pointed at the blue triangle representing the B-1B on the bottom of the square display. A civilian, former RF-4C back-seater, Garcia now worked for Martin Marietta in a support role as a systems specialist.

Gladstone hunched over the TACTS computer display used to monitor the aircraft flying over Fallon range. The screen's black background highlighted the bright yellow lines that outlined the valleys and mountains inside the test range like a topography map. The monitor showed a twenty-five-square-mile area, revealing the contour of the land and the aircraft flying in the airspace. The TACTS, using a series of highly advanced airborne and ground-based electronic instrumentation, was driven by high-speed software and computer technology. It was much like having a long-distance video camera hundreds of miles in the sky above Fallon. The general could see the area as if he were standing there himself. Originally developed to train top gun pilots, the TACTS was now used in all phases of testing and training.

He pushed his bifocals higher on his nose as a blue circle, an E-2C Hawkeye, came into view in the upper left-hand corner of the screen. Near the right edge were four red aircraft symbols, the F/A-18s acting as the bad guys, moving southwest. At the bottom of the screen, cutting across the dotted red outline of range Bravo-17 and on the edge of Echo Whiskey, the Arapaho 127 could be clearly seen.

"How long before hostile emissions?" Gladstone asked, not taking his eyes off the screen.

"Thirty seconds," Garcia answered.

Both men watched the B-1B snake its way north. The F/A-18s were now heading due south and east of the B-1B. Gladstone knew the Avenger, moving as fast as it was through the broken terrain, would make it difficult for the E-2C to locate it unless the Hawkeye was directly above the bomber.

"Contact. Hostile radar is on line." A red pulsing circle began to flash on the screen in the center of Echo Whiskey range.

The general nodded in approval.

Twenty-four thousand five hundred miles above North America, a SIGINT (signals intelligence) satellite, code number AFP-833, picked up the first faint electronic transmissions of a hostile I/J-

band fire control radar. The unmanned radar, operating on a wave-
length of 9,753 MHz, or 3.25 cm, was located in the central
section of Fallon's Echo Whiskey range. The satellite continued
scanning the sky for an enemy target. Its 32.3 billion-megabyte
memory cycled through its threat library in six seconds, identifying the emissions as a fire-and-control system capable of targeting and attacking low-flying aircraft.

Using a UHF radio command downlink, hopping across several
frequency bands a second, the satellite sent a coded burst of radio
waves toward the B-1B, notifying the aircraft's radar homing and
warning sensors of a threat operating eighteen miles to the north
bearing 347 degrees.

Gladstone's attention shifted to the smaller computer monitor on
the right side of the main screen. The monochrome display showed
a preliminary real-time readout of what electronic emissions the
AFP-833 satellite was beginning to detect. THREAT WARNING: I/J
BAND—3.25 CM—9753 MHZ. He watched the numbers for a
moment, making sure they didn't change. Through previous tests
he had learned not to trust the first set of data. As long as the computer was still cycling through its software, there was the possibility the data could change. He checked his watch. *If everything was
working as advertised, the satellite should be broadcasting confirmed data right about now,* he thought. Just then the computer
hummed as it processed information and displayed the words: CON-
FIRMED THREAT: I/J BAND—3.25 CM—9753 MHZ.

A smile came across his fixed, pudgy face. "Hot damn. I love
to watch this son of a bitch at work."

ESFAHAN, IRAN

Perijan Reza adjusted the mask covering her nose and mouth as
she walked across the computer microchip-manufacturing room.
Dressing in a white smock from head to toe helped to protect the
sensitive gallium arsenide chip-manufacturing equipment from
contamination. The room was extremely compact, no more than
ten meters square, and well lit, with bright white walls to aid in
reflecting the illumination. Buried beneath the surface, the building's low ceiling had been doubly reinforced with steel and concrete. The wall behind Perijan's work area contained a row of
four large glass windows that overlooked another larger manu-

facturing area. The windows allowed the chief engineer to keep a constant eye on Perijan.

An odd-looking device, about half the size of a small car, was used to manufacture gallium arsenide chips. It rested on a pedestal that was bolted to the floor, and was fabricated with high-quality stainless steel the Iranians had purchased from Germany. From the center of the machine a seven-foot hollow tube, three feet in diameter, extended out. Eight voltage regulators, in a circle around the outside of the tube, were used to increase or decrease the flow of electricity and to control the numerous mechanical parts. Half-inch-diameter pipes, containing liquid nitrogen and solid gold electrical wires, were intertwined along the side and top, with another large cylinder being welded to the upper-left side housing a vacuum pump. Several thick glass portholes were along the sides allowing the operator to see the process inside the chamber. All of this was connected to a specially programmed computer using high-speed Digital Equipment Alpha 21064 and a 64-bit processor operating at 300 MHz. The computers had been reprogrammed by Perijan to monitor the internal equipment.

Perijan took a seat behind the computer terminal and studied the data on the monochrome screen. It being late in the evening she was having a hard time concentrating on her assignment. Operating the equipment that was Iran's only source for gallium arsenide chips was tiring and monotonously unending work. The breaks allowed were minimal, but adding to her languor was the certainty the chips were being used in missiles manufactured in the same building for some devious military plan.

Perijan had been one of a handful of researchers involved in the development of the chip technology. They based their research and work on the theories of Leo Esaki, a Nobel Prize-winning physicist. Although his work was thirty years old, Perijan and the other researchers were able to build and improve on his computations. Their variant of the superlattice used layers of pure gallium arsenide interchanged with layers of aluminum-gallium arsenide that had been activated with silicon atoms to form a base crystal. Using a process she had studied at MIT known as molecular beam epitaxy, or MBE, Perijan had refined the manufacturing process, discovering a way to grow computer chip crystals one molecular layer at a time. This produced meticulously accurate superlattice computer chips. The procedure had to be carried out within a vacuum and under a liquid nitrogen shroud that froze out any impurities in the vacuum chamber. Using a computer to vary the temperature of the vacuum, Perijan could control the density of the crystal's molecular structure at the base level, producing an advanced ultra-high-speed computer chip that could operate at near room temperature. The breakthrough should have propelled her into Iran's scientific elite, but she was still treated as a second-class citizen. It had been nothing more than a burden to Perijan and her father, and she regretted having worked on the project at all. The revolutionary government began to watch her more closely. Her work as well as her personal dealings came under close military supervision and scrutiny.

Perijan's efforts no longer centered on research. She was forced to do hands-on work with the weapons and infrared optical guidance systems. Her strict routine at the plant was overseen by the chief engineer, Khalk Hikmet.

"Perijan, I need you," a gruff male voiced boomed over the intercom.

Perijan tapped a few keys, quickly saving the data before she left her computer terminal. The intercom was not designed for two-way communication, but even if it had been, she couldn't have asked for a minute while she came to a stopping point in her work.

She went down a short flight of steps and past a series of air filtration systems until she came to the assembly area. This evening only she and one man were working in the underground complex. She gazed across the room, taking note of four portable steel carts. Resting on top were odd-shaped black cruise missiles. Each of the missile's access panels was open and it appeared that chief engineer Hikmet was making adjustments to the optoelectronic computers, ones she and the other members of the team had designed more recently.

The team consisted of several people but only six, specifically chosen, were allowed access to the highly restricted area. The two-level complex was designed to be efficient, but security was the priority. New and innovative material was being installed on these missiles, and it was imperative not to raise suspicions on any satellite photographs. Therefore, a garage had been built on top of one of the buildings housing the cooling system. It took years and many trips to clear out enough dirt for the limited space necessary. Any materials needed were then lowered by crane to the missile construction room on the first level. From there they were lowered into the assembly room. This was where laser disk guidance systems were installed, tested and adjusted. When completed, the missiles would be hoisted up and loaded within the concealment of the concrete garage above. Trucks would then transfer the missiles to their specific destinations.

Perijan pulled the white mask from her face, waiting for Hikmet to notice her. He stood over one of the monitors used to test the optical laser guidance disks.

"Perijan, what is the rate of chip production for the past two weeks?" the chief engineer finally said, glancing up from behind his eyeglasses.

"I have been running at maximum production. Eighteen chips a day," Perijan answered. Each day she posted the number of chips that were produced, and Hikmet himself checked it. He also operated the testing equipment, verifying the chips' quality. The haggard man walked around the table to face Perijan.

"That is not acceptable. You must double that production."

"It cannot be done. I am making them as fast as possible," Perijan protested without thinking. It was not wise for her to speak out in such a manner.

"Do not tell me what can and can't be done. We have received new orders and I will see to it that you double the chip production." Khalk Hikmet came closer. Reaching out, he stroked the side of her face. Perijan brushed his hand away. "You will need to assist me in programming the missiles' laser guidance diskettes."

"I will report you if you touch me again." She spoke firmly, trying to sound fierce.

"I don't need any problems from you, Perijan. Do you understand? *No problems!*" Hikmet glared at her with his teeth clenched. "I can have your father thrown in prison for your lack of cooperation. I will only have to tell them that you are not following my orders." Perijan lowered her head as Hikmet continued. "Your father is not doing well; that is what I hear from the guards. Perhaps you think it would not bother him to be locked up for a while."

"Of course I will make the chips as fast as I can. If you would only let me work uninterrupted . . . I could get it done." Perijan's voice cracked. Hikmet smiled. He knew the Phalanx Dragon project would not be successful without Perijan and he'd have to be careful.

"Remember, I am watching your every move, Perijan." This time Hikmet's face was expressionless as he waved her away. "Go back to what you were doing."

Perijan turned and hurried out of the room. She felt the tears choking up in the middle of her throat.

FALLON NAS, NEVADA

"Threat . . . threat. Spike bearing zero one three. It's looking this way," Lieutenant Hooter Rawlings called out, referring to the hostile radar picked up by their threat sensors. The newly installed satcom multifunction RHAW display, an eight-by-eight-inch CRT located to the left of his standard threat panel, indicated an enemy radar had just started painting the sky out in front of the Arapaho 127. It was amazing, because the standard RHAW sensors on board the B-1B weren't showing a damned thing. The radar warning computers were being cued by a satellite in the blackness of space somewhere above him.

Hooter punched a button on his console, downloading and compressing the coded data from the satellite. The transmission sequenced through the B-1B's defensive computer system where it reprogrammed into a compatible program and fed into the number one AGM-88C HARM missile. The internal guidance system and threat library of the missile consequently was now programmed with the hostile radar's position, operating frequency and distance to target.

"Threat identified. Ready to launch, sir," Hooter radioed from his position behind Duke.

"Open bomb bay," Duke grunted.

"Bomb bay open," the offensive weapons operator answered, hitting a series of switches opening the Arapaho's forward weapons bay.

Duke compensated the big bomber as it yawed slightly to the right when the weapons bay came open, locking into place. Not taking his eyes off the horizon, he counterbalanced with a little left rudder, holding her steady at 600 feet above the desert.

"On my mark," he called out, throttling back slightly to reduce the bomber's airspeed. His eyes went from the horizon to the instruments. The B1-B was operating perfectly. He waited for his airspeed to drop below 550 knots before giving the order.

"Now . . . magnum," Duke ordered, pitching the nose up five degrees.

Suddenly, out of the corner of one eye Duke saw the bright flash of a rocket motor igniting and pushing the missile beyond the bomber. The HARM seemed to be floating out in front of the B-1B, waiting to gain airspeed and altitude. Then it raced away, leaving only a trail of white smoke.

"One down, one to go," Hodges said.

"Yeah," Duke muttered, paying close attention to manipulating Arapaho's low-level flight. Wiping the sweat from his face with the back of his sleeve, he pushed the bomber's nose back down and came level at 600 feet.

General Gladstone had begun to notice a sharp pain in his neck and back as he continued to stoop over Garcia's shoulder. He was practically on top of the man, watching the monitor. A new symbol had appeared on the screen. The HARM had successfully been fired, indicated by the bright, thin yellow line accelerating away from the B1-B.

"All systems operating. We should be seeing the number two threat any time now," Garcia whispered. The telemetry for the TACTS told him everything was going as scheduled.

"There it is," Gladstone pointed. A new radar threat blinked a red warning on the screen. A dotted red circle was flashing to the north and east of the first fire control radar.

North of Arapaho 127, speeding above the desert at Mach 0.98, the white and black AGM-88C HARM's "fire-and-forget" high-speed antiradiation missile's seeker head picked up the first waves of enemy radar emission. The I/J-band transmission steadily grew stronger, snaking the missile closer to the radar. The cool morning air aided in its smooth maneuvers.

Two miles from the target, the internal guidance computer instructed the front canards to pitch the nose up. Pulling 20 Gs, the AGM-88C streaked toward the horizon at a forty-five-degree angle, climbing 12,000 feet a minute. At the top of its climb, 3,000 feet above the target, the missile pushed over, making one more course correction. With its rocket motor burned out, the HARM moved through the sky powered by sheer inertia and the pull of gravity. It broke Mach 1 before slamming into the radar's wire mesh emitter antenna located on a flat rock hill. The intense heat of the explosion turned the radar into a fiery mass of molten metal.

"New threat, bearing zero four seven. Fifteen miles northeast," Hooter warned, examining his satellite screen. "This one's an H-band and I'm showing some ECM." Electronic countermeasures were being used to try to jam the B-1B's and the HARM's electronics systems.

The signal from the first radar faded from the threat screen. A wide smile crossed Hooter's face. "Threat one destroyed. Repeat, threat one destroyed."

"Copy, Hooter. Ready number two," Duke commanded. Once the second HARM was fired, he would close the weapons bay, jam the throttles forward and head back east toward Edwards AFB. There was no way the fighters could find them now. Arapaho 127 would win this one, hands down.

"Number two ready," Hodges informed, then scanned the sky. Duke checked his airspeed indicator. They weren't above 580 knots. He inched back on the stick, taking the B-1B up to 800 feet.

"Magnum!" Duke shouted, his eyes solidly on the horizon.

"Magnum," Hodges repeated.

Suddenly, the B-1B rocked back and forth.

"Uh." A thunderlike rumble echoed in the cockpit, and Duke grabbed the stick with both hands. A split second later, a violent tremor ripped through the B-1B. The bomber instantly yawed right and nosed over toward the ground, vibrating savagely. The instrument panel lit up like a video game, red and yellow warning indicators flashing all over the place.

"Ah shit! What the . . ." Hodges screamed from the right seat.

Fire . . . engine four . . . Fire . . . engine four, the female voice of the computer warning system filled the flight deck.

A blast of adrenaline nearly took Duke's breath away. He inhaled the oxygen from his mask, trying to clear his mind. The B-1B was out of control, angled down toward the ground. A blurry brown desert sand filled the cockpit windows. The altimeter was falling quickly, they were below 500 feet . . . 480 . . . 460.

"We're starting to roll," Hodges yelled, hitting the extinguisher button, not trusting the automatic system. Halon gas filled the engine compartment, killing the blaze before it could spread any further.

Duke's muscles tightened as he struggled to maintain his pull on the stick. With all his strength he kept it back and to the left, then pushed the left rudder, trying to align the aircraft. The bomber's roll slowed, but she was still descending at a high rate of speed. The control stick abruptly started quivering in protest.

"Prepare to eject," Duke shouted. "Prepare to eject."

"No way! We're going too fast!" Hodges argued as the flight deck began to shake. The Arapaho 127 was becoming increasingly unstable.

Duke chopped the throttles back to idle. He pushed himself back, trying to put more back pressure on the stick.

"Come on, baby. Get your nose up. Get your nose up!" he pleaded.

Fire . . . engine three. Fire . . . engine three, the computer warning erupted.

"Shut it down, Hodges! Shut it down!" Duke yelled, as his gaze left the cockpit window and skimmed the instrument panel. Only the number one and two engines on the left side of the bomber were still functioning.

"We're losing hydraulics," Hodges called out.

"I see it . . ." Duke's shoulder restraints cut into his arms as he continued to haul back on the stick without success.

"Five hundred knots . . . 495," Hodges rattled off the numbers. "Four eighty-five. Down to 300 feet. General, you're going to lose her! We're going down!"

The B-1B started to roll again, this time to the left.

"Sweep the wings forward with manual override," Hodges was shouting into his oxygen mask. He looked over at James to see if he had heard, but all Duke's energy was clearly focused on getting the nose up.

The B-1B was configured with its wings swung back for maximum high-speed low-level flight. With any luck, the aircraft would stabilize when the wings were extended fully forward.

"Tell me when we hit 300 knots," Duke commanded. "Prepare to eject."

"No! General . . ."

"*I said, prepare to eject!*" Duke bellowed and strained to see out into the distance. There in front of them was the broken outline of a hill. Either he nosed the bomber up in the next thirty seconds or they would have to risk ejecting at high speed.

The jet's airspeed hit 438 knots and she trembled, resisting efforts to save her.

"Yeah, come on, baby. Don't fight me," Duke coaxed. The bomber's nose was coming up and away from the horizon. He kept steady back pressure on the stick until the windows were filled with deep blue sky.

The Gs built as the B-1B rolled to the left, its nose pointed twenty degrees above the horizon. Duke felt himself being pinned deeper into his seat. Three Gs, then four.

"Trouble, sir." Garcia pointed at the B-1B TACTS computer readout. The electronic pod, externally mounted under the bomber's left wing root, was linked directly into the bomber's avionics packages. It was broadcasting that only two of the bomber's four engines were operating. The data indicated a rapid loss of hydraulic fluid and several malfunctioning electrical systems.

"What the hell is going on?" General Gladstone dropped to one knee, evening his vision with the screen.

Garcia scanned the telemetry. There weren't any electronic signals emitting from the second HARM. It was as if it never existed.

"I never established contact with the last HARM, General. My guess would be that it either collided with the Arapaho or blew up seconds after launch."

Gladstone picked up the phone, linking him directly with the control tower at Fallon NAS. He knew they would be receiving the same telemetry as Garcia.

"This is General Gladstone at Falcon in Colorado Springs. Are you copying what's going on?"

"Yes, sir, we are. S and R have already been notified." The Navy chief responded professionally, as if it were an everyday occurrence.

The general placed the receiver down, unable to break his watch on the screen. "Damn it, Duke, get the hell out of there."

ESFAHAN, IRAN

Perijan exited the weapons complex with two security guards escorting her. She filled her lungs with the cool, fresh air. Even their annoying presence could not dim the exhilaration she felt when leaving. Having been forced to work a second shift made her outside world seem less dismal by comparison.

Perijan climbed back into the van. She watched the routine of the prison guards patrolling the perimeter of the outer fence several yards away. In the distance she could hear the barking of the guard dogs. She wondered briefly if they were really as vicious as they sounded.

The motor vibrated the van's interior as they sped through the open gates. In twenty minutes she would be home. Perijan's thoughts turned to her father; the idea of him being ill and alone, without her by his side, left her feeling torn and empty. She longed for the day when the government would no longer control her every movement, but she was frightened by the unknown prospects that might bring.

She watched the side streets and buildings flash by and smiled slightly when she noticed the lights of Esfahan had come on. The trip was the same on the way to and from the prison. *Even the opposite sides of the street look the same*, she thought. Perijan rested her head against the cool window, then closed her eyes.

FALLON NAS, NEVADA

Duke and Hodges kept their eyes glued to the airspeed indicator. It fluttered at 350 knots. The laboring B-1B's nose was pointing up at a sixty-degree angle from the ground, altitude 2,300 feet. Instantly, everything seemed to revert to slow motion.

Duke stole a quick glance over at his copilot. Hodges was also working vigorously, trying to make sure the bomber's avionics didn't shut down.

"Shit!" Duke hollered at the same time his stick froze solid. The B1-B lost its primary and two backup hydraulic systems. The aircraft became an uncontrollable piece of metal in midair. It shuddered, then slid backwards, tail first.

"*EJECT, EJECT, EJECT!*" Duke barked, holding tight and keying his internal mike. The Arapaho 127 had flipped upside down and was spinning violently to the left. With each second the G forces built, as the plummeting bomber picked up airspeed, whirling for the ground. The force of the spin slammed him against the side of the cockpit wall, his helmet bouncing off the window.

"*EJECT . . . EJECT . . . EJECT!*" he repeated desperately to his crew. A deafening roar filled the inside of the cockpit. The air surrounding him turned a frosty white with condensation from the rapid decompression. The aircraft shook again with a second blast. The two backseaters were safely away from the aircraft.

"One . . . thousand . . . feet," Duke grunted, looking over at Hodges. He was nearly out of his seat with the pressure of the accelerating spin. Duke stretched out his arm. Straining, he caught hold of his copilot and helped tug him to a straightened position in his seat.

"Now, Major . . . get out!" Duke ordered, at the same time tightening his muscles, consciously pulling his arms and legs closer to his body. With all his strength he righted himself in the ejection seat. Closing his eyes, he pictured Katie, then pulled the yellow handle, arming the Weber ACES zero-zero ejection seat. The second immediate tug on the handle blew him out of the swirling aircraft.

The images of red and orange flames from the ejection seat's rocket motor filled his mind. Because the bomber was spinning upside down, the seat initially propelled him down and away from the plane. The sophisticated gyro sensed that it had punched out toward the ground, reversed thrust instantaneously and drove him up and away from the fast-approaching desert ground.

Duke separated from his seat and caught sight of the B-1B several hundred feet below him. It was spinning wildly, with black smoke streaming out from the tail end. Intermittent flames shot out of the right wing root when suddenly the remaining fuel exploded, producing a round fireball. A gust of hot wind blew past Duke as flying chunks of metal sliced through the air. Stunned and not quite believing what was happening, Duke watched the Arapaho 127 hit the ground. His mind slipped into a numbness as he fell. *My God, what happened? Did everyone get out?*

The tug of his parachute's shoulder harness snapped Duke partially back to consciousness. His chute had suspended him above the ground, and he snapped his head around to look for the other parachutes.

A shadow passed over Duke, and he glanced up in time to see a black object racing toward him. An ejection seat released from one of the weapons officers was tumbling down overhead. Duke tried to swing his body to and fro to move out of the seat's path. It all happened too fast. The edge of the seat smashed the left side of Duke's helmet, splintering it into a dozen pieces, and everything suddenly grew silent.

TEHRAN, IRAN

Sheik Bakhtiar closed the worn Koran and walked across his empty office. The ministry building was now quiet; the office clerks and personnel had gone home to their families. The peacefulness of the evening allowed Bakhtiar time to pray and think about the plight of his country.

The defense minister folded his hands as if in prayer and stared at the full-length painting of the Ayatollah Khomeini on the far wall. He examined the man's face, searching the painted eyes, crow's feet extended out from the corners. The cheering and chanting of Khomeini's name from huge crowds filled his mind. He remembered the era . . . yes, it was a time when the Muslim world had reached its boiling point with its disgust for the West. All Muslims were called upon to build a single nation constructed on the foundation of Islamic law. Khomeini had told his followers, "We are at war against the infidels. Take the message with you, carry it to every land. I command all Islamic nations, all Islamic states and all Muslims to join the holy war. There are many betrayers to be killed and destroyed. Many countries that must be rebuilt in the name of Allah. The Jihad must triumph."

Khomeini taught that the Islamic revolution did not recognize boundaries or statehood; their teachings should be spread throughout the world, whether it was welcomed or not. That was before the Gulf War had blanketed a great shame and humiliation on all Arab people. Bakhtiar had warned that the United States still held a great hostility toward Arabs and Muslims. The warnings fell on deaf ears. The Gulf War's malicious air campaign, followed by the furious destructive force of the ground war, confirmed Bakhtiar's beliefs. *Now the people are lost, set adrift by the massive evil power of the West.*

Sheik Bakhtiar was not sure how long the struggle could continue without a triumph. The Israelis had made peace with the Palestinians and now Syria had joined the peace process, turning its back on Iran. For the most part, Iran's worldwide terrorist operation had been a failure.

Bakhtiar had watched the operations fall apart under the leadership of Prime Minister Mahmoudi. The Beheshita camp in Karaj, west of Tehran, had once turned out 300 female terrorists a year ready to travel to America, Great Britain or other major countries in the world. Now it was nearly empty. The Manzarieh Park camp in Tehran, the largest and best equipped, had not graduated a class in the past year. The only organizations he could count on to defend the revolution were the 150,000 troops of the Pasdaran and the Islamic Revolutionary Guards Corp. Yet, if his country were headed for civil war, even these soldiers could not prevent it.

"Minister Bakhtiar," said Hassan Zadeh, who had entered the office quietly, "I brought you the information you requested."

Bakhtiar turned; his face appeared strained and creased by hours of contemplation. He looked directly into Zadeh's eyes. The guard continued without prodding.

"Prime Minister Mahmoudi is scheduled to leave in four hours. He will be flying to Syria to meet with representatives of the British government. He plans to open a dialog with the West."

Bakhtiar's eyes shifted as he took in this information. Zadeh was skilled at establishing contacts and retrieving intelligence. *So Mahmoudi has his own plan.* He was traveling secretly to Syria without the approval of the Ayatollah Abdol-Rasul Hanifnezhad. *He must be counting on the death of Hanifnezhad to push our country toward the West. He wishes to bury the revolution with our leader.*

"When will he return?" Bakhtiar's mind began to race.

"Two days from now. Tehran airport."

Bakhtiar paced the floor, his hands folded in front of him. "It is time to contact Major Dahawa. Mahmoudi is a traitor to the Muslim cause."

"Yes, sir. I will arrange a meeting for tomorrow." Zadeh waited for Bakhtiar's nod, then left the defense minister alone.

Bakhtiar felt a surge of renewed energy. He no longer was drained with worry and indecision; a youthful decisiveness had taken its place. This was what he had been waiting for. Mahmoudi's arrogance would be his downfall. The sheik opened the Koran, then closed his eyes, repeating the words in prayer.

FALLON NAS, NEVADA

"That's all the information I need right now. I may have more questions later," Admiral Bailey Hollings said, closing his notepad.

"Any word on General James?" Hooter Rawlings asked,

stretching out his legs. It seemed that every muscle in his body was beginning to stiffen from the ejection.

"He's got one hell of a concussion, but other than that he should be all right. The doctors are keeping him quiet and are going to watch him overnight." The admiral moved toward the door of the briefing room.

"Admiral, I'd just like to add that I believe General James did everything he could to save the aircraft. It's just that everything . . . well, everything happened so fast . . ."

"I appreciate your comments, Lieutenant. You needn't worry about the briefing anymore. I'll be sure to report everything just as you told me. I'm just damned thankful we didn't lose anyone." He was standing over the two systems operators and smiled at them. "Both of you can take a shower now and I'll have some clean flight suits brought over for you." He could tell by their expressions they were still pretty shook up.

"Oh, and there's a C-5B scheduled to leave for Edwards at 1300. I've told the pilot both of you will be on it."

"Yes, sir." The two men glanced at each other, then Hooter asked, "What about Hodges?"

Hollings lowered his head. "He's not doing well, I'm afraid. The doctors have stabilized him, but it's still going to be a matter of time before they know for sure." He looked up at the two men and continued. "We're not sure what happened, or why, but it appears he was injured when he ejected."

There was a moment of silence in the room; then the admiral said good-bye and left with three pages of debriefing notes tucked securely away in his briefcase. He had spent at least two hours taking information from the Arapaho's defensive and offensive weapons officers. Along with the computer telemetry from the TACTS, he was beginning to put together a picture of what had happened out over the test range.

The intense throbbing in Duke's head brought him to. His panic came racing back.

"EJECT . . . EJECT!" Duke shouted, sitting up.

"Whoa, General. Take it easy," a young man in a white medical smock said, placing his hand on Duke's shoulder. He gently urged him to lie down. A nurse hurried to the other side of the bed to help restrain the general should he become too agitated. "It's all right, sir. You're in the hospital now."

Duke let out a short gasp as his mind focused on where he was. He closed his eyes, sinking slowly onto the pillow propped below him. *The bomber, or was it the missile?* Duke reflected. *Something malfunctioned. We were out of control, going into an inverted spin. We were headed for the ground. I gave the order to eject.*

He blinked twice, trying to clear his vision, and looked up at the blurry images standing over him under the fluorescent lights. The doctor and the nurse went through their routine of checking his pulse and temperature, while Duke's mind continued to swirl. *I was in a test flight . . . HARMS. We were test launching HARMS . . . OH MY GOD.* He Pulled the thermometer out of his mouth and sat straight up.

"My crew, did . . . did everyone make it out okay?"

"General James, if you would please lie back down, I'd like to finish this examination. You're damned lucky you didn't break your neck—"

"Listen, shithead! I asked you a fucking question." Duke had grabbed the man by the lapels of his smock and was glaring, his jaw set. "Did everyone make it out okay?"

"I'm sorry, General . . . I'm only trying to . . ." the doctor began apologizing, when the stout older nurse stepped in.

"Now, General, you behave yourself, or the doctor will have to give you a sedative. Let go." With maternal firmness, the nurse took hold of Duke's wrist until he loosened his grip. "There, that's better. Now, if you mean is everyone still alive, yes they are. But you'll have to let us finish what we're here to do before you can start firing off questions. Now, open wide and let's see if we can get this done in a jiffy."

Duke became placid, somewhat satisfied knowing the crew was at least alive. On a chair in the corner of the room he spotted his flight suit and splintered helmet. More images came flooding back, and he realized that his head, neck and shoulders were burning with pain.

"How long have I been out?" Duke asked after the nurse had removed the digital thermometer. He glanced up, trying not to look so gruff.

"About three hours. Your injuries are minimal, but we're going to keep you overnight just in case there was more damage than we could detect with the initial exam."

The doctor wrote on the chart, avoiding eye contact. "If there are any complications I'll have to order a CAT scan.''

"Do you mind telling me now how the rest of my crew is doing?"

"Two have already been released. Major Hodges, however, was in critical condition and had to be transferred to Las Vegas General. The facility there is better equipped. I'm sorry I can't tell you more than that; you'll have to wait for Admiral Hollings." The younger man forced a professional smile, then closed the chart. "I have other patients, so if you'll excuse me, I'll be back to check on you in the morning."

"Sure. Thanks, Doc," Duke murmured, regretting his heated words. Tact wasn't one of his strong suits.

The nurse finished dabbing the cuts and scratches on the right side of his face with disinfectant. He was sure she was being extra rough to teach him a lesson, so he deliberately didn't wince, though it hurt like hell. She began wrapping gauze around his head, then interrupted his accurate thoughts.

"I usually wrap this stuff all the way down around loud-mouthed generals if I have to."

"I'll bet you do, and you probably have a few more tricks for the really unruly ones, don't you?" Duke snickered.

"That's right, and don't you forget it." She picked up the metal tray with the dirty bandages and turned to leave.

Duke, not wanting her to get the last word, called after her, "Oh I won't, *Florence*. It was Florence, wasn't it?"

ESFAHAN, IRAN

The strained, dry coughing brought Perijan out of a deep sleep. She threw off her covers, quickly making her way to her father's room. In the darkness she could see him lying on his back, straining to breathe. His chest heaved between short bursts of strong, forceful coughing, and his face was contorted with pain.

"Father . . . father. You must sit up." Perijan used all her strength to lift her father to an upright position.

"What is it?" her father groggily protested, as he pushed himself up, leaning against the headboard. "Did I wake you? I am all right, Perijan, I'm sorry."

"Father, you cannot sleep lying flat like that. You should sit up. The doctors said that would help stop the coughing." Perijan brushed his hair out of his eyes. The room had a heavy, musty odor, as if it had been shut up for a long time.

He feigned a smile. "Perijan, you mustn't worry about me. I am just a sick old man whose time has come. If I am to die . . . then Allah wills it."

"No, Father," Perijan said softly. "You must not talk like that. If I lose you, then I have nothing left in this world. I will be alone."

The doctors had diagnosed him to be in the late stages of emphysema. She adjusted the oxygen hoses, which ran from the small tank next to his bed, and the two open tubes inserted in his nostrils. She turned the oxygen one level higher, hoping it would allow her father to sleep soundly.

"Nonsense, my child. You have your whole life ahead of you. Someday you will find someone to love and care for you. You have done so much for me, and I have been unable to take care of you the way I should have. This country has nothing to offer. You can leave. I want you to go back to America. I think you liked it there, didn't you? You were so happy when you came home." His eyelids grew heavy and fluttered. "I have not been a good father to you . . . I'm sorry, Perijan."

"You don't know what you are saying, Father . . . you are just tired. Now, try to get back to sleep. It will be light in a few hours." Perijan leaned over and kissed him on the forehead. She pulled the blanket up to his shoulders, tucking it in under his arms.

"Good night, Father," she said in a whisper.

FALLON NAVAL HOSPITAL

"General James."

Duke opened his eyes. Admiral Bailey was standing next to him.

"Admiral . . ." Duke let out a yawn, only to wince.

"How's he doing?" Admiral Bailey asked the doctor, who had followed him into the room.

"Besides his concussion, some cuts and bruises. No broken bones, though, and there's no sign of internal bleeding. He's a little beat up, but he'll be all right. I'm going to hold him overnight for observation. I'll leave you two alone."

Admiral Henry Bailey pulled up a chair next to Duke's bed. Ten years his senior, Bailey had been working with the general sporadically for most of the year. The admiral was a former fighter puke with 140 missions. He flew F-4s off the USS *Constellation* during two tours in Vietnam. He reminded James of his wife's uncle, quick witted and always with a joke to share.

"Duke, I don't know of any easy way to say this. So I'm just going to say it. Pete Hodges might not make it. He's in critical condition." Bailey folded his hands and looked at the tile floor. "His neck is broken and the doctors don't think he'll walk again if he does pull through."

Duke sucked in a deep breath and let it out slowly. *If the bomber hadn't stalled, everyone could have gotten out safely.*

"He was married, right?" Duke asked.

"Duke, there's no need for you to—"

"I'll find out sooner or later, so just tell me now."

"Yeah. Wife . . . and a little boy. You might as well go ahead and beat yourself up all the way," Bailey added, looking up at Duke. "Anne Hodges hasn't been notified yet."

"The other two guys did make it . . . right?"

"Yes, they're okay. What the hell happened up there, Duke?"

"God, I don't know . . . everything was going as planned until we launched the second missile." His right hand went up to his throbbing head, trying to straighten out the events. "Then, shit . . . I don't know for sure. I think the damned HARM exploded prematurely, knocking out the number three and four engines. The telemetry can tell you more than I can. Have you reviewed it?"

"Yes, I've seen it," Bailey answered noncommittally.

"Well, is that what happened?" Duke was irritated at the admiral's hesitancy to give him the detailed information.

"You know I can't discuss that even if I wanted to. You'll have to wait for the review board's final summary."

"What? Damn it, if it was my fault, I want to know!"

"Duke, I think you're overreacting, but if you think you might have been responsible for something that went wrong up there, it'd be best if you tell me now." Bailey sat upright in his chair and assumed a more professional role. "You know it's my duty to report everything said to me by the pilots and the crew. With Hodges out, I'm relying on you and the data we can gather to get to the bottom of this mess."

Duke's face grew even grimmer as he looked down at the floor. "Of course I think I did it right. You think I want to believe I'm responsible for Hodges . . ." The words choked in his throat. He wasn't sure he could be man enough to live knowing he might never fly again.

Bailey backed down. "Listen, why don't you get some more rest. I'll come back and maybe your head will be a little clearer." He stood to leave, then glanced over at Duke. Perhaps he should hunt for the doctor and get some information on the general's emotional status.

Duke didn't move. He let his thoughts drift slowly in his mind. He didn't believe in luck, but he never discounted it either. For whatever reason, Duke was still in one piece and Hodges wasn't. Finally, he sat up and slid off the bed. The cold tile floor hitting his feet helped to calm him, as if numbing his sensations. Every muscle in his body smarted as he made his way to the bathroom. Duke looked in the mirror at the deep wrinkles and dark circles under his eyes. Time was catching up with him. The man looking back at him no longer seemed to know the other.

Maybe it's time to hang it up, Duke thought to himself. Being the youngest major general in the Air Force was a high-pressure position for him and his family. In some ways, even more so than when he was a B-1B pilot stationed at Ellsworth in South Dakota. He would turn forty-four in November and had already accomplished more in his career than most pilots ever hoped. His retirement would be a distinguished one even now. *We could move back to the Black Hills and buy that cabin in Spearfish Canyon I always wanted. Yeah right,* he thought, *Katie would kill me. Living year-round in a cabin. She'd put up with it in the summer, but four feet of snow six months out of the year and me underfoot would be too much for her . . . and me.*

"Oh shit!" Duke abruptly said aloud. "I forgot to call Katie." Any word she had gotten of the crash would be vague and deliberately hopeful. The military didn't want to unduly mislead relatives, but it had been known to happen that in emergency situations wires had gotten crossed or confused.

The agreement between the two of them was that Duke would call if he were able and that if she didn't hear from him, she could start to worry. He hoped that Katie wasn't overwrought waiting for a message. A disturbing picture of Anne Hodges erupted in his mind, and he hesitated before picking up the phone. He looked forward to hearing Katie's voice but knew she would sense something was wrong in his tone. At this point, Duke wasn't even sure if he knew what was going on. He finally lifted the receiver. When everything else was coming down, he knew Katie would be there.

Chapter Five

By late Tuesday evening, General Duke James had endured just about all he could take in a single week. He felt tired and beat up, and his self-confidence had been shaken more than any time during his career. Right now he wished he could beam himself home to a cold drink and the arms of his wife, probably in that order, but first he had to meet with Howard W. Chaniff, the chairman of the Joint Chiefs of Staff.

He glanced out the backseat window of the staff car at the streams of headlights. Earlier in the day he had caught a military charter out of Fallon, then a commercial flight to Dulles. The only annoyance on today's flight was seeing the *USA Today*'s front-page story of his B-1B going down in the desert. It seemed "The Nation's Newspaper" had decided that an Air Force test aircraft going down would sell a lot of papers.

Duke ran his hand over his brow, only to jerk in pain—he had forgotten about his bandages. The doctor said he would probably be sore for the rest of the week. Duke tried to ignore the traffic around him, looking at the lights of the night sky instead. His mind drifted back to the accident, once again trying to piece together the various bits of information. The past thirty-six hours were mostly a blur, and to say he wanted desperately to wish them away was an understatement.

The doctors back at Fallon warned him to anticipate a mild case of depression and to not expect any restful sleep for a few weeks. It would be best if he'd take some time off and perhaps even visit the base psychologist. The young doctor explained that it takes the subconscious a while to come to terms with the shock. It was all part of what the shrinks called posttraumatic stress disorder or some crap like that, Duke recalled. Pilots put it more simply: getting the *shit* knocked out of you.

Now on his way to meet with the chairman of the Joint Chiefs, he tried to remember his version of what was relayed to Bailey. Duke wanted to make sure it was the same story he had told the debriefers back at Fallon. Debriefings were a funny thing. After a while one's mind begins to remember how things should have happened rather than the way they actually did. That was one of the reasons debriefers always talked to pilots immediately after a mission or accident, not after hours or days had passed.

"Another five minutes, General."

"Thanks," Duke replied without enthusiasm. He closed his eyes and rested his head on the back of the seat. The good news was in another hour and a half he would be home with his wife and kids. *Maybe then this insistent throbbing will stop,* he thought.

THE PENTAGON

Duke walked slowly, taking the stairs rather than the elevator to the chairman's second-floor office. Although the Pentagon was active twenty-four hours a day, the volume of people traversing the corridors slowed down after six in the evening.

"Good evening, General James." A sharp-looking female Army major rose from her seat.

"Good evening. I have an appointment to see—"

"Yes. General Chaniff is expecting you, sir," the woman interrupted, obviously in a hurry to finish her duties so she could leave. She picked up the phone, letting the chairman know that James had arrived.

"He'll be with you in a moment. Please have a seat." She nodded toward the brown leather couch. "May I get you a cup of coffee?"

"No, thank you, I'm fine." Duke took a seat, folded his arms and tried to relax. The reception area of the CJC was businesslike yet warm. Besides the usual military artwork, portraits of past chairmen and famous generals, the walls also contained several wildlife prints—the obvious personal touch of the new chairman. Chaniff enjoyed the outdoors, which was one of the few things he and Duke had in common.

Officially, General Chaniff was Duke's direct boss, although James also reported informally to Philip Radford, the secretary of defense. Howard Chaniff had succeeded General Jack Dawson as chairman nine months earlier after Dawson completed his second term. Unlike Dawson, who had spent his career in the Air Force, Chaniff had come to the top spot in the military via the Army. He had a reputation of being honest and hard-nosed with street-smart instincts. Also, unlike Dawson, Chaniff not only understood the military but understood Washington Beltway politics, which was somewhat unusual for a military man. It was an asset that couldn't be taught at the war college, which was something to his credit, Duke thought. Not being a West Point grad and still fairly young, Chaniff had been a surprise pick when the President offered him the top position over six other four-stars who had been jockeying for the position. Pentagon higher-ups had made sure Chaniff had checked all the correct boxes outside and inside the Beltway while he climbed the career ladder. By doing so, Chaniff knew which egos needed to be fed and which couldn't be bullshitted. In his short time as chairman, and in a town where powermongering was a way of life, Chaniff managed to keep the military's mission narrow and focused, with the least amount of negative media attention possible. The last thing he wanted was any branch of the armed forces coming up with a black eye. Knowing this, there wasn't any question in Duke's mind why he was waiting to see Chaniff. It was only a matter of time before he found out just how pissed off the chairman would be.

"General Chaniff will see you now," the major said, slightly raising her eyebrows.

"Thanks." Duke knew she meant either to warn him or to set him at ease, but he couldn't tell in his state of mixed emotions.

"James. How are you?" Chaniff walked out from behind his rosewood desk with an extended hand.

"Oh . . . I'm a bit bruised here and there but otherwise all right." Duke consciously shook hands firmly. Chaniff wasn't smiling, and his face gave telltale signs of late nights.

The two men were about the same height, six feet; only the

chairman weighed thirty pounds less than Duke. Chaniff's seasoned cowboy look was complete with a long face, thin arms and
legs, and even a protruding Adam's apple. His graying hair stood
straight up in a standard Army crewcut fashion, and his rugged
complexion boasted crow's feet around his eyes from his years
of field command.

"How about a drink?" Chaniff asked abruptly, indicating he
had other things on his mind besides Duke's medical condition.

"Sure, I could use one," Duke answered, following the chairman back to a small bar next to his desk.

"Let's see. Scotch . . . is that all right?"

Duke nodded and watched as Chaniff filled two glasses with
ice followed by a couple of shots of Cutty Sark. Not Duke's
favorite, but it would do.

The carpet was the same deep chestnut from Dawson's days,
with only the chairs appearing to be reupholstered. The wall to
the left of the desk was filled from floor to ceiling with pictures
of Chaniff's career starting back in Vietnam. The wall to the right
was entirely hidden by a bookshelf. The other half of the room
was organized to look somewhat like a living area, with a couch
and two armchairs. In the middle of it all was an oak coffee table
with the latest copies of Proceedings and Air Force magazine
placed neatly on top.

"Well, Duke, you've had a hell of a week." Chaniff handed
him a glass, then walked over to one of the armchairs and ges-
tured for Duke to sit in the other.

"Yes, sir," Duke replied, not drinking from his glass. He
looked at the lights of the Washington and Jefferson memorials
out the window.

"I'm sorry to hear about Hodges, but needless to say I'm glad
you made it." Chaniff paused, putting his glass to his lips. "Can
you tell me what happened out there yesterday?"

Duke gave the chairman a brief summary of the events as best
he could, then stared into his glass. "I know you've read the
reports and it's all spelled out there."

Chaniff sighed. "Yes, I've read what you reported to Admiral
Bailey, and his own conclusion as well. I've also reviewed what
the two backseaters reported and have gone over the radar telemetry at least a dozen times. At this point, it's conclusive the second
HARM exploded, causing the fires in the engines. Unfortunately,
none of the reports can give us an accurate account of what hap-

pened to Hodges, but that was no fault of yours, Duke.'' Chaniff stopped again, this time looking directly at him. ''What I want from you is a no bullshit answer. Are you dealing with this, or do you need to take some time off?'' Chaniff's tone was even but strained.

Duke stared at the ice cubes in his glass for a moment, swirling them counterclockwise in the scotch. *Bailey must have listened to that overzealous, paranoid doctor,* he figured silently. *I shouldn't have popped off on him like that. They probably think I'm crackin' up.*

Finally, he cleared his throat. ''Sir, I'm not going to sit here and tell you that I'm not a little bothered by all this. I am responsible for the crew and if I could remember what was going on when Hodges and I ejected, I might feel better, but I do know I was doing my job. And I have to believe that I did my best to save the aircraft and get everyone out safely.''

''Well, we may never know, but right now I've got bigger problems of my own. Public relations people have been breathing down my neck and I've talked with at least ten congressmen— and the President, of course. They're all asking the same questions. What the hell happened? Are there more problems with the B-1B, and is the Air Force trying to hide something from Congress? Not to mention the damned press is having a field day with another botched military toy that costs the taxpayers money.''

''General Chaniff, if you've called me here to chew out my ass, you're a little late. I've already done that myself. The fact is, I'm qualified to assess B-1Bs and the testing of new weapons. Until proven otherwise, neither one is useless and I believe what happened was just a fluke. There's always the possibility of a weapons malfunction, and if you're worried if I'm capable of giving a reliable review, then . . .'' Duke tried to keep his tone measured, but his voice quavered and Chaniff interrupted.

''Hold on, General. I didn't mean to imply anything like that. But let's be honest with each other. You're not getting any younger, and by the tone of your voice, I'd say you're more than a little bothered. Flying is a young man's game. I know Dawson chose you for this job because you weren't afraid to get your hands dirty. But I need an adviser who's going to make solid choices, not embarrassing ones. Shit, this will set us back a year with the House Armed Services Committee. I don't need this when I have to fight for every red cent in the defense budget.''

"So what are you saying? Am I fired?" Duke said, not changing his expression.

"*No*, but I want you to take some time off. Think about where your career is going. Maybe you should consider taking a staff position here at the Pentagon. I'll see to it you get another star, and you can take your pick of field commands in a year or two. Besides, when was the last time you spent a weekend with Katie and the kids? Hell, you've served your country for a long time and have done it well . . ." Chaniff slowed, choosing his words carefully. "I just think you're wound too tight. Take some time to think things through . . . that's all I'm asking."

"Yes, sir. Is there anything else?" Duke asked coolly, looking at his watch.

"No, that will be all." Chaniff sighed, then rose as Duke set his untouched drink down and turned, leaving the chairman's office. He stood watching after Duke and cursed his job for having to question a general of such high caliber.

General Howard Chaniff looked at the wall clock across from his desk, watching the second hand tick off a few seconds. It was 9:16 P.M.; he had missed dinner . . . again. He had called his wife earlier, and she sounded disappointed but at least didn't nag him. By now she was probably sitting alone, curled up watching the AMC channel or on the phone with her sister. They knew when he took over the chairmanship it was going to cut into their time together. Chaniff just hoped he could settle into a more civil routine in a month or two. Right now, a ten-hour day sounded like a vacation.

Chaniff examined Duke's personal file one more time. The forty-three-year-old two-star's career started out as mundane as most did when working their way up the ranks. James had toed the line, following orders like every other flyboy in the Air Force. Most of the stats about the general were not only military knowledge, but had become public after a magazine article had been printed about the *Atlantis* shuttle mission James piloted a few years ago. Chaniff read over it anyway.

James wasn't an Academy grad, which certainly didn't set him on the fast track to the top. He had gone to school at Colorado State University, joined the Air Force a year after graduation and married, a must if an officer was to climb the ladder. *Well, he definitely has good taste,* Chaniff thought, staring at a picture in the file. Katherine James was a slender brunette with full shoulder-length hair and dark eyes. Her high cheekbones and olive coloring made him wonder about her ancestry. The expression on her face let Chaniff know she had acquired the same temperate confidence he had seen in many career officers' wives.

Chaniff looked at a recent picture of James and his family. He had three children, two boys and one girl. As a lieutenant, Duke copiloted B-52s before moving into the left seat of F-111s in the late '70s. He had also been assigned to work as an instructor pilot at Mountain Home AFB in Idaho, as well as at several overseas deployments. He spent eighteen months in Italy as a liaison for the Army, and in the early '80s James returned to the States to fly B-1Bs out of Ellsworth in Rapid City, South Dakota.

The chairman sat back, holding the file eye level. That was the beginning of Duke's career climb. He had piloted a prototype B-2 stealth bomber, code-named Nightstalker, into the Soviet Union, destroying one of their most advanced early warning centers. The mission was still classified as deep black, and Chaniff had only learned about it six weeks before becoming chairman. Duke then jumped to the astronaut corps, piloting the *Atlantis* on an ill-fated mission to rescue a Russian satellite. That mission had ended in the desert of northern Chad.

Well, James isn't afraid to try new career opportunities. I know quite a few officers who would prefer to follow the straight and narrow until they retired, then buy a condo on a nice golf course near a beach.

Chaniff understood why James continually put himself in the pilot's seat. It was one thing to evaluate a weapons system, tell the men flying the aircraft how to use it and write up a neat little report knowing your bosses in Washington would approve. But it was another to feel what it was like to fly the aircraft and have firsthand experience of the weapons being tested. James would always be surrounded by controversy, with his aggressive personality. *Hell, I guess I'd rather have a man like James advising me than some kiss-ass career bureaucrat who hadn't seen the outside of the Pentagon in ten years,* Chaniff thought, *and finished the rest of his scotch.*

ESFAHAN, IRAN

Perijan Reza sat alone in a sectioned-off corner of the underground weapons complex. She closed her eyes, the hum of electrical motors lulling her to sleep. After getting her father back to sleep, she had stayed awake the rest of the night, staring into the darkness. Perijan's thoughts kept drifting to her sick father, and she wished the day would end so she could return home.

The computer software sequenced a second time, and Perijan hit the keys and typed in a new set of commands. She watched the red and yellow lights, located on the side of the monitor, pulsating in rapid sucession, letting her know the optical hard drive was working.

The software program she was using had taken nearly two years to write and fine-tune. Perijan had designed the program to authenticate the quality of the holographic reflections imprinted on the storage disks by the infrared imaging camera. One of the principal problems she had encountered in developing the optical storage system was finding a photorefractive material that could store an electronic-charge pattern and at the same still be modified, copied and updated without losing the original image. She had found that by blending the precise combinations of some of the same materials used in high-speed semiconductors, 63.7 percent lithium niobate, 18.1 percent lithium tantalate and 18.2 percent potassium dihydrogen phosphate, a small dense photorefractive crystal could be produced. These crystals were then grouped in an array five inches in diameter, allowing them to be altered into a storage device using two intersecting 80-milliwatt output lasers. Once formed, the disks looked similar to a standard compact disk that could be purchased in any music store: round, silver and lightweight.

This crystal array allowed Perijan's computer system to produce a near-perfect holographic infrared image with an incredibly high memory speed. The holographic image could be imprinted or retrieved at over 160 megabytes of data per thousandth of a second. The only problem was she hadn't found a consistent way of testing the quality of the crystal storage arrays until after they had been encoded by the optical laser. Consequently, each disk had to be removed and tested after being encoded with data.

Perigan pressed the proper sequence of keys instructing the computer to compress a holographic image into digital form. Next to her workstation was a black box, an optoelectronic computer, approximately three times the size of an old-fashioned manual typewriter. The interior was packed with high-speed gallium arsenide microprocessors, gold and platinum-plated circuits and coils of optical fiber ribbons. She called it an "optical image amplifier"; in reality, it did nothing more than test holographic disks. Basically, the device transformed electricity to readable light patterns and back again using super-high-speed optical fiber ribbon and the gallium arsenide chips.

"I suggest you work faster." Chief Engineer Khalk Hikmet had walked up behind Perijan, stirring her out of her relaxed state.

Perijan froze and wondered how long the disgusting man had been watching her.

"You are taking too long. Now, speed it up." Hikmet moved closer until he was less than a foot away. He then placed a hand on her shoulder and smiled, showing his brown teeth. "Why is it, Perijan, that you always drag your feet? Is it because you do not believe in the cause? Maybe I need to motivate you."

"This process cannot be accelerated. You know that," she said softly, remaining perfectly still. "I assume you wish it to be done properly."

"Of course, Perijan," his voice more gentle this time because she didn't recoil from his touch. "You have another thirty minutes to complete the test and transfer the storage disks to me."

She looked up at her monitor just as it flashed, slowly materializing in color. A three-dimensional television-quality infrared image of a large ship appeared on the screen. The image was crisp and clean, with only an occasional wavy line or two. It looked like the massive hull of a supertanker.

"Very good." Hikmet grinned. He had removed his hand and was standing next to her now. "The quality is better than I expected."

The image remained constant for thirty seconds, telling Perijan the disk had captured it completely. She commanded the computer to make a backup copy. *A supertanker.* Perijan studied the image. This was the first time they had imaged a nonmilitary ship. Previously, she had tested only optical diskettes containing images of Saudi Arabian and Iraqi command and control structures, Kuwaiti naval destroyers and several dozen Western warships and aircraft. Perijan estimated that Iran had accumulated several hundred disks containing the IR holographic images of military targets. However, never were there any that were civilian.

I wonder what they are up to.

"There, that should do it," Perijan whispered under her breath as she watched the computer's LED readout flicker off, telling her the software program had stopped cycling. She reached over and shut off the workstation, then opened the black box containing the optical image amplifier.

Resting in the center compartment was a row of eight gray-and-white crystalline disks. Two of them were shiny silver but waxy to the touch, a result of the holographic storage process. She carefully removed the first two, holding only the edges, and placed them in a protective Plexiglas container.

Perijan quietly emerged from the work area. Hikmet had left her alone and was now standing over a nose section of a cruise missile. There were four missiles undergoing final assembly. Two of them still had open access panels. The area was well lit, and Perijan could see Hikmet inserting an optical laser gyration unit from across the room.

"I have finished," Perijan finally said, walking toward the chief engineer. She set the disks on a table a few feet away, then backed away.

Hikmet straightened up and checked his watch. *So she decided to complete the task without any other delays*, he thought.

"You confirmed the quality of the disks?" he asked gruffly.

"Yes. The images are complete."

Hikmet's thin lips curled into a smile. "Very well . . . you may go home now."

Perijan nodded. She turned and walked toward the front of the complex. Hikmet stared after her. To him she would always be beautiful poison. The last man who tried to seduce Perijan was put in prison and by now was probably dead. If she was going to have a relationship, it would be one that the government decided would benefit them. No one else would be allowed to interfere with their valuable possession, and as long as she continued to do her job and provide useful technologies, she would be protected.

I'm the one who should be getting the credit for this project. I have to keep her working or she would sit around all day and dream.

Picking up the disks from the table, he headed toward the back of the room. Lined up along the far wall, like large black logs, were the four cruise missiles. Hikmet had been working on two of the missiles for the past twelve hours, readying them for flight. All that the missiles needed were formatted disks for their guidance computers.

Hikmet removed one of the IR holographic disks from the black box, making certain he didn't smudge the surface with his fingerprints. Located six inches in front of the warhead was a miniature optical computer driven by two powerful gallium arsenide chips. The computer used two intersecting lasers to read the crystalline surface of the diskette. This produced the holographic image of a specific target. The cruise missile's IR targeting computer compared this image to a realtime optical image picked up through its IR-imaging nose camera. Once the missile was airborne, the two computers worked in unison to find the target. The system was passive and fast, allowing the missile to home in on a precise target within seconds.

The Iranian engineer snapped the disk solidly into place. If it jarred loose in flight, he would definitely take the blame. Hikmet closed the access panel, tightening it with four stainless steel screws. The missile could now be hoisted to the surface, where it would be fueled and mounted to an F-4E.

TEHRAN, IRAN

"This is the place. Drive around the back and stop at the door," Hassan Zadeh ordered the driver once they passed the front of a large warehouse. As the defense minister's personal bodyguard, Zadeh could use the car for the official and personal business of the minister. In either case, the driver was expected to perform his duties obediently and confidentially.

Zadeh glanced in the rearview mirror for anyone who might be trailing them. When convinced it was safe, he nodded for the driver to turn the black Mercedes-Benz down a long, narrow alley cluttered with piles of trash. The man maneuvered the car around the broken bottles, rotting boards and decomposing cardboard boxes.

Located on the southern edge of Tehran, in a dilapidated section of the city, the abandoned six-story building was once a clothing factory that had employed several hundred women and children. When one section of the third floor collapsed, killing twenty-one workers, the building was condemned. The plant was closed and people moved from the area in search of other jobs. The neighborhood was now a slum filled with vagabonds and tramps living in the vacant structures, eating from the piles of garbage.

The driver parked the car in a secluded spot behind the warehouse and turned off the ignition. Zadeh reached under his suit jacket, grabbing the handle of his Heckler & Koch P9S 9 mm pistol. The customized black rubber grip fit firmly in the palm of his hand. He flipped off the safety. Because of its unusual concealed double-action hammer, the P9S had a protuding indicator pin when cocked. Zadeh subconsciously would periodically stoke the pin to prevent any unfortunate accidents. He inspected the area before exiting the car. If someone should happen to spot them and take notice of their presence, it would be an ill-fated day for them.

Without speaking, he opened the car door and stood for a moment, his eyes scanning the area from behind mirrored sunglasses. Keeping his right hand on the pistol, he then proceeded inside the building through a broken metal door.

The building's interior was dark and shadowy. *Perfect location for an ambush*, Zadeh thought. Boards had been nailed across the windows, but streaks of sunlight cut through the air. The strange images were cast on the walls, making it difficult to probe the room for hidden dangers. Someone had taken a can of black spray paint and scribbled antigovernment slogans on the rough, worn walls. His every step echoed through the empty building. The floor was littered with splintered glass and large pieces of ceiling tile. Zadeh's keen sense heightened with the unavoidable noise he was making. If someone waiting hadn't heard the car, they had definitely heard his footsteps.

Eighteen miles from the center of the city, with the nearest government office three miles to the north, this was the perfect place for a rendezvous. But he also knew it would be the right place for a double cross. He crept down a long hallway leading to a larger room near the front of the building, in the center of which Zadeh could make out the shapes of a table and two chairs.

Suddenly, a subtle movement caught Zadeh's attention. A shadow had crossed the wall in the distance. He moved against the wall and slid down toward the floor, crouching. He pulled out his 9 mm, holding it with both hands straight out in front of him. Creeping toward the end of the hall and staying low, he squinted, straining to spot any movement.

There was more than one person moving about in the room. When Zadeh reached the end of the hallway, he stopped and straightened up. He could smell the odor of cigarette smoke. For a second he closed his eyes, trying to picture how the room would be laid out. He sucked in a deep breath, rotating around, and burst into the room with his pistol ready. His eyes swept the shadowy room in less than a heartbeat. He pointed his 9 mm, drawing a bead on the head of a man standing at the back of the room. There was just enough light for Zadeh to see the man's eyes open wide.

"What do you want?" The man slowly dropped his cigarette to the floor, crushing it with the front of his boot. He didn't seem startled at all by Zadeh's presence, much less by the fact that there was a gun aimed directly at him.

"Who else is here?" Zadeh asked, keeping his hands steady.

"No one. I chased a tramp out who had been sleeping on the floor," the man answered, motioning toward an exit. Zadeh leaned over, looking out a crack in the boards. He spotted a man clambering away down the sidewalk.

"You should have arrived an hour early to clear the place, Major Dahawa." Zadeh used the Iranian army officer's name to let him know he was facing his designated messenger.

"Yes, well, you probably should have done the same. But that is of no consequence now, is it?" The major reached in his pocket and pulled out another cigarette, lighting it. Zadeh could see the man could care less what he thought. "Lower your gun if you're not here to shoot me."

Zadeh brought the pistol to his side but left the safety off. Dahawa coughed and motioned toward the chairs.

Zadeh ignored the gesture as he watched the major walk out from the shadows. The man's wiry build fit the minister's description. His thin face appeared gaunt, even with his full, dark mustache. The hard eyes that bore into Zadeh's stare reassured him the minister had chosen the right person for this mission.

"I am here to offer you a deal if you carry out a priority mission," Zadeh finally said. "If you choose to accept, your wife will be set free from prison. The two of you may leave Iran or stay here with protection." Major Dahawa's wife had worked for a wealthy Iranian businessman in the northern town of Tabriz as a bookkeeper and private secretary. Three months ago she had been falsely accused of embezzling money from the man's business and was incarcerated. Major Dahawa's hard gaze didn't change. It was obvious he trusted no one.

"And what is the price?"

"You are to assassinate the prime minister." Zadeh spoke slowly, his deep voice barely audible. The two men stared at each other in silence.

The major was a Kurdish Muslim who had started his career in the army as a tank commander with Iran's 2nd Guards, or Imam Riza Brigade. At one point he worked directly for Bakhtiar as a special assistant. His assignment required him to provide the Supreme Defense Council with written reports on Iran's ability to fight another prolonged tank war against the Iraqi Republican Guards. He also worked on the prime minister's security staff, arranging armored transportation for members of Iran's ruling government. Consequently, Dahawa had firsthand knowledge of motorcade routes and the security pattern that the prime minister would be most likely to follow.

When the Kurdish Democratic Party announced it would no longer abide by Iranian laws, Dahawa was forced from the Iranian military.

If he refused to perform this mission for the defense minister, he knew Zadeh would have instructions to shoot him. And if he accepted and was caught, he would also be a dead man. Either way, life had not treated him fairly.

"What is the plan?" Dahawa broke the silence.

"Tomorrow evening the prime minister, returning from Syria, is scheduled to land at Tehran airport at 6:00 P.M. As always, his jet will park on the north side of the main terminal, away from the other aircraft." Zadeh's tone was even and calculated as he kept a watch on Dahawa's hands. "I have learned that he plans to drive directly to his residence from the airport."

"So only his standard security team will be in place," Dahawa thought aloud.

"Tomorrow morning I will have a messenger bring you a new uniform, a current security badge, a pistol and a rifle. There will be a car waiting for you in front of the Air France ticket counter." Zadeh pulled out a thick brown envelope and tossed it at the major, hitting him in the chest. "There is twenty-five thousand American dollars, two passports and two American driver's licenses. One is for you and the other is for your wife."

"And what about the airline tickets? What about my wife?"

"I will pick you up once the prime minister is dead and take you to a military transport aircraft. You will be flown to Bandar Abbas, where you and your wife have been booked on the first flight to Paris." Zadeh hesitated, wanting the man to understand the meaning of his words. "You will get your tickets and another twenty-five thousand only if the job does not bring attention to the defense minister."

"Of course, and if you double-cross me, I'll come after you next," Dahawa threatened.

Zadeh raised his pistol again, leveling it at Dahawa's head. "If you should be thinking of other options, I will see to it that your wife is killed, and if you fail or are captured, I will personally send a bullet through your heart."

"Death would only be a welcoming peace for my wife, and I have already died, so you cannot threaten me." With that, the major turned his back on the gun and slid between two boards, disappearing into the shadows.

The scent of roast chicken hung in the air as Perijan entered the kitchen.

"Father, why are you up? You should not be on your feet."

"When you come home so late, I know you are hungry and tired." Her father's voice was raspy, and he swayed a little as he stirred the contents in the pot on the stove. Suddenly, he slumped forward. "Help me, Perijan . . . help me to my room . . ." His voice trailed off. Perijan rushed to him, holding him up the best she could.

"Oh, Father . . ." She half-carried him while he staggered along. He closed his eyes once on the bed. His sweaty chest swelled and she could hear the strain of his breathing. Next to his pillow she spotted a white cloth blotched with dried blood.

"I am so sorry I had to leave you." She straightened his body, trying to make him more comfortable on the bed. His face was beaded with sweat. Perijan fought back the tears. "Papa . . . why didn't you call for help?"

"I called the hospital, but they didn't come. I felt better later . . . I didn't know where you were . . . I didn't know what else to do." His eyes began to fill with tears.

"They promised they would come, Father. They promised me they would send someone if you needed them." Perijan reached out and took hold of her father's hand. She could feel it trembling, and pulled the covers up around him. *I never should have trusted them. I should have been more forceful in demanding care for my father.*

"I will talk with them again tomorrow," Perijan said, her voice tranquil. "Everything will be all right. They can make you well again." Perijan did not believe her own words. She sat in a chair next to his bed, contemplating her demands. Her eyelids grew heavy and she fell asleep in the chair, not wanting to leave her father alone.

Duke James climbed into his Chevy Suburban and sat for a moment. He replayed the conversation with Chaniff over and over in his mind.

Maybe Chaniff is right, Duke thought. He had to be candid with himself. Spending half his life moving from air base to air base could be taking its toll. Matt, his oldest, was nearly twelve and Duke couldn't remember the last time he had taken him fishing or had gone to a ball game with him. Matt wasn't outwardly complaining or showing any signs of neglect, but Duke knew that before long his son would be a young man. Pam, being his only daughter, would always be daddy's girl, he thought. Sean was still at the age where Mom was the most important person in his life. And, of course, while he was off keeping the world safe from bad guys, Katie was left with all the responsibility and headaches. Perhaps she wasn't as happy as she appeared to be, either.

He started the engine, pulled out of the Pentagon parking lot and headed home.

Unlike most of the Pentagon brass, who lived in the Alexandria and Arlington areas a few minutes from work, Duke and Katie had selected the town of Stafford. Located thirty-five minutes south of Washington, the community was quiet and slower-paced than the cities and towns of the Beltway. In Duke's opinion, it offered a better atmosphere to raise their family. Duke liked the town; it even reminded him of the Black Hills when it snowed. The town was filled with pine and hardwood trees and the streets were always clean.

Katie and Duke had purchased a two-story brick town home with three bedrooms and a finished family room in the basement. Katie called it comfortable, but not their dream home.

There was a bike in the middle of the driveway, so Duke had to park on the street. He grabbed his flight bag and jumped out of the Suburban. He whistled loudly as he jogged up the brick walkway to the front door.

"Daddeee! Daddeee . . ." Sean, dressed in Disney's 101 Dalmatians pajamas, ran across the living room floor holding a crayon drawing. Duke dropped his bag and lifted the boy up, giving him a big hug and kiss. "Look what I made you, Daddy. It's a big plane."

"Why, thank you." Duke took the drawing and turned it, trying to tell which was the top of the paper. "You made this for me?"

"Yes, Mommy said your other big plane broke and she cried in bed, I heard her." Sean stuck out his lower lip and looked at the floor as if he were about to cry.

"Hey, kiddo, it's okay. I made it home and Mommy will be okay now." Duke gave Sean another hug, then put his lips together and blew on the boy's cheek. It made a loud noise and Sean laughed. "Can I take this one to work with me and hang it up in my office?"

Sean nodded.

Duke looked up to see Katie standing in the kitchen doorway. She was wearing a pair of faded Levi's with a wine silk tank top. The color accentuated her dark eyes and hair. Their eyes met and her lips curled into a tender smile. He wondered how long she had been standing there watching him.

"Welcome home, General," Katie said softly, her eyes watering.

Duke set Sean down and patted his behind, saying, "If you look in Dad's flight bag, you'll find a surprise."

The two met halfway and locked in a tight embrace. Neither one spoke a word. Duke stroked her hair and let the tension release from his body. He took her small face in his large hands and looked into her sparkling eyes and knew what she was thinking.

"I'm sorry, Katie. It scared the hell out of me, too," Duke whispered, pulling her close to him.

"I thought you'd never get home." Katie had cried all the tears she had the night before, not wanting Duke to see just how devasted she really had been. She grabbed Duke's hand and led him into the living room. He looked over his shoulder in time to see Sean pulling out a small plastic model of an F-16 Falcon. The boy began swishing the plane through the air while making jet engine sounds.

An open bottle of red wine and two glasses were on the living room table. Duke sat in an overstuffed chair, while Katie sat on the footstool in front of him, pouring the wine.

"Where's Matt and Pam?" Duke asked, taking a sip of wine.

"Over at Marilyn's. They're going to spend the night." Katie ran a hand up Duke's leg.

"Sean didn't want to go?"

"You know he doesn't like to do that yet, even at my sister's, who would feed him nothing but marshmallows and ice cream if he wanted." She paused, half-expecting Duke to make some wisecrack about her sister, as he normally did. "Well, I'll put him to bed early."

"You don't have to, I'll do it. I wish you'd let Matt and Pam stay, too. They wouldn't have been in the way." Duke gulped his wine and reached for the bottle to refill it.

"I'm sure Marilyn would drive them back . . ."

"No, I didn't mean that. I just thought they'd be here, that's all."

For a moment it was silence. Then Katie asked, "You want to talk about it?"

"Talk about what?"

"The crash. How you're feeling right now. Duke, you and I have been together too long to play the guessing game. Now, what's bothering you?"

"The fact is, Katie, I'm tired of answering the same damn questions over and over again. I'll tell you the same thing I've told everyone else. The missile blew up. After that the bomber went out of control and I did my best to get everyone out safely. Why Hodges . . ." Duke looked at the floor and put his hand up to his mouth, slowly moving it over his face as he sighed. "I don't know what to tell you. Why is everyone so worried about me? Hodges is the one you should be concerned about."

"I'll tell you why, Duke James. Just because you think you're some tough fighter pilot doesn't make you immune to emotions. They don't give you shots for that down at the base medical center, and you're just not behaving like yourself." Katie squeezed her husband's leg to emphasize her words.

"Not you, too. Did Chaniff call you?" Duke turned burning eyes on Katie. She knew she had hit a nerve but wasn't sure which one. "You think I need to *retire* . . . or maybe get a nice neat little consultant's job at A-1 Aerospace Corporation. Yeah, that's me. Suit and tie every day, with martinis after work. I can teach them how to talk military jargon and how to sell airplanes to the Pentagon and any chicken-shit country wanting to start a war. No emotion or strain in that line of work."

"That's not what I meant, and you know it."

"Well, I think Chaniff thinks so. He's told me to take a few weeks off. Think about my career. Katie, I don't want to sit behind a desk . . ." Duke's voice grew flat.

"Honey, slow down. Listen to yourself. You of all people should know that I wouldn't expect *you* to do that." Katie's good sense told her it was time to end the discussion. "Get up. Come on, march your butt up those stairs, mister, and I'll be up to run you a hot bath. I want you to get a decent night's sleep." She pulled him by his hands, getting him to stand, then pointed him in the direction of the stairs. "When you wake up in the morning and remember what you said, you're going to feel like a damn fool."

"You're right. Maybe that's what I need to do." Duke spun around and grabbed Katie by her waist. He closed his eyes and reached down, touching her soft hands. *Why do I always take things out on her.* "There's always a good woman behind every man," Duke said, then placed his mouth on hers and kissed her hard.

He left her startled, and walked out of the room.

"I love you, Duke," Katie whispered after a few moments.

Chapter Six

Major Raffi Dahawa thought over every minute detail of his plans
once more. One small mistake could mean failure and sure death.
Bakhtiar had been true to his word; the major had been cleared
to take the roof position on building 1701, overlooking the tarmac. The location was ideal for an assassination. The only problem was, Dahawa would be joined by a second security guard
before the prime minister's plane landed. That obstacle would
have to be dealt with in a quiet and effective manner.

He checked that his military camouflage fatigues were up to
regulation before climbing the stairs on the south side of building
1701. He didn't need an overly enthusiastic senior security officer
stopping him for something stupid like a misbuttoned shirt or
boots that weren't polished. A black beret neatly topped his head
and military-issue sunglasses hid his eyes. He had shaved and
trimmed his unruly mustache, and while that helped, his face still
remained hollow-looking.

Strapped to the right side of his belt was a black leather holster
containing a cocked 9 mm, along with several extra magazines
of ammunition. The other side held a two-way radio and a heavy
aluminum flashlight. From all outward appearances he was a
guard assigned to defend the prime minister. Even the photo ID
pinned to his left breast pocket was accurate in every way.

Slung under his left arm was a German-made G3SG/1 sniper rifle. The security forces carried AK-47s, AKS-74s and even some American-made M-16s. These weapons were openly displayed as a show of force.

The side entrance, located away from the main terminal, was used by foreign dignitaries and airline pilots. Dahawa knew it would be guarded by standard airport security personnel using metal detectors and X-ray machines. He had used the entrance before in his previous occupation and hoped no one would recognize him.

A blast of cool air hit his face as he opened the door and walked inside the air-conditioned building. He rolled his shoulders back and strode with confidence down the hallway, looking straight ahead. At the end of the hallway, several security guards milled around the X-ray machine. One of them turned and kept his eyes on Dahawa as he approached.

"You're here early," the guard said once the major got close enough. "The prime minister doesn't land for another three hours." He looked at Dahawa's security badge, then checked his face for a match. The ID read MASTER SERGEANT AL BATIN HUMAILA.

"Advanced detachment, you know the routine," Dahawa said, smoothly stepping around the metal detector. There wasn't any reason for him to go through it; they knew he was armed.

"An advanced detachment . . . of one?" the guard questioned jokingly, as the other's laughed.

"There's more of us. We just don't enter all at once," Dahawa answered, not cracking a smile, only staring at the guard. He showed no sign of emotion, and the men abruptly quieted down.

"Yes. We know." The guard gave the major the once-over and then said, "Allah be with you."

"Allah be with you," Dahawa repeated, marching away.

DAMASCUS, SYRIA

Prime Minister Mehdi Mahmoudi listened to the roar of the jet engines as the door of his A310 Airbus was sealed. Tucked neatly away in his briefcase were signed contracts spelling out the terms of three economic programs with Great Britain. In two and a half weeks, the first container ships would be arriving at Iranian port cities with shipments of food, medicine and clothing. As far as

Mahmoudi was concerned, he had just started his country on the first steps back to prosperity. He prayed to Allah that the hard-liners would give his plan a chance to work.

He buckled his seat belt, reaching for a pack of cigarettes despite flight rules prohibiting him from smoking during takeoff and landing. After two days of secret deliberations, he was nervous, tired and anxious to get back to Iran. He lit a cigarette and inhaled deeply.

"I must commend you, Mehdi. You have shown great courage. You have most likely just saved Iran from civil war. In thirty days the markets will once again have food." Akhbar al-Yawm, Iran's interior minister, spoke before yawning and taking a seat next to Mahmoudi.

Mahmoudi sighed heavily and turned to face Akhbar. "I hope you are correct, my friend. However, I am still concerned." He took a drag and then continued. "Many people will oppose what I have just done."

"Only the ones with their eyes closed. No government can stay in power with starving people in the streets," Akhbar reassured the prime minister. "Do you think the people will care where the food comes from?"

"It is not the people who have control of our weapons and military."

"So it is Bakhtiar who worries you . . . as always."

"Yes, Bakhtiar troubles me the most. I only pray that Allah will guide him to see this is the answer for our people and country." The prime minister set his chair back in a reclining position as the jetliner turned sharply onto the runway. He closed his eyes as the pilot ran up the engines and released the brakes. Thirty seconds later, the A310 lifted off the runway, turning southeast toward Iranian airspace.

Major Dahawa scrambled up the last set of stairs and onto the top floor of the building. This third-floor section contained a few offices and meeting rooms but was otherwise empty. The major had timed it so that the staff workers, who generally occupied this floor, had already left for home. His only concern now was the possibility of a cleaning lady or maintenance man nosing around.

Dahawa scanned right and left as he looked for a place to outline his next move, any place where he could hide before moving onto the roof. He hurried down a hallway, looking over his shoulder every few seconds.

Just ahead he caught sight of a door cracked open a few inches. Printed on the outside was ROOF ACCESS/CLEANING SUPPLIES. He opened the door a few more inches and looked inside. It was a small room, dark and crammed with buckets, mops and bottles. In the back of the room was a set of stairs leading to the roof. Dahawa had used this access once before to set up an observation post when a large party of Syrian emissaries arrived several years ago for talks on how to spread state-sponsored terrorism. He entered, closing the door securely behind him.

He checked his watch. The luminescent dial showed that the prime minister's plane wouldn't be landing for another two hours. He took a deep breath and let it out slowly before quietly climbing the stairs to the roof.

Defense Minister Bakhtiar paced before his cluttered desk. The evening sun had left his cramped office darkened, heightening his anxiety and tension. And yet for the first time he could feel the power inside him. He was just hours away from becoming the most powerful man in the Middle East. Once the prime minister was out of the way, fifty million Iranians would have no other choice but to turn to him for leadership. He would control the parliament and the military. Every Muslim religious leader would look to him for the authority and power he would control. But most of all, he could once again ignite the fires of revolution and save his country.

"You are sure Major Dahawa was seen entering the airport?" he asked Zadeh.

"Yes," Zadeh answered firmly. "Both guards at the southern entrance of building 1701 have confirmed it. Dahawa is there."

"And the rest of the plan is ready? You know what to do?"

Zadeh didn't answer. The defense minister already knew the answer. The questions and answers had been repeated numerous times.

"If this plan doesn't succeed . . . it will be your head," Bakhtiar grumbled, looking at the floor. He didn't mean it. Zadeh was more valuable alive than dead, especially now in the middle of a possible overturn in the government. There was no one else the minister could trust to protect him.

"It is time. I must go," Zadeh said, grabbing his AK-47.

"Yes . . . yes. Go." Bakhtiar waved his hands impatiently. He watched Zadeh leave the room. The defense minister immediately walked over and locked the heavy oak door. Although Zadeh left men posted outside, Bahktiar felt better with the added security. He would spend the rest of his time alone, thinking about the future of Iran and praying to Allah for guidance in the silence.

Major Dahawa sat perfectly still in the shadow of the large air-conditioning unit on the roof. The hum of the motor drowned out the noise around him, but still he had the advantage by being there first and maintaining a view of the entrance onto the roof.

He turned his head slowly, looking toward the west. The sun had just disappeared behind the mountains and he could see the landing lights of several aircraft as they lined up for final approach.

Dahawa pulled a six-inch knife out of his boot, clutching the hard rubber grip in his right hand. The blade had been sharpened on both sides, tapering to a sharp point. The bare metal had been anodized a dull black so it wouldn't reflect any light. He rubbed his thumb across the blade sideways, feeling the edge scrape his skin.

From his vantage point, he could see the entire layout of the airport. Below him to the west, the main terminal split into two concourses running north and northwest. Several of the jetways had airliners parked at them with luggage being loaded or unloaded. He could see the maintenance crews off-loading empty food carts and removing large plastic garbage bags. Several fuel trucks were under the jets, pumping JP-8 into their wing tanks.

Directly below him, the tarmac had been cordoned off with chainlink fence in preparation for the arrival of the prime minister. He took note of several guards posted around the edge of the fence.

Dahawa pictured where the jet would park. The twin-engine 310A would land out of the west and taxi to this section of the airport. Building 1701 had a separate entrance, on the lower level, leading to the tarmac. This allowed government officials to be dropped off or picked up by their vehicles without having to pass through the main terminal and crowds of people.

Suddenly, a man emerged from the doorway of the roof access. Dahawa stood tall so the man could see him.

"I am Sergeant Salum Jalluh. I have orders to—"

"I know who you are," Dahawa said curtly, not wanting to engage in small talk. "Take up a position over there, on the right corner."

"Yes, sir," the man answered under his breath.

Thirty minutes later, Major Dahawa remained crouched. He hadn't varied his position in the last half hour, and his legs were becoming cramped and tired. The setting sun had disappeared behind the western mountains, leaving a light red blush in the clouds. The dark shed enough light so that he could make out the objects around him.

To his left, Sergeant Salum Jalluh crept toward him. The only noise he made was that of the gravel grinding under his combat boots.

"The west side of the building is clear. It looks as if all the security forces are in place," Jalluh said, checking his watch. "The prime minister's plane will be landing in twenty minutes. Should I report in?"

"Yes. Confirm our position is secure and return to your post," Dahawa responded, looking out over the tarmac. He checked the location of the armed men around the fence.

Sergeant Jalluh pulled his compact hand held radio out of its protective holster. He extended the antenna and turned it on. The radio erupted with a crackling sound. Dahawa guessed the sergeant outweighed him by at least fifty pounds.

"Section seven is clear. Repeat. Section seven is clear and secure."

"*Confirmed . . . section seven is clear,*" the response crackled back several seconds later.

"Sector seven out." Jalluh released the mike key, replaced the radio in his holster and turned toward his spot on the roof.

Dahawa lunged at Jalluh from behind. He swung his left arm out in front of the man with all his strength, striking across the bridge of his nose and eyes, hoping to stun him. With his right hand clutching the field knife, he ripped the blade from left to right across Jalluh's throat. Dahawa felt the steel cut deep into the soft cartilage of the man's vocal cords as his body stiffened with shock, then pain. Dahawa brought the knife out and around, jamming it deep into Jalluh's back just below the rib cage. He hoped to sever a kidney or puncture the liver. He pulled the knife upward until he felt the resistance of bone and gristle.

"*Ahhh*," Jalluh moaned, grabbing his throat. He tried to yell, but all he made was a gurgling sound as the blood from his perforated jugular began to fill his throat. He coughed, spitting blood onto the ground before him. He felt the piercing pain of the knife in his back and gasped for breath. For a moment he blacked out, stumbling forward.

Dahawa backed up, expecting his victim to fall. There wasn't any doubt in his mind that the wounds were mortal.

Discipline and training took over, with only one thought filling Jalluh's mind. He had to stay alive. He swiveled to find Dahawa a few feet away. He could see the knife in his hand and the intensity in his eyes.

Dahawa raised the knife and charged one more time. He jammed the knife downward, trying to force the blade into Jalluh's neck. With a reflexing reaction, the sergeant's left arm flew up, blocking the attack. The bloodied tip of the knife was only a fraction of an inch from his neck. Gathering his remaining strength, Jalluh clenched his fist and jabbed it into the major's ribs. He heard the sharp crack as the force of the blow broke several bones.

Dahawa lost his balance and fell backward. Before he knew what had happened, he was lying flat on the ground. Several warm drops of Jalluh's blood hit his face as the man lunged over him.

Struggling to pull his pistol from its holster, Dahawa looked up to see wild, frightened eyes, then suddenly felt Jalluh's grip around his throat.

It was evident Jalluh was focused on one thing: he was determined to kill Dahawa before his wounds caused his own death. The sensation of Jalluh's thumbs pressing into his throat panicked Dahawa for a moment. He kicked and squirmed, trying to break free while grabbing the sergeant's hands to pull them away.

Suddenly, Jalluh's face became blank and his eyes rolled to the back of his head. He gasped and his grip loosened. Dahawa pushed the man's arms away and struggled to his feet. Jalluh's large limp body crumbled.

The major was breathing heavily as he wiped the blood away from his face and looked around. The entire engagement hadn't lasted longer than a few minutes. Dahawa slipped closer to the edge of the roof. The guards below had not moved from their spots. Dahawa retrieved his knife, wiping the blade clean on the dead man's pants. It was then he noticed that each time he moved

a sharp pain in his side shot through his body. *You bastard...
you broke my damn ribs.*

"You may proceed," the airport sentinel said after checking Hassan Zadeh's ID. Zadeh rolled up the window and dimmed the headlights. He headed down the single-lane road toward the VIP parking garage, checking his watch. The prime minister's flight was still en route. He had plenty of time to get into position.

He parked the car and looked around for anyone else in the garage. Once assured he was alone, he reached under his seat and pulled out an American-made Ruger .22-caliber automatic pistol. The sleek-looking automatic had an inch-and-a-half black silencer fitted to the barrel. Releasing the magazine, he rechecked the hollow-point bullets he had inserted, then snapped it back into the gun.

Major Dahawa didn't take his eyes off the blinking red and green wingtip navigational lights of the prime minister's aircraft. He watched the plane, waiting for the pilot to reduce power and turn right to taxi toward the rear of building 1701.

Dahawa crouched low, crept up to the edge of the roof. He closed his eyes, trying to push the intense pain of his broken ribs out of his mind. Every bit of movement sent daggerlike blasts of pain through the left side of the body.

He had dirtied his uniform in the earlier scuffle—the roof's tar was ground into his knees and elbows. He would have to think of an explanation should he be stopped and questioned by any guards.

Staying low, Dahawa cradled the sniper rifle in his arms. He was careful not to jar the matte black variable Zeiss 1.5x-to-6x low-light telescopic sight. The 60-mm objective lens allowed for maximum light-gathering power and could be used on short- to medium-range shots on well-lit nights. The front of the stock contained a bipod that stabilized the rifle for maximum accuracy. Unlike conventional sniper rifles, which were generally bolt actions, Dahawa was fond of the semi-and fully automatic G3SG/1, finding it to be reliable and precise. The rifle was heavy, at 12.2 pounds unloaded. He believed the mass added to the accuracy of his shots.

Dahawa was rigidly in place when the Airbus came to a stop and the ground crew hurried the portable stairs to the side of the plane. The sound of the jet's turbofans were fast becoming a dull whine, and the passengers would shortly be deplaning. He placed the scope's crosshairs on the exit door just behind the cockpit. On the tarmac to the right, two black armored limousines pulled up and the drivers jumped out to open the back doors.

"Three . . . 310 meters maximum," Dahawa muttered to himself, estimating the range. His rifle had been set to hit a target dead-on at 300 meters. He wouldn't have to compensate for added distance. He put the scope to his right eye, moving the rifle deliberately right and left. The light from the surrounding area cast enough of a glow so that he could see everything perfectly.

He winced as his side ached from the extended position of his arms. Trying to hold his breath, he realigned the sight after budging it slightly. A security guard climbed the steps, then stood at attention, waiting for the door to open. Dahawa steadied the rifle, concentrating on the man's head. A wisp of hair moved across the guard's forehead. Dahawa figured that a gentle breeze was blowing out of the south at four to five knots. At this short a range, it wasn't anything to worry about.

He slowly snapped the safety off with his thumb and shifted his forefinger to the set lever just behind the trigger. The tiny lever reduced the trigger pull to 1.247 kg of pressure, allowing for a clean shot. The rifle was loaded with standard 7.62 mm × 51 NATO ball ammunition. The full copper metal jacketed rounds were accurate out to 600 yards. One well-placed bullet could blow a man's head off six soccer fields away. Dahawa gently placed the tip of his finger on the edge of the cold steel trigger.

The pressure caused an uncomfortable throbbing in his side with every breath. Dahawa could still taste blood in his mouth, only it was fresh. It was his own. He looked down, examining his uniform. His fatigues were soaked with crimson, oxygenated blood. *Shit, a punctured lung*, he cursed.

He looked back through the scope, centering it on the open aircraft door. He blinked quickly a couple of times, trying to drive the sweat out of his eyes and clear his vision. Just then a man emerged from the Airbus. He was dressed in a Western-style business suit and carried a briefcase. Dahawa strained to keep his arms steady, but the pain was becoming intense.

Prime Minister Mehdi Mahmoudi crushed his cigarette into the ashtray and unbuckled his seat belt. He wished he could say it felt good to be back on Iranian soil, but it didn't. He wasn't looking forward to returning to his office; he knew signed agreements were only a start. Things would only improve when the Kurds put down their weapons and returned to their jobs and families.

"Mr. Prime Minister, your car is waiting for you." One of his aides stood patiently, ready to help him.

"Thank you," Mahmoudi answered, forcing a smile.

Prime Minister Mahmoudi, escorted by the aide, followed two administrative assistants out onto the platform and into the cool Iranian night. Akhbar al-Yawm picked up the minister's briefcase and was the last to exit. The prime minister grabbed the handrail as his assistant kept a firm grip on his arm. The low light made it difficult to see, even with the spotlights pointed at the stairs.

The minister of intelligence waited below for him. *I wonder where Bakhtiar is*, Mahmoudi thought.

"There you are," Dahawa whispered. He tried keeping the crosshairs on the man's head as he walked down the steps. The prime minister's head oscillated up and down with each step. Dahawa told himself to concentrate on the crosshairs. Nothing else should enter his mind.

A clean kill on the first shot—this was his only thought. Mahmoudi was nearly at the bottom of the steps. The crosshairs jiggled as Dahawa's hands shook. He was afraid to take a deep breath, already feeling lightheaded from the loss of blood. His vision blurred and thoughts spun inside his mind. The will to survive had started to take over, and panic erupted from his gut.

"*No, not now*," Dahawa pleaded to himself. For the first time, the fear of not being able to complete his mission flowed through him. The remote possibility that Bakhtiar would be true to his word and provide an escape for Dahawa and his wife was beginning to fade.

He closed his eyes for only a second, summoning every ounce of inner strength he could muster. The prime minister was standing on the tarmac at the bottom of the steps when Dahawa peered through his scope. He lowered the crosshairs, placing them on the base of the prime minister's neck.

Now, Dahawa thought. He gently squeezed the trigger and the heavy G3SG/1 sniper rifle lurched in his hands. The bright muzzle flash engulfed his view for a fraction of a second.

*   *   *

Prime Minister Mahmoudi stumbled forward, nearly knocked off his feet, as the unexpected force of the bullet ripped through his right shoulder blade, exiting out the front of his chest. The bullet pierced the upper section of his right lung, missing his heart by five inches.

"*Allah* help me . . ." Mahmoudi groaned, trying to stay on his feet.

The bullet, traveling at over 1,800 feet a second, then struck the Iranian intelligence minister, standing only feet away. The speeding projectile severed the man's second and third vertebrae, killing him instantly. His body crumbled to the ground.

Dahawa placed his finger back on the trigger, tightening his grip on the forearm of the weapon. Staring through the scope, he swept the rifle left and right, trying to find Mahmoudi in the confusion. The prime minister's bodyguards, reacting quickly, were now next to him, pushing his head down out of the line of fire.

The major prayed for an opportunity to get off one more shot. He caught sight of the prime minister's silver white hair and swiftly squeezed the trigger again.

"*Get down . . . get down!*" a loud voice boomed from the crowd. A guard worked desperately to shield the prime minister with his own body.

Mahmoudi's knees buckled under him as a second bullet streaked by his ear. It hit the guard's head.

A couple of men, unsure of where the shots had originated, opened fire, cutting down the baggage handlers fifty yards away. Mahmoudi was thrown into a limousine. He heard the muffled sounds of weapons fire and shouts as the door slammed shut. The car sped away, and the prime minister let the blackness overcome him.

Dahawa gritted his teeth, reaching over to pick up the two spent cartridges. A light gray smoke twisted out the end of the brass. On the tarmac, in the midst of all the pandemonium, no one appeared to be searching in his direction. Guards were screaming and running in all directions; no one seemed to be in charge. Just the same, he pulled the rifle close to his chest and rolled away from the edge of the rooftop. The confusion should give him enough time to escape.

Engulfed with pain, he used the stock of the rifle as a crutch, struggling to his feet. Once standing, he found that the upright position eased some of his labored breathing.

Dahawa turned, making his way to the doorway, the sound of racing engines and squealing tires filling the air behind him. He knew it was the limousine, racing to save the life of the prime minister.

He began to reach for the roof access door when it flew open. The major instinctively raised his rifle, pointing it at the man standing in the doorway. But he stopped short, recognizing the man's broad face and shoulders.

Dahawa did not have to ask Zadeh why he had come. He knew the answer and lowered his rifle, standing as tall as he could. There would be no point in trying to shoot his way out. It was certain the personal bodyguard of the defense minister would have a backup plan should he himself fail in his own mission.

"I only ask that you take care of my wife also, so that she may have peace," Dahawa spoke resignedly.

"Salam aleikom," Zadeh answered, raising the pistol and firing three muffled shots, each one hitting their mark.

Chapter Seven

Duke James poured himself another glass of Glenlivet, added two ice cubes, and looked out the picture window. The living room was beginning to look strange, filled with shadows and blurred images. He could barely see the outline of the furniture and the dark wood frames of the pictures on the wall. Already his body was becoming numb from the alcohol.

Well, James, I guess you owe yourself just one more. He took a big sip from the glass. *And you're going to pay for it in the morning.*

The kids were in bed and he could see from the lights on the staircase that Katie was still awake. The grandfather clock, a present from Katie's parents, broke the silence of the room with its constant tick, tick, tick. But it didn't matter right now. Duke just wanted to be alone. Alone with himself and his thoughts. Three days had past since the B-18 had crashed and he wasn't feeling any better.

He had a decision to make and he was the only one who could make it. Duke could pull himself together and fight this thing, telling Chaniff it was his job and he planned to do it, or he could fade away slowly, take the easy way out. For the first time in his life, the thought of getting out sounded good. He could do what he wanted when he wanted. He could even take Matt and Sean

108

to ball games on Saturdays, like a normal father, rather than be at the beck and call of his country twenty-four hours a day. After all, he had served his time, done enough for the good old U S of A Air Force. He'd given them twenty-one years, now maybe it was time they gave a little back. *Before I kill myself and a lot of other people with me.*

He sensed someone creeping down the stairs behind him. He didn't turn around.

"Duke . . . when are you coming to bed?" Katie asked, coming into view.

"I'll be there in a few minutes. Just give me a few more minutes," he said softly. He turned to look at his wife, who was dressed in a red nightgown. He really didn't want her to see him this way. He felt childish, sitting in the dark, getting drunk like a teenager stealing his parent's booze. He walked over and sat down in the chair next to the sofa.

Katie stared at him for a long while.

"I don't like this. Why are you doing this to yourself?"

"Doing what? I'm sitting here having a few drinks. What's wrong with that?" Duke's face clouded as he took another sip.

"A *few* drinks? This is the most I've seen you drink in the past ten years. My God, Duke . . . what's wrong? This isn't you." Katie sat down on the arm of the sofa.

"It isn't me . . . yeah this isn't me." Duke stood up. "Look, Katie, I'm really not in the mood for chitchat."

Katie grabbed his arm. "Duke, I don't care what you're in the mood for. You're behaving like a child and it's scaring me."

He turned away, losing his balance, but Katie caught him.

"I think you should talk to someone who can understand what you're going through."

"Like who? Who could possibly understand me . . . if you don't?"

"I'm trying, honey, but I can't." Katie stroked his head, running her fingers through his salty brown hair. "What about Willie?"

"No . . . it's none of Willie's concern. He doesn't know nothing." Duke's words were slurred.

"I don't believe that, Duke. I'm calling him in the morning. If you won't listen to me, maybe you'll listen to him."

"I just have a few things that only I can sort out." Duke stared straight ahead, still not looking at Katie. "Just leave me alone right now, okay? Just leave me alone.''

"Well, I'm going to bed. If you want to hurt yourself and act like a two-year-old, fine by me. I'll see you in the morning, General." Katie walked up the stairs and turned out the bedroom lights.

Well . . . I blew that one. She probably locked the door. Duke sat back down in the armchair to gaze out in the darkness. *She's right, I am acting like a prick. Why didn't she just tell me that? I think it would have made me feel better.* He swallowed the rest of the drink and tipped his head back on the chair. A moment later the empty glass slipped from his hand, hitting the carpet with a thud.

PATUXENT NAVAL AIR TEST CENTER

General Duke James parked his Suburban under a large elm tree, making sure most of its shade fell on the four-door truck. He sat for a second or two, his head pounding with a resounding throb. *At least Katie wasn't too hard on me.* The hangover was enough punishment for his behavior. Duke stepped out into the humid, summer afternoon air. *I'll be glad when it's fall*, he thought as he wiped the perspiration from his forehead.

The officer's club at Pax River Naval Test Center wasn't much different from any other air base across the country. It contained a bar and a dining room used mainly for lunches and receptions. The walls were covered with naval aviation artwork, scenes from World War II through Desert Storm. The officer's club did, however, contain some of the largest egos in the military—Navy test pilots. Duke thought they were only a tad smaller than the pilots' egos on the other coast at Edwards AFB.

Duke entered the building. He left his sunglasses on, knowing even the low light would bring tears to his eyes. It was just past 1:30 and most of the lunch crowd had already left.

"Duke, over here," a familiar voice called out.

Duke smiled. Seated in the corner, next to a picture of an A-6E Intruder screaming over the Iraqi desert, was Willie Quandt. It had been six months since he had last seen his colleague from NASA. The man's blond hair, tan face and white smile made a striking appearance from a distance. It wasn't until you came up close and noticed the deep scars on his face and saw that his eyes seemed to be hiding a mystery that you realized he was older than you first guessed.

Duke removed his glasses and slid them into his breast pocket before sitting across from Willie. They had known each other for five years and were closer than most brothers. Willie had recently retired from the Navy with the rank of captain and was now a primary test pilot for Lockheed, working with the Navy's team, testing and evaluating the Navy's version of the F-22 Lighting II fighter.

"How the hell are you, buddy?" Willie asked. The two shook hands firmly.

"Oh . . . I've been better."

"That's what I hear. Katie said something about a fight with a scotch bottle. Who won?"

"Right now I'd have to say the bottle did. Didn't have my wingman with me," Duke answered, smiling.

Willie looked up at the waitress hovering near their table. "I'll take a hamburger medium well with fries and iced tea, unsweetened. Hold the onions."

"Oh, I see you're still into health food," Duke said. "Make that two."

Willie looked at Duke, remembering they had been to hell and back in the desert. If it wasn't for James, he probably wouldn't be sitting here right now. He had a fairly good sense of why they needed to get together for lunch. The man sitting across from him wasn't the same one who had managed to keep cool-headed during a no-win situation. No, the fact they were meeting in the officer's club instead of on Willie's twenty-five-foot Mako fishing boat out in Chesapeake Bay, drinking beer and telling lies or trying to catch flounder and bluefish, was enough to make him concerned.

"How are you and Marcy getting along?" Duke asked to break the awkward silence. Marcy was Willie's latest girlfriend, or at least the last one Duke knew about.

"You're two behind, Duke. You missed Renee, and boy, she isn't any easy girl to miss. But I'm dating Wendy now. We'll all have to get together."

Duke shook his head, not really listening. "Yeah, we'll have to do that."

"Duke, why don't you quit playing macho and let's talk about you." Willie leaned forward and looked him straight in the eyes.

"It's written all over your face. You feel guilty as hell. In some way you're responsible for Hodges possibly being a cripple, not to mention that you've left Katie and the kids alone most of the time. You're wondering what kind of general, pilot, husband, father, and anything else you want to throw in, you've been."

Duke snickered, shaking his head. Somehow Willie hit it right on the money.

"Well, Hodges took his chances like every other pilot that straps into a flying machine—there are no guarantees. I wasn't there, but I'm betting you did everything right and then some."

"I just can't fucking remember, damn it. Maybe I punched out too soon and I could have helped him," Duke said exasperatedly.

"Shit, so maybe you did and maybe you didn't. But you've always been Mr. Air Force with the perfect service record. Why would you screw up now? Or is it you think you're too big a man to make mistakes like the rest of us Joes?" Willie paused, then less seriously, added, "You need to get your head together, buddy. I think that ejection seat hit you a little harder than the doctors think."

"Maybe what I need is another whack in the head."

Both men laughed, then stopped talking while their food was served. The aroma of their lunches warmed Duke's insides and his stomach growled. They both dug in and the conversation turned to past memories and the neverending talk of planes and technology.

Sitting across from Willie, Duke began to remember how lucky he was. Not so much for ejecting safely, but because even if he hadn't made it, at least he had lived more so far than some men would in their entire lifetimes. His wife and children did understand that, even though he was gone a lot, he was doing it for them. Duke knew if it wasn't for Katie's support, his career would not have excelled the way it had. He couldn't have been productive if Katie hadn't taken care of everything at home. Duke was beginning to understand that he wouldn't have done very much if it wasn't for her. He took another bite out of his hamburger. It was time to stop feeling sorry for himself.

TEHRAN, IRAN

"The bullet must have been a full metal jacket. It didn't cause as much damage as it could have." The doctor pulled off his latex gloves and dropped them in a disposal can. Operating on the Iranian prime minister was not necessarily a responsibility he relished, and he wasn't about to give anyone false hopes. "The prime minister is a lucky man. A few more inches to the left and his spine would have been shattered. He would be either paralyzed or dead."

"So, he will live?" Akhbar al-Yawm asked. His face, drained of color, was solemn.

"I cannot say that for sure. The prime minister lost a lot of blood and still has some internal bleeding." The doctor squinted, then rubbed his eyes. He had spent nearly twelve hours of intense surgery in the operating room. "I have put him in a drug-induced coma. He is not a young man . . . time is what his body needs to recover."

"You cannot stop the bleeding? Perhaps we should call in another doctor . . ." Akhbar spoke roughly.

"Of course you may do that if you wish, but I'm telling you the prime minister is a seventy-two-year-old man and he is very weak. There is only so much shock his body will take, and there is only so much I can do right now." The doctor's tone was firm and direct. "The next forty-eight hours are going to be critical."

"I need a more definite answer from you. What are we to expect? You're talking about the leader of this country," the interior minister pressed.

"Do you want percentages? Then I give the prime minister a fifty-fifty chance of pulling through. But I have seen men with a strong will survive worse conditions and I have also seen men with few complications give up and die." The doctor paused, then looked straight at Akhbar. "I suggest you go home and get some rest. There is nothing more you or I can do here."

Akhbar al-Yawm drew in a deep breath. The doctor was philosophizing, not realizing the importance of Mahmoudi's survival. With the prime minister in a coma and the head of Iranian intelligence dead, Sheik Bakhtiar was in charge. He not only controlled the military but could now issue orders without anyone of clear authority to challenge him. The only man who could command Bakhtiar's respect was the Ayatollah Abdol-Rasul Hanifnezhad, and Akhbar doubted the old man had the conviction. If only Allah would see to it that Mahmoudi would pull through before Bakhtiar could consolidate too much power.

Akhbar sat down in a chair in the empty waiting room. He

defiantly said to the doctor, "I will not be leaving. Let me know immediately when his condition has changed."

Bahktiar closed the drapes to his office windows and turned the volume of the television set up so the sound of static filled the room. If there were any electronic bugging devices in the room, the added noise would make them less effective.

The defense minister looked gravely at the Iranian air force colonel standing near the door. The man was one of only a few military officers Bakhtiar trusted. He motioned for the colonel to sit down close to him so they could talk.

"You are aware that the Kurdish rebellion is growing in strength," Bakhtiar stated.

"Yes," Colonel Alireza Rahavi answered.

"And what is your solution for the Kurds?"

"Give my squadron the order and we will stop their revolution," Rahavi snorted with confidence. "The leaders would be destroyed in one mission."

"I can assure you each member of the Supreme Defense Council shares your hatred of the Kurdish rebels and know how this is affecting our country. But, as before, our options are limited. With your airpower, Colonel, you would also kill hundreds of innocent women and children, and that, of course, is not our goal." Bakhtiar's eyes stayed fixed on the colonel's face. This wasn't the first time the two had discussed the repercussions of an air attack killing innocent people. Colonel Rahavi's men were well trained and disciplined, and the minister knew they would follow any order he gave without question. However, he was not as sure of Iran's military field commanders.

Bakhtiar crossed his legs and leaned forward. "We have given our country another option, one that would not be so barbaric. It is time for Phalanx Dragon to be used."

Colonel Rahavi's face hardened. His last two flight tests had been successful, but he had not guessed it would be utilized so quickly.

"Have all the ground tests been completed?"

"They have," Bakhtiar answered proudly. "Phalanx Dragon is operational and we now have 148 missiles. If I gave the command, we have the capability to manufacture a hundred more in a month's time." His lips curled under his stringy beard. "We have the means to become the most powerful country in the Gulf.

And Allah is on our side. The Phalanx missile will save our country from being ripped apart. The people will unite.''

Rahavi was quiet, listening to every word the defense minister said. He knew he was being called upon to execute the plan that would save his country.

"There is an enemy we can face that will bring our nation back together again." The minister's tone grew ominously deep, matching the fire in his eyes. "Only one force is so evil and powerful that our people will know they have no other choice but to join us in the battle or die. That evil is the United States."

"The United States . . . but, Sheik, I know Allah is on our side, yet I fear their forces outnumber us. It would be only a matter of time . . ." Rahavi spoke warily, not wanting to anger the minister. This was not what he expected to hear.

Bakhtiar shook his head, intent that the colonel understand his plan. "It is not as bold a step as you may think. I propose we first launch several missiles at tankers in the Gulf. We can destroy a few vessels carrying Saudi or Kuwaiti oil, effectively cutting the supply of oil to the world through the Gulf." Bakhtiar paused before continuing. "Because of the missile's stealth capabilities no one will know immediately who is responsible. The United States will undoubtedly react. I speculate they will send their Indian Ocean carrier task force into the Gulf of Oman. They will want to use their ships and warplanes to protect—how do they say—'vital interests' in the region. When the American forces arrive, we then attack them with our full force of missiles. It will be a revolutionary victory for the people of Iran. Our country can be united once again, and the shame of the Gulf War will be wiped away forever."

Rahavi, more optimistic, voiced his thoughts. "Yes, and with the American defense cuts limiting their forces in the Gulf, if we lure them in we could do hit-and-run attacks with few risks."

Bakhtiar smiled with Rahavi's comprehension. "This is not something I have taken lightly. I have asked Allah for guidance. It is the only way to save our nation." He placed a hand on the nearby Koran before speaking. "Colonel Rahavi, you are the highest-ranking officer assigned to this project, as well as a trusted patriot. I want half of your squadron of F-4Es armed with the Phalanx missiles at Esfahan. The missiles will also be deployed in our current Silkworm sites around Bandar Abbas and on our southern shore. We will have the capability to attack ships in the

Gulf without warning. My plan is to start operations in a few days. Will you and your men be ready?''

"We will be ready in twenty-four hours," Rahavi answered.

Bakhtiar stood, grasping the colonel's hand in his. "My plan is not to defeat the Great Satan. I only wish to wipe the shame of the Gulf War from our people and unite our country. Now, go. Return to Esfahan and prepare your men."

"Yes, Minister Bakhtiar," Rahavi replied. He nodded, then left the room.

Bakhtiar turned off the television and returned to his seat behind the desk. Finally, after all these years, he was controlling Iran's future. The responsibility weighed heavily on his mind but lifted his heart and soul to Allah.

Chapter Eight

Esfahan Air Force Base

Colonel Alireza Rahavi looked at the solemn faces of the three F-4E pilots and their backseaters as the crowded van arrived at the guarded hangar on the northeastern side of the base. The nervous silence led him to believe they all felt uncertain and cautious.

"Get to your aircraft and begin the preflight checks at once. We will be airborne in thirty minutes," Rahavi ordered.

They only nodded in response.

Located on the northern edge of the Zagros Mountains, 214 miles south of Tehran, the air base had been built during the last year of Iran's war with Iraq. Two 10,000-foot runways, one running north, the other south, crisscrossed the rocky Iranian desert landscape. The main section of the air base had been constructed on the eastern boundary of the Revolutionary Guard's army compound. It was home to the Iranian 153rd Mechanized Division. Sixty-four domed, hardened aircraft shelters housed the last two operational squadrons of American-manufactured F-4Es. There was a total of thirty-six aircraft.

Colonel Rahavi held a trusted position inside Iran's military. He had been chosen by Sheik Ali Bin Bakhtiar to train and lead an elite team of pilots whose missions were to defend Iran against outside attack. The colonel had also been the chief test pilot of the Phalanx Dragon project in the testing and evaluation of Iran's new secret stealth cruise missile.

The first three Iranian-manufactured cruise missiles he had been assigned to launch had exploded prematurely on the test range. But on every test flight, Iranian engineers learned something new, some small detail that they would work on diligently until it was corrected. The best engineering minds fine-tuned the engine propulsion systems and the computer guidance nerve center of each cruise missile, as well as the manufacturing equipment.

They then began installing state-of-the-art infrared optoelectronic sensors that would guide the missiles to their targets. The warheads also contained a shaped high-explosive charge large enough to destroy even hardened underground targets. However, the outer skin and shape of the missile, an exact copy of the one found in the desert after the Gulf War, was the breakthrough that would turn the balance of power in the Gulf. The lightweight graphite-based skin, with its honeycomb subsurface, allowed the missile to absorb the full spectrum of radar frequencies. This, combined with its angular shape, made it essentially invisible to electronic detection.

The colonel exited the van, stepping out into the cold dark night. He liked the air's bite, it seemed to revive his senses. Although it was 0320, he didn't feel fatigued. There was too much adrenaline pumping through his veins. He didn't acknowledge the driver and did not speak any other words to the pilots. The rest of the men fanned out behind him and headed for the aircraft shelters.

Rahavi glanced at the saluting guards. They stood erect on both sides of the hardened concrete hangar, their rifles ready. Thick steel aircraft bunker doors slid open, exposing the matte black finish of Rahavi's F-4E Phantom. The dark starry night and cool weather promised to be perfect for a flight to the Gulf.

Rahavi smiled as excitement overwhelmed any concerns he may have had earlier. In three hours he would return in triumph.

His jaw tightened as he waited for his jet to be pulled from the hangar. The ground crew was scrambling, making last second adjustments and securing the access panels. *Why isn't my fighter ready?* he thought. He didn't like last-minute modifications. That meant things weren't organized. Whatever was being done should have been finished hours ago.

"You have nothing to worry about," Chief Engineer Khalk

Hikmet said as if reading his mind. "Your aircraft is equipped and flight-worthy, Colonel. I have checked everything personally." It was very apparent the man enjoyed being in the thick of things. He was dressed in a heavy wool jacket and though he was tall, was still unimpressive-looking, with thinning gray hair and thick eyeglasses.

"And the missiles?" Rahavi asked, throwing a flight bag over his shoulder. He strode toward his fighter and Hikmet struggled to keep up with him. The two men stopped to stare at the two long cruise missiles suspended beneath the F-4E. Each one was bolted to a specially built weapons pylon. The pylons kept them tucked up neatly next to the aircraft's fuselage to reduce drag and fuel consumption.

"I made final calibrations to the tracking and homing heads an hour ago, and the optical tracking disks have been installed." The engineer placed a large hand on Rahavi's shoulder. "Just remember . . . do not release them above 350 knots airspeed. Do everything just as you did in the last test runs in the desert and you will succeed."

Rahavi took one last look at the angular-shaped cruise missiles, their bodies so unlike other missiles that it added to his confidence for success. He then turned abruptly and ascended the aluminum ladder, crawling into the cramped cockpit. He put on a skullcap, followed by a heavy brown camouflaged fiberglass helmet. The APUs kicked in with a thunderous roar, spooling up the twin engines. Rahavi flipped the avionics switch, sending a surge of electricity through the cockpit instrumentation. The fighter came to life in the stillness of the night.

The colonel knew why he had been selected for this project. Not only was he totally committed to the Muslim faith, but he had also studied and trained with the Americans before the revolution. He proudly returned to his country and joined the air force.

Rahavi was a captain when the Ayatollah Khomeini returned from France after his exile to change Iran forever. Purges followed, and many top air force officers were either killed or imprisoned. It left the military hollow and fractured. When Iran went to war with Iraq, the Revolutionary Guards formed an elite air force to protect the revolution. Because of his age and skill in flying, and of course his Muslim faith, Rahavi was allowed to follow his military career. Now, at forty-three, he was one of the most experienced and trusted pilots in the Iranian air force.

Colonel Rahavi connected his oxygen mask and radio before lowering the front canopy of the Phantom.

"Radio check . . . one, two, three." His backseater's voice broke the silence. Rahavi would fly tonight's mission with a young lieutenant, Haji Omrai. He considered Omrai to be one of the best radar intercept officers based at Esfahan. He was precise, dedicated and kept his mouth shut unless he was spoken to.

Rahavi studied the instrument panel one more time, making sure all systems were up and running. Hydraulic pressure was in the green fuel tanks fully pressurized and oxygen flowing. In his mind he reviewed the flight plan. Taking off to the north, he would climb to 15,000 feet, high enough to avoid the towering peaks of the Zagros Mountains, and head northwest for twenty minutes toward the city of Hamadan. His F-4E's TACAN system would then pick up a coded radio transmission guiding him to the Karan River. Turning south he would meet up with the other three F-4Es before following the river toward the Persian Gulf. They would keep their radar turned off and airspeed below 500 knots. Their flight path would take him within fifty kilometers of the Iraqi border. Chances were the Iraqis would be looking at them on their long-range search radars based at Qal'at Salih and Ali al Gharbi, but they would be well out of missile range. Within seventy-five kilometers of the coast, Rahavi would arm the two cruise missiles, launch them and break back east toward Esfahan, never leaving Iranian airspace. The other fighters would follow his lead, launching their weapons a few seconds apart.

When Rahavi was sure that the aircraft was functioning within operational parameters, he signaled to the ground crew that he was ready to taxi. He waited for the technicians to stand clear before easing the throttles forward and letting off on the brakes. He turned the Phantom toward the runway, listening to the sporadic static in his headset, then waited there for the other three F-4s to line up behind.

Without breaking radio silence, he advanced the throttles into afterburner, easing off the brakes, feeling the powerful turbojets force him back into his seat. Focusing his attention on the HUD, he watched the glowing green airspeed numbers quickly build to 175 knots. Using his right hand, Rahavi pulled back on the stick, pitching the nose of the F-4E up ten degrees above the horizon. The fighter flashed over the end of the runway as he cleaned up the gear and throttled back, taking the jet out of afterburner. In the rearview mirror, he could see the twinkling lights of Esfahan start to fade.

The afterburners of the number two F-4 lit up the sky as it raced down the runway and followed Rahavi into the sky.

The colonel put his Phantom into a slow climbing turn. A wave of relief came over him. He was in the air at last.

SHUHO MARU

The Japanese oil tanker *Shuho Maru* moved through the clear black night thirty-eight kilometers off the Saudi Arabian coast, heading southeast toward the Strait of Hormuz. Her massive hull pushed forward, creating a six-foot-high wall of dirty brown water as she cut through the ocean, making just four knots. As tankers go, she was among the largest, displacing over 258,000 tons of water when fully loaded. Leased to Overseas Shipholding Group, Inc., the *Shuho Maru* had been scheduled to sail at 0630. However, the ship's captain had bribed the Kuwaiti port authorities with two bottles of sake and five cartons of Marlboro cigarettes to allow his tanker to launch earlier than scheduled. He'd succeeded in being the first tanker to sail that morning out of Sea Island, getting a jump on the other six ships registered to leave the same day. Fully loaded with Kuwaiti heavy crude oil, the *Shuho Maru*, with her crew of thirty-two, had been pushed away from the open-water berth and had cleared the rock and concrete jetties two hours early.

"New heading of one six seven, reduce speed to one eighth." The captain's raspy voice cut through the silence of the bridge.

"One six seven, go to eighth," answered the tanker's pilot, as he moved the wheel right.

Captain Kerha Suakiwa stood, watching the compass swing around to the new heading. He walked up to the bridge's center window, squinting as he inspected the blackness off the bow. He couldn't see a thing, just the red and green flashing anticollision lights of an oil platform west of his position.

The captain put his hands on his hips and stared straight ahead. A small, feeble-looking man with a thin, stringy mustache and sunken cheeks, he wasn't a stranger to these waters. This was his twenty-third trip to Saudi Arabia in the *Shuho Maru*, and the feeling was the same each time. He wouldn't be at ease until his ship and crew had cleared the strait and was sailing in the open sea, toward their home port in Japan.

Suakiwa stepped back from the window and watched the radar scope for a few moments. He didn't like what he was seeing. The screen showed two small vessels cutting across the port bow eight kilometers to the southeast. Both had moved to the north, then stopped dead in the water for a few minutes. Now they were running parallel to his tanker. Each of the unidentified ships was cruising without any lights and not answering its radio calls. The radar return was small, telling the captain the two vessels were probably no bigger than a couple of hundred tons each. They were following each other, matching his speed of four knots.

"Steady as she goes," Captain Suakiwa said, noting the two ships' position, size and speed in his log. If they got too close and the *Shuho Maru* rammed one of them, it wouldn't be his fault, he sighed to himself. He walked over, poured himself a cup of hot tea and returned to his chair. It would be light in another forty-five minutes and the day promised to be clear. He could then get a visual on the fools.

Alireza Rahavi watched the altitude on the HUD hover near 15,000 feet. The colonel trimmed up his fighter for level flight, removed his oxygen mask and activated the F-4E's autopilot. He wiped the sweat from his brow as his eyes routinely swept the instruments, looking for red warning lights. To his amazement, the older fighter was operating perfectly. He wondered for how long.

"Any problems?" Rahavi asked his backseater, looking over his shoulder.

"No sir. All systems are operating."

"I want to know at once if any systems go down," the colonel ordered.

To the north, he could see the bright city lights of Arak drifting toward the aircraft. The landmark told him he was on schedule. He studied the instrumentation. The Dir and Nav dials, indicating direction and navigation, were still rock solid, showing he was maintaining a heading of 246 degrees.

"Colonel . . . right side of the aircraft," Omrai's voice crackled into his headset.

Rahavi's head snapped around. Through the canopy he could

see the navigational lights of three other Phantoms in a staggered formation.

The colonel didn't smile. "We should be picking up the navigational signal by now." The Phantom's TACAN system wasn't receiving the coded UHF navigational signals he needed to make his turn south to stay on course. He had been in the air for thirty-seven minutes; they should be picking up the radio signal by now. He knew the signal wasn't going to be very strong. It was feared the Iraqis would detect it, giving their enemy an opportunity to analyze and decode Iranian air force navigational signals. The thought that possibly he was flying too high crossed his mind.

Rahavi slowly moved the stick forward, pushing the jet's nose down two degrees. The other fighters would have to follow. His airspeed started to increase rapidly. Not wanting to overstress the pylons holding the missiles, Rahavi waited for the HUD to reach 420 knots before throttling back, descending gradually at 500 feet a minute. When the HUD's altitude indicator hit 11,000 feet, he hit the air brakes and began easing back the stick. Rahavi came wings level at 9,860 feet over the desert mountains. He could feel his heart rate increasing as more time passed.

A soft hum in his headset caught his attention. *That's it*, he thought, concentrating on the tone of the radio signal. The TACAN signal was being picked up by the navigational equipment and fed into his headset. The colonel watched the Nav needle swing to the top of the gauge as he banked to the south. He kept his airspeed constant at 530 knots, leveling the Phantom at 8,500 feet, heading 182. Reengaging the autopilot, he snapped the oxygen mask back into place. He sucked in a deep breath of cool air to help calm his nerves. The easy part of the mission was over.

The F-4E navigational computer showed that Rahavi was twenty-two kilometers from the max range launch point. He could see the glassy image of the river below him and the lights of Ahwaz in the distance. He would launch the missiles after passing over the city. If one of the missiles malfunctioned, he didn't want debris raining down on the area.

The cruise missiles' computers had already been programmed to fly at 10,000 feet for the first 100 kilometers. Once over the Gulf, they would drop to 1,000 feet and begin using a wide S flight pattern until acquiring their targets. The digital commands programmed in each missile's independent optoelectronic computers would essentially seek the outline of a tanker fitting the profile of the relayed image. It was the optoelectronic sensor and seeker head, located in the nose, that would methodically begin to search for its target. The eight-inch optical eye gathered enough light to detect and home in on a target even in total darkness.

Rahavi hit the dual switches, activating the missiles' internal computers and navigational systems. The fiberoptic system needed only a few minutes to warm up. The rectangular CRT, located on the right side of the instrument panel, showed that each missile was functioning within operational boundaries. Fuel was 100 percent, electronics were up and running. He flipped two more switches, commanding the small turbofan engines of each missile to spool up and begin to idle. The RPM meter for each fluctuated for a few seconds before stabilizing at 1,500. Next, he switched the optoelectronic seeker and navigational computers to standby. The laser-linked microprocessors would burn up if they weren't cooled by outside air supplied by an intake vent next to the nose cone. Once airborne and 1,000 feet away from the F-4E, the computers would automatically arm the 300-kilogram warhead and take control of the missile's flight.

"Ten kilometers to launch," Lieutenant Omrai said.

Rahavi keyed his mike three times, signaling to the other pilots that it was time to arm their missiles.

He throttled back, watching his airspeed begin to fall. He double-checked to make sure the air brakes were fully deployed, then killed the navigational lights. He estimated he was over the center of the city.

Rahavi tightened his grip on the T-shaped release lever located on the left side of his ejection seat. The mechanical delivery system would drop both cruise missiles two seconds apart. Not taking his eyes off the HUD, he put the Phantom's nose back on a heading of 183 degrees. *Thirty seconds to weapons release*, he counted down to himself.

He inched the throttles back further, watching his airspeed drop below 350 knots. He let it continue to fall until it reached 325 knots.

"Time to launch . . . five seconds . . . four . . . three," Lieutenant Omrai rattled off firmly. "Two . . . one."

One more check of the instruments told Rahavi that everything was ready. The city of Ahwaz was now behind him and the CRT flashed a red launch warning. It was time. He took a deep breath and pulled the lever once. The F-4E lurched upward twice as it was free of the first and then second 2,500-pound missile.

The colonel watched the black silhouettes of each missile against the pale morning sky as they began to streak toward the Gulf ahead of him. He jammed the throttles forward to follow the missiles, not wanting to lose sight of them. A coded electronic data link, hopping from frequency to frequency, between each missile and the F-4E's internal navigation computer told the pilot the two missiles were up and operating. As the missiles turned to dark specks and disappeared before him, he pulled up and away to the east, gaining altitude and airspeed.

"Esfahan center, this is flight two seven niner. ETA forty-four minutes. Repeat, this is flight two seven niner." Breaking radio silence once the mission was complete with the code two seven niner told the engineers on the ground and Defense Minister Bakhtiar that the first missiles had been fired successfully. Now all they could do was wait.

The lead missile nosed over and leveled at 9,980 feet. It traveled at 360 knots, on its way to 480. The cold, dense air gave the sleek radarevading missile added lift. Its fiberoptic gyroscope began to sense the slightest change in its flight path, sending a series of commands to the three tail-mounted fins, which worked in unison to keep the missile on course. The gyroscope had been programmed to guide the shooting projectile out over the Persian Gulf. Once twenty-five kilometers over the water, it would attack the target after authenticating the IR image stored in the computer's guidance system.

Fourteen minutes after separating from the F-4E, both missiles pushed over, heading toward the water. They followed each other in a loose formation 500 feet apart, and descended at 2,000 feet a minute. The internal navigational computers then activated the optical infrared seekers and homing heads of each missile. The steerable sensor heads, resembling eight-inch-diameter camera lenses, began to sweep the sky and water in a wide arc 180 degrees out in front. They would start their search pattern by turning to the east and then back to the west, covering seventy-five kilometers before turning back and searching in the other direction. The search would continue until a target was found or until the fuel levels of each missile ran critically low, at which point both missiles would nose over and fly into the water, destroying themselves.

Five minutes into the search, the optical seekers in the second
Iranian cruise missile picked up the faint outline of a tanker thirteen kilometers to the southwest. Using a laser designator, the
missile luminated the target, feeding the heading range and speed
of the ship into the NAV computer. The same data was shared
with the lead missile using a frequency-hopping data link. A split
second later the first and second missiles turned toward their target.

It was now light enough for Captain Kerha Suakiwa to see the
jagged horizon of Iran's mountainous east coast, but that was
about all. The dark, rolling sea blended into the distant coastline,
making it impossible to see anything with the naked eye. Picking
up a pair of binoculars, he struggled to detect the two ships still
off the port bow. After scanning the water, he finally gave up,
resigning himself to the fact that he would have to wait another
ten or fifteen minutes.

Suakiwa was beginning to feel tired and drained. As soon as
he made visual contact with the idiots off the port bow and things
looked safe, he would turn command over to the second officer.
He could then get something to eat and some much-needed sleep.
He folded his arms, slumped back in his chair and thought about
what he would have for breakfast.

Speeding out of the south after getting a positive lock, the lead
missile, traveling just under Mach 1, ripped into the lower section
of the bridge just below where Captain Suakiwa was sitting. The
missile's speed, along with its half-second delay fuse, allowed the
300-kilogram warhead to penetrate the two-inch-thick rust-stained
steel hull easily. The missile cut through several bulkheads and
into the mess hall, where a few seamen had gathered around a
coffee urn. There it exploded, vaporizing several decks in less
than a heartbeat's time.

A sudden flash of white light filled the bridge. Before realizing
what had happened, Suakiwa was dead, along with his crew. The
explosion was so intense that the entire upper section of the ship,
which overlooked the forward segment, virtually disappeared into
fire, smoke and flying debris.

The tanker rocked violently as the second cruise missile
slammed into the rear half of the vessel, just above the waterline.
Penetrating through the outer and inner hulls, the warhead entered
the aft cargo bay, filled with 26,000 barrels of heavy crude oil.

The resulting explosion buckled what remained of the gigantic tanker, nearly ripping her in half. A fireball one-quarter of a mile wide mushroomed into the sky, and the *Shuho Maru* began to burn.

Twenty minutes later, the sun was a ball of fire pushing itself above the horizon. To the east, a gray-and-white Iranian P-3F Orion marine surveillance aircraft came wings level out of a long banking turn. It was easy to see against the bright morning sky, long trails of black smoke pouring out of its four turboprop engines.

The pilot throttled back, keeping his aircraft a few knots above stall speed. Flying only a hundred meters above the pitching gray water of the Gulf, he dropped the right wing and began circling the burning wreckage. The *Shuho Maru* was listing thirty degrees to her port side. Flames and smoke could be seen pouring from the cargo holds and where the bridge used to be. The pilot looked for any life rafts in the water but didn't see any.

After circling the tanker three times, the copilot signaled he had used all the film in the 35-mm camera. The pilot increased power, turning the P-3 to an easterly heading back toward Iran.

Chapter Nine

ESFAHAN AIR BASE, IRAN

Mark Collins used his shirtsleeve to wipe the sweat from his eyes. The temperature inside the hangar was well over 100 degrees and still climbing. Even more distressing was the fact that it was only 8:30 in the morning. The hangar door was wide open for a possible desert breeze, but it wasn't working. Mark had a good idea that by noon his day would be over. The heat would drive everyone elsewhere to a cooler location.

Collins sat in the front cockpit of an F-4E. An APU (auxiliary power unit) hummed in the background, supplying electricity to the jet's avionics. He had just finished installing the computer software to operate the ALR-606 radar warning receiver, or RWR. The ALR-606 used a single processor and could handle up to four antenna/receiver warnings at one time. The warning data, threat type and direction, was displayed on the HUD. Before he activated the system, Collins needed to run the built-in test program one more time. On either side of the cockpit, standing on aluminum ladders, were seven Iranian technicians. They watched intently as the CIA agent took them through the process of installing and testing the latest computer software that drove the heart of the ALR-606 radar warning system.

In all honesty, Collins was impressed at the condition of each Iranian F-4E with which he had come in contact. He had expected

128

them to be in far worse condition. Most of the original parts had been replaced either by cannibalizing other F-4s or by purchasing parts on the open market. The CIA knew, and often secretly approved of the sale of parts and upgrades from such countries as Germany and Israel. Until recently, the Vietnamese had supplied the Iranians with spare parts they had captured after the U.S. pulled out of Saigon, but those stores had just about dried up. What surprised Collins the most was how the Iranians had been able to adapt new technologies to the F-4s they still had in inventory. If it wasn't for the fact they couldn't interface different software packages, Collins's assistance wouldn't be needed.

"All right, now you try it," Collins said to one of the technicians, an older man who called himself Mohammed Silimi. "Follow the exact sequence I just showed you without dumping the old data." Mark stepped out of the cockpit, changing positions with the man.

The Iranian technician started tapping on the computer keyboard. Collins could tell by his actions that he was intimidated by the small notebook computer and turned his head nonchalantly as the sharp whine of jet engines filled the air. Several hundred yards away, he caught sight of two ghost-gray MIG-29s making their way across the tarmac. He scrutinized the fighters for a few seconds, trying to see what kind of air-to-air missiles they carried. Iranian security had been unpredictable. The military guards were present only half the time he was on the base, allowing him to walk freely around the hangar area. They were also apparently preoccupied with other affairs. Rather than moving the F-4Es into one hangar, as was the original plan, Collins had been allowed to work in five different buildings.

Obviously, I don't look like much of security threat, he thought. He was using every opportunity to take mental notes on the aircraft the Iranian air force taxied past the open door. He paid careful attention to the weapons they carried and if there were any ECM pods strapped to the underside of the wings. So far Collins hadn't observed much out of the ordinary, which was what the CIA had hoped for, but his primary reason for being in Iran was still not achieved. Besides getting a fix on Iran's inventory of fighters, he was attempting to make contact with Perijan Reza, code-named Zenith. It was uncertain if she was still in the area, since contact had been lost for a while.

"Try it one more time." Collins spoke to the man patiently

and pointed to the F-4E's HUD display. The symbology was scrambled; the Iranian had misfed the computer program. The technician nodded and began again.

Collins wondered if the man was really focused on his work.

The assassination attempt was on everyone's mind, including Collins'. He was fortunate to have established his contact for the software sale prior to the attempt and that his whereabouts were accounted for, or he was sure the Iranians would be much more suspicious of his presence. The entire air base was buzzing with the reported fatalities of security guards, airport personnel and the injuries of a couple of personal aides. The latest news was that Prime Minister Mahmoudi was in critical condition somewhere in Tehran.

"That's enough. Let me show you one more time," Collins sighed, then sat back down in the pilot's seat, examining the F-4E's instrument panel. The Iranian had mistakenly disconnected the computer cable. He picked up his notebook computer and snapped the CPU-143/A digital air data computer relay cable into the back of it. The portable computer was now linked into the Phantom's air data computer, which in turn communicated with the threat-warning antenna. He tapped the keys, instructing the computer to activate the test program. If it worked, Mark would dump the new software into the F-4E's air data computer, bringing its threat-warning avionics up to Western standards. It was a trade-off that a few liberals might not understand, but it kept the U.S. abreast of an imminent threat. The HUD lit up.

"Now, let's pay attention this time," Collins said sarcastically as the technicians all nodded in response. "The first sequence starts with TEST RWR MODE/:*:82634." He tapped the keyboard without looking up.

THE PENTAGON

General Howard Chaniff, chairman of the Joint Chiefs of Staff, pulled the fax from his personal machine. It was the ninth one in the past twenty minutes. He read it quietly to himself while walking back to the conference table in his office. Stopping several feet from his chair, he looked up at the two men seated at the table. Philip R. Radford, the secretary of defense, was on his right and Bill Bishop, the President's national security adviser, was on the left. Both had shed their dark wool jackets and had loosened their ties. Their unkempt appearances gave away the fact that they had been sitting there for several hours.

Bishop was tall and athletic, with a full head of sandy-red hair. Radford, on the other hand, was short, stout and nearly bald. They both enjoyed a good game of tennis and played mixed doubles with their wives several nights a week.

Bishop glanced up at the general, his face asking the question.

"The count is now up to five. The Navy has just confirmed a fifth tanker was spotted burning thirty-seven miles inside the Strait of Hormuz. The vessel is dead in the water. The Saudis have several ships in the area and are attempting to rescue any survivors or pick up bodies." Chaniff sat back down and sighed heavily, placing the fax in the center of the table on top of the others. The transmissions had been sent from the commander of the United States Middle East Force, Vice Admiral Nelson Zachiem III, based on the command ship *LaSalle* docked at Mina' Sulman, Bahrain.

"Son of a bitch," Chaniff's raised voice crackled. "How the hell do five tankers blow up in the Gulf without any warning!" Secretary of Defense Radford groaned and pushed himself away from the table. Radford, a former Navy cruiser captain during the Vietnam War, began pacing the floor to control his irritation. His round face showed a hint of red from growing anger.

"They don't just blow up," Bill Bishop said harshly. "Something has to help them. I can't believe no one has seen or heard anything. This is just . . . absolutely preposterous!"

"Do you have any idea what this is going to do to the markets when they open?" Radford said, lost in his own line of thoughts. "Oil prices are going to skyrocket. There'll be pandemonium once the news breaks."

Chaniff didn't really hear either man. Right now he was in the information-gathering mode or, as he referred to it when he worked at the DIA, the sponge factor—trying to suck everything in and filter out the junk. The general had learned, and been taught, that seventy percent of the first few minutes' reports coming in from the field during a crisis were usually wrong. The percentage eventually dropped to zero, with each subsequent report becoming clearer and more accurate. However, the latest fax had been the third report in the past few hours and they were all saying the same thing. An assassination attempt had been made on Iran's prime minister and five tankers had mysteriously blown up in the Gulf. The picture was not becoming any clearer.

"*Why* the hell didn't the CIA give us some warning about this?" Bishop drummed his pencil on the table, looking between Chaniff and Radford. "Why do we have an intelligence agency if they can't give some sort of clue about potential terrorist threats?"

"I don't think this is the work of some terrorist group," Radford said, not wanting to start an accusation match. "Do you have any idea what it would take to blow up a tanker? I think it would be easy to point the finger, but that isn't going to take care of this problem." Besides, the secretary didn't have to remind anyone in the room that Langley had been spending most of its resources keeping tabs on terrorist groups since the end of the cold war. Al-Hudni controlled one of the Middle East's most powerful Shi'ite operations, based in southern Lebanon. The CIA was doing a good job of keeping him and his men in check, but the question still remained: at what cost to other operations?

"So, what are you saying, Phil? This is a state-sponsored attack?" Bishop asked.

"I'm inclined to bet on it," the secretary of defense replied, walking over to the large wall map of the Middle East. "And the likely candidates are Iraq and Iran. They have the most to gain from higher oil prices if the tanker traffic in the Gulf slows to a trickle."

"I agree, but the President's not going to do anything until we have some facts to back up any charges. Especially when we don't even know what the hell happened."

"Howard, you've been sitting there quietly. What's on your mind?" Radford asked.

Chaniff walked over to the map and pressed five red thumbtacks into the positions where the tankers had been hit. He then stood back and surveyed the area, deep in thought.

"Well, Howard . . . are you waiting for the wall to talk to you?" Bishop spoke impatiently, starting to drum his pencil again.

"I'm just trying to see if there is a pattern . . . Perhaps the ships . . ." The general stopped in midsentence. To his disappointment, it looked as if the ships had been hit randomly. Two of the tankers were up north near the Saudi coast, two others were almost in the center of the Gulf, and the last was near the Strait of

Hormuz. None of them were in central locations. "I just don't have enough information yet to give any sound reasoning. Once we get some information from the wreckage or some survivors, maybe we'll have something to go on."

Secretary of Defense Radford massaged his temples. "You're right, of course. We need more information, but we're still going to have to make a recommendation to the President." He walked over to the table and began gathering his papers. "Let's go home, get a few hours of rest and meet back here at 0600. Maybe by then something will be clearer."

"I disagree." Bishop caught the other two men off guard. "We need to make a move and make it fast. There's no question that these ships were attacked; by what or who doesn't matter at this point. If we sit back and wait without sending a clear message to the region, we're asking for a shitload of trouble."

"So, what do you want to do, Bill?" Radford asked, frustrated.

Bishop looked at Chaniff. "Where's our nearest carrier?"

"The *Abraham Lincoln* is in the Indian Ocean, about a day and a half away," Chaniff responded, knowing where Bishop was headed.

"I'm going to recommend that the President move the *Lincoln* and the rest of the task force into the Gulf of Oman as a signal."

"A signal to whom?" Chaniff asked.

"To whoever is attacking tankers in the Gulf." Bishop's face was contorted as he spoke.

"And what will their mission be?" Chaniff didn't back down. "Since we don't know what happened, we could be putting the carrier in the same danger as those tankers."

"When a carrier battle group enters an area and the F-14s and F-18s start patrolling the skies, it's amazing how fast attitudes change." The two men stood practically chest to chest; then Bishop shook his head and turned away, speaking more calmly.

"Okay . . . I'll see you two back here at 0600. I plan on having a briefing at 0645 sharp so we will have a response for the morning news." Bishop picked up his briefcase and walked toward the door. "Gentlemen, I'll see you in a few hours."

Radford waited for the door to close before he spoke. "He has the old man's ear more than anyone, Howard. By 7:00 A.M. that battle group will be sailing toward the Gulf. Mark my word."

"And what is the mission going to be? Who the hell is the enemy? What ships are we going to protect? Do I need to back up the Navy with some land-based fighters? Shit, we don't know crap right now.'' Chaniff took a deep breath and stared back at the map.

''Well, at least you're asking the right questions,'' Radford said sincerely. ''And in Colin Powell's words, 'there is no substitute for massive force.' That's probably good advice today.''

''I still don't like this, and Powell was in a different hot seat.''

''Well, you'd better get used to it. You and I are going to have to take the heat if the military screws up. Even if this wasn't our idea.'' Radford walked to the door, then stopped. He thought for a moment before speaking. ''You probably need to get someone over there you can trust, Howard. Someone who knows both Navy and Air Force operations. If this gets any uglier, we'll need someone to give us clear, no bullshit reports.''

''What about Admiral Zachiem?''

''No, I don't think so.'' Radford smiled. ''Obviously, you've never met Admiral Zachiem.''

Chaniff raised an eyebrow. It wasn't like Radford to blatantly say something negative about an officer.

''Don't get me wrong. Zachiem is a good Navy man, but that's what he is . . . *all* Navy. My advice to you is to get someone with a big ego but one that can be controlled. And he's got to be tough enough to compete with Zachiem, since he's going to be stepping on his toes.'' Radford opened the door. ''See you at 0600.''

Chaniff rubbed his hands over his face. *Great. I don't know what I'm dealing with and now I have to find someone who can fill Walter Mitty's shoes.* He needed a few hours rest and a hot shower. The chairman kept a clean set of clothes in his private bathroom closet, and the rest would have to be taken care of on the couch by the side of his desk.

Chaniff had been chairman of the Joint Chiefs for less than a year, and how he handled this crisis could determine the rest of his term. He needed to make the right recommendations to the President while thinking through all the options, but without being on the scene himself he didn't know what all the options were. Radford was correct about two things. Bishop would have the President convinced that moving the battle group was presently the best option. *And maybe Bishop is right*, Chaniff thought, sighing. But he also needed someone who would report directly to him, someone who knew that planes and black boxes couldn't solve all the problems.

A moment later he picked up the phone and dialed.

STAFFORD, VIRGINIA

"Duke . . . Duke . . . it's the phone." Katie nudged him and whispered, hoping the ringing hadn't awakened the kids.

"Yeah . . . I hear it." He sat up and fumbled in the darkness for the lamp switch next to the bed.

"Hello," he said groggily. He glanced over at the digital alarm clock; it read 1:21 A.M.

"Duke, this is General Chaniff. I'm sorry to wake you. We have a situation developing in the Gulf. I need you at the Pentagon at once."

"Yes, sir."

"My office. Forty-five minutes." The line went dead before Duke could ask any questions. He set the receiver down and stared back at the clock. *Shit, just what I needed to start my day.* Duke pulled the rest of the covers off and sat on the edge of the bed. *Why the hell does he need me? I thought I was on his shit list.*

"What is it?" Katie asked as she rolled over.

"That was Chaniff. He wants me at the Pentagon. In forty-five minutes." Duke's feet just touched the plush carpet when Katie reached over and pulled him back to her. They stared into each other's eyes a moment, then Duke kissed her tenderly.

"Better get going or I'll be making you late." She stroked his bare back with her fingertips.

"If I wasn't already in the dog house with Chaniff, I might take you up on that offer." Duke smiled, then kissed her again before getting out of bed. He turned away, not wanting to see the strain in her eyes. As always, the military seemed to come first.

"I'll make you coffee and something to eat."

"Thanks, but you don't have to get up if you don't want to." When she didn't respond, he continued. "It's probably just an admiral creating his own excitement. I'll be home in time to see the kids off to swimming lessons."

Katie smiled, knowing very well he probably wouldn't even be home for dinner. She got up, threw on her robe and went downstairs.

"Maybe we should try to get out Friday night," Duke called from the bathroom. "Just the two of us." He opened the door to add, "We'll go to that quiet Italian restaurant . . ." Looking around the room, he realized she was already in the kitchen and hadn't heard a word he'd said.

Forty minutes later, Duke James walked through the heavy gauge steel and glass doors at the River Entrance of the Pentagon. With his ID clipped to the front pocket of his Air Force uniform, he turned left onto the E-ring. He walked down one of the main corridors toward the courtyard, past several guards, and quickly climbed the stairs to Chairman Chaniff's second-floor office.

Duke wished that Chaniff had given him a few more details over the phone, something to chew on while he was driving. This wasn't the first time he had been pulled out of bed over some unforeseen world crisis, and as long as he chose to stay in the military it probably wouldn't be the last. Experience told him he would be walking into a roomful of overexcited commanders and expected to have answers to a lot of tough questions when he didn't even know what the crisis was.

He passed through the chairman's outer reception area and into his office. Chaniff was standing with his back to the door, looking at the large map of the Persian Gulf. Duke immediately noticed the red tacks along the shoreline and near the center. He looked around the office. They were alone, though it was apparent there had been others earlier. On the conference table was a sterling silver coffeepot and a plate of what looked like day-old donuts.

"Hello, General."

"Duke . . . thanks for getting here so quickly," Chaniff turned, greeting him and shaking his hand. His tired, bloodshot eyes and unshaven face made Duke wonder if the chairman had even been to bed.

"Grab a cup of coffee and I'll fill you in," Chaniff said, motioning to the table and then turning back to the map.

Duke poured a cup and listened, engrossed in every word Chaniff had to say. When he finished, Duke studied the map, just as perplexed. Then Chaniff cleared his throat.

"Duke, I need someone over there I can trust. Whatever the hell's going on is bound to be big and the information I get has got to be clear and precise."

"You want me in the Gulf? As what, your personal adviser?" Duke questioned, surprised by this new development, considering that a few days ago the general was not sure of his stability.

"That's correct. I want someone who understands joint operations and weapons systems. The situation is hot. I know I can count on you to cut through the bullshit. You won't be afraid to give solid recommendations." Chaniff looked directly at Duke as he spoke.

Duke's eyes narrowed as he listened to Chaniff stroking him while he was explaining his reasoning. There were at least a dozen other men with more experience for this type of assignment. *Why did Chaniff decide to give me the first shot at this?*

"I'm not as qualified as—"

"Don't play humble with me, Duke. I want you because you're not afraid to get your hands dirty. I don't need an ass-kisser or career builder out there when my butt's on the line. If you want me to stand here and blow sunshine up your ass because you're still insecure about Hodges, I don't have time for it. I think you made the right call on that one, and you know it. Now, either you want the job or you don't," Chaniff snapped, then took a deep breath. "If not, tell me *now* so I can make some other calls."

Duke's six-foot frame grew rigid at the chairman's outburst. He knew it was time to quit feeling guilty and get on with his work.

"When do I leave, sir?"

"Two hours. The transport is ready and standing by at Andrews right now, but I thought you might want to say good-bye to your wife and kids first." Chaniff shook Duke's hand and tried to grin but couldn't, he was too damn tired.

"General . . . you could have just given an order over the phone." Duke said trying not to smirk.

"I know. But I wanted to see your face. Make sure that the fire in your eyes hadn't been washed out yet." Chaniff slapped him on the back, then pointed to the door. "Get out of here, Duke. I need to get some sleep."

"Yes, sir. I'll be in touch when I land." Duke turned, his shoulders back and chest out. He was ready for another mission.

ESFAHAN, IRAN

"Minister Bakhtiar, I have Colonel Rahavi on the phone," the minister's secretary said over the intercom.

"Put him through." Bakhtiar's voice was light as he watched the television screen in the corner of his office. CNN was broadcasting live pictures from the Gulf. A large supertanker was burning, the *Shuho Maru*. Columns of black smoke were billowing out of several places along the top of the hull, and orange balls of fire exploded through a long tear in the ship's side.

"Colonel Rahavi. Do you have a final report?" he asked immediately upon picking up the phone.

"We have confirmed hits on five ships, Minister Bakhtiar. Seven of the eight missiles hit their mark. The number six missile, fired by aircraft number three, malfunctioned just after leaving the aircraft. The pilot succeeded in instructing the missile to enter the water, where it detonated."

Bakhtiar was quiet for a few seconds, watching the *Shuho Maru. The missiles had worked.* He smiled, inwardly jubilant. Millions were now viewing this evidence of their success.

"Do you have any other problems to report?" Bakhtiar asked, trying to keep his thinking clear.

"No, sir."

"Very well. You and your men have done well, Colonel."

"Thank you. We will wait for further orders, sir."

"I will contact Captain Behzad Moezi at Bandar Abbas. I want the Silkworm sites on-line in twenty-four hours. If I am correct, the Americans will move within the next few days. Good-bye, Colonel." He replaced the receiver and sat back in his chair.

The first shots of the second Iranian revolution had just been fired. Mahmoudi was finally out of the way and the military answered to him only. By the time the rest of the world figured out what had happened, it would be too late to stop him.

Bakhtiar suddenly leaned forward. His face felt hot and his breath was becoming short. Within seconds, his heart began palpitating rapidly, racing out of control in his chest. Zadeh, standing in his usual place behind the minister, knew something was wrong. The bodyguard reached into the desk drawer and pulled out a bottle of medication. He swiftly shook out two Inderal tablets and put the small blue pills into the minister's mouth. Grabbing a glass of water, he forced the minister to swallow. Once Bakhtiar indicated that the pills had gone down, Zadeh helped him to sit back in the chair. With uncharacteristic gentleness, Zadeh wiped away the water that dribbled from his mouth onto his chin.

Bakhtiar breathed heavily, angry at himself for becoming too excited. He couldn't let his country and people down now. Not at the beginning of a new era.

Chapter Ten

Tom Staffer, the CIA's deputy director for operations, or DDO, took a sip of his morning coffee and, shifting in his chair, flipped to the second page of the President's daily intelligence briefing. It was 8:10 A.M. and he had been seated in front of the President for the last thirty minutes. The briefing was a quick review of world events from the previous day and night, along with the CIA's opinion on how they would affect the security of the United States.

Bill Bishop, the President's national security adviser, seated next to Staffer, was anxiously following everything the DDO reported. He had already briefed the President over breakfast, but he wanted to hear what the CIA had to say.

"I don't like it when the CIA doesn't have answers to important questions, Tom." President Louis McEntire didn't attempt to hide his ugly mood. "If there is one area in the world where we *need* to know what is going on at *all* times, it's the Gulf. Am I correct?"

"Yes, sir," Staffer agreed. "And I believe we are doing our best to stay on top of the situations that arise, but there is only so much we can do."

"Frankly, Tom, I don't mind telling you I'm disappointed. How is that a supposedly 'superior intelligence agency' does not

139

know when something like this is about to happen . . . *and shit, you don't even know who's responsible!* I fought like hell when I was in Congress to make sure you guys got the best equipment . . . right?'' McEntire moved his hand up to emphasize his point. This would not look good with reelection coming up.

Staffer just nodded as the President blew off steam and vented his frustrations. Staffer had known Louis McEntire for a dozen years or so. He had been a representative from Arizona's sixth district before winning the Republican nomination and ultimately the presidency three and a half years ago. While a congressman, he had been a member of the House Permanent Select Committee on Intelligence and had chaired the Armed Services Committee. Staffer had come to know him through CIA briefings and casual encounters during cocktail and dinner parties. In Staffer's opinion, McEntire might be an efficient administrator, but he was hotheaded and tended to back down and reverse course when faced with strong opposition, particularly from within his own party. It wasn't a trait Staffer cared for, particularly in a President.

Now that his approval rating was below fifty percent, the talk inside the Beltway was that McEntire could lose reelection if he didn't start acting more like a President, specifically on foreign policy. The press was having a field day, and the President appeared to be a bit edgy, to say the least.

Staffer watched in silence as McEntire walked over to a sideboard to fill his coffee cup. Though the President was fifty-two years old, only a few years older than Staffer, his tan face and thick wiry black hair made him appear years younger. The only flaw was a slightly thick midsection, giving away his weakness for late-night snacks and Domino's Pizza. He had a flair for style and was usually seen sporting a Brooks Brothers tailored suit or perfectly matched casual wear. The President returned to his seat.

''If I am going to develop a policy, I need to know what's going on in the region.''

Staffer bit his tongue, wondering why there hadn't already been a policy established in the region. It seemed when things got screwed up, it was always the CIA's fault. If everything went right, the agency was just doing its job.

The President's attention shifted to a copy of *USA Today* on the corner of his desk. The latest ABC/CNN presidential campaign poll showed that the President's approval rating had slid another four points, now down to forty-two percent, in the past two weeks. He was now running neck and neck with the Democratic front-runner, Senator Jon Russell of Ohio. The headline picture was of Russell standing before a crowd of supporters in Chicago. He was blasting McEntire for his inept leadership on foreign policy and the economy. With the Republican National Convention just three weeks away, the President was starting to feel pressured.

"Show me what else you have on this." The President bit his lower lip as he looked through the briefing.

Staffer went on. "Sir, we received these photos from one of our reconnaissance aircraft about three hours ago." He handed over a series of eight-by-ten color photographs to the president, who passed them on to Bishop. "They're of the *Shuho Maru*, a Japanese tanker that exploded thirty-two miles off the Saudi coast in the Persian Gulf approximately seven hours ago."

"You're a little late, Tom," Bishop said mockingly. "CNN's been broadcasting pictures since I got up this morning. We've already seen this. Can't you show us something we haven't seen . . . like what happened before it exploded?"

"That's because it's the only ship that hasn't sunk yet," Staffer answered stiffly.

"The environmentalists are going to start screaming," was the President's only comment as he took off his glasses to rub his eyes.

"I already have the communication people working on a response, sir. Everyone knows environmental issues have been one of your priorities," Bishop intervened. "The press office will have an appropriate statement out shortly."

"*Spilled oil* is not what we should be concerned about, gentlemen." Staffer pointed to one of the pictures. "This was a very large explosion. Navy analysts at Norfolk believe the ship was hit by at least one, maybe two, antiship missiles . . . sea skimmers. You can see that the ship is burning in two distinct areas."

This caught Bishop's attention. "So, it was antiship missiles. Can you back it up with proof?"

Staffer fumbled through the pile to another picture. The photo was a closeup of the hull near the back of the ship. He pointed to a dark area about a yard square and ten feet above the waterline. It was very clearly a round hole, where something had impacted the tanker from the outside.

"If you look closely, you can see the metal curves inward

rather than outward. If this had been an internal explosion, the force of the blast would have pushed the metal outward. The Navy estimates the missile must have been traveling at near Mach 1, because it penetrated so deeply into the tanker's superstructure before exploding.''

''Were there any AWACS in the air?'' Bishop asked.

''Thirty minutes ago the Saudis supplied us with the computer tapes of an E-3 that was patrolling the area to the west. They reported no unusual aircraft or surface ship activity. I've already considered the possibility of an Iraqi-launched Exocet. But the E-3 didn't track one, so it's not likely.''

''Maybe if that E-3 had an American crew an Exocet could have been picked up,'' Bishop replied, still studying the picture.

Staffer was quiet; he couldn't disagree. Just because the Saudis had Western equipment didn't mean they could use it to its full potential.

''What about a Silkworm?'' Bishop asked, knowing that Iran operated at least thirty-five of the Chinese-designed antiship missile sites along their western coast.

''Silkworms are radar-guided. The Saudis didn't pick up any hostile radar transmissions, and neither did any of our listening posts in the Gulf.'' Staffer's tone was even as he continued. ''Besides, our satellites would have detected the boost phase of their launch.''

''Interesting.'' Bishop thumbed through the photos again.

''Since these shots were taken, the tanker has capsized. There is an oil slick about a half mile long that is burning out of control. Kuwait and Saudi Arabia still have search and rescue operations going on and are struggling to put out the fire. So far no survivors have been found.'' Staffer opened his black leather briefcase, preparing to leave since he had nothing more to report.

''And you say the other four ships have sunk?'' the President asked.

''That's correct.'' Staffer closed the case after collecting his papers. He waited to be excused from the session.

''What's your gut feeling, Tom?'' Bishop suddenly addressed Staffer. ''Is this some sort of terrorist attack?''

''It's too early to give an opinion. But I doubt any terrorist group could have pulled this off. Antiship missiles are fairly sophisticated, and you can't just haul them around in a truck or boat.''

Bishop looked at the President, then back at Staffer. "That's exactly what I think. We're dealing with something more dangerous than radicals. Mr. President, my recommendation stands. You should immediately give the order to move the *Abraham Lincoln* and her battle group into the area at once."

President McEntire nodded, making notes, and glanced at the national security adviser. "And what are they going to do there?"

"For right now I'd say they'd be there for intimidation purposes. We need advanced aircraft on patrol over the Gulf to show whoever's responsible we're not bluffing about keeping the shipping lanes open." Bishop then added firmly, "Defense Secretary Radford agrees with me. We need to move on this now."

"Okay, Bill . . . it's done. But I want you and Tom to find out who is behind this, ASAP. Flexing our muscle is one thing, but applying it is something else." The President handed the pictures back to Staffer, signaling the end of the meeting.

The expression on the President's face made Staffer wonder if he really understood what was involved in having tankers blown out of the water in the middle of the Persian Gulf for no apparent reason.

"Good day, gentlemen." Staffer stood quickly, exiting the Oval Office. He had problems of his own to worry about.

The President punched the intercom button on his phone. "Allan, get my press secretary in here at once." He wanted to alert the networks that he was ordering a carrier to the Gulf region at once so that the American people would know he was on top of the situation.

"Yes, Mr. President."

"Politically, this is a wise decision," Bishop said, smiling confidently. "The Democrats won't be able to criticize you for wanting to protect the United States' interests."

"I appreciate your worrying about the political ups and downs of this, but what I need from you right now is to make sure the CIA and everyone else involved at this point is doing their job. Unless you have anything else to add, I have other matters to attend to." McEntire brushed his adviser off, wanting to hear answers, not praise.

"I'll keep you posted, Mr. President." Bishop, chastised, picked up his belongings and left the Oval Office.

McEntire knew that ordering in a carrier would make him appear decisive and force his Democratic challenger to either support him openly or look unpatriotic. However, it wasn't Bishop's job to worry about politics. His responsibility was the well-being of the United States, and McEntire was concerned his adviser couldn't separate the two. At this critical time, the President worried that Bishop might not think things through thoroughly. Focusing on what looked best for a reelection could backfire and leave them all in a sinking ship, so to speak. *Well, Mr. Bishop, I hope you're right on this one. I don't need a foreign policy black eye right now.*

Walking past two blue-jacketed Secret Service men, Staffer exited the White House through the West Wing and climbed into one of the CIA's shiny black Cadillac limousines. A moment later, the limo turned onto Pennsylvania Avenue heading toward CIA headquarters in Langley, Virginia. Tom let himself sink into the soft leather seat, trying to organize the rest of his day. He still felt a bit uneasy giving the President's intelligence briefing. President McEntire was a difficult person to read, and Staffer didn't feel comfortable not knowing what was probably going through his mind.

Staffer's parents were wealthy, East Coast Ivy Leaguers and had sent him to Princeton, where he received a degree in law at the age of twenty-five. It was expected he would join the law firm of close friends and marry their daughter. To the dismay of his parents, however, he joined the CIA and married a waitress from one of the local hamburger joints. The rest is history, as they say: children, long hours at work leading to a divorce, then the drowning of it all with booze and cigarettes.

The job was what kept him going, and after twenty-seven years Staffer knew the CIA as well as anyone. The hard work and long hours paid off with a promotion to one of the upper levels in the agency.

Staffer's bulky build and dark looks were the stereotypical image of a CIA lifer. His intense eyes, set deep in a tanned face, were hard, but women found him attractive. Staffer had a definite, powerful demeanor, and the clubs in the D.C. area were full of young females searching for just such an older man.

The car phone rang only once before he picked up the receiver.

"Staffer here."

"Good, you're on your way back." It was Vance Edleman, the deputy director for intelligence.

"Yeah, what's up?" Staffer could talk freely, knowing the conversation was secure. Using a modified AT&T electronics signal scrambler, which electronically encrypted the conversation on a military UHF frequency, there wasn't any way the conversation could be picked up or recorded. Nonetheless, Staffer made it a point to keep conversations on the mobile phone short and general.

"We just got additional data on the tanker hits in the Gulf. Thought you might want to take a look at it. How long before you're back here?"

Staffer glanced out the window. "I'm just passing Arlington. Depending on traffic, I'd say about fifteen minutes."

"Good. Meet me in my office at 9:30. I have a few things I have to finish up first."

Staffer huffed as the line went dead. He looked at the receiver before replacing it. *Was everyone going to be acting like an asshole today?* he thought.

Staffer reached over and grabbed his unread copy of the Washington *Post* on the seat next to him. He opened it to the sports page, trying to take advantage of the quiet moment.

TEHRAN, IRAN

Defense Minister Sheik Ali Bin Bakhtiar finished his midafternoon prayers and shut the Koran, setting it carefully on the corner of his desk. A smirk came across his dried, cracked lips. He had left the television set on, with the sound turned down, to follow the news reported throughout the day. Once again the picture of an overturned tanker burning in the Gulf appeared on the screen. He quickly turned up the volume to listen.

I will cut the head off the infidels and they will never know what struck them. Just as he had suspected, the Western news agencies had quickly picked up on the story. Only in their incompetence they were reporting that several terrorist groups were suspected of the attacks, though none of them were taking credit yet. Bakhtiar felt himself growing irritated at the new reports.

"Minister Bakhtiar, I hope I'm not disturbing you," Akhbar al-Yawm, Iran's interior and security minister, said from just outside the door.

"No. You may enter," Bakhtiar answered, raising the remote control to mute the sound again.

"I am here to report on Prime Minister Mahmoudi's condition," Akhbar said tensely. "He is still in a coma."

"I'm sorry to hear that. I have prayed that Allah would let him rest," Bakhtiar said in a thick voice.

Akhbar stood for a long moment and stared at Bakhtiar. *I know I must be right. This man is not to be underestimated. Who else would have gained so much by the assassination of Mahmoudi.*

"Your mission last night was a success. Many tankers were destroyed," Akhbar spoke slowly, watching Bakhtiar's reaction.

"What are you talking about?" Bakhtiar asked, feigning bewilderment.

"Do *not* play games with me, Bakhtiar. I have many loyal people under my command. I know you launched cruise missiles last night. The mission was staged from Esfahan and took place only a few hours after the assassination attempt on the prime minister."

Bakhtiar sneered and his eyes hardened. He had never believed the quiet Akhbar would ever be a threat to him. The two had had few dealings together. *Perhaps he is only testing to see what he has to gain from my position*, Bakhtiar thought.

"You are a wise man, Akhbar. And you are correct, of course. The missiles hit their targets just as I planned and there were no problems. It was a victory for our country." Bakhtiar displayed the joy and pride he felt.

"You did this without consent from the other members of the Supreme Defense Council," Akhbar went on cautiously.

"Yes, that is also true. But how was I to know there would be an attempt made on Minister Mahmoudi's life? He and I had discussed moving ahead with these plans before he left. It simply could not wait."

"I do not believe that was the prime minister's wish. He had not seemed as anxious to use those missiles as you were."

"Well, perhaps you are not as well informed as you believe. The prime minister, Minister Marjid and I had a meeting on this very matter only days prior to his departure."

"Unfortunately, Minister Marjid was fatally shot during the assassination attempt." Akhbar was beginning to grow leery of his own safety, suddenly realizing how convenient Marjid's death had been.

"Yes, that was most disturbing." Bakhtiar lowered his gaze and shook his head in sympathy. "Minister Marjid's *Jihad* never wavered.'' He wanted to point out that Marjid had been loyal to the holy war that had to be won against the Kurdish rebels and the West.

"What is the next part of your plan?" Akhbar asked bluntly.

"We are now ready to expand the war against the Americans." Bakhtiar watched the man's face closely for his reaction to this news. "The order has already been given. Colonel Rahavi and his men will begin deploying the missiles to Bandar Abbas tonight. In forty-eight hours I expect the Americans will be bringing ships into the Gulf. When they do, their ships will be destroyed. All surface traffic will come to a halt. Mark my words . . . the West will squeal like pigs being slaughtered."

Akhbar looked Bakhtiar in the eyes, not wanting to appear overly surprised. "You have given the order . . . without the permission of even the Ayatollah Abdol-Rasul Hanifnezhad? Attacking unarmed tankers successfully once might be a victory, but attacking the American fleet could bring misery upon us." He paused. "With Allah's will I pray you don't destroy us," he added boldly.

"The responsibility is mine. You do not understand the power of our new weapon. It is Allah's will that Iran control the Gulf." Bakhtiar studied the man standing before him. He still could not figure out whether he was going to be trouble or not. "The prime minister's trip . . . you accompanied him. Perhaps you should tell me the details so that I may handle any matters that arise."

This surprised Akhbar and he backed away from Bakhtiar's desk, realizing his dilemma. He should never have started this line of questioning without being prepared, but now it was too late. The situation was already out of his control. Bakhtiar was getting exactly what he wanted: the power to lead Iran. Either he would succeed in saving Iran's revolution or it would be destroyed by his attempts. *I forgot about the contracts.* Akhbar took in a deep breath suddenly, remembering that he had proof that this war was not the prime minister's wish.

Bakhtiar stood from behind his desk. As he did so, Hassan Zadeh moved up beside him. He slipped his huge right hand under his suit jacket, placing it on the handle of his pistol. "Is something wrong?" Bakhtiar asked suspiciously.

"No . . . no, I'm sorry. I guess it's the strain of all that has happened. I have not had much sleep. Please excuse me." Akhbar, not waiting for a response, swiftly left the room.

Bakhtiar had only to look over at his bodyguard to get his message across. Zadeh left the room to find a trusted accomplice to follow the minister of interior and security.

Tom Staffer entered the private elevator in the CIA's basement parking lot that would take him directly to the seventh floor of the old building.

"Good morning, Mr. Staffer." His assistant, Heather Rice, smiled from behind her computer terminal as he walked past her desk.

"Good morning, Heather. Hold my calls, please."

"Yes, sir. Mr. Edleman's already called twice." She smothered a smile. Her boss was obviously having a bad day and it was only 9:15 A.M.

"I know. The damn traffic's put me behind schedule. But I wasn't going to meet him for another ten minutes. I'll try to answer some calls first." Staffer entered his office and threw his dark blue pinstriped suit coat on a nearby chair. He sat down at the desk and thumbed through the telephone messages.

Except for personal effects, such as pictures of his children and a mounted seven-pound large-mouth bass caught during a camping trip with his oldest son, Staffer's office wasn't much different from the other three deputy directors'. All were located on the seventh floor, down the hall from the DCI. Each had gray carpeting and dark brown paneling. On the left was a wall-length bookshelf filled with a variety of law books, novels and periodicals, everything from Civil War history texts to CIA and State Department briefing papers. Behind the desk was a computer terminal and three coded fax machines. The drapes were drawn and a large brass desk lamp added light to the somber and conservative atmosphere of the office.

"Tom, glad I caught you between phone calls," Vance Edleman said from the doorway.

"Yeah, but I thought we were on at 9:30."

"We were, but I don't want to be running behind the rest of the day."

"You're ahead of me—I'm already behind."

"Well, it's budget time for me. I'm briefing a group of congressmen at 11:00. We're scheduled to have lunch at Tempo. Want to join us?"

Staffer smiled. "No thanks. It'll be the same old story, only a different year. They have two questions, one—what are our plans for the next-generation space surveillance systems. And two— what kind of budget are we looking for and can we get by with a twenty percent cut without compromising our resources.''

Edleman shook his head, trying not to laugh. ''Yeah. I have to make sure I say all the right numbers or we won't get a damn thing. I hate this time of year.''

''Glad I'm not in on this one. All right. What do you have?''

Edleman took a seat, opening a dog-eared file and removing his notes. As deputy director for intelligence, Edleman was in charge of the analytical side of the CIA. His staff coordinated, consolidated and appraised the thousands of bits of information that flowed into the CIA each day. It was their job to make sense of the data collected in the field and from open sources.

Five years older than his counterpart at the DO, Vance Edleman was balding and thirty pounds overweight. He got along with Staffer probably better than anyone else in the building. He knew Staffer had a temper, but Edleman, having a mild manner, never took it personally. He generally let Tom go about his business without much interference, considering the daily rivalries of their departments. Occasionally, the two men would clash, but it was always over procedural differences, not philosophical ones. They knew they were both driven by the same mission.

''After you left this morning, we had a chance to go over the radar telemetry that was recorded from that Saudi AWACS operating over the western edge of the Gulf. I had Burnell plot ELINT data on a map so you could see it. It seems our Iranian friends had a P-3 orbiting above the *Shuho Maru* approximately four minutes after she was hit.'' Edleman handed Staffer a copy of the two-page report.

''Four minutes . . . huh, that's fast.'' Staffer studied the first page for a few seconds, then turned to the map. It was a simple black-and-white outline of the Gulf. A dotted line plotted the course of the Iranian P-3. It looked as if the aircraft had flown in from the southeast, circled the tanker three times and exited the area to the northeast, back toward Iranian airspace. Staffer shrugged. ''The Iranians are always flying operation aircraft in this area. I think you're being—''

''Not so fast, Tom,'' Edleman interrupted. ''The *Shuho Maru* was only thirty-two miles off the eastern coast of Saudi. I checked with both Air Force and Navy intelligence. The Iranians haven't operated an aircraft that close to the Saudi Arabian coastline in the last three years. The Saudis scrambled two F-15s, but the P-3 had exited the area before they arrived.''

Staffer leaned back in his chair. ''What are you telling me, Vance? The Iranians knew this was going to happen so they had an aircraft on standby? What about the other four tankers?''

''This is the only one they flew over. But the other hits could easily have been monitored from the shore or possibly from other surface ships.'' Edleman ran a finger over the map.

''So, are you saying . . . you think Iran is behind this?'' Staffer looked mildly surprised. ''If they were, would they be that stupid to give it away like this?''

''No . . . I wouldn't go that far yet, but I do think it's a hell of a coincidence. An oil tanker is hit by two missiles and the Iranian air force is circling above the burning ship before anyone else in the world knows what happened.'' Edleman closed the file. ''I also know we have limited agents on the ground in Iran. It's tough to guess what the bastards are up to with only satellites and radar telemetry.''

Staffer nodded knowing Iran's government and military had been extremely difficult for the Western intelligence agencies to penetrate. Even Mossad, Israeli intelligence, wasn't currently operating any agents on the inside. At least the CIA had had some successes. Staffer had been able to place two Pakistani students, both of whom had been recruited separately while studying in Britain, into one of Iran's guarded terrorist training camps. The Firuzkoor camp, in the desert near Tehran, specialized in teaching terrorists how to brainwash, control and activate suicide bombings. Distressingly, the CIA received only two reports from each man before they disappeared. Later, satellite pictures indicated the camp had been deserted. Staffer and his Middle East team still didn't have a clue as to what tipped the Iranians off, but it was obvious the two had come to an unfortunate end.

''I'll instruct my field officers to keep their eyes and ears open. But I need some help from your end. Have one of your information junkies give me a list of possible missiles that could have hit this ship. It may help us to narrow down what we're looking for.''

''You got it, Tom. I'll get Admiral Currie on it ASAP,'' Edleman said, leaving the room.

Directly in front of Staffer was a yellow notepad with a to-do list numbered from 1 to 7. So far this week the first three numbers were crossed out. The idea was to have the list completed by the end of the week and start a new one on Monday morning. Unfortunately, that never happened. He glanced at the pad in hopes he could cross another one off, but Edleman wasn't on the list.

On the right edge of his desk were three custom-made oak boxes designed to hold standard-sized paper. They matched the desk set an old girlfriend had given him one year for Christmas. The first box contained outgoing reports ranging from personal summaries, budget requests and expense reports to briefing papers on specific operations. The box beside it contained incoming field transmissions from a dozen or so world hot spots Staffer had particular interest in and wanted to stay on top of. They were written by CIA officers stationed at U.S. embassies and by CIA operation teams in the field. Staffer liked these firsthand reports because they hadn't been retyped or watered down. The third basket was for urgent correspondence, reports or requests that demanded his immediate attention. As was generally the case, this box was empty. Staffer grabbed the top document from the second in-box. Printed on white flash paper was a message from SPECTRA, the CIA's code name for Mark Collins.

AZVT3-SATCOM-TRANS   #724
PALACE   GUARD/SPECTRA   **IMMEDIATE**

- ESFAHAN AIR BASE. SECURITY HEAVY BUT NOT SUSPICIOUS.
- CONTINUING F-4 OPERATION. ESTIMATE IRAN IS OPERATING AT LEAST 36, REPEAT 36, F-4E PHANTOMS OUT OF ESFAHAN. HAVE SEEN A MIX OF MIG-29S, MIG-23S AND SU-24S. BASE IS CLEAN AND WELL ORGANIZED. SECURITY TROOPS ARE PROFESSIONAL AND ORGANIZED.
- START CONTACT ZENITH WHEN OPERATION IS SET.
- NEXT TRANSMISSION . . . 2000 HOURS LOCAL.

Staffer set the piece of paper down. The message had been received five hours ago after being decoded and hand-delivered to Staffer's office by one of the night watch officers. If the message had read FLASH or CRITIC, someone would have called him at home to wake him.

Collins's message had been short for a reason. It probably signaled he didn't feel comfortable giving a lot of detail at the moment. Collins's idea of impersonating a McDonnell Douglas engineer was a good one, but the Iranians would still consider him an outsider and that meant he would have limited access. The best Staffer could hope for was Collins's reestablishing contact with the young Iranian woman, Zenith. The last CIA officer to get this close to the air base was Edward Perry. Perry, operating as a medical equipment salesman from France, had worked in Esfahan for fifteen months when the agency abruptly lost contact with him. Before his disappearance, he had maintained regular contact with Zenith. She had supplied the agency with several detailed reports on Iran's growing computer capability.

If Collins could find her and reestablish contact, the operation could be called a success. The success rate of this type of operation was less than fifty percent, however. Staffer placed the field transmission under his notepad. Having Collins in Iran right now could prove to be beneficial.

Night fell quickly on central Iran. The blazing orange desert sun was disappearing behind the jagged Zagros Mountains, taking with it the intense heat, though the temperature was far from Colonel Alireza Rahavi's main concern. Hot or cold, the night was his friend and presently he planned to use it to transport twenty-four cruise missiles to the naval base at Bandar Abbas. He had received his handwritten orders from Defense Minister Bakhtiar twelve hours earlier. The orders were clear and precise. The missiles were to be placed in several of the secret fixed Silkworm sites that were scattered along the rocky coastline of southern Iran near the narrowest section of the Strait of Hormuz.

Rahavi paced back and forth in the tiny room he used as an office while working at the weapons site. Located in the basement of the complex, the room contained a standard metal desk and several sets of coded telephones all linked to Iran's newly installed military fiberoptic communications system. The new system was impossible to jam or eavesdrop on.

"All the missiles have been prepared for transport?" Rahavi asked Chief Engineer Khalk Hikmet, who was standing near the door.

"Yes. They should be loading the last few now."

Rahavi picked up one of the authority phones linking him directly to the command and control center at Bandar Abbas. It rang twice before being answered.

"Captain Behzad Moezi here."

"This is Colonel Rahavi at Esfahan. The missiles will be airborne in one hour. Is everything ready on your end?"

"I am prepared. My troops are standing by to transfer the missiles as soon as you land."

"And the sites? Are they ready?"

"As per your orders, Colonel."

"Very well. I will contact Defense Minister Bakhtiar after they are airborne."

Rahavi left the room with Hikmet following on his heels. The two walked down a long flight of concrete steps into the sub-basement directly under the weapons complex's final assembly room. At the end of a corridor, they stopped just before entering a large garage area. Three desert-brown military trucks with canvas tarps covering their rear halves were parked in a row. The colonel could see several dozen men, some of them driving electric carts, working to load long wooden boxes into the back of the nearest truck.

Rahavi rubbed his nose. The loading chamber reeked of dampness, sour mold and diesel fuel. The stench didn't seem to bother the chief engineer or the other men.

Hikmet shouted to one of the crew, an army lieutenant, standing on the loading ramp. "How many missiles have you loaded?"

"Twenty-three. We have only one more to secure."

Rahavi watched in silence. The reality of the situation came flooding over him, and he needed a moment to gather his thoughts. He had toiled with the engineers, computer programmer and other pilots to perfect each phase of research, development and now deployment of the Phalanx Dragon.

The last wooden box was being loaded. He watched the men's muscles strain as they guided the heavy missile off the cart onto the bed of the truck. It was secured with nylon straps for the short drive to the southern part of the air base. There they would all be loaded onto a transport and flown to Bandar Abbas.

Chapter Eleven

MINA' SULMAN, BAHRAIN

The jolt of the USAF transport jet's gear hitting the runway brought Duke out of his light sleep. He opened his eyes to the sight of bright white lights streaking past his window. *Oh shit, already.* Duke rubbed his grimy face. *Man, I could use a hot shower.* He brushed his short hair with his fingertips, hoping it helped make him look more presentable, as the aircraft wheeled around and parked next to a large aluminum hangar. He waited for the door to swing open before grabbing his briefcase and duffle bag and stepping outside.

"Welcome to Bahrain, General James," a short naval ensign with thick eyeglasses shouted over the jet engines. He added, "Admiral Zachiem has been expecting you, sir."

Duke felt a blast of warm desert air hit him in the face.

"May I take your bags, sir?"

"No, I have them," Duke laughed to himself, thinking the little guy probably couldn't handle them anyway. This was the first time he had flown into Bahrain. The base was awash in bright light from rows of floods lining the perimeter of the base. Several hundred yards away were four F-15s and two F-16s parked in front of the main hangar. The sight of the Air Force jets aroused him from his slumbering mood.

"This way, please," the ensign called out, waiting for him to

154

follow. Duke took only two long steps before he caught up with the young man who was leading him to a dark blue Chrysler sedan. He dumped his luggage in the open trunk and climbed in the backseat.

"How was your flight, sir?"

"No problems," Duke answered, smiling. *Why does everybody ask that same stupid question when you get off an airplane? One of these days I'm just going to say, well, it wasn't as good a ride as my wife gave me last night.*

"Admiral Zachiem asked that I give this to you, sir. It contains several short briefing papers on our operations here. It may help answer some of your questions before meeting with the admiral." The ensign handed Duke a two-inch-thick file.

This is short? Duke opened the file as the car started to move. *Either Zachiem is trying to impress me or he's trying to win the efficieny award—this is a joke.* He glanced over the first page listing the officers, ships and other personnel under the admiral's direct command. *An interesting way to start a briefing paper.*

Duke had heard a lot about Admiral Nelson Zachiem III while working at the Pentagon. The man was considered either a flaming asshole or a brilliant naval officer, but definitely a political man set on becoming the chairman of the Joint Chiefs. Duke figured he would form his own opinion based on personal experience. Not being a paper man himself, this briefing file wasn't a good sign. Duke had, however, with the permission and more than gentle urging of Chaniff, looked over the admiral's service file to get some insight.

Admittedly, Nelson Zachiem III's career had not always been on the fast track. He came from a long line of Navy officers, all of whom had graduated in the top ten percent of their class. His father, Nelson Zachiem II, skippered the light cruiser *Denver* (CL-58) during World War II and was part of an eight-vessel element that gained fame as the "Little Beavers," commanded by Captain Arleigh Burke. The *Denver* and her crew had fought in a number of furious naval engagements against the Japanese imperial navy including the battle at Empress Augusta Bay, in which the *Denver* sank the cruisers *Sendai* and *Myoko*. His father had also assisted William F. "Bull" Halsey in the strategic planning of the island-hopping campaign through the Central Solomons, from Guadalcanal to New Georgia. The man was recognized during and after the war for his courage, leadership and vision in defeating the Japanese in the Pacific.

Unlike his father's, Zachiem's career consisted of very little action. He served on several destroyers during the Vietnam War as a young ensign and lieutenant, although he never saw any actual combat. Through the late '70s and early '80s, Zachiem took desk assignments at the Pentagon and Annapolis, making sure he corresponded with the appropriate people within Congress and the military to spread his name and further his career.

It seemed that Zachiem's biggest career opportunity came during the Iran-Iraq war. The secretary of defense, Caspar Weinberger, transferred him to the Persian Gulf as his special assistant. Zachiem's job was to advise Weinberger on the formulation of U.S. foreign policy and strategy to use naval power to keep the sea lanes open. Zachiem drew up plans to reflag Kuwaiti oil tankers and escort them with U.S. warships when the war heated up in 1986. Iran's Revolutionary Guard boats were under the control of a small but powerful semi-independent group of mullahs who appeared to be willing to openly challenge the U.S. Navy.

The debate was heard all the way to the Armed Services and Foreign Affairs committees. The secretary testified in defense of Zachiem's plan to the dissatisfaction of many naval officers. He said that if the Navy couldn't operate in the Gulf, one of the United States' most critical areas of national interest, where could it operate? After a short and somewhat heated debate, Weinberger won out. On July 21, 1987, the first two Kuwaiti tankers to sail under the U.S. flag initiated Operation Earnest Will. Four U.S. Navy frigates, three cruisers and a destroyer escorted the tankers around the Gulf and the Strait of Hormuz. The plan was considered a success; for nearly a year U.S. warships patrolled the Gulf, with only a few minor incidents.

But then, on July 3, 1988, the USS *Vincennes*, an Aegis guided-missile cruiser, mistakenly shot down Iran Air Flight 655. The Airbus was carrying over three hundred civilian passengers and crew. As news agencies around the world showed the bodies of women and children being pulled from the water, the U.S. tried to explain how one of its most advanced ships could identify a large, slow-moving airliner as an F-14A fighter. Nelson Zachiem III was reassigned to the Philippines two days after the incident.

Duke closed the file and stared out the window. *And now Zachiem is back in the Gulf as commander of the U.S. Middle East Task Force. It will be interesting to see how he handles this sit-*

uation. There wasn't much question that Zachiem was smart and had extensive experience.

Duke felt the car slow as they turned onto the naval base and drove past the security gate. Up ahead to the right, he caught sight of the USS *LaSalle* moored at the dock. She was outlined in white lights against the dark sky. The Bahrain government allowed the U.S. to station the ship at Mina' Sulman, rationalizing that it was not a permanent base of operations and the U.S. could be asked to leave at any time. Of course, in reality the Bahrain government hadn't any intentions of asking the U.S. to leave. American warships and aircraft regularly used the island nation to practice Gulf exercises, and the U.S. presence gave the tiny country a sense of security.

"General James, we'll be using the gangplank on the right, sir."

"I'll follow you, Ensign. That way I won't get lost." Duke stuffed Zachiem's file into his briefcase.

Duke exited the car to the smell of salt water mixed with diesel fuel. He could hear the sound of the ocean in the distance as well as water slapping the hull of the *LaSalle* fifty feet away. The ship, a former amphibious transport, still wore the traditional white paint of U.S. Navy ships serving as flagships in the Gulf region. Displacing 14,650 tons of water fully loaded and 500 feet long, the ship loomed in the dark night, appearing even larger than she actually was.

Duke walked across the gangplank and into the interior of the ship. He wondered why the admiral hadn't been waiting at the gangplank to greet him. After a series of turns down several narrow hallways, he found himself standing outside Admiral Zachiem's quarters.

The ensign knocked on the door twice. "General James here to see you, sir."

"Thank you." Duke smiled as the young ensign opened the door for him. The admiral's muffled voice bidding entry sounded gruff.

The ensign closed the heavy metal door after James ducked his head to step inside. *Well, here goes nothing*, he thought. He squinted, adjusting his eyesight from the brightly lit hallways. Surprisingly, the chamber was extremely cramped and poorly lit.

"Admiral Zachiem . . . Duke James." He held out his hand to the man standing before him.

"General James, welcome aboard. It's a pleasure to meet you." Zachiem took the extended hand and smiled.

"Nice to meet you also, Admiral."

Duke had pictured a smaller man, not the nearly six-foot, broad-shouldered naval officer before him. Zachiem's brown eyes were indifferent and shallow lines framed his forehead, cutting down across his cheek bones. His head was topped with plenty of gray-and-black hair, which was short on the sides and neatly combed on top. A pair of wire-framed reading glasses rested on the end of his long, narrow nose.

He began to feel claustrophobic. To a man used to looking out at the entire sky, this situation could prove to be bothersome. On the admiral's desk were several neat stacks of paper. Against the wall was a tan leather couch and directly next to that a wooden table with a coffee machine on top. The glass container was half-filled with brown liquid.

"Sit down, General. You must be tired." Zachiem pointed to the couch. He then sat behind his desk and crossed his legs before speaking. "So, I hear Chaniff asked you to come here to watch me, to make sure I don't screw things up."

Duke chuckled, caught off-guard by the question. "Excuse me?"

"I'm well connected at the Pentagon, General James, not to mention that I have been dealing with the politics of the military a lot longer than you. It's quite obvious you were sent here for a reason. I would just like to know where you stand." The admiral's expression was cool to the point of being arrogant.

Duke sat upright on the edge of the couch. He knew why the admiral had motioned for him to take this seat—it was lower than the chair and Zachiem was able to look down on him. "If you think my being ordered to advise the chairman on this situation is a way of watching you, then you need to take that up with General Chaniff."

"Let me cut to the chase, General." Zachiem leaned forward. "I command the Middle East task force. I have more experience in this part of the world than ninety-nine percent of the officers in the military. Five tankers were hit by God only knows what, and I don't need an Air Force two-star down here getting in my way."

"I see. I'm not here to get in your way, Admiral. I have my own job to do and I don't need you getting in my way, either.

Until I am ordered to do otherwise, you can expect me to join you during any defensive or offensive operations." Duke stood. He could feel his face flushing with irritation. He understood why Chaniff wanted someone here.

"So long as you understand you can observe all you want but I call the shots." Zachiem's face and tone hadn't changed. He might as well have been talking about the weather. "As long as you can manage staying out from underfoot we'll get along just fine."

"I'll be getting out of your way right now, Admiral. That is, if it suits you to order someone to show me to my quarters." Duke was too tired to banter and decided he'd need more rest than he'd thought. "I'll be in the CIC tomorrow . . . at 0600," Duke added after Zachiem had buzzed for the ensign.

"It was nice meeting with you, General. I hope your quarters will suit your needs."

Duke had to fight the urge to smash that look right off his face.

AZRAQ AIR BASE, JORDAN

Mark Collins had been in Jordan for nearly six hours. *Five hours and fifty-five minutes too long*, he told himself. Even with sunglasses on, he had to put his hand to his forehead to shield the bright setting sun from his eyes. A slight breeze ruffled his hair when he took his baseball cap off to wipe away the sweat. He continued to study the cloudless blue sky for a twin-engine Iranian transport jet.

Collins brushed more sweat from his upper lip and ran his fingertips through the six-month-old beard covering his face that he had grown for this operation. Feeling the perspiration building underneath the whiskers, he wondered why anyone would ever want one. The whole situation was becoming more uncomfortable with each passing second.

"I'm going to give these jerks another fifteen minutes and then call it quits," he grumbled to himself. Having to travel to Jordan to receive CIA shipments bound for Iran was awkward and annoying. However, it was the only way the CIA could cover its tracks. The items were flown from Turkey on Jordanian military transports. Collins, being the middleman, made sure the shipments arrived intact and then accompanied the Iranians back to Esfahan. This also helped him to keep tabs on the goods.

I know the bastards really need this stuff, Collins reasoned, worried they might not show today, which would mean he would have to come back tomorrow. Behind him, resting on the tarmac, were six wooden pallets wrapped in black plastic. Each contained American high-performance jet aircraft spare parts for F-4Es, including the AN/APG-66J radars and avionics upgrades along with electronic jamming pods. Collins knew these parts weren't available on the open market. The Iranians didn't have much of a choice. Either they bought them from Collins or their American-made jets flew without them, downgrading their ability.

"There is your airplane," Hafiz Kansi, the Jordanian arms trader snarled sarcastically through a partly open window in his parked Honda limousine. The engine was running, along with the air conditioning system. The fact that Collins was baking in the overwhelming heat rather than sitting in the car amused the Jordanian.

In the distance, a white-and-gray high-winged aircraft made a slow banking turn out of the east and leveled on final approach. The aircraft grew larger and louder coming in closer, before touching down, a puff of blue smoke exploding from under the landing gear. Collins watched it turn and taxi toward him on a secluded part of the runway.

Collins turned to look at the fat-faced Jordanian. He didn't like or trust Kansi. As Middle Eastern arms traders went, Collins considered Kansi worse than average, right next to the scum of the earth. The man rarely bathed and had a foul odor, a mix of alcohol, acrid aftershave and tobacco. Collins could see cigar smoke escaping through the open window of the limousine.

He turned back to the Russian-built transport, speculating that the pilots were being cautious when he couldn't see any movement around the aircraft. The waves of heat radiating off the wings and engine cowlings made him feel even more hot.

"All right, what are you assholes waiting for?" he cursed under his breath. It could be this wasn't the bird he was waiting for and even if it was, it wouldn't be the first time Iranian pilots, not liking the looks of things on the ground, decided to turn around and fly back to Iran empty. Sometimes they didn't show up at all. Collins tried not to fidget, worried he might make the possibly suspicious pilots more nervous.

The transport finally taxied to a stop several hundred yards away, but its engines were not powering down. The aircraft didn't have any markings that were standard procedure for an Iranian arms transfer. The plane was odd-looking, even for a Russian design. It had two large engines mounted on top of its wings near the fuselage, with a stubby body airframe for hauling cargo. Collins folded his arms. He would have to wait until they made the first move.

After working on this project for the past eight months, he had made amazing progress, considering he was trying to penetrate the Iranian military. He hadn't expected to be this far into the operation for another year. The CIA had failed at almost every other covert attempt at establishing a contact deep inside the military structure. So Collins, along with the CIA's Middle Eastern station chief and Tom Staffer, the DO, had come up with a new straightforward strategy to get someone placed inside Iran.

Collins had assumed the name of Kiram Kahman and spent six months in St. Louis undergoing a rigorous training program from McDonnell F-4 Phantom technical engineers. He also attended classes to learn everything he could about the Phantoms. At night, a team of CIA briefers instructed him in Turkish and Middle Eastern customs, as well as the Islamic religion.

After Collins had a thorough understanding of their culture and knew the F-4E inside and out, he flew to Konya AB in Turkey, where he began to work as a McDonnell Douglas technical representative assisting the Turkish air force in the their F-4E upgrades. It took him only three months to get to know almost everyone at the base. He especially concentrated on befriending Shi'ite Muslim fundamentalists, letting them know he was sympathetic to their cause, particularly toward Iran. This part of the operation was essential. His cover had to be backed up by people at the air base. If anyone asked if Collins really did work at Konya, the question could be answered without hesitation—yes, they remembered him well.

The CIA, with help from Mossad and Egyptian intelligence, had flagged an Iranian businessman named Ali Fesseghi earlier in the summer. Through two separate sources in the Turkish government, the CIA learned he covertly worked for SAVAMA, the Iranian intelligence service, brokering weapons and information between Iran and other Middle Eastern countries. He had developed an international reputation as a shrewd and clever dealer. Before the Iran-Iraq war, Fesseghi had worked in a family business as a food exporter. Seeing an opportunity, he switched to arms sales when Iran's munitions ran desperately low during the mid-1980s.

During one of Fesseghi's trips last fall, the Iranian made it known he was interested in acquiring, legally or illegally, F-4E upgrades and spare parts, as well as locating someone who had the technological experience to aid in their operation and installation.

Acting on this information, Collins traveled from Konya to Istanbul and checked into Fesseghi's hotel. He deliberately ran into Fesseghi, striking up a conversation every time he could. It took Collins several days of casual conversation before Fesseghi became comfortable with him. The Iranian spoke English extremely well and Collins knew enough Farsi to get by and make Fesseghi feel relaxed. By the end of the week, Collins let the Iranian know he had technical and computer experience and access to American weapons and spare parts. There was no need for him to say they were for sale; in this part of the world almost everything was for sale if the right price was offered.

Persistently and professionally, Collins explained that he had been treated unfairly by the Turkish air force because he was a Muslim. Turkey was rapidly switching from F-4s to F-16s, and his services would not be required any longer. Finally, the day before Fesseghi traveled back to Iran, he supplied Collins with the name of a Jordanian arms trader, Hafiz Kansi, who might be interested in doing business. To Collins's gratification, Fesseghi also gave him a handwritten list of Phantom parts Iran was interested in obtaining.

The next month, Collins succeeding in making contact with Kansi. The CIA had a computer profile of the man, making it easy to contact him. At first he sold the Jordanians simple things, such as upgrade antennas for the AN/ALR-46 RHAW receiver and TACAN systems or Midas 4 gun blast diffusers and MK 111 antiskid brakes. The parts were pulled from Turkish F-4 inventories, the serial numbers were removed so they couldn't be traced and the computer records were then altered. The spare parts were flown from Konya to Azraq Air Base, Jordan. Collins forged Turkish purchase orders and shipping vouchers, stating the pallets contained automobile and truck components. All Collins then had to do was bribe Jordanian export agents into not inspecting the cargo before it was transferred to an Iranian aircraft. The entire process sounded much more complicated than it actually was. He

ad learned Turkish, Jordanian officials were generally lazy and
most of what he needed could be accomplished with the right
amount of money. However, just the opposite was true when it
came to the Iranians.

Collins had made sure the Iranian air force got only a taste of
what he could offer them, but hadn't sold anything of substance.
Until today. Iran was extremely interested in upgrading their F-4
radars with Westinghouse AN/APG-66Js. These were powerful
look-down, shoot-down pulse-Dopplers that the Japanese operated
in their fleet of F-4EJs.

Without warning, the jet's engines spooled up and the transport
swung around. Mark Collins winced as the sound of the Antonov
An-72's two turbofans stung his ears. He had been waiting on the
tarmac too long. His white shirt was wet with perspiration and
clung to his skin. The transport taxied toward him, slowed and
came to a stop. Collins waited as the back of the aircraft opened
and the pilot shut down the engines. A moment later a tall, well-
dressed man emerged from the rear of the aircraft and walked
toward Collins. Following him were a half dozen armed men
dressed in Iranian military fatigues. The man carried a black briefcase and wore wire-framed sunglasses. Collins recognized Ali
Fesseghi instantly.

"Mr. Kahman . . . it is nice to see you again." Fesseghi smiled.
Collins returned the amenities and kept his eyes fixed on Fesseghi.

"Come, let us go for a walk as my men load the aircraft. I
assume you were able to meet our needs." Fesseghi pointed in
the direction he wanted to walk, away from the aircraft.

"More or less. This isn't like shopping at a department store,"
Collins said sarcastically, trying to play his part. He looked over
his shoulder. Hafiz Kansi, the Jordanian arms dealer, was waiting
for Fesseghi in the car.

"I know that my country is happy with the work you have
been doing," Fesseghi said, looking off in the opposite direction.
"You have managed to supply us with very important upgrades
and are very discreet." Fesseghi paused, then added, "Almost
too discreet."

Collins let Fesseghi's last comment linger for a while before
answering. He wasn't sure if the Iranian was on to him or was
just fishing.

"The fewer people who know about me, the better. The Mus-

lims supporting me in the Turkish air force are not anxious to b
exposed. How do you think the U.S. Air Force would react
they knew F-4 parts were being sold to one of their enemies.''

"This world of arms selling can make a man rich, possibl
make him want too much. He could get greedy then . . . get care
less."

"Or killed," Collins added. "He would be a foolish man
do such a thing when he is getting handsomely paid already."

"Yes, he would. I must go now. Mr. Kansi and I have othe
business to attend to. Here is your payment, Mr. Kahman. I hop
you have a safe journey back to Iran." The man handed Collir
a thick envelope, then added, "I know we will have many mor
dealings in the future."

"Of course," Collins said, accepting the envelope, and the tw
parted.

Collins looked back at the Iranian aircraft. The men in fatigue
were loading the last pallet. They would be leaving in a fe
minutes.

A gas-powered forklift was spitting black smoke as the ma
chine struggled to pick up the pallet containing a Westinghous
AN/APG-66J pulse-Doppler radar unit. The radar system, de
signed for McDonnell F-4 Phantoms, had been carefully wrappe
in thick black plastic sheets to protect it from weather an
blowing debris. Its microelectronics were extremely susceptibl
to contamination from dirt and other airborne pollutants. Th
more obvious reason for the protective wrapping, of course, wa
concealment from the casual observer but it would also arous
suspicion in someone with a trained eye.

"Let's speed it up. We don't have all night," Collins shoute
over the noise of the forklift. "I want this bird airborne in twent
minutes." The forklift operator didn't respond as he downshifte
and chugged slowly up the rear loading ramp of the AN-7
Coaler.

Collins surveyed the area after Kansi and Fesseghi sped off i
the limousine, making sure no unauthorized personnel were wit
nessing the loading of the fourth and final radar system. He coul
see several Jordanian military police patrolling the hangars to th
west, but their presence didn't reassure him much.

Collins scratched the skin beneath his scraggly beard as th
forklift disappeared inside the aircraft. One of the guards ha
stopped a few yards away and was watching the activity. Collin

stared through his mirrored sunglasses until the guard walked on. Even though several high-ranking members of the Royal Jordanian Air Force were supporting the operation and assisting with the transportation, it would not be wise to trust them completely.

So far the operation had gone off without a hitch. *And now I need to contact Zenith*, he thought. He walked to the rear and peered inside. Three men were hurriedly securing the last radar unit to the floor of the four-engine cargo plane. They stretched the heavy nylon straps to fasten the awkward pallets in place, tethering them to the steel tiedown rings on the floor and walls of the fuselage.

"The cargo is loaded and ready for transport, Mr. Kahman," one of the load masters said to Collins. He waited for the men to exit the cargo bay before continuing up the ramp. He inspected the entire payload as he made his way past the radars toward the flight deck.

"Close this thing up and let's get going," Collins said firmly, ready to get something to drink.

The pilot hit a set of switches on his instrument panel and a moment later the AN-72 came to life as its high-performance engines began to turn.

Collins felt the hum of hydraulic motors kicking in as he watched the cargo ramp slowly close. He ran his fingers though his hair, relieved it had taken only thirty minutes to secure everything.

Collins took a seat behind the bulkhead that separated the flight deck from the rest of the aircraft. He slipped on a helmet, strapped himself in and folded his arms in an attempt to get comfortable. The inside of the Coaler vibrated as both jet engines came to life and the AN-72 started to taxi toward the end of the runway in preparation for takeoff.

Maybe I can get some sleep, Collins thought, leaning his head against the wall of the fuselage. The pilot advanced the throttles and the transport lumbered down the runway, jostling Collins.

Chapter Twelve

Rear Admiral Hal Currie, Sr., ran the scenario through his mind for what seemed like the hundredth time. It was Friday afternoon and he still didn't have the answers he had been looking for. On the one hand, the photographs clearly showed that at least one and possibly two antiship missiles had hit each ship the morning of July 26. The Navy pilot who had taken them several hours after the attack had done a good job making sure they were clear and crisp, particularly the one of the *Shuho Maru*. There wasn't any question something had impacted the ship above the waterline, and it must have been traveling at a high rate of speed. On the other hand, there were probably a half dozen missile systems in the world capable of doing such damage. Any nation in the Gulf region could be operating one.

Currie rubbed the bridge of his nose beneath his thick glasses and closed his eyes. Saudi AWACS radar hadn't detected anything out of the ordinary the morning of the attack. Currie preferred analyzing data collected by American AWACS crews. The Saudi operators were trained but weren't very reliable or efficient. The admiral had checked and rechecked the computer disks. Even if the operators had missed the missiles snaking their way toward the tankers, they should still show up on the backup diskettes. Nothing was on them, no signs of an enemy aircraft, a hostile search or acquisition radar, and there weren't any military surface vessels in the area.

Admiral Currie stared back at the computer screen thinking how he would word the last few sentences of his CIA report. He had come in early to finish it and was now running late. The extra time didn't produce any answers.

"Currie here," he answered the phone.

"Hal, this is Vance."

"I'm finishing it right now," Hal said, knowing what Edleman, the director of intelligence, wanted.

"Sorry to push you, but I'm meeting with Staffer and Brady in fifteen minutes. I need that report." On Friday mornings at 10:00 A.M. both deputy directors, operations and intelligence, met with the DCI. It wasn't a formal meeting in which an agenda was followed, rather, the three men discussed problems in general terms. Specific questions were handled one on one behind closed doors.

"Well, I'm going to tell you up front, Vance, you're not going to like it. I don't have any conclusive answers." Currie let out a sigh, signaling his frustration. "I just don't have enough data or time."

"Well, let's just see what you've got. It's Staffer and Brady you should be worried about. I'll see you in ten minutes." The line went dead.

The Directorate of Intelligence used a sixteen-member board of analysts known as NIOs (national intelligence officers). Each was responsible for an individual issue or geographical area. Hal Currie had been given a tough assignment. His responsibilities covered the Middle East and warning, nuclear proliferation and strategic weapons. In simpler terms, he analyzed and compiled every shred of data the CIA collected on Middle Eastern countries, where they were getting their weapons and which ones were operational. Currie then drafted a National Intelligence Estimate, explaining what a country's military capabilities were and the potential threat to the U.S. and its allies. This report was given to the DCI, who added his views, before it was delivered to the President.

He typed the last few words and twenty seconds later pulled the three-page report off the laser printer, signed it and headed up to Edleman's office.

*   *   *

Tom Staffer was already seated at the conference table in Tony Brady's office. In Staffer's opinion, Brady's lavish office looked like a corporate boardroom. But then Brady looked more like a successful investment banker than a career intelligence officer.

The DCI had a full head of silver hair, which he combed straight back, making sure it was never out of place. He wore only custom-made monogrammed white dress shirts with button down collars, and even though he was a bit overweight the director covered it well with tailored double-breasted suits. His year-round darkened skin tone was due to a local tanning salon serving an exclusive crowd.

Behind Brady's elaborate mahogany desk were dozens of plaques and certificates from his early days in the FBI and CIA, as well as a diploma from Harvard Law. Brady had graduated magna cum laude and joined the Washington-based law firm of Williams, Colly and Boatwright in 1952 at the age of twenty-five. Two years later, he enlisted in the FBI before moving on to the CIA in 1985 as director of intelligence. The paneled walls surrounding Brady's desk were covered with Southwestern and American Indian artwork. The built-in bookcases were neat and well kept, but every inch was crammed. Brady had only one real hobby and that was information—he was a reading machine with a particular interest in U.S. history. It was known that he read forty books or magazines every few weeks. He could devour an 800-page chronicle on the Civil War in one day.

Staffer thumbed through his notes. He was scheduled to testify before the Senate Intelligence Committee on Monday, so the DCI would have more ground to cover than usual. Brady always liked to make sure Staffer was well briefed on all CIA operations when he appeared before the committee.

Brady was on his phone and from the conversation it sounded as if someone from the State Department was picking his brain about Iran. Staffer could tell by the man's expression he was growing annoyed with endless questions. The DCI rarely bothered to hide his emotions. He had served too long in Washington to worry about what anyone thought of him.

"Yes, I'm meeting with Staffer and Edleman next. If they have anything to add, I'll call you back." Brady put the receiver down a little too roughly, then poured himself a cup of fresh coffee.

"More bad news?" Staffer asked, knowing Iran was the topic of the day and that was generally always bad news.

"Yeah. Prime Minister Mahmoudi is still in a coma and their defense minister, Sheik Bakhtiar, just addressed their parliament." Brady shook his head. "The State Department's all shook up. It seems the sheik's declared Iran will not allow a stronger U.S. presence in the Gulf and has called for a renewed revolution. Did you have a chance to listen to the translation?"

"Yeah, I listened," Staffer said.

The door opened and Vance Edleman walked in. "I apologize for being late, gentlemen. One of those mornings."

"I know. Tom and I were just discussing your favorite part of the world." Brady smiled, motioning for him to join them.

Edleman drew a tight-lipped smile in agreement as he sat down, setting his note pad on the table.

"Gentlemen, the State Department, White House and Pentagon are all on my back. I need some hard intelligence as to what is really going on in Iran. All we have to go on right now are satellite photos, CNN reports and watered-down intelligence reports from damn Mossad. I don't have a handle on what's really happening, and I don't think either of you do either. Tom . . . how long has it been since you've been able to place an operative to give us some solid intelligence?" Brady's tone was growing gruff as he continued. "And I don't mean who's sick and who's a homosexual. I'm talking about finding out what their intentions are, hard intel. Like the shit we used to do during the cold war. Or has everyone forgotten how we used to really spy?"

Staffer didn't answer the question. Brady already knew the answer. It was one of the most discouraging parts of Staffer's job. The Kremlin had been easier to penetrate than Iran's Supreme Defense Council; they were such a tightly knit group of religious zealots.

"Hell, oil tankers start blowing up off Saudi Arabia and we still don't know who or what caused it." Brady looked at both men, hoping he had gotten his point across. As difficult as it was, he still expected his people to find a way to get the job done.

"Well, unfortunately I don't have any answers for you today either," Edleman said sliding a copy of Admiral Currie's report across the table to both Staffer and Brady. "I picked this up from Currie about fifteen minutes ago. It's inconclusive, except for the fact that we know the tankers were hit by two antiship missiles; Currie couldn't ID what kind."

Staffer reached for the report and started glancing over the first page. Currie had listed all the possible missile systems. Iran operated Chinese-manufactured Silkworms—they had several dozens batteries along their western coastline around the naval operations center at Bandar Abbas. Two other possibilities were Russian Kh-35s, code-named Harpoonskis, or the Kh-31P, code-named Krypton. Iraq had both systems and MiG-29 fighters to carry them. Both Russian missiles fly at near supersonic speeds and have a warhead large enough to kill a tanker. However, each was radar guided. There just wasn't any evidence of radar transmissions in the area.

Staffer spoke, looking at Edleman. "This is going to make things tougher. I was hoping Currie could—"

"Of course . . . we all were hoping for answers, but there aren't any right now." Edleman's expression was guarded.

"This may be one we don't solve right away," Brady interrupted. "Give me something in writing on why you think Iran isn't about to use military force to help its international position. I'll need it by this afternoon if I'm going to calm down the State Department." Brady stood. "Gentlemen, I'll talk to you after lunch."

"I have one other thing," Staffer insisted. "I received word from Spectra. He's penetrated the air base at Esfahan in central Iran."

"Spectra. That's . . ." Brady looked at the ceiling, his mind racing.

"Mark Collins. He's operating as a McDonnell Douglas engineer."

"And?" Brady asked.

"We now have someone on the inside."

"Well, why didn't you say so? What have you learned?" Brady sat back down, feeling hopeful.

Staffer didn't answer. He lowered his head, realizing his mistake. *I should have kept my mouth shut.*

"For christsake, Staffer, don't shit me." Brady's eyes lit up. "I don't want to wait to hear about it until you have something to report. I don't have time for this . . . you're acting like an amateur. I'll talk with both of you this afternoon."

Edleman got up quickly, wanting to leave before the DCI grew angrier. As soon as he left, Staffer put Currie's report into his notebook, then slowly exited the room.

Shit, that was stupid. Brady was right and Staffer knew it. If he had one failure in his position as DO, it had been penetrating Iran's central government in Tehran and its military. Sure, he had placed several field officers in smaller cities, such as Mashhad near the Russian coast and Zahedan west of Pakistan. The officers had recruited plenty of low-level agents, usually military factory workers and government personnel who were disgruntled with the government. But the intelligence they turned over never gave the CIA any insight into what was really going on inside Iran or any of its terrorist training groups. The last solid information he received came from the computer specialist, Zenith, and that was a year and a half ago.

"Chairman Chaniff called while you were out," his assistant said when he walked back into the office.

"Thanks." Staffer closed his office door and glanced over to the television set. CNN was airing a report on Iranians burning an American flag and waving signs denouncing the U.S.

He hit the remote, turning off the TV.

THE WHITE HOUSE

"Please listen to me, Mr. President. This campaign doesn't need a foreign policy fumble. We can't afford it. The Democrats will jump on this if we don't make the right decision. You need to let our allies and the American people know we're not going to sit back and let the goddamn Iranians threaten the stability of the region." Bill Bishop, the President's national security adviser, stood in the center of the Oval Office with his hands on his hips. "One carrier task force isn't enough. You need to order the Navy to sail another battle group into the area."

"I agree with you, Bill," the President said, "but I don't want to be accused of running around saying the sky is falling. The headlines would be PRESIDENT MCCHICKEN LITTLE SAYS THE GULF IS FALLING." He swirled the ice in his afternoon bourbon and water.

Bishop loosened his tie and walked over to the nearest window. Advising the President on national security during an election year, especially when they had differing opinions, was the toughest part of his job. Bishop knew the President better than anyone in Washington and had been his closest confidant and friend for the past twenty-two years. He recalled the day they first met. Bishop was a lawyer completing a ten-year career in the Army, and McEntire had hired him to advise his Phoenix-based construction business how to work with local officials on preserving the desert landscape around the Superstition Mountains. At the time, it was an original approach to dealing with environmental concerns and it had earned Bishop's respect.

"Speak up, Bill. I hate the silent treatment."

"Mr. President . . . I know I'm supposed to keep my mouth shut about domestic policy, but you can bet your ass I'm right on this one. You'd better be ready to fight back." *And you're going to lose this election if you don't start listening to me.*

"Bill, calm down. Give me a little credit for knowing what I'm doing here."

"I just don't want this one to blow up in our faces, Louis. The Republican leadership doesn't want you to show any sign of wavering. They view this as a perfect opportunity for you to show the leadership you're capable of—headstrong, with a vision."

"Tell the Republican leadership to shove it. This isn't the first time Iran's threatened the security of the Gulf. They do it about every six months or so. Everyone should stop a moment to think about it instead of panicking. I still think it's best to focus on attacking the Democrats on domestic issues. Besides, our conventions are coming up in two weeks and we'll get a boost then." President McEntire took another sip of his drink. He'd decided the day was over and wanted the alcohol to numb some of his frustrations.

"Louis, I thought you agreed to address this Iranian thing this afternoon. It doesn't look good to cancel a press conference. It makes you appear to be indecisive or incompetent."

"I did agree, but I took it off the agenda until I have more information. You don't want me to get on national networks saying something happened but we're not sure what, do you? No, I don't want to focus on this until the *Abraham Lincoln* arrives in twenty-four hours. Then I'll decide on reinforcements and a press conference. Besides, I didn't want to say anything until I read the CIA briefing. I made an ass of myself last week for not having all the facts straight on one small uprising in China. And wasn't it you who suggested I have all my ducks in a row before making any *more* foreign policy statements?" The President respected Bishop for wanting to help him make the right decisions, but he felt it necessary to put him back in his place from time to time.

"Yes, it was." Bishop tried to temper his tone.

"I'm not going to make the same mistake twice. I asked the CIA and Pentagon both to get me some solid information on Iran by tomorrow morning so my press secretary could have it released before the evening news."

"Well, that may be too late, Louis. You should call a press conference for tomorrow morning. Otherwise people may start thinking you're not on top of things or that you don't care. The news about the tankers has already been out for too long."

"And say what?" McEntire laughed. "The networks will see that it's a campaign ploy and make that the headlines instead. No way, Bill, just drop it. I'm not going to do that." He paused, then sighed, saying, "If you want to worry about my campaign, I suggest you spend your energy working with my chief of staff on fine-tuning travel arrangements for the next two weeks. I don't want to be on the road more than six nights before the convention, so you'd better make sure they're worthwhile stops. I want to be well rested and ready to go after the convention."

"All right, you're going to do what you want to do anyway, but you just remember who told you about jumping on this thing right away. Go ahead and take the rest of the day off. I'm going back to my office and see if I can get a handle on things myself." Bishop's tone was somewhat harsh but without another word he turned, leaving the President alone in the Oval Office.

McEntire looked at the closing door. If Bishop was correct, and his track record said he usually was, the Democrats would try to use this Iranian issue as a sign of weakness. He might end up dropping a few more points in the polls and he couldn't afford to do that. Yet the President knew the alterative would be to react strongly, which could escalate the situation. After all, Iran's leaders did have their backs against the wall with the Kurdish uprising. *Maybe all they need is to let off some hot air and shoot their mouths off for a while*, he thought.

Chapter Thirteen

Colonel Alireza Rahavi watched the last truck as it snaked its way up the winding single-lane dirt road toward the top of the mountain ridge. The road was crude—two ruts cut through the boulders and thick dried underbrush of Iran's coastal mountains. Maintaining the road wasn't a priority, since it was only used to transport Chinese-made Silkworm missiles or radar equipment from site to site. And that wasn't done very often.

Rahavi watched the truck stop and back up to a brush-covered opening in the side of the mountain. Several men rushed to the rear of the vehicle and began unloading the last eight stealth cruise missiles. Well camouflaged, to conceal it from satellite imagery and Western reconnaissance aircraft, the dome-shaped entrance led to a series of eight tunnels and hardened underground bunkers. Each bunker housed two HY-4 coastal defense Silkworm missiles. An improved version of the HY-2G, the surface-to-ship missile, the HY-4s were capable of hitting targets 135 kilometers away using a passive IR guidance system.

However, even these new versions of the Silkworms were obsolete. The missile's large size and radar signature could easily be detected and tracked once in the air. If HY-4s were used to attack ships, American surveillance satellites using infrared and electronic sensors could pin-point the launch sites in seconds. This would not be the case with the new cruise missiles taking their place. Once the replacement missiles were inside, the Iranians would have twelve hours to deactivate the Silkworms before bringing the new missiles on line, ready for operation.

"You men, speed it up," Rahavi shouted at the top of his lungs. He didn't want any of the trucks to be photographed by a reconnaissance satellite. Even though heat emissions may be picked up, he knew it was best to avoid positive identification.

Bakhtiar would be very pleased indeed when Rahavi reported that the missile transfer had been successful. Everything was going just as scheduled.

Esfahan, Iran

Well, here we go again, Collins thought, as he exited his hotel room, making sure he closed the door tightly behind him. He reached into his jacket pocket, touching a half-used roll of masking tape and a small plastic tube called a dead-drop device, or concealment chamber. The dark olive tube was hollow and pointed at one end with a screw-off watertight cap at the other. Inside was a handwritten ambiguous note. Collins planned to use this in an attempt to make contact with Zenith.

Good God, don't let me screw this one up. Collins hesitated, waiting for the nervous emotion to pass. He closed his eyes, remaining still as he clutched the doorknob of his hotel room. It wasn't a feeling Collins was unfamiliar with; in fact, he had been trained to deal with it. His psychological instructors back at Langley had warned him that sooner or later a field officer would find himself becoming tired and undisciplined. Particularly one who operated in a far-off place for a long period of time, alone and without the support of other officers. Collins mentally refreshed himself by taking a moment to think over his goal. He reminded himself to be keenly aware of everything and more alert. If he planned to complete his mission and live to tell about it, it was of the utmost importance that he feel confident at all times.

Once relaxed, Collins left the doorway and headed toward the lobby. He could hear the sounds of people laughing, and the warm smell of food filled the air.

The Iranians had done a good job of keeping track of him the three previous times he had made his way to the open market for dinner and entertainment. Of course, Collins had wanted them to follow him. He was hoping to establish a boring enough routine so they would become lax in their work. After all, following a man to watch him eat dinner and read the local newspaper night after night would put anyone to sleep.

As he entered the lobby, he tried to pick out which set of goons would be on duty tonight. It was becoming a test of his skill—could he have them made before it was too obvious? *Maybe it would be the fat and thin pair, the ones who trailed me the first night.* He got his answer a second later. Seated in the back of the room, near the entrance to the kitchen, were two men who quickly glanced away as Collins entered. One was a tall, thin man with a shaggy mustache, the other, shorter and very stout. Both men wore baggy clothes, Collins guessed, to hide their concealed weapons.

Lucky me. I get Laurel and Hardy again tonight. This should be fun. Collins tried not to snicker or look at the two men.

"Mr. Kahman, your taxi should be here in a few minutes," an elderly man said from behind the hotel desk.

"Thank you. I'll be eating at Maharajah Restaurant and I won't be gone long," Collins said loudly enough for the two to hear. He tipped the desk clerk and walked outside. He felt his stomach rumble with hunger. *I wonder what the special is tonight.* He longed for a juicy steak, baked potato and hot apple pie.

"Bring it down, slowly . . . carefully," a tired-looking sergeant said as he guided the last of the cruise missiles over the horizontal railmounted launcher. Constructed from aluminum and steel, the launcher was basically a narrow cart, a third of the length of the missile. Each cruise missile rested on the launcher, which functioned as a stable platform.

Clutching a handheld controller, the sergeant pressed the buttons that operated an overhead electric hoist. The motor strained as it maneuvered the final missile into position.

"To the right . . . swing it around. Hold it steady. Now . . . it is in place." The sergeant tapped the red button, lowering the 2,500-pound cruise missile into a set of aluminum and rubber supports. Almost immediately, two other men began to bolt a small solid rocket motor to the base of the launch cart, while another started the tedious task of wiring the missile's thrust and guidance controls into the command and control network. The rocket motor would be used to propel the heavy missile down the long tunnel to the opposite side of the bunker. It would allow the missile to reach a sustainable flight speed in just a few seconds.

"This is the last one, sir," the sergeant said, wiping the sweaty dirt from his face and eyes. "When this one is wired, all twenty-four missiles need only to be fueled before they are operational."

"Good work." Colonel Rahavi nodded.

"My men are exhausted. Permission to grant nine hours of rest, sir."

"Very well. Have the trucks return to Bandar Abbas, then tell your men to stand down. We will resume operations at 0600," Rahavi directed. "Make sure they get plenty of food and water. They earned it today."

Rahavi watched as the final adjustments were made to the last missile. He, too, felt weak from lack of nourishment and fluids.

We have made much progress, he told himself. He was standing in the final bunker, number twelve. Fourteen hours ago they had started the same time-consuming process in the first bunker, a half mile to the east. Now it was dark and they were nearly finished.

Rahavi searched the bunker to make sure everything was in place. All twelve bunkers were simple structures, fifteen feet by twelve feet. Constructed with five-foot walls of steel reinforced concrete, each room was located a minimum of thirty feet under the rocky ground overlooking Iran's shoreline. The ceilings were low, only six feet, and the work area was just large enough for two or three men to maneuver comfortably. Two low-voltage halogen bulbs supplied the only light, giving the chamber a yellow glow.

Once it became evident that Iran could indeed build a missile invisible to radar, the next problem was how they would launch it. Aircraft was the logical choice. The missile could be launched from high altitude while the fighters were still inside Iranian airspace. However, aircraft could be detected on radar, and the advantage of surprise would be lost.

The Iranians had learned that during the Gulf War it had taken Iraq as little as fifteen minutes or as much as six hours to set up and launch a Scud. The Scud launches were dependent on crews of men, some of whom proved to be very efficient while others were inept. Scuds are far less sophisticated than cruise missiles, so relying on crews was not feasible. Rather than using standard erectable launchers, the Iranians had developed and constructed permanent underground launch sites. Using hard-rock miners from the northern mountains, it had taken eighteen months to blast a bunker and tunnel complex from beneath the jagged shoreline.

What made these bunkers different from all the others scattered across Iran were the tracks bolted onto the floor. Running down each side of the chambers were a set of heavy iron railroad tracks, resting on which, in the back of the bunker, were two low-profile launch platforms. These platforms were secured to the tracks with standard train wheels. Each track led to a five-foot-diameter tunnel approximately fifty feet in length. In effect, the Iranians had designed the tunnels as miniature runways. Because of the country's steep and rocky shoreline, the end of each tunnel overlooked a sharp drop-off. Well camouflaged from detection, the outside exits to each launch site were nearly impossible to see from ship patrols or aircraft. A cruise missile could be launched by accelerating on the platform down the tunnel, reaching a high speed in a matter of seconds. The platform would remain stationary at the end of the track while the missile glided off into the air, and it could conveniently be wheeled back to its original position inside the tunnel ready for another launch.

It only made sense that Iran's new missile from the Phalanx Dragon project should be placed as close to the shore as possible. Once airborne, its flight time to a target would be cut.

The colonel ducked his head and walked down the nearest tunnel. He could hear the hollow echo of his boots as he made his way to the opening at the other side. The tunnel was void of any light. As his eyes adjusted, all he could see was the flickering light of a few stars shining in the fast approaching night sky at the other end. When he reached the opening, Rahavi stood for a moment. He could now feel a cool breeze whistling past the opening. He noticed the roots of a few plants growing inside the shaft and hanging down in front of the opening. He reached up and broke them off.

Rahavi's eyes swept across the strait. In the distance, the running lights of at least ten ships, moving in both directions, caught his attention. From the brightness of the lights, he guessed some of the ships were large tankers while others were smaller container vessels. Several hundred feet below him were the waters of the Gulf. He stood silently, watching and listening to the waves crashing against the rocks.

Finally, my country is ready to control what is rightly ours. No longer will the Persian Gulf be controlled by the West.

"Stop here, at the corner." Mark Collins ordered the taxi driver, tapping him on the shoulder.

The driver grunted a response and the car came to a stop near a side street. Collins handed the man 1,500 rials and glanced back before exiting the vehicle to see the headlights of his trail several hundred yards away. *Better keep up. I decided to walk the rest of the way.*

Collins put his hands in his pockets and briskly walked toward the main street a hundred yards ahead of him. He wanted to get a feel for the layout of the interconnecting streets and alleys in this section of Esfahan. CIA satellite photos showed the Iranians used the street as a main thoroughfare to cross the northern part of the city. He also remembered seeing military vehicles in several of the pictures. It was becoming more and more evident to Collins that even after seeing neat and clean satellite photos run through image-enhancement programs, the actual ground was still different from what he had pictured in his mind. The CIA's toys had their place, but they were no substitute for an agent's firsthand experience. He had to wonder what other surprises were in store for him.

Before reaching the main intersection, he took notice of a vacant lot off to his right. He would walk right past it. *This is the field. Zenith lives only two blocks from here.* This was the place where Perry made his dead drops. The small lot was between an automobile shop and an abandoned store. It was filled with weeds, busted lumber and a couple of stripped American cars from the late 1970s. It was a flawless place to run this type of operation.

Collins fought the urge to turn around and see if the two men were still following him. He was sure they were. He finally reached the main street of Esfahan's open market. Both sides were lined with shops and peddlers. Cars and bicycles sluggishly made their way through the crowds. He stayed on the sidewalk, dodging his way through the crowd toward the Maharajah Restaurant.

"Good evening. A table for one?" the waiter asked, recognizing Collins, who had become a regular customer.

"Yes . . . and could I have an outside table tonight? Near the street, please?" Collins asked.

"Certainly," the man nodded, leading Mark to a small table in the corner. The waiter picked up the extra table setting, then handed Collins a menu.

Just what the doctor ordered. The table was right next to a rusty iron fence separating the café from the street. He had a clear view of everything around him. Collins moved the chair so that he was facing toward the street. Looking up just then, he caught sight of a dark gray, dust-covered BMW slowly passing by. The car contained the two Iranian goons. Collins moved his head exaggeratedly right and left, as if looking for someone, making sure they saw him.

"May I get you something to drink?" the waiter asked.

"Water's fine. Do me a favor—I have to use the restroom; hold this table for me." Collins handed the man twenty dollars' worth of rials. "I may be a while."

"Yes, sir," the man said, smiling.

Collins slipped into one of the restroom stalls and locked the door. He took off his dark blue sports jacket and turned it inside out. The jacket was now tan. Next he reached inside the pocket and pulled out a black wig, placing it on his head. He removed a pair of silver wire-framed glasses from his breast pocket and put them on. Mark looked in the mirror, making sure the part in his wig ran down the center of his head. The curly natural black hair of the wig made him look ten years younger. The changes made a sufficient difference in his appearance so that they'd have to look long and hard to know it was him.

Collins walked through the café with an air of confidence and went back onto the street. He turned left and picked up his pace. He had practiced this routine using the satellite imagery a dozen times back in Langley.

The CIA operated a huge indoor training facility outside Langley, roughly the size of a football field, and fondly referred to as "the playground." The dull windowless building contained ten dome-shaped rooms, each equipped with three-dimensional video equipment. The brains of the system was a Cray 4-MP supercomputer, which rested on an eighteen-ton slab of granite. This was done to isolate it from the building's vibrations. The Cray had access to over 46,000 magnetic and CD-ROM disks supplied from seven giant silos, known as the seven dwarfs. The disks stored millions of images from satellite photos, allowing the computer to pull and use any file available. The result was a high-quality 3-D cartoonlike image that allowed a CIA officer to practice driving or walking anywhere in the world. The simulation allowed the Delta Team to practice hostage rescue missions, even supplied them with the thickness of walls they might have had to blast through.

When Collins reached the corner, he stopped. Driven down into the sidewalk was a ten-foot-high aluminum light pole. It had been painted black, and a large gaslight sitting on top illuminated the area. *This is it.* Collins knelt down and acted as if he were tying his shoelace. On the side of the aluminum pole he could barely make out the residue of old masking tape. A feeling of relief came over him. This was the same pole Perry had used.

Mark glanced up, casually looking around for anyone who might be watching him. He removed the tape from his pocket, quickly tearing off two strips, then placed the strips horizontally on the north side of the pole. This was all done in a split second.

Collins checked his watch. He had been away from the café for three minutes but still had one more chore to complete. He waited, making sure the street was clear of cars before he slipped into the vacant lot. He stepped over a large patch of dead weeds, staying close to the building and in the shadows. The field was just like Perry had described it in his last report before disappearing. Only Collins didn't remember any mention of two abandoned cars in the back section. *Okay, don't worry about that.*

He walked toward the northwest corner. A weathered wooden fence, broken in several places, separated the lot from an alley. Collins knelt down and removed the dead drop device from his pocket. He pushed it into the ground next to the corner fence post, adjacent to the building. The plastic cylinder could be retrieved from either side of the fence.

Collins stood and rapidly made his way out of the lot. He was light on his feet, careful not to step on any glass or make too much noise. Checking his watch again, he noted that it was now eight minutes that he had been gone.

Collins walked as innocently as he could back to the restaurant. Once inside the restroom, he removed the wig and glasses, stuffing them both into a side pocket, and reversed his jacket again. The entire drop had taken him just under twelve minutes to complete, two minutes less than he had practiced back in Langley. Before exiting, he double-checked himself. It would be stupid to forget something after making a successful dead drop.

He strolled to his seat outside. Nothing appeared to be out of the ordinary, and he felt relieved. He picked up the menu and smiled up at the waiter. It had been much easier than he had thought it would be. Sipping his water, he seemed only slightly interested in his surroundings. The Iranians weren't in clear view at the moment, but he was sure they were out there somewhere.

"Would you like to order now?" the waiter asked, appearing with his pad in hand.

"Yes," Collins said, only glancing at the menu for a moment. "I believe I would."

ESFAHAN, IRAN

Perijan Reza tried to hide her tears from the two guards inside the van. It was again early morning, the sun just cresting the mountains, and they were driving their regular route east toward Esfahan air base and the prison complex. Perijan had only managed to sleep a few hours the night before. The doctor had come again, but her father was still keeping her awake with fits of coughing and choking. The medication they gave was only to comfort him, and was not even managing to accomplish that. Perijan knew the drugs would not cure him, but had hoped they would at least ease some of his pain and discomfort.

The sleepless nights and long days were taking their toll on her emotions. Her eyes watered easily on and off throughout the day, and the slightest irritations seemed to be extreme. She knew in her heart her father was dying and was distressed they would not allow her to spend more time by his side.

Perijan turned her head to the window as she tried to hide her puffy red eyes. The alleys and side roads flashed by. Several people were lying in the street and on the sidewalk, sleeping like animals. Grown men curled up inside doorways with newspapers used as blankets.

This is the great Iranian revolution. Money is spent on building weapons, but they can't spare any to feed and house their own people. Perijan clenched her fists in the folds of her robe and shook her head in disgust. Out of the corner of her eye she caught sight of a familiar light pole. It startled her. It had been almost eighteen months. But there, about a foot above the sidewalk, were two horizontal strips of masking tape. Just as before.

Her heart beat unevenly as she wondered why after all this time the message would be there. She had deduced that her contact had either temporarily left or met with an unpleasant fate. But as the months passed she knew the latter was more likely. The obvious occurred to her. Someone else had arrived. The American government was reestablishing contact with her.

There couldn't be a more awkward time for this to take place. Suddenly, an awful possibility erupted in her mind. What if it wasn't the agent's replacement? What if her own government had figured out the details of the drop and were trying to catch the other person involved? Could it be that they tortured the agent and he told them? Her heart beat wildly and she feared the guards would notice she was becoming more distraught. *No*, Perijan thought, attempting to calm herself. *No one knows. An American is back and I must make contact with him. And if it is a trap, what do I have to lose now, anyway?*

She turned her head to lean against the window as she usually did during the ride. *I will have to remember to behave as I always do and not raise any suspicions.* Tonight, after the sun went down, she planned to sneak out in the dark and return to the field. Iran would pay for what it had done to her family.

THE WHITE HOUSE

Allan Manning, the chief of staff, stood next to Bill Bishop, the national security adviser. Having arrived at the same time, both men were waiting at the entrance to the President's second-floor private study. Manning knocked twice on the solid wood door, making sure it was just loud enough to catch the President's attention.

"Come in . . ." President McEntire covered the mouthpiece of the receiver and at the same time motioned for the two to enter the study. He then swiveled his chair around, turning his back to them and continuing with his discussion on the phone.

Located next to the First Couple's bedroom, this was where the Chief Executive spent most of his time when he wasn't in the Oval Office or on Air Force One. Richard Nixon and Franklin Roosevelt had used the room as a bedroom, and Jackie Kennedy had a small plaque placed above the fireplace mantel reading THIS ROOM WAS OCCUPIED BY JOHN FITZGERALD KENNEDY DURING THE TWO YEARS, TEN MONTHS AND TWO DAYS HE WAS PRESIDENT OF THE UNITED STATES. JANUARY 20, 1961—NOVEMBER 22, 1963. President and Mrs. McEntire had decorated the study with their own furniture from Arizona.

The President continued to talk on the green phone. It was the one designated for secure person-to-person calls to heads of state because it would scramble and encrypt the conversation. *I wonder who's bending the old man's ear*, Manning pondered, still standing in the middle of the study with Bishop. He continued to suck on his pipe as he glanced at CNN. Slouched over with his right arm resting on top of his protruding belly, Manning was often said to resemble Mr. Magoo, the cartoon character, with his bald head and large round nose.

The President finished his conversation and turned toward the men, gesturing for them to sit.

"That was the Israeli prime minister. He's calling an emergency meeting of his cabinet first thing in the morning. Their intelligence indicates the Iranians might be planning some sort of military move." The President leaned back and rolled his chair away from the desk. "With Mahmoudi out of the picture, they feel the more radical members of the Iranian government have the opportunity to attack the Kurds in the north. And if that happens, then Iraq could counterattack, sensing a weakness." McEntire ran his fingers through his uncombed hair. *Why couldn't they have waited until after the damned election*, he thought morosely.

"I think Mossad's overreacting," Manning said, crossing his legs. "It's still too early to tell what's going on over there. We haven't received a solid confirmation on Mahmoudi's condition or the missiles involved. And don't forget that the British prime minister informed us of his negotiations just prior to the shooting. I think we need to give them time to sort through their own problems before assuming they're up to no good."

"Well, I'm beginning to think I have to assume the worst." The President's voice was irritable. "Prepare for any situation that could end up causing a big commotion."

"I share your frustration, Mr. President. I know Mahmoudi wasn't totally hostile toward the West, and with him in power we had a chance of keeping the Gulf region somewhat stable. But if the defense minister, Bakhtiar, should be taking his place, it could be we have a serious problem. What little we know about him is definitely not favorable." Manning looked over at Bishop, waiting to see if he would agree. "Bill, what do you think?" he asked, knowing he had probably already stepped on the man's toes.

Manning had jumped in first on what was considered Bishop's turf—foreign policy and how it affected the security of the United States.

"I agree with the Israelis' assessment that Iran may use this assassination attempt to attack the Kurds, possibly with air power and armor, not just ground troops this time. But we don't need the Israelis stirring things up. You need to tell them to back off, Mr. President. I'm not surprised the Israeli prime minister is up in arms and ready to jump to conclusions. After all, it's his job to be concerned with Israel's security. But they're not equipped to handle it the way we are. And, as I have said, Iran and Iraq are the most unstable countries in the region."

"So, what are you suggesting?" Manning asked, wondering what words of wisdom Bishop had already relayed to the President.

"I'm not suggesting anything. I am merely stating facts. Since we're dealing with the Iranians, it is undoubtedly something to be worried about and we should be reacting to this immediately." Bishop stared Manning down, waiting for him to contradict all or part of his statement.

"Well, there is some truth to that . . . but I'm also concerned about the possibility we could end up being the ones overreacting if we were to do anything more than we already have. The *Abraham Lincoln* is deployed there and I believe that is presently signal enough to the guilty party." Manning looked to the President, uneasy about igniting tensions further.

"I agree. But shit, I need some help here, gentlemen. Can anyone tell me what is the perfect solution to this dilemma? I'll be damned if I do react and damned if I don't."

"Let's back up a minute here and go over the real facts," Bishop said, opening his briefcase and pulling out a half-dozen faxes from various sources, including Mossad, British Intelligence, and the CIA. "They all say the same thing."

"And what might that be?" Manning asked.

Bishop looked at the top one. "From Mossad—they've received reports of some minor troop movements in the north, nothing major yet. The British are reporting the same thing."

"And the CIA?" the President asked. "What is Brady saying?"

"Brady was the last one I talked with before coming over here. He's getting his information from the same source as everyone else—at this point, basically CNN. We're waiting for satellite photos right now. Our early-warning satellites would have picked up the infrared signatures of any major armor movements. We know that isn't happening.''

The President shook his head and laughed sarcastically. ''That's just great. How am I going to make an informed decision?''

''Mr. President, the information you need isn't going to come from satellite passes. There isn't much we'll know, unless you think the Iranians are going to tell us what's going on. That's just the simple truth.'' Bishop grew even more sober. ''Whoever is in charge over there right now is going to be on edge. There could even be a military coup attempt or a Shi'ite leader could start another religious cleansing campaign. Mahmoudi was considered a moderate, by Iranian standards, at least, and we know he had a lot of hardline enemies. My advice is to issue a statement condemning *any* military movements. We have to let the Iranian military know we're prepared to step in if they try anything. Send a strong signal to Iran's religious leaders that the United States will not tolerate its actively anti-Western government. And if I may speak frankly, sir—''

''That's bullshit,'' Manning interrupted, shaking his head. ''Any moves on our part might be perceived as—''

''Go ahead, Bill,'' the President insisted.

''We can use this to boost your standings in the polls. Show the country you are in charge of the situation and that you can handle any crisis efficiently. The Democrats will have to scramble to keep up.'' Bishop finished, thinking, *Come on, Mr. President. You're running for reelection. Show some balls.*

''So, you basically think I can settle all this by threatening them?'' the President asked, not sure he was following his national security adviser.

''No, not threatening . . . just taking a firm stand. If Mahmoudi dies, we don't need a hotheaded radical taking his place. You can tell the Iranian people that all Americans grieve for their turmoil, but we also have interests in the Gulf.''

President McEntire was quiet for a moment. If this was handled properly, with the right diplomatic touch, maybe Iran would . . . hell, *could*, change course. Mahmoudi had made the first move, realizing the U.S. wasn't the Great Satan. But was another military signal necessary when the prime minister's fate wasn't decided yet? It was possible that whoever replaced Mahmoudi would also be a moderate. But that wasn't very likely. *This isn't an issue I'm going to drag into the campaign*, he decided.

"I want a statement issued before the morning news shows go on the air saying we condemn the shooting and our prayers go out to the people of Iran in hopes that Mahmoudi recovers." The President continued, looking at Manning, "Allan, at noon I want another statement issued restating our commitment to the security of the Gulf region. And at the same time I'm ordering all our aircraft and Navy assets in the area to stand down at once."

"Stand down?" Bishop asked.

"That's right. I don't want anything in the air for the next forty-eight hours." McEntire spoke firmly without turning his gaze on Bishop. "I want to give everyone some time to cool down."

"What about the *Lincoln* and her battle group? They're scheduled to enter the Gulf in twelve hours," Bishop protested. "Shit, and what about the tankers?"

"I didn't say to withdraw the *Lincoln*. I just don't want the Navy to provoke any hostilities."

Manning smiled, knowing the President was sending two signals at the same time, a classic foreign policy strategy. One signal was to the American people, saying he was a tough-minded leader and would not tolerate U.S. interests being threatened. The other was to the Iranian military, saying he didn't want any conflicts. Manning just hoped both messages would be received and understood. When Jimmy Carter sent unarmed F-15s to Saudi Arabia after the Shah fell, it took ten years to patch up the political damage of such an ineffective gesture.

"That's all I want said, or done, right now." McEntire stood and waited for the two to follow his hint, then walked them to the door. "I have a few more phone calls to make. Good night, gentlemen."

"Good night." Manning walked down the hallway toward the stairs, with Bishop keeping up next to him. The atmosphere between them was tense.

"I know you'd rather I didn't speak my mind, Bill, but I believe it's in the country's best interest that the President look at all sides of an issue, politically and strategically."

"Well, politically and strategically speaking, *Mr. Manning*, I think it's in the best interest of U.S. security if you just did your job and let me do mine,'' Bishop replied heatedly.

"I wish it were that simple, but I haven't yet figured how polls and Democrats scrambling around affect national security,'' Manning answered as they reached the foot of the stairs. They glared at each other a moment, then turned and walked in opposite directions without saying another word.

The day had dragged on slowly and Perijan was more than relieved to finally be home. She had worried that Hikmet would notice there was an unusual tension about her, but he hadn't shown up at the laboratory today.

The house was silent and she walked in quietly, not wanting to disturb her father if he was sleeping. She entered the kitchen to find her father slouched in a chair at the table with steaming tea cupped in both his hands. The clear plastic tubes were loose around his face and his eyes were closed.

"Papa, are you awake?'' Perijan walked over to him, speaking softly. She adjusted the oxygen and his eyelids fluttered open. "How are you feeling?''

The old man smiled, his face tired and worn. "I am fine, my child. I must have dozed off for a moment . . . I wanted some tea.''

Perijan lovingly smiled back and placed her hand over his, letting him know the tea was right there.

"Oh, yes. I fixed it myself, didn't I. I told you not to worry so much. I am able to take care of things while you are at work.''

"Oh, Papa, I know you can take care of yourself. I am so pleased to see you up.'' Perijan leaned over and kissed him on the cheek. "Did Sunita come and fix you lunch today?''

"Yes, but you mustn't bother our neighbors. I can . . .'' Her father sipped on the warm liquid and coughed lightly.

"She wants to help. You be nice, Papa, and let her cook for you. You know she was Mama's friend and wants to do what she can,'' Perijan answered, walking into her bedroom to put away her duffel bag. The queasy feeling she had felt since early morning, after seeing the tape on the light post, had not left her stomach. Hanging up her uniform, she only went through the motions of her daily routine. Everything was feeling uncertain, as if she were watching herself in a dream.

In a few hours the sun would be down. She would slip out and it would be revealed who was trying to contact her. She longed to tell her father of the messages and what she was doing. But she knew it might put him in danger. Besides, his mind would come and go; she couldn't trust that he wouldn't say anything if questioned. They probably wouldn't bother with him since he was a sick old man, and Sunita would more than likely take him in if something were to happen to Perijan. At least that's how she reassured herself.

"I will make you dinner. Then you must go back to bed and rest. You may be feeling well enough to get up for a while, but you shouldn't do too much in one day."

"I will stay up with you . . . and talk like we used to when your mama was alive. Your mama would know what to do. You should have someone to talk to. You never have any friends or go out . . ."

"Now, Papa, you know better than that. I am fine by myself. I do have friends; I get to see and talk to them at work. Now, don't worry. Besides, I have a lot of reading to do tonight." Perijan stroked her father's hand, thinking this could be the last time she saw him if she were wrong and it wasn't the American government trying to reestablish contact with Zenith.

Chapter Fourteen

By this time tomorrow, all Muslims, particularly Shi'ite Muslims, will no longer be looked upon as weak radicals unable to oppose the infidels in the West. The bitterness, scars and malice that all Arabs felt from our defeat in the Gulf War will be over. No more would Muslims bow their heads and look the other way in shame because of who we are and what we believe. Allah's great revolution will live because Allah wills it to live.

Defense Minister Sheik Bakhtiar watched as the Ayatollah Abdol-Rasul Hanifnezhad's wheelchair was pushed into the Supreme Defense Council's dark ground-floor chamber in the ministry building. Bakhtiar felt a change in the room as the most powerful holy man in Iran came closer. Hanifnezhad's omnipotent presence sent a warmth to everyone. It was written, and Bakhtiar believed, that Hanifnezhad communicated directly with Allah. There was no doubt that he was infallible in all his actions and decisions.

"Allah be with you," Bakhtiar said, bowing his head in deep respect to the ayatollah.

"Allah be with you," Hanifnezhad whispered back in a weak, frail voice.

The ayatollah's fifty-year-old son pushed Iran's religious leader to the back of the conference room, stopping at the end of the

190

table. He carefully locked the wheels and remained standing behind his father as if at attention.

It had been only a month since the last time the two men had met, but now Bakhtiar barely recognized the man. Dressed in traditional clerical robes, the man appeared to be only a shadow within the heavy folds, almost skeletal. The ayatollah was listless. His face was sunken in yellowing skin, the sockets around his blind white eyes were a lifeless gray with thin red veins crisscrossing them. His shoulder-length hair was no longer silver, rather a dingy gray, thinning and oily. The beard that once covered his face was nearly gone, leaving patches of whiskers. The man's bony hands rested on his Koran.

The defense minister took short, determined steps as he walked to the front of the room. Everything had not gone as planned. Mahmoudi wasn't dead yet. The man had been lapsing in and out of a coma.

It doesn't matter, Bakhtiar thought. *Mahmoudi is still out of the picture*. And now Bakhtiar controlled the military, without any interference from anyone.

He glanced about the room. Two of the council chairs around the square table were empty, those of the prime minister and the minister of internal security, Marjid. *Let them wonder why for a moment longer*. Bakhtiar had rehearsed his speech a dozen times in his head, anticipating every objection.

"Major Dahawa, it has been discovered, is a traitor. A traitor . . . working for the CIA. My security forces searched his apartment several hours ago. They found these along with American-made weapons and ammunition." The sheik threw several documents down on the table.

Scattered were an American passport and three rolls of American money, tens, twenties and hundred dollar bills all tightly bound with rubber bands.

"This file was found, along with pictures of an American woman. I presume she was his wife. He has a family living in America. Also found were detailed instructions for an escape after the assassination of Prime Minister Mahmoudi." Bakhtiar flipped the file folder open and tapped on the top paper. "Here is the map showing an escape route into Saudi Arabia. He was to board one of their tankers at Abadan and sail to the port of Al Qatif, where an American aircraft would take him back to the United States. Do you understand what this means? The CIA has killed one of the highest-ranking members of this government. They have attempted to kill our prime minister.''

"We have many enemies.'' Hanifnezhad answered from his wheelchair. ''Many enemies.'' His dull eyes were looking in the direction of Bakhtiar but not directly at him.

"Israel and the PLO have made peace. We stand alone against the Great Satan. The Arab world is afraid to challenge America for fear it will be cut to shreds like Iraq. If the revolution is to continue, we must unite our people. Unite them with a war against the West.'' Bakhtiar glared at each man seated around the table, speaking gruffly.

"Many people will die if you challenge the United States,'' the minister of the interior said. ''And there are other ways to unite our people.''

"Many people die in our streets *now*,'' Bakhtiar retorted scornfully. ''The Ayatollah Hanifnezhad and I have prayed to Allah many days. And I know of the other ways you speak of. They are the coward's ways. They will shame us further. Our country will be destroyed by the evils of the West if you open our doors to them. Allah has given us the means to unite our people—the Phalanx Dragon has been a success. The Great Satan is still baffled by its power. I ask permission to proceed with the revolution while time is in our favor.''

"You are a *fool*. We will never win a war with the United States. The parliament will never agree to this,'' Adnan Hanifnezhad, the ayatollah's son said, shaking his head in disbelief. ''This weapon of yours was used against defenseless tankers. How do you know what will happen when it is matched up against the Americans' armory?''

Bakhtiar looked at the man. Adnan Hanifnezhad resembled his father in many ways—long face, drooping eyelids and a crooked, pointed nose. Adnan had studied Islam at the holy city of Qom and planned to follow in his father's footsteps. But at this moment Adnan Hanifnezhad was not an ayatollah.

"The parliament will do whatever your father says. My goal is not to defeat the Americans, just bloody their noses. We are a *divided* nation. The Iranian people must have a common enemy to fight and unite against. *We have the means to challenge the Americans in the Gulf. We must use our weapons to save the revolution!*'' Bakhtiar pounded his fist on the table, his voice escalated to near-hysteria.

"*The Dragon came from a weapon that was made by the Great Satan. How do you know it was not meant to be our destruction?*" Al-Yawm stood, his voice matching the defense minister's.

"I have ordered our aircraft and missile sites to arm and stand by. The missiles are ready. They can be launched tonight if it is your wish." Bakhtiar ignored the outburst, searching the ayatollah's face for the will to continue the revolution.

"Iran will *never*—"

"Bakhtiar speaks the truth," Hanifnezhad said feebly, interrupting the man. "Minister Bakhtiar is correct . . . the Ayatollah Khomeini would not be afraid to strike the West to save Iran. An armed revolution will save our people this time, as it saved them before."

Al-Yawm was not sure how the news of signed contracts with the British would be received, but felt it urgent he now reveal their existence. "Pardon me, your holiness, but Prime Minister Mahmoudi came to a resolution to end the fighting through the West—"

"Enough." The old man raised a trembling hand, speaking harshly. "I have heard enough. There will be no more talk of dealing with the West."

"Everything is ready." Bakhtiar stared warningly at Al-Yawm before continuing. He turned and pointed to a map behind him. Small red pins protruded from Iran's northern coastline along the Strait of Hormuz. "Our surface-to-surface sites are armed with the stealth missiles, and Colonel Rahavi commands a squadron of F-4Es at Esfahan armed with the same missiles. We can destroy half of the American battle group before they ever know who is attacking them."

"The revolution must continue," the Ayatollah Hanifnezhad muttered. His head then bobbed up and down as he closed his eyes. "Iran will never give up the revolution."

Bakhtiar stood rigidly still. The ayatollah had seemingly given his consent. Knowing he could not go against his father's wishes, Adnan quietly unlocked the brakes of the wheelchair and pushed the ayatollah out of the room.

"*Do you know what you have just done?*" the minister of the interior asked.

"I have just saved Iran from a long and bloody civil war," Bakhtiar answered, his burning eyes staring hard at the man.

"I pray to Allah you are correct." Al-Yawm stood from his chair and walked out of the room.

The sun had been down for many hours and the clear night sky was dotted with white stars. Perijan Reza kept her head covered and down. She was too frightened to look around to check if she was being followed. The five-minute walk from her home already seemed an eternity. She wanted to appear casual and therefore strained to walk at a normal pace. The streets and market area were relatively quiet, but Perijan was still worried that someone would be suspicious of her walking alone this late in the evening.

She turned onto Hheyabun-e Modarres Street but before entering the alley couldn't fight the urge to look right and left, searching for anyone who might be following. A flood of memories came back to her. Just as before, the alley reeked from the lingering odor of urine and rotting garbage. The sharp pungency of the smell turned Perijan's stomach. The shadows, cast from the nearby streetlights, exaggerated the murky outline of the broken furniture and empty boxes littering the alleyway. Perijan tried to examine each detail, looking for any movement or anything that might signal trouble.

Up ahead, not more than thirty yards away, she could see the weathered boards of the fence separating the alley from the vacant lot. Not much had changed since the last time she had walked down the road at night over a year and a half ago, except the buildings were in worse condition and more trash had been left outside to decompose in the weed-infested lot.

Perijan reached the end of the alley and stopped. She pivoted in a small circle. If anyone was waiting for her, this would be the place. She tried to listen for any sounds, but was too nervous to concentrate. Deciding that if she had been followed this far it was already too late to explain her presence and that the only thing they might learn was where the message was hidden, Perijan held her breath and, as bravely as she could, bent down, reaching under the fence next to the corner post. She felt around in the dirt for a piece of string or leather.

It should be next to the post. Next to the post on the opposite side. She froze. Her fingers felt something cold and hard—a coarse piece of nylon string tied in a loop. She rang her forefinger through the loop and pulled the six-inch cylinder out of the ground.

Perijan straightened and turned back to the alley. Her eyes scanned right and left. In the distance, she saw the shadow of someone walking past on the sidewalk. Her heart skipped a beat and she shoved the plastic cylinder into the pocket of her chador. She slowly began to return the way she came, carefully strolling over to the light post at the corner. Standing next to it, she fumbled and dropped a book she had brought along. Stooping down and spreading out her chador to help hide her actions, she used her fingernail to peel away the two pieces of tape from the light post. Perijan retrieved the book and walked a little way before lowering her hand to her side and letting loose the crumpled tape.

Collins turned the key and heard the lock snap. He pushed on the door; the edges always caught on the frame. The room was dark but in the streetlight streaming in through the thin curtains he could see his bed was unmade, just the way he had left it.

As he entered, however, Collins noticed some things were not in place. Someone had been in his room. He had expected Iranian security forces to search his belongings, but it wasn't until now that it was done so obviously. The movable brass handles on his top dresser drawer were no longer pointing up the way he had intentionally set them. The bottom drawer wasn't even shut.

He walked into the bathroom and turned on the light, immediately noticing the contents of his shaving kit had been dumped out, then haphazardly thrown back in.

The only items that would incriminate him were the ones he carried in the false bottom of his briefcase: the wig, glasses and two sets of fake IDs, each with other names. And, of course, there was his computer. *Well, maybe now they'll leave me alone for a while.* Collins left the bathroom to see an inch-long roach scurry across the floor and disappear under the bed.

"Hello, Mr. Kahman. I see you have arrived safely." Ali Fesseghi smiled, knowing he had startled Collins. The man was sitting in a straight-back wooden chair that was tucked into the right corner of the cramped room.

Collins spun around, cursing himself for being so stupid.

"You should be more cautious and lock your door," Fesseghi said. Collins smiled, remembering he had heard the lock snap open. "I must apologize for the accommodations. However, they were the best I could arrange under the circumstances."

Rather than wearing a business suit, Fesseghi was dressed informally—black wool pants, leather dress shoes and a turquoise patterned shirt open at the collar. For the first time Collins noticed a thick gold chain around the man's neck. An obvious measure of his success.

"They'll do," Collins answered politely. He could see that Fesseghi was holding his briefcase. *Well, this is the moment of truth.* The case contained his notebook computer. Hidden in the software were CIA files, maps of Esfahan, Tehran and other Iranian cities, along with a low-power satcom uplink so he could communicate directly with CIA headquarters in Langley. If any of the file codes were deciphered, they would automatically erase. But that wouldn't do Collins any good if he needed to contact headquarters or transmit information.

"Good. I'm glad you're not a man who is hard to please." Fesseghi stood and walked over to the bed, placing the briefcase on it. He was quiet a moment, his eyes fixed on Collins. "We must talk. As you are aware, someone has gone through your room. I'm sure that you understand the necessity for these actions. There are people in the military, at this base, who are not pleased with my government's decision to bring you here."

"This was your idea, not mine. I can be on the next plane out of here." Collins's mind was now up to speed. He stepped back into the bathroom and washed his face. Blotting his face with a hand towel, he stood in the doorway.

"We have inspected your personal items and everything seems to be in order. However, I understand there is some confusion with an item in your briefcase." Fesseghi tapped the top of it with his index finger, waiting for a reaction.

Collins threw the towel on the sink behind him before responding. He thought for a minute. Fesseghi was showing his true colors—a SAVAMA intelligence officer. However, if the Iranians had found the encrypted CIA satcom program and data files concealed inside the computer's hard drive, he would probably already be dead. Someone would have put a bullet between his eyes. Possibly they hadn't found anything and Fesseghi was just testing him. Collins figured if he backed down, the Iranian might take it as a sign of weakness, that he really was trying to hide something. He had to take a chance and hope it worked.

"And what item would that be?" Collins asked, walking over and opening the briefcase. "I didn't expect you to treat me like a spy. I was under the impression we had a business relationship.

I have nothing to hide. See for yourself.'' He pointed at the open case, its contents exposed. "This computer contains the technical files I've needed to work on your F-4s and nothing more.''

"Remove the computer and turn it on," Fesseghi demanded. Without any hesitation, Collins removed the 6.2-pound Hewlett-Packard notebook from its protective cover, flipped up the view screen and punched in the access code, turning the machine on. The battery kicked in and a surge of electricity ran through the microprocessor. *I hope some idiot hasn't screwed this up*, he thought.

After a few seconds Collins punched in the code accessing the computer's hard drive. He then pulled up the data he would need to repair and program the AN/APG-66J radar pulse-Doppler look-down, shot-down radar. He scrolled down the file, stopping at a part he hoped the Iranian would be familiar with. Collins pointed to the data.

"This is one of the internal schematics for the radar you purchased.'' He hit the control key twice, zooming in on a section of the radar directly behind the phased array radar panel. The diagram showed several black boxes, along with a wiring layout and the position of several circuit panels. "This shows the location of every circuit, every microprocessor—a complete wiring blueprint. This program will allow me to bring every one of those radars on line, and it has enough power to test each fighter's avionics before it ever gets into the air.'' He tapped the keyboard a few more times, changing the active matrix color screen. It now showed another section of the radar's internal workings, this one a detailed picture of electrical leads.

Fesseghi studied the screen for a few moments. He could clearly see the radar's outline. Each of the black boxes was coded with a computer number and looked as if it could be referenced for more detailed information. Across the bottom of the screen were rows of numbers and written instructions on installing replacement parts.

"I hope whoever checked my system knows what they're doing and didn't damage any of my programs. They were developed by McDonnell Douglas to be used by F-4E engineers. If I lose any of it, I can't do my job . . . and I can't go out and buy another one. That means I won't be able to fix your radars.'' Collins acted as if his feathers were more than a little ruffled and stared at Fesseghi. "So I don't like anyone messing around with my computer. This is how I make my living. It'll cost you a pretty penny if it's destroyed.''

"You should not get so worked up, Mr. Kahman. I just wanted to hear your explanation myself," Fesseghi replied indignantly. "We cannot be too careful. I'm sure there is nothing wrong with your computer." He turned to leave, then smiled at Collins. "I apologize if I startled or upset you, but I'm sure you understand that I am only doing my job."

"Of course, I understand." Collins shut down the computer, placing it back in his briefcase. He could feel his heart racing and insides rolling at the same time. Fesseghi wasn't an idiot. He hoped he would be as lucky the next time Fesseghi challenged him.

Collins placed the briefcase on the dresser. *Well, at least I'm over the first hurdle.*

Perijan crept through the dark apartment, not wanting to wake her father. A single flickering candle on the kitchen table cast just enough light for her to see the way. As she passed through the kitchen, Perijan could hear her father's strained breathing. She stood next to his door a moment, making sure he was sleeping soundly. At least he wasn't coughing.

Her mind swirled with a thousand thoughts as she entered the privacy of her bedroom and drew the heavy canvas drape across the entrance. In a natural desire for security, she craved the isolation and solitude of her cramped room. She lit a large beeswax candle resting on the dresser and sat on the edge of the bed, waiting for her eyes to adjust before pulling the plastic cylinder out of her pocket and unscrewing the cap.

Perijan hesitated, feeling disloyal and a little guilty. Once she removed the paper rolled up inside, she knew the feelings of despair for her country would disappear. Hope would replace those emotions. She wondered if it was only a fantasy. Her hatred for the revolution had not faded in the past few months. If anything, it had boiled and festered, growing more intense. Her family was destroyed by the revolution and she had no desire to have children of her own when she watched children begging for food in the streets daily. At that moment, Perijan decided to help the United States once again.

She unrolled the paper carefully, holding it gingerly in her hands. Whoever it was attempting to contact her would no doubt be the CIA, she knew. They wouldn't know she no longer worked in research and development and was being watched more carefully.

She held it up next to the light of the candle. The thin waxy paper told her the message had been written on pyrofilm, specially coated paper that would burn in a flash if exposed to an open flame.

ZENITH. ARE YOU STILL WITH US?

Perijan stared at the letters. The handwriting was neat and the message simple and ambiguous. She brushed the corner of the paper by the candle's flame and watched as it was consumed by fire.

Opening the bottom drawer of her dresser, she pulled it completely out. In the back, behind a simple board that had been tacked in place, was concealed her supply of pyrofilm. The compartment was a simple design they had taught her to construct before she left America.

She thought a moment about how to write what the CIA would want to know using the fewest words. Perijan neatly wrote her reply, rolled up the paper and placed it in the cylinder. Tomorrow night she would slip back into the night, returning the cylinder to the same place.

She blew out the candle and crawled into her cool bed. She knew that sleep wouldn't come this night, but not because of her father.

Mark Collins locked the bathroom door but left the light off. He turned on his computer and several seconds later the screen filled the small room with just enough light for him to read the keyboard.

He quickly connected a flexible rubber-coated copper antenna cable to the computer's mouse port. Going to the window above the toilet, he made sure no one was lurking near the building. The alley was dark and the streetlights across the road were too far away to cast any light in his direction. He gently forced the window open a half inch, uncoiled the wire and fed the antenna outside, letting it dangle against the side of the building. The wire would act as an uplink and downlink antenna, enabling him to transmit data directly to the CIA in Langley via a Defense Department communications satellite parked over the Persian Gulf.

Okay . . . let's make this fast. Collins sat down on the toilet and went to work. He typed CD/SATCOM *.* UPLINK TRANS and pressed the enter key. This told the system he was sending a message, not receiving one. The hard drive began to cycle as it pulled the coded communications program from the rest of the software. Thirty seconds later the screen flashed CDMA, for code division multiple access, telling Collins it was safe to begin typing in his message.

The system was one of four the CIA operated and had been designed for worldwide communications. It was developed by modifying Motorola's civilian Idirdium personal phone network. Inserted inside Collins's computer was a Hewlett-Packard HP-95LXC processing chip combined with an Ericsson GE Mobidem (mobile modem). The encrypted low-power signal generated by his computer could pick up and retransmit by a number of means, mainly ground stations, satellites and ocean-based sensors. K-band frequency was used in the uplink and L-band in the downlink. The signals could be bounced off any country's standard microwave network, essentially allowing Collins to communicate with the CIA in real time if need be.

However, tonight's transmission would be "send only," and he planned to keep the message short and sweet. When he finished, he hit the control and F10 keys, electronically compacting the transmission into a radio transmission that would last a fraction of a second. The software program then coded and scrambled the message, feeding the electronic pulses into the main microprocessor. When the screen blinked READY, Collins sent the single-channel microburst communication, capable of transmitting over 50,000 bits of information a second, to the satellite overhead.

Collins shut down the computer and pulled in the antenna, coiling it into a neat ball. His next thoughts were of sleep. Tomorrow would be here before he knew it, and the Iranians would be expecting a full day's work. He slid the computer under the mattress and crawled under the cool sheets. He could hear the barking of a dog in the distance and he closed his eyes, thinking about the time change. He figured it was nearly two o'clock in the afternoon back home.

Chances were Christine, his wife, was putting their daughter down for her afternoon nap. In the back of every CIA officer's mind is the possibility of losing a loved one or not being home during a family crisis. Collins had heard numerous tales of officers who returned to Langley after being in the field for a lengthy time to discover that a parent, spouse or even son or daughter had died. In an attempt to be prepared for the unknown, Christine and he had discussed what to do if the worst should occur.

Collins had spoken to Christine before he left Turkey, three weeks ago. Hell, he hadn't seen her or his little girl in four months, and it was beginning to wear on him. Love of country, duty and honor were great, but there was a lot to be said for holding your wife each night in bed. He couldn't help but wonder if everything was all right. He hoped his daughter, who was not yet two and a half, still remembered him. When he returned home, he doubted she would. Kids were funny about that, they forgot quickly. God must have planned it that way. Made them resilient until they were old enough to take care of themselves. He smiled, thinking of ways to win her affection all over again.

The thought of walking downstairs to call home flashed through his mind. *Yeah, right, Collins. Get stupid and you might not even make it home.* There was a rumor a while back that an agent thought he could get away with just dialing to hear his wife's voice and not speak. But even the lobby phone had been tapped. The agent was dead in twenty-four hours. Collins wondered if some of the rumors they were told in training were just scare tactics but had decided they were plausible enough that he wouldn't chance it. After all, the Iranians had put him in this hotel for a reason, and it wasn't for a vacation. They were watching his every move.

Chapter Fifteen

The CIC (Combat Information Center) was bathed in a light blue pulsating light radiating from the twenty-four various-sized display consoles lining the walls. The room was larger than Duke James had pictured, but it still seemed cramped from the immense amount of communications and computer equipment that had been jammed into the thirty-by-forty-foot chamber. The operators at the computers were seated shoulder to shoulder, and Duke could smell the faint odor of sweat and strong coffee.

In essence, the CIC on board the *LaSalle*, berthed permanently at Bahrain, served as the nerve center for all naval operations in the Middle East. The ship was in constant contact with all U.S. and NATO vessels, as well as various Air Force and Marine elements operating in the region. The ship could also communicate with every U.S. command center around the world and was tied in with the Pentagon and the National Command Authority via satellite and backup ground communications.

The *LaSalle* employed an advanced version of the LINK-11 data relay system to stay in touch with all combat ships. The LINK-11 utilized a series of coded frequency-hopping UHF and EHF radio transmissions, allowing the commander on the *LaSalle* to see exactly what each ship was viewing on its radar screens anywhere in the area. The system was also tied into the Navy

202

E-2C and Air Force E-3C AWACS patrol aircraft, giving it the means to control a battle over the entire Gulf region from a central location. The room was dominated by four sixty-by-sixty-inch display screens arranged in a semicircle. Outlined in white, each screen showed a separate portion of the Gulf region, along with each country's military and naval bases.

Duke could see the air traffic in the region and the surface ships sailing through the Strait of Hormuz. The merchant ships, a mixture of tankers, freighters and container vessels, appeared as yellow rectangles and U.S. warships were marked in green. Any potentially hostile ships would appear as orange and turn red if they became a threat. On the screen to the far right, Duke could see a cluster of U.S. ships heading northwest.

The *Abraham Lincoln* and her battle group were now 300 miles southeast of the strait, ten hours out. However, that wasn't where everyone was focusing their attention. Steaming ahead of the *Lincoln* was an Aegis-class guided cruiser, the *Shiloh*, and the destroyer *John Young*. Zachiem had assigned the *Shiloh* and her crew the task of clearing the area south of the strait by identifying and dealing with any airborne or surface threats.

Duke knew the *Shiloh*-operated Aegis system, which had been designed for fleet defense and could hit high-flying aircraft as well as fast-moving sea-skimming cruise missiles. The ship's sophisticated SPY-1B detection system was designed around four antenna panels, each containing 1,100 stationary phased array radars canted at a fifteen-degree angle. Each tiny radar produced a narrow, high-resolution beam that was electronically focused or steered for continuous 360-degree coverage. The data collected by each radar was then fed into the ship's central UYK-43B computer, where it was filtered and integrated into the fire control system. The system could engage over 120 fast-moving airborne threats, simultaneously targeting each with air-to-air missiles.

Duke was seated in an area normally reserved for VIPs and high-ranking military brass, although he was sure Zachiem didn't consider him high-ranking or a VIP. Several feet directly behind the commander's seat and elevated several feet above the main floor, he had an excellent view of the entire CIC. Duke had spent the majority of the last two days in the CIC getting a feel for Navy operations. He was starting to feel restless and fidgety, and hoped everything would blow over soon and Chaniff would order him home. Sean's birthday was in ten days and he didn't want to miss it, again.

"*Shiloh* reports no hostile surface threats in the area, sir," one of the chief petty officers reported. "And the skies are clear."

Duke watched Zachiem finish filling his coffee cup and walk back toward his seat. The admiral had been in the CIC for the last ten hours and was starting to look tired. Duke wondered how long he would stay at his post. *It's your show, Admiral. Kill yourself if you want, but pretty soon you're gonna be wound so tight you'll snap.*

"Very well. Confirm the transmission," Zachiem grunted. "Is the *Shiloh* detecting any radar transmissions?"

"Just the standard, sir. Iranian civilian air traffic control and surface ship radars south of Bandar Abbas. No military frequencies."

Zachiem stood for a long moment, taking several sips from his coffee.

"I'll be in my cabin. Contact me if anything changes." Zachiem glanced over at Duke. "It's going to be another three hours before the *Shiloh*'s in range of the Iranian coast. You can stay here if you want. I'm going to get some rest."

Duke nodded. "Thank you. I might stick around a little while longer, then get some shut-eye, too."

"I'll have one of my officers wake you at 2300 hours, or sooner, if you'd like," Zachiem offered, setting his cup down.

"No, thank you, that won't be necessary," Duke answered coolly, looking at his watch. It had a built-in alarm and he'd rather rely on that than the admiral. Zachiem turned on his heel and exited the room. Duke got up to take a closer look at the CIC since the admiral wouldn't be around to look over his shoulder.

USS *SHILOH*

The guided-missile cruiser USS *Shiloh* slowed to sixteen knots as she sliced through the dark turquoise water sixty-two miles south of the Strait of Hormuz. Sailing on a northwesterly heading, the 9,600-ton Ticonderoga-class cruiser left a trail of boiling water in the darkness. Two thousand yards behind her, the *John Young* also slowed, making sure she didn't overtake the larger cruiser.

"Slow to ten knots heading three-two-niner," Captain Carter

C. Parkington of the *Shiloh* ordered from his raised seat, two decks below the main bridge.

"Ten knots . . . heading three-two-niner, sir," came the reply.

Parkington folded his legs, trying to get comfortable in his worn leather seat. He had just awakened from a sound four hours of sleep. He was thankful for the rest, knowing the next eighteen hours would be filled with more than the usual stress of command. The time it would take them to get through the strait and into the open waters of the Persian Gulf would tax him and his crew to the maximum.

"Any air traffic?" Parkington asked, looking at the tactical air screen.

"One Comair to the north, sir. Iranian flight zero-three-four . . . bearing three-four-niner. The log book shows it as an A340 Airbus . . . destination, Paris," the combat systems coordinator responded. "I'm also showing two F-18s to the south."

Parkington nodded, his attention now focused on the multicolored radar information display screens that showed all surface and air activity. The four screens had the capability of superimposing computer-generated maps covering up to 2,000 nautical miles of any coast in the world. Parkington could also zoom in on an area less than eight nautical miles long.

The display screens used special symbols for each type of target—aircraft, surface ships and submarines—all plotted opposing geographical coordinates and shoreline contours. On the left, the picture had been zoomed so it covered 230 square miles, plotting the position of the carrier task force the *Shiloh* was attached to. Parkington could see the carrier *Abraham Lincoln* along with the escort ships thirty-eight miles to the south of their current position.

The cramped, windowless Combat Information Center had a prismatic hue from the four larger and twelve smaller radar screens that provided most of the light that danced across the walls and floor of the steel-reinforced chamber.

The captain, a twenty-three-year veteran of the surface navy, watched the console operators manipulate their computer keyboards to get the most out of the Aegis SPY-1B radar system. Five years from his planned retirement, Parkington was sitting where he had strived to be most of his career—commanding the most complex and sophisticated surface ship in the U.S. Navy, an Aegis cruiser. It was a command post every Annapolis graduate aspires to hold; however, only a few can ever reach the position. If he could only grow more hair and didn't have to fight the battle of the bulge, a battle his wife reminded him he was losing, he'd feel like he had it all.

Parkington adjusted his ball cap and thick glasses and watched a superimposed computer image of the *Shiloh* making its way toward the coast of Iran. This wasn't the first time he had sailed his ship this close to the Iranian shoreline. Power projection was one of the things the Navy did best, and the U.S. liked to remind Iran occasionally that the sea-lanes would always be protected. Sixteen months ago, Parkington had taken his ship through the Gulf and into the Kuwaiti port at Sea Island. Sailing in the Gulf then had also been tense, but this time he could clearly feel the heightened anxiety in his crew.

"Fifty miles to Iranian territorial waters, Captain," Chief Petty Officer Sam Farland, the ship's combat system coordinator, reported.

Farland sat next to the SPY-1B radar operator. Parkington considered him a jack of all trades, and contrary to the popular saying, Farland *was* the master of all of them. Farland's main assignment put him in charge of doctrine statements. This was the data collected by the SPY-1B radar, which he prioritized, deciding what should appear on the radar screens for the captain and crew to see. He switched them on or off when required or revised them as conditions changed. Using his ten years of experience, Farland knew what information was needed and when to display it—whether to display air traffic only, with or without interference, and if the data should be filtered or not to eliminate false targets caused by atmospheric ducting, in which radar waves bounced off the atmosphere.

"Forty-seven miles to Iranian territorial waters, Captain," Farland reported again.

"Steady as she goes," Parkington said, looking at Farland. Both men were thinking the same thing. The captain was planning to take the *Shiloh* to the edge of international waters, just outside Iran's territorial twelve-mile limit. As the *Shiloh* neared the strait, the sea-lane narrowed considerably, and if the Iranians were looking at him from their shore positions, high above the Gulf, Parkington was betting he could get them to turn on their surface-to-surface acquisition and targeting radar, allowing his crew to plot their positions. These radars controlled Iran's Silkworm missiles, and it was safe to assume where there were radars, there were Silkworms.

I want to be sure those bastards know we're out here, Parkington thought to himself.

"Contact, sir. I'm showing two long-range radars sweeping to the northwest."

"Give me an ID, Mr. Farland." Parkington adjusted his position in the chair, his eyes narrowing in thought. *Well, that didn't take long. Maybe the bastards are looking for a fight.*

Farland held up his hand, waiting for the threat library's software to cycle. "We have positive ID, sir. Computer showing two radars . . . an FPS-100 and an FPS-113 system. There's a good chance we're in range for them to track us."

"Location?" Parkington asked.

"Fixed positions, sir. Both are near Bandar Abbas. My guess is they're located in the mountains above the base." The petty officer pointed at the port city of Bandar Abbas on the display.

Parkington signaled his approval of Farland's speculation by touching the rim of his cap and nodding once. The ship's intelligence officer had been right. Iran operated several large radar sites above their naval base at Bandar Abbas. The radars had been built during the Shah's regime and were part of a national surveillance system called "Seek Sentry." The system was never totally completed, yet the CIA had obtained satellite pictures over the past few years showing the Iranian military working on the sites. They had refurbished enough of the radars to supply Iranian commanders with a workable early-warning and tracking network.

What bothered Parkington was the fact that the radars also controlled a number of smaller sites scattered along the coast. These sites, mainly TPS-43s and ADS-4s, were linked to the Silkworms, as well as SA-2 and SA-3 surface-to-air missiles hidden in rough mountains above the coast. Naval intel had identified five of the sites, but Parkington was smart enough to know there were probably more that hadn't been detected. The CIA had also reported the Iranians preferred moving the missiles at night using heavy trucks, making it nearly impossible to know which sites contained missiles and which didn't.

"Reduce to seven knots and sound general quarters," Parkington ordered.

"Seven knots . . . general quarters."

"Sam, give me an air update."

"Just the two Hornets to the south of us," Farland answered.

The captain looked up at the screen. It was clear except for the flashing blip of two fighters.

"Steady as she goes." Parkington spoke calmly, wanting his crew to remain alert.

ESFAHAN, IRAN

Colonel Alireza Rahavi taxied away from the hangar as the canopy of his F-4E locked into place, shutting out most of the noise from his two turbojets. Turning his oxygen mix to a hundred percent, he blinked hard, hoping his eyes would adjust to the darkness more quickly. He tapped the brakes and brought the fighter to the edge of the taxiway, waiting for instructions from the tower. After examining the cockpit instrumentation one more time, he decided everything looked good: fuel, oxygen, hydraulic pressure and engine temperature.

"Tower, this is flight 875 ready for takeoff."

"Flight 875. Use runway three five left," the sound of the controller's voice crackled through his headset. "Maintain runway heading to flight level 200. Wind out of the southeast at five knots."

"Confirmed. Flight 875 . . . runway 35 left . . . rolling," Rahavi radioed. He lined the fighter up with the center line and pushed the throttles forward slowly, feeling every subtle vibration of the jet as the engines quickly built up. He released the brakes and the fighter, fully loaded with fuel, sluggishly started to move down the runway like a freight train trying to build up a head of steam. The colonel watched the aircraft's gauges, his eyes flashing from the HUD and the cockpit dials every few seconds. When he was confident the jet was operating normally, he jammed the throttles all the way forward, feeling them snap past the afterburner grooves.

A second later his head was jerked back as the huge fighter's velocity increased, its tailpipes glowing orange. Rahavi and his aircraft were airborne.

BANDAR ABBAS, IRAN

"Turn left, heading one-six-niner. Your target is forty-four miles out. Maintain 2,000 feet." The Iranian ground control officer spoke slowly and clearly. He watched the electronic symbol, representing the P-3 Orion, make a leisurely turn to the south on his amber-colored scope.

Iranian Naval Captain Behzad Moezi leaned over the radar display screen and studied the images. On the edge of the scope were two inverted triangles identifying the radar returns of unknown ships sailing to the southwest. He had been tracking them for the past twenty minutes as they methodically made their way toward the Iranian coast and the Strait of Hormuz. Moezi had a good idea what the ships were. By their speed and their electronic emissions he believed them to be military and probably U.S. However, with his limited sensors he could only be sure with a visual or verbal verification.

"How long before that P-3 gets into the area?" Moezi asked, straightening up. He looked around the dark control center. The room was quiet except for the hum of electrical equipment and the occasional static of the radio. Six other technicians sat at their posts monitoring everything from ship-to-shore radio transmissions to SAM sites around the base.

The bearded radar intercept officer didn't look up. "The P-3 is currently forty-three miles out. They should be tracking him now."

"Keep the channel open. I want to hear everything that's happening out there," Moezi ordered, folding his arms.

"Squawking mode II ... 1100. I believe it's a P-3," Farland warned as he watched the unknown target approaching the *Shiloh* on the radarscope. He had been following it for the past three minutes; it had taken off from Bandar Abbas and made a series of turns before heading out to sea and straight for the *Shiloh.* The IFF transponder showed that the aircraft was military. The only question was its intentions.

"Current position?" Parkington asked.

"Forty-two miles out and closing, sir. They want to find out if we're naughty or nice," Farland answered, grinning uncomfortably. He could feel the thick air and hoped the joke would lighten things up. It didn't.

"Forty miles and closing," he added a few seconds later. That wouldn't give them much time to react if the unknown aircraft was armed with antiship missiles.

"Warn him off, Mr. Farland," Parkington ordered, knowing he might have waited too long.

The petty officer changed radio frequencies to the one all aircraft were required to monitor while flying over the Gulf.

"Unknown aircraft on course of one six niner, speed two fiver four, altitude two thousand feet, you are approaching U.S. naval warship operating in international waters. If you maintain current course, you are standing into danger and will be subject to U.S. Navy defense measures. Repeat, you are standing into danger. Request you change course to two two fiver . . . change course to two two fiver." Farland looked over his shoulder at Parkington. If the aircraft didn't respond, Farland would repeat the message and wait another thirty seconds.

Once repeated, the standard reaction to an unanswered response was to bring up the ship's fire control radar and illuminate the target. If it didn't change course then, there wasn't any question in Farland's mind that Parkington would attack the aircraft.

"U.S. naval warship, this is Iranian patrol aircraft. Understand your request. Will change course to two two fiver. Repeat. U.S. naval warship, this is Iranian patrol aircraft. Understand your request. Will change course to two two fiver." The Iranian pilot's English was broken but understandable.

"Well, they now know we're out here *and* who we are," Parkington said, knowing at night it was difficult to get a positive visual ID on surface ships. But the Iranians were clever enough to fly one of their aircraft at his ship, forcing him to identify himself. If his ship had been a civilian vessel, the P-3 could have flown right over it and never been challenged. "The next move is up to them."

Duke jumped at the sound of knocking on his cabin door and glanced at the glowing dials on his wristwatch. *Shit, I just fell asleep an hour ago*, he thought grumpily. It was now a few minutes past midnight.

"Yeah . . . just a second." Duke flipped on the light before putting on his pants. He opened the door to the sight of the same neatly dressed ensign who had escorted him on his arrival. *Man, don't these guys ever eat or sleep?*

"The *Shiloh* has just warned off an Iranian surveillance aircraft. Admiral Zachiem thought you might be interested in how the Navy handles such operations, sir," the man said in monotone.

Sure, he'd just like to tell Chaniff I slept through a military engagement.

"Lead the way," Duke said, buttoning his shirt and shoving the tail into his trousers.

A moment later he walked into the *LaSalle*'s CIC. Zachiem was standing behind one of the technicians, watching the display screens.

"Is there a problem, Admiral?" Duke said sarcastically.

"No, it's being handled. The *Shiloh* just waved off an Iranian P-3. Standard procedure, that's all." Zachiem didn't bother to turn around. "But if you want to know the ins and outs of naval operations, you're going to have to move a little quicker. It's over now."

Duke climbed the steps to his seat. "Why don't you just fill me in and give an update, please." His tone was direct and to the point.

Zachiem turned and strolled back to his seat. "The *Shiloh* is now forty-two miles from the Strait of Hormuz. An Iranian P-3 challenged her and was waved off. That's all. It happens all the time."

"And why wasn't I notified sooner?" Duke asked, knowing the answer.

"Because you were asleep, General. If you're going to sleep, you're going to miss a few things." The ends of Zachiem's mouth curled into a slight grin.

Duke folded his arms. *This is the last time you're going to make a fool out of me, Admiral.*

Colonel Rahavi brought his F-4E Phantom out of a long banking turn and came level at 18,000 feet, heading ninety degrees, due east. He throttled back, reducing his airspeed to 270 knots, and pushed the nose up two degrees. At his current speed and altitude, the fighter's fuel gauges showed he had enough gas to stay in the air for another three hours.

The colonel had been flying in a large circle 120 miles north of Bandar Abbas for the past thirty minutes. His orders had not changed, and he was growing impatient.

"Bandar Abbas center, this is flight 875," Rahavi radioed. "Request mission update."

"*Copy, 875. Maintain current heading and altitude. We'll advise time to descent.*"

"Copy, Bandar Abbas center. Maintaining current heading," he answered bitterly.

Rahavi unhinged his oxygen mask, letting it dangle from his helmet. He could see the city lights below him and the clear night sky was filled with stars. The colonel felt somewhat uncomfortable—he was flying alone. The cockpit behind him, used by the radar intercept officer, was empty and he was having to operate the radio and navigation controls by himself. It was decided that for this particular decoy mission it was not necessary to risk the lives of two pilots.

"Flight 875, take a heading of 194. Gradual descent to flight level four thousand."

Rahavi, exhilarated, snapped his mask back into place. "Confirmed, Bandar Abbas; 875 descending." *It's about time.*

He adjusted his shoulder harnesses and lap belt, making sure they were snug. Rahavi knew his mission would be purely defensive. His F-4E didn't carry any weapons, just additional fuel tanks under each wing. Rahavi was planning to use his fighter as a decoy, flying it straight at the lead American ship. The tactic was to draw the ship's attention away from the real attack from the missile sites at Bandar Abbas. The ground controllers would guide him to the target, but he would have to use his own skills to turn away before an American surface-to-air missile or fighter blew him out of the sky.

Rahavi rolled the Phantom right and pushed the nose down five degrees, throttling back. The big fighter responded quickly as the firm push of 3 Gs forced him back into his seat. He watched the altitude click off the right side of the HUD at the rate of 2,000 feet a minute.

"New contact, sir . . . bearing zero niner one." Farland tapped the computer keyboard, making sure the Aegis software wasn't playing tricks on him. "Altitude twelve thousand and descending."

"Descending?" This caught Parkington's attention. "What's the range?"

"Seventy-two miles . . . ten miles north of Bandar Abbas," Farland answered. "And I have a negative IFF reading on both civilian and military channels."

"Speed?"

"Three hundred ten knots."

Parkington brushed away the perspiration forming around the

corner of one eye. "Could it be a commercial airliner landing at Bandar Abbas?"

"Checking now, sir." Farland thumbed through the latest Iranian airline flight schedule. It didn't show any commercial aircraft landing or taking off after 10:40 P.M. "I am not showing anything. It could be a transport jet."

Parkington got up from his seat and walked over behind Farland. He could see the unknown aircraft symbol ⌐•⌐ showing the position of the plane. "Give it a track number."

"Yes, sir." Farland tapped the keyboard, assigning the number TD 3335 to the aircraft. The number appeared next to the unknown aircraft symbol.

"Let me know if it breaks the fifty-mile barrier." Parkington returned to his seat. "Ensign, bring me a cup of hot coffee."

Captain Behzad Moezi dialed the direct line to the command post of his western missile sites. The phone rang twice, then the commanding officer answered it.

"Lieutenant Salem here."

"Lieutenant, this is Captain Moezi. We are tracking two targets bearing one seven seven approximately fifty-three miles from your position. I want sites two and three operational in fifteen minutes with two missiles each."

"Yes, sir . . . fifteen minutes . . . two missiles at each site."

"I will download navigational data and launch instructions from this command post." Moezi hung up the phone. Fifteen minutes was pushing it. His men would have to work fast to warm up the missiles' internal electronics and laser guidance gyros.

Each of the missiles' navigational computers would be updated just before launch, putting them on a preplanned path to the target area. Once in range, each missile's internal infrared sensors would take over, guiding the missile to the surface ship with the largest IR signature. The missile's entire flight would be totally passive. There was no way the enemy would know it was being launched on.

"Targets now fifty-one miles south."

Moezi didn't respond. His mind was with the missile crews preparing for the launch.

*   *   *

"That's it, sir. He just crossed the fifty-mile mark," Farland said.

"Code the prick as hostile and warn him off, Mr. Farland," Parkington barked.

The petty officer did as he was told, commanding the computer to designate the target as hostile. The symbol $\wedge$ appeared next to the code number TD 3335.

He keyed his mike. "Unknown aircraft on course of one niner three, speed two fiver four, altitude seven thousand feet and descending, you are approaching U.S. naval warship operating in international waters. If you maintain current course, you are standing into danger . . . repeat, standing into danger . . . and will be subject to U.S. Navy defense measures. Request you change course to one fiver zero . . . repeat, one fiver zero." Farland changed frequencies and repeated the message over the military air distress channel.

"Status report," Parkington requested.

"No response, sir. Aircraft is now forty-three miles out and passing through 6,000 feet. Speed 320 knots."

"Try the international channel," Parkington grunted.

Farland repeated the warning without any response.

"Anything on IFF?" Parkington asked.

"Negative on both Mode II and Mode III channels."

"Damn it. What's the bastard trying to do?" Parkington stood. "Helm, increase speed to twenty knots and bring us around to zero one four." The captain wanted to point his ship directly at the approaching aircraft to reduce his radar signature. Suddenly, the ship turned sharply to the right and several loose clipboards and coffee cups slid onto the floor, filling the CIC with unneeded noise and confusion.

"Target now level at 5,000 feet. Range, thirty-nine miles. Speed, steady at 312 knots." Farland, oblivious to the noise around him, looked over at the captain. "Should I illuminate the target, sir?"

"*Only* on my order, Mr. Farland. Let's complete this turn and see what happens." Parkington's back was rigid as he steadied himself by his chair.

"The *John Young* is asking permission to engage target," the senior communications officer reported.

"Negative. We have priority on target. Tell Beckworth this one's mine."

"Target now thirty-six miles and closing," Farland called out. "Speed, 330 . . . altitude, 4,500 feet."

* * *

"Bearing one niner seven. Thirty-six miles out. Engage radar."

Colonel Rahavi keyed his mike twice, confirming the transmission. He leveled his F-4 and activated the autopilot at the same time. Using his left hand to reach behind the throttles, he turned the Phantom's radar from standby to on. He then waited for the lime-green scope, located in the upper center of the console, to flash to life. When it did, he switched the radar from scan to seek, hoping to lock onto the target.

The experienced pilot wrapped his right hand around the stick and adjusted his grip on the throttle handles. The trick would be to break away a split second before the American warship fired on him.

"Son of a bitch!" was Farland's first response. *"Threat . . . threat.* I'm showing a hostile radar sweeping from the north. That bastard just illuminated us."

"Lock up a missile and prepare to fire," Parkington said hurriedly.

"Range, thirty-three miles and closing." Farland hit a series of keys on the keyboard, calling up the ship's surface-to-air engagement radar. He used a small half-dollar-sized ball next to the keyboard to manipulate two small computer-generated cursors over the target. When the cursors were in place, he pressed the ball, locking the radar onto the target.

"Confirm radar lock . . . target TD 3335." Farland's thumb hovered above the launch button.

The high-pitched shrill in his helmet meant only one thing. The F-4E's RHAW sensor had just picked up an enemy radar painting his aircraft. Within a second, the tone changed again, telling Colonel Rahavi that the radar had just locked onto his fighter. He strained, trying to pierce the darkness for the flicker of a bright light that would tell him from which direction a missile had been launched.

"Shit." Rahavi groaned, as he yanked the stick to the right, then back, putting his fighter into a 6 G maximum turn. He held the stick with both hands and watched his compass heading swing around to 023 on top of the HUD. A heavy, sharp, burning pain cut into his body as the Phantom sliced through the night air, completing the 180-degree turn.

He came wings level and thrust the throttles all the way forward until he felt the force of the afterburners kick in. Inching the stick down, he allowed the fighter to accelerate to over 500 knots before leveling out at 2,000 feet above the ocean.

Rahavi looked in the rearview mirrors, seeing the yellow glow of his engines. If a missile was following him, he couldn't see it.

The yellow "weapons ready" symbol flashed on the computer screen to tell Captain Moezi that the most current navigational data had been dumped into the four cruise missiles' targeting computers. He double-checked the rest of the data one more time, making sure each of the missiles was indeed ready to launch.

"Site two and three are cleared for launch," Moezi's communications officer stated. "All systems are up and ready."

Moezi sucked in a deep breath, fully aware of what he was about to do.

"*Now*," he whispered under his breath, and pressed the launch button four deliberate times. He quickly adjusted his radio headset. "Confirm each launch."

"*One away*," came the report from site number two. "*Two away*."

"*Negative on number three*," the third missile site radioed. There was a short pause. "*Four away*."

Moezi looked back at the radar screen. The American ship was now turning away from the coast forty-five miles out. Three missiles were in the air. He estimated it would take them eight minutes to travel the distance.

"Make sure those radio channels are kept open," he ordered.

"No other aircraft in the area, Admiral," one of the *LaSalle*'s petty officers reported. "*Shiloh* reports the target is leaving the area."

"Signal the *Shiloh* job well done. Tell Parkington I have a bottle of scotch waiting for him when he comes ashore," Zachiem said, smirking.

Duke leaned forward, studying the display screens. The entire encounter had lasted less than ten minutes. The crew on the *Shiloh* seemed professional and well trained. The aircraft had approached to within thirty-five miles before it turned away. Duke had to admit, he was impressed. Even if Zachiem was an asshole, maybe he still knew what he was doing.

"Welcome to the Gulf, General James." Zachiem looked arrogantly over his shoulder. "As you can see, playing chicken has a whole new meaning here."

"What was the purpose of that ploy?" Duke asked, wondering if it would end up being a stupid question.

"Probably nothing. I think the Iranians will leave us alone now that they know we are ready. If you want to return to your cabin . . ."

"Thanks, Admiral, but I think I'll stay put for a while." Duke folded his arms and leaned back. He had decided to stay until the sun rose. *No use going to sleep if all the action happens at night*, he thought.

Chief Petty Officer Sam Farland rubbed his sweaty hands on his trousers as he watched the overhead display. The unidentified aircraft was now heading back for Iranian airspace. There wasn't any question in his mind the target had been a fighter. It had painted the *Shiloh* with a powerful J-band radar. This told Farland it was either a MiG or one of Iran's older F-4s.

"Speed, 408 knots. He's hauling ass. We scared the hell out of that guy." Farland laughed as the radar blip crossed over the coast and began to climb. "Skies are clear, sir. I'm not showing any other targets."

"Good job, men." Parkington removed his cap and scratched the back of his head. "Cancel general quarters. Reduce speed to ten knots."

Farland glanced at the radar display screen twice, not quite sure what he was seeing. A hostile target symbol emerged on the screen only to disappear a second later. The symbol showed a target two miles off their stern. Farland sat up as two more symbols appeared and faded out in the blink of an eye. The first thought that crossed his mind was that the *Shiloh*'s radar was somehow malfunctioning. Why would it be flashing intermittent hostile aircraft warnings? Either there was something out there or there wasn't.

"Captain . . . something strange is happening." Farland pointed to the screen, as Parkington came to stand by his side. "Watch the screen." Just then three symbols appeared for a split second.

"Sound general quarters." The memory of the rumors of ghost missiles hitting the five tankers entered his mind. "Are you show-

ing a malfunction?'' he asked, knowing the Aegis system wasn't
perfect.

"Negative, sir. It's as if—''

Suddenly, the ship rocked violently back and forth. A thunderous ripping sound could be heard coming from the stern, and
Parkington grabbed hold of Farland's chair.

"*Holy shit* . . . what was that?'' The captain regained his balance and keyed the ship's internal intercom. "Bridge . . . what the
fuck is going on . . . did we hit something?''

"Negative, sir, we—''

Parkington heard the loud sound of static while the ship rocked
a second time. The lights in the *Shiloh*'s CIC flashed on and off
for a few seconds, then all the display screens went down.

"Bridge . . . damage report!'' Stunned, Parkington heard the
sound of fire bells ringing and men shouting.

"We've been hit, sir. Lookout reports two missile hits,'' Farland shouted over the growing confusion.

"*Son of a bitch*!'' Parkington, coming to terms with the situation, was thinking furiously. "I want a damage report now.''

"Damage to the engine room and lower decks . . .''

"Farland, get on the radio. Tell the *John Young* we've been
hit with probable casualties.'' Captain Parkington surveyed the
CIC. The faces of his crew were ashen and blank.

Chapter Sixteen

President Louis McEntire drummed his fingers on the top of his Oval Office desk, staring at the patterned blue carpet. A lukewarm cup of black coffee sat on top of the morning's first edition of the Washington *Post*. The bold headline read 52 AMERICANS KILLED IN MYSTERIOUS GULF ATTACK. A large picture of the USS *Shiloh*, smoke pouring out of two massive holes in her hull, dominated the front page.

Bill Bishop, The NSA, entered the room hastily.

"Mr. President, I just got off the phone with Admiral Zachiem. He's reporting the *Shiloh* is no longer in danger of sinking and the fire should be contained in another two or three hours. The *John Young* has her under tow." Bishop sat down in one of the armchairs across from the President.

"What's his analysis of the situation?" the President asked solemnly, not looking up.

"Zachiem believes it was an Iranian attack. He monitored the entire sequence of events from the *LaSalle*."

"I assume he can back that up?" Allan Manning, the chief of staff, questioned as he joined them in the room.

"General Chaniff will be here in a few minutes. I would prefer he give the details," Bishop answered, not bothering to address Manning. He opened his briefcase and pulled out several files.

The National Security Council had adjourned for an hour so each man could shower and grab a quick bite to eat. The council had agreed to meet in the Oval Office at 5:00 A.M. to get out of the hot and stuffy situation room.

"How long before she makes it to port?" the President asked, finally looking up.

"Four . . . five hours, sir," Bishop said, reviewing the notes he had scribbled on a yellow pad. "They just passed through the narrowest part of the strait and are now on their way to Dubai. The hospital ship *Comfort* is in the area, and the most severely injured are being helicoptered off the *Shiloh* as the rescue crews reach them."

McEntire shook his head. Dressed in a shiny blue and green jogging suit, he had not changed since being awakened in the middle of the night. The President had followed all of the events. His face was unshaven and his red, weary eyes beneath uncombed hair said enough about the way he felt.

In morbid relief, McEntire was glad the death toll had finally been agreed upon. Over the past eight hours solid data had been hard to come by, and between the intervals of news he had prayed silently for the numbers to stop. The numbers had slowed, and while there would probably be another few added to the casualty figures, once the commotion was all over, it would be nothing drastic.

"I want the name of each man killed." McEntire's eyes watered and his voice was shaky. "And the phone number for each of their families . . ."

"Mr. President, that could take all day," Bishop interrupted. "The military is more than capable of handling this. Besides, most of the families are already being notified. We need to focus on what the hell is going on out there!"

"I don't give a shit how long it takes, Bill! These men have died for their country and that is the least I can do, the very least," McEntire fired back, then paused a moment to regain his composure. "Allan, clear my schedule for this."

"Yes, sir." Manning nodded, not wanting to look at Bishop, because he knew they would probably have words later. He didn't want to start an unnecessary debate in front of the President.

"Mr. President, we can't afford to sit back and hope that whoever is attacking our ships in the Gulf stops. I believe you need to let the American people know that whoever attacked the *Shiloh* will pay for it, and pay for it dearly. I don't think there is any possibility that it is anyone other than Iran, and we need to punish them. Otherwise, it's going to be a long, hot summer and we're all going to be out of a job in November." Bishop had stood and was pacing in front of the President's desk. "Just postpone your press conference from 7:00 to 8:00 A.M. instead of canceling it. Then reschedule the Republican congressional caucus meeting to tomorrow afternoon. That should give us enough time to gather the information we need to come up with a tough statement, and you can still contact all the families."

"Tough statement . . . I'm not going to say a damn thing until I know what we're dealing with," McEntire said, wondering if Bishop just needed to get some sleep. "The last thing I need is to go off half-cocked and make a mistake."

"I disagree. We shouldn't wait. The *Lincoln* is now only four hours away. We can have aircraft patrolling the skies at a moment's notice. And did you see this?" Bishop snorted. "The bastards have a poll out on this already." The national security adviser pointed to an article on a Washington *Post*/ABC poll reporting his popularity even with the Democratic challenger. "By the end of today the press will have you losing the next election by a landslide. And to top that off, each network is running some sort of commentary on the way the *Shiloh* had been allowed to be attacked. You know how dangerous speculation by the press is—this morning I've heard predictions of everything from the start of another Gulf war to a new wave of terrorist attacks to one suggesting we're hiding information to protect a military blunder."

"Wait . . . slow down," Manning said, shaking his head at Bishop. "I agree with the President. We don't need to be saying anything that's not confirmed. Chairman Chaniff, along with Brady at the CIA, can put together a military game plan within twelve hours if need be, but I think cooler heads should prevail here."

The President placed his head in his hands, sighing heavily. Right now he was wondering whose butt he could chew out for not having the information he needed to make a decision. The helpless feeling he had had when the tankers had been destroyed was multiplied to the point of being overwhelming. If the elections were tomorrow, he'd probably vote for the other guy himself. *Let someone else deal with this shit*, he thought fatalistically.

"The biggest criticism you're about to face is the perception that your foreign policy is in disarray." Bishop had continued to ramble on while the President was lost in his thoughts. Manning only stared while he listened, thinking Bishop should be on the campaign committee, not the NSC. "Your critics are saying it's a lack of leadership. And, of course, they want to know why you ordered an American warship into harm's way. I know that sounds like bullshit, but that's what the questions are right now in the press."

"Well, wasn't that your doing? Advising the President to send in a battle group before we knew what the dangers were?" Manning broke into the one-man conversation.

"Yes, it was, and now we know just how serious this is, don't we? When before we could only guess . . ." Both men stopped at the entrance of General Chaniff and Tony Brady, the DCI, into the office.

"I hope you have some more information for me," the President said without any formalities.

"Yes, sir, I do." Chaniff was the first to speak. He walked over to the President, holding a pad filled with notes and several eight-by-ten color photos, which he placed on the desk. "The Navy is ready to confirm that three sea-skimming missiles hit the USS *Shiloh* at 0212 hours local time. The missiles were fired from near Bandar Abbas, Iran. However, at this point we don't know exactly what type of missiles they were. One of the missiles struck the stern of the cruiser near the engine room. One hit the upper deck aft of the deckhouse, beneath the rear-looking radar antenna."

"You said three missiles hit the *Shiloh*. What about the third?" the President asked.

"That missile didn't explode entirely, it just burned the fuel from its engine. The warhead didn't detonate and is still intact. The Navy has several explosive experts attempting to dearm it now." Chaniff leaned over the desk and pointed to the area of the ship where the missiles hit. "We were lucky the third missile didn't go off. The ship could have been split in two, killing everyone in the CIC. As it happened, Captain Parkington and the senior officers are still alive. The majority of the casualties were below deck near the engine room."

The President looked at the pictures in a confused state of anxiety. "How in the hell did this happen? Can you answer that? Why didn't they fire back?"

"Well, sir, I can't answer as completely as I would like, but we're starting to piece some things together. First of all, the *Shiloh* tracked two separate targets last night before she was hit. The first was an Iranian P-3 patrol plane. The second one was believed to be an Iranian fighter. Radar telemetry shows the ship was hit a few minutes after the second aircraft turned away." Chaniff's voice was raspy and his throat felt like sandpaper. He'd done a lot of talking recently.

"Okay. There were two aircraft in the area. But how did three missiles hit the most advanced cruiser in the world?" the President asked slowly, irritated.

"That's the one question I can't answer yet, sir. We do know the *Shiloh*, as an Aegis-class cruiser, is designed to shoot down aircraft and sea-skimming cruise missiles, but the radar data indicate that whatever was fired at her wasn't detected until about fifteen seconds before impact. The crew and computers didn't have time to knock down the missiles."

"So the system malfunctioned?" Bishop asked.

"No, the Aegis system was working perfectly," Chaniff answered. He hoped if he went slowly enough the information would sink in and he wouldn't have to repeat any of it.

Exasperated, the President sighed heavily while throwing out his arms. *"Then how the hell did this happen?"*

"Unfortunately, I'd have to say that Iran has a new weapon," Chaniff said grimly.

"What . . ." Bishop stood, aware of the implications.

"As I said, we know the missiles were fired from somewhere near Bandar Abbas, an Iranian naval port." Chaniff held up one hand to finish without interruption. He nodded toward the pictures in front of the President. "The *Shiloh* was hit on the starboard side. I've checked with NORAD, and they detected four very hot heat signatures leaving the coast of Iran approximately eight minutes before the *Shiloh* was hit. The heat signatures didn't last long, only a few seconds."

"The CIA confirms that, sir," Brady jumped in. "One of our KH-14s also detected four very small IR signatures leaving the Iranian coast. Our guess is that they were small rocket boosters of some kind."

"I knew it was the Iranians. I just knew it had to be them."

Bishop almost smiled, but no one was paying attention to him.

"The Navy believes one of the missiles malfunctioned and veered off course," Chaniff said. "The other three hit the *Shiloh*."

"What kind of missile could defeat an Aegis system?" Bishop asked, his face wrinkled in puzzlement.

"One with low observation characteristics," Brady answered.

"Low observation?" The President was tired and irritable from lack of sleep. "Shit, talk English. What does that mean?"

"It would have to have been some sort of radar-defeating missile, sir," Chaniff said unfazed.

"No way . . . they don't have the technology for that," Allan Manning protested.

"Then you explain what happened out there. They either have them or they've bought them." Chaniff's face was stern and his voice louder. "I have fifty-two dead men and a billion-dollar ship burning in the Gulf. Every bit of data I've seen so far points to the Iranians' possessing a missile that defeats radar."

"That's nonsense! Are you telling me—"

"Shut up, Allan. Let the general talk," McEntire said.

"The only missile capable of doing this would be one of our stealth AGM-129 advanced cruise missiles."

"What kind of guidance system did this missile use?" Bishop asked, too involved in the conversation to enjoy Manning's being reprimanded.

"They could be radar guided," Chaniff said, keeping his eyes on the President. "The *Shiloh* did pick up hostile radar transmissions from the target it was tracking, but other than that they only picked up the usual transmissions—surface and air traffic."

"If you can prove the Iranians are behind this, my advice is we move the *Lincoln* and her battle group in close enough to hit their base at Bandar Abbas," Bishop said. "Destroy the missile sites. We need to knock the crap out of them."

The President looked at his national security adviser, fighting the temptation to explode uncontrollably. "If they can hit one of our ships, what makes you think they can't hit the others?"

Bishop didn't answer. The look on his face told everyone he had opened his mouth before thinking.

Philip Radford, the secretary of defense, walked in and took a seat. "Sorry I'm late, sir. Where are we?"

"Past all the details. Now we just need to decide what to do."

Chaniff leaned over, speaking quietly to Radford as the President sat pensively.

"I am ordering the *Lincoln* to stay put until we know more about this." McEntire wrote a few notes to himself on a pad before speaking again. "Manning, you get on the horn to the State Department and tell them to issue a formal protest to Iran and anyone else that may be involved, *with some very strong language.*" The President then turned to Radford. "Philip, you keep our forces on alert and make sure all U.S. naval and civilian ships stay clear of the Iranian coastline until further notice."

"Yes, sir," Radford replied.

"Now, Mr. Brady." McEntire stood up from his desk and looked directly at the DCI. "Why in the hell doesn't the CIA know anything about this? Those missiles had to come from somewhere. If there was a transaction, you guys should have been on top of it." The President spoke with a definite trace of disgust in his voice.

The DCI took a deep breath before answering. "Iran has always been a tough environment to operate in and get solid intelligence. There is only so much we can do when we can't get inside. I don't have any other answer for you."

"The CIA can spend $35 billion a year but you can't tell me who's blowing up ships in one of the most important regions in the world." McEntire shook his head. He desperately wanted more conclusive information. "That's a pile of shit, and I don't buy it. I want your men out there like mosquitoes on a hot summer day. Someone has information on this, and you'd better be finding out who the hell it is and what they know. Check the Russians, the Chinese, whoever else might have missiles for sale. It's your job to know this crap."

"Yes, Mr. President. I already have some of my best people on this. I've requested that Navy intel back us up so we can piece this together as fast as possible. You just have to believe we're doing the best we can. I'm hoping we will know something within the next few days," Brady said, thinking of Staffer's mention of Collins.

President McEntire leaned back in his chair. *I just want to know for sure before I get into a big mess. Why the fuck can't someone just give me one definite answer!*

"Okay . . . I want something tangible I can believe in. Chaniff, get me some proof that Iran is indeed behind this. I don't care how you get it, just get it. Brady, you and your people get me answers on what and why ASAP. I don't care what you have to do, just get me solid verification of what the hell is happening behind the scenes. Once we have that, *then* I want attack plans drawn up. Those sailors' deaths won't go unavenged." McEntire jotted more notes on a tablet before looking back up. "Allan, have those names and numbers ready for me right away." He looked around the room one more time. "I'll see you in twenty minutes. I'm going to take a shower."

The President left the Oval Office, and the security council sat silently with their thoughts.

CIA HEADQUARTERS

Tom Staffer stood stiffly in front of his boss, Tony Brady. The DCI's face was hard and pale, matching the displeasure in his voice. Staffer knew that no matter what he said, nothing would satisfy Brady right now. It was obvious Brady was trying to pick a fight to vent off steam, but Staffer wasn't in the mood to play mind games, so he just stood there and took the heat.

"I have Hal Currie analyzing the satellite data and Aegis radar telemetry right now . . . along with the Navy. I've also contacted Colonel True and Major Tackett at DARPA. They're going to be working with Currie after the *Shiloh* docks. Navy intel has a team of experts on the way to the Gulf right now." Staffer reached into his pocket for a cigarette, then thought better of it.

"I don't care if you have to shut down every other operation in the CIA, Tom. I want answers and I want them fast," Brady said bluntly. "Do you understand me? The old man bit off a piece of my ass and I'm not walking back in there empty-handed."

"Yes, I understand," Staffer answered. *And the sooner you let me out of here, the faster I can get to work.*

"Make sure you contact Collins tonight. I want him to try to find out the following." Brady scribbled a short message on a piece of paper and handed it to Staffer.

Tom looked at the note, then at his boss. "Collins may not report in tonight, but I'll put it on the satellite."

"Well, shit, don't you have a set schedule of when officers are going to report in? Some type of system so you know when to expect to hear from them?"

"No, sir, but I'll definitely consider that."

"Good. What's your schedule the rest of the week?" Brady asked.

"I've cleared everything except for the Senate. The Intelligence Committee is meeting tomorrow and I'm scheduled to testify," Staffer replied, looking at his watch, wondering how much longer this was going to take.

"Damn it, their timing stinks. Keep your answers about Iran vague. The committee's going to hammer you about what we're doing and I don't want a fucking mess. You think you can manage that?"

"Yes, sir." *Easier said than done, though.*

"I just hope Collins really is in a position to help us." Brady rubbed his forehead. "If not, then you pull him out and get someone else in there. Put someone aggressive in there."

Staffer didn't respond. He just continued nodding his head and saying "yes, sir" now and then.

"Tom, I mean it. You need to turn the heat up on this one. I've never seen the President so hostile toward the CIA." Brady's face was rigid. "If I go down, you'll go with me."

"I understand."

"And I want you to start briefing me twice daily," Brady added before concluding. "Now get *with* it, Staffer. Get me some results."

"You got it." Staffer immediately walked out of the director's office before another word could be said. *That meeting with the President must have been a doozy. What the hell,* Staffer thought, taking a cigarette out and lighting it. He glanced down at the piece of paper in his hand, then opened it and started reading. Brady had listed three items: (1) Is there talk of Iran purchasing or developing new weapons? (2) Where are they deployed? and (3) Could they be manufacturing radar-evading missiles? Obviously, the director wanted verification, other than Chaniff's word, that the missiles that hit the *Shiloh* couldn't be detected and that the ship's equipment hadn't malfunctioned. If the military was trying to cover their asses and leave the CIA holding the bag, Brady would find out, then hang somebody's butt out to dry.

In his office, Staffer sat down and lit another cigarette. He took a sip of cold coffee before rereading Brady's note and running it through the paper shredder behind his desk. *Shit, is it possible Iran has come up with a stealth cruise missile?* He knew the U.S. had lost at least one Tomahawk cruise missile over western Iran in the spring of 1993. Pentagon planners were forced to fly their missiles over the Zagros Mountains because the Iraqi terrain was so flat that it was nearly impossible to target a missile's flight path using its satellite digital scene-matching software program. During the attack, one of the twelve missiles fired at Iraq's intelligence compound near downtown Baghdad had gone down. The Pentagon assumed that it had exploded when it hit the ground, but satellite photos never confirmed this. *If the Iranians got their hands on that missile ... or at least parts of it ...* Staffer dismissed the thought. Even if they did, he knew an Aegis's radar was sophisticated enough to detect and hit sea-skimming missiles. There had to be something else.

Staffer took one last drag from his cigarette and crushed it. It would be dark in Iran in a couple of hours. Collins should be returning to his hotel room soon. Staffer needed to get down to the CIA's satcom department and put together a message.

"Heather, hold my calls." Staffer then slipped on his suit jacket.

Bill Bishop entered the President's private study located off the Oval Office. McEntire was seated at his desk, his sleeves rolled up and his tie loose at the neck. A half-eaten sandwich was on a tray next to him. Bishop waited for the President to acknowledge him before speaking.

"Louis, this just came through from the State Department." He handed the President a sheet of fax paper. "It's from the Turkish embassy in Tehran. Prime Minister Mahmoudi died two hours ago."

The President slumped back in his chair and slipped off his reading glasses. He didn't bother to look at the fax. "That means Bakhtiar is in charge."

"Yes, sir ... at least until new elections can be held." Bishop leaned against the doorway. "But that's not what worries me. Bakhtiar just made a speech from Khomeini's tomb site. He's claiming the CIA is behind the assassination of Mahmoudi and it *was* Iran that attacked the *Shiloh*."

"What—" The President sat up.

"Bakhtiar is calling on all Iranians to join him in attacking the United States. The exact word he used was *Jihad*, a holy war. He said if any more U.S. ships come near the Strait of Hormuz, they will be hit with this new power from Allah and sunk." Bishop's tone was slow and measured.

"I see." McEntire ran his fingers through his hair, thinking.

"I don't think he's bluffing, sir. The CIA's brief psychological profile indicates the man is focused and determined on one thing only—the continuation of Iran's revolution. If that's correct, then with Mahmoudi out of the way there's no one to stop him."

"Well, actually, this just makes my job a little easier now. At least we know who the enemy is," the President answered, sighing. "You find out what 'new power' they're launching at our ships and where the weapons plant is. Once we know that, then Bakhtiar will think twice about threatening us."

"As soon as we learn something, I'll let you know." Bishop nodded, not arguing this time.

ESFAHAN, IRAN

Mark Collins handed fifty rials to a young man selling newspapers outside his hotel and took a copy of the Tehran *Times*. He tried not to stare at the headline for more than a few seconds. It was a fairly objective source, considering he was in Iran, for world events. Mark also bought a copy of the Muslim fundamentalist *Hezbollahi Kayhan International*, which slanted everything toward its radical view. If anyone was watching his purchases, he didn't want to slip up by making a simple mistake. It also helped to give him a better insight into the people he was dealing with.

Collins tucked the newspapers under his arm and walked through the hotel lobby. The air was hot and stuffy; either they deliberately turned off the air conditioning in the mistaken belief they would save themselves money or the unreliable electricity was out again.

"I'm going to need a taxi in about thirty minutes," he informed the man behind the counter.

"Yes, Mr. Kahman. The phones aren't working, but I'll get one for you."

"Thank you." Collins tipped the man and restrained himself from asking why nothing in this hellhole worked. He looked around the lobby. Seated in the corner, next to a miniature palm tree, were the two Iranians assigned to follow him. They were both reading magazines, trying to be inconspicuous. Collins pretended not to notice and headed upstairs to his room.

Locking the door behind him, he sat on the bed and opened the *Times*. "My God . . . I can't believe this," he said under his breath. *The bastards are claiming responsibility for this; how could this happen?* He scanned the front page. *Fifty-two Americans dead . . . and the Iranian government is warning the West to stay clear of the Gulf or more ships will be attacked.* Collins studied a picture at the top of the page of Defense Minister Sheik Ali Bin Bakhtiar. Bakhtiar was posed on the steps of the Khomeini shrine on the southern edge of Tehran near Behest-e Zahra, holding a copy of the Koran in the air. A second photograph showed a crowd of several thousand people standing before the sheik. The caption read:

LEADERS CALL FOR ALL IRANIANS TO UNITE AGAINST
THE WEST.

Collins next looked at the picture of the USS *Shiloh.* He could see it was an Aegis-class cruiser. *How in the hell did they pull that one off? No wonder the base was so active today,* he thought, trying not to panic.

He checked his watch, then quickly picked up the computer and walked into the bathroom. Once more, he carefully fed the cable antenna outside the window. Flipping open the screen, he tapped on the side of the computer, impatiently waiting for it to warm up before punching in the commands. If he was right, there would be a message waiting for him. He tapped in SATCOM CONFRM; the software cycled, and he typed RECV. Collins felt the hard drive vibrate, knowing it would take a minute for the coded transmission to be verified by the DoD satellite parked over the Middle East. A few seconds later the screen jumped and a message appeared:

DODSATCOM TRANSMIT VV-DOWNLNK*.*/5032-CC9
TO: SPECTRA   FROM: CRYSTAL PALACE

1] AEGIS-CLASS CRUISER ATTACKED. PRIMARY INTEL
   SHOWS MISSILES WERE LAUNCHED FROM BANDAR
   ABBAS. CONFIRM IRANIAN USE OF RADAR EVADING
   CRUISE MISSILES.
2] CONFIRM MISSILE PURCHASE OR MANUFACTURING.
3] IDENTIFY SOURCE IF PURCHASED.
4] *EXTREMELY* IMPORTANT FIND AND CONFIRM
   LOCATION OF WEAPONS.

He read the message twice, memorizing the data, and confirmed the transmission before deleting it from the screen. He then folded the antenna and slipped the computer back into its cover. *"I'm surprises they didn't ask for the defense minister's shoe size and blood type,"* Collins said and cursed. He removed a piece of flash paper and neatly wrote a coded message outlining what the CIA needed to know. The code, a series of five-digit groupings of numbers, used a mathematical key converting numbers to letters. It was impossible to break without using a modern supercomputer. Zenith had been given the key. If his earlier drop had been picked up, as he prayed it had been, then maybe she would be able to answer several of the questions.

A few minutes later Collins climbed into a taxi with the two Iranians in tow and headed for the Maharaja Restaurant. As the car pulled away, he noticed that his trails didn't appear to be in any hurry. *Good, they're starting to tire of this routine. I can make the drop without worrying about them being suspicious.*

"Staffer here."

"Collins confirmed the transmission." It was the director of intelligence, Vance Edleman.

"How long ago?"

"About two hours. We just got the electronic dump off the satellite." It was three minutes after six.

"Thanks for letting me know." Staffer sighed, relieved. *Well, Mr. Collins, I sure hope you can dig something up.* He then realized he didn't even know if Collins had managed to reestablish contact with Zenith yet. *One thing is for sure, when things start happening around this place, they all happen at once.*

The summer evening was cooler than normal, filling Esfahan's bazaar with many people. The crowd made Perijan feel more comfortable. It would be easier to disappear among the people strolling about in the marketplace. She had placed her message by the fence the night before and hoped the messenger had time to retrieve the drop earlier.

Perijan waited for the sun to disappear behind the buildings before turning into the alley. The long shadows caused the same eerie distortions of the garbage and broken boxes piled up behind the buildings.

She looked over her shoulder twice, checking for anyone in

the area. With her head down, she made her way into the alley. Behind her she could hear the voice of a young child calling for her mother. When she reached the vacant lot, Perijan knelt, feeling the warm earth for the hard plastic top of the cylinder. Her fingertips felt it and she swiftly yanked it out of the ground, slipping it into her pocket. The sound of footsteps on the gravel behind her made Perijan freeze. She remained still for a moment, not wanting to stand too quickly and appear alarmed. She slowly straightened up, then turned to face two Revolutionary Guards.

"What are you doing here?" The guards were approaching from the street. It was still light enough for Perijan to see their faces. Their expressions were more curious than distrustful. They were dressed in brown desert combat fatigues and were carrying rifles as well as side arms.

Perijan's heart pounded and she tried to swallow before speaking.

"I said what are you doing here?" the youngest guard blurted out again, lowering his AK-47 and becoming annoyed.

Perijan managed to swallow. "I was walking through the alley."

"Why do I think you are lying? What were you doing on the ground?"

"I am not lying. I was walking home . . . this is a shortcut and . . . and I saw this." Thinking quickly, she reached in her pocket and pulled out several rials. "They were scattered on the ground . . . there." She pointed to the side of the building.

The young man smiled, showing his rotten front teeth. He walked up and looked in Perijan's hand. "Ah, this could be evidence of a crime. I should probably take it and save you the trouble it could cause." He snatched up the bills and stuffed them into his pocket. Then he took notice of her half-hidden face.

"You are a very brave woman to be walking through here in the dark. Why does your husband allow this?"

Perijan didn't answer. She didn't like the look in his eyes. They were wild and reckless.

"I don't think that's what you were doing here. I think you are looking for something else. Maybe a man. Were you looking for a man to walk you home?" The guard reached up and tried to touch her face.

Perijan stepped back, nearly falling down. "I told you . . ."

"That's enough. Leave her be." The older guard laughed.

"Come with me. I will be your husband." The younger guard ignored him and moved closer.

"That's enough." The older man stepped in front of Perijan, shoving the other guard out of the way.

"But I was just—"

"I know what you were doing. I said, leave her be." The guard twisted around to face Perijan and said gruffly, "Go home now. Go home to your family. You should find a safer shortcut home."

The two guards laughed as they watched Perijan scurry out of the alley. She clasped the cylinder tightly within her pocket and breathed heavily, trying to catch her breath before she got home to her father.

Chapter Seventeen

"Watch your footing, General, and follow me, please," Lieutenant Michael Horton said.

Duke zipped his green nylon jacket to his chin and pulled up the collar. A cool evening breeze was blowing out of the southeast off the Gulf and low clouds hung in the sky. Overhead the shrill cry of seagulls could be heard as they circled over the *Shiloh*. Their hideous call added to the macabre scene.

Duke followed the stout lieutenant across the gangplank and onto the rear section of the docked cruiser. He stood for a second and surveyed the damage. The first missile had impacted the cruiser just above the waterline on the port side of the stern, severely damaging the engine room and several of the ship's weapons systems. The deck was scattered with pieces of burnt and destroyed equipment. Duke could see where the crew had cut holes in the deck to vent gases and smoke.

Four Harpoon canisters were lying end to end near the *Shiloh*'s rear five-inch gun. They were charred black and twisted from the heat. Directly in front of the gun were the vertical missile launchers. About half the subdeck cell housings for the ship's Standard-MR SM-2 surface-to-air missiles were gone, melted in a bizarre mass of steel and aluminum. Five of the white missiles were strewn about the deck in several pieces. Duke assumed that the

234

intensity of the fire was strengthened by the missiles exploding rocket motors. The wind shifted and the strong odor of scorched plastic and charred metal filled the air, burning his nose.

"Have they removed all the bodies?" Duke asked, not believing the ship had lost only fifty-two men.

"Yes, sir."

"Okay. Where's Admiral Zachiem?"

"This way, General."

Duke followed as they walked toward the aft deckhouse. He continued looking over the wreckage and saw where smoke and heat from the second missile hit must have started an intense blaze in the upper section of the ship. The fire had discolored the outer surface of the ship's superstructure, turning the gray paint to a deep black. Several members of the crew were busy painting, trying to get the outside of the *Shiloh* back to her original color. The Navy's pride would make sure the ship was as close as possible to her original condition before she was docked at a friendly port.

Large areas of black soot above the doorways and portholes were evidence of the fire and smoke damage inside. They walked onto the helicopter landing pad, approaching the deckhouse. In front, the mangled wreckage of a helicopter sat like a piece of abstract art. One of the missiles had torn through the LAMPS III hangar, obliterating almost everything there.

The lieutenant entered the hangar, with Duke directly behind him. Several rows of portable lights were suspended from the ceiling, illuminating what was now a darkened crater. They both descended a make-shift staircase into a room about twenty by thirty feet wide. Or, at least Duke thought it was about that size—it was hard to tell because of the lack of light. The entire chamber was littered with incinerated steel conduit, wiring and other indistinguishable objects. Water was still dripping from the ceiling, leaving puddles scattered over the floor. Large cables strung across the left wall, many of them broken or melted together, swayed unsteadily. Several portable fans were near the entrance, helping to freshen the rancid air inside the room.

Damn . . . what a mess. Duke rubbed his nose and eyes, which were watering from the lingering smoke.

In a far corner of the room, he made out the shadows of a half-dozen or so figures. He figured the taller man to be Zachiem.

"Over here, General."

Duke made his way through the debris and joined the group, taking a spot next to the admiral. Two floodlights were pointed toward the opposite corner of the room. Resting on the floor was an eight-foot section of what appeared to be a missile. The outer body was scarred and dented, partially charred. Two technicians were kneeling next to it, their bodies covered in protective clothing and their faces sheltered by clear Plexiglas visors.

"So, this one didn't explode," Duke said to no one in particular. "At least we had one bit of luck. Have you located the guidance system?"

"No. This is the midsection. The explosive team removed the warhead an hour ago." Zachiem pointed to the segment of the missile nearest the wall. "They estimate it contained roughly eight hundred pounds of explosives."

Duke shook his head.

"Right now we're making sure all the electronics are disconnected before we move the damn thing," Zachiem said coldly. "The bastards are going to pay for this."

"It's dead, sir," one of the technicians called out. He flipped up his visor and wiped the sweat away from his forehead.

"All right, General James, come take a look at this. I want you to tell me what you make of this thing's outer skin." Zachiem and Duke walked over to the missile, and the admiral pointed to a portion that wasn't burnt.

Duke crouched down to get a closer look at the missile. It was apparent that it wasn't a standard design. Rather than being round, as he expected, the body appeared to have been triangular with circular edges. A small section that hadn't been disfigured by the heat was exposed. He reached out and touched the skin. The surface felt hard and slightly waxy at the same time. *Possibly some kind of soft, semipliable plastic*, he thought. The skin was a quarter of an inch thick.

He grabbed a broken section and bent it toward him. Directly underneath the exterior, Duke could see a three-inch-thick honeycomb structure with diamond-shaped chambers that were filled with a coarse rustcolored powder. He used a fingernail to dig out a small amount of the powder. After rubbing it between his thumb and forefinger, he tasted it.

"It's salt," he said, looking up at Zachiem.

"Salt? What are you talking about, man?" Zachiem snorted.

Duke stood up and stared at the admiral, then pulled him aside.

They were out of earshot of the technicians before he spoke again.

"That powder is a radar-absorbent material," Duke explained in a hushed tone. "The outer surface is a graphite. I've seen this used on our own stealth aircraft and missiles."

"Do you realize what you're saying? Are you sure about this?"

"That's a stealth cruise missile."

"Bullshit."

"There's no bullshit about it, Admiral. Don't think I wouldn't like you to take the heat for this, but that's why your ship didn't pick it up on radar until it was too late," Duke replied firmly.

"Is it one of ours?" Zachiem asked, thinking it would be better to have a reasonable explanation of how something like this could happen.

"No, I don't think so. The skin is similar, damn similar, but the shape is definitely not one I've ever seen." Duke looked back at the technicians waiting for the admiral's order to have the missile removed.

Zachiem sucked in a deep breath, held it and exhaled. "If what you're saying is true—"

"You need to get this thing to Wright Paterson ASAP. The research facility there can test and verify its characteristics."

"Oh, I don't think so, General. The Navy is set up to do the same research and that's who's going to run the tests. I've already made arrangements to have it flown to Norfolk to be analyzed, anyway. But thanks for the information. It may prove to be useful." Zachiem turned away abruptly. "Speed it up, men. I want this missile out of here in twenty minutes."

Duke put his hands on his hips. He was speechless. Zachiem's bullshit attitude was beginning to wear thin. The man was agreeable long enough to get what he wanted, then turned into a complete jackass, and apparently for his and the Navy's benefit only. He was difficult to read and impossible to predict. Chaniff called this one right. *All right, Admiral Zachiem, you do it your way. Just don't expect me to be bailing you out or giving you any more info*, Duke thought, then muttered an obscenity under his breath.

"I'll be on base if you should need me to help fill you in on anything else, Admiral," Duke said, then strode back to the temporary staircase. He walked up into the open, hoping to get a breath of fresh air, but the burnt smells were still around him. He began to mull over his next move.

It was understandable that Zachiem would want to try to redeem the Navy. After all, one of their best systems had failed to protect the ship. The admiral saw the incident as one giving the Navy a black eye. Duke was sure he would be on the phone to Chaniff in the next hour, recommending a Navy plan of attack on the missile sites once they were found and identified.

Maybe this wouldn't be a Navy problem for long, Duke reasoned. There wasn't any way the Pentagon was going to risk sending a carrier battle group in close enough to attack Iran. Especially if there were stealth missiles involved. That meant only one thing to Duke—the Air Force would be needed for a deep strike hit. When he returned to the base, he would start formulating his own ideas to report to Chaniff when the time came.

THE PENTAGON

Located in room 4C-956, in a secluded top-security section of the Pentagon, the National Reconnaissance Office was virtually dead quiet. Only the hum of computers and the buzzing of fluorescent lights kept Hal Currie company while he continued to work steadily. He rubbed his face, then looked back at the computer screen. He yawned. Currie didn't mind the quiet while he worked; he concentrated better without the distractions that went along with a full office. After several hours of silence, however, he would welcome any kind of noise to help keep him awake.

The fourth-floor Pentagon offices, housing the NRO, weren't as accommodating as Currie's CIA office. The carpet was a dirty gray, the furniture looked to be 1960 vintage, the ceiling tiles were stained yellow and brown from years of cigarette smoke and water damage and the chairs weren't the most comfortable he had ever sat in.

However when analyzing satellite photos, Currie preferred to work at the Pentagon because the photographic enhancement software was state-of-the-art. It was linked via fiberoptic cable to the National Photographic Interpretation Center in Washington, D.C. He had access to their database and the latest intel coming off the CIA's recon birds.

The analyst shook his head a few times, forcing himself to wake up. Currie elected to study the satellite photos alongside the computer nerds at the NPIC to help give him a better perspective. The raw imagery coming off the KH-14 was of better quality than most home movies. Besides, Currie recognized that the computer's added capabilities to find targets was a must, particularly targets in the vast desert. Missile sites were always well camouflaged.

He jumped when the phone next to his desk suddenly rang.

"Hal Currie," he said, glad for the interruption in his work.

"Hal, Mitchell Burnell here." Burnell worked at the NPIC and was in charge of the Middle East satellite imagery. An ex-Marine colonel, Burnell now made his living managing a department of thirty-five photo interpretation specialists.

"What are you doing still at work, Mitch?"

"Oh, just trying to save your ass . . . again."

Currie laughed.

"It's the luck of the Irish that's come to rescue you this time. A high-pressure system blew into the Gulf about six hours ago, bringing with it clear skies, cool breezes and temps in the low mid-fifties. And guess what else?"

"I don't need a weather report," Currie replied excitedly. "Just tell me you have some clean shots."

"Bingo. I've run them through the filters twice and, man o'man, are they sharp. Some of my best work yet."

"Great! How soon can I see them?"

"How about in thirty seconds? I'm feeding them to your mainframe now."

"Thanks. If it wasn't your job, I'd owe you one, but maybe I'll buy you a burger anyway," Currie joked, then hung up the phone. He was appreciative that Burnell had stayed long enough to amplify the KH-14 shots.

He tapped the keyboard several times, pulling up the menu. Several seconds later a new file appeared.

That's it, Currie thought, pulling the file out of the mainframe and onto his wide-view monitor. The screen flashed several times before a three-dimensional color picture of the area around Bandar Abbas appeared. He could see the Iranian port city, along with a section of Gheshm Island to the south.

"Damn! Mitch was right. This is clear," Currie whispered under his breath. If the Gulf War did one thing, it instructed everyone in the world, specifically the Arabs and North Koreans, it would be imperative to hide military equipment from U.S. reconnaissance satellites if they wished to maintain their secrecy. Consequently, the CIA and Pentagon, with a lot of help from the

Advanced Research Projects Agency, developed an extremely advanced sensor system using a sophisticated range of multilayered networks to battle this new obstacle.

The system basically combined a multispectral optical system with the CIA's best 100-400-MHz synthetic aperture radar. By applying a simple detection algorithm and side-scanning radar, the new computer program allowed them to detect tanks and mobile missiles camouflaged in dense vegetation, among rocks or in mountainous terrain. Advance recognition schemes were used in the program by comparing 10,000 to 50,000 stored images of a single area. It relied on a "fuzzy logic" processing program and other artificial intelligence techniques to detect changing conditions. The software also filtered "speckle noise," echoes caused when a radar sweeps a rugged area. The echoes cause grainy images that impair detection.

Okay, let's start here. Currie wanted to begin with a section he was familiar with. He had surveyed a certain area several times over the past two years. The Iranians had built several crude roads through the area, most of them ending near the coast. The roads were actually one-lane dirt trails and could only be used by four-wheel-drive trucks and jeeps.

Currie had watched them move large dump trucks in and out of the area at night. This led to the conclusion that they were constructing something. Unfortunately, the CIA had never been able to identify what. But Currie now had a good idea. The bastards had constructed underground bunkers that were secure from satellite detection.

He used a mouse to zoom in on an area five miles west of Bandar Abbas. His plan was to first focus on a section of coastline twenty miles west of the Iranian port. He clicked the mouse twice, narrowing the screen onto a rocky point leading out about a half mile into the ocean.

The terrain was very mountainous, with deep rocky ravines, steep box canyons and very little vegetation right up to the ocean. He could see the blue water of the Gulf breaking into white waves as it hit the jagged coast. Tapping the mouse several more times, he ordered the software to zoom to an elevation of 10,000 feet. Several hundred yards from the shoreline he could see a flat area; it looked white, having been cleared of topsoil and leveled manually.

Currie had previously identified the spot as a launch site for mobile Silkworms. However, the area was void of vehicles. He zoomed in further, to an altitude of 2,500 feet. Moving the mouse left and right, he found the road leading to the mobile site. It was nothing more than a trench filled with rocks. The optical picture, combined with the synthetic aperture radar, indicated that no one had traveled on the road for quite some time. The radar had an 0.023-meter resolution, allowing him to easily see that the trail was void of tire tracks, footprints and the impressions left by helicopter landing skids.

Currie sat back. *Interesting.* The Iranians had fifteen such sites scattered down the coast. The one he was looking at, in Currie's opinion, would be the best from which to launch missiles.

He followed the dirt road north for about a thousand yards, stopping when he suddenly noticed there was a junction. It made a sharp turn to the west while the main road continued north. This trail was even more rugged and entered a very narrow section of the mountain. It was bordered by large rock cliffs on both sides. Currie leaned closer to the screen. He could see the very faint three-dimensional images of treadmarks in several places. He tapped the FI0 function key three times, zooming in on the trail. Suddenly, the screen brightened. *Sure as hell; there it is, plain as day.* Currie was irritated for not picking it out sooner.

The tire tracks of several large trucks could be seen in the soft sand and mud, along with the footprints of several dozen men. He realized what the Iranians had done. The road, having made a second sharp turn next to a large outcropping of rocks, entered a constricted ravine, there making another sharp turn south. Basically, a U-turn.

The outcropping was being used as cover for a tunnel. The trucks were being driven into the tunnel a half mile away from the coast so they would not be detected by U.S. surveillance ships. And there was no way coastal reconnaissance aircraft could detect it unless they were right on top, and that would mean violating Iranian airspace.

Now all Currie had to do was find the underground launch bunkers. The previous satellite photos picked up four simultaneous heat signatures leaving the coast. That would mean there were at least four definite sites. He got up from the chair, revived, and filled his coffee cup. It was going to be a long night. A very long night.

ESFAHAN AIR FORCE BASE

Colonel Alireza Rahavi stood motionless as he surveyed the late morning sky and the runways in the distance. To the west, a fast-moving thunderstorm partially hid the sun, allowing him to remove his sunglasses for a moment. From his position, north of and several hundred meters above the main part of the base, he could see most of the hardened aircraft shelters that dotted the landscape like anthills. The structures protected his force of F-4E, F-14A and SU-24 bombers, along with ten advanced MiG-29 fighters.

Iran's minister of defense was an hour and fifteen minutes late, and the colonel could feel himself growing thirstier and sweatier with each passing minute. Nonetheless, he knew it would be better to endure the blistering heat than to not be present when Sheik Ali Bin Bakhtiar arrived.

Colonel Rahavi paced slowly in front of two concrete-reinforced single-story buildings. The windowless structures were close together in a secluded, half-mile-square area inside the maximum-security prison complex. They housed the missile manufacturing facility. The buildings were painted a light beige with blotches of brown in an effort to make them less vulnerable to attack. Rahavi doubted the crude camouflage could fool anything, especially a sophisticated aircraft with infrared detection equipment. What really protected the structures, besides the fact that they were a well-guarded secret, was a complex system of well-hidden surface-to-air missiles. The radar and SAM network around Esfahan was more advanced and complicated than any system in Iran, including the one in place around Tehran. Colonel Rahavi personally placed the multilayered air defense himself.

He stopped and watched well-armed Revolutionary Guards patrolling between the two fences with the aid of dogs and motorcycles. His eyes then followed the fences to one of the guard towers, where he kept his gaze until he saw movement.

A convoy of five cars was moving across the air base to the south, preceded by an Iranian air force pickup truck acting as escort. The convoy turned left toward the prison section of the air base, staying on a narrow single-lane asphalt road. The first car, a Volvo sedan with flashing headlights, was followed by two black Chevrolet Suburbans with dark security windows. The fourth vehicle was a large four-door Mercedes sedan trailed by a desert-camouflaged armored personnel carrier. A turret-mounted heavy machine gun could clearly be seen.

When Defense Minister Bakhtiar travels, he doesn't take any risks, Rahavi thought. The colonel knew there were many people who would prefer to see Bakhtiar dead, but he doubted they would challenge the firepower that traveled with him.

Several minutes later the vehicles passed through the prison's fortified gate and slowed to a stop fifty meters in front of Rahavi. The colonel walked up to the Mercedes and stood at attention. Several security guards dressed in Western-style clothing with dark mirrored sunglasses exited the Suburban carrying AK-47s and Uzi submachine guns. After deciding it was safe for the minister, one of them nodded to the driver.

"Minister Bakhtiar," Colonel Rahavi said, saluting as Sheik Ali Bin Bakhtiar stepped out of the car.

"Colonel Rahavi. It is good to see you." Bakhtiar stood for a second surveying his surroundings before moving toward Rahavi.

"I trust your trip was pleasant," Rahavi said, as he turned and started walking next to the defense minister toward the nearest building.

"It was pleasant, if you consider riding across the hot desert for seven hours pleasant," Bakhtiar said sarcastically.

"You should try flying, Minister. It is much faster and I am here as proof it is safe." Rahavi knew the man was deathly afraid to set foot on a plane.

The two men didn't exchange any more words as they continued toward the main structure. Bakhtiar's security personnel kept up, surrounding him on all sides. The shorter and rounder heavily dressed minister looked odd next to the trim and fit colonel. Rahavi had known the defense minister for five years. They shared the same faith, and he believed the minister was willing to die for Iran and Allah. For this Rahavi respected him, even if he didn't fully trust Bakhtiar, who publicly seldom hid his dislike and skepticism of Iran's forces. He was still blaming them for many of the country's internal security problems. He also didn't have any military experience and knew very little of tactical or strategic strategy.

Two guards opened the door and the men entered a small, brightly lit entryway. A solemn-looking security officer was seated behind a thick Plexiglas window. The colonel showed the man his ID, and the heavy steel door leading inside the complex opened.

"You know the procedure. Your men must remain here. This is a secure area," Rahavi reminded the minister.

Bakhtiar stared at the colonel for a moment, then nodded and signaled to his guards to remain in the outer area.

"This way." Rahavi led the minister toward a stairway at the end of a narrow hallway. After descending a long set of compact concrete steps, they turned right and entered a room. It was Rahavi's underground office. The air was cool and stale in the crude room. It contained only a desk, two chairs and several telephones. It was obvious the room wasn't used very often.

Colonel Rahavi took a seat behind his desk and watched the defense minister sit in one of the chairs before him. The old man sat for a long moment, trying to catch his breath. He accepted a glass of water and took one of his heart pills. Once rested, he finally spoke.

"The Supreme Defense Council is ready to further our attack on the West. How soon can you and your air crews be ready to strike the American carrier?"

Rahavi sat up perfectly straight in his chair as a swell of apprehension shot through his body. This was not what he had expected to hear from the minister. He and his men would now be expected to fly at a carrier to deploy the missiles out over the sea. Shooting missiles from launch sites at a cruiser fifty miles offshore was not as hazardous.

"You are asking me to attack—"

"I am asking nothing," Bakhtiar interrupted roughly. "It is a direct order. The United States is not going to sit back and do nothing about our assault on their ship. Only a fool would think they will not retaliate. That is why we must attack first. Hit them again. Take away their will to fight!"

Rahavi looked into the old man's eyes. He knew it would be foolish to argue. The sheik's face was set and hard.

"Again, I ask you . . . how soon can you and your men be ready to attack the American fleet?"

The colonel drew in a long breath, his mind racing. A carrier controlled over eighty aircraft, of which more than half were fighters. Rahavi would have to strike the target with his best fighters and saturate the battle group with as many missiles as possible. Even then there was no guarantee he could get within the minimum distance of his missiles. He wondered if the defense minister honestly understood what he was demanding.

"Are you ready to absorb the losses we will take attacking the Americans?" Rahavi asked. "The Iraqis tried to fight the Americans. Their country is still in ruin."

"The Iraqis went to war. I am talking about a lightning-fast strike that will catch them off-guard."

Rahavi turned his head and snorted. "I doubt the Americans will be caught off-guard again. Just because it happened once doesn't mean—"

"I know what it means. It means Allah is on our side. Now, how long, Colonel Rahavi?"

"At least three days . . . possibly four."

Bakhtiar's head snapped back and his eyes closed for a few seconds. "You have three days."

"I may need more—"

"That's all the time you have. Three days from today an American carrier will be resting on the bottom of the ocean. And our people will be united once again." Bakhtiar leaned forward, staring hard into the colonel's eyes.

May Allah be with us, Rahavi thought. *And may I and my men be better pilots than the American forces.*

Now, show me what you plan to do and how you will destroy their ship," Bakhtiar said smiling, looking at the map tacked on the wall.

WASHINGTON, D.C.

Tom Staffer walked casually down the hall toward room SH 219 of the Hart Office Building, carrying a dark burgundy leather briefcase. He wore his favorite Brooks Brothers dark gray pin-stripe suit with a teal silk tie, a Father's Day gift from his daughter. The suit felt comfortable and he generally wore it when testifying on Capitol Hill.

Although Staffer was required by law to answer all questions on covert operations, he knew he still needed to be very careful about the words he chose. He had learned a long time ago that politicians were of a very different breed. Most had chameleonlike personalities, changing with public opinion polls; and now that the cold war was over, many of the Senators considered the CIA extra baggage that should be pared like the rest of the military.

"Good morning, Mr. Staffer," a young woman, part of the Capitol Hill police, said.

"Good morning," Tom replied, entering the main chamber. The large room, where the Senate Select Committee on Intelligence met, was one of the most secure installations in the U.S. government. Congress appropriated several million dollars a year to make sure the room was bug-and soundproof and that it was electronically swept every other day. Shielded by vaulted doors and constructed of steel to deflect electromagnetic waves, it was actually a room within a room, elevated on all sides to aid in the inspection for bugs. The security team even went as far as filtering the electrical supply so that electronic emissions couldn't be picked up and recorded.

The chamber itself was divided into smaller rooms, and each looked like most of the other conference areas on the Hill—dark brown walnut paneling, brass doorknobs and light fixtures, wine carpet and mauve-covered chairs. The walls were pictureless; for the most part the testimony chambers were sterile and boring. Staffer figured that was done on purpose, to not distract the people giving testimony.

This morning, the director of operations would be testifying in the main conference area. Designed in the shape of a horseshoe, with a map of the world on the wall behind the senators, the room had been constructed with a public address system. A special, more powerful, system had been installed when William J. Casey had been the DCI during the Reagan years. Casey had a bad habit of mumbling his lengthy answers to questions, hoping the senators would grow tired and move off subjects he didn't want to talk about.

Staffer set his briefcase on the table and scanned the group. It appeared that most of the senators had arrived.

"Go ahead and take a seat, Mr. Staffer. We'll be starting in a few minutes," Paula Jenrette, the Democratic senator from Colorado, said pointedly. The senator chaired the committee and was commonly referred to around the CIA as the "Queen Bee." She had a sharp tongue and fast wit, making her almost impossible to verbally spar with and come out unscathed.

Staffer nodded slightly and caught her looking keenly at him. He wasn't fazed; he had dealt with her before and managed to hold his own. Jenrette was a tall, fairly attractive woman with light, reddish hair who always dressed in stylish clothes. Staffer guessed her to be in her late forties, maybe early fifties. He did know that Jenrette wasn't a friend of the CIA or the military and wasn't afraid to publicly criticize either establishment. She had never voted for a weapons system and complained constantly about the lack of women in high-level military and government jobs. She looked upon the CIA as a haven for white, Ivy League males and did her best to challenge the agency and its history whenever she could. Fortunately, the other members of the committee were less hostile and tended to keep Jenrette in check.

Staffer sat down and pulled out his notes, waiting for the senators to stop milling around the front of the room.

Out of the corner of one eye, Perijan caught sight of an Iranian air force officer entering the rear section of the computer assembly room. She recognized the man, although she didn't know his name. He had inspected the complex many times and Hikmet, the chief engineer, seemed to respect him very much. However, this time the officer somehow looked different. His face was rigid, eyes intense, and he walked with a stiff arrogance.

He stormed directly into Hikmet's corner office, closing the door behind him. She watched Hikmet stand up from behind his computer as the man immediately began talking. Hikmet rushed over and lowered all the venetian blinds around his office.

She felt her insides roll over. This had something to do with the attack on the American ship; Perijan was sure of it. The second message she had retrieved urgently requested any knowledge of the attack and the missiles involved, specifically data on the guidance systems and the missiles' origin.

She picked up a tray of computer chips and walked across the room. Very carefully, she rolled a chair across the bare floor toward Hikmet's office. When she was five feet away, Perijan stopped and sat. She was close enough to see the shadowy silhouettes of both men through the thin slits of the blinds. They were standing with their backs to her, facing the wall. She thought hard, trying to remember the office's layout. *They're discussing the map of the Gulf above Hikmet's desk*, she surmised. She could barely hear their voices through the closed door. Pretending to be concentrating on a chip, she strained to hear what was being said.

''. . . our P-3 reconnaissance aircraft are keeping track of the American fleet. They are located here . . . 380 miles from Bandar Abbas.'' The colonel's shadow arm pointed to the wall.

"We will not have the option of getting an infrared signature to target the carrier." That was Hikmet.

"It cannot be done. There is no way the Americans will allow us to get that close. The P-3s are being escorted away as soon as they get within a hundred miles of the carrier. You will have to develop a different way to target the ships."

"I can't—"

"You must. My aircraft are to fly in three days. I will not allow my men to fly in without each of those missiles programmed to hit that carrier."

"The missiles have a range of only sixty miles. You will never get close enough."

"My pilots *will* get close enough . . ."

Perijan moved nervously away from the office. Their raised voices were becoming argumentative, and she worried that one of them would come out of the office soon. *They must be planning to attack again in three days. And they will use the missiles.*

She walked back to the opposite end of the room. The computer terminal was still on, but she didn't pay attention to the screen. Her thoughts were on getting this information and the information requested, to the CIA before Iran killed more Americans and started a war that would also kill her own people.

If only I had been able to keep up contact, none of this would have happened.

The only person who had access to the classified information on the missile system was Hikmet. Perijan had been in his office on only one occasion, and she had never seen anyone else in the room. The man was paranoid and many times even locked the door when he was in there alone. The room contained three metal file cabinets that were both secured with large bolt locks on the side and standard locks on each drawer. She was sure any files he had were kept in the secured cabinets. *The computer,* Perijan thought, *is my only hope.* She judged she might be able to access some information through Hikmet's computer. She slipped two empty 3.5-inch floppy disks into her white lab coat.

Perijan glanced up from her computer monitor when both men exited the office. They were still talking and were preoccupied with their conversation. Within a few moments they had walked toward the back of the complex. A moment later they disappeared up the stairs.

Now, Perijan . . . go. She forced herself up and rushed toward

Hikmet's office. The light was still on and the door was slightly ajar—he hadn't remembered to lock it. Taking a deep breath, she pushed the door open.

Her eyes swept across the room rapidly as she tried to take notice of every possible detail. Hikmet's desk was cluttered with papers, files and engineering books; she resisted the temptation to look through the files. Just as she had expected, the file cabinets were locked.

Perijan hurried to the computer, knowing that was her only option. Slipping a disk into the drive, she tapped the keyboard to call up the main menu. It wasn't the same menu she used. Scrolling through it, she stopped at AUTO CAD:/INFRARED SYSTEM.

Let's see what this is. She tapped the F1 function key, and ACCESS DENIED began to flash on the screen.

Perijan felt her breath growing short. She would have to have access to the main program on the hard drive, bypassing the security program, and that would take some time. She looked around for Hikmet. She knew she would have to hurry.

Staffer had just finished briefing the senators on eight different covert CIA operations that were going on in the world. He had intentionally saved Iran for last.

One of the ironies of covert operations was that CIA officers have been trained to cheat, lie, steal and break the laws of foreign governments in order to get crucial, accurate information. Then Staffer was expected to sit before a group of skeptical senators and convince them that all the clandestine dealings were in the best interest of the United States' national security. No wonder the CIA was looked upon with a cynical eye.

Tom Staffer took a drink of water, reviewing his handwritten notes. He felt his mouth going dry again a few seconds later. Staffer had been in the CIA for nearly twenty-five years and by far this was the toughest part of his job. Sitting before fifteen senators and their aides, answering question after question, wasn't much better than having a root canal without Novocain. And by the looks on their faces, Staffer could tell that several were out for CIA blood. *I hate fucking election years*, he thought. *Everyone wants their name in the paper.*

"Mr. Staffer. I have a few questions about your Iran operations now." Senator Paula Jenrette adjusted her glasses and stared at him over the top of them.

All right, here it comes. Give me your best shot.

"Why didn't the CIA know anything about the attack on the *Shiloh* before it happened? Isn't this the sort of thing we have the CIA for, to give us some warning before a terrible catastrophe such as this happens?"

"As I've previously stated, Iran has been a very difficult environment for us to infiltrate," Staffer answered. "They are extremely protective of their government and military."

"And on whose advice did you decide to sell them advanced jet fighter radars and spare parts?"

"Senator Jenrette, the radars and spare parts we are selling Iran are advanced for them, but are not considered frontline inventory in the West. We made a joint decision with the Pentagon to offer Iran a product they could use in order to get one of our officers inside one of their military installations. It's not the first time this tactic has been used, and it won't be the last. This method goes all the way back to World War II."

"I'm well aware of that, Mr. Stafford," Jenrette retorted a little heatedly. "My concern is that you and whoever was involved in this transaction are attempting to withhold vital information from this committee to cover up an error in judgment. And because of it, fifty-two Americans are dead."

"I'm sorry, Senator, but I fail to follow your line of thought." Staffer cocked his head, looking directly at her.

"Then let me explain it to you, Mr. Staffer. I have information, from a high-level military source, that the *Shiloh* was illuminated by a powerful airborne radar just before it was attacked. And that radar operated on the same frequency . . ." Jenrette paused and looked at her notes for a second. ". . . A J-band, I believe, as the radar system you are selling them. Is that correct, sir?"

Shit, how the hell does she know that? Stafford maintained his composure. "I can't confirm that, Senator. I'm not a radar expert."

"Well, can you confirm that the electronic countermeasure equipment the CIA has been supplying to the Iranians can be used against U.S. radar detection equipment?" Jenrette grilled.

"Possibly some of our older systems, but not an Aegis system, if that's what you're trying to refer to," Staffer rebutted.

"Mr. Staffer, you just informed us that you're not a radar expert. I find it strange you know the answer to that question and yet don't know the radar frequency of a missile that has destroyed several tankers and one of the military's cruisers. Now, it seems odd to me that you come before this committee to recommend an operation without telling us the whole truth.''

"The CIA has—'' Staffer began, but was quickly cut off.

"I remember sitting in this very same room as a junior senator a dozen or so years ago when the CIA told us the same story about Iraq.'' Jenrette removed her glasses and folded her arms, leaning forward. "At that time, the CIA was telling us we needed to sell arms to Iraq because they were at war with Iran, and Iran was a greater threat. Do you remember that argument, Mr. Staffer?''

"Yes, I do. And at the time I believed that was the correct decision.'' He knew where the senator was headed, and he didn't like it. She was trying to paint him into a corner and put words in his mouth. It was more than possible that by the end of the day the CIA could look like the bad guys.

"Yes, but no one stopped to think that we were arming a nation we might have to go to war with in a few years. And Americans died in that war, didn't they, Mr. Staffer? I see the same thing happening here, and it's my job to make sure the CIA doesn't make another mistake. What kind of results have we seen from this sale? Nothing but dead Americans again!'' Jenrette exploded angrily.

Staffer's face turned red with her outburst. She had managed to completely misrepresent a necessary tactic for the U.S. to stay abreast of world strategic affairs.

"Yes, to date it would appear the success has been minimal. However, we now have—''

"Minimal is a poor choice of words, Mr. Staffer. I'd say *zero* is more like it. And now the Iranians have some of our equipment.''

"Just a minute, Senator, if you'd let me finish.'' Staffer's tone was mild as he regained his self-control. "One officer has already died trying to acquire critical military intelligence in Iran and we have only recently been able to get another in place to extract high-level data. Now, I would not consider that a waste of time and effort, and in light of current events this officer will be more than beneficial.''

"Sir, are you suggesting that despite the loss of tankers and a cruiser, not to mention the casualties, this operation should continue? It is clearly obvious to me, and I would think everyone

else in this room, that enough damage has been done in the nam
of national security."

"That's an extremely simplistic view of the world. The Unite
States doesn't have permanent enemies or friends, Senator, jus
permanent interests. I stand behind what we are doing in Iran
And, if I remember correctly, you were one of the members o
this committee who voted to allow this covert arms sale to pro
ceed. It was the only way for us to penetrate the last hostile natio
in the Gulf," Staffer said with a touch of abrasion. "That is wha
our goal was and that is what we have done. This operation ha
been successful, and now you want to end it when the real payof
is just about to begin?"

"I voted to allow the sale of low-level defense weapons sys
tems. Radars that can be used to attack American ships don't fal
in that category. And if you wish to deem an operation that ha
cost fifty-two American lives successful, then you and I hav
entirely different views of the world," Jenrette replied, shufflin
her papers back together.

"Do you mean to tell me you think—"

"I'm the one asking the questions, Mr. Staffer, not you." Jen
rette donned her glasses and masterfully shifted the conversation
"Now, what specific information have you obtained from thi
Iranian operation?"

Staffer stopped, realizing the senator had accomplished he
goal. *There's no doubt about it, she's good at what she does
Queen bee, my ass—she's a black widow.*

"Nothing."

"Very well. I move for a vote to discontinue the funds for thi
operation before another American gets killed," Jenrette spoke
assuredly, looking around the conference room. "Do I hear a
second?"

Staffer examined each of the senators. His only hope was tha
the committee was mostly comprised of conservative men, ever
though the trends in government jobs were looking optimistic fo
liberal women.

"I second the motion."

"All those in favor of discontinuing the funds say aye." Staffe
sat on the edge of his seat as a few hands went up and "ayes'
rang out.

"All those opposed." The senator counted the votes, unruffle
by the fact that the motion was obviously defeated.

Maybe next time I'll send Heather to tackle Jenrette, Staffer thought. *She'd probably do a better a job than I just did.*

Jenrette remained seated once she was finished announcing the outcome. Then she spoke unwaveringly, going out on a limb. "When we adjourn, I am writing a letter to the President expressing my dissatisfaction with the CIA's handling of this matter. And I challenge my colleagues to do the same."

"I move we recess for lunch," one of the other senators said. "Second."

Staffer closed his folder and stood to leave the room. Jenrette was glaring at him with narrow eyes.

"I'm not going to give up on this, Mr. Staffer." Her expression let him know she was dead serious. Just because the committee hadn't backed her didn't mean there weren't other avenues of retaliation. It would take a lot of effort and bull-headedness, but Staffer knew Jenrette well enough to know that she was more than capable of that. He just wondered from what direction her next move would come as he walked out of the room, not responding to her hostility.

Chapter Eighteen

Come on . . . cycle faster, Perijan pleaded inwardly. The base software on the chief engineer's computer wasn't processing the data on the hard drive quickly enough.

"There," she whispered. Touching the arrow-down key several times, she highlighted AUTOEXEC.SEC, the security file. The screen blinked, showing the root files. She had avoided the password. Next, she reaccessed the main memory and pulled up AUTO CAD:/INFRARED SYSTEM. She waited for the file to be dumped into the computer's RAM. After the hard drive's green light flashed off, she copied the file onto the empty disk. This took only fourteen seconds, but it seemed like an hour.

One more. Scrolling the menu, she stopped on COMPLEX:/BLUE-PRINT. Snapping in a new disk, she pulled the file into the memory and repeated the procedure. After thirty seconds, the hard drive cycle light flickered out and the words NOT ENOUGH MEMORY flashed on the screen, telling Perijan the disk was full. She didn't dare risk the time it would take to get another disk.

Perijan removed the disk and placed it in her pocket, then made sure the file Hikmet had been working on was back on the screen. She was walking over to the door, when she suddenly saw the legs of a man descending the stairs at the other end of the room. It was Hikmet.

254

* * *

"This session of the Senate Select Committee on Intelligence is officially closed," Paula Jenrette said, striking a gavel on the wood table. The senator turned off her microphone and neatly replaced her notes along with a stack of files in her briefcase. She turned to her aide, whispering, "Call my husband and tell him I'll be about fifteen minutes late for dinner."

"Yes, Ms. Jenrette," her personal assistant, a young male University of Colorado graduate, answered.

Jenrette stepped off the raised platform and looked over at Staffer, catching his eye. "Mr. Staffer, do you have a minute?" She headed straight for Staffer, not waiting for him to answer.

"Sure," Staffer grunted.

"I just want you to know this isn't personal. I honestly believe the CIA is way off base on this one. There are ways to infiltrate a country other than selling weapons that have only one purpose and result," Jenrette explained somberly.

"Most of the systems we've sold Iran are defensive, Senator," Staffer responded, picking up his briefcase. "They're not designed to be harmful themselves. It's the people that use them that are dangerous."

"Why can't the CIA use more creative means to get intelligence? Maybe if you recruited a doctor or a—"

"Ms. Jenrette, we're talking about the Iranian military," Staffer cut her off. "Not a hospital. How would the CIA look to you if we sent in men or women who weren't equipped for this type of operation and they were killed? We'd be even bigger bad wolves, wouldn't we?"

"You're living in the past, Tom. It's time to start changing." She shook her head.

"I'm doing my job the only way I know how. If you think that if we sit back and do nothing, then all this chaos will stop, those rose-tinted glasses of yours are affecting more than your vision."

"I know you think I'm being unrealistic, but it's men like you that fuel the fires of the wars that exist in the world today. I just wanted to see if there was any chance you would have an open mind and listen to reason. I see that I was sadly mistaken. Good day, Mr. Staffer," Jenrette replied, pulling her briefcase off the desk and stalking away. She made a definite impression with her perfect posture, and Staffer couldn't help but wish she was on his side.

Shit, he suddenly thought. *What did I just do? Staffer, you idiot, when are you going to learn to keep your mouth shut? If Brady finds out I got into a sparring match with her, he'll have my head on a platter.* The director of operations knew it was best to keep your opinions to yourself. Especially when it came to the feely, touchy type, because they were the ones who usually caused the CIA the most grief.

Staffer headed out of the Hart Office Building. The hot, steamy summer air that blasted his face felt good compared to the recycled air conditioning of the committee's conference room. He noticed Senator Jenrette climbing into the backseat of a Lincoln as her aide shut the door. He chuckled as he read the sticker on the bumper: VISUALIZE WORLD PEACE. *I wish that was all I had to do to get the job done,* he thought.

Senator Jenrette was looking out the window at him. She smiled but didn't wave, and the car sped off. The senator was busy with her own thoughts. *By this time tomorrow, the CIA will be wishing it had never begun this operation,* she mused. *And better yet, the President will have to explain why his foreign policy was responsible for the deaths of fifty-two Americans. And all this only a week before the Republican convention.*

Perijan ducked down below the window, hoping Hikmet didn't see her. Crawling on her hands and knees, she made her way into the main computer assembly area as fast as she could. Behind her she could hear Hilmet's footsteps approaching fast.

Perijan looked up. She had stopped next to one of the workstations. Resting on the edge of the desk was a small metal tray she knew contained a dozen or so computer chips. She reached up and grabbed it, scattering chips on the floor in front of her.

"What are you doing?" Hikmet inquired harshly.

Perijan stopped and looked up. She was still on her knees. "I dropped some of the computer chips."

Hikmet looked around, his eyes going from Perijan to his open office door, then back to Perijan. He stared at her for a long moment before finally gesturing with his hand. "Get them picked up . . . *now.*" Hikmet walked into his office and closed the door.

Perijan lowered her head and closed her eyes, fighting the urge to cry. Her hands and arms trembled uncontrollably. She bit her lip to regain some composure. *That was too close,* she told herself. Picking up the chips, she returned to her desk. In forty-five minutes she could go home and be with her father.

BAHRAIN AIR BASE

"I understand how the Navy feels about this, General. Hell, I'd probably feel the same way. But from what I've seen of Zachiem and his method of operation, I'm not that impressed. The man doesn't want help or advice from anyone. He's a one-man show." Duke James spoke candidly with Chaniff via one of the dozen or so secure military channels used to transmit data into and out of the region.

"I know that, Duke. That's why I sent you. Zachiem has his strengths, but I also know he has just as many weaknesses," Chaniff responded, then asked, "Have you had a chance to look over the Navy's report on the missile hit?"

Duke picked up the report from naval intel. The words CLAS-SIFIED SECRET were printed across the front cover in large black letters. It was the preliminary report on the missile found inside the *Shiloh*, and Duke had just finished reading it.

"Yes, sir."

"And what do you make of it?"

"Sounds like the bastards got their hands on stealth cruise missiles, all right," Duke answered, tapping a pencil on top of the report. "And from what I could tell, they're damn similar to ours."

"That's the consensus at the Pentagon also. And believe me, everybody's jumping now. Stealth missiles . . . shit, I still can't believe it. Do you think they bought them or that they could have figured some way to manufacture the damned things?" The general posed the question without really expecting an answer.

"Well, somebody better be figuring that out real soon." Duke sighed, shaking his head. "What's our next move till then?"

"The President wants to explore two options. The first is to strike Bandar Abbas in retaliation for the *Shiloh*. The second is to wait until we have solid intel of the weapons' locations, then destroy them. Hell, we don't even have any idea how many they have right now." Chaniff's tone expressed the dilemma of not having anything to work with.

"Sounds like the spy guys need to hustle."

"They are. Oh, I've already signed off on your request for additional aircraft. The President and Radford agreed with your thoughts on being prepared for a counterattack. So the F-16s you requested should be in the air by now.''

"And the F-15s?"

"The C models are coming from Germany and the Es from Great Britain," Chaniff answered, then paused. "I want you to get back over to the *LaSalle*, too. I'm calling Zachiem next and I want the two of you to discuss this report. I've scheduled a flight to Bahrain tomorrow morning so I can meet with both of you. I know he can be hard to deal with, Duke, but we're stuck with him for now and I'm expecting a full briefing on how we can counter this new missile. I need you to work together."

"No problem, sir." Duke hung up the phone. *Yeah, no problem*, he thought. *I've just got to convince Zachiem that I've got Navy blood running through my veins. When are these arrogant SOBs going to realize the military is one big team and we all have got to work together.* He put on a fresh shirt and a clean pair of pants, snatched up his briefcase and walked out of his quarters toward the waiting staff car.

CIA HEADQUARTERS

"Edleman asked that I review this with you," Admiral Currie said, standing in the doorway of Tom Staffer's seventh-floor office holding a thin file. His face was pallid and his eyes puffy red.

"Yeah . . . come on in," Staffer said, thinking the man looked like an actor from *Night of the Living Dead*. He fumbled with his half-smoked cigarette, finally grinding it out in the ashtray next to his phone. He smoked more since trying to quit in the last week than he had in the last six months.

Currie pulled a chair up next to Staffer's desk and sat down, keeping the file folder on his lap.

"Hold my calls, Heather," Staffer said, hitting the intercom button. "When was the last time you got some rest, Hal?"

"You sound like Edleman. Are you two going for the mother of the year award? I'll get some sleep when I have this thing nailed . . . and I'm almost there." The admiral removed from the file six black-and-white satellite images and laid them out in a neat row in front of Staffer. "Take a look at these."

Staffer studied the pictures for a few seconds, then said, "Let me guess, the Iranian shoreline?"

"That's right, and I'm eighty percent certain I know where the missiles that hit the *Shiloh* came from."

This got Staffer's attention. "Show me."

Currie pointed to several places on each of the photographs. They were extreme closeups of areas no more than a couple of hundred square meters across. Though the photos were somewhat blurry, the director of operations' experience told him he was looking at stretches of rocky shoreline dotted with large boulders, twisted dead trees and dried brush piles. Here and there he noticed clumps of weeds that appeared to be alive, although everything else around them was dead. Staffer focused on the places Currie had circled with a white grease pencil. The shaded impressions didn't seem out of the ordinary other than the fact they were larger than the other dark spots on the pictures.

"I wish these were clearer, but even with a resolution of three inches the details are unmistakable." Currie picked up a ballpoint pen and began to use it as a pointer. "These dark zones are outlets from manmade tunnels. They're approximately four feet in diameter."

"Yeah . . . ," Staffer said, not sure if he was seeing it correctly.

"Don't worry about seeing it right away. It took me and four other people from the NPIC eight hours to identify these launch tunnels. Hell, I didn't see them the first twenty times I looked at these photos. We had to run the resolution to the finest setting before we finally caught them." Currie yawned, rubbing his eyes.

"Launch tunnels . . . underground launch tunnels?" Staffer asked, piecing the information together.

"That's right. We've located eight of them and there are probably more. My guess is they've built a large underground network to house their new missiles. And I'd have to pay them a compliment. The Iranians have done a damned good job of concealing the exit holes." Currie paused, then added, "If it wasn't for that new 3-D software program, we never would have spotted them."

I'll have to remember to tell that to the Senate Select Intelligence Committee—money put to good use, Staffer thought, not taking his eyes off the photos. The dark spots could be tunnels, all right, but that didn't convince him this was where the missiles had come from. If Jenrette was going to be breathing down his neck, he didn't want another CIA screwup on his hands.

"Do you have any other evidence that these are launch sites and not just tunnels?" Staffer reached for his last cigarette, then threw the package at the wastebasket. He missed.

"Yes, sir. I knew you'd ask me that, so I had NORAD supply me with an IR overlay. It showed the exact location of the hot spots they picked up the night the *Shiloh* was hit. They line up perfectly with four of the launch sites." Currie picked the package up and tossed it straight into the basket, turning to smile while waiting for Staffer's reaction.

"Great job, Hal!" Staffer smiled.

"And that's not all. I calculated the flight time for a cruise missile, traveling at Mach 0.98 with an altitude of twenty-five feet above the ocean, to fly from this point to the *Shiloh*'s location at the time of the hit." Currie paused, smiling even wider.

"And—"

"It would take exactly eight minutes, thirteen seconds for the first one to hit its target," Currie answered. "It was eight minutes, twenty-two seconds from the time NORAD detected the first IR bloom to when the *Shiloh* was hit."

"Okay, ground-based missiles hit the *Shiloh*. But what about the tankers, how were they attacked? There were never any IR blooms detected by the satellites."

"Now, remember we're dealing with what the Navy believes to be some kind of stealth cruise missile. My guess is they have two versions, one surface to surface and the other air-to-surface. That's why the Saudi AWACS didn't reveal anything. The missiles came off an aircraft, not a ground launch, so there were no heat signatures from rocket boosters to detect."

"So we're dealing with a double threat," Staffer said, thinking out loud.

"You got it," Currie agreed, then asked hopefully, "Vance said you have an asset placed in Iran now. Have you received any data from him?"

"He's reestablished contact with the operative working in Eshafan," Staffer answered. "She's been transferred to a weapons complex, but that's all we have right now. We're just playing the waiting game. As soon as I know anything, you'll know."

"Okay. I've got to run, but I'll leave these copies with you. On the backs I've marked the latitude and longitude of each launch site. I'll be back at my office in about an hour or so."

Staffer took in a deep breath after Currie left. He placed the satellite pictures in a pile in front of him and wondered what Collins was doing at this very moment. Things were happening fast, and Staffer couldn't help but worry about the younger man being in a dangerous situation. He recalled his first encounter with Collins as an eager analyst, smiling at the thought. He checked his watch: 2:15 P.M. Collins wouldn't be transmitting for another four hours.

ESFAHAN, IRAN

The sun was setting in a cloudless deep blue sky and the calm winds promised to aid in cooling the temperature outside. But Perijan Reza thought of nothing but getting safely inside her home as she walked up the stone pathway. The day had left her drained and she prayed it would be a peaceful evening.

Her first thought was to check on her father. She closed the door and entered the shadowy confines of his room. The blinds were pulled shut as usual, and the room was hot and stuffy. *Oh, Father,* she thought, as her eyes slowly adjusted to the darkness. *Why do you insist on keeping the window shut and not letting the light in.* She considered opening them, then realized she couldn't wait to shut herself up in their home either.

Perijan sat on his bed. He was lying with his back to her. An old gray wool blanket covered half his body. She could see his large hand resting on top.

"Hello, Father. I'm home," Perijan whispered, taking his hand in hers. She leaned over and kissed him on the cheek. His skin felt cool and dry, not hot and clammy as she had expected. "Father?" she whispered a little louder, squeezing his hand.

A surge of panic swept through her. "*Father* . . . please answer me. Wake up!" She grasped him by the shoulders and using all her strength pulled him toward her. His limp body was too much for her to handle and fell back on the bed. She rolled him onto his back, then gasped at the sight of his open eyes staring up at her.

"Father . . . Father!" she shouted, grabbing him around the neck. "Don't die, Father . . . please don't die."

Mark Collins didn't spot the car with the two goons and wondered if they had decided to just wait for him to return to the hotel. The crowd was smaller and he could see where several of the shops had already closed for the night. He had intentionally waited to leave later, deciding to vary his routine to avoid suspicion should it ever beome necessary.

"Your usual table, sir?" the waiter asked, as Collins entered the restaurant.

Collins nodded, following the young man to his regular seat next to the sidewalk.

"The lamb is exceptionally good tonight. I have saved you a choice portion."

"Thank you. That would be fine, and I'd like some water," Collins said casually, looking around. Up the street, to the left, he spotted the gray BMW approaching. The car slowed, then drove off. The waiter set his glass on the table. Collins immediately emptied the glass and requested a refill. A good reason to excuse himself to go to the restroom later on.

Perijan wiped the tears from her eyes as she slumped against the wall next to the bed. She held her father's arm, sobbing feebly.

"I'll always love you, Papa . . . I'm going to miss you," she said softly. Looking up, she noticed that the light filtering through the blinds had a bluish tint. The gaslights had been turned on to illuminate the streets. Night had come to Esfahan. She wondered how long she had been sitting in the dark.

Perijan stood. Her knees felt weak and her stomach queasy and numb. She had known this day would come; she just didn't realize it would hurt so much when it did. Her last family member was dead, and she was left alone.

She entered the bathroom and washed her face with cold water. A thousand thoughts ran through her mind at the same time. *Now they don't have anything to hold over my head . . . the government can't force me to work for them.* She dried her face with a towel, feeling strangely relieved that they could no longer threaten to harm her father.

What are you thinking? she asked herself. *If the Revolutionary Guards learn of his death, they will report it to Hikmet. He would have me penned up like an animal, kept under his constant supervision, and I would still be forced to work at the plant.* Perijan's relief turned to fear and resentment.

She walked back into the bedroom and looked at her father again. Carefully, she began removing the oxygen hoses from around his face. *Oh Father, what am I to do?* She covered him with the blanket, praying to Allah to care for her father. *There is nothing I can do for him now . . . he is in a better place. No more suffering.*

Perijan stopped. She reached into her pocket and pulled out the two computer disks. *Yes, there is something I can do for my father.*

Chapter Nineteen

ESFAHAN, IRAN

Perijan adjusted the chador covering most of her face. Rather than walking through the bazaar and doubling back down the alley as she usually did, she was approaching the alley from the opposite side.

She checked her watch as she rounded the corner into the alley. She had been instructed to always make the drop before 10:00 P.M. and it was now 10:30. *Pray Allah that I have not missed the messenger.* It was prearranged that if for some reason she couldn't make it to the vacant lot, she was to try again the next night. But Perijan did not want to think of having to wait another day with the disks in her possession.

Mark Collins, his curly dark wig on straight and glasses resting squarely on his face, exited the restaurant. He walked swiftly through the dining area and into the bazaar, turning left toward the alley. He didn't see the BMW parked at the end of the street. He had waited to leave until after he had completed his meal. It was a few minutes past 10:30. If the tails returned, they would see he had asked for a cup of hot tea and should be back at his seat soon.

Collins walked rapidly but not so fast that people would notice him. He paused for a few seconds, looking around, and didn't move into the dark confines of the alley until he felt comfortable. He could see the tape was off the lamppost again, telling him another drop had been made.

The sound of gravel crunching under his feet echoed off the buildings as he moved toward the vacant lot. He had already made up his mind that this would be the last time this drop would be used. He had left new instructions in the drop container for a rotation using several drop points rather than just one.

Reaching the vacant lot, he stopped and bent down as if to tie his shoe.

Across the street Perijan stood straight in an effort to see over the people milling around. She tried to appear as if she were waiting to meet someone as she watched the alley. Several people had walked past it; however, only one had entered the alley, a bearded man of medium build wearing a wrinkled tan sports jacket.

She had followed him as he headed down the path but lost sight of him in the darkness.

This is a foolish idea, she told herself. *You will never find him. It may not even be that he will show up tonight. Perhaps he has already been here and left.*

Perijan fought back a swell of panic moving through her. The same man exited the alley and turned left, walking away from her. Her legs strained to keep up with the man's longer strides. She twisted her way around several people, hoping she wasn't drawing too much attention. The pounding in her chest and head blocked out the shouts of doubt running through her head.

In a desperate move, she was almost running as she caught up with him in front of an open-air restaurant.

"Mister . . . ," she heard her voice say, not sure how she had managed to talk at all.

"Yes." Collins, startled, glanced down at the woman before resuming his search of the area for the gray BMW.

"I . . . I . . . ," Perijan stuttered, not knowing what to say. Iranian women were prohibited by law from talking with strangers, much less strange foreign men. She felt as if everyone in the market was watching her.

Collins, ready to dismiss her before the goons returned, hesitated, noticing the birthmark above her right eye. Her face suddenly looked strangely familiar—the eyes, the soft skin. A nagging feeling kept him from turning away and leaving her. She appeared to be frightened and desperate.

"You must help me," Perijan finally whispered, hoping she was not mistaken that this was the American messenger.

"I'm sorry, but I must be going," Collins replied, seeing the BMW coming around the corner ahead. He glanced at her one more time, then started to walk away.

Perijan stood, not sure what to do next. She felt a wave of fear and panic overtake her. This was her last hope. Tomorrow she would be a prisoner and never have the chance to be free again. *Allah, help me. Say something, Perijan . . . say something.*

"American, look at me. You must know me." She ran up next to Collins, pleading.

Collins looked back, but he forced himself not to break stride.

"My name is—"

"Shut up!" Collins hissed out the side of his mouth. He spun around and faced the stunned woman, then spoke more softly. "Don't say a word. Just follow me and try not to look so suspicious." He cursed his luck as the BMW drove directly past them. They walked into the restaurant one after the other.

USS LA SALLE, BAHRAIN

Duke entered Admiral Zachiem's official quarters in time to hear the phone being hung up. Zachiem was seated next to the far wall. Resting on the table were two glasses and a half bottle of scotch.

In the two days he had worked with Zachiem, Duke had learned one important thing—Nelson Zachiem III was a manipulator. The man was determined to get his way, no matter what, and it didn't seem to make any difference who he ran over in the process. On top of that, he was obsessive about being a Navy man. The admiral didn't hide the fact that he considered the Navy responsible for American security in the Gulf and Duke was just in the way.

"That was General Chaniff." Zachiem used his foot to move the chair across from him away from the table. Duke accepted the somewhat polite gesture and sat down. "He's scheduled a flight out of Washington first thing in the morning. He wants to meet with both of us at 1500 hours tomorrow. It seems the CIA has dug up some more information and he wants to brief us personally."

"Yes, I know. I spoke with him about half an hour ago," Duke informed him, wanting to get the edge.

"I see. Would you like a drink, General James? I think we should have a talk."

"No, thanks," Duke answered, wanting to stay alert.

"Suit yourself," Zachiem replied, pouring himself a glass of scotch, no ice. "Regulations prohibit alcohol on board Navy ships. But rank does have a few privileges . . . doesn't it."

Duke didn't respond, watching the admiral take a large gulp.

"Nothing like Irish blended scotch. A bottle from my father's collection. A birthday gift." Zachiem swallowed the last bit left in his glass, then swiveled around in his seat to face Duke. "I want you to know I've recommended to Chaniff that the Navy hit the military base at the Iran port city of Bandar Abbas in forty-eight hours in retaliation for the attack on the *Shiloh*."

"I see," Duke said slowly.

"I've already instructed the *Lincoln* to begin prestrike operations. She'll start to move in closer as soon as it's dark."

"If you've already decided this, what would you like to talk about?" Duke asked curiously.

"Well, I believe you already know since you apparently spoke to Chaniff before I did," Zachiem sarcastically retorted, then continued when Duke only stared back silently. "Chaniff suggested that you might be able to advise me. The Navy will need some help from the Air Force, General, mainly your AWACS capability."

"Advise you on what? It looks as if you have everything under control."

"You did read this? I had a copy sent over to you." Zachiem pointed to the intel report.

"Yeah, I've read it."

"Our investigation team at Norfolk estimates the missiles' range at between eighty and a hundred miles. Obviously more if it's launched from an aircraft. It carries a warhead weighing roughly eight hundred pounds and attains a speed of just under Mach 1. Our radar tests show the missile can only be tracked with low-frequency radars. The *Shiloh*'s SPY-1 system operates on an F-band covering 3,100 to 3,500 MHz. That's why they didn't detect the missile until it was too late. We're reprogramming some of our systems right now to deal with this threat," Zachiem said confidently. "There is no way I will allow this to happen again."

"Don't bet on it, Admiral." Duke could stay quiet no longer.

"What if the Iranians have several classes of missiles? Ones that will defeat different radar bands? What then?" The two men stared at each other for a long moment.

"That's why you will be advising me on the best way to strike Bandar Abbas," Zachiem said defensively.

"My advice is that you wait until we have an adequate force in the region to—"

"That's a typical Air Force response, General. Would you have us just sit around and wait until more people are killed and more ships are sunk? We have an adequate force *now* and it's the *Lincoln*. The fucking Iranians hit one of our ships, General James, one of our best ships. I do not intend to sit back and do nothing. You yourself know the Air Force has limited resources in this area. It would take you at least two weeks to gather the firepower I have on one of my carriers."

Duke didn't bother to argue. He knew by Zachiem's tone and insistence he had made up his mind. "I'll just state my concerns to Chaniff when he arrives."

"Fair enough." Zachiem responded more calmly this time. "I wish you'd share a drink with me, General. You're starting to make me nervous. I'm wondering if you're a team player." The admiral poured himself another shot of scotch, then without waiting for Duke's reply poured some in the other glass.

Duke left the scotch untouched on the table in front of him. He crossed his legs and sat back.

"Duke, I want you to know there's another side to me you haven't seen yet," the admiral went on. "I am a team player, though it may seem at times that I am only concerned with the Navy."

Is this your way of apologizing? Duke asked himself. *Or are you trying to charm me?*

"I know you're sitting there thinking I'm an asshole, and you're probably right. You and I got off to a bad start, and it was my fault. I just want us to start over. Bury the hatchet, so to speak." Zachiem raised his glass at Duke.

Duke swirled the scotch in his glass, not accepting Zachiem's salute. *You just need me to sign off on this little plan of yours so that Chaniff will let you have your way. That's all you want.*

"My gut tells me the President isn't going to wait too much longer. And I want him to know that when he does make a decision, the Navy is willing and ready." Zachiem paused, looking intently at Duke. "James, I'd like to know the Navy can depend on you for support. I want you on my team."

Duke forced himself not to laugh at the admiral's arrogance. "What the hell is attacking their port going to accomplish?"

"It will teach the bastards not to fuck with the U.S. Navy again," Zachiem blurted.

"Well, my gut tells me that's just what the Iranians would like us to do, attack their port, kill some innocent women and children. Give them a reason to curse the West and possibly get our ships in close enough so they can sink a few more of them. What makes you think they won't hit us again? And I doubt changing a few radar frequencies is the only answer." Duke shook his head in bewilderment. The two sat in tense silence thinking about what the other might do next.

Collins headed for the back of the restaurant. Perijan apprehensively stayed a few feet behind him. When he reached the restroom, he glanced in all directions, making sure no one was around. He then hastily grasped the young woman by the arm and pulled her inside, closing the door. She cowered away, unsure of his intentions. Collins held a finger to his lips, then whispered, "You shouldn't have done this. You've put us both in danger." His mind raced. He did not want to frighten her any more than she was, but he was unable to hold back his anger.

"I have brought you some valuable information. They plan to attack in three days . . . and they will use the missiles again." Perijan was relieved that this was the messenger, but also worried that he would not understand her situation. She reached into the folds of her chador and pulled out the two computer disks from a pocket. "These have a layout of the complex, where the missiles and guidance system are being manufactured. It is all the information I've been able to obtain." She stopped, realizing she was talking very fast and might be confusing the American.

"Perijan, if they catch us together I'm a dead man. Do you understand that? I'm dead, and so are you." Collins spoke quickly as he took the disks and shoved them down his pants. He noticed that her face flushed and she turned her head. "You've got to leave this place now," he went on. "A security team has followed me here. If they see you . . ." He pulled off his black wig, stuffing it inside his jacket pocket, then removed the glasses and shoved them in the breast pocket.

"My father is dead." Perijan's eyes watered and her voice was breaking as she spoke. "As soon as they know this, they will take me away. I will not be able to help you anymore."

Collins stopped straightening his hair and turned to face her. "Please don't feel that I would only help you because you are beneficial to us." He reached out, touching her gently on each shoulder. "I'm sorry, but you have to understand—"

"*No*. You must understand, American. I want to get out of Iran. I want to go to America," Perijan insisted, tears streaming down her face. "They have nothing to hold over me now. They will make me work or I will die in prison."

Collins didn't have time to argue. He had already been away from his seat too long. "Listen to me. Do *not* go to work tomorrow. Tell them you are sick . . . something."

"Yes," Perijan agreed, wiping her face and nose with her chador.

"I am staying at the Kowsar Hotel. Meet me there at ten tomorrow night, after it's dark. Can you do that?" Collins asked.

"Yes . . . yes. I will be there." Perijan nodded adamantly.

"Okay. Count to fifty and then leave. Look straight ahead and don't make eye contact with anyone," Collins ordered. Without another word he slipped out the door and was gone.

Perijan did as she was told. Five minutes later she returned home, locking the door behind her, and fell into a chair. The tears came openly now and she placed her head in her hands, sobbing in the darkness.

Collins had been back in his hotel room for over an hour. When he had returned to his seat, one of the tails was pacing around outside the vehicle while the other appeared to be relaxed in the driver's seat. Collins deliberately sat long enough to drink two cups of tea and read through his papers. He hoped that was enough time to ease any concerns.

He had spent the last forty minutes in the small confined bathroom, and his legs were cramped from sitting on the edge of the toilet. The computer programs Perijan had supplied him were much more complicated than he had expected. It had taken his machine approximately thirty-eight minutes to run the software, compress the message and electronically encrypt it.

MESSAGE RELAY READY flashed across the bottom of the screen. Collins hit the enter key and watched the green lights under the screen flicker as 2.35 million bits of information cycled off the hard drive to the orbiting satellite in short 3.6-second microbursts.

When the lights stopped flashing and the hum of the hard drive faded, Collins felt himself become more relaxed. A few seconds later the screen surged and a message appeared.

DODSATCOM TRANSIT VV-DOWNLINK*.*/96RWQ-CC909
TO: SPECTRA   FROM: CRYSTAL PALACE

1] CONFIRM LOCATION OF IRANIAN CRUISE MISSILE LAUNCH SITES ALONG COASTLINE WEST OF BANDAR ABBAS.
2] SURVEILLANCE SATELLITES HAVE LOCATED EIGHT POSSIBLE SITES.
3] LONGITUDE AND LATITUDES TO FOLLOW.

Collins watched as a black-and-white map of the region appeared on the screen, along with the latitudes and longitudes. He quickly jotted down the numbers and studied their positions, memorizing them.

Beep . . . beep, the computer sounded. Collins looked at the flashing light under the screen. The battery was getting low. He had only three minutes of power left. Shutting down the machine, he closed the lid, then stood and stretched his legs. He plugged the battery charger into the wall and connected it to the computer, then walked over to the bed and fell onto it, exhausted. His mind was on a thousand things at once.

Perijan was foremost. How was he going to lose his tails to speak with her and how could he possibly help her? Then there was the new information the CIA was requesting. He rolled over and looked at the alarm clock next to the bed. The second hand wasn't moving. *Great*, Collins thought, *the electricity is off again.* His last thoughts before dropping off to sleep were of his wife. He wasn't sure if he was dreaming, but he thought he had called her name out loud.

"They're on final, sir," the air traffic control officer reported, pointing out the left side of the darkened control tower.

Duke James shifted his gaze away from the dancing green and blue air traffic control lights to the black desert sky. He caught sight of four bright white lights lining up in a short string to the north. The American fighters had just turned on their landing lights.

"Advise Colonel Naylor to meet me in the main hangar after he lands," Duke ordered.

"Yes, sir."

Duke watched the aircraft lights for a few more seconds as they continued their descent, then climbed down the winding stairs in the rear of the control tower to the flight line. The night air was warm and he felt a breeze blowing off the Gulf, bringing with it the scent of salt and seaweed.

Walking toward the nearest and largest hangar, he heard the roar of jet engines in the distance behind him. He turned to see the first F-16 touch down. A few seconds later another of the sleek single-engine jets hit the runway.

Duke stopped in front of the open hangar and waited for the first F-16 to shut down its engines. One of the ground crew clamped a portable ladder onto the side of the aircraft. The canopy began to open and the pilot started to unbuckle himself.

Duke had asked for and received permission from General Chaniff to start assembling a strike package of available combat aircraft in the area. Zachiem was right: it would take the Air Force at least a week to put together as large a group of fighters and bombers as the Navy already had deployed on one of its carriers. But he wanted to be prepared if the Pentagon decided that a deep penetration into Iran was needed. As far as he was concerned, only the Air Force would be capable of providing that type of strike package and accomplishing the desired goal.

The four aircraft that had just landed had flown in from Incirlik AFB in Turkey. They were part of a newly formed SEAD team stationed there. SEAD, or Suppression of Air Defenses, was an Air Force program using F-16s as lead aircraft for a force package intended to decimate enemy air defenses during high-risk missions. Over the next eight hours, a mix of EF-111s, F-15Cs, F-15Es and F-16s would be landing to complete the team. He had also requested two KC-135 tankers and one E-3C AWACS.

"Hello, Colonel," Duke said to the pilot who was sauntering toward him.

"It's been a while, General," Naylor responded, taking off his flight gloves. He smiled and extended his hand. Colonel Naylor was the skinny cowboy type—all legs without an ounce of fat anywhere. His upper body was well muscled, however, and his chest looked almost too big for his flight uniform.

It had been just over a year since the two men had last seen each other. Naylor was known in the Air Force for his reputation as the best Viper driver in the world. The two had become close friends while Naylor was attending fighter weapons school at Nellis AFB in Nevada, not far from Las Vegas. Duke had learned that Naylor loved fishing, to the point that it didn't matter what was caught at the other end, and that was the beginning of weekend trips to Lake Mead for stripers and large mouth bass. They would spend their Sundays doing what Duke liked best: sitting in a bass boat drinking beer, catching fish and talking about flying.

"I was *damn* glad to learn it was you heading up the squadron, Eddie." Duke shook his friend's hand.

"*Damn* glad to be of service, General," Naylor said and grinned.

"You know why you're here?" Duke asked, as they walked inside the hangar.

"I have an idea."

"Good. I have a few things I want to run by you. Hope you're not too tired." Duke spoke energetically, feeling in his element. It was good to have someone around who would understand his strategic planning.

Chapter Twenty

"Funeral arrangements have been finalized. Mahmoudi will lie in state for five days. He will then be buried at Behesht-e Zahra cemetery," Akhbar al-Yawm said somberly as he looked out Minister Bakhtiar's office window. He did not want to face the man and see that there was no remorse.

"Very well," Bakhtiar replied with a grunt from his desk.

Al-Yawm turned and faced the defense minister. Bakhtiar looked smug and confident seated at his desk and busily writing. Al-Yawm was certain now that the sheik had something to do with Marjid's and Mahmoudi's deaths. He was also aware that Bakhtiar was having him followed, and had to therefore be discreet. Any irrational moves might cause him to join the former members of the Supreme Defense Council.

"Senior members of the parliament are calling for new elections immediately. Many questions are being asked, and they are openly challenging your authority."

"Let them challenge me. In a few days my work will be complete. They can hold as many elections as they please after that." Bakhtiar stood and walked over to the picture of the Ayatollah Khomeini at the other end of the room.

"What are you saying?" al-Yawm asked as he watched the minister move away from him.

"What are your security forces reporting?" Bakhtiar ignored the question. "Have the riots stopped?"

"Yes . . . they have stopped."

"And the people? Are they talking of the West and the danger our country now faces?"

"There is talk of war. The fear of going to war again is on everyone's mind." Al-Yawm became irritated at not being able to make sense of the older man's line of thought.

Bakhtiar turned. "Tell me, is Iran ready to defend itself against the West? Are the people ready to die?"

"To defend against the West? To die . . . for what?" al-Yawm asked perplexedly.

"Defending Iran and saving our people from corrupt foreign morals and distorted values. The West . . ." Bakhtiar stopped and glared at the interior minister. "I do not have to explain my actions to you. Out of my office!" he shouted. "Out of my office!" Zadeh came to the door immediately, indicating that if al-Yawm did not leave on his own, he would be more than happy to assist him.

CIA HEADQUARTERS

"It's marked 'Critic' and it's from Collins," Heather said, handing Staffer a brown eight-by-ten envelope.

Staffer looked up from his desk and took the packet. "Critic" was the CIA code used to notify computer operators receiving an incoming transmission to give it precedence over all other satellite communications.

He removed the papers quickly, thumbing through them. The first fifteen pages contained several detailed outlines and computer diagrams of an optical relay unit, along with illustrations of a missile's nose section. The last dozen or so pages included a blueprint of what looked like a prison complex. Staffer wasn't sure, but he assumed the complex was near Esfahan. He checked the downlink code at the end of each page. The transmissions were only eighteen minutes old.

"Does Edleman have a copy of this?"

"Yes, I do," the deputy director for intelligence said as he entered Staffer's office.

"What do you make of it?" Staffer asked.

"Well, considering it took the NSA thirty minutes to decode

it, I'd say it's fairly significant.'' Edleman closed the door. "It looks like your man Collins got ahold of some Iranian computer disks. He transmitted the raw data in a three-second burst. We then had to piece it back together.''

Staffer smiled slightly; Collins deserved a long vacation when he got back. Maybe a raise, too. He looked back at the transmission.

"I have several people looking at this,'' Edleman said, "but it seems the first section is an outline of a passive IR detection system. The second part is a breakdown of a manufacturing facility. I'm having Burnell pull our most recent satellite photos right now, but it looks like it's outside Esfahan.''

"Holy shit! So the bastards have been building these things. How in the hell did they manage that?''

"There's more. Collins says they're planning another attack two and a half days from now. The pricks want to sink the *Lincoln*.'' Edleman was bent over Staffer's desk, using his arms to support himself.

"How soon can you and your rocket scientists decode this and get it to Chaniff?'' Staffer began counting the days the military would need to either counterattack or be prepared with a damn good defense.

"I've got my best men on it, including Currie. I'm pushing them to have this completely broken down and understood within the next four hours.'' Edleman glanced at his watch. "The weapons complex layout is fairly simple, though it may take some time to get a handle on this other stuff.''

"Send a copy of this over to the DIA. I want their input as well.'' Staffer looked at the map of the Middle East hanging on the wall. He calculated the difference in time zones—it now was midnight there. He wondered what Collins had done to get this information.

"Collins is coming out . . . with the girl,'' Edleman said, as if reading his thoughts.

Staffer looked back at the first page of Collins's transmission. At the bottom was a quick synopsis of the circumstances, along with the route Collins planned to follow with Perijan in order to exit Iran by dawn the next day.

"It looks like he'll hit the coast in eighteen or twenty hours. I'll inform the Navy to move one of their subs into the area.'' Staffer was biting his lower lip in thought. Pulling a spy out of a hot spot was hard enough without trying to take one of the locals, too. Their disappearance usually caused more alarm.

"We may still need him there," Edleman differed. "Shit, Tom . . . look how long it took us to get him in place."

"I don't care. If the Pentagon decides to hit this place, I don't want one of my men near it. Besides, our informant knows who Collins is now and she wants out. If they catch on to her, he'll be next, and I don't want a dead officer on my hands." Staffer shook his head.

Edleman looked at Staffer's face and knew he'd better back off. "It's your call. At least we got this much. I'm going back to my office. When I have some more information, I'll let you know."

"All right. I'll put together a report after I've read through this. Thanks, Vance." Staffer lit a cigarette, leaned back in his chair and picked up the pile of papers. Collins was Staffer's primary concern right now. He understood what the information meant to everyone else, but that was his man with his butt on the line and Staffer felt responsible for his safety.

Collins would have to get his hands on some transportation, possibly even steal a car, then travel 170 miles over paved and dirt roads to get to the coast. A young woman tagging along would definitely make him more vulnerable. They wouldn't have more than eight or nine hours to make an escape, and that included bypassing any Iranian security checkpoints set up along the way.

Once they reached the coastline, Collins would follow a pre-arranged set of instructions, activating an FM-encrypted homing signal. By then a Navy Seal team would have penetrated the narrow strip of land west of Bandar-e Deylam on the Iranian shoreline to extract Collins and Perijan Reza.

Staffer spun around and used the computer mouse to click up the menu file on current naval operations in the Gulf. He then called up the Navy covert action file to see which submarine was currently on patrol. The *Key West* was in the area. Staffer knew the skipper of the Los Angeles-class nuclear sub *James D. Hill. I better get on the horn to Navy and have this all figured out before I go to the top,* he thought.

THE PENTAGON

There was a reason the secretary of defense's office is one floor above that of the chairman of the Joint Chiefs. Whenever Chaniff wanted to talk with the secretary, a civilian, he had to climb up the stairs. This simple gesture was believed by some to help clarify the fact that the military was required to answer to the elected officials. General Chaniff breezed past the marine guard outside the secretary's office and entered the small waiting area.

"Secretary Radford is expecting you." The receptionist jumped up to open the solid oak door to Radford's office. Chaniff didn't reply.

"What do you have?" Radford asked just as the phone rang. He held up one hand, signaling Chaniff to wait. "This is Radford. Hello, Mr. President." The secretary pointed to one of the chairs in front of his desk.

Chaniff sat down, placing file folders and a rolled-up map of the Middle East on his lap. He watched Radford's expression, trying to figure out what was being said on the other end of the line. The secretary was slumped over his cluttered desk looking haggard and annoyed. The shades were slightly open, offering a partial view of Arlington Cemetery. *Quite appropriate*, Chaniff thought.

"Chaniff's in my office right now, sir," Radford said. "Yes, I'm sure he's read the CIA report." The general nodded. Radford didn't fit the stereotypical image of a Washington bureaucrat. He hadn't finished college, his only degrees being honorary ones from Yale and UCLA. Yet he was considered to have one of the sharpest minds in McEntire's cabinet. Radford was older than the President and resembled an overweight cowhand from a western movie, with a double chin, large belly and scraggly gray mustache. His scruffy appearance bothered many of the straight-laced, starched-collar types in the military. However, it didn't annoy Chaniff in the least. The general had followed the secretary's career since his years as a representative from Texas, and he knew Radford was probably the best friend the military had. He was well respected on Capitol Hill and very few senators and representatives ever confronted him on issues concerning the defense of the United States.

"Understood, sir." Radford hung up the phone. "You know who that was."

"The old man," Chaniff answered.

"Yeah." Radford got up from his seat and poured himself a glass of water. He then dropped in two Alka-Seltzer tablets and drank it before they were completely dissolved. "The President's in a meeting with Bishop, Brady and several members of Congress. It seems the latest news from our friends in the CIA has everyone jumping through hoops,'' Radford said, blinking and rubbing his eyes. ''Damn it . . . I could use a drink right now.''

''He wants your recommendation,'' Chaniff said, second-guessing his boss.

''You got it. I'm supposed to have my fat ass sitting in the Oval Office in twenty minutes. So make this fast.'' Radford stroked his forehead, his face showing the strain of a headache.

''This is the information we've needed, sir. I now have a hard target, not just a few Silkworm sites along the coast.'' Chaniff spread the map across Radford's desk. The hard target was the manufacturing facility, located at an altitude of 6,500 feet. ''The weapons plant is located here, on the northern edge of Esfahan. Ten years ago the Revolutionary Guards tripled the size of Esfahan air base, adding two more 10,000-foot runways, hardened hangars and a new training facility. They also built a maximum-security prison to hold political dissidents. The blueprints obtained by the CIA show the missiles are being built in an underground facility, approximately 150 feet below the surface, inside the prison yard.''

''What are you saying? It's inside a prison complex?'' Radford asked, still puzzled.

''Yes, sir,'' Chaniff replied. He removed several eight-by-ten black-and-white KH-14 photos from their protective sleeves and set them in front of the secretary. ''The CIA pulled these from their library an hour ago. They're six months old but the best we have.''

''Great. Nothing like up-to-the-minute intel for the President,'' Radford said sourly, knowing the President was going to hit the roof on this one.

''This shows the Esfahan air base from an altitude of 10,000 feet. We know Iran's air force operates two full squadrons of F-4Es and a mix of F-14s and MiG-29s. Some of their best pilots are stationed here, and it's the most heavily defended base that Iran currently operates.'' Chaniff pointed to a set of buildings clustered together on the north side of the city, next to which were two black runways cutting across the desert.

''What sort of air defenses?'' Radford asked.

''We're trying to get a handle on that now, Mr. Secretary. So far the CIA is telling me they've located a mix of SAMs—

SA-2s, 3s and 6s, along with mobile triple As.''

"And what about the new shit our friends, the Russians, have been selling them?'' Radford was not liking what he was hearing.

"The CIA is working on that too, sir. But that's going to take time. SA-10s and 12s are mobile. It's tough to pinpoint those launchers in mountainous terrain.'' Chaniff reached for the last of the photographs. "These are close-ups of the base and surrounding area. This is a close-up of the weapons complex. We believe it was built at the same time as the prison, about eight to ten years ago. That's why the CIA didn't locate it. Fairly clever, really.''

Radford folded his arms. "Sneaky bastards. Sounds like something the North Koreans would do.''

"Precisely. And that's why we need to turn this place into a burning hole in the ground. We can't afford to let Iran build more of those missiles,'' Chaniff said and sat down.

"All right. What's your plan, General?'' Radford inquired, jotting furiously on a pad.

"We hit them with a two-pronged air attack. The first assault will be carried out by the Navy, launching A-6 Intruders supported by F-18s and F-14s. They'll launch from the *Lincoln* with orders to destroy the missile sites west of Bandar Abbas before dawn. Our main attack will be a package of Air Force jets staging out of Bahrain. Their job will be to take out the weapons complex at Esfahan.'' Chaniff reached into his briefcase and pulled out two blue file folders. The words OPERATION: BLACK THUNDER were written across the front of each. "Page one outlines the aircraft required for the mission. I've already given General James permission to start pulling the jets and pilots he's going to need. And as you know, the *Lincoln* has been on a heightened state of readiness since the *Shiloh* was hit. She can launch on the President's order.''

Chaniff watched the secretary of defense scan the first two pages of the mission brief, flipping back and forth. "At the present time,'' Chaniff continued, "we have four F-16C air defense suppression aircraft on the ground at Bahrain. Two EF-111As and four F-15Cs and Es are scheduled to land in the next fifteen hours under cover of darkness. The Saudis will let us use one of their E-3 AWACS, and two KC-10 tankers are being diverted from Diego Garcia.''

"Why aren't you using any F-117As? I would think the stealth is ideal for this mission," Radford asked, clearing his throat.

"General James is advising against deploying them." Chaniff saw the question on Radford's face and answered before it was asked. "The stealths have a limited payload, and I also have my doubts the F-117s would be able to keep up with the strike package once it got over enemy territory. They're just not fast enough."

Radford nodded in agreement. That was Chaniff's job—to know his military equipment's capabilities.

"We considered cruise missiles, but they don't carry large enough warheads to destroy a hardened underground target. The F-15Es will have to do that with multiple 2,000-pound bomb hits." Chaniff picked up the loose photos on Radford's desk and pointed to the map. "Esfahan is located about 170 miles from the coast. It is surrounded by high mountains and steep, rocky canyons. Iran has scattered air defenses and search radars along their coast and border with Iraq, but there is no way they can cover all the airspace. James plans to have his strike package fly at low altitude, avoiding radar, destroy the weapons complex and get the hell out of the area before they know what's hit them." Chaniff sat back down, adding, "I've ordered an RC-135 Rivet Joint reconnaissance aircraft to start operations at once so we can locate any holes in their radar network."

"Fourteen aircraft . . . that's not much firepower." Radford was skeptical.

"We're using our best aircraft and pilots. Believe me, it's more than enough muscle, Mr. Secretary. We're talking about a single target. I've spoken with James extensively, and he wants a strike package that is fast and flexible without a lot of confusion." Chaniff managed an uneasy smile.

Radford rubbed his chin, looking at the ceiling for a few seconds. He wanted to be more than prepared when he walked into the meeting with the President. He then asked, "The President's going to want to know how many aircraft and air crews we're going to lose."

"The Navy should have the lightest casualties. DIA computer models show they might lose one, maybe two, A-6 attack jets to ground fire . . . triple As. We shouldn't lose any fighters unless the bastards get lucky." Chaniff swallowed. He disliked this part of his job. "The Air Force is a different story, of course, because they'll be going all the way in to take out the complex. Worst case puts the losses at five or six jets with as many as ten pilots captured or killed. It just depends on what they run into once they get over the target."

"And civilian losses?" Radford asked.

"Hard to say. But it shouldn't be more than a handful . . . I'd say a dozen."

The secretary leaned back in his leather chair. "I only have one problem with this, Howard. It's your choice of command personnel."

"Duke James is—"

"It's not James I'm concerned about," Radford interrupted. "It's Admiral Zachiem. He's going to fight you tooth and nail on this. The good admiral's going to try to make this a one hundred percent Navy show."

"He already is." Chaniff nodded in agreement.

"I've known Nelson for twenty years. He's a good man, but he's about as pigheaded as a Wyoming rancher. And if we need anything now, it's cooperation and teamwork, not solo acts."

"I agree. That's why I'm flying to the Gulf to personally brief Zachiem and James," Chaniff said determinedly. "And I'm prepared to relieve him of command if he gives me any trouble."

"Good." Radford stood. "I'll give you a call if I need your help selling the President on this."

Chaniff handed the secretary six more copies of the operations plan. "Good luck." He mocked a salute, then turned, leaving Radford's office.

Chief Engineer Khalk Hikmet had just finished supervising the loading of eighteen more cruise missiles onto two flatbed trucks for transport to Bandar Abbas. Eight more were being hauled the short distance to the air base so they could be secured to the weapons pylons of the F-4Es.

He was now alone in the lower level of the complex. Hikmet sat down, feeling exhausted and closed his eyes, listening to the soft hums of the overhead fan and the computer. He had been working for the last twenty hours straight, with nothing to eat and only water to quench his thirst, and was ready to return to his apartment for a hot shower, a plate of rice and several hours of well-deserved sleep.

He turned to the computer to call up the main menu before shutting down the machine for the night. He watched the screen flash for a few moments, his mind wandering.

The menu cursor flashed over COMPLEX:/BLUEPRINTS. Hikmet forced himself to concentrate. He hadn't used that program recently. He scrolled down the menu coming to the file containing the program for enriching the missile's fuel blend. Entering the program, he saw where he had completed his work eight hours ago. Someone else had been in the blueprints file.

Hikmet, curious and anxious, pulled the program in COMPLEX:/BLUEPRINTS onto the screen. His eyes went to the top, checking the logout time. It showed 16:14. His mind jumped. *Where was I at 16:14 this afternoon,* he thought anxiously. He felt his body tremble with fear for not being more cautious. *I was with Colonel Rahavi.*

Then it occurred to him. Perijan. She was the only person near his office during the day, and when he returned from his meeting with the colonel the door was open. He tapped the keyboard, dumping the file back into the hard drive. *What other files was she looking at?* Enraged, Hikmet scrolled through the menu, quickly accessing each file to look at the exit times. When he reached AUTO CAD:/INFRARED SYSTEM, he froze. This file had been accessed just a few minutes before the other. Perijan was looking for exact data, and she would be the only one with the ability to circumvent his security program without tripping the alarm. His face grew red with uncontrollable fury.

Hikmet slammed his right fist onto the intercom, nearly breaking the small plastic box. "I want a security team here at once!" he shouted. His outrage was more from his distress that Perijan had jeopardized him as well. If Bakhtiar knew he had left the door unlocked, he would never see daylight again. Hikmet began thinking of another explanation for how Perijan gained access to his office.

Staffer started on his second pack of cigarettes. That was the problem with working in the CIA—he always had about a dozen reasons to stall his pledge to quit. At least this vice wouldn't impair his judgment.

"It's some sort of highbred IR detection system," Admiral Currie, seated across the conference table from him, said. "And a damn good one. I had the boys in research run it through the Cray twice to make sure we didn't miss anything."

"Hal, I hope you're not saying what I think you are," Staffer said, picking up one of the detailed computer drawings. "The Iranians can't have something you and your silicon-brained buddies can't figure out, can they?" Staffer was annoyed.

"No, it's not quite that," Currie said, ignoring Staffer's remark. "They've just done a few things in a totally unconventional way. And they've built an IR detection and seeking unit better than anything we have in the West. Look at this." Currie pulled one of the black-and-white drawings from the pile. "This is the nose section of the Iranian missile. The seeker head is a copy of a standard WGU-10/B infrared imager used on our Maverick missiles, only it's nearly twice as large. My guess is it can pick up a faint heat source a couple of hundred kilometers away on a clear night. Directly under it is a laser transmitter and receiver. But that's where the similarities end. Now take a look at this." He placed another drawing on top.

"Well, it's Greek to me. What the hell is it?" Staffer said, holding the drawing one way and then another.

"This is the part that worries me," Currie answered. "This is the scanner/infrared imager unit. Directly behind it is the computer guidance system. They're using a fiberoptic laser computer with gallium arsenide-based chips to synchronize the IR imager, laser range finder and radar altimeter. The scanner converter isn't the digital version, which we still use on ninety percent of our systems. It's a damn laser!" He shook his head. "On top of that, they're using an optical storage device with a huge memory able to distinguish one target from another. That's another reason why the *Shiloh* was hit and the *John Young* wasn't."

Staffer was quiet for a long moment. "I want you to get this data to the Pentagon at once."

"It's being done right now. Edleman and I also have a team looking at ways to counter this thing."

"Shit, this is unreal." Staffer looked up as the door opened. Standing in the entrance was Tony Brady.

"Tom, may I see you? We need to talk," Brady said soberly.

"Yeah, we're finished. Hal, thanks for the good work. You guys keep on it," Staffer said, getting up to leave. He followed Brady down the main seventh-floor hallway into an empty conference room usually used to brief congressmen and other VIPs.

"The White House got a call from ABC about twenty minutes ago," Brady said while he turned on the TV and adjusted the sound. "They're going to break a major foreign policy story at the top of the hour and the CIA's going to be involved.''

"What's it about?'' Staffer asked, sighing.

"They wouldn't tell us. I only know the topic is going to be the unauthorized sale of weapons.''

"Are you thinking what I'm thinking?'' Staffer asked, recalling Senator Jenrette's smile as she drove off.

"I sure am.'' Brady answered.

"*. . . We now join Amy Asbell outside the CIA. Amy, what can you tell us about the alleged illegal weapons sale to Middle Eastern countries which is being conducted by the CIA and the Pentagon?*''

"*Well, Peter, ABC has learned that the CIA has been involved in the illegal sale and transfer of highly advanced technical equipment to Iran and possibly other countries in the region.*''

Staffer stared, captivated by the television. The reporter was standing outside the east entrance to the CIA, her red, white and blue scarf blowing in the afternoon breeze. Behind her, the glass-enclosed guard station acted as a backdrop.

"*Earlier this afternoon, briefing papers were supplied to our Washington office detailing a covert CIA operation in which advanced radars and electronic weapon upgrades for American-built F-4E Phantoms were sold to Iran.*'' The screen showed three computer-generated images of CIA documents. "*At first, White House Press Secretary Drusilla Spaigh denied any knowledge of the operation, but she has since told us the President and his top aides are now looking into the report to see if any laws were broken.*''

"That *fucking* bitch. I can't believe she squealed to the press,'' Staffer said, knowing the senator was the only possible source.

"Shut up, Tom,'' Brady grunted. "I want to hear this.''

"*Amy, you said these are weapon upgrades for F-4 Phantoms. I assume these are the jets that the U.S. sold to Iran when the Shah was still in power?*''

"*That's correct, Peter. Many of those aircraft are now over a quarter of a century old and would need the upgrades if they are to keep up to Western standards.*''

"*Can you tell us how long this has been going on and why it is we would sell weapons to Iran?*''

"*According to a reliable source in the Senate, this operation was initially set up about a year ago and was designed to sell F-4 upgrades as part of a plan to win Iranian confidence and*

generate feelings of goodwill. However, it is now believed the
CIA is possibly using this operation as a cover to expand the sale
of weapons, including advanced radars . . .''

"A cover to expand what?" Brady bellowed. "What kind of
blarney is that! Damn it! And didn't that bitch from Colorado
stop to think she just put one of our officers in danger? Collins
could be a dead man! Tom, you'd better . . ." The DCI turned
and realized Staffer was already out of the room. Hal Currie was
standing motionless in the hallway with his arms full of documents. Brady walked over and slammed off the television with
his fist, breaking the plastic knob.

"There's got to be a way to contact him," Currie said, joining
Brady in the room. "Some way of warning him."

"It wouldn't matter even if we could contact him," Brady said.
He looked at his wristwatch, quickly calculating the difference in
time. "How long do you think it will take the Iranians to figure
out who's been selling them F-4 parts? The fuckers watch CNN
just like everyone else." He felt ready to explode.

Currie stood not saying a word, watching Brady pace across
the room.

"Don't you have something you should be doing? Damn it to
hell, get busy! Staffer can't do it all by himself! We're not going
to leave Collins to be dragged through the streets by the damn
Iranians!" Brady stormed out of the room, deciding he'd better
wait to cool down before he spoke to Senator Jenrette.

Chapter Twenty-one

ESFAHAN, IRAN

Perijan wiped the tears from her swollen eyes and rolled over in bed. She stared into the dim light filtering through the curtains of her room. The stale air was hot and still. From somewhere outside she could hear the wail of a stray cat, the eerie shrieks penetrating the thin walls of her apartment.

She couldn't sleep. Her mind was spinning with a hundred thoughts. Perijan peeled off the sheet and dressed herself in an ankle-length navy blue skirt and white blouse. She walked to the bathroom and splashed cold water on her face, trying to clear her mind. *Allah help me. I need your strength,* she prayed. Her mind drifted to her dead father in the next room. She hoped he was now in peace.

Perijan walked slowly through the dark apartment and sat down in her father's favorite chair. It still smelled like him. She buried her face in her hands, trying not to think.

Perijan froze and looked up. She heard the muffled sounds of several car doors slamming. None of her neighbors owned cars, making the sound unusual, particularly in the middle of night. She rose and hurried to the front door, making sure it was locked. Guardedly, she pulled the curtain back and looked outside. Across the street, a hundred feet away from the nearest streetlight, were two cars with several men standing around them. A third vehicle pulled up and turned off its headlights. She could tell by its silhouette that it was an armored personnel carrier. Within a few seconds, seven or eight men could be seen standing in the center of the street.

"Those are soldiers . . . Revolutionary Guards. They must have learned about the computer!" Perijan panicked, muttering to herself. She quickly made her way back into her bedroom, where she grabbed her chador and reached into the top drawer of the dresser for a small leather satchel filled with 20,000 rials. Perijan dropped to her hands and knees and crawled to her bed. She pulled the rug aside and fumbled for a small box under the dirty wooden floor, the only possessions she would take from home.

She dashed to the back door and searched the outside. Seeing no one, she ran out into the alley and quickly hid along an extended wall of the neighboring apartment, using her chador as a blanket of cover. She cowered in the darkness to await the men approaching her door from each side.

They stood motionless before it for a moment, then all at once burst through. She peered out from her cover and seeing the alley was clear, rushed on toward the next building, stopping only long enough to catch her breath.

The sounds of men shouting and cars being started were echoing in the alley as she continued working her way out of the area.

Mark Collins felt a bead of cool sweat run down the side of his face and drop off. The tingling feeling forced him out of a shallow sleep. He stretched and yawned, looking for the glowing face of the alarm clock on the nightstand next to the bed. It wasn't there. He looked out the window and realized the normally bright hotel sign was also dark.

Damn . . . the electricity is still off. Collins guessed the temperature of the room was near a hundred degrees. That wasn't all that was giving him a fitful sleep, but in order to get some rest he tried to keep his mind off Perijan.

He finally got out of bed. He was hot, sweaty and tired and needed a cold shower.

Thoughts of Christine and his daughter filled his mind as he let the water run over him. *When I get out of this shithole, I'm going back to a nice desk job*, he told himself. He then wondered if he'd ever get home, but quickly dismissed the idea as paranoia. *What could possibly go wrong*?

After dressing, Collins grabbed both of his false Iranian IDs and placed them in his back pocket. Closing the door, he walked out into the lobby. The two goons were sleeping in chairs in a corner. He walked outside. The night air was cooler than his room and felt good. A brisk forty-five-minute walk would help him get his mind cleared. He turned right and strolled down the empty street.

TEHRAN, IRAN

Defense Minister Sheik Ali Bin Bakhtiar stepped into the main room of his apartment. Standing at the door was his personal bodyguard, Hassan Zadeh. "Well, come in, Zadeh. What is it? What could possibly be going on that is so important you must disturb my sleep at this hour?" Bakhtiar said, wrapping a robe around himself.

"Colonel Rahavi has reported that Hikmet informed him someone has copied certain computer files." Zadeh stood with his chest puffed out, as if he had run all the way to the apartment.

"What? What do you mean, certain files? Which ones?"

"Structural plans to the weapons complex at Esfahan, along with details of how the guidance system of the Phalanx Dragon functions. He is now concerned the mission may fail."

"This is an outrage! Who . . . who has betrayed the revolution?" Bakhtiar asked, trying to control his rage.

"The girl, Perijan Reza," Zadeh answered without emotion.

"The woman. She should never have been trusted in such a position. I warned Hikmet of this, but he refused to listen to me." Bakhtiar moved toward the entrance of the apartment. He could see the headlights of his waiting car and two guards standing nearby.

"Let me dress, then I will go to the ministry building," Bakhtiar ordered. "I will have to attend to this myself."

Propping herself up with both arms, Perijan gently lowered her legs into the darkened confines of a tunnel opening. She looked around one last time, seeing the silhouettes of two men running past. She had decided the sewer tunnels would be her best choice for an escape. That is, if the fumes didn't overcome her.

You must do this, Perijan, she told herself. Closing her eyes, she fell the last few feet down the shaft. Spider webs covered her face as she slipped into the tunnel. She let out a brief gasp but fought back the urge to scream. Reaching out, she grabbed some debris from around the area and haphazardly concealed the tunnel's entrance.

Ducking her head, she crawled on her hands and knees down the sewer tunnel. It was pitch black and the putrid smell of mildew and rotting animal carcasses turned her stomach. Perijan forced herself to concentrate on staying alive and just getting to the other end. She had been in the tunnel once before. When they were children, her brothers had dared her to go through with them. She recalled the tunnel would run straight for twenty feet or so, then make a slight turn to the left. It would angle downward and stop somewhere under the center of the street, on top of the main sewer line.

The tunnel was curving to the left and she felt it starting to slope downhill slightly. The air was changing from moist and hot to a damp cool. She kept one end of her chador up to her nose as the smells grew stronger.

By now her heart was pounding in her chest so hard she could barely inhale. Her breath was becoming short, and she felt herself starting to panic. The darkness and constriction of the tunnel were beginning to overwhelm her, and she wished to be out in the open.

The image of her father sitting at their kitchen table flashed across her mind. Suddenly she remembered his good friend Tufayli. He and his family were friends of Perijan's. His boys were the same age as her brothers, but he too lost his only sons in the revolution. His wife, unable to cope, had taken her own life. They had not seen him for some time, but Perijan felt certain that if he were still around, he would help her escape.

"Yes, Father . . ." she whispered, wondering if he had sent her that message from wherever he was. Determined now, Perijan lowered her head and crawled as fast as she could, nearly hitting her head against the end of the brick tunnel.

The entrance to the storm sewer was covered with several layers of garbage bags. She clawed at the bags, violently ripping them away. As she did, the main tunnel filled with the rancid smell of human waste and the sound of running water. She countered the sudden reflex to vomit by breathing through her mouth and climbed into a large concrete pipe. She guessed the storm sewer was four feet in diameter, just barely large enough for her to stand stooped over.

Up ahead she could see the soft glow of streetlights filtering down through the drains located by the curbs above her. There was barely enough light to lead the way. The high-pitched squeal of rats behind her forced Perijan to move forward rapidly. *Now I have to find my way out of this place*, she thought, and hurried on.

Ali Fesseghi swept the room with his flashlight. Two other guards carried kerosene lanterns, which cast a yellow glow throughout the small hotel room. The bed was unmade and clothes were still hanging neatly in the closet. Nothing seemed out of place, but the man he had known as Kahman was not in the room.

"Look what we have found here," a bearded middle-aged security guard, having ripped the bottom out of a suitcase, said. He held up the black wig and glasses. "Look what else is here. They're hollow. Used to—"

"I know what they're used for, stupid!" Fesseghi said between gritted teeth, seeing the tubes used to pass documents. "I want one of you to stay here. If he should return, bring him to me."

Fesseghi unplugged the computer and exited the room, with the guard following. He needed to find the American or his own neck would be on the line. He walked to the front lobby. The two tails were standing there, trying to appear alert, when it was obvious they had been snoozing only moments earlier.

"They say he has not left the building all night," a Revolutionary Guard said once Fesseghi reached them.

"Is that so? Well, you idiots, he is not in his room!"

"We were here the whole time and he never left," the fatter man stammered.

"Then perhaps you let him walk out of here without following him."

"No, no . . . it isn't that way at all. We were taking turns watching and I was sleeping. It was his turn to stay awake and watch . . ." The skinny man began professing his innocence and trying to blame his partner. "Why, you pig!" the other said, and the two lunged for each other. The guards quickly pulled them apart.

"Imbeciles! You have let him go! For how many nights has

this been going on?'' Fesseghi was beyond the point of being rational. "Take them, take them away!" The two guards grabbed the men by their arms and dragged them outside.

"What does the desk clerk have to say?" Fesseghi asked, as he stalked over to the counter.

"He says he was asleep also, but only for a few minutes."

Ali Fesseghi slammed his left fist onto the front desk, causing the clerk to jump back shakily.

"I do *not* believe you! How much did the American pay you to keep your mouth shut?" Fesseghi demanded. "Is it enough for you to lose your life . . . because that is what is going to happen."

"I . . . I don't know what you're talking about. I fell asleep, but only for a few minutes. I beg you and Allah to believe what I say. I speak the truth. I am only an old man. I have tried to do what you have asked me to do," the frail man pleaded, his voice quavering.

Fesseghi looked at him in disgust. The clerk's white hair was unkept and oily; his yellowing teeth were broken and chipped, and his thin, wrinkled face looked pitifully helpless as he stood stooped over, trying to defend himself.

"I am paying you to inform me of any unusual happenings in this hotel. You know that the two guards have fallen asleep and yet you do not let me know. You are not to be trusted. Tell me what else you know!" Fesseghi snarled.

"I know nothing. He must have—"

"Shut up!" Fesseghi looked around. "Who gave this fool this assignment?" No one answered. Fesseghi turned to the lead Revolutionary Guard. "Have the entire building searched—every single room. Is that understood? I want him found!"

"Yes, sir."

"Replace the old man. If this happens again, I'll hold you responsible. I'm returning to the air base," Fesseghi said, squeezing the handle of the computer case he was carrying. "When you find the American, be sure he is brought to me immediately."

"Yes, sir."

"Well . . . start your search NOW!" Fesseghi shouted, as the man quickly hurried away.

*   *   *

Perijan brushed her hair out of her eyes and stood up after squirming out through the storm drain. She was relieved to be back out onto an empty, shadowy street. She realized she was dirty and smelled from walking through the storm sewer. *It doesn't matter*, she told herself, *at least I can breathe clean air again.*

Perijan guessed she had crawled two miles. She was now southeast of her apartment, near the old bus station. Sighing, she thanked Allah, thinking it would be easier finding a taxi near the station than waiting for one to drive by. But then she stopped, wondering if that would be one of the first places they would search for her. Still, she needed transportation.

Making sure her forehead and neck were covered, Perijan walked rapidly toward the bus station. She hoped she could find the American in time to warn him. If they were onto her, it was very possible they were onto him as well. Ten minutes later, Perijan rounded the corner and saw the lights of the bus station ahead. She slowed her pace, taking in the surroundings. A single streetlight illuminated the loading area in front of the station.

"There's a taxi," she breathed aloud. Several people were climbing out of a plain blue Ford sedan. Waiting until they had retrieved their luggage and paid the fare, she approached the driver when he was climbing back into the car.

"Taxi . . . I need a taxi," Perijan announced only audibly enough for the man to hear.

He turned toward her. "I am off duty now. I've had a long night and must go home."

"I will pay you," Perijan said, her hand trembling slightly as she held out 3,000 rials, double the going rate for an hour-long ride.

The driver studied the money in her hand, then looked up at her face. "I will take you. Hurry and get in."

Perijan gave him the money and scrambled into the back seat. She averted her eyes, seeing that the man was staring at her in the rearview mirror. He was undoubtedly wondering what a young girl was doing out in the middle of the night . . . alone. She felt compelled to say something.

"Take me to the Kowsar Hotel. My husband has just returned from many months of military duty. SAVAMA says I can see him," she said, hoping the man didn't notice her clothes or the door.

The driver grunted and pulled away from the curb without another word or glance.

THE PENTAGON

It had taken Tom Staffer an hour to set up a meeting with General Howard Chaniff. *It's probably a good thing it did take that long*, Staffer thought. At least he had cooled down enough to think straight and formulate a plan.

"General Chaniff will see you now, Mr. Staffer."

"Thanks." He entered the chairman's office and closed the door.

"Mr. Staffer." Chaniff greeted him and they shook hands. "I understand you have a problem that we might be able to help you with."

"I hope so, General. One of my men's life depends on it. Mind if I use this?" Staffer pointed to a bulletin board on the wall.

"Be my guest."

Staffer removed and unfolded a forty-eight-by-forty-eight-inch laminated black-and-white satellite topography map from his briefcase, pinning it on the large board. In the upper right-hand corner was the city of Esfahan, with every road, bridge and building shown in precise detail.

"I'm going to get right to the point. As you know, we have a CIA officer in Iran and his cover's been blown. I'm here to recommend an Echo mission to get him out . . . alive." Staffer's tone was one of urgent demanding rather than asking.

"So you know where he is?" Chaniff asked, surprised.

"His precise location, no. Not right now," Staffer replied. He watched Chaniff fold his arms and glance at the map. He didn't like the chairman's expression.

"All right. What do you have in mind?"

"With every CIA operation we have several backup plans for these types of emergencies." Staffer cleared his throat and turned to the map. "Collins has orders to proceed to this location if he's discovered or if things begin to look shitty. And I'd say that it looks more than shitty from where he's sitting.

"Located fifty miles southwest of Esfahan and just north of the town Shahr Kord is an abandoned silver mine." Staffer tapped the map with his knuckles. "The Iranians haven't used the mine for six years. Collins has orders to make it to this area in the first twenty-four hours of a crisis. He'll wait there for two days. If we don't get a team in to rescue him, then he's to try to make it to the mountains north of Haft Gel. He will wait there for another forty-eight hours before heading to the coast." Staffer finished and looked at Chaniff.

"You're asking me to send a special forces team 150 miles inland to extract one of your officers, who you don't even know for sure will be there, when they have probably figured out we'll be trying to get him out?" Chaniff shook his head. "No way, Tom . . . it's too risky. Especially with this new weapon of theirs."

"This entire area is full of steep ridges and mountains. The aircraft can sneak in under radar at night. There's a dirt road just below the mining camp. Satellite photos show it's long and flat enough for a C-130 to land. I'm not talking about more than thirty, forty minutes on the ground." Staffer's voice was more urgent now. He became quiet, knowing that the general was thinking.

Staffer understood Chaniff's reaction. The CIA was calling on the military to clean up one of its dirty little messes, again. The military had a bad taste from CIA Echo missions, Echo being the code word for "extraction." Off the record, Air Force, Navy and Marine pilots called them Ejection missions. Staffer recalled that during the cold war, military pilots, primarily from the Air Force and Marines, would penetrate Soviet and Chinese airspace with specially modified helicopters and light fixed-wing aircraft. Their missions were to try to rescue CIA officers and agents who needed to get out of the country fast. Even though the missions were generally conducted near the border, Pentagon records showed the success rate was less than thirty percent, and many pilots lost their lives while making the attempts.

"This isn't a simple snatch-and-grab, Tom. My men would have to be in Iranian airspace for at least three hours with slow-moving aircraft. I'm sorry, but there's no way I can authorize this." Chaniff shook his head. "I can't risk it."

Staffer sucked in a deep breath and held it before speaking. "During the Gulf War, we routinely rescued pilots deep inside Iraq. This would be the same sort of mission. Hell, General, all I'm asking for is a couple of Pave Low choppers supported by one or two C-130s. They can follow your strike team into the country. If the Iranians discover them, the aircraft can turn and get out.''

"The difference Mr. Staffer, is we generally had a good idea where the pilots were located. In all honesty, your man could be dead by now.'' The general's voice grew coldly formal. "Now, I really—''

"His name is Mark Collins. He's a friend of mine and he has a family.''

"I don't want to hear this. Every man I send out there has a family.'' Chaniff placed his hands on his desk and folded them, looking directly up at Staffer.

"I know Collins. He's not dead and they're not going to capture him.'' Staffer was beginning to feel angry that Chaniff wouldn't even give an inch. That was why he had come up with so many options. At least one should work. "If there's a way out, he'll find it and I need someone to be there when he does. You must be able to meet him at one of those three checkpoints.''

"General James is having a hard enough time putting this mission together without worrying about a side show—''

"James is in charge of this operation?'' Staffer interrupted.

"Yes. He's commanding the Esfahan strike package.''

"Then all I ask is that you at least get his opinion,'' Staffer said, certain that if Duke learned it was Collins trying to get out of Iran, he would pull the strings necessary for an Echo mission. He hated it when people used their influence for family or friends, but knowing that Collins's life was on the line made him appreciate the opportunity.

Chaniff's thin lips came together. "All right, Mr. Staffer. I'll agree to that. But I want a complete mission outline before I leave for the Gulf in four hours.'' He paused. "No, on second thought, I have a better idea. Go home and pack your bags. You're going with me.'' Chaniff stood, walking Staffer to the door.

"What?'' Staffer asked, staring at the general in disbelief.

"If this mission of yours ends in disaster, the CIA's going to be the fall guy, not the Air Force,'' Chaniff answered.

"I'll see you in four hours.'' Staffer smiled with confidence.

Collins ducked between two buildings as a second black Mercedes sped toward the hotel. He checked his watch, 4:18 A.M., and wondered what was happening. Only government officials or wealthy Iranian businessmen drove 300SEs, and Collins doubted much business was being conducted at this time of the morning.

Staying low, he made his way to the rear of the two buildings and hopped over a wire fence leading to an alley that intersected the main street fifty yards from the hotel. Staying in the shadows, he carefully approached the edge of the street, then knelt down and looked to his right. The electricity was back on and the hotel's yellow-and-red neon sign was on. Parked in front were several Mercedes and one armored personnel carrier. Several men with AK-47s strapped across their backs were standing near the entrance to the hotel.

Oh man, I'm up the creek now . . . and without a paddle, he thought, and cursed softly. He studied the hotel, searching the rows of windows along the second floor. His room would be the seventh window. *There it is. Light's off.*

Two men emerged from the hotel, climbed into the personnel carrier and drove off. Collins allowed himself to breathe a little easier. If they were looking for him, they wouldn't be driving away. Something had happened, but it didn't have anything to do with him. Collins felt reassured.

Before standing, he glanced at the second-floor window one last time. He saw something—the curtain moved and the silhouette of a man passed the window. His heart skipped a beat. *Thanks, buddy. They're in my room, all right. Son of a bitch, how could this happen? There is no way they could have known. I've done everything the right way.* His mind flashed to the computer. *The bastards are going to get their hands on it. They've probably torn everything else apart by now. I just hope the auto-destruct blows someone's hands off.*

He moved a little farther into the alley, still keeping his eyes on the hotel. *I'll have to find a way to contact Zenith.*

"Drop me across the street from the hotel, please," Perijan said as forcefully as she could. The taxi driver grunted something, then slowed and swerved to the right.

Perijan surveyed the area around the hotel. The gas streetlights illuminated the area fairly well. She immediately noticed several men in civilian clothes and two soldiers standing outside. Two of the men were smoking cigarettes. Only two cars were parked along the street, and everything seemed quiet. *It isn't that unusual to see soldiers at all hours of the night*, Perijan reminded herself.

The taxi came to an abrupt stop. She remained seated for a few seconds, trying to muster the courage to climb out of the car.

"This is the place. I want to go home," the taxi driver said and turned in his seat.

Perijan opened the car door and got out.

Collins watched curiously to see who was getting out of the beat-up taxi. It seemed strange that someone would be arriving at four o'clock in the morning. Then, seeing it was a woman, he scrutinized her more closely. It was hard to see her features since her chador covered her completely. The woman stayed on the corner, moving her head left and right, as if looking for someone.

When she turned in his direction Collins caught a glimpse of her face. He realized at once that it was Perijan. Without a second thought, he stood up and walked out of the alley away from the building. He tried not to run as he moved swiftly down the stone sidewalk toward Perijan.

"My sister . . . I am over here," Collins blurted out, hoping the guards wouldn't pay attention to them.

Perijan twisted around and caught sight of a man approaching her. It was too dark for her to make out his features, but she did notice he had a beard and was wearing a white long-sleeved shirt. Her first thought was to get back into the taxi and order the driver to take her away. The man had not yet driven off and appeared to be waiting to see what she was going to do. Frozen and indecisive, Perijan stood while Collins approached.

Out of the corner of one eye she saw one of the guards throw down his cigarette and start to move toward her. A second guard swung his AK-47 around, pointing the assault rifle in her direction.

Stricken with fear that they had recognized her, Perijan jumped back into the taxi and shouted to the driver, "*Go . . . Go!*"

"Taxi . . . wait, taxi!" Collins yelled at the top of his lungs. He knew the guards heard him that time and no longer tried to be unobtrusive. Unconsciously, he had broken into a dead run to catch Perijan and the taxi. The car was only fifty feet away. The driver turned around and looked at him.

"Stop! That is my sister," Collins called out, waving his right hand in the air.

"You . . . stop or I'll shoot," one of the guards shouted at Collins from across the street.

Collins could see the man shoulder his rifle. Just then a puff of blue smoke erupted from the tailpipe of the taxi. It was pulling away from the curb. Collins sprinted up to the left-side passenger door as the car sputtered, picking up speed. Grabbing the handle, he threw the door open and jumped inside. His body hit Perijan's, knocking her to other side as she let out a gasp.

"What is happening? What is happening?" the driver shrieked, stepping on the accelerator.

"Just drive! Go before they shoot us all!" Collins ordered.

They heard the sharp crackling sound of gunfire. The back window exploded as several bullets fragmented the glass, sending shards flying onto both Collins and Perijan. The frightened driver slouched and jammed his foot on the accelerator. Collins ducked as a dozen more bullets ripped into the back of the car. He felt the engine rev and the car swerve right. The wheels spun throwing up rocks and gravel.

"Are you okay?" he asked Perijan, trying to help her steady herself in the seat.

"Yes . . . yes," she said, looking at his face, then realizing who he was.

Straightening, Collins could see that the driver was turning down a narrow side street. "Turn right at the next intersection," he instructed. "And you'd better move this thing a lot faster if we're going to get out of here."

"I . . . I can't . . ." the driver moaned, then slumped over onto the wheel. Two deep red spots spread on the man's shirt.

"Oh, shit. Perijan, help me." Collins grabbed the steering wheel in time to keep the car from hitting a row of trash cans. Using his other hand, he pulled the driver by the collar, forcing him onto the passenger seat. Perijan awkwardly tried to help but was truly stunned by the whole affair. Collins threw his legs over the seat, sliding down to take control of the car. A moment later they exited the alley, and Collins turned right onto Kehandezh Street. They were now headed west, away from the city.

Defense Minister Sheik Ali Bin Bakhtiar slammed the teacup in his hand down on the saucer. Both pieces of china shattered, and he immediately used his arm to swipe them onto the floor.

"They let the CIA scum slip through their hands!" he shouted. "I will not tolerate this incompetence! I want this man caught, put on trial and hanged in public for all to see." His voice cracked with anger.

"Ali Fesseghi is heading up the search," Hassan Zadeh said, walking back in after calling someone to clean up the mess.

"Fesseghi is the fool who allowed this man into our country to begin with," Bakhtiar sneered at his bodyguard.

"We must assume the girl and the American spy are working together," Zadeh cautioned. His muscular body stiffened as he considered what he would like to do to them both.

"This man and this woman must be caught, Zadeh," Bakhtiar said calmly. "I am sending you to Esfahan. You will assist Fesseghi in the capture of the two spies." There was a moment of silence as the defense minister thought through the implications of this new development. "This has changed everything. No doubt the Americans know of our plans." He picked up the phone linked with Colonel Rahavi's private quarters at Esfahan Air Base.

"Rahavi here."

"This is Minister Bakhtiar. Listen to me very carefully. You are correct that the mission plans need to be reconsidered under the circumstances. The girl who got into Hikmet's files is working with an American spy. I want you to accelerate your preparations and attack the American fleet within twenty-four hours, before they have time to act on the information they have received."

"My aircraft will not be—"

"They must be ready!" Bakhtiar shouted. "You have your orders!" He hung up the phone.

Minister Bakhtiar felt his heart palpitating. He reached into his top drawer, removing two of the bright blue Inderal tablets. "Get me some more tea," he demanded, and realized his guard had already done so. "Then be on your way. And Zadeh? Don't disappoint me."

ANDREWS AIR FORCE BASE

Tom Staffer looked out the window of the C-21A Air Force jet transport and noticed that a slight rain was hitting the tarmac. It had been a long day, but he didn't feel tired. The pilot advanced the throttles and the eight-passenger aircraft swung around, heading for the end of the runway.

"Would you like something to drink, sir?" an Air Force staff sergeant said, holding a stainless steel coffee pot.

"Yeah . . . sure," Staffer answered, taking a cup. He looked over at Chaniff. His head was leaning against the side of the fuselage, his arms folded. *Hell, we're not even in the air yet and he's asleep*, Staffer thought. He took a sip of the coffee, feeling it burn his tongue.

"Did you bring the mission profile?" Chaniff asked with his eyes closed.

Staffer tapped his briefcase. "Both a hard and soft copy."

"Good. When we get in the air, have the sergeant transmit it to James." Chaniff put a small pillow under his head. "You might as well relax, Tom. It's going to be a long plane ride."

"Well I'm a little uptight right now," Staffer replied.

"How long you been in this line of work?" Chaniff asked.

"Twenty-four years."

"And you haven't learned yet that worrying doesn't change anything?" Chaniff reclined his chair, never opening his eyes. "I personally find that I do some of my best problem-solving when I sleep."

"Well, you sleep and I'll worry. Between the two of us maybe everything will turn out all right," Staffer said and returned his gaze to the window as the jet came to a brief stop. Then he watched the blinking runway lights start to flash by as the jet soared up and became airborne. It banked to the left, climbing.

Collins turned down a side street and used the parking brake to slow the car so the brake lights wouldn't come on. In the rearview mirror he saw several vehicles streak past two streets away.

"There's a place. Next to that pile of boxes." Perijan pointed to a heap of garbage stacked next to the side of a building.

Collins pulled up next to the pile and got out of the car. He opened the passenger door and picked up the driver by the arms, hauling him over to the debris. Collins laid him on his side and quickly covered the man's body so he couldn't be seen by a passerby. Then he climbed back into the car as Perijan sat up front. Collins looked into her eyes, wishing she didn't look at him so helplessly. "You could have gotten us both killed."

Perijan blinked. "They came for me. I knew they must have learned about the computer disks . . . I didn't know what else to do."

Collins let out a long breath and rubbed his face with both hands.

"I didn't mean to bring harm to you," Perijan said uneasily.

"It's not your fault. I just need to think." Collins scratched his beard.

"If they find us . . . you know they will kill us." Perijan's voice cracked.

"Yeah, well, they're not going to find us. Listen, we need to find some other transportation. They're going to be looking for this taxi." Collins contemplated their dilemma as he put the taxi into gear, pulling away.

"I know where we must go. Turn right at the next main street and stay on it until we get to the highway," Perijan advised.

"Why didn't I think to just ask you where we should go?" Collins smiled and wheeled the car around, pushing the gas pedal to the floor. The taxi accelerated sluggishly, its engine shaking and vibrating from lack of maintenance. "Where are you taking us?"

"South of town, to a friend of my father's. His name is Tufayli. He will help us," Perijan said quietly.

Collins checked the rearview mirror again to make sure no one was following them. His first instinct was to head for the main highway leading out of town. They needed to get to the mining camp as soon as possible, and he reasoned it would take the Revolutionary Guards an hour or so to set up a road block. *First things first*, he forced himself to think rationally. *We have to find a new car and put together a plan.*

"I hope this place is close," Collins said. "It's going to be light in another hour." He was feeling apprehensive.

Chapter Twenty-two

BAHRAIN AIR BASE

Bathed in pale blue light, the Air Force command and control center at Bahrain had been designed to maximize a limited amount of space. Located thirty feet below the ground near the control tower, the chamber was jammed full of computers, radios and radar monitors in a very neat and efficient manner. General Duke James stood in the doorway and watched the mix of men and women at their workstations. Along the far wall were the communication consoles, including an encrypted satcom uplink and downlink, connecting them to the Pentagon and national command authorities.

The right side of the room contained six large blue computer-generated screens, with technicians seated in front of them. Each displayed a different region of the Gulf. The center screen showed flashing blue, red and green symbols representing all the aircraft and ships in the region.

Duke looked to his left at Colonel Eddie Naylor, who was seated at one of the computers. He poured himself a cup of black coffee and walked over, taking a seat next to Naylor.

"Good morning, Eddie."

"No, it's not, General," Naylor said, continuing to tap with a rapid hunt-and-peck method on a keyboard.

"Oh yeah?" Duke asked, caught off-guard. He watched the

changing data and waited for Naylor to fill him in.

Naylor reached over and ripped a long report off the printer. He handed the sheet to Duke.

Duke glanced over the report, barely able to read it in the low light of the command center. He felt the blood slowly rushing to his face. "All this ordnance should have been here twelve hours ago." He shook his head, not holding back his frustration. "I requested AGM-88Cs, not the B model. And GBU-10Bs, not 15s. Hell, for this mission 500-pound bombs are worthless."

"Yeah, well, I have more good news. The GBU-28 bunker busters you requested haven't left Incirlik yet, and some idiot shipped us optically guided rather than laser-guided Mavericks." Naylor was just as frustrated as Duke.

"Damn it! Chaniff assured me we would get everything I requested within twelve hours. Everything should be on the ground now. What about the aircraft?"

"I really do have some good news there. The 15-Cs and EF-111As arrived four hours ago. The maintenance crew's giving them a final once-over before loading the missiles on the Eagles. The E models are in the air." Naylor looked at his watch. "They should touch down in forty-five minutes, an hour max."

Duke's jaw hardened. "I can have the best aircraft in the world, but if I don't have bombs to drop, it won't matter. Get on the horn. I want every bomb and bullet I requested in the main maintenance hangar in six hours, and I don't give a shit if they have to fly them in from the States!"

"It's being done, sir," Naylor said, shaking his head. Duke had requested him for a reason, and he just proved it was a sound choice. Naylor had started straightening out the mess instead of waiting for an order.

"Good. I want this thing rock solid as soon as possible. You have the mission profiles ready?" Duke asked.

"Just about. I'm waiting for one more transmission from our friends at Langley and I'll have them wrapped up."

"All right. I'm going to get something to eat," Duke said. Naylor returned to the computer.

"General James. This transmission just came through from General Chaniff." A young female lieutenant handed Duke a report. The front page outlined its contents.

Duke quickly scanned the document. *Son of a bitch . . . Collins is in Iran.*

ESFAHAN, IRAN

The sun was a glowing ball as Mark Collins and Perijan Reza
came to the end of a single-lane dirt road. Collins slowed the car.
It wasn't what he had expected. Located at the base of a rock-
covered hill on the outer edges of Esfahan, and surrounded by a
makeshift chain-link fence, their destination looked to be a miniature junkyard. He guessed the fence encircled five or six acres.
Along the back of the property were four broken-down tractors,
with flat tires and dead weeds ringing them. Their green paint
was bleached from the scalding desert sun. In the center of the
lot were several cars propped up on cement blocks, none of which
contained windshields. Against the fence were a couple more;
these looked to be in fairly good shape. In the nearest corner,
surrounded by several dented washing machines and air-
conditioning units, was a small, weathered house. Five large television antennas sprouted from the roof.

Collins pulled up next to the gate and shut off the engine. A
cloud of dust settled behind the car. The air was still and everything appeared quiet. "You're sure about this?" He looked at
Perijan.

"Yes. He will help us." Without hesitation, Perijan exited the
car.

"Do not tell him who I am. Just say we're friends," Collins
instructed, deciding to stay in the vehicle.

"I understand."

He watched her walk up to the door, knock and go inside.
I hope she knows what she's doing, he thought. He began surveying the surrounding area.

Colonel Rahavi stepped out of his staff car and slipped on his
sunglasses. Dressed in pleated light olive pants and a paler olive
shirt, he walked into the main hangar at the Esfahan air base. He
stood for a second or two and observed the maintenance crews
at work.

Along the far wall, parked in an organized row, were eight
F-4E Phantoms. Their twin canopies were raised and dirty gray
radomes opened, exposing their radars. Several maintenance personnel were gathered around each jet. Rahavi could see that most
of the avionic access panels were open and thick black cables
dangled from each of the fighters as the crews checked the elec-

trical systems. Stacked next to the jets on heavy custom-made steel weapons racks, covered with black canvas tarps, were the cruise missiles. Three maintenance men were starting to attach the first black missile to the fighter nearest him. He watched a hydraulic lift raise the missile to the weapons pylon under the right wing.

"I wasn't expecting you, sir," the senior maintenance sergeant said, saluting him.

"Status report," Rahavi barked, not returning the salute.

"We are running two hours ahead of plan, Colonel. Ten F-4s are loaded and ready. The other aircraft will be ready to fly on schedule."

"And the air defense fighters? What is their status?"

"Twelve F-4s are now operational. I personally supervised the loading of each air-to-air missile. We just have to fuel them." The sergeant was obviously proud of his accomplishments.

"That is not good enough," Rahavi grunted.

"I have followed your orders, sir. Everything has—"

Rahavi held up his hand, cutting off the man. "There has been a change of plans, Sergeant. I order you to have all fighters, including the MiGs, armed and ready for combat in eighteen hours."

"Eighteen hours? I will need twice the men. I . . . that will be . . ." the sergeant protested, then stopped, knowing it was better to keep his mouth shut.

Rahavi only stared at the man, then looked back at the nearest F-4Es. He knew it would be impossible to have all the jets ready for combat in eighteen hours. But if he pushed the sergeant and the ground crews to the limit, he might have just enough fighters to complete the mission. At least, that's what he hoped.

"Move the MiG-29s and the F-14s into the hangar. I want them armed and put on alert at once." Rahavi folded his hands behind his back and started walking down the flight line. "I will brief the pilots in six hours. I expect a full update in four hours." He turned around. "Do you understand me?"

"Yes, Colonel . . . I understand."

Rahavi strode back to his staff car.

Hassan Zadeh checked to make sure his pistol was cocked and securely placed in its shoulder holster before entering the security office at Esfahan Air Base. He buttoned his sports jacket, covering the pistol and his broad chest. Walking up the gravel pathway, he tried to anticipate what he would encounter once inside. Zadeh suspected that Ali Fesseghi would be cautious on his arrival, and rightfully so. After all, it was Fesseghi's poor judgment that allowed the American to intrude on one of Iran's most secure air bases. Men making lesser mistakes were routinely disposed of quietly in the dark of the night.

Zadeh flashed his ID at the two guards standing outside the door.

"You may proceed," one of them said.

Zadeh entered the building. Most members of Iran's armed forces and internal security team thought of him as being more than Bakhtiar's personal bodyguard. Some considered him the second most powerful man in Iran's military because of his access to the Supreme Defense Council's innermost secrets. Zadeh didn't discourage the rumors. He used the perception to his advantage, letting military officers and senior members of SAVAMA know that in the past Bakhtiar had called on only him to accomplish missions of extreme importance to the revolution and to Bakhtiar's political career.

Zadeh rounded the corner and entered a protected section of the building. Seated at a desk, dressed in a black Western-style business suit with a white shirt and gray floral tie, was Ali Fesseghi.

"Mr. Zadeh. I was informed of your arrival just minutes ago," Fesseghi said, standing up but not offering a hand to greet him.

"I understand you have still not located the American spy or the girl." Zadeh spoke bluntly in answer to Fesseghi's own rudeness.

"That is correct, but I can assure you the American will be found . . . along with the traitor," Fesseghi said, confidently sitting back down.

"How can you be so sure?" Zadeh asked. He studied Fesseghi's face. Fesseghi had a refinement about him, an air of confidence that Zadeh had only seen in the eyes of Western businessmen.

"All of my people have been notified. She only has a few places to run to, and besides, I know women." Fesseghi smiled, bringing his fingertips together and raising them to his lips. "All of her belongings were left behind. I am certain she will return to her apartment. Her father was found dead. She probably left to find comfort with friends, but will have to take care of his burial. She would need someone to help her make those decisions. It is a weakness women are born with. They cannot think for themselves.''

Zadeh was quiet for a few seconds, taking in what the man was saying. ''And the CIA spy?'' he finally asked.

''I searched his hotel room personally. I located his computer. And now I plan to—''

''Mr. Fesseghi,'' a male voice boomed over the intercom. ''Chief Engineer Hikmet has secured the computer. He is ready for you.''

''I will be right there,'' Fesseghi said and stood up. ''Your timing is exceptional, Mr. Zadeh. We are ready to access the American's computer software. Hikmet has deactivated the auto-destruct mechanism.''

''And what do you expect to find out from this software?'' Zadeh asked.

''I expect to find out what information he has acquired from the traitor. I would imagine that would be of importance to someone in the military. Perhaps we may also learn of his whereabouts or escape route,'' Fesseghi speculated, making his way down the hall, with Zadeh silently walking alongside.

''It is safe. Tufayli is here.'' Perijan stood outside the car. ''He will help us escape. You are to open the gate and park the car over there.''

Collins hesitated, looking at the area Perijan had pointed to. He slowly got out of the car and began pushing the heavy gate until it swung back. He searched the inside of the yard. Not seeing anything unusual, he jumped back into the Ford, drove fifty feet inside the junkyard and parked between an old pickup truck and a 1975 Chevy Impala with its engine removed. Getting out, he threw several handfuls of sand and gravel on the hood and trunk to hide its color and make it look as if it had been parked for a while.

Collins followed Perijan up the front steps of the house, which up close looked more like a shack. He guessed the dwelling would be in need of repair and as he entered, his suspicion was confirmed. The house contained only one room, with a dirt floor and a broken window. There was a rug, but the accumulation of dirt on top made it hard to see. The room was full of worn furniture and several wooden crates were used as tables. Collins could hear the rattling hum of a fan, yet the room was still hot and the air smelled stale.

"Tufayli, this is my friend. His name is . . ." Perijan stopped, realizing she didn't know the American's name.

Collins's eyes were slowly adjusting to the dark room. Seated in the corner, bent over in a wooden rocking chair, was an old man. He had gray hair and a long beard hanging to the middle of his chest. His eyes were light yellow.

"My name is Kiram Kahman," Collins said. His attention drifted to the rest of the room. Stacked up on a makeshift platform were five battered radios. Collins couldn't be sure, but he believed they were shortwave radar transmitters and receivers.

"Perijan tells me you need help. The Intelligence Service is looking for you." The old man was hard to understand. His voice was gruff. "I knew her father. I remember Perijan when she was a child." He reached out to hold Perijan's hand and patted it fondly. "You may use whatever you need."

"Do you have a phone?"

"No, just my radios. But I suggest you do not try to use them. They monitor my transmissions."

"What about a gun?"

"I do not own a gun. It is against the law."

"We'll need a car and a change of clothes. And if you could spare some food and water, we could use it." Collins knew the first two requests, especially, were too much to hope for, and paused to wonder if he was being too direct.

"It is yours," Tufayli replied.

"I'm going to need a mirror and razor. Perijan, gather the food and water. I want you to dress in men's clothes. You'll need a hat, too."

Perijan nodded and hugged the old man.

"You must hurry, child," the old man muttered, getting up from his chair. "They will be setting up roadblocks soon. Come, I will help you get started."

Hikmet removed the protective Plexiglas visor from his face, stripped the leather gloves from his hands and wiped the sweat from his brow, letting out a labored sigh of relief. Hanging around his neck was a heavy fireproof smock that would shield his body from a sudden explosion. On the table in front of him were parts of the American's computer, along with several screwdrivers and pliers. Hikmet had removed the screen and opened the back of the unit, exposing the internal workings.

"The explosives were very well hidden." Hikmet pointed to a small silver box. "I thought at first this was a backup hard drive. There is enough plastic in this unit to kill a man."

"Now what?" Ali Fesseghi asked.

Hikmet scratched the side of his head. "It will take some time to decode their programs. I can't make any promises. The Americans are very clever. I wanted your approval before I access the hard drive . . . it may erase all the programs."

"NO! I want all the information that is in that computer," Fesseghi demanded.

The room fell silent as Hikmet slipped off the smock and picked up the main section of the computer. He turned it over in his hands. "I must return to the weapons complex. I will need the computers there to help me." He looked up at the two men.

"I will accompany you," Zadeh said.

Duke James took a sip of bitter, lukewarm coffee. Seated next to him at a rectangular conference table covered with several dozen satellite photos were Nelson Zachiem and Tom Staffer. Howard Chaniff filled his coffee cup and sauntered up to a map of the Gulf on the wall. His face looked gaunt and his eyes were red. Duke guessed it was from the time change and the stress of putting together this type of mission.

"You have all read the mission specifics of my plan to attack the Iranian weapons plant," Chaniff began. "President McEntire and Secretary of Defense Radford have signed off on it. The purpose of this meeting is to iron out any concerns you may have and fine-tune the final details. Once that is done, I want your mission commanders briefed, ordered to get some rest and ready to fly at 0300 tomorrow morning."

Duke watched the lanky general look around, his gaze stopping at Zachiem. "Admiral . . . any comments?"

"Yes, sir. I think the Navy is getting the shaft on this one. It was our ship that got hit. It should be our planes that take out the weapons plant," Zachiem said in a flat, even tone.

"I've assigned the Navy to two primary missions, Admiral. They're the ones you requested—the launch sites west of Bandar Abbas and shooting down any enemy fighters that take to the air and challenge the strike force,'' Chaniff responded firmly.

"That was before the CIA learned of the weapons complex. Hell, General, as we speak the Iranians are planning to attack my carrier battle group again. We have every right to defend ourselves. My pilots are ready to fly right now. And I think we should hit them first instead of waiting for them to make another move.'' Zachiem's voice was raised slightly but still in control.

"That's *exactly* why you need to hold aircraft in reserve, Admiral. What are you going to do if they send a squadron of fighters toward the *Lincoln* and half your interceptors are inland?''

"I have enough aircraft as well as surface-to-air missiles for both missions, sir. If the Air Force wants a piece of the action, they can provide air cover over the target.''

Typical Navy arrogance, Duke thought. *That's the type of thinking that gets the military in trouble. Why must he always have center stage?*

"Sorry, Nelson, the subject is closed . . . and not open for discussion. The main target will be hit by Air Force F-15Es. They're faster than your A-6s and can fight their way out if need be.'' Chaniff looked at Duke. "James, anything on your end?''

"All my aircraft, pilots and maintenance crews are on the ground, but I still don't have all the smart bombs I've requested,'' Duke said, feeling Zachiem's icy stare directed at him. "If the GBU-28s aren't on the ground in the next six hours, my F-15Es will have to hit the target with GBU-27s. The 27s are only 2,000-pounders, and I won't be able to guarantee the target will be destroyed.''

"All the more reason for letting the Navy strike the weapons plant. We can saturate the site with 2,000-pound bombs,'' Zachiem interrupted.

Chaniff ignored the admiral. "You'll have your bombs, Duke, if I have to go back and fly them here myself.'' Chaniff looked at the admiral. "Any more questions?''

Zachiem sucked in a deep breath, puffing out his chest. "No, sir.''

"Good. Admiral Zachiem, I'll meet you in the CIC on board the *LaSalle* at 0200. If you run into any snags, let me know at once.'' Chaniff walked over and sat down, dismissing the admiral.

Zachiem stood. "I'm not happy with this decision, General. And my commanders are going to be furious. We deserve to hit Iran right between the eyes.'' He paused. "But I'm also aware of the fact that my duty as a soldier is to follow orders. We'll complete our part of this mission and we'll do it damned well.''

''I know you will, Admiral,'' Chaniff said.

''Duke. I'll see you when this is over.'' Zachiem reached for his hand. ''Good luck.''

''Same to you, Admiral.'' Duke returned the handshake, noticing the admiral had called him by his name for the first time.

With that, Zachiem left the briefing room. Duke waited until the door was shut before turning his attention to Staffer.

''Have you had any transmissions from Collins?'' he asked, concerned that they might be too late.

''No, we haven't,'' Staffer replied, his gaze down on the papers in front of him.

''Son of a bitch!'' Duke ran his fingers through his hair.

''Have you had a chance to act on my request for an Echo mission?''

Duke glanced at Chaniff, then back at Staffer. ''Yes, I have. The pieces are coming together right now,'' he said slowly.

Staffer drew a tight-lipped smile.

''Whoa. Wait a minute. I didn't authorize any of this yet,'' Chaniff protested.

''I know that, sir. But when you hear what I have in mind, I know you won't be able to disagree.'' Duke stood and walked over to the wall map. ''Air Force intel has analyzed every shred of electronic intelligence gathered from the RC-135 flights along the Iranian coast. The bad news is Iran has done a good job of updating their air defenses along the coast. Eighty percent of the systems they've purchased from the Russians are now operational, and we think they may be paying Russian technicians to operate some of the systems.''

''Well, let me guess what the good news is. The Russians are our friends, so they won't fire if we wave a flag?'' Chaniff challenged.

''Now, just hear me out a minute. Every area has double or triple radar coverage. Except for here.'' Duke pointed to an area on the map. ''This section is covered by only one radar . . . a fifteen-year-old Soviet P-35M. Our data show it's been updated and controls several SA-2 and SA-8 missile batteries. The radar is located on a rocky bluff above the coast city of Bushehr. A half mile to the west is a heliport used to ferry technicians to and from the SAM sites. My plan is to send in a special forces team to capture that radar station.''

"Capture it? Shit, Duke, I can tell you I don't like this plan already.'' Chaniff shook his head.

"So, if you capture the radar station, the Pave Low choppers and C-130 can penetrate Iranian airspace unopposed,'' Staffer said.

"That's right.''

"Say what? What are you talking about?'' Chaniff decided he'd best open his mind a little if Staffer understood what Duke meant.

"We capture the site at 0300, an hour before the Navy strikes their first targets at Bandar Abbas. The C-130 and Pave Lows will cross first, followed by the rest of the strike team. As the target is being hit, the C-130 will touch down a few miles south of where Collins should be—the abandoned silver mine north of Shahr Kord. It will be night, which of course will make it difficult to see the aircraft on the ground. If Collins is in the area, we'll get him out.'' Duke's speech and mannerisms exuded so much confidence that no one would have a hard time believing that that was exactly what was going to happen.

"He'll be there,'' Staffer said firmly.

"The C-130 and Pave Lows can then take off and egress over the same route followed into the country. When they're safely out of hostile territory, the special forces team can blow up the station and hightail it out of there.'' Duke returned to his seat as he concluded the plan.

"What's your backup plan, then?'' Chaniff was beginning to think it wasn't such a bad idea.

"We don't have a lot of other alternatives. If I order my people to knock that radar site out or jam it, every Iranian air defense commander will know we're coming. Our other option is to try to sneak in under their radar coverage. That's fine for the F-16s and F-15s, but the C-130 and the Pave Lows are too slow. We could try it, but if we're detected there will be hell to pay all the way to the target and all the way back. And since my butt will be one of those on the line, I'd prefer that didn't happen?''

"What does that mean? You're commanding the mission?'' Chaniff asked.

"This Echo mission is for volunteers only. And I'm the best possible volunteer to lead the mission,'' Duke answered.

"Bullshit. I won't authorize it, Duke. I want you here on the ground."

Duke looked straight at Chaniff and spoke evenly. "Maybe you don't understand, sir. I owe Collins one, and I'm not going to leave him out in the desert."

"I know what he did. He played a big part in getting you and the *Atlantis* crew out of that Chad mess. I can read classified reports just as well as anyone else." Chaniff looked at Staffer. "And I also know why Staffer wanted you to make the call on this. Shit . . . he knew you'd react this way."

Staffer raised both hands in the air. "I knew he'd find a way to get Collins out, but I didn't have anything to do with Duke thinking he's a he-man. He was born with that affliction."

"General, it really doesn't matter who's out there. We can do this mission, and I need to be out in the field with the men." Duke's tone was soft and sincere. "All I'm requesting is a single C-130 and two Pave Lows. We're talking about eighteen ground troops and a handful of pilots. They all know the risks and they've all volunteered. By God, General, would you leave one of our pilots behind if you thought there was a damn good chance you could reach in and pluck him out?"

Chaniff sat pensively, searching both men's faces. Flying in mountainous desert terrain, at night, was one of the most demanding missions in the military. Duke really couldn't blame the general for his concern, but there wasn't any way he would back down. The bottom line was he believed he could do it and therefore had to.

"I'm going on record as being against this mission. But I'm not going to stop you, Duke." Chaniff stared at Duke. "But if any of our men come home in black bags, you'll be responsible."

"I know that. I always have and always will." Duke's somber answer was meant to reassure the general he was not going into this mission without complete understanding. The thought of Hodges crossed his mind, but he knew it was all part of the job.

Chaniff reached the door first. "I have some phone calls to make. I'll be in my quarters if you need me."

Staffer and Duke stood at the same time and looked at each other a moment before smiling.

"Thanks, General James." Staffer clasped his hands. "Mark's a good man. I'd hate to lose him."

"I just hope he's in that silver mine when we get there. If not,

I'd hate to have to go find him myself.'' Duke caught a slight glimmer of worry in Staffer's eyes.

"I pray to God he's there, too," Staffer replied. "I pray to God."

Chapter Twenty-three

Mack Collins rubbed his smooth face and looked in the mirror. He felt somewhat relieved without the coarse whiskers but at the same time felt strangely exposed. He then took the scissors and trimmed his hair, shortening the bangs to his scalp.

"Everything is ready," Perijan said. She was dressed in black wool trousers, a cotton flannel shirt and tennis shoes. The clothes were several sizes too big for her, making her body look thin and frail.

"Food, water and extra clothes?" Collins asked.

"Right here." Perijan pointed to a couple of canvas bags and two plastic jugs.

Tufayli walked over, giving Perijan a hug. "It has been many years since I have seen you. You have grown to be a very beautiful woman. May Allah guide you both to safety." He looked over at Collins. "At the edge of the yard is a black Volvo sedan. It has gas in it and is my best car. Take it. There is a road map under the seat." He reached in a drawer and pulled out a large ring of keys, removing one.

"Thank you, Tufayfi," Perijan responded, returning the hug. Her eyes watered, but there were no more tears left in her to cry.

"Which way do you plan to go?" the old man asked as he walked them toward the door.

316

Collins hesitated before answering. "North, to the Turkish border."

"Stay on the side roads. Alternate between routes 34 and 52 until you reach the city of Hamadan. The Kurds control most of the countryside to the north. You can use the main roads once you're north of Hamadan." Tufayli returned to his rocking chair out of breath. "Now, go . . . before they come here looking for you."

Collins grabbed the food and water, leading Perijan out of the house.

After closing the gate, he put the 240 Volvo in gear and drove away from the junkyard. The car felt sound. *Better than the taxi, at least,* he thought. The air conditioner didn't work, but the gas tank was three-quarters full and they were on their way. For that much, he was thankful.

"Turn right here. It is the road to Turkey," Perijan said when they came to the first main road. Collins turned left, heading south.

"But that way is north."

"We're not going to Turkey. That's just what I told your friend," Collins answered, putting on his sunglasses.

"Why? You do not trust him?"

"That's right. There are only three people I trust right now. You, me and my mother, and she's not here. So you better try to understand we're on our own from here on out." Collins brought the speed up to seventy-five kilometers an hour. "Did the old man see the other clothes you put in the bag?"

"No. I took them from a dresser in the back of the room," Perijan answered, perplexed by Collins's line of thought.

"Good. Climb in the back and change clothes."

"Why?" she asked, dismayed that he would even make such a suggestion.

"*Do it.* Or maybe you would like me to take you back if you trust him more than me," Collins insisted.

Perijan, obliging, crawled into the back. Sinking as low as she could onto the floor, she meekly began changing her clothes.

Collins studied the two-lane highway as it stretched out in front of him. For an instant, the clear blue desert sky touching the jagged mountains in the distance reminded him of New Mexico. The black pavement ran straight for what looked like ten or twenty kilometers. The road then twisted up the mountainside. On the other side was Shahr Kord and the mining camp. *Now we just have to get past the checkpoints*, Collins said to himself.

Tufayli sat behind the shortwave radio transmitter and waited for the circuits to warm up. It had been twelve years since he had seen Perijan. She still seemed a small and innocent child to him. *What was she doing with that strange man? And why hadn't her father helped if she was in trouble? I knew when I heard he had allowed her to go to the United States for schooling that it would end up being trouble*, he thought. He felt peculiarly disloyal doing what he knew he must do. There was a time when he would have helped without question, but the world was confused and chaos was taking over in the cities. Living in the country, he had managed to isolate himself from the shame and filth. He had to go into town only for supplies and necessities. There were rumors that his mind had gone, but almost everyone just left him alone.

Slipping on the headset he listened to the static while randomly turning the transmitter knob, his blurry eyes preventing him from seeing the numbers clearly. The authorities in Esfahan would pay him handsomely for the information, but the authorities in Tehran would pay him even more. He would have money and food to make it through the next winter.

"Tehran receiver three five seven. Tehran receiver three five seven. Do you copy transmission?" Tufayli radioed.

There was no reply.

"Tehran receiver three five seven . . . do you copy?" Tufayli repeated.

"*This is a military channel. Advise you stop transmitting at once.*"

"This is Tufayli Sabri. Patch me in to your commander. I have important information."

"*Oh . . . it's you, old man. How many times have you been warned to stay off this channel? And the commander isn't in— you'll have to speak with me.*"

"I said, I have some valuable information," Tufayli said, oblivious to the man's scorn.

"*Tell me what it is and I'll let the commander know as soon as he returns,*" the voice said, attempting to appease the old man.

"No. You tell your commander to radio me when he returns. I will be standing by." Tufayli took off his headset and turned the volume to high so he could hear when his call was returned.

The fools don't know that a young woman's life may be at stake here, he thought. *They think I am only a stupid old man. Well, I'll show them.*

BAHRAIN AIR BASE

"How are they coming, Captain?" Duke asked, walking to the edge of the hangar.

"We're putting the last coat of paint on them now, sir," Captain Skip Watson answered, looking at the two Bell 206 Jet Ranger helicopters. Two maintenance technicians were busily spraying the tail section of the nearest chopper with a dirty brown paint. It had taken the crew only three hours to transform the dark green 206s to the two-tone brown-and-beige color scheme used by the Iranian air force. The green, red and white Iranian flag had also been efficiently painted on the side of the pilots' doors and beneath the engines.

"It's been a while since I've flown one of these babies," Watson said and smiled. Watson was assigned to the Air Force Special Operation Command based in Hurlburt Field, Florida. This was exactly the type of missions AFSOC pilots were trained for—moving special operation teams, such as the Green Berets, into and out of covert areas. The twenty-eight-year-old Air Force pilot looked old for his age. Nearly bald, with a graying mustache, his blue eyes and youthful smile added to his laid-back country mannerism. The man appeared to be so relaxed, Duke was curious if he was ready to go.

"You can handle it?"

"No sweat, General." Watson paused. "I was still in flight school when Desert Storm broke . . . missed all the action. This may be my first shot at combat, but I won't be screwing things up."

"Your orders are clear, Captain. If the Iranian ground controller questions anything about the IFF transponder code you're using, terminate the mission," Duke reminded him decisively.

"You don't have to worry about me taking any unnecessary chances. I have no desire to be a dead hero. The commander told me you wanted someone who can stay in control in a hot spot, and that's me. Takes a lot to get me worked up." Watson stood assuredly, talking in a lackadaisical manner.

Duke, amused that the pilot was so arrogantly cocky, just lis-

tened. He wondered if at one time he also sounded so conceited
"Get some rest, Captain. I'll see you in the briefing room a
0130." Duke's face remained stern, though he felt concerned for
Watson. It would take more than his positive outlook to see him
successfully through the mission.

"Yes, sir." Watson started to walk away, then added, "If i
makes you feel any better, I did graduate at the top of my class.'

Duke nodded, thinking that sitting in the classroom was a
whole lot different from flying in combat.

"It says all cars must stop," Perijan said, reading the road sign
"It's a checkpoint," she added nervously, waiting to hear wha
Collins planned to do.

"All right, try not to act so fidgety." Collins surveyed the area
for possible escape routes. "How much money do you have?"

Perijan dug through her leather purse. "Not very much . .
about 20,000 rials."

"Take half of it out and hide it." *I hope 10,000 is enough fo
these guys to look the other way*, he thought. He checked himsel
in the rearview mirror.

The car crested a slight incline and Collins saw blinking yellow
and red lights mounted on top of a shiny metal shack in the
distance. He wasn't close enough to see if any guards were standing along the road. For an instant he thought about turning around
and heading back toward Esfahan. *Maybe there's another way to
get to the silver mine. A back road somewhere that isn't on the
map. No . . . the longer we take, the more time security forces
have to be looking us. Keep your head, Mark, don't lose it now.
Just play it slow and cool.*

He slowed the car just as a white Mercedes with darkened
windows breezed through the checkpoint from the opposite direction. Collins was now close enough to see one of the guards
waving it through.

"Let's hope we're as lucky," Collins said.

"We won't be. That was a government official."

Collins looked over at Perijan, making sure her hair was pulled
up inside the black baseball cap covering her head. In his opinion
she didn't look much like a young man. Her skin was too clean
and eyes too bright. He just hoped the guards wouldn't get close
enough to notice. "Remember, don't say a word," Collins cau-

tioned. "You're my brother and we're on our way to Ahvaz for business."

Hitting the right turn signal, Collins pulled over and stopped fifty feet from the metal shack. He could now see two guards, each armed with AK-47s and side arms. One was standing next to the shack, while the other was on the side of the road. The nearest guard walked over and motioned for Collins to roll down his window.

"Let me see your ID," the man grunted from behind a greasy beard. He wore sweat-stained green army fatigues and a black beret. Collins guessed him to be in his late thirties. His skin was very brown from standing long hours in the desert sun.

Collins reached into his breast pocket, pulling out the false ID and passport with pictures of him clean-shaven. His occupation was given as Turkish rug trader.

The guard looked at the picture, then at Collins, flipping the pages of the passport back and forth several times. He then stared at the Turkish ID examining both the front and the back.

"You remain here," the guard said. He walked over and showed the IDs to his partner. Occasionally, while they were talking, each man would look over at Collins.

"What are they doing?" Perijan whispered.

"He knows that since I'm a rug trader, I probably have money. But he's probably worried that because I'm a businessman, I may know government officials," Collins speculated, then added, "They're trying to figure out if there's a way to get money without getting into trouble."

Finally, the first guard walked back over to the car. "Who is this?" He pointed to Perijan.

"He is my brother," Collins said in Fazi. "I am teaching him the family business."

"Where are your rugs? You sell rugs . . . where are they?"

"I am not selling this trip, just buying. They are shipped to my warehouse in Turkey."

"Receipts? Where are your receipts?" the guard asked, his tone becoming more belligerent.

"I do not get the receipts until I buy the rugs. You may see for yourself. We have only money to buy rugs." Collins picked up the leather satchel without thinking. His heart leaped as he hoped it didn't look too feminine.

The guard snatched the bag and stood upright. "I will have to inspect this."

Collins felt a long drop of sweat roll down the side of his neck. There wasn't enough money to buy rugs, but Collins hoped it wouldn't matter. When you're stuck with grunt work out in the middle of nowhere, if a little gravy came your way most people would take it. Chances were they could have cared less if Collins was lying or not, as long as they got something out of the deal.

They sat silently as the two guards huddled together, occasionally glancing back toward the car. Their voices became escalated, and one of the guards began shaking his head and pointing in their direction. The other guard remained close to the shack, while the first stormed to the car. "Get out!" he bellowed, and pointed his rifle at Collins.

"I have done nothing wrong," Collins protested, alarmed. "I am a guest in your country. This is not how a businessman should be treated."

"OUT!"

Collins, mentally going over his options, quickly did as the man commanded. He opened the car door and the guard stepped back. Part of his training included overpowering someone with a gun pointed at him. However, it was best to have the patience to wait it out and make certain that was the only recourse. "Your government will hear of this," he threatened, hoping that the man would back down.

"Open the trunk. I must see what is in it."

Collins opened the trunk and pointed to the canvas bags. "There . . . you can see. All we have is food and extra clothes." If the man got close enough, it would be the perfect opportunity—they were obscured from the view of the other guard. "Go ahead. Look at them."

The guard only stood where he was and spoke irritatedly. "You have no rugs?"

"I told you, I'm looking to buy rugs this trip, not sell them." Collins consciously made eye contact with the man and sounded annoyed by his stupidity.

"There is nothing in here. You may get back in your car," the other guard ordered, having walked up alongside his partner to return the small leather purse and ID.

Mark stared at both men a moment. They both stared back as if daring him to create a disturbance.

"Thank you," Collins finally said, then returned slowly to his seat. Perijan was looking directly ahead, and he could see she was trembling slightly.

He started the car, not looking back at the guards still standing at the back of the vehicle. Once they were out of view, Perijan opened the purse and let out a high-strung laugh. "It was all a diversion. They did it to steal the money. I was frightened they were going to just shoot us there. I have heard of such things happening in the desert."

"Bastards," Collins snorted. "They didn't have to be so rough." *Scared the shit out of me*, he thought to himself, as he clenched the steering wheel.

TEHRAN, IRAN

"I believe the American and the girl are traveling together," Akhbar al-Yawm reported. He stood in front of Sheik Bakhtiar's desk. The minister had his arms folded and was staring up at him.

"You tell me nothing new. I have already received this information."

"You have definite proof of this information?" al-Yawm asked suspiciously.

"I have many resources," Bakhtiar answered vaguely.

"What else have you learned, then? Why have they not been brought in for questioning?"

"They were to be heading north to Turkey," Bakhtiar said, smirking, "but I believe that information was given only to mislead us. The Americans are very clever, but not as clever as I am. Do you think I would just let them escape?"

Al-Yawm didn't answer the question. The defense minister appeared only to be annoyed with the issue now, acting as if it was of no major consequence.

"It does not matter where they go. Every checkpoint around Esfahan has been alerted. It will be impossible for them to get by any of them."

"You have spoken with the leader of the Kurdish resistance?" al-Yawm asked, concerned about the possible retaliation should the two manage to avoid capture.

"Yes. He has agreed to help locate the spy and traitor." Bakhtiar's expression changed from smugness to one of callous delight. "And the cowards in the parliament, the ones who just days ago opposed me, they are now quiet.''

Al-Yawm knew Bakhtiar was correct. They weren't saying a word. In a matter of weeks, Bakhtiar had become the most powerful man in Iran. No one would dare resist the change he was currently forcing upon the country. And if they did, it was known that Zadeh, though he was only a bodyguard, now had the means with which to carry out the minister's wishes without being questioned.

"So, al-Yawm. Do you still oppose what I do for Iran?'' Bakhtiar asked, his eyes narrowing.

"You have nothing to worry about from me, Bakhtiar, nothing,'' al-Yawm replied obediently. "I know you control Iran.''

Bakhtiar nodded. "Very good. I am pleased we have come to an understanding.'' He turned on the television set, not bothering to acknowledge the man's departure.

You will make a mistake, al-Yawm thought, as he walked away from Bakhtiar's office. *And when you do, I will see to it you are removed from power forever.*

It was late when Hassan Zadeh entered Khalk Hikmet's underground complex for the fifth time in two hours. Resting on the table, next to Hikmet, was the American's computer. The keyboard and screen had been removed and were lying next to the main housing. Zadeh could see the interior workings of the small machine. The rows of circuit boards, miniature microchips and hair-thin black wires looked neatly placed, but he wondered how such tiny pieces could be of any importance.

Several cables were connected from the back of the machine to Hikmet's larger desktop computer. Zadeh sat down several feet behind the chief engineer, impatiently watching him manipulate the keyboard. Hikmet had been trying to break the American program and was having limited success.

"What progress have you made?'' Zadeh demanded.

"This is much more difficult than I first believed. The Americans are very innovative.'' Hikmet didn't look away from the monitor. The screen was filled with unreadable lines of computer code.

"Minister Bakhtiar will not be pleased if you cannot produce any information,'' Zadeh warned.

"You do not understand what is involved. This is a delicate machine. I have accessed the American's hard drive and can in-

spect each program, but now I am looking at each line of computer code . . . for each program . . .'' He paused, annoyed by the
man's distraction. "There is more than just the primary and
backup files. They have coded special files within the main program. It is like they are camouflaged . . . a piece here and a piece
there. I have written a simple program trying to isolate the pass-
key code, which will copy the program onto a hard disk. This
must be done one line at a time.'' He tapped the key-board, scrolling down the screen. "It may take me an hour or it could take
weeks to find what I need. One must have patience to work with
this type of intricacy.'' Hikmet suddenly held up his left hand.
"Wait. I believe I have isolated some sort of variance. It could
be one of the programs.''

"What is it?'' Zadeh pressed.

"I do not know yet.'' Hikmet touched the screen. "See right
here. This line is written in another type of program language.
It's hidden between these two lines of data.''

"Can you not understand what it means?'' Zadeh asked, now
bent over Hikmet's shoulder and looking at the monitor.

Hikmet didn't respond. He scrolled the coded data to the top
of the page. Pressing control F3 and F10, he copied the data onto
the B drive. After the disk stopped cycling, he punched another
set of buttons and called up the program. The monitor flashed for
several seconds. Then a black-and-white map of Iran appeared.

"Praise Allah. It is a map showing each one of our military
bases,'' Hikmet said in disbelief. He tapped the F10 button and
the screen flashed again. This time it showed a close-up of downtown Tehran, with all its streets and the location of each government building, including the ministry building.

"Keep looking. There must be something more here than
maps,'' Zadeh blurted. "And work faster. It will be dark soon.''

It had taken Collins and Perijan nearly six hours to travel the
winding mountain road and drop into the valley below. According
to the odometer, they had traveled only 68.3 kilometers since
leaving Esfahan. Though the sun was now low in the desert sky,
the outside temperature was easily still over a hundred degrees.

Collins took a short drink from the water jug and handed it to
Perijan. The highway, if one could call it that, was in need of
repair. Rarely were both lanes open at once—either one lane
or the other was obstructed with debris. There were boulders or

abandoned cars and trucks, many of them stripped and burned. This forced everyone using the highway to share one lane, a problem that was compounded by the fact that many trucks used the road.

He watched the temperature gauge hover around the red mark. The car was overheating from the extreme heat and the stresses of driving slowly on the winding road. He just hoped the Volvo's cooling system would work long enough to get them to the mining camp. As they came to the base of the mountain, Collins pulled over and turned off the ignition.

"Why have we stopped?" Perijan had removed the baseball cap to readjust her hair.

"The engine is running hot and if this thing overheats, it's going to be a long walk." He closed his eyes a moment and tried to get his bearings. He had driven to the silver mine twice while training in the CIA simulator. *The turnoff should be only a dozen or so kilometers down this road*, he tried to remember. *That is, if the satellite photos were accurate.*

"Are you all right? Do you need to rest?" Perijan asked, disturbing his concentration. She wondered if he had fallen asleep.

"No, I'm fine. I was just thinking." Collins started the car and turned back onto the highway. Since leaving the checkpoint, Perijan hadn't spoken more than a few sentences, and that was just to answer his questions. Collins, preoccupied before, now considered what was going through her mind. She was so solemn. He then noticed that she was clutching a small box. He didn't recall seeing it and wondered about its contents. The way she held it deterred him from asking.

"I know you must be frightened," Collins said soothingly and forced a smile. "Leaving your family and friends behind is a very brave thing to do. But we're going to make it out all right."

"I do not have a family anymore."

"I'm sorry," Collins answered, feeling stupid for not remembering the data on her. He recalled that Perijan's mother and brothers were dead and that her father was very ill. Trying to lighten the conversation, he changed the subject. "If help doesn't show up tonight or tomorrow night, we'll move closer to the coast. We have a prearranged pickup spot, and I know they'll be coming soon."

"You are certain they will come? How will they be able to get past my country's military?"

"Yeah, I'm certain they'll be coming," Collins lied, using a shirtsleeve to wipe the sweat from his brow. He wasn't sure what was involved in this whole mess, and it could be that it would be too risky to send a team after him. "You see, there are these special forces teams. They're trained soldiers who actually get excited about sneaking into hostile territories at night and pulling out helpless CIA officers. They've got all sorts of equipment and firepower to get past any military. A mean bunch of guys."

"I have heard of such men," Perijan spoke timidly, remembering that it was said these soldiers were brutal and would kill innocent women and children.

"You don't have to worry about them. You're with me. They won't harm you." Collins thought that maybe he should just keep his mouth shut, realizing he had alarmed her. "Help me look for a dirt road. It should be on the left side of the highway near those foothills."

Ten minutes later Perijan pointed to two weathered ruts veering off to the left. "Is that what you're looking for?"

"That must be it." Collins glanced over at the area, then stepped on the brakes. The car shuddered to a stop. Tire grooves were cut into the desert, but they hadn't been used for quite some time. Rocks and dried weeds filled the ruts, and he couldn't detect any fresh tread marks in the sand.

He shifted the Volvo into low and started up the hillside, scanning the mountain for a building or something that would indicate the old mining camp was nearby. The road wound right and left for a few kilometers before crowning the top of a steep hill. Collins stopped and looked into the shallow valley below. He now knew why CIA planners had chosen this place. The mine couldn't be seen from the highway and if need be helicopters could easily land. The road turned sharply to the left and was straight for several hundred yards.

The terrain was void of trees and large rocks. Partway up the mountainside he spotted five buildings of various sizes clustered in a small area. The metal roof of one of the structures was gone and the windows of the buildings were broken. From the distance, one appeared to have three garage doors, and Collins hoped they would be able to hide the car there. *Perhaps the miners had left some supplies behind, too*, he thought.

As they approached, he could see large, reddish-brown piles of mining tailings scattered here and there and an old diesel-powered dump truck parked near the largest building. It was then he noticed the first hints of vapor beginning to appear from beneath the Volvo's hood. The car was overheating.

"Okay. Let's find a place to hide this car. Then we need to check out those buildings to find a safe spot to rest."

"This is where they will meet us?" Perijan asked.

"Yeah, this is it." Collins sighed, breathing a little easier. "We'll stay here for two days. With any luck, we'll be out of here before too long."

"But how?" Perijan was still baffled as to how anyone could accomplish such a feat.

"You'll see. The CIA and U.S. military can do anything once they put their minds to it," Collins said, trying to sound confident. *I just hope they've decided to put their minds to it.*

Duke James paced in front of the large wall map of the Persian Gulf. Also hanging on the wall were KH-12 and KH-14 satellite photos of the areas around Esfahan and Shahr Kord. Small red dots on each photo marked the location of known SAM and triple A sites. Yellow triangles were also scattered, showing probable mobile missile sites.

Duke waited for the last flight leader to be seated before starting the briefing. The room was small and crowded, which allowed him to see each man's face. He had conducted many mission briefings and felt that sometimes their expressions divulged more than the questions they asked, or didn't ask. In the corner, to his right, General Chaniff sat solemnly. Every man in the room took notice that the chairman was present, although they tried not to be obvious.

"All right, gentlemen, let's get started," Duke said flatly. The room fell silent and all eyes were on him.

"The mission tonight will involve four elements with four very different objectives. The first element will be handled by our friends from the Navy. The carrier *Abraham Lincoln* is stationed 220 miles off the Iranian coast. In six hours they are scheduled to launch an air strike package against Iranian coastal targets west of Bandar Abbas. Navy Seal teams are already on the ground and will guide the A-6 Intruders to their targets. Their objective is diversion; they will pull the Iranians away from the main strike force coming in from the west." Duke turned from pointing out the directions on the map and looked around the room.

"The second element will be commanded by Captain Watson and his special forces team. Their mission will be to capture and control the radar site at Bushehr, holding it for three hours. If this part of the mission fails, the rest of us will not fly. The Navy will go ahead and strike their targets, but we'll sit tight." Duke looked at Watson. "Are your men ready, Captain?"

"Yes, sir," Watson answered assuredly.

"The third part of the mission will be under my command. Once the radar station is under our control, two MH-53J Pave Lows will penetrate Iranian airspace flying low level and supported by a single C-130 Herky bird. We will land here, a few miles north of Shahr Kord." Duke indicated the location of the Iranian town. "This is an Echo mission and that's all I can say." Duke was now looking at the lead Pave Low pilot. "Your pilots ready, Hank?"

"They're going over the final details now, sir. We'll be ready to fly," Major Hank Brown said in a deep Southern drawl.

"Well, that leaves the fun part to you fast-movers," Duke said with a smile. "Colonel Naylor will conduct the briefing for the final element of the mission."

Eddie Naylor stood and walked to the front of the room. His sturdy frame and disciplined appearance added to the sober atmosphere.

"After General James and his team are across the border, a Saudi E-3A AWACS will move into position off the eastern coast. They have been flying the same pattern for the last week and a half, so the Iranians shouldn't suspect anything. The only difference will be that this time the AWACS will have an American crew on board. Their call sign will be 'Terminator' and their eyes will extend to about ten miles from the target. The final leg of the mission we'll be on our own." Naylor looked around the room, making sure everyone was following him. "The E-3 will only contact us if they see any trouble coming our way. Our GPSs should lead us to the target without any problems.

"My package of four F-16s, call signed 'Coors,' will lead into the country. Our objective will be to take out any SAM operators that get stupid enough to challenge us. The EF-111As will follow, call sign 'Hammer.' If everything goes as planned, they will only be needed at the target. The F-15Es will bring up the rear and the F-15Cs package will clean the skies of enemy aircraft. Your call signs will be 'Mustang' for the Es and 'Marathon' for the

Cs. I want you to keep your pilots under 1,000 feet until we get deep inside Iran. Remember, if there is any trouble, the AWACS will pick it up.''

Major Michael Leonard, lead pilot for the F-15Cs, shook his head in disagreement. ''My men aren't going to like that, sir. We need to be above 10,000 feet to be effective. Otherwise we're going to be climbing toward targets rather than hitting them from above.''

''I understand your concern, Major, but to attain our objectives we must remain undetected for as long as possible,'' Naylor explained. ''After the Es start their target run it won't matter. I'll need your team on top to cover for any MiGs or F-4s taking off from Esfahan air base. Intel reports the Iranians have a few F-14s that are still operational. Details are sketchy as to what missiles they may carry, so if those Tomcats do become airborne, you'll need to take them out first. MiG-29s should be secondary threats, and F-4s after them.''

Naylor turned to Lieutenant Colonel Robert ''Snake'' Baker. ''Bob, you and your pilots will only get one pass at this thing. We're not planning to stay around and do any sightseeing.''

''You just keep the SAMs and triple A guns off our backs. We'll need two minutes over the target . . . that's all.'' Baker, a large, barrel-chested Academy grad, spoke as if this were routine.

''After you drop the bombs, I want you up top to help Leonard in the air-to-air role.'' Naylor finished and turned to Duke.

''All right, that's it,'' Duke said, looking straight at each man. ''I want each of your pilots in his bird an hour before takeoff. Good luck, men. Breakfast is on me when you touch down.''

Naylor walked over to shake Duke's hand. ''Good luck, General. And keep your head down.''

''Oh, I plan to,'' Duke said, catching Chaniff's eye. ''Mr. Chairman, sure you don't want to come along? We can make room in that second Pave Low.''

Chaniff shook his head. ''Wish I could. But someone's got to stay home and protect the women.'' He looked at Duke, then Naylor. ''You two know the routine. Be sure your men watch each other's backs, and just come home without any holes.''

''Yes, sir,'' Naylor answered. ''Without any holes.''

Chapter Twenty-four

ESFAHAN, IRAN

Colonel Alireza Rahavi stood in the darkened control tower of the Esfahan air base watching the dark silhouettes of two twin-tailed MiG-29s taxi into position at the end of the east runway, listening to the controller's instructions.

"Flight four four three. This is the tower. You are cleared for take-off. Wind calm at one to two knots. Maintain runway heading to flight level zero two zero."

Both MiGs' dual tailpipes turned a deep orange as the 29s kicked into afterburner and streaked down the runway, becoming airborne in a matter of seconds. The colonel watched them until they disappeared into the darkening eastern sky. To the west, Rahavi caught sight of landing lights as two other aircraft lined up on final approach. "F-14s?" he asked.

"Yes, sir," the controller responded.

"Tell the pilots to taxi to the fueling area after they touch down. I don't want any time wasted taxiing to the hangars first."

"Yes, sir."

Air operations were proceeding smoothly. MiG-29s and F-14s were alternating patrol of the airspace above Esfahan. However, Rahavi still didn't allow himself the privilege of feeling comfortable. That would only come after all his aircraft had returned safely from destroying the *Lincoln*.

"I will be in the command bunker," Rahavi announced, as the first F-14 touched down and slowed to a stop.

SHAHR KORD, IRAN

Perijan sat huddled alone in the corner of what used to be a maintenance garage. The ten-by-ten-foot chamber had only one window, which was broken, and a single door. She sat on a wooden chair that must have been used with a broken metal desk that was overturned in the middle of the room. The concrete floor was cluttered with weathered papers and layers of dust and dirt. Perijan suspected that vandals had come here after the government had pulled out of the camp. She stared out the window, a thin wool blanket folded neatly on her lap. In a few more minutes it would be completely dark and she wouldn't be able to see the brown landscape and jagged rocks surrounding the mining camp. In a way, she felt more secure now that night was falling. The darkness could be a friend, making it difficult for the Revolutionary Guards to continue their search and locate them. It could also be their enemy—the rapid drop in temperature could make it impossible to stay warm and find comfort.

Feeling a chill, Perijan unfolded the blanket and threw it around her shoulders. The hunger pains that rumbled in her stomach were only a minor discomfort. The American had been gone for the past two hours, checking the other buildings, and she was beginning to get worried. She closed her eyes and tried to think of something else. Her dead father came to her thoughts first. What had they done with his body? Would they bury him next to her mother or have him cremated? She wished she would have been able to say good-bye, tell him one last time how much she loved him. Perijan felt tears welling up in her eyes. The penned-up emotion was about to overflow deep inside her. She raised her hands to her face and began to sob.

Suddenly, she heard footsteps and a whisper. Looking up, she could see the dark outline of a man. "Allah help me," she cried out.

"Perijan . . . it's me. Are you all right?"

Perijan quickly wiped away her tears. "You scared me . . . I, I was worried."

Collins set a round canister, a square box and a dirty cloth sack down on the ground.

"I thought maybe something had happened to you. I wasn't sure what I should do." She spoke quietly, wishing she didn't feel so frightened.

"I wasn't gone that long, Perijan. It just seems that way," Collins said, his tone reassuring. "And if anything does happen to me, you stay put for two days. If no one comes, then go to the coast north of Bandar-e Deylam. Take all the supplies you can and wait. Someone will come." He wasn't positive, but he wanted her to feel as if she had options other than just depending on him. "Do you understand that?"

"Yes." She paused a moment, then asked, "What did you find?"

Collins squatted down. "Every building but this one has been ransacked. Two of them don't even have interior walls—everything's been stripped away. But I did find these hidden away in one of the mine shafts about a half mile from here. It's a kerosene heater with about a gallon of fuel. It should help us keep warm. Come help me try to light it."

Collins decided he had better start getting Perijan used to being resourceful. They moved toward the broken desk. Collins swiveled it around, then lifted it so it was standing on edge in the corner and would deflect the light away from the window. He took the lid off the heater while Perijan carefully filled it with kerosene. The odor burned her nose as several drops hit the floor. It was quickly becoming too dark to see. She watched the American pull out a small propane lighter and hold it at the base of the heater.

"This thing is pretty beat up. I don't know if it's going to work." Collins primed the heat again, turning the on/off knob to maximum. "Tilt it forward, Perijan."

She leaned the heater forward, and he flicked the lighter on one more time. The heater flashed on in a blur of blue flames. He adjusted the fuel flow knob and a soft yellow light filled the room.

Collins pulled a hammer and a handful of nails out of the sack he had set next to the kerosene. Taking one of the blankets given to them by Tufayli, he tacked it over the window, securing it on all sides.

Perijan warmed her hands a few minutes, then removed some cans of food from the sack and opened them. She set the cans on top of the heater, stirring them gently. After they were heated slightly, she handed Collins one of the cans and a spoon.

"Ah, dinner in a can. My favorite." He sat down next to Perijan and started to eat. He felt uncomfortable with her continued silence but didn't know what he could say to get her to relax and open up.

They ate in awkward silence, each lost in thought. When they were finished, Perijan took the spoons, wiped them off and returned them to the canvas sack. Collins smashed the two cans and neatly disposed of them so as not to leave any evidence that they had been there. When he returned to sit by the warmth, Perijan suddenly spoke.

"Are you married?" she asked, staring at the yellow flames dancing at the base of the heater.

"Yes," he answered, surprised at the frankness with which she now talked. "And we have a little girl."

"Who takes care of them while you are away?" Perijan looked up into Collins's eyes. The sorrow he saw there left him only with pity for the way of life she and her people suffered.

"Well, she takes care of herself mostly. But before I leave I ask friends to check in on them to see if they need anything, and money is taken care of. It was difficult the first couple of times, but we've got it figured out now."

Perijan shook her head, not sure she understood what it meant to be independent in such a way, without a male family member close by. Then she realized she was truly alone. She should be going to some distant relative and asking him to take her into his family and protect her honor. "Allah has blessed her with you. I do not know what I will do . . ." Her eyes watered and tears began streaming down her face. She hid her shame, burying her face in her hands. Collins sat for a moment, stunned by the abrupt release of emotion, and watched her body shake with sobs.

"Now, it's going to be all right, Perijan." He walked over to her. "That's something my government will help you with once we get back to the States. You're tired and we've had a long day." He caressed her arms and gently lifted her off the seat, making a place for her to lie on the floor next to the heater. "There. Now, you go to sleep and don't worry anymore. I'm here and nothing is going to happen tonight."

The heater felt good and Perijan curled up, suddenly exhausted. For the first time in many years she felt somewhat secure and safe. The American was a good man. He had not tried to take advantage of her, or to treat her like the government said American men would. He was still speaking soothingly to her and stroking her arms to quiet her sobs. As her eyelids grew heavy and her thoughts dimmed, she was aware that Collins was a man of honor and integrity, someone she had hoped to find one day. A moment later she was soundly sleeping.

BAHRAIN AIR BASE

Master Sergeant Ricky "Vasquie" Vasquez felt the chopper vibrate and the interior fill with the sound of thunder as the Bell 206 Jet Ranger lifted off the ground and headed out over the ocean.

I hope this bucket of bolts holds together, he thought. He tightened his lap belt and watched the flashing white, red and blue lights of the air base disappear from the window ahead of him. They were fifty feet above the water, flying in a northeast direction.

Resting on Vasquez's lap was an M40A2 sniper rifle. He reclined the heavy stainless steel barrel against his shoulder, making sure nothing touched the AN/PVS-4 Starlight scope. The twenty-nine-year-old sniper appeared older than his years. Long hours in the sun on the shooting range and on training missions had lined his face. His dark skin and eyes accentuated the rough look.

Vasquez was assigned to the Special Operations Command Head-quarters attached to the 82nd Airborne at Fort Bragg. Being a sniper was the only duty he had served during his entire military career. When he wasn't on an assignment, he evaluated newly trained rangers' rifle scores for possible admission into the Weapons Training Battalion, a fancy name for sniper school. He had earned a reputation as being one of the best during Desert Storm. Later, that reputation turned into legend, and many of his buddies believed him to be the next Carlos Hathcock. Vasquez rarely missed, even while aiming at a target 1,500 yards away in windy conditions.

"Hey, Vasquie, you ever get airsick on that rifle of yours?" First Lieutenant Max Rath shouted. He was seated across from Vasquez.

"Nope."

"You ever get airsick at all?"

"Yeah," Vasquez hollered back. "But never on my buddy."

He patted his rifle. "Usually it's on the guy across from me."

"Smart-ass." Rath laughed.

Vasquez joined in, shaking his head at the first lieutenant. Rath was his partner, the scout and spotter of the two-person sniper team. They had been a team for five years.

Once the radar site was secured, it would be their job to make certain no one approached the area. Rath and Vasquez would keep the bad guys away long enough for the reinforcements to stabilize the site area. Their duties were clear and precise: Rath spotted trouble and Vasquez eliminated it.

Vasquez felt the helicopter bounce up and down as the 206 cut through an air pocket. He adjusted his night vision goggles, making sure they were squarely on his head.

"*Twenty-five minutes to target,*" the pilot's voice informed them over the intercom.

P-35M RADAR SITE, BUSHEHR, IRAN

Lieutenant al-Shira fought back the urge to sleep as he stood and started to pace around the confining concrete-walled room. A small, thin man with high cheekbones, the lieutenant looked haggard since he hadn't shaved in a week. As he did each night, he was commanding the coastal defense radar station located above the town of Bushehr. And as usual, everything was quiet and boring.

The concrete structure, lacking any form of ventilation, remained hot and sultry during the night. Al-Shira looked forward to the time when he would return to the day shift. He could be with his wife and children in the cool evenings and only deal with the sweltering heat during the day. But that wasn't scheduled to happen for another two months.

"Report," he ordered, as a matter of routine.

The two sergeants assigned to monitor the radar equipment didn't move or answer. They were slumped over in their chairs, and he wondered if they had even heard him.

"I said *report,*" al-Shira said loudly.

"Section one clear."

"Section two clear."

He walked up behind the two men to glance over the scopes himself. They were both older than he was, with many years of experience. Al-Shira didn't question them about their report or slowness in responding.

BADGER TWO, 206 JET RANGER

"There you are," Captain Skip Watson said to himself. The first faint warning hums from his RHAW equipment filled his headset. The long-range Soviet-made radar was sweeping them from the northeast. He studied the instrument panel. The dials and gauges appeared green and white through his night vision goggles. A round dial, located above his right knee, showed the radar was sweeping his chopper from a bearing of zero four niner.

He keyed his mike. "Badger Two . . . Badger Lead. You copy?"

"*Copy, Lead.*"

"Stay below fifty feet," Watson ordered. "I don't want them seeing us until we're fifteen miles out."

"*Roger, Lead. I'm with you.*"

Watson didn't want to give his Iranian friends any extra time to ask questions or make telephone calls once he popped up on their radar screens. He had rehearsed his speech several dozen times and just hoped he had the accent down. If not, this was going to be a very short mission.

His eyes went to the mission clock: 0142. They were right on time.

BAHRAIN AIR BASE

Duke rubbed his hand along the side of the MH-53J Pave Low III special operations helicopter, feeling the rough two-tone light-absorbing paint. Above him, the heat radiating off the right engine waved upward into the rapidly cooling desert night air. Three floodlights bathed the half-mile-long tarmac, casting long shadows across the black concrete. Duke could see through the open hangar door that the ground crews were putting the finishing touches on the fighters.

The general was dressed in a green flight suit, with a Sigarms 9-mm automatic pistol, along with three extra magazines, strapped to his waist. Under his left arm he carried a brown camouflaged helmet and his flight bag.

"I just received the latest weather report," Chief Warrant Officer Steve Newall, the pilot of the Pave Low, said. "There's a large sandstorm moving through central Iran. With our current flight plan, intel reports we should miss it by twenty miles. Other than that, we're good to go in five minutes, sir.''

"All right. Spread the word. I want everyone on board and strapped in within two minutes," Duke responded.

"Yes, sir."

Duke stood back from the chopper, giving it the once-over. The MH-53J Pave Low III, was even more immense at night than during the day. No wonder the pilots referred to it as the Battlestar Galactica of helicopters. It was an impressive machine and many pilots were intimidated by its size. Unlike the sleek jets Duke was used to, the chopper, with its instruments and sensors bolted to the side and nose section, appeared as if it would be awkward and clumsy once in the air. He knew, however, that the chopper had been packed with the most advanced electronics and IR sensors in the world. It was the only bird capable of penetrating deep into enemy territory. With a crew of six and a maximum takeoff weight of 50,000 pounds, the Pave Low III could fly at treetop level during the night, avoiding radar at speeds in excess of 240 knots.

The Air Force had designed the chopper for covert operations, giving it a range of over 1,290 miles with jettisonable fuel tanks. It was operated by the 21st Special Operations Squadron based at RAF Alconbury, which fell under the command of Air Force Operations Command based at Hurlburt Field, in Florida's panhandle. Duke knew the pilots from the 21st SOS by reputation only. They were dedicated, hard-working and very good at what they did.

He walked around to the front, eyeballing the second Pave Low parked a hundred feet away. That chopper would be used as a backup only if the first became inoperable or was shot down. It would carry only its crew, additional medical supplies and extra ammunition. Behind it sat a Special Operations AC-130U Hercules, commonly referred to as "Spectre." The four-engine modified cargo plane would fly a race track pattern over the mining camp when the ground crew went in to extract Collins. Painted a matte black, with an unearthly picture of a skeleton firing a minigun and using a crescent moon as cover, the AC-130U carried an imposing amount of firepower. It was armed with three guns—a 25-mm Gatling gun, 40-mm cannon and 105-mm howitzer. With all-weather capability, the Spectre could pin down enemy troops at night, allowing special ops teams to get into and out of an area without many losses, most times with none.

Duke looked up to see a large, flat-faced Army Ranger walking toward him with a determined stride. The man's broad chest, narrow waist and muscular legs reminded Duke of a college linebacker. He recognized the man as Lieutenant Chuck LaCoss, the squad leader for the Rangers who had volunteered for the mission.

"My squad is loading now, sir," LaCoss stated in a deep voice.

"They've been fully briefed?" Duke asked, looking at him squarely.

"Yes, sir. We've reviewed every shred of satellite imagery. If the CIA officer is in the area, we'll get him out," LaCoss said confidently. "My men will sweep the area in twenty minutes. We'll be back in the air within thirty."

"Good." Duke watched the lieutenant stalk back toward his troops, helping to toss several more bundles of equipment onto the chopper. Duke had met him only six hours ago and already decided he liked him. Chuck LaCoss was down to earth with a dead-serious attitude. Duke knew he probably would never be the life of a party, but he appreciated the squad leader for a mission like this one.

Eighteen Rangers started climbing inside the Pave Low. Each man's face was covered with black camouflage paint and each wore a camouflaged helmet with night vision goggles, or NVGs, mounted on top. Their upper bodies were covered with thick black SPECTRA bulletproof armor, and they were armed to the teeth with rifles, rocket launchers and communications gear. There was no talking or commotion as they uniformly ascended the small ladder into the chopper.

Duke lifted himself into the cockpit of the MH-53J and took his place in the center seat between the pilot and copilot. A moment later the six massive rotor blades began slowly twirling in the air. As the momentum picked up, they filled the flight deck with a clamoring noise. Duke slipped on his helmet, plugged in his microphone and allowed himself one last thought of Katie and the kids before they took off and he gave his full attention to the mission.

BADGER TWO, 206 JET RANGER

"Yeah, I see it," Captain Skip Watson answered his copilot as they skimmed fifty feet above the water. The green outline of a giant tanker was approaching fast below and out front, filling his

NVGs. It was bathed with numerous white spots and Watson could easily make out the floodlights along the bridge and bow of the ship. He snapped the stick right, working the rudder pedals, and nosed the chopper up another hundred feet. The massive hull of the supertanker flashed by to his left, missing the helicopter by the length of a football field. As if racing over the Persian Gulf at 160 knots just above the water at night wasn't dangerous enough, they also had to dodge tankers.

Watson pitched the chopper's nose down, losing altitude quickly and picking up airspeed. He panned his head right and left, taking in every detail around him. The cool water looked a dark olive green, with an occasional lighter green blur appearing in an expansive area. Out the left window he could see Badger Two, his wingman, about fifty feet away, paralleling his speed and altitude.

In the distance, the white lights of Bushehr twinkled out at him. The pulsing tone in his helmet had turned to a clear drumming sound. He was surprised they hadn't challenged him.

"Okay Badger Two, it's time to play ball," Watson radioed.

"*Copy that . . . we're with you, Leader.*"

Watson flipped on his navigation lights and climbed through 500 feet. He swung the nimble chopper around until they were headed straight for the radar site. Once again he pitched the chopper's nose down, this time allowing the rotor blades to reflect a strong stream of radar waves back toward the Iranian early-warning site.

P-35M RADAR SITE

The sergeant blinked several times, then rubbed his eyes to make sure he was seeing the black screen correctly. Amber lines cut across the bottom half of the scope, showing the jagged coastline. On the left, a yellow triangle told him a surface ship was making its way north toward Kuwait. But now two green triangles were also pulsing, heading straight for the coast.

Damn it; where did they come from? He was certain that section of the scope was empty only a second ago. Well, *almost* sure of it. Could he have dozed off? He tapped the computer keyboard, checking his equipment. The targets were moving fairly slowly telling him they weren't fighters or bombers making a high-speed run at the coastline. From their speed and altitude they looked to be small single-engine aircraft or helicopters. He cleared his throat before speaking.

"Lieutenant, I'm tracking two unknown aircraft bearing two six five degrees. Altitude, 520 feet and climbing, speed, 140 knots, range . . ." The sergeant didn't look up at his commanding officer. "Range, thirteen miles."

"*What* . . . thirteen miles? Where did they come from?" Lieutenant al-Shira sputtered in disbelief. He leaned over the sergeant's shoulder, studying the radar screen.

"I don't know, sir," the pudgy-faced sergeant replied, staring at the military and civilian flight schedules tacked to the nearby wall. "There is nothing on the regional flight plans. They . . . they just appeared out of nowhere."

"Damn it, Sergeant, I should have been notified sooner." Lieutenant al-Shira rubbed his hands together.

"Should I try to establish contact, sir?"

"No, I will," al-Shira barked. "I don't need any more incompetence." The lieutenant knew it would be his head on a stick if anything went wrong. He picked up the headphones and placed them over his ears. His eyes were focused on the changing radar data. The IFF transponder code was blank. Whoever was out there didn't want to be identified.

The lieutenant tuned the radio to 243 MHz, the military air distress frequency, which was monitored by all aircraft in the Gulf. He keyed the mike. "Unknown aircraft bearing two six fiver . . . altitude, six hundred feet and climbing, speed, one hundred forty knots. You are approaching Iranian airspace. State your intentions or turn away. You are advancing into danger." Al-Shira immediately changed frequency to 121.5 MHz and repeated the message over the international air distress frequency.

Captain Watson inhaled deeply and felt his mouth go dry. "Well, we're going to see if those boys in the Super Snooper earned their pay this week." He felt a stirring in the pit of his gut.

Three days earlier, an Air Force RC-135 had recorded the distress signals from an Iranian training jet south of Deyyer, along Iran's central coast. The emissions were decoded and analyzed, telling Air Force intel officers which radio frequencies and IFF codes the Iranians used. Watson now planned to use the same IFF transponder and radio codes to land at Bushehr. It should work if the code hadn't been changed in the past seventy-two hours.

His eyes swept the instruments, making sure the radio was tuned to the proper frequency. "This is Iranian special operations flight zero zero five. Requesting emergency landing beacon," Watson said in practiced Farsi with a thick accent. "Acknowledge . . . this is Iranian special operations flight zero zero five. Requesting emergency landing beacon."

Lieutenant al-Shira paused, trying to sort out the facts. This was the first time he had ever come across this kind of situation. His mind raced, trying to remember the procedure for emergency landings.

"Turn to radio frequency Zulu November Alpha," he radioed. "Repeat, Zulu November Alpha." That was the code name for the classified Iranian radio channel used for special operations. It was changed randomly.

Here goes nothing. Watson changed the digital radio dial to 201.5 MHz and keyed his mike. "This is Colonel Birjand of the 3rd Special Forces Air Corps. I am returning from a mission and experiencing mechanical problems. Request permission to land at once."

"*Negative, flight zero zero five. Not without an authority IFF code. Permission denied.*"

Watson lifted the protective cover over the IFF transponder switch and flicked it on. "Transmitting code now. I urgently need that landing beacon turned on."

In the left-hand corner of the radar screen, the number TNX473 flashed. The red letters pulsed every other second.

"That's a current IFF code, Lieutenant," the communications sergeant said, breathing a little easier.

"*Repeat. This is Colonel Birjand of the 3rd Special Forces Air Corps. Request permission to land. I have a chopper leaking turbine oil . . . engine is overheating. Estimated flight time, three minutes.*"

"Range, eight miles and closing, sir. Speed is now 153 knots. They're climbing, but slowly."

"*Repeat. This is flight zero zero five . . . we are returning from a classified mission carrying sensitive equipment and personnel.*"

I demand permission to land . . . NOW."

Lieutenant al-Shira's mind swirled. Iranian regulations were detailed. The base at Bushehr was considered classified and that meant restricted access only. Granting landing permission to an aircraft was prohibited, even with the proper codes, without contacting his commander at Ahwaz first. *But then again, where else would a special forces helicopter land?* he asked himself.

"Contact regional command," the lieutenant finally decided.

"This is Colonel Birjand. I demand clearance to land at ONCE! Do you hear me? Who is in charge there? I can't keep this helicopter in the air much longer."

"Six miles and closing."

"There is no response from regional command yet, sir," the second officer reported. "It takes at least a minute to bring the SA-2 acquisition radars on line."

"I know how long it takes," Lieutenant al-Shira snapped. He paused only a moment longer. "Turn on the landing lights to pad one. And make sure a security detail is on hand to assist me when they land." He keyed his mike.

The two Bell 206 Jet Rangers streaked over the coast at 1,000 feet, continuing their climb toward the radar station. They were low enough for Captain Watson to make out the crowded rows of apartment houses and single-room shacks along the coastline. *Fifteen seconds and we turn back*, he thought, his eyes gliding between the mission clock and the Plexiglas window.

"Either this guy is playing it smart or he's having to look it up in the rule book," said the copilot.

"You just be ready with the flares and chaff," Watson demanded.

"Flight zero zero five. This is Lieutenant al-Shira. Take a heading of one six six. Emergency landing beacon is on frequency Oscar Romeo . . . repeat, Oscar Romeo."

"Copy. We are coming in."

Watson wiped the sweat from his upper lip. He turned on the exterior lights, illuminating the Iranian flag. At the same time the needle inside the TACAN swung around to the top, indicating he was on course for the station.

"I see it, Captain. On top of the hill." The copilot pointed toward a cluster of lights that had just appeared straight ahead of them. "Well, it's the end of the first quarter. Score ... U.S., seven, camel drivers, zippo." He hit the button, turning on the smoke generator. Watson banked his chopper before dropping the nose and heading for the radar station.

Chapter Twenty-five

ESFAHAN, IRAN

Colonel Rahavi walked down the last flight of stairs into the underground control center. The walls were lined with sandbags, and steel beams ran across the ceiling to reinforce the chamber. Located several hundred meters from the air base's main control tower, the Command Operations Center housed twenty of Iran's best-trained communications and ground control intercept officers. It was from this site that Rahavi would command his squadrons of F-4Es as they prepared to attack the American fleet.

He stood in the entryway for a few seconds and scrutinized the center. The horseshoe-shaped room had been built with the help of French air force technicians. It had been constructed to survive several direct hits from Western smart bombs, although Rahavi seriously doubted it could withstand a direct attack from the West's latest weapon, known as a bunker buster.

The French had also sold and helped install one of their most advanced air defense computer systems as part of a swap for a cheap price on oil. The code name for the systems was NARI, which was Iran spelled backwards. The French had divided Iran into four air defense zones, each with a strategic defense operations center that controlled the SAMs, air defense guns and fighters in the zone. The control structure was very similar to the one the French had helped build for Saddam Hussein before the Gulf

345

War, the only difference being the Iranian system was more advanced, using secure fiberoptic cables, which were impossible to jam, to link each of Iran's long-and short-range warning radars. In addition, the data from each of the four centers transmitted to the COC, where it was displayed on a single screen in the rear of the room. From this center, Rahavi could call up radar telemetry for every section of the country, allowing him to track all aircraft flying above 2,000 feet in mountainous terrain. Below 2,000 feet, ground clutter interference made it impossible to track anything. It was a flaw he didn't care for but knew he had to live with for the time being.

The colonel moved next to the senior communications officer, a fifty-year-old sergeant with a thick beard and bald head who had worked with Rahavi for over ten years.

"Status report, Sergeant Lidaz," Rahavi snorted, hands behind his back.

"Two MiG-29s are currently on patrol to the north of us." He pointed to two blue triangles making a slow turn to the northwest. "To the south I am tracking three civilian airliners and one cargo plane."

"What is the condition of our fighters?" Rahavi demanded.

"Twelve F-4Es configured for air-to-surface operations. They are armed with cruise missiles, fueled and ready. Eight F-4Es are fueled and ready for flight escort. They are armed with air-to-air missiles. The pilots await your orders, sir."

Rahavi studied the large radar screen. It was centered on the southern portion of Iran from Esfahan to Bandar Abbas, including the Strait of Hormuz. Any American aircraft patrolling the skies south of Bandar Abbas would also be displayed on the screen.

"Our P-3 patrols are reporting the American carrier is now 157 miles southeast of Bandar Abbas," Sergeant Lidaz reported. Both men knew the F-4s would have to fly fifty miles over the ocean before launching their missiles.

One hundred miles, Rahavi thought. He had hoped the Americans would have moved the *Abraham Lincoln* closer. He wondered how many fighters would be shot down by American interceptors before reaching their target.

"Give the order to launch the aircraft," Rahavi said finally. He picked up the authority phone, linking him with Defense Minister Bakhtiar.

P-35M RADAR SITE, BUSHEHR, IRAN

Lieutenant al-Shira stood erectly on the edge of the landing pad and searched the night sky. He could hear the rhythmic sounds of two helicopters approaching from the southwest. Standing beside him were five soldiers, their AK-47s ready.

"There they are," one of the security team shouted and pointed up. All eyes looked in that direction.

Appearing over the edge of a distant hill, two choppers made their way toward the radar site. Thick black smoke was trailing behind the lead helicopter. The sound of its engine surged and sputtered.

"Stand back," the lieutenant shouted excitedly. "He may have to crash-land."

Captain Watson twisted the throttle back and forth, simulating an engine in distress. A quarter of a mile away he could see the well-lit concrete pad with two large white circles painted in the center marking the landing spot. Approximately fifty yards to the south he caught sight of a dirt road twisting its way up the mountain, ending at the radar site. In front was the concrete building used to control the early warning radar and a half mile farther, sitting on the highest point in the area, was the large wire mesh radar antenna. It was slowly rotating in a counterclockwise direction.

"Badger Two . . . Badger Lead. I'm going to touch down first. You follow thirty seconds behind."

"*Copy, Leader. We'll be thirty seconds off your tail.*"

He keyed the internal mike. "We have company down there, men. I want you to be alert and ready. If they start to play rough, hit back hard and fast." He switched the interior lights from a soft green to red, telling the Rangers in the rear half of the chopper they were headed for the ground.

Watson banked sharply to the left, then right, as if the chopper was hard to control. He was now close enough to see the faces and uniforms of the soldiers below him. The armed men were Iranian special forces, dressed in brown fatigues and black berets. *Well, I guess I'd have been insulted to be greeted by anyone of less experience and ranking*, he thought.

The 206 hovered above the landing pad for a few seconds, the thick black smoke swirling around the chopper. Watson felt the right skid hit the ground and then the left as the rotor wash kicked up a thick cloud of sand and dust. He throttled down, letting the helicopter's blades slow.

A short and lean Iranian air defense lieutenant approached the side of the chopper. Behind him, two guards pointed their AK-47s at the window.

"This is one hell of a welcoming committee," Watson's co-pilot said as he unstrapped himself from his seat and removed the NVGs from his helmet. Within thirty seconds, the second chopper touched down, throwing more dust and dirt into the night air.

Colonel Rahavi watched as the last group of F-4Es appeared on the large radar screen, heading south and gaining altitude. After a few minutes, the four planes joined the lead group. The colonel knew they were air defense fighters. The F-4Es had been divided into two groups. The first group consisted of eight F-4Es, call signed Blue Flight. It was their mission to keep the Americans from shooting down any of the F-4Es armed with the stealth cruise missiles. The second group, twelve F-4Es armed with two cruise missiles each, was the main strike package. Their call sign was Gold Flight.

The two flights continued to move south in two tight formations spaced a half mile apart. The air defense fighters were cruising above the F-4Es armed with the missiles. It would take them forty-five minutes to reach the coast and another fifteen to get into range to launch their missiles.

"Blue Leader . . . this is Command Center Esfahan. Do you copy?"

"*Copy, Esfahan. This is Blue Leader.*"

"ETA to coast . . . forty minutes. Skies are free of hostile aircraft," Colonel Rahavi reported.

"*Copy, Esfahan. All aircraft report normal operations. We are proceeding to first way-point. Blue Leader out.*"

Rahavi looked back at the screen as the fighters slowly inched their way farther south. Twenty aircraft against an American carrier. Being able to get close enough to launch the missiles, then turn back without being detected, would be the key to the pilots' survival. Rahavi knew this might appear to be cowardly by American standards, but the odds were not in their favor and the end results would be all that mattered.

*   *   *

"Lieutenant, I am Colonel Birjand," Watson said in Farsi, stepping out of the chopper. His brown khaki Iranian uniform was sweaty and dirty. He wore his helmet to disguise his light-colored skin. On his shoulders were the green-and-red-checkered symbols of a special forces full colonel.

"Yes, Colonel. Wel . . . welcome," Lieutenant al-Shira stuttered as he saluted.

"My helicopter is in need of repairs. I must use your communications center," Watson demanded, as he strode toward the smaller lieutenant.

"Colonel . . . may I see some ID, sir? This is a restricted base." The man's voice broke.

"My men and I are returning from a mission into Iraq. You must not let anyone know we have landed here." Watson ignored the man's request. "I must use your radio to contact my commander. Take me to the control center *now*. And have these guards bring my men some water."

"I cannot do that, sir." The lieutenant cleared his throat and stood in front of Watson. "Not until I see your identification."

Watson stopped. Two security guards standing behind the lieutenant pointed their rifles at him. Fifteen feet away, three other guards pointed their weapons at the chopper.

Master Sergeant Ricky Vasquez already had his rifle shouldered and had placed a round in the chamber. He thumbed the safety one more time, making sure it was off. Seated inside the chopper, he leaned against the back of the fuselage, using one of the jump seats as a rest to steady his heavy-barreled supressed sniper rifle.

"On three," one of the Rangers whispered, as he knelt next to the chopper's cargo door. "One . . . two . . . three!"

In a flash, two other Rangers swung the side cargo door open. Vasquez only had to shift his rifle a few inches to center the crosshairs of the Starlight scope on the farthest guard's head. He tapped the trigger, feeling the silenced rifle jump. Only a muffled sound could be heard as the bullet shot out from the barrel. He immediately chambered another round.

That's one, he thought, pivoting the rifle to the next target. He placed the crosshairs squarely on the second guard's face and pulled the trigger. The man's head flew back just before his body crumpled to the ground.

That's two. He chambered another .308 round, sweeping his

rifle to the left. Just then two other Rangers, using suppressed 9-mm Uzis with laser sights, took out the other guards. The Iranians hadn't gotten off a shot.

The lieutenant heard a moan and turned in time to see two of the guards drop only seconds apart. Stunned, he turned back to see Watson pointing a pistol directly at his head. He froze and remained motionless until the short episode of gunfire was over. All five men lay in crumpled heaps on the ground.

"Turn around and put your hands on your head," Watson ordered once he received the signal it was safe to move.

The lieutenant did as he was told. Watson walked up from behind, put his pistol in the Iranian's back and removed his side arm.

"You men . . . secure this area. Vasquez and Rath, get on top of that hill and make sure no one comes up the road," Watson shouted to the soldiers exiting the choppers.

"Now, take me to the command center before you end up like your friends over there," he said to the lieutenant in his best Farsi.

"Let's go, Vasquie," Lieutenant Max Rath said, adjusting his black skullcap and grabbing his gear and his M-16. Rath was three years older than Vasquez, but shorter and with a smaller frame. His facial features were more like those of a history teacher than someone who was part of a sniper team. Walking across the landing area to make their way up the nearby hill, they looked like an odd couple.

The other members of the assault team were moving the bodies away and securing the area. Rath was silent, not taking notice of the commotion. He glanced at Vasquez, waiting for his partner to be ready to talk. They had been together long enough that he knew Vasquez's thoughts were ones of sorrow for the wives and children of the men he had so quickly shot down. It was not easy for him. He had once confided to Rath that he said a prayer of contrition after every operation. He didn't know if it would help when his time came, but it made him feel better.

The two-man team started up the crest of the hill. It was covered with small rocks and boulders, allowing for good concealment. They planned to stay on the hill for only three hours, so additional camouflage and cover wouldn't be needed. The dark of the night and surprise would be their defense against any intruders on this mission.

Rath reached into his backpack and pulled out a handheld Starlight spotting scope mounted on a small tripod. He turned the scope on to let it warm up and started scanning the area around the radar complex. The Iranians had built the command building about a hundred yards from the edge of a rocky cliff overlooking the town of Bushehr. The helicopter landing pads were near the rear of the building. As with most of the desert, the area was void of plant life and the nearest trees were several hundred yards away. He trained the scope right, focusing on the dirt road below them. Other than by air, it was the only way to get into or out of the radar complex.

"Okay . . . we're clear," Rath said aloud.

Vasquez was spread out on the ground next to his scout, the barrel of his rifle resting on his backpack.

"Better get out your radio and set up a link with Watson," Rath ordered, returning to the scope.

Captain Watson followed the Iranian lieutenant into the radar command center. The room was much smaller and more crowded than he had expected. It was long and narrow, with the electrical equipment stacked next to the nearest wall. He could see the lights from the display screens reflected off the faces of the Iranian operators seated at their posts. They were oblivious to what had just happened on the landing pad.

"Move away from the consoles," Watson ordered, letting the two sergeants see his pistol.

The two turned and stared at Watson, then looked at their lieutenant in disbelief.

"Do as he says or he will kill us now." Lieutenant al-Shira, sweating with fear, spoke harshly. The sergeants moved away from their consoles, keeping their hands in sight.

"Take them outside and tie them up. Make sure they're out of the way," Watson ordered. "Jones . . . Petersen, man these posts."

"Yes, sir." Two special forces technicians slid behind the radar and communications consoles.

"Contact Coyote three four," Watson said. "Tell them the objective is under our command. The mission is a go and kick ass."

"Yes, sir."

"I do not know what you are planning, but you will never get away with it," al-Shira stated defiantly.

"You'd best keep your mouth shut. The only reason you're still alive is that I might need you for something later on," Watson said bluntly. "So start praying to Allah that if I do need you, you're smart enough to help out . . . or I might just leave you here looking like you were more than happy to cooperate."

Al-Shira only stared back in response. He understood what the captain meant.

MH-53J, COYOTE THREE FOUR

Duke James watched the pilot bring the big chopper level as it came out of a long banking turn three hundred feet above the Persian Gulf. They had been in the air fifteen minutes and were now in a holding pattern outside the range of Iranian search radars, off the northern shore of Bahrain. He looked at the mission clock. Watson and his men should have captured the radar base ten minutes ago. Duke's MH-53J only had fuel to maintain the holding pattern for thirty minutes, with enough in reserve to reach their objective. If they had to, the pilot could call for a tanker to top off their tanks, but that would take time—time they didn't want to spare.

"Coyote Three Four . . . Badger Leader here. Do you copy?"

"Go ahead Badger Leader," Duke answered the radio call.

"Objective Kilo Hotel is secure. Repeat, Objective Kilo Hotel is secure. No fatalities."

"Hot damn, Badger Leader. Good work. We're on our way."

"Copy, Coyote Three Four. See ya on the way out. Good luck."

"Put the pedal to the metal. We're on our way," Duke said, ready for their part in the mission. He felt the massive power of the Pave Low's engines spooling and heard the deafening whine of the turbines as the chopper picked up airspeed, heading for the Iranian coast. It would take them forty-five minutes to reach their objective. Right now that seemed like an eternity, but Duke knew that very shortly it would all transpire much too fast.

Chapter Twenty-six

USS *La Salle*

The command center was quiet, just the standard radio chatter, yet Tom Staffer could feel the trepidation in the air. For the past two hours he had watched the glowing yellow symbols representing the *Abraham Lincoln* and her battle group. They were now 118 miles south of Iran. The display screen to the right listed the aircraft in the air, along with their call signs. Admiral Zachiem paced the floor down in front of Staffer and General Chaniff, who was seated next to him in the rear of the room.

Staffer watched the steam rise from his styrofoam cup of coffee as he thought about Mark Collins. Being stuck behind enemy lines was a nightmare most CIA officers would only discuss among themselves, if they talked about it at all. He wondered how Collins was doing, where he was at the moment and what was going through his mind. Staffer sat down next to General Chaniff, took a sip from his cup and looked at Chaniff, amazed that he could sit still for so long.

"The last A-6 just launched off the *Lincoln*. They'll hit the first way-point in ten minutes," Zachiem announced, turning to face them. "We have two E-2C Hawkeyes moving to the north section of the battle group. When the Iranians move, we'll see 'em."

"Sir, we just received word from Coyote Three Four," the communications officer said. "Badger has secured their objective."

"Well, that's good news. Now let's hope they hold it until your man can be rounded up," Chaniff said to Staffer, then called to Zachiem, "What's the status of the main strike package?"

"Colonel Naylor has just given the order for the EF-111As to take off. They should all be airborne in the next five minutes," Zachiem responded in his usual monotone.

"Very well. Now all we can do is wait," Chaniff said and finally stood up.

Yeah, wait. Staffer checked his wristwatch. They should be on the ground in about an hour, just before the main strike force hit Esfahan. He folded his arms and slumped in the chair. It was going to be a long hour.

A-6E INTRUDER, SHREDDER LEADER

"Strike . . . Shredder Leader Two Seven. Do you copy?"

"Shredder Leader . . . Strike . . . We copy, Shredder."

"Holding at way-point one." Lieutenant Commander Bert Cummings throttled back and pitched the nose of his fighter bomber up two degrees. He banked to the left, keeping the big plane at 12,000 feet.

"Roger that, Shredder Leader. Keep channel open and wait for further orders," came the response from *Lincoln's* CIC.

"Copy, Strike . . . Shredder Leader holding." Cummings dropped his oxygen mask from his mouth. He felt his blood start to boil and swallowed hard, trying to keep his temper under control. "We're also burning fuel. Just in case you're wondering, Strike . . . that's what keeps this baby in the air. No fuel . . . no fly," he said irritably to no one in particular.

"I knew I should have had beans for dinner," his bombardier/navigator, Lieutenant Jason George, who was seated next to him, said with a slight laugh. "Then we'd have lots of gas."

Cummings laughed and he checked his instruments, making sure the fighter bomber was functioning properly. The lieutenant commander would lead a four-ship strike package against the two launch sites located west of Bandar Abbas. Eight other Intruders would hit the sites to the east. Their plan was relatively simple: Navy Seal Teams had already penetrated the Iranian coast and pinpointed six launch sites. At 0247, the Seal teams would begin illuminating the targets with portable AN/PAQ-1 laser target designators, riflelike devices capable of illuminating a target up to

4,000 feet away with an invisible laser. All Cummings and his bombardier/navigator had to do was find the reflecting laser beam, lock onto it and drop their four GBU-12 Paveways. The homing mechanism in the nose of each bomb would guide the Paveways to the target by following the reflecting laser.

Navy intelligence, with the help of the CIA-controlled satellites, had detected a number of SA-6 missile batteries along the Iranian coast. An EA-6B Prowler would jam the SAMs' radars, but that would alert the Iranians that an attack was about to occur or was already in progress. Cummings knew the trick would be to get all his bombs on target the first pass. And, of course, hope the F/A-18Cs and F-14As flying MiG-cap above him kept the enemy fighters off his back.

Cummings's attention returned to the HUD. He chopped the throttles further, cutting his airspeed to 190 knots. Through the HUD, he could barely make out the lights of a ship cruising west five miles in front of him. It was nearly impossible to see anything without the aid of the bomber's forward-looking infrared system. Cummings looked at his navigator, who was staring at the FLIR scope. "See anything?" Cummings asked.

"Nope, just salt water and seagulls," Lieutenant George answered.

BAHRAIN AIR BASE

Colonel Eddie Naylor watched the ground crew pull the red-flagged safety pins off the last of his six AGM-88C HARM missiles. They then quickly moved to his wingtip-mounted AIM-9M Sidewinders, pulling the pins and making sure the air-to-air heat-seekers were ready. Naylor checked his weapons panel; it showed all the missiles were wired to his computer. He hit a switch on his throttle, changing the weapons' computer from air-to-ground to air-to-air mode. The HUD responded instantly with the correct symbology.

The colonel flashed a thumbs-up and waited for the canopy to close on his F-16C before easing back the throttle. He released the brakes and taxied away from the hangar toward the south end of the runway. Three additional F-16Cs, the rest of Naylor's SEAD (suppression of air defenses) team, were waiting at the edge of the runway.

As the colonel taxied toward his takeoff point, he watched the last two F-15Es soar into the dark sky, their afterburners bright blue and orange. He swung his sleek, single-seat F-16C around, lining it up on the right side of the runway. His wingman glided into position next to his left wing.

"Tower, this is Coors Leader. Ready for takeoff," Naylor radioed.

"Roger, Coors Leader . . . you're cleared for takeoff."

"Copy, Tower. You with me, number two?"

"I'm right on your wing, Lead," came the response.

"Coors leader rolling."

Naylor advanced the single throttle forward just short of the afterburner groove. The fighter's 23,830-pound thrust engine quickly spooled up, pushing the jet down the runway. Naylor's gaze focused on the HUD, and he watched the symbology change rapidly. At sixty knots he jammed the throttles forward, past the afterburner groove. The added thrust forced him deep into his seat as the F-16C picked up speed. When the HUD hit 160 knots, he gently pulled the stick back, lifting his fighter into the air.

BUSHEHR, IRAN

"What is *that*?" Watson asked. A sharp, piercing noise cut through the radar command center.

"It is the priority phone," Lieutenant al-Shira said, his voice tight and strained.

"And who would be calling?" Watson asked, keeping his pistol leveled on the Iranian.

"It is regimental command." Al-Shira swallowed hard.

The phone buzzed again. *Damn it*, Watson cursed to himself. He cocked the hammer on his gun and raised it to the man's head.

"Okay, Lieutenant, here's the deal. You pick up the phone, tell them what they want to hear and I'll let you live. If you screw up and say something stupid, I'll blow your fucking brains out. You understand me?"

"Yes . . . I understand." Al-Shira shook his head nervously.

"Good. Now, pick it up." Watson put the barrel directly on al-Shira's temple so he could feel the cold steel.

"Bushehr . . . site one. Lieutenant al-Shira speaking."

Watson drew closer to the lieutenant's ear, pulling the receiver down slightly so he could hear the voice on the other end.

"Lieutenant al-Shira, this is Sergeant Tabas at headquarters. Your relief team will be arriving two hours later than planned.

They are having mechanical problems."

"Yes, Sergeant . . . I understand," al-Shira answered, hanging up the phone.

"What time will that be?" Watson asked.

"They were scheduled to be here at 0600, but now it will be around 0800 if they can get the problem solved in time," al-Shira lied. The relief squad was actually scheduled to arrive at 0400, possibly putting them at the site at 0600. Al-Shira hoped they would catch the Americans off-guard and recapture the base.

"You had better not be lying to me, Iranian," Watson grunted.

"Sir. Here they come." Sergeant Jones, seated at the radar screen, pointed to a cluster of green triangles on the outer edge of the scope.

"Okay . . . take this thing off line," Watson commanded.

"Yes, sir." Jones had already studied the radar's control panel. He flipped a series of five switches and powered down the system. A moment later the radar screen faded, going from amber to black.

"All right. They have five minutes to clear the area." Watson nodded to the man at the communications equipment. "Petersen, make sure that radio channel is open. I want to hear what's going on out there."

"Yes, sir."

Watson didn't want the Iranian radar down any longer than five or ten minutes. He reasoned that a few minutes could be explained away as a brief malfunction, something that could be handled without outside assistance, but longer than that might be inviting company. He doubted the Iranians were that efficient, but he didn't want to chance a technical team being sent in to help repair the radar.

"Sit back down, Lieutenant," Watson ordered, noticing the man was still rigidly standing in the way.

F-16C Coors Leader

Colonel Naylor noted the lime green image of the lead MH-53J Pave Low III chopper on his FLIR monitor in the upper center of his cockpit. He could clearly see the glowing image of its two hot engines and whirling rotor blades. The LANTIRN (low-altitude navigation and targeting, infrared, for night)-equipped jet allowed the colonel and his team of SAM hunters to maintain high speeds and low altitudes at night while attacking targets, and also permitted him to distinguish friendly aircraft and avoid mid-air collisions.

Naylor's four F-16Cs were in a tight formation, less than two hundred feet apart. They were trailing two EF-111As. A hundred yards above him were the F-15Es and F-15Cs, also flying in tight formations. The Pave Lows were leading the strike package in-land followed by the AC-130U gunship.

He keyed his mike. "Coyote Three Four . . . Coors Leader. All present and accounted for."

"*Roger, Coors Leader. Three minutes to feet dry.*"

Naylor recognized General James's voice crackling over the radio. "Roger, Coyote Three Four."

MH-53J, Coyote Three Four

Duke studied the blurry green Iranian coastline through his night vision goggles. Strapped on top of his flight helmet was one of the most sophisticated night-imaging systems the military had ever produced—the AN/AVS-6(V)1. The system, which looked like something out of a science-fiction movie, consisted of a small replaceable battery pack with a toggle switch that turned the goggles on or off. The battery wires coiled around the front of the helmet, providing power to the NVGs, which were fastened to the front of the helmet visor.

Duke estimated they were seven miles out. The city lights of Bushehr were now evident, showing up as off-white smears. The murky green shadows of mountains and rocky hills lining the horizon were also laid out in front of him.

He adjusted his lap belt, making sure it was snug. Once they began to fly over land, the ride would change drastically. Rather than skimming across the flat ocean, the pilot would engage the Pave Lows' terrain-following radar, keeping the chopper at 200 feet above the not-so-flat desert. Their Sunday afternoon drive would turn into the Indy 500 without any pit stops.

The main segment of the strike package would streak ahead of the Pave Lows and AC-130U. If everything went as planned, those aircraft would be hitting the weapons site a few minutes after Duke and the choppers touched down at the mining camp.

For a moment the coast appeared beneath the Pave Low. He could see the waves rolling over and crashing onto the rocks.

Instantly, the pilot put the chopper into a steep climb, forcing it to gain altitude and airspeed.

Duke keyed his mike. "This is Coyote Three Four . . . we are feet dry. Repeat. This is Coyote Three Four . . . we are feet dry."

USS *LA SALLE*

"Confirm the transmission," Zachiem ordered his communications officer. The admiral looked over at Chaniff. "The main strike package just crossed the coast. Phase one is over without a hitch. I'm ordering the Intruders to hit their targets now."

Chaniff only nodded his head, then leaned forward, studying the radar screens inside the command center. Two groups of four blue triangles, Navy air superiority fighters, were flying a racetrack pattern north of the *Abraham Lincoln*—F/A-18C Hornets and F-14A Tomcats flying BarCAP (Barrier Combat Air Patrol). It was the fighters' job to make sure nothing came too close to the carrier. To the west, four F/A-18Cs and two EA-6B Prowlers were escorting the A-6Es as they broke into two groups, preparing for their run at the coastal targets. The main strike force was just moving into position off Saudi Arabia's eastern coast.

Chaniff looked up at the mission clock, then scrutinized the main screen. *I don't like it that everything is so quiet,* he thought. *You'd think they'd be expecting something.* Other than the Navy's battle group, a few oil tankers to the west and three commercial flights to the northeast, there wasn't any other surface or air activity. It was as if the Iranians had put their heads in the sand.

"When did we lose contact with that last Iranian P-3?" Chaniff asked.

"Two and a half hours ago. It dropped out of AWACS coverage at 2325 hours," Zachiem answered.

Chaniff's eyes narrowed. The Navy's two E-2C Hawkeyes were also moving north, but it would probably be another ten to fifteen minutes before they could detect airborne targets.

"How many fighters do you have in the air flying BarCAP, Mr. Zachiem?"

"Eight, sir. Four F-14s and four F-18s."

Chaniff contemplated the situation for a moment. "Give the order to up four more F-18s."

"Sir, with all due respect, eight fighters can handle anything the Iranians—"

"Just do it, Admiral," Chaniff cut him off, not liking the nagging feeling in his gut. "If eight can handle whatever they have, then twelve should be able to do the job even better." He looked at Staffer. "If your Mr. Collins is correct and Iran was planning an attack, then they're going to want to do it early. They could be betting that your man didn't get the information to us, but I'll lay odds that they'll opt for not allowing us time to prepare a defense."

Staffer didn't respond.

Chaniff looked back at the main display. He heard Zachiem ordering the *Abraham Lincoln* to launch more fighters. "There's something about that P-3, too," he added, then was quiet, speculating on his own and hoping Staffer was doing the same. This was the challenge of war—outguessing your enemy.

ESFAHAN, IRAN

"I cannot wait any longer," Hassan Zadeh said from behind Khalk Hikmet. "You have been working for almost eighteen hours, and all you have found are maps and worthless computer information. Work faster or get someone else in here who knows what he's doing."

"*No one* else can do this!" Hikmet shouted. "I cannot concentrate with you bothering me. Why do you not go outside and wait?"

"Because you are not to be trusted. How did top-secret information get into the hands of that woman?"

Hikmet slowly rose from his chair. The chief engineer was just as tall as Zadeh, but he wasn't nearly as wide or well conditioned. "No man talks to me this way." Hikmet, tired and overworked, had finally reached his limit. "I am no traitor. I have worked on this project from the beginning and without me, it wouldn't have gotten as far—"

Zadeh reached out, grabbing Hikmet by the throat and cutting off his air supply.

"Stop this. Stop it, I say!" Ali Fesseghi stepped between the two men. "We are not going to find the American if we do not cooperate. Zadeh, step away. Do as I say!"

Zadeh shoved Hikmet away from him. "I have killed men for less."

Hikmet rubbed his throat, staring defiantly at the two of them.

"We are all just tired," Fesseghi said. "But we mustn't give up yet. There is still work to be done."

"Tell the fool I'm doing the best I can," Hikmet muttered.

"Hikmet, sit down. Return to your computer. Zadeh, I suggest that you get something to eat, and some sleep as well," Fesseghi said firmly.

"All I need is to know the location of the American. And I am wasting time waiting for information that may not even be on the computer," Zadeh snapped.

Hikmet let out a long breath, feeling his pulse settling back to normal. He sat back down and rubbed his fatigued eyes before starting to study his computer screen again. *Fesseghi is right. I am so tired, I can barely think,* he thought. He scrolled the screen forward, stopping at the beginning of the next set of computer codes. *This is impossible. It will take me weeks to break these codes.*

Hikmet focused on the center of the monitor. He squinted and cocked his head to the right. In the middle of the screen he detected a slight variation from the file pattern. The program's line code was out of sequence. The numerical symbol 27<<*.*>>72 didn't seem to belong with the remainder of the program. He moved the cursor, highlighting the numbers. He pressed control F3 and F10. The screen flickered.

This is a large file, Hikmet thought. He copied the data onto the B drive. The chief engineer watched the monitor flash as the data was transferred onto the hard disk. After a few seconds he recalled the data, bringing it back on the screen.

Without warning, the smaller computer made a muffled beeping noise. Hikmet glanced at it before looking back at the main screen. Written across the top was this message:

DOWN-LINK DODSATCOM TRANSMIT VV-DOWNLINK*.*/ 78DDFQ-CVO883
TO: SPECTER FROM: CRYSTAL PALACE

1] PROCEED AT ONCE TO RECOVERY POINT ALPHA.
2] EXTRACTION TEAM EN ROUTE FOR RECOVERY.
3] GOOD LUCK.

Hikmet's heart pounded with the rapid taps he made on several more keys. The screen flashed again. Within seconds, it filled with another map of Iran. Only this one was of the central part of the country and it was in color, with a red circle pulsing over the town of Shahr Kord.

This is it, Hikmet said to himself. He zoomed in on the map, seeing if he could pinpoint the exact location of the pulsing. "Fesseghi . . . Zadeh, come quickly. See what I have found," he shouted.

Both men, roused from their sullen moods, rushed over and stood behind the engineer.

"This must be a CIA satellite downlink transmission," Hikmet said, pointing excitedly to the screen.

"It only looks like another map to me," Zadeh said skeptically.

"Can you focus closer on that pulsing symbol?" Fesseghi asked.

"I don't know . . ." Hikmet worked at manipulating the program. Once again the monitor blinked and the map grew smaller. Hikmet cursed and started over again. The town of Shahr Kord was now in the lower left corner. Northeast of the town Hikmet could see a number of small buildings clustered together near the base of mountain ridges. A single road twisted its way into the area from the main highway. The pulsing red dot was originating from the center of the buildings.

"I know this place," Zadeh said slowly, beginning to believe that the engineer had indeed found something. "It's an abandoned silver mining camp, about fifty miles from here. Yes, this is probably where the CIA pig is headed." Zadeh started to turn.

"Wait. You can't be sure of the that," Fesseghi argued.

"What else could it mean? That is the rendezvous. I am certain of it. The Americans are going to try to pull him out from under our noses." Zadeh's chest puffed up with determination. "Fesseghi, gather your best security troops and get me some helicopters *at once*. We will leave in ten minutes. I will not allow the American and the woman to escape."

Fesseghi stared at the screen, studying the location of the camp. Then, without another word, he left the room.

Hikmet stood looking at Zadeh. "I hope you see what a little patience can do. It is not wise to be so hot-tempered."

"I would suggest you think of how being patient may have delivered secret documents into the hands of the enemy. It has still not been discovered just how this woman was able to penetrate your office and computer, Hikmet. And you have not yet seen my temper. Bakhtiar will want to speak with you when I return." Zadeh slipped on his jacket, looking appropriately vicious for the hunt that was about to begin.

Chapter Twenty-seven

A-6E Intruder, Shredder Leader

"This is Hawkeye on guard. Shredder Leader ... proceed to main objective. Repeat, proceed to main objective."

"Copy, ... Shredder Leader inbound," Lieutenant Commander Bert Cummings responded, as he caught sight of his wingman a hundred yards away.

"You with me, Shredder Two?" Cummings radioed, changing frequencies.

"Right on your wing."

"Three and Four?"

"Three's in."

"Four's in."

"Okay ... follow me down," Cummings instructed. "We'll hit the IP in five minutes."

It had been predetermined that the IP, or initial point, would be an unmanned oil rig located 42.3 miles off the north shore of Oman. Cummings and the other three Intruder pilots would join up and fly over the rig at precisely 0340 hours. They would then maintain a constant air-speed of 310 knots for thirty-two minutes while flying at 500 feet above the ocean. This gave them time to synchronize their flights and hit their targets at precisely the same time, 0412. If one of the Intruder's synchronizations was off and one target was hit before the others, the air defenses along the

363

coast would be alerted and begin their counterattacks. The chances of a completely successful mission would then decrease greatly.

Cummings tugged at his oxygen mask, securing it snugly around his face. Adjusting his grip on the stick and throttles, he eased his bomb-laden Intruder into a slow left-hand turn, feeling the rolling pressure of two Gs come across his body. He watched the lime green numbers on the HUD. His altitude was dropping and airspeed climbing as the Intruder shot down toward the black ocean below. At 8,000 feet he rolled the bomber upright and throttled back, keeping the jet in a shallow climb.

F-4E BLUE LEADER

Major Kuh Gahar methodically checked the instruments of his F-4E every thirty seconds. He sat upright and perfectly square in the fighter's worn ejection seat. The major had been personally chosen by Colonel Rahavi to lead the strike force out over the Gulf of Oman. A month into his fortieth year, he had trained with Rahavi for over a decade. In many ways the major's life paralleled that of the Colonel. Neither man had a family and neither desired one. Their entire existence was dedicated to flying jets and serving the revolution. Tonight's mission would certainly earn the major a promotion, and he would shine in the eyes of the Supreme Defense Council.

The HUD told Gahar he was speeding over the desert at 350 knots at an altitude of 2,500 feet; every gauge and dial glowed brightly inside the Phantom. One thousand feet below his fighter, flying in groups of four with their navigational lights burning, the twelve F-4Es of Gold Flight banked slowly to the right.

The Iranian strike package had just passed its second way-point, the city of Bam, and was now on a heading of 165 degrees, southeast. The major had intentionally kept the group at low altitude. He was using Iran's interior mountains to hide their presence from the probing eyes of American AWACS radars. He knew that tactic wouldn't last forever, but wanted to at least give them an edge.

Major Gahar had rehearsed the attack a hundred times in his mind. Iranian P-3 long-range patrol aircraft had been monitoring the location of the American battle group for the last three days. Their latest intelligence placed the *Abraham Lincoln* roughly 112 miles southwest of the Iranian coast, north of the Tropic of Cancer. The plan called for the fighters to stay on their current heading for another 243 miles before crossing the coast west of Chah Bahar. Major Gahar would then give the order to drop their wing tanks, go into afterburner and head for the American fleet at high Mach speed. They would catch the Americans off-guard and launch their missiles before the Great Satan could bring its powerful interceptors to bear. It was Gahar's mission to lead his group of F-4Es against any American fighters or defenses.

"Navigational update," Gahar grunted.

"Currently five miles east of Bam. ETA to the coast . . . thirty-one minutes," Gahar's backseater responded.

The major's head twisted to the side. He could see the city lights of Bam passing on the right. "Let me know when we're twenty miles from the coast," he ordered.

A-6E INTRUDER, SHREDDER LEADER

Bert Cummings watched the HUD click off his altitude. When his Intruder hit 3,000 feet, he popped the air brakes and used both hands to ease back on the stick. He watched the G meter—2 . . . 3 . . . 3.5. The A-6E groaned, but responded smoothly, the nose coming up and away from the water. The firm bite of 3.5 Gs pushed his body deeper into the hard vinyl ejection seat. At 1,000 feet he leveled the A-6E, the pressure oozed out from his body. The jet's large windscreen filled with the sparkling of a million stars.

"Take a heading of three four seven," Lieutenant Jason George advised, watching his instruments.

Cummings did as he was told, banking the bomber right a few degrees. He centered the stick as the compass heading, located on top of the HUD, stopped on 347 degrees. They were heading northwest.

"You should be picking up the lights of the oil rig any second," George advised. "It's two miles out, coming up on the right." The A-6E jolted up and down as it shot through an air pocket rolling off the ocean.

"Tallyho, right one o'clock," Cummings said. In the distance he could see the flashing red warning lights of the rig's drilling mast. His eyes went to the mission clock. They were running a few minutes ahead of schedule. They would have to join up and circle the rig one time to make sure they passed over the IP at 0340.

"Two, three and four. This is Lead. Form up on my left wing." Cummings throttled back, reducing his airspeed to 260 knots. He strained to look over his left shoulder as the other three A-6Es swung around in tight formation.

P-35M RADAR SITE, BUSHEHR, IRAN

"Jonesy, bring this son of a bitch back on line," Captain Watson exclaimed, looking at his watch.

"One Iranian radar coming back on line, sir," Master Sergeant Kirk Jones said as he tapped the proper sequence of control buttons. The electrical power started to flow through the paint-chipped gray control panel.

Watson watched the round radarscope slowly turn from black to amber.

"It's free of targets, sir. They must be ten miles inland by now," Jones reported.

Watson looked over at the communications panel. "Anything on the Iranian military channels?"

"Just what's standard for this hour of the night," Petersen said, adjusting the radio receiver. The small Iranian headphones looked funny on the Ranger's large shaved head. "Weather . . . transfer order . . . nothing for this base."

"What are you planning to do here?" Lieutenant al-Shira asked. His tone was much weaker now. "My country will not stand for this. I know who you are . . . American special forces. What are you planning to do? Take over my country?"

"Only in your dreams, Lieutenant. We're just here for a friendly visit. Check out your equipment. You know, the usual," Watson answered, walking over to the Iranian lieutenant and pulling out a pack of Marlboro cigarettes. He took one out, stuck it between his lips and lit it. "Care for a smoke?" Watson offered it to the Iranian officer. "Come on. If I was going to kill you, I would have done it by now."

Lieutenant al-Shira looked at Watson, then raised his cuffed hands and took the cigarette. Watson took out another one for himself and lit it. The two men watched each other, not saying a word, as they smoked their cigarettes.

MH-53J, Coyote Three Four

A two-lane dirt road flashed below the big chopper, as the terrain-following radar forced the nose down to follow a steep sloping rock canyon. The Pave Low III leveled at 100 feet above the desert and gained airspeed as the pilot felt it roll right and left, moving around a group of large rock-covered hills. Duke observed the Special Operations pilot deliberately work his head left and right to use his NVGs to look for power lines and other hidden dangers in the darkness. The AN/APQ-158 radar managed to keep the chopper from hitting the sides of hills, but it couldn't inform a pilot if he was flying in the correct direction or up the wrong canyon. For that, the pilot relied on a sophisticated navigational system of INS gyros and a satellite-controlled GPS. Following a trail of preprogrammed way-points superimposed on a movable map, he would know exactly where he was at all times.

The pilot, Chief Warrant Officer Steve Newall, didn't look the part of a stereotypical Special Forces flyboy, at least not in Duke's opinion. He was a man of medium build, with a long pointed nose and a gaunt face. He sported a neatly trimmed mustache and regulation white-wall haircut. When he flew, Duke thought, it was as if his entire being were controlling the 50,000 pounds of whirling aluminum, steel and electronics. When he moved, the aircraft moved with him.

Several miles away Duke could make out the lights of the Iranian city of Borazjan reflecting into the sky. He forced his eyes from the horizon of the FLIR unit directly in front of him and observed the greenish desert landscape drifting out in front of him as they weaved their way northwest.

"The number one turbine is running a little hot," the copilot warned from the left seat.

"Yeah, I see it," Newall replied, his eyes flashing back at the instrumentation. "Let's keep an eye on it."

"We should be hitting the main highway any second," Duke said, keying the internal mike. Strapped to his knees were detailed CIA satellite photos showing five-square-mile sections of Iranian landscape. It was his job to help the pilot locate the landmarks to keep them on an accurate course. "It should be on the back side of the next ridge."

The Pave Low pitched up, forcing Duke back into his seat. He felt the engines surge as the chopper climbed to peak a windswept ridge.

A half mile away, in the center of a long valley, ran an unmistakable dark green line—a paved highway. It was void of traffic.

"There it is. Highway one one six. Runs all the way to Shiraz." Duke's tone was even and serious.

Newall disengaged the TFR and banked the Pave Low left, cutting across the highway. They would parallel it for the next three minutes before breaking back due north.

"Coyote Three Five . . . you with me?" Newall radioed.

"*Roger, Three Four . . . right on your fuzzy green little ass.*"

"Spectre, you with me?"

"*Roger, above you to the east.*"

Newall looked over at Duke. "General, how we doin'?"

Duke looked at the next satellite map on his right knee. "In two and a half minutes the highway will bend right. After we pass it, bank left, heading three five five degrees." The next landmark would be an Iranian military microwave tower. He lifted his NVGs. The soft green and red light of the Pave Low's cockpit allowed him to see they were on course, slowly making their way north. He ran his finger over the vinyl-severed photos pinpointing their current position.

F-4E BLUE LEADER

"Twenty-one miles to the coast, sir," the backseater warned.

Major Kuh Gahar snapped his oxygen mask back into place and tightened his lap belt. A second later he heard the soft hum of the RHAW equipment telling him an American search radar was somewhere in the distance. He had hoped they would have at least made it to the coast before being detected by the American AWACS.

The major put his fighter into a steep climb, gaining 3,000 feet of altitude quickly. At 4,900 feet he leveled the fighter and reduced his airspeed. "Activate the radar . . . low power setting," he ordered.

Gahar watched the radarscope, located directly below the HUD, flash on. The top center of the scope filled with the blips of a dozen aircraft. The chief part of the Iranian strike force was below him and a mile out in front.

"All aircraft . . . all aircraft. This is Blue Leader. Execute mission. Repeat, execute mission," Gahar ordered the F-4s under his command.

He pulled the emergency release lever, dropping his two underwing fuel tanks, and jammed the throttles all the way to afterburner. His head snapped back as his F-4E accelerated.

Major Gahar put the jet into a climb, 2,000 feet a minute. He banked slightly, seeing the glowing orange tailpipes of the fighters streaking for the coastline below him.

"Allah be with all of you," he said under his breath.

A-6E Intruder, Shredder Leader

Bert Cummings relaxed his grip on the throttles as his Intruder sped past the northern coast of Oman just 500 feet above the water. He could see the bright multicolored lights of six oil platforms in the night.

Shredder Flight was now twenty-seven miles from the Iranian coast. He banked to the left, taking a new heading of 225 degrees, and nudged the throttles forward, maintaining 310 knots.

"Let's hope our buddies on the ground are ready," Cummings said to his copilot, referring to the Navy Seal teams. "When we hit twenty-one miles out, let them know they're going to have company in six minutes."

Lieutenant George switched his radio to a classified frequency covering three separate UHF bands. He waited thirty seconds, then opened the channel. The computer-controlled radio transmission hopped from frequency to frequency at random intervals, making it impossible to intercept or lock onto the transmission. If an enemy did home in on one of the frequencies, they would hear only a partially coded transmission.

"Leonardo . . . Shredder. We are inbound in five minutes. Do you copy?" George radioed.

There was no response.

George cursed under his breath. If the Seals had been discovered, the mission was going to end without any action. He gave Cummings a concerned look, then repeated the call.

"Ah . . . copy, Shredder Leader. This is Leonardo."

"You guys awake down there?" George radioed.

"We are on target and ready to rock and roll. Take a heading of two three one degrees. We'll guide you to the target."

"Copy, Leonardo . . . Shredder Flight inbound and hot to trot. We'll be at the target in six minutes," George said casually. He let off on the mike and spoke to Cummings. "Well, they're on the ground. Hope they can shoot straight.''

"Shredder Flight, this is Shredder Leader. We have our guys on the ground. Let's make sure you put those bombs on the target, not their heads," Cummings radioed.

"*Roger, Leader. We copy.*"

"We just hit way-point three," George called out. It was time for them to increase airspeed and make their bomber run.

"Shredder Two . . . here we go." Cummings sucked in a deep breath of cool oxygen and inched the throttle forward. He banked the blunt-nosed bomber to the west and dumped the nose, watching his airspeed climb past 360 knots.

"Twenty miles to target," Lieutenant George said, watching the FLIR.

Cummings leveled his bomber at 700 feet. *I should be picking up shoreline lights any time now*, he thought. A drop of cold sweat rolled down the back of his neck. "Anybody looking at us?" he asked.

"I'm showing one hostile radar bearing east of our current position," George said, checking his threat panel.

"Damn. I hope those Prowlers are in position. I don't want to play hide-and-seek with a fucking SAM," Cummings said dryly. He let his Intruder drift down to 600 feet before leveling it again.

Thirty-seven miles east of Shredder Leader's position, a lone ghost-gray EA-6B Prowler made a slow bank 500 feet above the rolling ocean. The pilot kept his aircraft just above stall speed, coming around to a new heading of 225 degrees. The Electric Intruder was now heading west along the southern coast of Iran. After leveling the jet, the pilot picked up a few knots of airspeed and began to climb.

The ECMO-3 (electronic countermeasures officer), seated behind the pilot, scanned the multifunction display situated between his knees on the control panel. The Prowler's AN/ALQ-99A EW system showed a single high-powered medium-range radar fifty-eight miles away. It was sweeping the sky every eight seconds. A continuous-wave H-band, the radar could pick up and track the eight attacking A-6E Intruders once they closed within ten miles of the coast. That meant Iranian air defense missiles and gun sites had a little over two minutes to sweep the sky, locate and lock on to the slow-moving bombers.

The Prowler was on station to make sure that the radar didn't do just that.

"Bring her around to two four five degrees," the ECMO-3 ordered, not looking up from his display.

The pilot did as he was told, gently moving the stick right.

"All right, assholes. Now you see us . . . now you don't," the ECMO-3 grinned. He toggled the switches, activating the Prowler's high-speed electronic jamming system. A steady stream of H-band radar waves burst from the Prowler's fin-tip mounted radome. Two seconds later, the emissions from the Iranian coastline stopped. From experience, the ECMO-3 knew the hostile radar scopes were now filled with fuzzy white lines.

"Four minutes to target," Lieutenant Jason George said into his oxygen mask. The flashing yellow light on his threat warning panel told him the radar was now being jammed.

"Okay. I'm taking her up to 2,000 feet," Cummings said, pulling back on the stick. At the same time, he advanced the throttles, not wanting the bomber to lose any airspeed. The Intruder's twin engines whined as she pushed higher into the sky.

"Leonardo . . . this is Shredder Leader. Three minutes out and inbound. Time to light the fire," George radioed.

"*Copy, Shredder . . . target on fire in ten seconds*," the Navy Seal responded.

Wearing a black insulated dry suit and flat black camouflage face paint, the 190-pound Navy Seal crawled on his belly across a small outcropping of sandstone rocks and dried bushes. Lieutenant Commander J. W. Parbel, the Seal team's senior commanding officer, raised the AN/PAQ-1 laser target designator and planted it firmly on his right shoulder. Looking through the scope of the riflelike device, he scanned the hillside. He stopped on a four-by-four-foot hole on the other side of a deep ravine.

Centering the crosshairs on the dark image, he depressed the trigger, sending a three-inch-diameter invisible laser to the target. The digital readout told him the target was 312 yards away. Parbel kept the laser designator steady on the target.

"Two minutes thirty seconds to target," George called out.

"Okay, Georgie boy. Time to work your magic." Cummings

readjusted his grip on the Intruder's stick.

George dropped his head into the IR scope. Using his left hand, he controlled the target recognition and attack multisensor located under the nose of the Intruder. The round sensor unit began to pivot, providing George with real-time television imagery of the target area. The TRAM system's integrated laser and FLIR sensors included a multiplemode target recognition system. This allowed George to see the aim point, at the same time picking up the reflecting beam of the targeting laser. He could then zoom in on the target area and guide the weapon system's crosshairs over the objective, locking onto it.

"Come on . . . where are you?" he muttered to himself. "Give me some more altitude."

Cummings responded by pitching the Intruder's nose up three degrees and increasing their airspeed.

George carefully moved the TRAM to the east. He was looking for a pulsing beam of white light from the Seal's target designator. They were close enough for him to be picking it up.

Cummings was growing anxious but remained silent, not wanting to distract his bombardier.

George zoomed in to the glowing IR image of the jagged, rocky coastline of Iran. The lieutenant hoped that by gaining a few thousand feet of altitude, he would pinpoint the target faster.

"Three thousand five hundred," Cummings called out.

Come on, you bastard. Where are you? George swiveled the TRAM to the west a few degrees. This time he caught sight of a faint white spot coming from what looked like the edge of a narrow ravine. He focused on it to determine if it was the laser. The bright light was pinpointed on a dark spot surrounded by several large boulders. *That must be the entrance to the launch tunnel.* "Confirmed target. Take a heading of 227," George told his pilot. "Keep her level."

"Roger, two two seven," Cummings said, repeating the heading.

George felt the bomber move slightly to the right as he wrapped his hand around the controller on top of the weapons panel between his knees. Using his right forefinger, the lieutenant manipulated the throbbing crosshairs until they were directly over the target. He then pressed the set button, locking the laser tracking mechanism onto the reflecting laser. The crosshairs stopped pulsing and turned a solid ghostly white, telling him he was locked onto the target.

"Thirty-nine hundred feet."

"Two minutes from target. Take us up to five thousand," George ordered. "Leonardo . . . Shredder Leader. We have laser lock. Weapons drop in thirty seconds."

"*Roger, Shredder.*"

MH-53J, COYOTE THREE FOUR

"What the hell is that?" On Duke's IR display, a giant green cloud was roiling toward the chopper, seemingly devouring everything in its path. It looked as if the entire desert was disappearing several miles in front of them.

"Shit! Those air brains back at base told us we wouldn't be running into any sandstorms," Newall said, disengaging the TFR and forcing the chopper up to 1,000 feet.

"Well, at least we're inside," Duke cracked. "I wouldn't want to be out in the middle of that shit."

"It's hell on equipment, though. I just hope we don't have to set her down to change the filters." Newall opened a channel so he could talk with the rest of the crew. "This is the flight deck. We're about to enter a sandstorm. Everyone tighten your restraints and hold on. We're in for a little ride."

Duke continued to watch the approaching cloud just as the Pave Low was pelted by a strong gust of wind. In an instant, the chopper's windshield was covered with tiny bits of rock and sand. The chopper jolted up and down, and the sound of the wind and bursts of sand mixed with gravel striking the aircraft surrounded them. Newall sat stiffly in his seat, holding onto the throttle and fighting to control the chopper.

"What about the others?" Duke asked, looking at Newall's grave face.

"I don't want to break radio silence unless we have to. We're just going to have to watch our instruments and hope everyone makes it out. There's no way to keep track of everyone in this shit."

"Then what?" Duke asked, sounding irritated.

"Usually these last only a few minutes," Newall responded.

"And if it doesn't?"

"General, right now I just hope this chopper holds together."

He pointed to the instrument panel and the backup GPS unit. "You keep your eyes on this and help me watch the FLIR. It's the only way we're going to stay on course."

Duke took a deep breath and did as he was instructed just as the Pave Low vibrated violently, struggling to cut through the sand. An uneasy feeling swept over him. He had enough experience to know that even the best-designed military hardware wasn't perfect.

The Pave Low relied on its enhanced navigation system, or ENS, which linked the chopper's twenty-odd navigational aids together. All their readings were filtered into the chopper's mission computer, then organized and merged using all the compass readings, radars, gyros and computer map displays. This was done every few seconds, giving the flight crew an up-to-date readout of where the Pave Low was at all times. In Duke's view, it was just a best guess. No matter how sophisticated, an electronic brain was only an electronic brain.

Duke studied the FLIR and radarscope video screens. The FLIR screen was glowing bright green, with a half dozen symbols superimposed over the infrared images. In many ways it resembled the HUD of a jet fighter, only it was smaller and located on the instrument panel. On the lower left edge of the display, Duke saw the number 2—the number of Coyote Flight's next way-point. The right side contained a white bar, which floated up and down to indicate the chopper's altitude, and a thin strip on the top, which indicated their compass heading. The upper left corner displayed their ground speed, while the distance and time to the next navigational way-point were clicked off in the upper right corner. Wobbling in the center of the display were a number of parallel white lines showing the helicopter's relationship to the horizon. To stay on course, the pilot matched up a white dot with crosshairs in the center of the screen.

Duke looked right and watched Newall maneuver, working the cyclic and collective sticks. Their airspeed had dropped to under 110 knots. *Come on, baby . . . let's hold together*, Duke thought.

Lieutenant Commander Cummings' stomach turned over with anxiety and excitement. There was a rumor that carrier pilots thought landing on a rolling and pitching deck, particularly at night, was more stressful than flying combat. In Cummings's opinion, that was bullshit. When he was landing no one was attempting to shoot him down, and he didn't have to have steady nerves like he did while waiting for his bombardier to get their bombs on target.

They were now four miles from the Iranian coast. There was nothing on the threat warning panel. The RHAW equipment wasn't detecting any hostile radars, either. *Maybe this one is going to be a freebie*, Cummings tried to convince himself.

"Fifteen seconds to drop. Give me some airspeed," George said, his face buried in the IR scope.

"You got it." He knew George was making sure the bombs had enough speed to reach the target. But this would also make their bird more vulnerable to any idiot on the ground with a gun or slingshot. Cummings dropped the nose and jammed the throttles forward. He watched the airspeed steadily climb.

"Ten seconds to weapons release. Maintaining target lock, start your turn," George ordered.

Cummings rolled the Intruder right at a forty-five-degree angle. The HUD clicked off the airspeed: 380 . . . 385 . . . 390.

"Four . . . three . . . two . . . one. *Drop*."

Bert Cummings smashed the weapons release button on his stick two quick times. The Intruder shuddered as two pairs of GBU-12s Paveway II 500-pound laser-guided smart bombs fell from the weapons pylons, forcing the jet to pick up a few knots of airspeed. The pilot continued to bank the Intruder to the right, away from the target.

"Leonardo . . . Shredder Leader. Four live ones in the air. We're outta here," George grunted.

"*Copy, Shredder.*"

Several hundred feet below the A-6E, the four unpowered GBU-12s pushed over, heading for the ground at 512 miles an hour. Angular front-mounted fins stabilized their trajectory. The silicon laser detector array, attached to the nose section of each bomb, locked onto the reflecting laser light a mile and a half away. Divided into four separate quadrants, the seeker head was controlled by a miniature computer that received signals from each quadrant and in turn drove the four control fins. If the computer wasn't receiving the same amount of reflected energy from all four quadrants, it would command the control surfaces to steer the nose of the bomb toward the aim point. As a result, the seeker unit kept the bomb pointed directly at the target at all times.

The four bombs, clustered in a tight fifty-foot radius, made two midcourse corrections as they sped toward the ground. They arced left five degrees, then right two degrees, before drawing a clean fix on the laser below. Twenty-one seconds after weapons release, the first GBU-12 hit the ground only four feet from the launch site opening. A fraction of a second later, the other three bombs hit, blowing a hole forty feet deep in the side of the mountain. The launch tunnel collapsed in an explosion of fire, smoke and rocks. A small brushfire erupted as a wave of flames spread up the ravine.

"Hot damn! We nailed that sucker...dead on!" Lieutenant George exclaimed.

Cummings kept his attention on the HUD.

"There they go..." George wrenched around to watch three different explosions on the mountainside behind his bomber. The other Intruders had hit their targets within a few seconds of each other.

"Holy shit! Look at that!" George bellowed. "They're throwing all kinds of shit up into the air."

The sky had lit up with strings of triple A gunfire. George could see yellow and red tracer rounds and the twisting bluish-white fire trails of handheld SAMs trying to locate a target spurt into the night sky like brilliant fireworks.

Cummings keyed his mike. "Strike...Shredder Leader. Objective Alpha is an Elvis. Objective Alpha is an Elvis." Alpha was the code for a hit, and Cummings used the term Elvis to notify his commanders on board the *Lincoln* that if anyone had been near the target area, they were dead, just like Elvis.

"*Copy, Shredder Leader. Good job.*"

"Okay, we're heading home, Georgie," Cummings said, pushing the throttles to the stops.

"You don't want to stay and watch the entertainment? Let's go back through there just for the fun of it," George said, as they both took a brief glance back at all the commotion in the air.

"If I want that kind of excitement, I just need to go home after being gone for six weeks," Cummings said, jinking the Intruder right and left. "Besides, I've had tougher days on the practice range."

"Yeah, they always fire live SAMs at you on the practice range," George joked.

*   *   *

Hassan Zadeh grabbed a 7.62-mm Dragunov sniper rifle from the weapons rack. He jammed three loaded magazines into his belt and walked toward the waiting chopper, snapping a fourth thirty-round clip into the assault rifle. Zadeh chambered a round and clicked on the safety. He was dressed all in black: jumpsuit and combat boots.

Two twenty-three-year-old Bell 214 Hueys, their navigational lights flashing, were being readied for takeoff near the farthest hangar. As Zadeh came closer, he could hear Ali Fesseghi shouting orders at a half dozen Revolutionary Guards climbing into each helicopter. The side cargo door of the farthest chopper closed as the pilot prepared for takeoff.

"I have briefed the men," Fesseghi shouted over the roar of the engines and whirling rotor blades. "They have been instructed to take the American and girl alive, but if either resists, the guards should kill them."

"NO! I want both of them *alive!* Minister Bakhtiar must learn the details of the American operation," Zadeh shouted back.

"These men are trained, Zadeh. I suggest you let them do their job." Fesseghi climbed into the dark interior of the chopper and sat behind the bulkhead separating the cargo hold from the flight deck.

Zadeh sat next to him. "If the American dies, I will hold you personally responsible, Fesseghi."

"You already hold me responsible," Fesseghi retorted. He looked at Zadeh before strapping himself in. *It is only by Allah's will that I should escape death now*, he thought. Fesseghi knew the only reason he hadn't been dealt with yet was because time had not allowed Bakhtiar and Zadeh to decide his fate.

Zadeh didn't take his eyes off Fesseghi as he ran his arms through the shoulder restraints and tightened his lap belt.

One of the ground crew slammed the cargo door, sealing out some of the noise. "I have instructed the pilot to follow the highway to the mining camp," Fesseghi told Zadeh. "It is the safest route."

Zadeh hit the side of the bulkhead with his fist. "Let's get going. Get this thing in the air!" he shouted.

"It's confirmed, sir. Six launch sites have been hit west of Bandar Abbas. No word on casualties," the Iranian communications officer said from behind the blinking red and yellow lights of his console.

"Cruise missiles or aircraft?" Colonel Rahavi shouted. His face was bright red as he stared at the radar screen. *Why didn't our air defenses pick up anything?*

"Unknown, sir. Long-range radar's empty and I'm receiving reports of our coastal SAM radars being jammed a few minutes before the attack."

"That means they used aircraft." Rahavi paced the back of the COC and stared at the concrete floor. *What are the Americans doing?* "How many of our interceptors got into the air?" Rahavi asked.

"None, sir."

"None . . . *none?* What were they doing down there? We should have fighters combing the skies for American aircraft!" Rahavi bellowed, picking up the phone. He looked at the screen. The Iranian strike force was just crossing the coastline eighty-seven miles east of Bandar Abbas. They would be launching their missiles in another twelve minutes. Rahavi stopped, setting the phone back down. "I will deal with the cowards at Bandar Abbas later." His voice cracked with anger. "Right now I have a larger battle to win."

Chapter Twenty-eight

E-2C HAWKEYE, SPLINTER 207

Lieutenant Brian O'Malley didn't shift his attention from the four-color radar screen as the sluggish twin-engine turboprop came out of a long banking turn and circled above the *Lincoln* at 28,000 feet. It was O'Malley's job to monitor the E-2C's sensors. In the center seat at the combat information radar panel, he looked for enemy aircraft trying to penetrate the outer defensive perimeter. Tonight, however, the only things on his scope were bright green circles—symbols for friendly aircraft turning away from the Iranian coast. They had caught the Iranian air force with their pants around their knees. Not a single fighter had come up to meet the attacking A-6s.

O'Malley, a round-faced Irishman from upstate New York with a lust for fast food and cold beer, ripped the wrapper off a candy bar and shoved one end into his mouth. He felt the pilot level the aircraft, as the E-2C started to head south toward the back side of the carrier battle group, and took another bite from his candy bar. The top edge of his screen showed the southern tip of Iran, including the port of city of Bandar Abbas. The irregular border, showing up as a thin yellow line, faded with his radar coverage to the east. He had positioned three groups of fighters between the Iranian coast and the *Lincoln* to intercept any Iranian fighters that might take to the air from Bandar Abbas. It was now three minutes after the attack and he was mildly surprised that Iran had not sent any fighters into the air. He watched the electronic symbols, representing U.S. fighters, fifty-five miles south of the Iranian coast. Each group was flying in a loose, oval, racetrack pattern. He had instructed the fighters to remain silent, flying with their radar off to avoid detection. The four aircraft on the far left were F/A-18Cs flying at 24,000 feet, the group in the center were F-14As operating at 28,000 feet. The last four, F/A-18Cs flying at 18,000 feet, were now escorting the A-6Es away from the coast.

O'Malley finished off the last of his candy bar and reached for his water bottle. He was glad he had brought provisions.

F/A-18C MICHELANGELO SIX ONE

The soft hum of the twin jet engines gave Commander Frank K. Calloway a sense of security as he scanned the night sky looking for anything that might be an aircraft. He twisted around, making sure his wingman was still in sight, as he guided the single-seat, split-tailed fighter to a new heading of 220 degrees.

Calloway, a thirty-eight-year-old-former Annapolis defensive end and F-14A pilot, had listened to the radio chatter as each group of A-6Es came off their targets and headed back to the *Lincoln*. Knowing his companions had completed their mission without any losses allowed him to relax a little. But he knew it was now his turn to make sure none of Iran's high-speed fighters tried to sneak in behind the slower-moving A-6s. Intruders were a fine old aircraft, but there was a reason their flight crews affectionately called them "Cement Trucks." They could carry a large load of bombs, but they were sluggish and would be an easy target for any of Iran's more advanced aircraft.

The commander, a veteran of thirty-four Gulf War missions over Kuwait and southern Iraq, loved to fly at night. The black desert sky and bright city lights allowed him to see out into the vastness of what seemed like forever. He had learned during the war that his Hornet's powerful AN/APG-65 radar was extremely effective, allowing him to lock up and kill targets without having to see them with the naked eye. On the night of January 23, 1991, Calloway had shot down an Iraqi MiG-23 with an AIM-7 Sparrow radar-guided missile as it tried to attack a group of Air Force EF-111As escorting a strike package. It was his only kill of the war, but the sight of the exploding MiG beneath his fighter was as clear now as the night he fired the missile.

Calloway slid the stick right and brought the Hornet to a northerly heading. He watched the HUD and leveled the fighter, keeping his airspeed at 340 knots and altitude at 24,000 feet. The vertical fuel gauges told him he could stay in the air another hour. By then any threat from the Iranians should be over.

E-2C HAWKEYE, SPLINTER 207

Brian O'Malley wadded up the candy wrapper and shoved it into the side pocket of his flight suit. Just as he looked up, a warning tone sounded in his headset, notifying him that an unidentified target had just appeared on his scope.

"What the hell?" O'Malley's face grew white and his jaw dropped. On the upper right edge of the radar screen he saw five, then six, then eight yellow triangles moving south at a high rate of speed.

"I'm picking up a new set of targets to the north—"

"I *see* them," O'Malley said, cutting off the radar operator. He watched the data starting to appear on the radar screen. There were eight targets flying in two four-ship formations at 8,000 feet, heading 187 degrees at 450 knots. The computer had already plotted them on an intercept course for the *Lincoln*. Just as O'Malley put his finger on the microphone button, he saw several more targets appear. These were flying at 18,000 feet a little behind the first wave.

"THREAT . . . THREAT. All aircraft . . . all aircraft, this is Hawkeye on guard. Multiple targets. bearing zero zero niner. Repeat, multiple targets bearing zero zero niner." O'Malley wiped away the sweat that was starting to bead on his forehead. He now counted twenty aircraft speeding toward the *Lincoln* at Mach 1.

USS *LASALLE*

Zachiem spun around, looking directly at Chaniff and then Staffer. "I'm showing twenty aircraft heading south at high speed."

Chaniff stared at the largest display screen. "Well, the bastards have balls after all. I have to hand it to them."

He knew enough about air combat to understand what was

happening. The CIA had been correct. Iran was doing exactly what Staffer's man had reported. Navy intel estimated Iran's cruise missiles had a range of only fifty miles, maybe sixty if they were launched from air-craft. Iran's air force was trying to get close enough to the American battle group to launch a salvo of stealth cruise missiles.

"How long before they're in range to launch their weapons?" Chaniff asked.

"Five, six minutes," Zachiem answered.

"Damn it. That's not much time," Chaniff cursed.

"Give my fighters five minutes," Zachiem said. "They'll sweep the skies clean."

Chaniff sat back down. *I hope you're right*, he thought. *I hope you're right.*

F/A-18C MICHELANGELO SIX ONE

"Copy, Splinter. Michelangelo to the rescue," Commander Calloway answered, sucking in a deep breath. "Michelangelo flight . . . this is Leader," he radioed the three other Hornets. "You guys heard the call. Let's haul ass."

"*Copy, Leader, this is Mich One Seven. I'm with you.*" It was Calloway's wingman, Lieutenant Commander Kip "Roadkill" Karson.

"*Mich One Eight's in.*"

"*Mich One Nine's in.*"

Calloway didn't respond for a few seconds, as he tried to sort things out. Twenty targets were forty-five miles north of his position and closing fast. They were flying at two different altitudes, indicating a classic attack pattern—air-to-air fighters flying above fighters configured for surface attack. Michelangelo Flight was the closest group of fighters to the bandits. Four F-14As were thirty miles to the west, but it would take them at least three minutes to get into position to fire their weapons even if they flew at maximum speed. Calloway's Hornets, being the first to engage the bogeys, would take out as many of the aircraft as possible before the F-14As arrived.

"Attack pattern bravo . . . repeat, attack pattern bravo," Calloway ordered. The other three pilots fanned out in a straight line spaced a half mile apart. Once in position, they turned on their powerful radars to find and lock on to the enemy below. Each of the F/A-18Cs was armed for air-to-air combat. They carried six AIM-7M Sparrow radar-guided missiles on wing and fuselage pylons, and two wingtip-mounted AIM-9M heat-seeking Sidewinders. Calloway's strategy would be simple: Close in on the enemy at a high rate of speed. When in range, launch the missiles, downing as many Iranian aircraft as possible. They would streak past the attacking fighters, turn and regroup behind them. By then, Calloway figured the F-14As would be in position and they could sandwich the Iranians between two groups of American fighters.

"Turn to a heading of zero one zero degrees," Calloway radioed. "Go to burner . . . let's *haul ass*, men!" He jammed the throttles to the stops, and his fighter accelerated into the darkness.

F-4E BLUE LEADER

Major Kuh Gahar's radarscope showed the airspace in front of his fighter patrol was clear of targets. He smiled to himself. In four minutes they would be close enough to launch their weapons. They would then break back toward the safety of Iranian airspace.

"This is Blue Leader to all aircraft. Arm your weapons and stay alert." The major released the microphone button and listened to the static in his helmet. He gazed at the HUD, keeping the jet level. He let his fighter drift a few feet below 18,000 on a heading of 187 degrees.

"Sir, I'm picking up several targets at extreme range," his backseater said.

Gahar's eyes swiftly went to the scope. Two faint dots were in the upper right section. "Range . . . heading?"

"Unknown. They're at the edge of detection. It's going to take me a few seconds."

Gahar watched the sweeping beam narrow as his backseater focused the Phantom's AN/APQ-120 radar, trying to get a fix on the targets.

"Two more targets to the south, sir."

"I see them." Gahar snorted at his earlier belief that there were not going to be any complications. "Update, Lieutenant."

"Four targets . . . range, forty-two miles. Altitude . . . 24,000 feet. They're on an intercept, closing at 1,100 knots. Negative on IFF."

"This is Blue Leader. Enemy aircraft closing from the south.

Blue Two, Three and Four are with me. The rest of Blue Flight stay with Gold Flight," Gahar radioed. "Break now." The major banked his F-4E to the right, maintaining 18,000 feet.

F/A-18C Michelangelo Six One

"Okay, Mutants, let's light 'em up." Calloway hit the control switch, turning his radar from standby to active. He then set the Hornet's powerful look-down, shoot-down radar to max range, sacrificing detail for distance. The radar screen filled with the symbols of twenty targets. Four were moving toward them at high speed.

"Leader, this is One Seven. I'm picking up a hostile radar to the north."

"Copy, One Seven. Leader has it." Calloway boosted the power level of the RHAW equipment. A soft hum in his headset told him a powerful J-band air-to-air radar was sweeping the airspace out in front of him.

"Commander, those bastards are trying to lock up on us."

Calloway heard the warning from his wingman, Lieutenant Commander Karson. "One Seven, take the two bogeys to the east. I have the pair to the west. One Eight and One Nine, take the main body," Calloway called.

"Copy, Leader," Karson replied.

"Copy, Leader," called One Eight and One Nine.

E-2C Hawkeye, Splinter 207

"Donatello Flight . . . this is Splinter. Get your ass in gear. Those Hornets need some help," Lieutenant O'Malley roared into his radio. Donatello was the call sign for the F-14As under his control.

"Copy, Splinter . . . we're at Mach 1.3 and moving. Tell those Hornet drivers to keep their pants dry. The big boys are on the way."

O'Malley watched the four symbols representing the F-14As dash toward the upper part of his scope. He double-checked to make sure each aircraft was broadcasting the proper IFF signal. The last thing he needed was F-14As shooting at F/A-18Cs.

"Michelangelo Leader . . . Splinter. Help in two minutes."

"Copy, Splinter . . . turning to engage."

F-4E Blue Leader

The threat warning panel on the left side of Major Kuh Gahar's instrument panel flashed on. The small square box contained several rows of colored plastic lights. The top row flashed yellow, telling him an enemy radar was now sweeping his fighter from somewhere in the distance.

Three minutes to weapons launch, he reminded himself. His eyes involuntarily swept the cockpit, looking for warning lights. Hydraulic pressure was steady and his engines were running within normal temperatures. He checked his fighter's weapons-select button. It was set to launch the four American-made AIM-7 Sparrows mounted to the belly of his F-4E.

The twenty-year-old missiles had recently been updated with new solid-fuel rocket motors and guidance systems, including radar seeker heads and warheads, purchased from Egypt in exchange for intelligence on Syrian terrorist operations. Major Gahar had fired several of the updated Sparrows during the closing months of the Iran-Iraq war. He downed one high-speed Iraqi MiG-25 after it had flown over western Iran on a reconnaissance mission.

"Climb to flight level two thousand," Gahar ordered. "Fire on my order only."

F/A-18C Michelangelo Six One

Commander Frank K. Calloway knew from experience that his radar could detect small targets, such as F-16s and F-18s, as far away as fifty-three miles on a clear night without any electronic interference. During mock engagements he had even locked onto an F-14A fifty-eight miles out. However, combat was an entirely different matter. The targets on his radarscope were flying at him head on, which reduced their radar cross section. He would have to wait for the targets to close to within thirty miles before locking up his radar. He could fire his first missile at twenty-six miles out, or closer if he thought he could get away with it.

"*Michelangelo Six One . . . Splinter.*

"Copy, Splinter. Go ahead."

"*Bogeys now heading one niner seven. Closing at 1,130 knots at angels twenty. They're running with radars on trying to find you.*" Angels 20 meant the enemy was at 20,000 feet.

"Copy, Splinter . . . we're tracking them."

"BVR weapons clear . . . repeat . . . BVR weapons clear."

Calloway clicked his mike twice, confirming the transmission from the Hawkeye. BVR stood for beyond visual range, meaning he now had permission to attack the bogeys with radar-guided missiles.

His eyes went to the small radar screen. The nearest bogey was now in the upper third of his scope, close enough to try to lock onto. He changed his radar's mode to track-while-scan. Calloway's F/A-18C could now track ten targets, displaying eight of them on the scope. The commander painstakingly moved the twin cursors across the radarscope, centering them on the closest target. He depressed the lockup button and moved on to the next target. The HUD flashed and a small square box appeared, showing the position of the first bogey. *Gotcha*, Calloway thought. He just had to keep the target in the center of the HUD and wait for his missiles to lock up. "Mich One Seven . . . this is Leader. I have the two to the west."

"Copy, Leader. I'm on the two to the east. Lock up in ten seconds."

"Take 'em on my signal," Calloway ordered. The first target was twenty-nine miles out, twenty seconds from maximum launch range. Calloway felt a surge of energy shoot through his body as he neared the target.

F-4E BLUE LEADER

"Allah be with me," Major Gahar whispered, as his threat warning panel flickered from yellow to red. An American fighter had just locked up on his Phantom.

"Distance to target," he demanded from his backseat radar intercept officer.

"Twenty-eight miles, sir," his backseater answered. "Two thousand feet above us."

"Give me radar lockup now."

"We're still not in range, sir. We need to get within twenty miles."

Twenty miles . . . we'll be dead by then. Gahar jinked his F-4E right and left, pulling several hard Gs to see if the radar would stay locked onto his jet. Coming level at 21,240 feet, the major looked back at the threat warning panel. The flashing red light terrified him, and he was beginning to lose his confidence. The American fighter was somewhere in the distance.

"Six miles to lockup," his backseater called out.

Major Gahar strained, looking for a burst of light that would indicate the enemy had launched a missile from above. He pictured an American pilot doing the same thing, scanning the skies. Only he knew their equipment was better and they could attack. him from a longer range. If he was going to break the American's radar lock, there was only one way to do it.

Gahar pressed the weapons release button on his stick twice, sending two AIM-7s from beneath his fighter. In his haste, he forgot to shut his eyes. The Sparrow's bluish white rocket blinded him. Jamming the throttles into burner, Gahar nosed his F-4E up ten degrees and started to climb.

F/A-18C Michelangelo Six One

The steady pong, pong, pong of the Hornet's RHAW equipment told Calloway an enemy radar was looking for him. His eyes went from the HUD to the F/A-18C's threat panel. An airborne radar was sweeping his aircraft but hadn't locked up. The bridge of his nose tickled as a droplet of sweat stopped at the edge of his oxygen mask.

"*Threat . . . threat. Missiles bearing zero one fiver.*" Calloway's heart thumped and the adrenaline raced as he listened to the call from the Hawkeye. Off the right side of the F-18's nose he thought he saw the flash of two rocket motors igniting and starting for his aircraft. However, he couldn't be sure. The lights of the Iranian coastline made it hard to distinguish the flash of a missile. He blinked hard, straining to detect the slightest spark of moving light.

"You see anything, Roadkill?" Calloway radioed his wingman.

"*Negative, Leader . . . negative,*" Karson responded apprehensively.

"Shit . . ." the Commander said under his breath. The HUD told him the nearest target was still twenty-five miles away. From twenty-five miles, it would take an enemy missile under a minute to reach his jet. And it had been ten seconds since the call from the Hawkeye.

He had a choice. Calloway could ignore his radar warning

equipment and turn hard right to get perpendicular to the enemy radar beam. It was a standard maneuver used to break the missile's radar lock by getting lost in electronic clutter. Or he could stay on course, believing the fighter somewhere out in front of him was trying to draw him off with a missile shot.

All right, you bastard. I'll play chicken with you, Calloway thought, letting his fear turn to anger. At this range, he judged the enemy fighter would have launched a radar-guided missile. A heat-seeker, which was smaller and more maneuverable, didn't have the range. That meant the enemy pilot would have had to have a solid lock.

Calloway let his Hornet drift up to 24,800 feet before coming level. He listened for the tone in his headset. It turned from a faint hum to a piercing shrill, signaling a radar lockup. The HUD told him they were closing in at 1,180 miles an hour, more than Mach 2, range, twenty-four miles.

Come on, baby ... come on. Stay locked up. The tone inside his helmet was now even stronger. He watched the range to target click past twenty-three miles. He brushed the weapons release button with his thumb for assurance.

"Fox one," Calloway radioed, smashing the launch button. A split second later he closed his eyes as the F/A-18C quivered. The first missile fell from the rail under the right wing. Dropping his head into the cockpit, he moved the cursor on the radar screen until it was centered over the second target. He pressed the weapons release button a second time.

"Fox one." Calloway's cockpit once again lit up with a bright white light.

"*Fox one ... fox one*," Michelangelo One Seven radioed. Four AIM-7M Sparrow missiles streaked toward their targets, following a steady stream of reflecting radar waves.

E-2C HAWKEYE, SPLINTER 207

"*Fox one ... Fox one.*" Lieutenant O'Malley heard the call as two more Sparrows left the launch rails of another F/A-18C. He breathed deeply and tried to relax while keeping his eyes fixed on the radar screen. Eight more American fighters were speeding toward the mass of enemy targets clustered at the top of his radarscope.

"Strike, this is Splinter," O'Malley called, radioing the *Lincoln.*

"*We copy, Splinter. Go ahead.*"

"We need some help up here . . . pronto."

"*Roger, Splinter. More fighters on the way. Hold tight.*"

O'Malley didn't like the odds. The enemy fighters were seventy-three miles from the *Lincoln*. And in his book that was too damn close.

F-4E BLUE LEADER

"Twenty-one miles and closing," Major Gahar's backseater advised. "We should have radar lockup any second."

"I need radar lockup now! Lockup, damn it!" Major Gahar shouted at him. The American fighters sweeping his aircraft had not turned away as he had hoped. The steady throbbing sound in his helmet warned they were bearing down on him.

"*Missiles right, one o'clock,*" came the call from one of the other F-4Es.

Gahar's insides jumped. He desperately searched the sky to the left for the telltale signs of rocket motors burning. He blinked repeatedly, still trying to clear his vision. After a few seconds he spotted two bright white licks of flame coming toward his aircraft. The flames were growing closer with each beat of his heart. *Allah is great. Allah is good.*

"Blue Two, this is Leader. Break on my command." Major Gahar's mouth went dry as he spoke. Horrified, he watched the glowing white fire of the two missiles' rocket motors fade and burn out. He made a mental note of their last location before they disappeared into the darkness. It would be like trying to dodge a knife flying through the air while blindfolded.

"This is Blue Leader. Break right," he grunted. Using both hands and all his strength, he snapped the stick of his F-4E to the right and hauled straight back. Reaching up, he hit the chaff button two quick times before the strain of mounting G pressure pulled his arm down and away from the console. Two churning balls of radar-thwarting foil exploded out from behind his fighter. The big jet labored as he forced the nose to the west.

Gahar watched the G meter climb to 4 . . . 5 . . . 6. Finally, at 6.5 Gs, he held the stick firm and watched the compass heading swing around to 270 degrees. He was now heading due west at

420 knots. Before he came out of the turn, he dropped the Phantom's nose to pick up lost airspeed. He would need the velocity if the Americans fired on him again. When the HUD hit 460 knots, he came level at 19,300 feet and looked over his right shoulder.

"Allah save them!" his backseater shouted.

Both pilots watched stunned as two orange fireballs erupted off the their right wing. The American missiles had hit two of their marks. The spheres of fire appeared for only a few seconds before dispersing in a flash. Gahar watched several pieces of flaming wreckage spin toward the ocean. A sick feeling swept over him. Gahar's wingman and another F-4E had just been shot down. He searched for any chutes, knowing it was impossible to see anything in the darkness.

"Splash one . . . Splash one," Calloway radioed. His breath was short and fast, as the realization of what was happening started to sink in. The image of the farthest bogey faded from his radar screen. He looked up in time to see two bursts of orange light and the spinning wreckage of two fighters a dozen miles in front of and below him cartwheel downward.

"*Fox one . . . Fox one.*"

Calloway heard the call of two more F/A-18Cs sending their missiles into the air. Off to the right, he caught sight of three long streaks of fire shooting through the darkness. His radarscope was now a mass of confusion, friendly and enemy fighters starting to merge into one group. He figured he could get one more shot off before passing the enemy and turning to engage from the rear.

"Splinter 207, this is Mich Six One. Give me a vector," Calloway hollered into his face mask. "I need another target . . . *now.*"

"*Roger, Michelangelo Six One. Turn right to a heading of zero four niner. Four bogeys at angels eight . . . speed, 450 knots.* They're all yours, Commander."

"Copy, Splinter . . . Mich Six One. Back on the hunt."

Calloway rolled his fighter to the left and dropped his nose over, picking up airspeed. Two . . . four, and then six new targets appeared on his radarscope. They were grouped together in tight formation. The distance to the nearest target was eleven miles. Slowing the radar's cursor across the screen, he locked on to one of the fighters in the center of the group.

"Mich One Seven, you with me?" Calloway radioed his wingman.

"*Roger, Leader*," Karson answered readily.

"Cover my ass. I'm taking her down."

"*Copy . . . I'll stay high and behind you.*"

Reacting on reflexes, Calloway jammed the throttles into afterburner and pushed over into a 2-G negative dive, slicing back to the right. The prickling pain of blood rushing to the upper part of his body forced him to ease off the stick.

Come on . . . lock up, he coaxed the radar. An instant later the tone told him his missiles were picking up the reflecting radar emissions of enemy targets below his Hornet. He was descending at 470 knots. Calloway took the Hornet out of afterburner and popped the air brakes, watching the HUD click off his airspeed. When he was below 430 knots, he hit the weapons launch button on the top of the stick.

"Fox one . . . Fox one," he announced, as a third and fourth AIM-7M tore away from the underside of his fighter. Two missiles were now speeding toward their target at Mach 3.4.

USS LaSalle

General Chaniff's jaw hardened as he watched the first wave of F/A-18Cs race for the enemy targets on the center display screen in the CIC. Small yellow lines indicated air-to-air missiles maneuvering toward the enemy. It was difficult to understand the grunts and groans of the American pilots as they communicated with the Navy E-2C orbiting a hundred miles south of the combat zone. From the look on Zachiem's face, the chairman could tell not everything was going well.

"Three Iranian fighters are down," Zachiem said. The computer symbols representing the enemy fighters had disappeared from the radar screen.

"How much longer before those F-14s get into position?" Chaniff asked. He was now pacing the floor behind the admiral.

"A minute . . . at the maximum." Zachiem didn't look away from the screen. "We don't have enough fighters in the air. There are going to be some leakers."

"Leakers?" Staffer asked, getting up to join the men standing facing the screen.

"That's right. Leakers. Unless we knock the shit out of them in the next five minutes, some of those fighters are going to leak past our air defenses.''

"Alert the *Lincoln* and her battle group. I don't want them caught off-guard this time."

"They already know it," Zachiem responded coldly. The crew aboard the *Lincoln*, as well as the other ships in the battle group, were watching the same information. Ten miles north of the *Lincoln*, the Aegis-class cruiser USS *Princeton* sailed a crisscross pattern, acting as sentinel. If any stealth cruise missiles penetrated the outer defense layer, it would be her responsibility to knock them down.

The Navy had made several minor adjustments to the ship's SPY-1B radar. The radar now operated on the lower half of the F-band frequency, and the computer software had been calibrated to pick up the slightest amount of reflection. With the redefinition, many of the operators were seeing false targets because of added background clutter. Navy rocket scientists believed that would enable the SPY-1B radar to detect and intercept any missile, even one with a radar cross section smaller than a bumble bee.

Chaniff had his doubts, because the new system was untested. If his background as a field officer had taught him one thing, it was that when a weapons system broke down, nine times out of ten it was due to the electronics.

The chairman folded his arms and looked at the floor. The thought of more dead sailors made his stomach queasy.

Chapter Twenty-nine

F-16C Coors Leader

Colonel Eddie Naylor watched the engine temperature of his F-16 climb a few degrees before falling back. The gauge fluttered just below the red line, then drifted lower for a few seconds before increasing again. He hoped the cause was just the added stress of the fighter's engine having to chew up and spit out the sand that was whirling around his aircraft. If it did climb a few more degrees, he might be forced to turn around. It was something he didn't want to do.

Naylor's passion in life was flying the nimble little fighter. His wife often joked she would come in second if he ever had to choose between them. He had started his career as a second lieutenant flying large F-105s and later transferred to F-4s as the Vietnam War wound down. He had hoped to command a squadron of F-15s after graduating from war college. When told he would be flying F-16s, he was disappointed, but only until he flew one. He now commanded a squadron of the most maneuverable and versatile jets in the world. Air Force pilots referred to the sixteens as Vipers, not Falcons, which was the official name. Their ability to turn violently, hitting the pilot with over 9 Gs, was the reason.

If Naylor had to make one complaint about his jet, it was that it had only one engine. If it showed any sign of failing, he didn't have any other option but to haul ass back to base.

The turbulent sandstorm hadn't relented. The strike package had been flying through it for the past thirty-two minutes and had reduced their airspeed. Naylor's GPS system, located on the right side of the instrument panel, told him he was now fifty-three miles southeast of Esfahan. They were fifteen minutes behind schedule, and the colonel was starting to have doubts they would make it at all.

Naylor recalled one sandstorm he had flown through during Desert Storm. That mission was during the day and it was like trying to navigate through thick mud with a hangover. It could be done, but you hurt all over the whole time you were doing it and you swore never to do it again. After he had landed, AWACS told him the sand cloud extended into the sky to an altitude of 18,000 feet and ground teams had clocked winds in excess of sixty miles an hour. There wasn't any doubt in Naylor's mind that this storm was larger and more powerful.

With his eyes firmly on the HUD, he pitched the nose up several degrees, forcing his fighter to climb through 8,000 feet. The aircraft lurched suddenly.

Shit! I don't like this, he said, holding on. The LANTIRN system was worthless. The IR scope was a mass of dark green swirling images. The sand and dust made it impossible to see anything. He knew if he stayed above 8,000 and on course, he wouldn't run into any unexpected surprises, like the side of an Iranian mountain. The only good news was that he doubted Iranian radars could cut through the gunk, so they were free from radar surveillance.

"Coors Leader . . . Hammer Two Two. You copy?" Hammer Two Two was one of the two EF-111As that would be needed to jam Iranian radars and communications channels once the air assault began.

"Hammer Two Two . . . Coors Leader. Go ahead."

"Colonel, my TFR radar is going squirrelly on me and I'm slowly losing hydraulic pressure. There's no way I can make it. Request permission to RTB," one of the pilots anxiously radioed, wanting to return to base.

"Roger, Hammer Two Two . . . RTB," Naylor responded. Well, it had started. He wondered how many other fighters would be heading back because of foiled weapons systems or radars. *Son of a bitch 'n sand.*

Esfahan, Iran

"Sir, long-range radar shows we just lost a third F-4. Should I give the order to pull back?" the communications officer asked.

"NO! Instruct the flight leaders to reduce altitude and move toward the launch point at maximum speed. We will not quit!" Colonel Rahavi's face was bright red and stiff with a mix of anger and conviction.

"Yes, sir."

"Get four more MiG-29s in the air at once," Rahavi ordered. He spun around and stared at the air tasking officer. "I want this base protected!"

"Yes, sir . . . four more MiG-29s."

Rahavi scrutinized the rest of the command center. It was quiet, with only the sound of computer keyboards being tapped and the muffled chatter of pilots talking with the ground controllers.

"Colonel, receiving reports we lost another fighter. That makes four down." The thin-faced communications officer relayed the data in a dull, lifeless voice.

"I *know* how many that makes. What is the status on the F-14s? I want them in the air at once." Rahavi rolled his shoulders back, as if readying for a prize fight.

"I have given the order to have them fueled. They should be airborne in ten, fifteen minutes," said the air tasking officer.

"That is not fast enough! I want them in the air in two minutes. Instruct the pilots to set up a patrol radius of a hundred miles around this base. They will fly 5,000 feet above the MiG-29s. Anything entering the airspace without the proper IFF codes I want shot down immediately."

"Yes, sir."

The Americans had hit the launch sites west of Bandar Abbas, catching the air force completely off-guard. Now his fighters were flying into a wall of American fighters. Rahavi couldn't do anything for the F-4Es, and he wasn't sure if he had made the right choice by ordering his pilots to press the attack. But if the Americans were also planning to attack the weapons plant at Esfahan, he would have a surprise or two waiting for them. His best pilots would be in the air.

"Are you detecting any aircraft in the area?" Rahavi asked again.

"No, sir." The radar technician pointed to a bright pulsing blotch on the amber-colored scope. "But I can't see anything to the south-west. There's a huge sandstorm moving through the area."

"How long before it dissipates?" Rahavi snapped.

"Unknown, sir. But it should move out of our radar coverage in twenty to thirty minutes."

Colonel Rahavi studied the technician's smaller radar screen. He had flown through sandstorms before. It could be done, but it was hell on equipment. If the Americans were out there, they would be paying a high price in pilot stress and equipment.

"Keep me posted," he grunted, deciding it was not an immediate threat.

E-2C HAWKEYE, SPLINTER 207

"Splinter . . . Donatello Leader. Confirm targets to the north . . . confirm targets to the north," the lead F-14A pilot radioed O'Malley, who was already looking at the situation. After the first attack on the enemy fighters by the F/A-18Cs, the bandits had broken into four groups. Two groups were below 8,000 feet and heading south. None of those targets had been shot down. The other two groups had split, one going east and the other west. The F-14As had come in from the west at supersonic speed and were now in a position to fire on the enemy. However, they didn't want to be blowing their fellow F/A-18Cs out of the sky along with Iranian fighters.

"Donatello Leader . . . Donatello zero three. Turn left, heading zero four niner. Two targets to the north of your position at angels eighteen," O'Malley ordered. "Go BVR and engage."

"Roger, Splinter . . . BVR."

O'Malley looked back at the left side of his radarscope. Two more AIM-7Ms were speeding toward the farthest group of four bandits. The enemy fighters were at 7,890 feet and descending, while Michelangelo Leader was descending through 11,300 feet, covering his wingman's six o'clock position.

"Shit . . . there's a bad guy on your tail," O'Malley said under his breath, watching a single bandit coming around at 22,000 feet, its altitude steady, picking up airspeed. Michelangelo Leader and his wingman, Mich One Seven, now had bogeys ahead of them and behind them. Not a good situation to be in.

"Fox three . . . Fox three."

"Fox three . . . Fox three."

O'Malley's attention went back to the F-14As that had just entered the theater. The numbers below the F-14A aircraft symbols showed their call sign and IFF codes. The double "Fox three" call notified him they had launched AIM-54C Phoenix air-to-air missiles. He watched the missiles accelerate, their active terminal homing radars each locked onto a target. The Phoenix missiles, which weighed nearly half a ton, hit an airspeed of Mach 4.2 in a matter of seconds. They made several course changes before impacting three more enemy fighters. One of the missiles missed, pushing over and disappearing off the scope. O'Malley pictured the Phoenix's massive 133-pound fragmentation warhead ripping through an Iranian fighter.

"Splash one MiG . . . splash two MiGs," came the call from the lead F-14A.

"Splash number three . . . splash number three."

O'Malley keyed his mike. "Donatello zero four . . . Donatello zero five. Turn right to one six four. Target the bandits at angels seven."

"Copy, Splinter . . . angels seven."

F-4E BLUE LEADER

"Turn left to three four seven," Major Gahar's backseater instructed. "I'm picking up a target below us."

The pilot did as he was told, pushing the stick left and throwing the throttles forward to full military power. The F-4E sliced through the night sky at a forty-five-degree angle.

"You should be picking him up . . . to the left, to the left," the backseater grunted under the pressure of the Gs.

Gahar glanced from the radarscope to the HUD, hoping to get a glimpse of the American fighter flying in afterburner. It was no use; he couldn't see a thing in the blackness. When the HUD hit 347, he came wings level and pushed the nose down a few degrees, watching his airspeed increase. Suddenly, a bright green spot appeared on his scope.

F/A-18C MICHELANGELO SIX ONE

"Hot damn . . . that makes two," Commander Calloway shouted into his empty cockpit. A second fighter exploded five miles from his Hornet. The explosion was a bright blue that quickly turned a deep orange; the changing color told him the missile had hit one of the jet's fuel tanks. His eyes went to the second Sparrow as its rocket motor burned out. He waited for another explosion but didn't see one. Unknown to the commander, the missile had lost its lock a half mile from the target. The Iranians were filling the air with chaff and had succeeded in confusing the American radar. The Sparrow had locked onto a ball of chaff heading for the water below.

"Shit . . . it missed," Calloway cursed, caught up in the momentum of the fight. He banked his fighter to the right, leveling the Hornet at 11,300 feet. He was down to two Sparrows and two Sidewinders. He caught sight of three enemy fighters turning below him, their afterburners glowing bright blue. They were heading to the north, away from the *Lincoln*.

"Splash one MiG," Calloway roared, not realizing he had hit an American-made Iranian F-4E. "This is Mich Six One . . . that makes two." Calloway pulled back on the stick, forcing the nose of the F/A-18C into a steep climb. His G meter jumped to 6 as he rapidly gained altitude to rejoin his wingman, Roadkill Karson. They could then plan their next move and Calloway could go for number three.

Major Gahar listened to the chirping sound of his Sparrows, trying to lock up on the target below him. He tapped the right rudder, which swung the F-4E's nose around four degrees. The radar targeting box, now in the center of the HUD, showed the American fighter directly in front of him. *This should be an easy shot.*

"Range . . . two point three miles," his backseater called out.

"I can't get a lock!" Gahar knew he only had a few seconds to fire before the American turned away from him. *I'm too close for Sparrows.*

"Range two miles and closing."

Gahar switched from AIM-7s to AIM-9 Sidewinders. Slung under each wing were two of the heat-seeking missiles. He listened to the growl of the super-cooled seeker heads and tried to lock up on the hot spot directly ahead of him. A split second later the tone changed to a solid, even shrill.

"Now you will die," Gahar snarled. He hit the launch button twice, sending two AIM-9s toward the target. As the missiles streaked away, Gahar put his fighter into a hard left turn and forced the nose down. He had managed to get some vengeance and would head back toward the safety of Iranian airspace.

"Gold Flight, this is Blue Leader. Launch your weapons. Repeat, launch your weapons."

"Mich One Seven . . . *Threat, threat!* Break right," O'Malley shouted into his microphone. An Iranian fighter was at the Hornet's six o'clock, two miles behind it. He watched, startled, as two yellow streaks curved toward the American fighter.

O'Malley sucked in a deep breath and held it. He cursed himself for waiting too long to warn the Hornet. The missiles were only seconds away.

Calloway's F/A-18C broke through 15,000 feet. His airspeed was increasing even though he was climbing at a seventy-degree angle with full military power.

Hearing the call from the Hawkeye, Calloway's head snapped right to left as he looked for the inevitable signs of a missile launch. Somewhere above him Roadkill Karson was preparing to engage with an enemy fighter.

"Hold on, Mich One Seven. I'm on the way." Calloway jammed the double throttles into afterburner, risking a rear attack from the fighters below him. The Hornet's twin engines kicked in, shoving him firmly back in his ejection seat. But as the words left his mouth he saw two missiles, their fiery white plumes streaking across the sky above him at a high rate of speed.

"*Watch your six . . . watch your six, Roadkill!*" Calloway screamed. But it was too late. The commander watched in dread as the first, then the second missile impacted into his wingman's aircraft. It all happened in the blink of an eye.

"*EJECT . . . EJECT!*" Calloway shrieked, then breathed more quietly. "Get out of there, Kip."

Three thousand feet above him and to the right, a small orange fireball erupted, followed by a larger explosion. The back of his wingman's F/A-18C exploded into several pieces of flying, burning debris. Calloway watched for the sign of an ejection seat motor pushing its pilot away from the wreckage. He waited . . . but didn't spot one.

Calloway keyed his mike. "Splinter, this is Calloway. Get S and R out here on the double and give me a fucking vector. I want that son of a bitch."

"*Mich One Six . . . Splinter. Take a heading of three four two.*

Bogey is heading away at high speed. Altitude, 17,000 and descending.''

Calloway didn't acknowledge the Hawkeye as he rolled his Hornet upside down and pushed over, topping out at 19,000 feet. He grunted hard, not allowing the stress of the Gs to push the blood from the upper part of his body.

The bastard's heading north . . . back to Iran, he thought. He flipped the fighter over, coming wings level at 19,340 feet. Keeping his F/A-18C in afterburner, he watched his airspeed increase past 450 knots. Out of the corner of one eye he caught sight of several more missiles racing through the night sky at unknown targets. He resisted the urge to turn and see if any missiles were coming at him. The glow of the afterburners would impair his night vision.

Calloway forced the image of his wingman's exploding fighter from his mind but couldn't shake the enmity boiling deep within him. *I'm going to kill this prick.* His eyes went to the radarscope. Below him and speeding away, he caught sight of the enemy pilot.

"Okay, asshole, now it's your turn," Calloway snorted. He dropped the nose of his Hornet, picking up valuable airspeed. He locked his fighter's radars onto the bogey. Range, 5.4 miles; Closure, -114 knots. The enemy jet was outrunning him.

Major Gahar looked over his shoulder. His Phantom's radar-warning equipment told him an American fighter was behind him, sweeping his F-4E, but the afterburners made it impossible to see anything. Gahar swept his instruments; the radarscope was clean. If other Iranian fighters were retreating, they weren't out in front of him. The threat warning panel flashed yellow and his fuel tanks were below the one-third mark.

"Ten miles to the coast," the radar intercept officer called out.

"Keep an eye out for missiles," Gahar warned his backseater. His attention returned to the HUD. He was cutting through the sky at Mach 1.3 and climbing. To the east, the major could see the first signs of the sunrise. In twenty minutes it would be light enough to see. He wondered how many of the fighters had been able to get their weapons airborne.

Gahar had speculated many times what it would be like to face the Americans in battle. Now he knew. They were fierce fighters who used special tactics to gain the advantage quickly.

*   *   *

Calloway heard the lockup tone become even and steady. He closed his eyes and tapped the launch button on his stick two times. Only this time nothing happened. The Hornet didn't shudder with the force of the missiles leaving their underwing pylons. He hit the button again and again. The same response . . . nothing.The Sparrows wouldn't leave their rails.

"Damn it! I can't believe this shit!" Calloway said. *There must be a malfunction in the launch mechanism.* The enemy target was not 6.8 miles away. He had two options. He could turn away. Or he could try to target the bastard with heat-seekers. That would be a long shot, but worth taking for some satisfaction, he thought.

Calloway turned his radar off and hit the switch, calling up his wingtip-mounted AIM-9M Sidewinders. Focusing his eyes out to infinity, he tried to catch sight of the jet's afterburners. Calloway had only intended to use the heat-seekers for close-in combat. While Sidewinders were designed to hit targets out to fifteen miles, they were rarely used outside of five miles.

The tone in his helmet changed to a high-pitched pulsing. It wasn't a sharp piercing shrill like it should be. The target was fading.

This one's for you, Kip. He punched the weapons release button twice. The two AIM-9M Sidewinders left their wingtip rail launchers a split second apart. Calloway watched them for a few seconds before pulling up and away to the right.

"Burn, baby, burn!" he yelled into his cockpit, releasing some of his emotion.

"Bingo fuel . . . bingo fuel," a soft female computer voice sounded in his helmet.

"Yeah . . . bingo fuel. That's how I feel right now, bingo fuel." Calloway tone was dull as the finality of his loss hit him. He had just enough fuel to get back to the *Lincoln* or the nearest tanker. "Strike . . . Mich Leader. I'm at bingo fuel. Heading home."

"Copy, Mich Leader."

The commander glanced in the direction of his missiles one last time. He couldn't see them; the Sidewinders had faded into the murky night. He trimmed up the Hornet for level flight and dialed in the radio frequency used for emergency search and rescue. "Michelangelo Six Seven . . . do you copy?" Calloway radioed.

There was no response.

"Michelangelo Six Seven . . . This is Mich Leader. Do you

copy?'' He listened to the crackling static. Calloway closed his eyes, feeling them burn with sweat. A sick feeling swept through his body.

"Ah, roger, Mich Leader. This is Michelangelo. I copy you man, I copy you."

"Kip . . . Hallelujah! You're alive, you Wyoming sheep-chaser. Are you all right?''

"Yes, sir . . . except I think my leg is broken . . . and I'm freezing to death."

"Hold on, buddy. S and R is on the way." Calloway laughed. "Is your emergency homing transmitter working?"

"Yeah, I think so."

"Good. I want you to wait ten minutes, then turn it on along with your strobe light. The choppers should be in the area by then."

"Roger . . . ten minutes. Commander?"

"Yeah."

"Can you wait out here with me until S and R picks me up? It's pitch black and I can't see a damned thing."

"Sure. I'll wait with you, Kip. I'm not going anywhere." Calloway smiled and unlatched the oxygen mask from his helmet. He could hear the quivering in Karson's voice and knew it wasn't caused just by the cold water. "Splinter . . . this is Mich Lead. I need a tanker to meet me out here to refuel."

Seven miles to the north, the solid-fuel rocket motors of the AIM-9Ms burned out as the Sidewinders closed in on the target. The missiles, traveling at a velocity of Mach 2.8, pushed over as the front-mounted canards made subtle adjustments, twisting right and left. The miniature guidance computer kept the nose pointed at the strongest heat source in the night sky, the glowing tailpipes of the escaping F-4E.

The force of the first explosion rocked the Iranian fighter as if it had hit an invisible brick wall in the sky. Major Gahar's helmet smacked the side of his F-4E canopy, nearly knocking him unconscious. The AIM-9M had impacted his fighter above the left horizontal stabilizer, nearly blowing it off. The F-4E's rudder jammed and immediately the jet started to lose hydraulic fluid. Fragments of the warhead ripped into the left engine, cutting the fuel line. Unknown to the pilot, the engine compartment began to fill with kerosene.

Gahar pulled the throttles back, taking the big fighter out of afterburner as he tried to force the stick down and right. The F-4E trembled in protest, barely responding. The maneuver was too little, too late. The second Sidewinder streaked past within ten feet of the right side of the Phantom, close enough to detonate the warhead's proximity fuse, which showered the Phantom with steel shrapnel. The cockpit flashed with the bright light of the blast and the Plexiglas shattered. A heartbeat later Gahar felt the sting of freezing air rushing in. He wrenched around, seeing the lifeless body of his radar operator slumped over the instruments, his head bobbing. The young man's neck and the side of his face were a mass of blood and torn flesh.

"Allah help me," he prayed. Gahar watched his instrument panel light up with red and yellow warning lights. He worked at moving the stick left and right, but it was heavily sluggish and hard to push. He forced himself to think. The fighter was still heading north at 012 degrees. In a few minutes he would be able to make out the Iranian coastline. If he could reach the coast, he could at least eject safely over land.

The Phantom was rapidly losing altitude. His HUD showed he was down to 7,569 feet and losing 3,000 feet a minute. *Just hold on, hold on.* Preparing to punch out, Gahar made sure his restraints were tight. He shut down the left engine and changed his radio frequency to that of the Bandar Abbas air base. He thought he could see the coastline ahead. *Two more minutes . . . that's all I need.*

"Bandar Abbas, this is—"

Major Kuh Gahar never completed the sentence. Deep inside the fighter, sparks from the right engine had started a small fire in the rear section. In a few seconds it had spread to the left engine compartment, which was full of leaking fuel. A fireball ripped the F-4E into several pieces. Gahar's last sensation was that of heat surrounding his cold body, warming him.

Chapter Thirty

BELL 214 HUEY

Hassan Zadeh was seated in the cargo bay of the chopper. Through dirty Plexiglas windows, he could see the lights of Esfahan fade as the American-built Huey banked sharply to the left, throwing the men around like matches in a box. The chopper vibrated wildly, the rivets seeming ready to burst from age and lack of maintenance. They were skimming across the desert at less than 100 feet, with navigational lights on. The high-pitched whine of the engine indicated the pilot was pushing the helicopter as fast as it would go. Zadeh cursed that the machine should hold together, or someone would pay. He gave no thought to the fact that he might be in danger. He was convinced that he would still be around to punish whoever was responsible. They still had to climb the mountain toward the mining camp.

Zadeh turned on the battery pack of his Soviet-designed night vision goggles. The pack was fairly large and resembled a pair of rubber-coated binoculars with a slot for two C-size batteries. Several wires ran down the side of the goggles, supplying power to the light-gathering lenses. He waited for the red LED light to switch on, telling him the NVGs were up and running. He raised them to his eyes and scanned the interior.

Seated next to him, Ali Fesseghi bounced with every jolt. Along the sides of the chopper, holding assault weapons ranging from AK-47s to 9-mm Sterling submachine guns and bearing side arms, were eight Revolutionary Guards. Each man wore desert-brown camouflage fatigues void of any patches or unit insignias and a Russian helmet. There wasn't any question in Zadeh's mind the men were well trained. Revolutionary Guards were assigned to each military base in Iran. It was their job to ensure that the military remained loyal to the religious leaders in Tehran. The guards had been trained by Syrian and North Korean commandos. Not only were these men loyal, they were also physically and mentally tough.

"Believe me, Zadeh. When we hit the ground, these men will know what to do," Fesseghi shouted, as if reading his thoughts. "I've seen them in action."

"Then I suggest you don't get in their way. Or mine, for that matter," Zadeh smirked. "You wouldn't want to be responsible for another blunder, would you?" He then turned his attention back to the window. He trusted only one man to complete this mission—himself.

MH-53J PAVE LOW

"If we're not out of this shit in five minutes, General, I'm calling it quits," Chief Warrant Officer Newall said, scanning the chopper's instruments. "Flying at night is dangerous enough without having to put up with this crap."

Duke felt the special forces helicopter pitch up and down as the terrain-following radar guided it up and over a small group of hills. "Yeah? And fly through this stuff for another forty minutes all the way back? No way. We keep moving forward. We're only twenty-five miles from our objective."

"I've never flown through soup this thick." Newall's usually calm tone was anxious. He was experienced enough to know what he was talking about. "She's only a machine, General, designed to take only so much stress. We have eighteen men in the back, and I'm not about to risk their lives to save one man."

"Neither am I. But I say we move forward. This is the best cover we could have asked for." Duke turned his head right and left, using his NVGs to search for any signs they would break out of the sandstorm soon. Every now and then he could see through the wind and sand, catching sight of the ground or a nearby hill.

"Like I said, General . . . five more minutes," Newall answered.

Duke knew in all truthfulness the pilot was probably right. He had been flying high-performance aircraft his entire life and had never been in a storm this severe, either. But he believed that sometimes you had to push a little to find out just what your aircraft could handle.

"Coors Leader . . . this is Coyote Leader," Duke called. "How are things topside, Eddie?"

"Level at eight thousand. No change, Coyote Leader. I'm still in the middle of it."

"We're going to give it another five minutes. If we don't break out of this, I want you to climb to the top until you do. We need to know how far this storm reaches," Duke ordered.

"Copy, Coyote Leader . . . five minutes."

"Five minutes and then we go topside," Duke said, resolved. "Not back. I don't care if we have to climb to 30,000 feet."

Newall was quiet.

Duke flipped up his NVGs. He could see the rigid set of Newall's face as he scanned the instruments. The man was busy worrying about flying the chopper and didn't argue with the general. There wasn't any doubt in Duke's mind, though, that if the special forces pilot thought his ship was in danger he would turn around anyway, order or no order.

USS *LaSalle*

The symbols of two more enemy aircraft disappeared from the primary display screen in the CIC. A dozen American fighters were now engaging the Iranians at several altitudes. The display showed that several groups of F-18s and F-14s had turned away and were now heading toward the *Lincoln*.

"That makes nine down, sir," Admiral Zachiem reported. He walked over and stood next to Chaniff and Staffer. Only three enemy fighters were still moving south; all the others had turned back.

"Any word from James and the rest of the main strike force?" Chaniff asked.

"Nothing in the past twenty minutes," Zachiem said. "Their last report said they were still heading north but were in a large sandstorm."

"Damn it. That's what sank us in '80 when we went in after the hostages. Makes you wonder if the Iranians can control the weather," Chaniff commented, rubbing his forehead.

"Well, they don't control the weather, and we have better equipment now, sir," Staffer added confidently. "They'll make it."

"They damn well better, Staffer. Or I'm hanging a failed Echo mission around your neck when the shit hits the fan in Washington."

Staffer turned to Chaniff and spoke clearly. "You don't have to worry. If it does fail, I'll take more than the responsibility."

Zachiem looked at both men, then shook his head and walked back to his station in front of the display screen. He understood what it meant to have your reputation and career on the line for something you believed in strongly. At that moment, Zachiem expressed compassion for Staffer by turning his back on him and allowing him to meet Chaniff's stare without any witnesses. The screen showed that the last of the enemy aircraft had turned and were now trying to head north. Two F-14s were in pursuit, firing the last of their missiles.

"That's it. They're retreating," Zachiem announced, breaking the silence behind him.

"How close did they get to our ships?" Chaniff asked.

"Sixty-eight miles, sir."

"If five of their fighters were able to let loose with two missiles each . . ." Chaniff paused, contemplating the situation. "Then ten missiles could be headed for the *Princeton* and possibly the *Lincoln*. Admiral, get on the horn to Captain Wright at once. Warn him that ten stealth cruise missiles could be coming his way. ETA three minutes."

"Yes, General." Zachiem was already putting on the radio headphones.

"I hope to hell those Navy rocket scientists know what they're doing," Staffer said. "If not, the *Princeton* won't be able to find and lock up those missiles. Then . . ."

"I know," Chaniff grunted in disgust. "This is a hell of a way to find out."

"General," Zachiem interrupted. "The *Princeton* reports picking up four, possibly five, air-to-ground radars several minutes ago."

The room had been clamorous with activity. But all was soon

silent as the men in the CIC waited for the fates of the ships and their crews to be resolved.

USS PRINCETON

''Confirm the transmission and bring her around to zero one four. Full speed,'' Captain Nathan Samuel Wright barked from his chair in the center of the room. ''We'll give them a moving target.''

The captain was overweight, and though he was sitting upright it appeared that he was slouching in his worn leather chair. His droopy eyelids covered half his soft gray eyes, and his expression never changed—just the tone of his voice shifted to suit the occasion.

Wright had been the XO when the *Princeton* hit a moored mine during the Gulf War. The ship's stern heaved twenty feet into the air as the shock wave from the 380-pound underwater explosive pushed the rear half of the ship out of the water. Crippled by the explosion, the ship's engines had shut down. The keel had been cracked and her Aegis radar was inoperative, leaving the *Princeton* dead in the water and defenseless for two hours. Wright remembered every detail as if it were yesterday. Now in command, Wright was determined that this would be the day the *Princeton* redeemed herself.

He shifted in his seat and unconsciously heaved a sigh. His head was cocked to the side as if straining to hear the slightest noise. The CIC had become a hushed chamber awash in blue light and flickering multicolored displays. Each technician was sitting behind a console working the computer controls. The knowledge that the *Shiloh* had recently played the same game and lost was burning in each of their minds.

''Mr. Alvarez, any hostile targets on your radar screen?'' Wright said abruptly.

''Negative, sir. I'm tracking three F-18s returning to the *Lincoln*. All other hostile aircraft have regressed the area,'' Lieutenant Juan Alvarez, the *Princeton*'s combat systems coordinator, replied, sitting at his console. He monitored the ship's SPY-1B long-range radar. The LINK-11 data relay system was taking in information from every ship in the battle group, as well as the E-2C circling overhead, and displaying it on the four screens in the CIC.

Captain Wright studied the tactical display screen, checking the *Lincoln* to the south of their position. The carrier was heading northwest; she had turned into the wind to recover her aircraft. The top part of the screen showed the Iranian coastline.

Wright didn't have any illusions of what his Aegis cruiser was capable of during combat. In an offensive mode, the cruiser was unbeatable, but in a quasi-war environment, in which the enemy could potentially strike first, the *Princeton* could be very vulnerable.

"You know the procedure, Mr. Alvarez. Find those ghost missiles if they're out there." Captain Wright was speaking slowly and calmly, as if this were routine.

"Yes, sir," Alvarez answered. He continued tapping the keyboard, changing the antenna focus of the forward phased-array antenna. Located on the front of the ship's main superstructure, hundreds of small, narrow, high-resolution fixed radar beams were sweeping the airspace north of the cruiser in rapid succession. Alvarez commanded the computer to drop the beam's search slant fifteen degrees so that the radar could see and get a fix on any incoming targets streaking toward the *Princeton* at extremely low altitude. With the new radar setting, a low-flying missile would be detected at a greater range even if it was flying a few feet above the ocean. He tapped a few more buttons, trying to filter out the clutter as the radar beams began striking the water ten miles in front of the ship.

"Beam angles at seventy-five degrees," Alvarez reported. "We're going to cut our range by a third, Captain."

"Do it, Mr. Alvarez," Wright grunted.

"Yes, sir. Boosting power to maximum. Radar frequency changing to 3,109 MHz." The SPY-1B radar was now operating at the low end of the F-band radar spectrum. If the Navy research team at Norfolk was correct, this new frequency should be able to penetrate the graphite skin of the Iranian missiles, allowing the system to detect and lock onto any incoming stealth missiles.

"Status, Mr. Alvarez." Wright shifted to the edge of his chair.

"System is on automatic, sir. But my scope is clean. I don't see a thing."

"Make sure the fire control teams are standing by. Heads up," Wright instructed, not wanting anyone to get unduly relaxed. He needn't have worried, though. No one in the CIC was the least bit relaxed as the ship continued north at twenty-eight knots.

MH-53J Pave Low

The hissing sound of the rotor blades cutting through the air ended a few seconds after the Pave Low suddenly broke out of the sandstorm and into the open. The chopper's main IR screen immediately filled with the greenish glow of the desert night. Duke could once again make out large rocks and bushes as the chopper sped 100 feet above the desert at 110 knots.

"All right, General. Let's confirm our location and complete this mission. It'll be light in half an hour and it's not a good idea to be flying this fat lady in broad daylight. She makes a nice round target," Newall chattered.

"You just worry about making up for lost time. I'll get us where we're going," Duke answered, while he studied the satellite maps on his knees and the global positioning system. The chopper's system showed they were five miles east of a long series of broken, rocky hills. If they were on course, they would fly over a two-lane paved road in another two minutes. It ran northeast toward the city of Shahr Kord. As he watched the screen, it flickered several times before fading to black.

"Damn it, we just lost the GPS."

"Shit." Newall keyed his mike. "Coyote Two, this is Leader. We just lost GPS . . . take the lead."

"Copy, Coyote Leader. We're a quarter mile behind you. Moving to the lead."

Duke flipped to the third photograph before finding the one he needed. If the GPS was correct before it went off-line, they were eighteen miles southwest of the mining camp and six miles from Iranian highway H-23. They needed to bank right to find the highway. "We're still on course," Duke insisted. He watched as the image of Coyote Two filled the IR screen. The whirling green blades of the chopper and glowing white heat radiating from the engines cast a menacing portrait of the giant helicopter moving through the night.

"General, we're going to be touching down in ten minutes. Better let LaCoss know," Newall said.

Duke carefully unstrapped himself from the engineer's seat and made his way past the wall separating the flight deck from the Pave Low's large cargo bay. Using handholds mounted on the fuselage, he climbed into the rear section of the chopper and sat down next to Special Forces First Lieutenant Chuck LaCoss. The cargo bay was bathed in red light. The Army Rangers were seated with their weapons across their laps. The upper half of each man's face was covered by NVGs, making it impossible to see their eyes. Duke preferred it that way.

"Lieutenant, we're ten minutes from touchdown," Duke said over the loud whine of the turbine engines.

"That storm put us behind, General. I hope your boy is already in place and waiting." Lieutenant LaCoss tapped his watch set to the mission time. "That twenty minutes we were allowed to be on the ground is now fifteen. If he doesn't hear us coming, we'll have to go through each of those buildings and—"

"I'll go in with you," Duke shouted impulsively.

"I can't allow that, sir. We can get the job done. I'm just letting you know that even if he isn't located, we will leave the area as scheduled . . . and if you're thinking that just because you're out there we'll stick around a few more minutes, you're wrong. We're taking off on time." LaCoss emphasized his words, tapping on his watch again. "I can't have my men walking around in daylight bare-assed."

"I don't give a damn about your schedule, Lieutenant. When we land, I'm going with you." Duke looked straight at LaCoss. He decided that he'd feel better doing something than just sitting and waiting inside the chopper. "And if I have to, I'll pull rank."

LaCoss shook his head and shifted his gaze down to his specially designed Rocky Eliminator boots. "Fucking generals all think they're Sergeant Slaughter," he breathed under his breath.

"Did you say something, Lieutenant?"

"Yeah, you'll need this," he said and handed Duke a tube of black grease paint. "I don't suppose you brought your own gun?"

Duke answered with a grin.

"Well, you think you can handle an M-16?"

"It's been a while, but if I can handle you, I'm sure I can manage," Duke replied, smearing the camouflage paint over his face, neck and hands.

"We'll see if you still feel that way when we land. You better stay right with me, got it? I don't give a shit if you do outrank me. When we're in the field, I'm in charge and I won't have you screwing up this mission."

"I'll be right on your ass, Lieutenant." Duke stood up and his sturdy frame towered over LaCoss. "By the way, I taught Sergeant Slaughter everything he knows."

ESFAHAN, IRAN

"That is correct, Minister. The Americans did hit the launch sites west of Bandar Abbas approximately twenty minutes ago." Colonel Rahavi was standing at attention as if the defense minister was in the command room at Esfahan with him.

"How many of your fighters were able to launch their weapons?" Bakhtiar asked.

"Five missiles were launched."

"*Five!* You assured me they would be able to launch twice that number."

"Under the circumstances, sir, I regard the mission as a success. Ten of my F-4Es were shot down and only one flight crew has been recovered. Your plan to attack the Americans has decimated this country's fleet of fighters." Rahavi stood his ground.

"It was the American spy, I know it. He will pay for this."

"The fighters are returning to base now. When I receive more information, I will give you another report," the colonel said without asking whether they had located the American or the woman. His mind was on the fighters and the men on their way back, as well as on those who weren't.

I have lost eighteen of my best pilots. Ten aircraft were shot from the sky. My men have sacrificed enough, Rahavi thought. This would be the last time he would follow the orders of a crazy man. He would keep the fighters patrolling around Esfahan for only another hour.

USS *PRINCETON*

Lieutenant Juan Alvarez dropped his head and made one more adjustment to the computer controls. A slender man with soft features and black eyes, the lieutenant had joined the Navy right out of high school, planning to let the government pay for his college through the GI bill. That was seven years ago, and now he couldn't picture himself doing anything else.

Alvarez had spent the past five years learning every aspect of the SPY-1B radar system. Now he was having to rethink some of the basic strategy used to defend the ship. The radar had been reconfigured to detect the slightest electronic reflection. The data could then be fed through the ship's weapons computers and the SM-2 SAM system could be updated in seconds. The lieutenant had his doubts, though. As far as he was concerned, the *Princeton*'s radar had been fine-tuned to the point where they would be targeting every seagull within a hundred square miles. There were only so many benefits to being able to pick up every little moving target.

"I need a better angle. Bring her around to one one four slow to one half," Alvarez ordered.

Captain Wright nodded his approval.

"If there's anything out there, sir, we should be picking it up." Two minutes had passed since they had received the warning from the *LaSalle*.

"There, sir, to the starboard." Alvarez pointed to the main viewing screen. The symbol appeared—an unknown target moving in a southerly heading.

"Confirm," Wright ordered.

"It's a target, but it's weak," Alvarez said steadily, unaware of anyone else in the room. "Speed, 530 knots. Altitude, twelve feet. Range, seven miles and closing. Forty-five seconds to engage."

Three more unknown target symbols appeared on the screen.

"That makes four . . . no, five." Alvarez quickly glanced back at the captain, then turned his full attention to the screen.

Wright reached over and switched the fire control key from standby to active, engaging the ship's antimissile defense system. The *Princeton*'s fire control computer immediately locked onto the five targets, illuminating them with F-band radar waves.

"Confirmed . . . we have five targets, Captain. Converting from unknown to hostile," Alvarez warned. "Two off the port side, three to starboard." The lieutenant breathed in deeply, sitting back. He had done his job. It was now up to other members of the crew and the Aegis's computer system.

The computer symbology changed from ⌐•⌐ to Λ and tracking numbers were assigned to each target.

"Permission to take the targets," the missile systems supervisor requested.

"Permission granted. Take the bastards," Wright said loudly.

The MSS stood up. He tapped a series of buttons instructing the SPY-1B radar to fire two missiles at each target. The words SELECT WEAPON flashed on the bottom of his screen. Making sure he didn't get ahead of the sequence, the officer tapped the Standard-MR SM-2 button, calling up the ship's arsenal of medium-range SAMs designed to shoot down aircraft and cruise missiles at a range of two to ninety miles. "Missiles armed. System is on auto-sequence," the MSS confirmed.

"Range, five miles," Alvarez alerted. "One minute to impact." He knew the closer the missiles flew to the *Princeton,* the more difficult they would be to shoot down.

Without warning, the CIC of the *Princeton* shook. Alvarez swallowed hard, feeling the cruiser shake a second and a third time as the SM-2s exploded out of their launch tubes located on the ship's bow.

"Missiles away," Alvarez announced.

The bow of the *Princeton* lit up with flying sparks and white smoke. The sealed hatches of the vertical launch canisters blew open, exposing the fiery plumes of rotor motors igniting. Ten surface-to-air missiles thrust their way into the night air, climbing slowly at first and then accelerating. The SAMs climbed to an altitude of 200 feet before pushing over and heading for their targets. Located in the nose cone of each missile, a tiny radar-seeking device began to search the sky for subtle traces of reflecting radar beams bouncing off the solid internal parts of each cruise missile.

"I recommend we fire again, sir . . . sending four missiles at each target," Alvarez advised. "The radar return is extremely weak. The SAMs will have trouble tracking the targets."

"Do it," Captain Wright ordered, immediately trusting Alvarez's assessment of the dire situation.

F-16C Coors Leader

Colonel Naylor leveled his F-16C at 2,000 feet after coming out of the sandstorm. His LANTIRN system was functioning again, allowing the colonel to see the desert below his aircraft as it sped toward the objective.

Naylor wasn't feeling any easier about the mission, however. Yes, only one fighter had returned to base because of the storm, but now they were eighteen minutes behind schedule. The weapons complex should already have been bombed and they should be heading home at Mach 1. He decided to risk breaking radio silence to make certain everyone was on track.

"All aircraft . . . this is Coors Leader. New orders. We hit the IP in two minutes. Anyone not able to continue the mission needs to report in now." Naylor listened for a response but didn't get one. "All right. Three minutes over the target. That's it. Do it and get the hell out of there. See you on the ground."

Naylor moved the stick right, putting his F-16 into a slight banking turn. He made sure he stayed below a group of sandstone mountains to the west. His RHAW equipment was picking up the faint whisper of an Iranian radar sweeping to the northeast. As long as he stayed below the tops of the mountains, the Iranians would have a hard time finding them.

The colonel pictured in his mind what was happening. He was sure the E-3C, call sign "Terminator," had by now moved farther east. The American AWACS would be sweeping the Iranian skies, checking for any hostile aircraft. The rest of the strike package was strung out behind him over a couple of miles, no doubt scattered unevenly because of the storm. Each pilot knew the IP, or initial point, was an Iranian radio transmitter located twenty-two miles south of Esfahan. They would form up at three different altitudes and cross over the transmitter together.

The lead F-15E, piloted by Robert Baker, would move out first, accompanied by Coors Three Three. It was Baker's job to take out the main power grids supplying electricity to the air base, as well as the backup system. Thirty seconds after that objective was complete, the EF-111A Ravens would begin jamming the Iranian radars in the area. Naylor and the other two F-16Cs of Coors would swoop in from the south, firing their HARMs at any SAMs trying to illuminate the strike package with surface radars. The F-15Cs would stay on top using their radars to hunt for MiGs, while F-15Es pounded the weapons complex with laser-guided bombs. The plan was to hit the Iranians with a savage attack, catching them off-guard. Naylor couldn't help but wonder, since they were behind schedule, just how surprised the Iranians were going to be.

The colonel throttled back as the blinking red lights of the transmitter came into view four miles ahead of him. He leveled his F-16 at 1,900 feet and pitched the nose up as his airspeed fell. One scan of his instruments told him everything was functioning.

Here we go, he said to himself. He rocked his fighter left, catching the winking navigational lights of his wingman in his peripheral vision.

USS *PRINCETON*

"Twenty seconds to SAM impact," Alvarez called out, his tone dry and lifeless.

"Zoom in on sector two seven," Captain Wright ordered. The second display to the left jumped several times, then filled with thin white lines showing the flight paths of the ship's missiles as they tracked the incoming cruise missiles. The SAMs curved right and then left as their radar-seeker heads attempted to stay locked up on the weak reflecting radars bouncing off the Iranian missiles. Some of the countermissiles weaved off course, their seeker heads losing the weak lock.

The CIC had become hushed and tense. All radio transmissions had stopped.

"Come on, you bastards . . . take them out," someone called out from the opposite side of the room.

"Phalanx on automatic," someone else shouted, referring to the ship's last-ditch defense against low flying cruise missiles, a 20 MM Vulcan Cannon designed to shoot down cruise missiles seconds before impacting the ship."

"Ten seconds to SAM impact."

"Take a heading of zero zero nine. Keep us pointed straight at them." Wright was gripping the sides of his chair unconsciously.

"NO!" Alvarez said abruptly, protesting. "That may affect the radar return."

"*Belay* that order," Wright said quickly.

"Five seconds, sir." It was Alvarez again. "Three . . . two . . . one. They should be converging."

The images of the SM-2 SAMs merging with the hostile target symbols filled the tactical display screen.

Four miles north of the *Princeton,* the sky flashed with exploding warheads and flying metal. The first three American missiles found their marks. The two lead stealth missiles exploded, cartwheeling into the ocean. Shrapnel from one of the *Princeton*'s SAMs tore into a third missile a quarter of a mile away, igniting its fuel tank. Two seconds later the fuel supply exploded, vaporizing the missile in a small fireball.

"One down . . . two down," Alvarez called out as the symbols disappeared from the screen. He blinked the sweat from his eyes.

"Come on . . . ," Wright whispered.

"Three down."

The IR guidance system on the fourth stealth missile detected the white flashes a mile ahead of it. The intense light caused its IR and computer guidance systems to temporarily overload. The missile automatically pitched up ten degrees, gaining altitude, and the computer's software began to cycle over again, trying to regain the proper flight profile. When the missile leveled at 100 feet, it began to swing east away from the *Princeton*. Before it could complete the turn, two SM-2 SAMs impacted its side, destroying it.

"Four down." Alvarez studied the screen, waiting for some of the data to clear. "It looks like we've got a leaker," Alvarez said, alerting the captain that one of the missiles was making its way toward the *Princeton*. It was coming from the south at a high rate of speed.

"Forty seconds out . . . ," another officer called out.

"Range, 3.6 miles."

"Ready the flares," Wright ordered.

"Flares ready."

The captain waited for the symbol to move closer to the ship.

"Thirty seconds, Captain." Alvarez said anxiously. "It's closing on us fast."

"Full spread . . . *now!*" Wright barked.

Lieutenant Alvarez punched the flare desperation button on the right side of his control console. From just above the MK-36 SRBOC chaff launchers, one on each side of the ship, a series of small explosions jettisoned several dozen magnesium IR decoy flares high into the air. Burning at different temperatures, covering a 1-to-8-micron range, the flares were designed to fool the seeker heads of IR-guided missiles.

"Fifteen seconds."

"Hit it again, Mr. Alvarez," Captain Wright commanded more calmly.

MH-53J PAVE LOW

Newall disengaged the TFR, and the big Pave Low pitched up and down as he wrestled for control of the ship.

"Turn left ten degrees," Duke instructed. "Do you see it?"

"Yeah . . . I have it," Newall replied unruffled.

Cutting across the desert like a thin green ribbon was highway H-23. It was void of any traffic except for a small herd of camels and goats gathered around what looked like a watering hole. The other Pave Low banked to the northwest, coming parallel to the road while maintaining an altitude of 250 feet.

"Not so close, Coyote Two," Newall said out loud to himself. "We just need to follow it, not drive on it."

"Fifteen miles from touchdown. I'm picking up the lights of Shahr Kord." Duke watched the green glow of the horizon grow slowly brighter through his NVGs.

"Anything on the RHAW equipment?" Newall asked.

"Negative. I'm not reading any SAM or triple A radars in the area," the copilot responded.

"All right . . . I'm going to stay a half mile east of the road. Keep a lookout for any traffic."

"The strike force is poised to hit the weapons center in five minutes. We need to be on the ground before the first bomb hits," Duke reminded the pilot.

"We will," Newall answered assuredly and pitched the chopper up several degrees, banking to the left.

USS PRINCETON

The fifth and final missile didn't vary from its course. Its computer guidance program had a solid lock on the pulsing IR image of the *Princeton* one mile directly ahead of it. As the missile closed, the image became stronger, filling the entire laser storage disk with the heat signature of the Aegis-class cruiser.

"Seven seconds . . . six seconds."

"One more time, Mr. Alvarez." Captain Wright was mentally preparing for the situation should the missile strike the bow section of his ship.

Lieutenant Juan Alvarez did as he was told, punching the decoy flare button one more time. He looked up just in time to see the hostile target image merge with that of the *Princeton*. The missile was only seconds away from impact.

As the missile closed to 100 feet, the IR picture the laser computer system had been locked up on began to blur and distort from the various heat sources. The last volley of flares was more than the missile's guidance computer could handle. Its filtering system hadn't been designed to screen out a barrage of changing IR signatures. The cruise missile nosed over and hit the water fifty feet in front of the *Princeton*.

The force of the explosion rocked through the ship and all on board braced themselves. Captain Wright began shouting orders: "All stop . . . all stop!"

"All stop," came the response.

"Damage report," Wright bellowed.

Alvarez, who had fallen on the hard steel floor, picked himself up immediately and slipped on his radio headset. He held a hand to one side of his head, pressing the speaker closer to his ear. The ship's communications channels were filled with the chatter of everyone reporting to the CIC at once. Finally, he heard something he could understand.

"Lookout reports the missile struck the water near the starboard bow." Alvarez closed his eyes. "No reports of water entering the ship, or the breach of structural integrity; only minor injuries are being reported."

"There's damage to the five-inch gun and the forward MK 26 missile launcher. The blast knocked them clean off their mounts," the XO reported, looking at the captain.

"Engine room," Wright said, pressing the intercom button. "Damage report."

"We have a few scrapes, but other than that everything's A-OK down here."

"Good . . . give me fifteen knots." Wright leaned back in his chair as if there was never any danger. "Take a heading of one three zero. Mr. Alvarez . . . send a message to the Golf Bravo telling them we just shot down five Iranian cruise missiles." Golf Bravo was the code name for the Middle East Task Force commander.

"You got it, Skipper," Alvarez smiled, as he picked up the authority phone linking them with the *LaSalle*.

"Then make a copy of the computer tapes and transmit them to Zachiem. The professors back at Norfolk will want to take a look at them." Wright continued giving out the routine orders and didn't appear to be rattled in the least. "Oh . . . and Lieutenant Alvarez."

"Yes, Captain?"

"Good job."

"Thank you, sir." Alvarez wasn't sure, but he thought he could make out a slight grin on the captain's somber face. He returned his attention to his work.

Chapter Thirty-one

E-3C AWACS, TERMINATOR

"They just hit the IP," Master Sergeant Albert Adams said soberly to himself. "They're twenty-two minutes behind schedule."

"That storm really screwed them up. Keep me posted," Lieutenant Colonel Patrick Connor replied. The colonel was the E-3C's combat information officer.

Adams pushed the black military-issue glasses higher on his nose and ran his fingers through his curly brown hair. He stayed focused on his multi-purpose SDC (situation display console). The square-jawed "scope dope" habitually scanned the four-color screen trying to spot anything unusual. The black background of the display console highlighted the superimposed green lines of Iran's western border and the northern section of the Persian Gulf, along with the central interior of Iran. It was as if he were looking at a moving electronic road map.

On the right side of the display, Adams watched the blue triangles which, along with their IFF transponder codes, represented the strike package of F-15s, F-16s and the single EF-111A. The other EF-111A had turned back during the storm. The fighters had just converged, at varying altitudes, over their IP. He had lost contact with the Pave Lows and C-130 about six minutes ago as they flew behind one of Iran's interior mountain ranges.

Assigned to the 963rd AWACS (Airborne Warning and Con-

trol) Squadron based out of Tinker AFB, Oklahoma, Adams and
the rest of the crew had deployed to a classified air base thirty-
seven miles northwest of Riyadh, Saudi Arabia, four days earlier.
They weren't strangers to the Saudi base. This was the second
time in the last nine months they had been assigned to work with
the Saudi air force, helping fine-tune their air crews on the operating skills required for air-to-air surveillance and interception.
However, this night they weren't flying with any Royal Saudi
officers.

Flying the same orbit they had flown for the last week, a racetrack pattern at 42,000 feet over the extreme eastern edge of Saudi
Arabia, the E-3C's powerful pulse-Doppler radar scanned the airspace deep inside Iraq. The only difference was that this wasn't
a practice mission and Adams didn't feel any fatigue. Too much
adrenaline was pumping through his 140-pound frame. He had
been tracking several Iranian fighters above Esfahan. They were
on the very edge of his coverage, making them nearly impossible
to keep track of all the time.

Adams looked around and noted the tension on the other men's
faces. He was glad to see that he wasn't the only one feeling
uneasy inside the fuselage of the converted 707 jetliner.

The interior was alive with red, yellow, blue and green lights
bouncing off the walls from the display screens. Thirteen operators, huddled together, watched a variety of Hazeltine high-
resolution multipurpose consoles. They monitored everything
from ECM (electronic counter-measures) to the fighters' essential
avionics and communications channels. The rear half of the aircraft was fitted with a galley, bunk beds and a toilet. The cockpit
was nothing more than that of a standard 707 with a few modifications for secure communications and data processing computers. Above the aircraft, a Westinghouse APY-1 liquid-cooled
radar rotated clockwise at six revolutions a minute, sending out
a steady stream of pulse-Doppler radar waves. The thirty-foot-
diameter radome also served as an aerodynamic flaring, giving
added lift to the aircraft.

Adams felt the big four-engine jet bank to the left, then come
wings level. They were heading ninety degrees, due east. The
pilot throttled back, reducing the AWACS' airspeed by several
knots, which would allow them to stay in the air a few minutes
longer.

"All right, gentlemen . . . one minute to showtime. Heads up,"

Lieutenant Colonel Patrick Connor's gruff voice boomed through Adams's headset. It was his job to make certain that everyone was doing their job properly and to prioritize the threats.

Adams swallowed hard and took a deep breath, trying to slow his rapid heartbeat. *Stay calm,* he told himself. *Do it just like you always do it. That's what got you here.* Even though he was only twenty-nine years old, the sergeant had over 2,300 hours of experience guiding aircraft through the sky. He was inexperienced, though, when it came to directing fighters in actual combat. A comment by one of his first instructors back at Tinker entered his mind: "Keep the blue triangles from running into the other blue triangles and you'll do just fine." *I hope it's going to be just that easy.*

"Any bandits to the northeast?" Connor asked, kneeling down next to the sergeant. Connor looked the part of a weathered Air Force colonel. Short-cropped gray hair and deep wrinkles, from hours of exposure to the desert sun, ringed his rigid face. His hard, seasoned eyes didn't give away any emotion whether he was laughing or screaming his head off because someone screwed up. Yet tonight Connor's tone was filled with an emotion Adams couldn't define.

"None, sir," Adams replied. "The two targets I was tracking headed south. I lost sight of them three minutes ago. Probably scared stiff and won't be back."

"Don't bet on it," Connor chided him, looking at the screen. "Keep an open mind as well as open eyes. Where is Coors Leader?"

"Right here, sir." He pointed to a small blue triangle heading northeast.

"Those SEAD aircraft are going to be the most vulnerable. Make sure you have at least one F-15C covering them at all times."

"Yes, sir." Adams felt the colonel's hand give him a slight pat on his back. "Okay, Coors Flight . . . I've got ya covered," he said loudly enough for Connor to hear.

F-15E MUSTANG LEADER

"It's time to rock and roll." Lieutenant Colonel Robert Baker heard the call from Coors Leader. *"Mustang Leader, do your stuff. Coors Three Three stay with him."*

"Coors Leader . . . Mustang Leader. We're moving."

"Mustang Leader . . . Coors Three Three. I'm on your ass."

"Here we go." Baker quickly twisted around to glance at his weapons systems operator, who was seated directly behind him in the cockpit of the Strike Eagle. His backseater, First Lieutenant Dennis Summers, didn't look up. His attention was firmly focused on the four multifunction displays located along the top of the cockpit instrument panel.

Baker watched the radio transmitter flash under his fighter. He banked to the right and pointed the nose of the F-15E toward two irregular hilltops in the distance. The colonel had been flying the Strike Eagle for six years, though he had missed the Gulf War. The Air Force had assigned him as head F-111 instructor pilot at Cannon AFB in New Mexico. Now, the thirty-nine-year-old Floridian was about to maneuver his fighter bomber through the mountainous terrain south of Esfahan and take out two power relay stations.

Keeping the Strike Eagle level at 200 feet, Baker watched his airspeed steadily increase past 400 knots. When the HUD showed 410 knots, he throttled back a fraction of an inch and let the big fighter float up. Off his right wing he could see the flashing navigational lights of the F-16C only a hundred yards away. Baker felt better having the smaller single-engine fighter flying escort. Unlike his F-15E, which was loaded with a mix of GBU-10B 2,000-pound laser-guided bombs and AIM-120 AMRAAM missiles, the F-16C carried only one type of external weapon—under each wing were three AGM-88C HARM missiles. Acting as bodyguard, it would be Coors Three Three's job to locate and destroy any SAMs or triple A threats in the target areas.

Baker had been around a few F-16C SEAD pilots while training back at Seymour Johnson AFB in North Carolina. In Baker's opinion, the men flying the F-16Cs were a different breed. They tended to be cocky and extremely sure of themselves. Baker figured it was all part of their training. After all, their mission was to find and locate enemy defenses by having hostile radars sweep and lock up on their fighters.

"Two minutes to target," Lieutenant Summers said. "Turn left, heading three five five. Take her up to three hundred."

Baker banked his F-15E left, watching the heading change on top of the HUD. In the distance he could see the glowing lights of Esfahan filtering over several irregular hills.

USS *LaSalle*

Staffer lit another cigarette, his fifth one in the last thirty minutes, and blew smoke out his nose. Tired of coffee, he finally gave in to his craving for nicotine. The center display screen now showed the center part of Iran, with Esfahan in the upper left-hand corner.

"Damn it! Why can't we see what's going on?" Chaniff screamed.

"They're below radar coverage, sir. Our AWACS will only be able to pick them up once they climb above 2,000 feet," Zachiem explained patiently.

"How long before sunup?" Staffer asked.

"Thirty-five, forty minutes."

"Shit. That sandstorm really screwed things up." Staffer put out his half-smoked cigarette, took a seat and watched Chaniff continue to pace back and forth. He wished the general wasn't acting so nervous. It added to his sense of dread. *Maybe he always acts this way*, Staffer thought. He reached for another cigarette. *What I really need is a damn shrink to explain why I put myself through this kind of shit.*

SHAHR KORD, IRAN

The black CIA staff car pulled up in the driveway of Mark Collins' Arlington, Virginia home. The street was quiet and the sprinkler sprayed the lawn. Yes, it had to be a staff car. The men getting out were wearing black suits and dark ties. Their eyes were covered by sunglasses and their faces were stern. *No . . . no, I'm not dead. Don't tell them I'm dead.* Standing in the doorway of his home was his wife, Christine. She opened the door slowly. She invited the men in shakily and picked up her daughter. Tears began streaming down her face. *No, Christine, no . . . I'm not dead.* The words wouldn't come out. No one was aware of his presence. He reached out to grasp his wife and was suddenly alone in the middle of a desert. He searched for some familiar sight and began running, his footsteps pounding the air.

Collins's body jerked as he stumbled in his dream. He came to and bolted upright. His mind began to clear and he realized it was only a nightmare. *Yes, only a dream. This whole thing is a nightmare.* He wiped the cold sweat from his face and breathed deeply, calming his nerves. The desert night had turned frigid, and Collins felt a chill as the cool air hit the perspiration running down his back.

The thumping he had heard in his dream continued to sound off in his mind. *No . . . wait. I'm not dreaming . . . that's real. What the . . .* He recognized the sound immediately. Helicopters were approaching or were close by.

"Perijan, get up," he whispered.

"What?" Perijan woke instantly, as if she weren't sleeping anyway.

"Shhhh. We have company." Collins put a finger to his lips.

Her face grew rigid and fear covered it. "It is them. They know we are here—"

Collins gripped her shoulder firmly. "Shhhh . . . I don't know. But we'd better move out of here until we know for sure." He glanced at the kerosene heater. It was still running but not giving off much heat. He stood up, feeling every muscle in his body scream in protest.

"Where will we go?" Perijan asked.

"Away from this building." Collins pulled her to her feet, then bent over and turned off the heater. He yanked the blanket down from the window and used it to move the heater away from the warm air surrounding it. He hoped the cool air would engulf it quickly so their presence could not be detected. "Come on . . . grab your gear, let's get going." Perijan was frozen in her spot and Collins feared she would be of no help to him when he needed it most.

The pounding of chopper rotor blades increased in volume. Collins figured there was more than one helicopter. The sounds indicated they had circled the camp and were now coming in to land.

Hassan Zadeh felt the skid bars of the Huey touch down. He slid out of the shoulder harnesses and pulled back the cocking lever of his AK-47, jacking a live round into the chamber of his assault rifle.

"You men, fan out," Ali Fesseghi shouted over the thunderous noise of the chopper blades. "We're going to search the buildings first. If we don't find anything, we move into the foothills. The American and the woman may be hiding in one of the mine shafts."

Zadeh stayed in his seat as he watched the Revolutionary Guard commandos jump out of the chopper. He was the last one to exit the Huey. Ducking his head, he could feel grains of sand pelting his face. To his left, the commandos linked up with the men getting out of the second chopper, and they started moving toward the nearest building a hundred yards away.

"If they are here, we will find them." Fesseghi held a hand to his mouth so Zadeh could hear him.

"We've landed too close, you fool. They could hear us coming," Zadeh sneered, irritated with Fesseghi for his stupidity.

"We didn't have time to waste by landing miles away. It will be light in twenty minutes and we will have the rest of the day to search for them."

Zadeh didn't respond to Fesseghi's reasoning. He watched the man stalk off toward the commandos fanning out in front of them. *Landing twenty armed men in the middle of an abandoned mining camp and ordering them to assault the buildings isn't a plan. It is recklessness and too aggressive for any surprise.* If the American was clever enough to get this far, he would have had a backup plan for just such an attack. Zadeh decided to move on his own instead of wasting time following the orders of an idiot. His first strategy was to simply put himself in the place of the American. *Now, where would I go if I were trying to hide?* He raised his Russian-designed NVGs to his eyes and scanned the base of the mountain. He could see the openings of several shafts and caves that the miners had blasted into the side of the mountain. A smile came across his face. If he were going to hide, it would undoubtedly be up there, among the rocks and debris. "Fesseghi . . . come with me," Zadeh ordered, jogging up next to him.

"I have—"

"I said, come with me." Zadeh's tone informed Fesseghi that he was not to be argued with. "You will be of no use to the men going through the buildings. We can finish the task sooner if we spread out on our own." *And I can keep my eye on you at the same time.*

"Nothing on the RHAW. They don't know we're out here," Lieutenant Dennis Summers said over the F-15E's internal intercom.

"Well, it won't stay that way for long," Colonel Baker replied. "Welcome to Esfahan."

Summers felt his shoulder harnesses dig into the upper part of his arms as Mustang Leader shot over the last series of hills. His eyes were fixed on the FLIR, watching the images change. The city of Esfahan filled the eight-inch multifunction display.

The jet banked left as the pilot tried to keep the fighter on the edge of the city at only 200 feet. The FLIR filled with a maze of streets and buildings packed closely together. They were of all shapes and sizes, from traditional Arab structures to stone huts. The streets were narrow and he could see only a few streetlights.

"Take a heading of three seven four," Summers directed.

The twenty-six-year-old WSO was only three months away from making captain. He had been recruited by the Academy to play football, never intending to make the Air Force a career. "One minute to target. Kick her up to 5,000 feet."

"Five thousand . . . here we come," Baker alerted.

Summers grunted as five quick Gs hit his body. The F-15E seemed to pull up into an almost vertical climb. In a few seconds, every early-warning and SAM radar in a ten-mile radius would be looking at them. Summers knew it would take the Iranian radar operators a few minutes to figure out what was going on. By then the first target would be a smoldering pile of fire and smoke. With a little luck, they would take out the second power transfer station before any of the SAMs became airborne.

"Forty-five hundred," Baker called out.

"Three miles ahead and to the right," Summers said loudly, his eyes glued to the FLIR. The satellite photos Summers had studied showed the power station was located on the north side of the city, only a mile from the main gate to Esfahan AFB. He had to find a cluster of small stone buildings standing by themselves at the end of a dirt road. Air Force intel officers speculated the buildings were some sort of religious training facility. North of the buildings was a mosque, which would help in locating the target.

Come on, baby . . . where are you?

MH-53J PAVE LOW

Collins should be able to hear the low rumble from the Pave Lows, Duke speculated as he studied the cockpit instrumentation. He changed the FM radio frequency to the emergency channel that Collins was supposed to be monitoring and keyed the mike two distinct times. Duke didn't want to say anything, fearing any Iranians in the area could be listening in. He keyed the mike again two quick times and waited.

"No response," Duke reported to the pilot.

Newall worked the cyclic stick, keeping the chopper level at 200 feet and their forward airspeed pegged on 210 knots.

"There they are," Duke said calmly. The chopper's FLIR was locked onto the rectangular images of several buildings in the distance. "That's the mining camp."

"You got a picture, Coyote Two?" Newall radioed.

"Negative."

"To the left . . . at the base of the farthest set of hills," Duke told the other aircraft. He listened to the crackling of the radio.

"Yeah . . . we got 'em on Kodak now," the pilot of Coyote Two radioed back.

"Circle the camp once, then put down south of the buildings. We'll follow you in," the general instructed. He looked at Newall. "I'm going with the men on the ground when we land."

Newall raised his eyebrows as if Duke had lost his mind.

"Keep a radio channel open with the AC-130U," Duke added, not answering the man's look.

"Don't worry about us. I'm going to sit here with the engines running reading my latest issue of Aviation Leak," Newall joked, glancing at him again. "You just hurry and find your man so I can be back at base in time for breakfast."

"Shit . . . we're late for the party. Looks like we have company." Duke touched the screen. In the upper section of the display were the radiant green specks of heat signatures. "What do you make of it?" he asked.

"I don't know. Trucks maybe. We need to get closer," Newall replied.

"All right. Set us down west of the buildings, out of sight of those vehicles. I'm going to order the Spectre in to check things out." Duke keyed his mike to instruct the AC-130U to circle the camp.

E-3C AWACS, Terminator

"I want an update. Where are the F-15Es?" Colonel Connor asked as he leaned over Master Sergeant Adams.

Adams looked back at the radarscope. The strike package was

on the outer edge of his coverage, at the upper edge of the screen. He could see the outline of the southwestern part of Esfahan. Three groups of blue triangles were clustered together at different altitudes. Cutting across the screen were bright yellow lines representing the various mountain ranges crisscrossing the Iranian landscape. The interior mountains made it difficult to keep track of all the aircraft. If they dropped below 2,000 feet, Adams lost them.

"Mustang Three, Four and Five are here." Adams pointed to three blue triangles clustered together southwest of Esfahan. He caught the glimmer of the radar lights in the colonel's eye. "The F-15Cs are 3,000 feet above the Es, and the F-16Cs are a mile to the south at 2,500 feet."

"What about Mustang Leader and the Pave Lows?" Connor asked.

"I lost the Pave Lows about fifteen minutes ago. They disappeared behind this mountain range." Adams touched the screen. "Mustang Leader should be over the western edge of Esfahan. Naylor gave the order for him to bug out a few minutes ago."

Connor examined the scope. Each of the triangles was slowly moving toward the edge of Esfahan. "Are you picking up any SAMs?"

"No, sir."

"Where are those fighters you were monitoring?"

"They're still to the north." Adams touched the hard metal edge of the scope. "I could use some more altitude to get a wider scope."

"I'll order the pilot up to 48,000." Connor straightened up. "That should give you a few more miles of range."

F-15E Mustang Leader

"Check right two o'clock," Colonel Baker's backseater called out. "Forty-five seconds to weapons release."

"Tallyho . . . I see it. Target the son of a bitch." Baker looked at his FLIR on the lower left side of the instrument panel.

Summers had located the mosque, zoomed in on the road running next to it, then followed the road to the power transfer station a mile away. The whole process had taken only ten seconds. Summers then called up a patch map of the area. With his radar in map mode, he moved the cursor around the display, stopping on the center of the station. The target was easy to pick out, the radar image having the clarity of a black-and-white photo.

"Target lock," Summers said. The Strike Eagle's invisible targeting laser, located on the underside of the fighter, was now illuminating the center of the station with a three-foot-diameter laser beam.

Baker quickly scrutinized the IR image of the station now being projected on his HUD. He hoped that Air Force intel was right and he wasn't about to blow up a switching station for one of Esfahan's residential areas. He could clearly see several dozen rows of transformers and the steel structure used to house and support them. Thick electrical wires connected each of the transformers, and several large black metal boxes dominated the center of the network. A tall wire fence surrounded the complex and there were blinking lights on the corners.

"Fifteen seconds," Summers said.

"Holding steady at 5,100 feet, speed, 412 knots." Baker's attention quickly flashed to the right side of the cockpit windscreen. *I can't believe this,* he thought. Off to the right he could now see the flashing runway lights of the Esfahan air base. The Iranians still hadn't swept his fighter with a single hostile radar.

"Five seconds to target."

Baker moved his thumb to the red weapons-release button on the stick. The MAX RANGE symbol flashed on the FLIR, telling him he could release the laser-guided bombs at any time and they would have enough energy to hit the target.

"Two . . . one. Let her rip, Colonel."

Baker waited two more seconds, then tapped the release button. At the same time, he banked the Strike Eagle to the east. The fighter fluttered slightly as a single GBU-10B Paveway was released from the right side of the aircraft. Baker kept steady pressure on the stick, not pulling more than 3 Gs.

The guidance computer mounted inside the bomb's laser seeker head had already locked onto the reflecting light beam. It instructed the bomb's canards to bank to the left as it glided toward the transfer station at over 500 knots.

The colonel didn't shift his attention from the HUD. He kept the belly of the fighter pointed toward the target. Ten seconds later, Baker saw the sudden smudge of the bomb streak across the HUD. From what he could tell, the bomb impacted the target about ten feet left of the center. The BLU-109, which was the bomber unit minus the guidance system, penetrated the steel structure surrounding the transformer before exploding. The FLIR screen blinked off for a few seconds as the bright flash of the explosion blinded the system.

Baker leveled the F-15E and turned around to see the churning orange fireball rise up into the sky. As his eyes returned to the HUD, the lights in the northern part of the city went dead. An instant later the runway lights at Esfahan faded, as did the rows of lights inside the air base.

"Alpha Nevada . . . Alpha Nevada," Baker radioed. "Lights out." Alpha told the rest of the attacking fighters that the first target had been hit. Nevada meant it had been destroyed.

"It's not one of our fighters, sir," the radar operator said.

Colonel Rahavi watched the electronic symbol. The radar image had appeared less than two minutes ago and wasn't transmitting an IFF code. The radar indicated it was flying at 5,000 feet above the northwestern section of Esfahan. Rahavi thought possibly it could be one of his fighters in trouble, or possibly a fighter from another air base trying to make an emergency landing.

"All fighters are accounted for, sir. That's not one of our jets."

"Radio a warning and then bring up the SAMs. If he doesn't answer, I want it shot from the—" Colonel Rahavi stopped. The radar data began to dull as the lights in the CIC flickered on and off. A second later the entire room fell dark. The battery-powered emergency spotlights in the rear of the CIC came on, allowing Rahavi to see three men trying to leave their stations.

"Sit down! I did not give the order to evacuate this complex," he screamed. "Get back to your posts, *now!*" Rahavi looked over at the senior technician. "Go to backup power," he demanded.

"Switching now, sir."

"Hammer Two One . . . this is Coors Leader. Start the music," Colonel Naylor radioed.

"Copy, Coors Leader . . . Hammer Two One will be in station in thirty seconds. Music in thirty."

"All aircraft, this is Coors Leader. Hit the target in two, repeat, hit the target in two. Heads up and keep this channel open." The colonel spoke slowly and clearly, enunciating his words carefully.

Naylor jammed the throttle forward, feeling it snap past the afterburner groove. He pulled the nose up fifteen degrees and watched his airspeed and altitude climb quickly. The strike package was five miles west of the target. They would come in at 2,000 feet and hit the complex, breaking out to the south over the city. His fighter flashed over a narrow two-lane highway. The night sky had now turned a light gray in the east. Naylor didn't like the fact that they would be coming off the target just as the sun was rising, but they were already committed. There was no turning back now.

"Spike . . . left . . . nine o'clock far," Summers warned.

"Yeah, I hear it," Baker called, his eyes sweeping the cockpit instruments. The RHAW equipment was filling his headset with different levels of electronic activity. It sounded as if a hundred radars were sweeping the skies from all directions.

"Hey, Magnum guy . . . you hear that?" Baker radioed Coors Three Three. The Strike Eagle's RHAW equipment had just determined that the hostile radar was sweeping the left side of the aircraft. The search pattern wasn't random; it was rapidly and repeatedly passing over the F-15E. He glanced at the warning dial, seeing that the radar's signal was fading. Baker wanted to make sure the F-16C had picked up the signal nonetheless.

"Mustang . . . Coors Three Three. I have it."

"Roger, Three Three. We're moving to secondary target. Cover my ass." Baker banked his jet back to the north and dropped the nose, picking up additional airspeed. Surprise was no longer on his side. Baker now had to use his F-15E's speed and massive striking power to hit the next target.

Keeping the throttles just short of afterburner, Baker leveled his jet at 4,000 feet and watched his airspeed climb past 430 knots. The added speed pressed him back into his seat. The secondary transfer station was located on the other side of the air base, at the bottom of a small rocky hill. The SAM network around the Iranian air base was now on full alert.

"Come on, Lieutenant, we don't have all day," Baker complained. "Where's that last target?"

"Come left five degrees . . . I should be picking it up."

Baker heard the warning tone in his headset change from a soft hum to a crackling buzz. Another SAM site was painting his fighter from the east. This one operated on a different frequency.

"Shit. We have another SAM looking at us." The warning

tone of the RHAW equipment sounded like an SA-6 search radar. Baker instinctively jerked the stick right as a barrage of triple-A fire filled the air to the left of his Strike Eagle. The orange tracer rounds reached with fingers of twisting light up past his cockpit window.

"Son of a bitch, that was close," Baker exclaimed, leveling the fighter at 4,800. "If you don't want a ground tour of Esfahan, you'd better find that fucking target," he ordered.

"Hold tight . . . I'll get it." Summers concentrated on the FLIR. Manipulating the IR camera, he shifted the image to the right, looking for one of the landmarks he had memorized before leaving the ground. The area around the air base was nearly void of roads, buildings and vegetation. A sick, rushed feeling came over Summers. "I can't find it, sir." He grew queasy and unsure of himself.

"Okay . . . I'm taking her up to 6,000 feet. If you can't locate it in another minute, we're out of here," Baker grunted. He pulled the stick back, forcing the Strike Eagle to gain more altitude. In the distance he could see several SAMs streak into the air. Their bluish-white plumes of fire lit up the gray sky. *The F-15Es should be just starting their target run,* he thought.

"Colonel, I've isolated the problem. The main power transfer station is no longer functioning," one of the senior technicians reported to Colonel Rahavi.

"Why isn't that backup power on yet?" Rahavi snarled in disgust.

"Secondary power coming on line now, sir."

The colonel paced nervously, listening to the radar and communications officers talking among themselves.

The lights in the Iranian CIC blinked on in rapid succession. A few seconds later the large screens filled with bright lights. Only they weren't displaying radar data. The displays were a mass of confusion.

"Get this system back on line. Radio the fighters that we're under attack!" Rahavi's voice boomed throughout the underground complex.

"It's no use, sir. We're being jammed and I can't burn through it . . . it's too strong," the radar warning officer said, tapping his computer keyboard. The two dozen early-warning and surveillance radars used to supply the CIC with coverage were broad-

casting nothing but garbage. The words POWER FAILURE kept
flashing on the screen.

"Sir, all frequencies are jammed. All I'm getting is static."

"Keep trying. I want every fighter that is flightworthy in the
air at once." Rahavi moved closer to the main radarscope. It was
still filled with white wavy lines. The pattern on the scope indicated the Americans were jamming his radars from close range.

"This is central command . . . this is central command. We are
under attack. Request assistance from all fighters . . . request assistance," the communications officer radioed.

"Underst . . . central com . . . we're . . . inbound . . . ," the voice
of a pilot sounded through the command center.

Chapter Thirty-two

SHAHR KORD, IRAN

Collins estimated they had traveled three hundred yards up the hill to the west of the main building. Even though his eyes had adjusted to the darkness, he still couldn't move as fast he wanted to. They were half-jogging, but the ground was littered with large boulders as well as debris left behind from the mining excavations.

"Come on, Perijan," Collins urged, holding her by the hand and pulling her over a four-foot-high mound of dirt. They both slid into a shallow ditch and he forced her head down as he lay on the ground, making sure they were completely out of sight. She rolled over next to him, breathing heavily.

"Don't move," he whispered. "We need to get our bearings."

Collins stayed still for a few seconds to regain his composure. *Maybe they're Americans. Maybe I'm doing all this for nothing*, he told himself.

He turned over on his belly and slowly pulled himself to the edge of the ditch. There still wasn't enough light for him to make out what was happening below or who had landed. He strained to locate the choppers. The flickering of several lights caught his eye, and he sensed that men were moving toward their position but he couldn't focus on anything solid.

The wind was calm and he distinctly heard the crunch of gravel

435

under footsteps. *Damn it! If I could only see those choppers.* Collins knew that the only American chopper with the capacity to extract forces from deep inside enemy territory was the Pave Low. He closed his eyes and listened. The pilots hadn't killed the engines, so the rotor blades continued to whip around.

The MH-53J Pave Lows had six rotor blades and they made a well-defined sound penetrating the air. Collins had flown on a Pave Low only twice, both times while training with the CIA special antiterrorist team in North Carolina. The methodical beat of the choppers below him didn't belong to Pave Lows. *Besides,* Collins reasoned, *I would be seeing some type of signal—a fluorescent green light stick or a strobe.*

Collins took a deep breath and let his tired body slide back into the ditch. Looking west, he could see the ditch disappearing into the darkness. Maybe there was something at the end of it, some place to hide. *Damn, I wish I had my computer maps with me.*

"Come on, Perijan. We must keep moving." Collins looked at her and was worried. She was pale and lifeless, as if she had given up hope. He knew that was the worst condition to be in if you were on the run.

"I can't move. I'm too tired. They aren't going to stop until they find me." Perijan sat without budging and didn't look up. She caressed the box clutched in her lap, the one he had noticed earlier in the car. "Go on without me. It is not really you they want, only me."

"Horse manure, you can do it. And they want both of us." Collins walked over and picked her up by her arms. "If they get you now, they'll know I'm here, too. So get up and let's get moving." He pulled her toward him as they made their way along the ditch.

"I am sorry," Perijan said softly. "You are right. I will try harder."

Collins let go and kept walking. He felt like a jerk being so tough on her but knew their lives depended on it. He had gone about thirty feet and was waiting for Perijan to catch up when he lifted his hand for her to stop. She closed her eyes for a moment, expecting the Revolutionary Guards to bound into the ditch. When she opened her eyes, Collins's head was twisted as if he were straining to make out sounds in the distance.

The noise grew louder and more apparent. Rotor blades were

thrashing through the air. *Shit*, he thought. *Another chopper coming out of the west. More Iranians from the opposite side of the mining camp. That's all we need.*

"Let's go," he urged, waving her closer to him.

"We have a change of plans," Lieutenant Chuck LaCoss shouted to the eighteen Rangers seated in the cargo bay of the Pave Low.

Duke was seated across from the special forces commander as the Pave Low weaved the last mile to the landing zone.

"On the approach, the pilot spotted two choppers on the ground to the east of us," LaCoss continued. "We will be landing a half mile from our objective. The Spectre will provide air cover as we make our way to the buildings."

"How many men are on the ground?" one of the Rangers asked.

"Don't know that. You've got thirty seconds to get your asses out of the chopper. We'll be using attack plan Juliette. The mining camp will be directly over the nearest hill to the east." LaCoss looked around the cargo bay, his eyes resting on each man for a second. "Fifteen minutes, gentlemen. That's all the time we're going to have on the ground before we lift off. I want the area swept in ten."

"Yes, sir," each Ranger grunted.

"All right. Check your radios and your NVGs. And remember, no unnecessary chatter." LaCoss sat back down, making several last-minute adjustments to his own gear.

"What happens if they've already captured him?" Duke asked the lieutenant.

"General, I don't have time to explain to you how we operate. If you're going along, just follow my lead. We'll deal with it if we have to when we're on the ground," LaCoss barked. "I hope you're ready for some excitement. We're dropping into a hot LZ."

Zadeh shifted the heavy SVD sniper rifle from his left hand to his right. He could hear Fesseghi panting several yards behind him, attempting to keep up. The two men were now halfway up the side of the mountain. Below them, moving from building to building, the guards continued their own searches.

Zadeh panned his head right and left, using the NVGs to take in every detail. The terrain was steep with shallow ravines cutting into the hard dirt. He stopped to stand on what looked like a shallow man-made gully that ran east and west of his position. The ditch was filled with rocks and other debris. He guessed it had been dug to catch rubble tumbling down the mountainside from the mines above him.

"Do you hear that?" Fesseghi asked between breaths once he had caught up with Zadeh.

"Hear what?" he asked, irritated that the man wasn't concentrating on finding the American and the woman.

"Helicopters . . . I hear helicopters."

"Those are our choppers," Zadeh snorted back.

"No. Listen, it's coming from a different direction. Did you call for reinforcements?"

"No, we are the only ones." Zadeh searched the sky to the west. Without warning the ground vibrated. The deafening roar of turbofans filled the night air.

"Oh Allah . . . it is the Americans!" Fesseghi blurted.

Zadeh snapped his head around. The image of a C-130 filled his NVGs for a second before it banked to the left and disappeared in darkness.

"Follow me," Zadeh grunted, breaking into a fast climb.

F-15E Mustang Leader

"This is Mustang two . . . November Oscar November."

"Copy . . . Mustang three is in from the northeast."

"Mustang four in from the northwest."

Colonel Baker listened to the chatter in his headset. November Oscar November was their code for "now or never." The other three Strike Eagles were lining up for their run on the weapons plant. "Remember, one pass and haul ass," he ordered.

Baker rolled the fighter ten degrees to the left. They were now skirting the southern edge of the Esfahan air base at 6,000 feet, airspeed, 380 knots. He looked over his shoulder, trying to pick up any details of the base below him.

"Negative on the target, Colonel. I can't find the son of a bitch." Summers' voice was filled with frustration. "Those satellite photos aren't worth a crap. Take her up to 10,000 and I'll see if I can locate it on the radar."

"Shit," Baker said under his breath. The secondary power grid should have been destroyed over a minute ago. They were going to throw the timing off the entire strike cell.

All at once the airfield began lighting back up a section at a time. Baker jerked his head left, watching the runway lights flicker on.

"Their emergency power system must have kicked in," Summers said, distracted and discouraged.

"That's it, buddy. We're outta time and outta here," Baker said, resigned to the fact his WSO wasn't going to find the target. "Coors Three Three . . . we're off the target. Take a heading of two two five on the egress."

"*Copy, Mustang Leader. Coors Three Three at angels two . . . a mile behind you.*"

Baker put his fighter into a gradual right-hand turn and drove the throttles forward, increasing his airspeed. *In two minutes it was going to be over with*, he thought.

"Spike right one o'clock near. Shit, it's over the fence . . . break right!" Lieutenant Summers shouted. An SA-6 radar had just locked up on the Strike Eagle. The backseater caught sight of two rocket motors igniting several miles away.

Colonel Baker blinked before jamming the stick hard right. The F-15E shuddered under the stress of a sudden 7.5-G turn. The fighter rolled right, cutting across the sky and leaving white contrails of condensed water vapor streaming off its wingtips. Baker used all his strength to inch the throttles forward just short of afterburner. He groaned, feeling the pressure of the Gs hit his body.

"Chaff . . . chaff . . . chaff," Summers grunted, letting his pilot know he was sending out a flood of radar-confusing foil.

"Do you see it . . . you see it?" Baker felt the burning sensation of bile moving up his throat. His G suit hissed, compressing around his stomach and upper legs to keep the blood from pooling in his lower body.

"I got 'em!" Summers shouted out. "Right eight o'clock. Looks like they're tacking us." He turned his head to the right, trying to follow the SAMs. Their fiery plumes made them easy to see against the graying sky. The radar-guided missiles accelerated quickly, pushing over toward Mustang Leader.

Baker leveled the fighter at 5,500 feet, letting the Gs fall off. In the turn he had dropped 500 feet but picked up forty additional knots of airspeed. He was now flying across the SAM's radar beam, hoping to get loose in the return clutter. He was angry at himself for being too high.

"Coors Three Three, this is Mustang Leader. I need some help up here," Baker radioed. "Two SAMs are trying to fly up my butt."

"*Roger, Leader . . . I have you covered.*"

Baker banked his fighter to the left so he could see the SAMs. He estimated they were several miles out and closing.

"Get ready on the chaff," Baker ordered.

"Don't worry. You just fly this bitch out of here." Summers watched the SAMs closing. "One mile. Four o'clock."

"Hold tight." Baker adjusted his grip on the stick and throttle, not taking his eyes off the lead missile. He planned to duck under the first one, break back to the left and dive away, hoping the second would pass over him.

"Half a mile, closing fast," Summer advised. "*Do it!*"

"Chaff . . . *now*," Baker moaned, snapping the Strike Eagle to the left and dropping her nose. The HUD instruments spun, trying to keep up with the violent maneuver of the aircraft. The G meter jumped from 1 to 6.5 in less than a second. Baker felt his sweaty back press against the hard vinyl seat as he watched the first SAM streak past. Several hundred yards overhead and traveling faster than Mach 2, it appeared more like a blur than a thirty-foot-long air-to-air missile.

"*Coors Three Three . . . Magnum, Magnum.*" Baker heard the call from the SEAD fighter somewhere below him. The F-16C had just launched two HARM missiles at the radar antenna directing the SAM.

"More chaff," Baker ordered, keeping track of the HUD and the oncoming SAM. The HUD read 2,900 feet. His airspeed was down to 320 knots. He had just enough energy for one more hard turn.

"Three thousand yards," Summers warned, eyeballing the SAM.

"That HARM is never going to make it." Baker kicked the F-15E into afterburner and rolled left into a dive at the same time. Three negative Gs slashed through his body, and his eyes felt as if they were about to burst. With the nose of the fighter pointed down thirty degrees, Baker watched his altitude click off: 2,800 . . . 2,400 . . . 2,000 . . .

He lost sight of the missile as it broke over the top of his fighter, heading for the ground ahead of them.

"Hot damn! We did it!" Summers called out, laughing nervously. His arms were straight out in front, bracing his upper body on the cockpit sill.

Baker didn't respond. He was busily righting the Strike Eagle from her roll. At 1,600 feet he came wings level, then yanked the stick back, popping the air brakes. The HUD read 1,357 feet.

It's going to be close. He had both hands on the stick and was straining to get the nose of his aircraft up from her vertical dive: 1,000 . . . 800 . . . 500 feet.

Summers, realizing their new dilemma, was silently urging his pilot on. The fighter started to respond: 400 feet, speed, 275 knots. The G meter climbed to 5 and hovered there as Baker applied more pressure to the stick.

"Come on, baby, come on," Baker prodded his aircraft. The F-15E, answering his plea, leveled out for a few seconds and then obediently shot straight up into a steep climb. Instinctively, Baker moved the throttles forward as they rose. A white flash from the right side of the cockpit told him the HARM had just impacted the SA-6 antenna. The RHAW warning tone faded from his headset, confirming the assumption.

Unknown to Baker, only four hundred yards from where his fighter bottomed out, an Iranian ZSU-23-4 antiaircraft gun swiveled around. The operator locked the dual track in preparation to fire. The microwave target-acquisition and fire-control radar switched on, locking onto the climbing fighter. The Iranian gunner inside the turret watched the target appear on his scope. He centered the crosshairs and pulled the trigger, sending a burst of 23-mm armor-piercing rounds into the air. The first few dozen tracer rounds ripped into the back and tail sections of the Strike Eagle. The aircraft jumped as if hit repeatedly by a huge hammer. This was accompanied by the ear-splitting sounds of tearing metal.

Baker and Summers were caught unaware and were stunned by the attack. The stick immediately became hard to move and began to vibrate. Baker scanned the instruments; several red lights were flashing on. The onboard computer took control, automatically keeping the jet in the air by compensating for the change in aerodynamics.

Several more bursts of fire darted past the canopy ahead of them. The gunner had lost his range. Baker leveled out upside down at 2,500 feet and then flipped the Strike Eagle over. The left engine was out and hydraulic pressure was slowly following. There was also a good chance one of the internal fuel tankers had been ruptured.

"Terminator . . . this is Mustang Leader. Primary objective is Alpha. Secondary is Charlie. I've taken a hit, heading for home plate," Baker radioed the AWACS.

"*Copy, Mustang Leader.*"

Baker kept his only engine in afterburner and watched the HUD creep up to 403 knots. It was as fast as he was going to go. He flew at 3,000 feet southwest toward Bahrain.

"Any damage on your end?" Baker asked Summers, turning around. A shot of dread went through his body. He could see the blood darkening on his WSO's suit.

"It's all right . . . I think I can make it till we get back," Summers said in reply to his pilot's shaken face.

"Just hold on, buddy, I'm going as fast as I can." Turning his attention back to the aircraft, Baker once again implored for mechanical loyalty. "Come on, sweetheart. You've already saved us once today. Give me a little more."

"Let's move it!" Lieutenant LaCoss shouted as the Pave Low hit the ground with a hard thump.

Duke unbuckled the shoulder harness and dropped his NVGs over his eyes, flipping them on. The red light inside the cargo bay turned a glowing green. The other Rangers were already standing, ready to exit the chopper. The hydraulic motors that opened the cargo ramp whined. A cloud of dust whipped around inside the cargo bay. Duke stood, a loaded M-16 across his chest, and followed the Rangers as they ran out of the chopper. He held his breath, not wanting to inhale the dust being kicked up by the Pave Low.

"Right, heads down," LaCoss said into his radio.

Duke waited for the lieutenant to come even with his left shoulder before moving away from the chopper. Under his helmet, mounted with Velcro strips, was a miniature radio headset with an earpiece. It operated up to ten miles away on EHF (extremely high frequency) radio bursts. The unit was connected to a small microphone, which coiled around to the front of Duke's mouth, allowing him to talk with each member of the team as well as the Pave Low and Spectre pilots.

"Take up position off the right flank," LaCoss instructed

Duke. "Make sure no one comes in behind my men."

Behind them the Pave Low took off and banked to the south, joining up with the second chopper, which was hovering 500 yards away. Duke glanced around to see the black image of the chopper disappear, then ran hunched over behind the lieutenant.

"There are two Hueys on the ground due east of the mining camp. I count eight men on the outside, more in the buildings." Duke listened to the AC-130U pilot and watched LaCoss slide in behind a set of boulders. Duke did the same, keeping his rifle pointed in the direction of the mining camp. The rocks were situated on a small mound overlooking the buildings slightly below them. Duke propped himself up so he could see what was happening and watched as the Rangers made their way toward a building.

"We're picking up some sporadic small arms fire. The bastards know we're up here. I'm climbing to 3,000 feet."

Duke heard the sharp crack of gunfire echo in the distance. He strained to hear from which direction it came. "We need to make sure they don't radio for reinforcements."

"Hit the choppers," LaCoss radioed. "Hit the choppers."

"Copy, ground. Spectre to rescue. Coming around in twenty seconds."

"Fireworks in twenty . . . fireworks in twenty," LaCoss radioed to the rest of his team.

Duke hunkered down. He had never seen an AC-130U in action but guessed it would be powerful.

"Where are the F-14s and the 29s?" Rahavi asked loudly.

"It's difficult to confirm their location. I can't burn through the jamming," the CIC's senior radar technician responded.

"Sir, I'm picking up a radio transmission from the search team at the mining camp."

"Put it on the speaker."

"Command center Esfahan . . . we are under atta—"

The colonel was silent for a moment before he realized the transmission had been cut off. He gave an immediate order. "Vector two MiGs to that camp."

As the words left his mouth, a rumble rolled through the command center. Rahavi looked up as dust fell from the ceiling. The specks hit his eyes and he blinked. The ground shook a second,

third and fourth time. The colonel looked around the room, not
showing any fear. He knew the men were waiting for his reaction.

The resonance of the chopper faded as Collins made his way
farther west. He heard the sound of the multi-engine turboprop
circling overhead and gunfire erupting somewhere behind him.
He cursed under his breath, unable to see what was happening.

Keep going . . . don't stop yet. He turned around to check on
Perijan. She was managing to keep up, but her expression was
one of misery. He wished they could end this nightmare soon.
The sky to the east suddenly filled with the fiery red streaks of
tracer rounds streaming toward the ground. A 25-mm Gatling gun
racked the desert night with over 3,000 rounds a minute. The short
bursts sounding like a chainsaw cutting the night sky.

"Perijan . . . stay down," Collins warned, crouching even
lower to the ground. He glanced back toward the cannon fire just
as two large explosions shook the ground. Once the air cleared,
he could see that the Iranian choppers were on fire, lighting up
the entire area. Several men were running away from the exploding aircraft as pieces of debris shot into the air.

"They're here . . ." Collins excitedly reached for Perijan's arm
and felt her trembling.

Perijan only stared up at him, tears welling in her eyes, the box
clutched tightly to her chest.

"There is another pair of helicopters ahead of us." Ali Fesseghi
searched the sky as he spoke. "I can hear them."

"Shut up," Zadeh hissed. He placed one knee on the ground
and surveyed the area around the burning wreckage of helicopters
below him. Bursts of machine-gun fire followed by shouts and
screams brought his attention to the right. Through his NVGs, he
could see that a firefight had begun with the Revolutionary
Guards.

"We do not stand a chance against the Americans. We should
give up our search and hide in the hills until they are gone,"
Fesseghi suggested, thinking there were probably more Americans on the way.

"You coward. I will not allow that spy and traitor to leave the
country unpunished."

"We have been ambushed, you fool." Fesseghi's voice was
ragged and harsher now. "This will get us nowhere. Minister

Bakhtiar would want us to report back to him to receive our new orders."

"Minister Bakhtiar has already given his next order . . . and it was not to have both of us report back to him." Zadeh raised his gun and fired two shots into Fesseghi's heart. "Now I will have to finish this job on my own. You could have at least found the traitor you hired," Zadeh sneered at the dead man, then swung round and stood up, fury burning in his eyes. He could no longer hear the helicopters, but bursts of gunfire continued to echo from below. He put his head down and started running down the ditch toward the choppers he had heard.

LaCoss looked at his watch and then at Duke. "They've been out here for eight minutes. We're sticking to the timetable. Reinforcements are probably on their way now."

Duke didn't answer. He felt helpless, not knowing what more they could do to locate Collins. The chatter in his radio headset told him the Rangers had swept through each of the buildings, fighting off the resistance as they did so. One Ranger had already been wounded. Seven Revolutionary Guards had been captured and a few were still cornered in one of the remote buildings, while the others had run into the hills to the north. However, none of the Rangers had found Collins.

"Two minutes . . . I'm calling them in now." Lieutenant LaCoss wasn't going to waver on his decision.

Duke only continued to scan the area in a desperate last hope. He knew he couldn't ask LaCoss's men to risk their lives any more than they already had by entering a hot LZ.

"Coyote Leader . . . this is Bobcat Leader. It's time to boogie. Let's move out." LaCoss radioed.

"Copy, Bobcat Leader. Coyote inbound."

Within a few seconds Duke could hear the Pave Low's rhythmic beating coming toward them.

Collins came to the end of the ditch, his heart racing in his chest. He knew he was practically dragging Perijan along, but didn't want to let go of her arm for fear she'd get too far behind. They were standing at the edge of a small hill that gradually sloped downward. It was now light enough for him to see the black profile of several groups of large rocks in the distance.

He searched north and south for an entrance to an old mine

shaft, another set of buildings, anything they could take cover in.
But he didn't see anything. On the horizon he could barely make
out another hill he estimated to be a mile away. *Well, maybe we
can make it there. Something will be on the other side of it.*

"Do you hear that?" Perijan whispered.

"No . . . what is it?" Collins answered, unable to hear anything
but the pounding in his head.

"Helicopters . . . they are coming back this way." Perijan
strained to hear from what direction they were coming but
couldn't tell.

Collins forced himself to stop breathing so he could listen.
Dirty sweat was dripping from his face, and he wiped it away
with the sleeve of his shirt. The sound of rotor blades became
louder. He wasn't sure if it was wishful thinking or if he could
trust himself, but it sure as hell sounded like a Pave Low.

"Perijan, if we don't make it to that chopper before it takes
off, we could miss our last chance out of here. Understand?"

She nodded her head and the two of them began running along
the ditch.

"I count sixteen." LaCoss watched his men work their way
across the hill, covering each other in pairs.

"There are the last two . . . to the left, three o'clock." Duke
pointed, then quickly scanned the entire area one more time.
Damn it, Mark. Where the hell are you? A thought ran through
his mind that Katie must feel this same powerless frustration when
he left on missions.

"I see them." LaCoss dropped his NVGs. He could feel the
vibration of the Pave Low as she set down a hundred yards away.
He knew he wouldn't want to abandon one of his men, but would
still have to if other lives depended on it. "General, time to move.
It's getting too light out here to be safe." LaCoss put his hand
on Duke's arm. "Come on. They're waiting for us."

Duke couldn't speak as he swept the NVGs left, then right one
last time. He had to be sure before he went home empty-handed.
"Wait . . . I see another man."

"Everyone's been accounted for, General," LaCoss said, sliding his NVGs over his eyes again. The last group of Rangers was
climbing into the Pave Low.

"Lieutenant . . . to the right at two thirty. Do you see him?"

Duke had unconsciously stood in his effort to make out the image. "It's Collins. I'm sure it is."

LaCoss panned right, then stopped when he unexpectedly did see a man. "I see him . . . but I don't like it."

Duke studied the ghost-green image for a few more seconds. A man was hurrying toward them with a young boy or woman, it was hard to tell, following close behind. The two were running and stumbling along the way. Studying him a little more, Duke could tell he was wearing civilian clothes.

"That's Collins. I'm going after him." Duke lurched forward only to be stopped by LaCoss's firm grip.

"Like *hell* you are!" LaCoss exclaimed. "That's all I need— a dead general." LaCoss dropped his arm, and just as he did Duke stepped away from the safety of the rock and broke into a dead run toward the man.

"*Shit!*" LaCoss cursed, following after him. They both swerved left to right, back and forth, perfectly, as if they had trained together. If the lieutenant wasn't so angry, he might have admired the general's natural skills.

Zadeh was at the edge of the ditch. The sky was a dark morning-grey and he could clearly hear the helicopters ahead of him.

The Americans are going to great lengths to save one of their people, he thought, irritated that he might not have his vengeance. Both choppers resting on the ground were massive, much larger than he had expected. The swirling cloud of dust rising up around the birds seemed to add to their mystery. Zadeh bent over to examine the sand in front of him. There were footprints leading down the hill.

So . . . you did just what I thought. Zadeh smiled. *Allah grant me this one vengeance for the sake of our country.* They had no other place to hide.

Lying flat, he steadied the vented stock of his sniper rifle on the soft dirt. Flipping up the dust covers that protected each end of the rifle's scope, he began to scan the area below him. Within a few seconds he spotted the shadowy images of men climbing into the helicopter. The 4x scope gathered enough light for him to make out a target. He worked the action back on the Dragunav sniper rifle, chambering a 7.62-mm round. The American would not escape. He shouldered the weapon and placed the rubber cup over his eye.

*   *   *

Collins spotted a man bolting out of the darkness ahead of him. *I pray to God you're an American, whoever the hell you are.* He stopped moving and sucked in a long breath.

"Perijan, stay directly behind me," Collins whispered as he let go of her hand. He was speaking hurriedly but didn't want to frighten her any more than she already was. "We have company. I see a man moving toward us."

"Allah save us." Perijan's eyes grew wider, and Collins worried for a moment that she might either faint or run off in the other direction.

They both froze. Collins waited until he thought the man was close enough before speaking. "I'm unarmed," he shouted in a loud voice and raised his arms.

The man slowed to a jog and swung his weapon around, keeping it out in front of him.

At thirty feet, Duke's vision in his NVGs was still unsteady. The man had shouted something, but Duke couldn't understand what he had said and still couldn't make out the man's face well enough to recognize him. Duke stopped his approach, sensing LaCoss had come up even with him. He glanced over. The lieutenant had leveled his M-16 at the man's head.

"Fire *only* on my order, Lieutenant," Duke commanded flatly. He then turned toward the man, flipping his NVGs away from his eyes.

"Identify yourself," LaCoss shouted. *"Now!"*

"We are unarmed. Don't shoot us," Collins said, and stood without budging an inch, knowing that many officers had been killed through such misunderstandings.

"Who's that behind you?" Duke asked. He took a few cautious steps toward the two. The man's English was thick with an accent. He did sound like Collins, but Duke felt that he couldn't be certain.

"She's an Iranian. She is with me."

"Have her step around where we can see her." LaCoss stood his ground. *"Damn it, have her put her hands up!"*

"Perijan, just come around and put your hands in the air slowly," Collins said without taking his eyes off the two men in front of them.

Shakily, Perijan came from behind and raised only one hand,

still clutching her box in the other.

"Let's move it, General," LaCoss said impatiently. "This place is going to be crawling with Iranians any second."

"All right, both of you come on down slowly. Stay out in front and head for that chopper." Duke and LaCoss spread out, enabling them to get an angle on either one should they make a sudden move.

Zadeh snapped the safety off his rifle. The black duplex crosshairs were easy to see against the grayish beige earth of the desert. He estimated the chopper was 120 yards away, an easy shot.

At the bottom of the scope he could see four people running toward the last chopper on the ground. He estimated they were fifty feet from the helicopter. *They will have to slow down before climbing in*, he reasoned.

Zadeh's thin lips curled into a smirk. He rested the crosshairs on the ramp at the entrance of the helicopter.

Duke and LaCoss followed behind the two who were running toward the waiting Pave Low. Two Rangers had come out on LaCoss's order to await the new passengers. They stood ready at the rear cargo ramp.

"Quickly . . . inside," one of the Rangers shouted, motioning with his gun. The other was scanning the area behind Duke and LaCoss.

Now! Zadeh held his breath and pressed his forefinger to the trigger. The crosshairs were centered on the image of two people clambering up the chopper's rear ramp. He applied a little more pressure to the trigger. The rifle jumped back and the barrel leaped upward. The muzzle flash obscured the image in his scope. He readied for another shot.

Collins slipped scurrying up the ramp, and Perijan stepped over in back of him to avoid his fall. Suddenly, her body jerked forward and she let out a loud moan. The box she had been clutching flew up in the air, its contents scattering onto the ramp and desert sand. Collins let out a gasp as she fell over on top of him. The 180-grain bullet struck her in the spine just below the shoulder blades.

"*Shit* . . . she's hit!" one Ranger yelled. Two others immediately crouched in their spots, their guns level as they searched for the source of the shot.

LaCoss and Duke heard the call through their headsets. Duke turned to see the lieutenant responding by lowering his rifle and squeezing off several three-round bursts in different directions. *"Go . . . go!"* LaCoss shouted to the general. "Get her inside and order the pilot to take off."

The two Rangers raised their M-16s and started firing in a 180-degree arc. Duke reached the ramp and picked up the woman.

"Mark, get up! Move off the ramp!" he yelled, cradling the woman in his arms. He had suddenly realized that the man was indeed Collins. The two Rangers were already on the ramp, covering their commander. Collins had scrambled up and LaCoss had leaped onto the ramp just as another shot rang out from the distance. LaCoss suddenly fell back onto the ground. The rear cargo door had already begun to close and the Pave Low was lifting off the ground.

"Stop! Man down! Stop!" one of the Rangers yelled, as he sprang up and began shooting wildly in a half-circle above the lieutenant's body.

Duke had seen LaCoss fall back. He threw the woman into Collins's arms and rushed down the ramp, jumping out just before it closed. LaCoss lay on the ground sweeping his rifle back and forth but not firing. The bullet had hit him in the upper part of his thigh.

The chopper, committed to takeoff, lifted off and had to level before it could be set back down and its ramp opened. The noise and dust caused the two men on the ground to huddle together. LaCoss realized it was the general. "Are you fucking nuts or what?" he shouted, trying to keep an eye on the area around them.

"I figured since I outrank you, I'd better save your ass, Lieutenant." Duke put himself directly behind the man, keeping his weapon up and panning in all directions, ready to fire at the threat.

Zadeh, his vision narrowed by the scope, fired three more rounds at the moving helicopter, not aware there were two men on the ground. He watched it lift off the ground. *The damned infidels.* He wished he had been able to shoot the woman as well as the man. Moving the scope from his eye and standing, he cursed the traitors and the rest of the Americans who had escaped.

*   *   *

Duke stayed low, scanning the area, when he caught sight of movement on a ridge in the distance. Through the swirling sand of the chopper rotor wash, he could see a man holding a rifle.

All right, you bastard . . . you're mine. Duke shouldered his M-16. Using his thumb, he changed the selector from semiautomatic to a three-round burst. He leveled the sights, centering them on the upper section of the man's body. The sand made it difficult to see the target.

"Let's go, General!" Duke heard someone shout.

Duke ignored the call. *Come on . . . come on.* He waited for a break in the sand. Suddenly, the silhouette of the man became clear. He pulled the trigger twice, firing off six quick rounds. At the same time he saw a stream of bright orange tracers fill the air from above him. The ripping sound of automatic weapons fire cut through the sound of the chopper engines. The backup Pave Low was hovering two hundred yards away, fifty feet off the ground, its mini-guns blazing.

Duke dropped the M-16 and watched the image of the man crumble to the ground. Behind Duke, Coyote One swung back around and set down a few yards away. As the ramp opened, two Rangers raced out behind the general. "We've got him," they said, as they lifted the lieutenant up and carried him onto the chopper. Duke followed them, still surveying the area, not sure if the sniper was dead.

Chapter Thirty-three

E-3C AWACS, Terminator

Colonel Connor keyed the internal intercom, linking him with the flight deck. "Take a new heading of three four zero. I want to be closer to the Saudi border. And damn it, we need some more altitude." He turned his attention to Sergeant Adams. "Where is Mustang Leader?"

"I don't know. After his last radio call I lost him behind these interior mountains." Adams pointed to a thin yellow line on the scope showing the outline of the mountains running to the southwest.

"Terminator, this is Mustang Two. Alpha Nevada . . . Alpha Nevada."

"Mustang Three . . . Alpha Nevada . . . Alpha Nevada."

"Mustang Four . . . Alpha Nevada . . . Alpha Nevada. That son of a bitch is a burning ball of fire."

"Copy, Mustang flight. Bring 'em home." Adams turned to the colonel. "Confirmed, sir. Each of the other Strike Eagles are reporting positive hits on the weapons center." Adams watched the blue triangles moving quickly toward the center section of his screen before they also vanished behind a mountain range.

"Vector Marathon Seven, Marathon Eight and Coors Leader to cover the Pave Lows and Spectre," Connor ordered.

"Understood, sir." Adams wished he'd thought to suggest it himself. The colonel was right. Without the cover of darkness to conceal them, the slower-moving aircraft would need some additional cover. He keyed his mike.

USS *LaSalle*

"Mustang and two F-15 from Marathon packages just hit the coast," Zachiem said. "Mustang Three is reporting six solid hits on the weapons compound with secondary explosions. That place is nothing more than a burning hole in the ground."

Staffer stood stiffly, waiting to hear the news of the ground team. Eight blue triangles were crossing the coastline, heading for Bahrain at a high rate of speed.

"Any casualities?" Chaniff asked.

"One. Colonel Baker in Mustang Leader is reporting his WSO is hit."

Chaniff's face hardened. "Make sure they have priority clearance."

"Well, it seems they got your man, Mr. Staffer. And an Iranian woman is with him. She's been shot and is in critical condition. Lieutenant LaCoss is hit in the leg, but he's all right." Zachiem pointed to the location of the two Pave Lows and the AC-130U on the screen.

Staffer could hardly believe it. The AWACS was tracking the aircraft flying almost due west toward Bushehr. He could see the two blue symbols representing the jets above the choppers. The Spectre was five miles out in front.

"What's the chopper's ETA?" Staffer finally asked.

"They should cross the coast in eighteen minutes. But don't start celebrating too soon. They're not out of the fire yet," Zachiem added. "I'd say forty, forty-five minutes until they touch down."

"I'm going to the air base." Staffer had had more waiting and tension than he could stand. "I want to be on the ground when they land."

"All right," Chaniff dismissed him, still having important matters to worry about. "I'll meet you there later."

Staffer didn't hear the general's last words. He was already lost in his own thoughts and had grabbed his suit jacket, heading out the door of the CIC.

ESFAHAN, IRAN

"The American AWACS just changed radar frequencies," the threat warning officer announced from behind his computer console. His tone was low and even, without a sense of alarm.

"Colonel Rahavi, I'm picking up sporadic radio reports . . . the weapons complex has been hit," the communications officer continued, even though the colonel hadn't asked for additional information. "Reports also coming in that most sections are currently on fire, but I'm unable to confirm this."

Rahavi picked up the phone that linked him directly with the compound. The line was dead.

"Try the backup radio," he ordered.

"Trying, sir, but the radio is also out."

Rahavi stood, contemplating his options. The radar screens in the CIC were coming back on line. The jamming had faded and the hissing that had filled the secure Iranian radio channels was nearly gone.

"Colonel, radar is tracking two targets twenty-eight miles southeast. Altitude, 14,000 feet . . . speed, 390 knots," the radar operator confirmed.

"Notify the SAM sites." *It has happened,* Rahavi thought. *The Americans have hit the weapons site. They have flown in under radar coverage and destroyed our secret weapons plant.* He felt the rage boil inside of him.

"Major Kiamha. You are in charge," he said firmly. "Have my driver bring my car around." He turned, walked to the back of the command center and climbed up the stairs.

"I can't . . . I can't feel anything," Perijan said weakly. Her body trembled. Her eyes were wide, but they were no longer filled with fear. Only confusion.

"You're going to be all right. Just try not to move," Collins reassured her. He had placed a rolled blanket under her head and sat next to her, wiping away the sweat. He watched the Marine doctor put an IV into her arm. Then he looked at Collins and shook his head.

"Mark, you need to buckle up," Duke said. "It's going to take us forty-five minutes to clear Iranian airspace. The ride could get wild." Duke glanced at the Iranian woman. The medics were securing her to the cot.

One of the Rangers leaned over to Collins once he was seated and buckled in. "Here's what's left of her box." Mark stared at the torn cardboard box for a moment before accepting it from the Ranger. It looked frail in his hands, just as she did.

"She's the one; she did all the tough stuff," he said to Duke and the Rangers sitting around him. "I mean, she got us the information on the weapons complex and helped get me to the mining camp." His eyes watered. He didn't really understand why he felt so emotional. The box made him think of his own little girl and the memories she would save one day. He was glad to be going home. "I don't really know her . . . she's just so young and she doesn't have any family left . . ." He stopped short, choking on his thoughts more than his words.

"We know, Mark," Duke sighed, then got up from his seat and headed for the flight deck.

Collins looked back down at Perijan. Her eyes were closed and she was speaking her parents' names softly.

"I'm sorry." The Marine medic stared hard at Collins. "There's not much I can do. The bullet broke her back. She—"

"Just make sure she's comfortable, Doc," Collins said, handing him the box. "She'll want this next to her. It's all she has left, so please be sure it doesn't get lost in the shuffle."

"Colonel, take a look at this." Adams pointed to two red enemy aircraft symbols on the upper left corner of his screen. The symbols were in a tight two-ship formation coming out of the north. They were Iranian fighters.

"Son of a bitch! Give me an ID," Connor snapped.

"Speed, 390 knots and increasing. Altitude, 6,700 feet. Climbing at 2,000 feet a second. I'd say they're Fulcrums, sir; the data fits their performance profile."

"Great . . . *fucking* MiG-29s!" Connor's mind swirled. *Two lumbering Pave Lows and an AC-130U will be fishbait for a pair of Fulcrums.* The enemy fighters' pulse-Doppler radars were capable of separating large electronic images from the ground clutter in a matter of minutes. They would lock onto the targets and kill them in no time at all.

"Damn it! They spent too much time on the ground." Connor knew it wasn't anyone's fault that the sandstorm threw them off schedule and he shouldn't dwell on what he couldn't change. One sign of a good soldier was his ability to adapt and improvise.

"Can you tell if they're searching for a target?"

Adams's eyes swept across the AWACS electronic detection equipment. If the MiG's J-band pulse-Doppler radars were sweeping, his instruments weren't detecting it. "Negative, sir. My guess is they're being controlled by one of the ground radars near Esfahan."

"Where are the Pave Lows?" Concentrating, Connor bent over to get closer to the screen.

"They should be right here." Adams pointed to a small group of yellow lines. "Behind this group of mountains. I'm also showing some SAM radar activity to the north."

"Any other enemy fighters?"

"No, sir." Then he quickly added, "At least not on the scope." Adams didn't need to know what SAMs were in the area. Air Force intel had confirmed the region was covered with SA-6 SAMs, along with several dozen high-altitude SA-10s. Older SA-2s were also scattered to make it a little more interesting, depending on which side you were on, of course. On top of that bad news, the latest CIA report stated the Iranians had reinforced the area with ZSU-23-4 radar-guided triple-A guns.

"How long before the MiGs are in firing range?"

Adams calculated for only a second. He didn't need to use his computer. "At their current speed . . . three minutes. But if they're carrying long-range missiles, they could fire in one, two minutes."

"Contact Marathon Seven. Advise him of the MiG threat and advise Coors Leader of the SAM threat."

"Yes, sir." Adams keyed his mike to make radio contact with the westernmost flight of F-15Cs.

Duke strapped himself back into the center engineer's seat of the Pave Low, plugged in the radio cord and tightened his shoulder harnesses. He glanced out the window, seeing brown desert mountains on either side of them. The Pave Low was following Iranian Highway H-23 back toward the coast.

"What's our status?" he inquired once settled.

"One hundred ten miles from the coast. Thirty-two minutes of flying time. Terminator has ordered two F-15s and an F-16 to escort us out," Newall replied, working the collective pitch lever that moved the chopper up and down. "General, we're sitting ducks out here in daylight. Every asshole with a rifle is going to be shooting at us."

"Is that part of the tour guide speech, or are you trying to say something?" Duke asked sarcastically.

"Yeah. I recommend we abandon the original flight path and use the backup plan," Newall said without taking his eyes off the desert landscape. "It will cut seven or eight minutes off our flight time."

Duke flipped open the plastic-covered insertion map. It sounded good, but he knew there had to be a catch or they'd have been flying that route in the first place. A blue line showed their primary flight path into and out of Iran. It had been carefully plotted using CIA satellite photos, allowing the Pave Lows and AC-130U to avoid most of the SAM sites in the area. Duke ran his finger along the secondary extraction route marked in red. Rather than weaving through the mountains, where they could hide from enemy radars, the secondary route took them over flat terrain. Newall was correct. They could fly faster over the flat terrain and it would cut a few minutes off their flight time. But they would also have to skirt several SA-6 and SA-2 sites north of Bushehr.

"Decided you need to get in on the action, too, dodging SAMs?" Duke asked, as he felt the pilot force the chopper up a short rocky hill and down the other side.

"I'm for getting our asses out of here ASAP. I figure we've been here longer than we should have. We can leave the SAMs to the SEAD guys," Newall answered.

Duke thought for a moment. The Pave Low was crammed with electronics and radar-jamming antennas, not to mention a full crew. They also carried twice the chaff and flares of a normal aircraft. "All right, let's do it." He keyed his mike. "This is Leader . . . go to flight plan bravo . . . repeat, flight plan bravo."

His attention returned to the windscreen. The jagged outline of a sandstone mountain ridge came to an abrupt end several miles away. The desert then flattened out into a series of rolling hills. He estimated they would break into the open in thirty seconds. "When we clear that ridge, keep us at 500 feet and put the pedal to metal," Duke advised.

F-15C MARATHON SEVEN

Major Bud "Stud Dog" Cole leveled his single-seat fighter at 14,000 feet. His eyes were fixed on the glowing symbology of his fighter's HUD. Coming wings-level out of a long banking turn, Cole eased the stick right, then left, until the W-shaped steering symbol was pointed southwest at 210 degrees. Five miles ahead of and below him were the Pave Lows and the AC-130U. He and his wingman were heading south-west away from Esfahan, making certain the Iranian airspace ahead was clear of enemy fighters. The sky around him was a light gray and the few stars that could still be seen were fading.

Cole grew restless after being in the sky for over an hour and a half. His fighter was carrying a little over half its original fuel and was fully loaded with a mix of four AIM-7 Sparrows and four AIM-9 Sidewinder air-to-air missiles. All he needed now was a few bad guys to engage so he could stay awake.

The major, a former F-4E jock, had been flying F-15Cs for the past five years. His command style was down-to-earth and straightforward. He preferred to let his men know where he stood on all issues, including social and military ones, and he tried to keep the bullshit of command to a bare minimum.

He snapped his oxygen mask back into place. "Marathon Eight, state your position," he radioed.

"Level at angels fourteen, heading two two one. I'm five hundred yards off your wing, Major," came the response from Marathon Eight, piloted by Captain Ronald "Laser" Thompson.

"Copy, Laser. Increase separation to 2,000 yards and be ready to rock and roll."

MiG-29 FULCRUM

"Multiple aircraft are bearing two two three degree. Two targets . . . speed, 390 knots; altitude, 13,800 feet and descending. Estimated range, thirty-two miles. Three targets to the southwest now bearing two one niner degrees . . . speed, 180 knots, altitude, 500 feet." The ground controller's voice crackled through the pilot's headset.

"Understood," Lieutenant Colonel Ahmad Jihbari radioed. Flying at 9,000 feet over the southeastern edge of Esfahan, he banked his fighter five degrees east and dropped the nose to pick up additional airspeed. Studying his empty radar screen, the pilot pictured the scenario. By their speed and altitude, the low-flying targets were probably helicopters. The aircraft above them were no doubt fighters providing cover for their escape. He could either turn and engage the fighters or take out the slower-moving choppers first. It was an easy decision.

"Two . . . this is Leader. Turning left heading two two three. Engage high-altitude targets," the colonel radioed his wingman.

"Understood, Leader."

Jihbari switched the fighter's powerful NO-193 multimode pulse-Doppler from standby to full power. The four-and-a-half-foot-diameter antenna immediately filled the airwaves with a stream of powerful J-band radio waves as he began the search for the enemy aircraft.

"Marathon Seven . . . Marathon Eight . . . This is AWACS on guard. Turn right heading one one seven. Two bandits approaching at angels niner."

"Copy, Terminator. Marathon Seven on the hunt," Major Cole radioed.

"Marathon Eight is in."

Cole's eyes swept the morning sky in front of him before he banked back to the right. He would have to catch up with the Pave Lows later. He watched the compass heading on top of the HUD swing around to 117 degrees before he came wings level at 13,000 feet. He pushed the throttles forward until his airspeed hit Mach 1.3, then throttled back, taking his big jet out of afterburner. Easing the stick forward and lowering the nose a few degrees, he let the pull of gravity help maintain his supersonic flight.

"I hope those AWACS operators don't have their heads up their butts," Cole said under his breath; he was no longer guarding the Pave Lows. The fighter's radar warning receiver indicated that two MiGs were ahead of him and his wingman. The high-pitched shrill of the RHAW equipment cutting into his headset was becoming more distinct as they approached. The alerted MiGs were now using their radars to try to find a target. *Not very smart*, Cole thought. A pulsing J-band had a tendency to show up like a fat woman in a bikini contest. Well, their stupidity was his good fortune, and Cole wasn't going to argue with anything that made him look good. He keyed the radio mike button on the throttle.

"Terminator . . . Marathon Seven. You copy?"

"Roger . . . we copy, Marathon Seven."

"I don't want those MiGs to know we're out here. Guide us

to within fifteen miles. We're going in like a mother checking on her sleeping baby.''

"Roger, Seven . . . turn right heading one zero three. Bandits thirty miles out; altitude, 10,000 feet closing at 920 knots."

"Copy, Terminator . . . Marathon Seven turning to engage." He changed radio frequencies. "Laser, this is Stud Dog. Kill your nav lights. We're going in silent."

"Roger that, Dog."

Lieutenant Colonel Jihbari leveled the MiG-29 at 8,950 feet, at the same time brushing his thumb across the launch button on the control stick. Tucked cleanly under each wing root were two long range AA-7 Apex semiactive radar-homing missiles. The missiles, manufactured by the former Soviet Union, were designed to destroy a target out to 25 miles. At least that's what the Soviet tech manual said. Jihbari knew better. He had fired a dozen of the missiles during the war with Iraq and experience told him the AA-7 was effective only inside a range of 18 miles. And even at that range it worked only fifty percent of the time.

Two orange circles were near the top of his radarscope. The MiG's radar was picking up two targets at an extreme range. His eyes moved to the HUD; two radar missile-tracking symbols were now moving across the MiG's glass HUD.

Jihbari concentrated on lining his MiG up with the nearest target. He dropped the nose of his aircraft and throttled into afterburner. The fighter jumped forward as the burners pushed the MiG beyond the speed of sound. His eyes jumped from the HUD to the smaller radar screen. He waited for the distance to close. The MiG-29's radar continued to track the invaders as he rocketed through the sky at Mach 1.4, the computer successfully filtering out the background clutter and electronic countermeasures. "Two miles . . . ," he whispered to himself. In the distance, out in front of him, were two American enemy aircraft. Jihbari felt the energy pump through his veins. He tapped the radar lock button on the throttle.

When the range to target readout hit 18 miles, Jihbari closed his eyes. He tapped the launch button twice, sending two radar-homing air-to-air missiles toward the target. He waited a few seconds before looking out the cockpit window. The bright silver fire of the solid-fuel rocket motor of each AA-7 lit up the sky around him as they raced straight ahead. He looked back at the radarscope. The enemy aircraft was now only 17.5 miles out.

One thousand feet from the MiG, the warheads of each missile armed and the radar seeker heads locked onto the steady stream of reflecting radio waves coming off the lead F-15C team. In just under five seconds, the missiles had accelerated to over Mach 2.5. Jihbari watched as they both pushed over, disappearing under the nose of his fighter.

"Threat . . . threat!" Adams reported excitedly into the microphone of his headset. Two yellow lines moving away from the MiG sped toward Marathon Seven. The bastards had launched.

The F-15C's RHAW equipment told Cole an enemy radar had just locked up on his fighter a second before he heard the call from the AWACS. A tingle went down his spine. A moment later, two distant white specks of fire caught his attention. He knew instantly they were air-to-air missiles. He watched them for a few seconds accelerating across the light blue morning sky. Then, as if someone had turned off a switch, the missiles' rocket motors burned out and he lost sight of them.

"Two can play at this game," Cole shouted. Touching the selector on his throttles, he switched from AIM-7Ms to AIM-9Ms. He hit the weapons launch button on his stick, sending two of the heat-seeking missiles away from his fighter. The Sidewinders shot straight ahead and began weaving back and forth, looking for a heat source to lock onto.

With the missiles safely away, Cole called, "Break right." He snapped the Eagle into a 6-G right-hand turn, tapping the chaff and decoy flare button on the stick. The horizon of the desert cut across his cockpit window.

Jihbari caught sight of the missiles coming toward him. Instinct took over.

"Break left," he groaned into his microphone.

Without thinking, he banked to the left and dropped his nose, gaining more airspeed. He moaned under the pressure of the turn as he felt 8 Gs crushing his body. He forced the stick forward, letting the Gs fall off to 4 before hitting the chaff and flare button. The airspace behind his jet filled with a dozen missile-deceiving decoys.

As he turned to the north, the MiG's powerful radar lost contact

with its target. The two AA-7 radar-guided missiles no longer had
a reflecting beam of electronics guiding them.

Jihbari throttled back into military power, catching sight of the
enemy missiles as they continued to the northeast. They would
miss his fighter by several miles. Banking back to the southwest,
he put the MiG into afterburner again. What had happened then
hit him. In the confusion he had become separated from his wingman. He looked right and left before seeing another dark gray
MiG a mile to his three o'clock. He throttled back, punched open
his speed brake and waited for his wingman to rejoin him. *I will
find the Americans again*, he thought, watching the radarscope.

*"Marathon Seven . . . Terminator. Fifteen miles to bandit. Take a
heading of zero four two."*

"Copy, Terminator, zero four two . . . here we go. You with
me, Eight?" Cole asked.

*"I'm with you, Major. Let's knock the shit out of him and get
the hell out of here."*

"Activate your radar . . . now." Cole leveled his fighter, turning the F-15C's APG-63 radar to full power. He knew it would
take a few seconds for the pulse-Doppler to find and lock onto
the targets. Punching a set of buttons on the side of the control
panel, he cleaned up the HUD so it would show only the alphan-
umerical information he needed to attack the bogeys.

"Shit hot . . . there you are!" Two targets appeared on his radar
screen. "Contact, you see them?" Cole asked his wingman.

"Yeah, I have them."

"I'll take the leader. You have the trailer," Cole ordered. Using the target designator button on the closest throttle handle, Cole
moved two small cursors over the bright dot representing the target. He depressed the TD, locking his air-to-air radar onto the
target.

Cole blinked as the HUD's radar target indicator box flashed
on. Slaved to his radar, it allowed him to know the exact position
of the enemy aircraft. The radar had taken only two sweeps to
locate and lock onto the target. He watched the MiG move across
the heads up display. "I have the one to the north," he radioed,
smashing the stick right and putting the fighter into a hard, sweeping turn. The sudden pressure of 4 Gs pushed his arms down and
pinned his body deeper into the seat. He rested his thumb on the
launch button. In ten seconds he would be in position to fire.

*   *   *

Jihbari knew he would have to maneuver his MiG in closer to lock up the four AA-8 Aphid infrared missiles hanging off his wings. He pushed the stick right and down, and jammed the throttles forward, dropping the nose. The stress of several Gs rolled over his body. His plan was to accelerate toward the target, fire his heat-seekers and race for home.

When the HUD hit 5,000 feet, his headset filled with a high-pitched tone. The MiG's radar warning equipment had picked up a threat. Jihbari leveled his fighter, throttled back and looked at the instruments. The directional threat indicator showed the radar was behind and above him to the northwest. The tone became even and steady. An enemy radar had just locked up on his fighter. The thought of breaking away entered his mind.

Hold steady, Cole told himself, as his eyes swept the instrument panel one more time. *No problems.* There was a minimum of electronic emissions—only that of the AWACS and the MiG's radar. He decided to fire just one AIM-7M Sparrow. He might need the other three later.

"Fox one," the major radioed, shifting his gaze below the cockpit sill for a second.

"Fox one," called his wingman.

Cole watched his missile rocket away, leaving an eerie white trail in its wake. A second later his wingman's Sparrow raced past, arcing to the east.

"Praise Allah," Jahbari whispered into his oxygen mask. In the distance he saw two bright flashes. He watched them for a few seconds to make sure they were streaking toward him and not his wingman. The bluish-white color of the flames told him they didn't come from an Iranian aircraft.

He keyed his radio. "Break . . . break." He jammed the stick back and right, forcing his MiG up to 6,000 feet in a fraction of a second. His wingman was on his own. Jahbari kept his eyes on the missiles. One broke high and away, obviously following his wingman. The other looked as if it were tracking his fighter. He knew that at any moment its rocket motor would burn out. When that happened, he wouldn't be able to see it. He felt his mouth going dry.

Jahbari adjusted his grip on the stick and waited. His timing had to be perfect. His eyes stayed focused on the bright burning rocket motor streaking toward him. There wasn't any question it had locked up on his fighter. Four miles out and closing fast, he estimated it would impact his MiG in under thirty seconds.

Now, if its motor would just stay lit long enough for me to follow it . . . damn, Jahbari cursed. The flame burned out. All he could see was a trace of fading light. His insides rolled over. He would now have to guess when to break. He closed his eyes for a few seconds and tried to picture where the invisible projectile was heading. Even if the missile didn't hit his aircraft, the explosive force of the warhead could send enough shrapnel into his MiG to bring it down.

Jahbari opened his eyes. "Five . . . four . . . three . . ." He calculated that the missile was a half mile from his aircraft. "Two . . . one, *now*," he grunted, jamming the throttles forward into afterburner and moving the stick hard right. The MiG snapped into a hard 8-G slicing turn as it nosed up and over the oncoming missile. Jahbari tightened the muscles in his legs and stomach, trying not to black out from the painful bite of the G forces. He kept steady pressure on the stick for what seemed in the gray morning light like an eternity, though it was only ten seconds. He pushed it center as the compass on top of the HUD swung around to a heading of 270. Jahbari was now heading back toward where the missile had been fired.

"Praise Allah!" Above him, a mile away, he saw the sudden flash of an explosion. A half second later the sky lit up again. The realization that his wingman had just been hit shot through his mind. From the size of the fireball, he doubted the man had ejected.

"I will kill you," he shouted into his cockpit.

"Splash one MiG . . . splash one MiG," Cole's wingman called out.

The American major wasn't as lucky. He watched his missile blow past the target on his radar screen. The enemy pilot must have known he was under attack and turned at the right time.

"All right, asshole. Got lucky once, but you're still mine." Cole pushed the dual throttles forward just short of afterburner. The target was now only five miles out, heading toward him. He waited for the HUD to flash the weapons lock symbol. This time he hit the red launch button twice, sending two AA-7Ms on their way. The F-15C shook and the cockpit lit up as both missiles sprinted off their rail launchers.

Jahbari knew he was in deep trouble. Two bright flicks of fire were accelerating toward his position. He quickly scanned the HUD and instrument panel as his mind raced. His heat-seeking missiles weren't sensitive enough to lock up on the heat emissions from an aircraft head on and it would take a few seconds for his last radar-guided missile to lock up, seconds he didn't have. He swallowed hard, knowing he had only one choice. Switching the weapons selector from AA-7 Apex to AA-8 Aphid short-range missiles, Jahbari punched the launch button two times. Shoving the stick left, he rolled his fighter over, pushing the nose toward the ground and picking up airspeed. Out of the corner of one eye he saw both missiles accelerate to the west.

Hitting the chaff and flare buttons, Jahbari sent five bundles of foil and a dozen magnesium flares streaming from the underside of his MiG. He watched the altitude dropping at 4,000 feet a minute as his fighter broke through Mach 1. At 1,500 feet he pulled the stick back, popped the speed brake and brought the nose up quickly. Jahbari watched the G meter climb: 3 . . . 4 . . . 5 . . . 6 . . . 6.5. His body was being pressed into the hard ejection seat.

At seven Gs, the Fulcrum started to pull up from the steep dive. Jahbari tried to move his other hand onto the stick but couldn't. The pressure from the G forces had it locked in place. His eyes glued to the HUD, he watched his altitude: 1,000 . . . 800 . . . 500. The nose still hadn't come up.

"Allah save me," he pleaded. When the HUD hit 200 feet, Jahbari closed his eyes. The image of his wife and two-year-old boy flashed through his mind the instant his MiG slammed into the ground.

"Threat . . . threat." Cole heard the AWACS' call a few seconds after he spotted the missiles heading toward his aircraft. He instinctively pulled the stick back, taking his fighter up and away from the oncoming missiles. As he did so, the F-15's radar lost contact with the MiG-29 in the ground clutter. The seeker heads in both of his AIM-7 Sparrows no longer had a steady stream of reflected radar waves to home in on.

Cole gained several thousand feet before rolling his fighter over, searching the airspace under him. Below and to the east, the two missiles sped away, snaking back and forth.

"Where's that son of a bitch?" he shouted.

He looked back at the radarscope, dropping his nose. If he could reacquire the target, maybe it wouldn't be too late to redirect his missiles. "Terminator . . . Marathon Seven. Give me a vector to that target."

"Negative, Marathon . . . target is no joy."

Cole clicked his mike twice, confirming the transmission. Righting his fighter, he swung around to a heading of 114 degrees. He dumped the nose ten degrees and watched his airspeed quickly climb past 390 knots. When the HUD hit 7,500 feet, he looked to the left. Rising up off the desert floor was a black column of smoke. He knew what had happened. The MiG had flown into the ground.

"Break off, Cole," the major told himself. He eased the stick back, putting his F-15C into a gradual climb, banking to the southwest. "Marathon Seven . . . breaking through ten thousand. You with me, Eight?"

"I'm with you, Seven. Off your left wing."

Cole wiped the sweat from his face with his sleeve. Five hundred feet away he watched Marathon Eight level his fighter. He smiled, knowing his wingman had been backing him all the time.

Chapter Thirty-four

MH-53J PAVE LOW

"Papa, where are you? Papa . . . I can't see you." Perijan yelled out, panicked. Collins glanced over at the doctor, who nodded his approval for him to be by her side. Collins ran his hand across her forehead. She looked ghostly pale and he wondered if she was still breathing.

"Perijan, it's me. We're almost to a hospital. Just don't give up . . . think about the new life you'll be starting," he said soothingly while he brushed her hair from her face. He hadn't realized how beautiful she was until now.

Perijan's eyes fluttered open. "Thank you . . . thank you for helping me escape," she whispered. Collins had to lean over her to hear the soft-spoken words. He was getting ready to answer when her body became limp. "Oh, God . . . Doc, you better come take a look," he called.

After a few moments the doctor looked up and put his hand on Collins's shoulder. "I'm sorry, sir. There was nothing more I could do."

Collins shook his head, then said, "I know."

He watched the Marine medic take the green wool blanket and pull it up, covering her face. It didn't matter. The picture of her lying there was still vivid in his mind. *Why is it that some people are born into nice homes and can go their whole lives without anything sad happening, but then others . . . yes, others,* he thought. *They just get a raw deal from the beginning.* He felt his eyes filling with tears but fought back the urge to cry. The Rangers had their heads hung low as if they understood what he felt.

''Do you want her box?'' the medic asked kindly.

''No, she's held onto it through this whole mess . . . she should have it with her during her final escape.''

The medic just nodded, not fully comprehending his meaning.

Collins felt the Pave Low pitch up and down rapidly, nearly tossing him to the ceiling. He grabbed a hand strap and closed his eyes, resting his head against the bulkhead.

BUSHEHR, IRAN

''Do you see it?'' Lieutenant Max Rath asked in a hushed tone. He could see a large cloud of dust being thrown into the air as vehicles moved up the road toward the Iranian radar site.

''Yeah . . . I see it,'' Vasquez whispered back. He looked through the scope of his sniper rifle. ''I'd say two, maybe three trucks.''

''Captain,'' Rath radioed Watson, ''this is Lookout One. We have company . . . moving up the road.''

''We need a few more minutes. Those choppers are still fifteen minutes out.''

''I count one . . . two . . . three. Three trucks, Lieutenant,'' Vasquez reported. Through his scope he could see the dual-axle brown-camouflaged trucks moving up the road. The cargo sections were covered with canvas tarps. ''I'll bet my left nut it's a relief team.'' He looked at his watch. ''Yeah, in thirty minutes it's going to be six o'clock.''

''Confirmed, Captain. We're looking at three trucks.'' Rath watched them slowly come around the base of a rugged hill. He heard the drivers downshift and begin the long climb to the radar station.

''I need five minutes, Lieutenant. Give me five more minutes.''

''Copy, Captain. Five minutes,'' Rath said skeptically.

''Let me guess. He wants us to wait another five,'' Vasquez growled. ''He's been saying that for the last forty minutes.''

''Something's not right. The strike cell must have run into trouble,'' Rath reasoned.

''I'll tell you who's in trouble. We are. The sun has been up for fifteen minutes and I feel like I'm at a party without any clothes on. The deal was we'd be out before first light. Well, first light happened twenty minutes ago and I'm still sitting on an Iranian dirt pile.''

''Well, the Plaza was booked, and hell . . . it isn't that bad. If you weren't here, you'd probably just be in bed sound asleep with your wife . . . or maybe that round barmaid you've been hitting on back in Fayetteville,'' Rath joked while scanning the road below them with 8x30 binoculars.

''My wife better not ever hear you—''

''Shut up. Here they come,'' Rath warned, lying back down.

Vasquez shouldered his rifle. ''I wonder how fast that first truck can go with a flat front tire.''

''Take a heading of two four three.'' Duke looked off to the right, seeing a narrow series of hills about five miles away. Returning his gaze to the satellite map, he compared the photo with the landmark. They were right on course. He returned his gaze to the FLIR, watching the flight symbology change.

Newall was maintaining a flight level of 200 feet, only having to pitch the chopper up and down slightly as they crossed the flat terrain.

''We have a couple of SAM sites coming up on the right,'' Duke said before checking the radar's warning lights. None of them were lit up.

''All's quiet on the western front. Let's hope it stays that way,'' Newall said. Off to the left he could see Coyote Two flying a hundred yards away and a little above them.

On a high, windswept desert ridge fifty-two miles southwest of Esfahan, an SA-6 Gainful launch battery sat quietly with its target-acquisition radar turned to standby. Each TEL contained three SA-6 SAMs. In the center, a single Straight Flush target engagement radar, its antenna pointed south, was parked next to the Ural 375 command and control vehicle.

Four miles to the east of the SA-6 site, inside a small concrete building that housed a P-12 acquisition radar, NATO code name Spoon Rest-A, five Iranian technicians started hitting a series of switches, warming up the electronic circuits. The command bunker controlled a Chinese Hong Qian HQ-2J air defense missile system, a more advanced version of the Soviet SA-2 system. Iran deployed the two systems together to provide overlapping coverage.

The radar operators, one at each of the SAM sites, listened to their radios. The order had just been received for them to activate the radars. A number of low-flying enemy targets heading southwest had been detected.

"Twelve minutes to the coast," Duke called out. He could feel the anxiety building the closer they got to safety.

"Shit, trouble!" Newall yelled, seeing two radar warning lights flash on followed by a third and fourth. The Pave Lows were being painted by two hostile radars to the north.

"Yeah," Duke sang out. He looked right, toward several rolling hills. The Iranians operated a large refinery twelve miles to the north and the SAMs were no doubt in place to protect it.

"Give me an ID," Newall said, dropping down to 100 feet.

"Hold tight . . . it's running through the threat computer." Duke activated his mike. "Coors Leader, we have trouble. SAMs right three o'clock."

"Copy you, Coyote Leader. I'm picking them up."

F-16C, COORS LEADER

Eddie Naylor watched the HARM targeting system display located below and to the right of his F-16C's HUD. The multifunction display was linked directly to his fighter's AN/ASQ-213 radar threat precision direction finder. The system had been designed to identify each radar threat in the area, prioritizing for the pilot which site to attack first. The number one threat was red, and so on. Under each square, targeting information appeared, including heading, location and distance to the target.

"Come on. Where are you?" Naylor complained. It actually only took the computer fifteen seconds to cycle through the threat library. A moment later a red box appeared on the threat screen. BAND: G * HEADING: 023 * RANGE: 7.3 MILES * SYSTEM: SA-2 GUIDELINE.

He banked to the right, snapping the jet into a quick 6-G turn. As the HUD clicked off his heading, he pulled the stick back, climbing from his cruising altitude of 2,500 feet.

In Naylor's mind, flying a SEAD fighter wasn't much different from playing a game of cat and mouse. His job, after all, was to try to get an enemy SAM site to turn on its tracking radar and lock up on his F-16. He did this by flying above the aircraft he had been assigned to protect, making sure his jet was the first to be targeted. Once the SAM site did lock up on him, Naylor would fire a HARM, which followed the radar beam to the antenna and destroyed it.

"All right, assholes, here I am. Come and get me," Naylor said into his empty cockpit.

The SA-2 radar-tracking officer watched the cluster of targets to the south of his position. He tapped on his computer keyboard, trying to get the software to break out a single target so it could be locked onto. The Chinese HQ-2J system allowed the Fan Song radar to track six targets at the same time. However, he was more concerned with just locking up one of the enemy aircraft.

He looked at the scope, making sure none of the blips were displaying Iranian IFF codes. He then changed the radar frequency from 4,905 MHz to 4,990. Looking back at the screen, he saw a single target coming straight for his radar site—speed, 420 knots; altitude, 3,000 feet and climbing. He pressed the red lock button next to his computer keyboard. An X symbol appeared over the nearest target. The Fan Song radar had just locked up.

"Permission to fire," he said confidently.

"Fire when ready," said the lieutenant in charge.

Vasquez centered the crosshairs on top of the truck's tire. "Range?" he asked.

"Three hundred thirty meters. Wind out of the southeast at four to six knots," Rath reported. "No sweat, Vasquie."

Vasquez paused until the truck was directly ahead of him on the narrowest section of the single-lane road. He tightened his grip on the trigger, waiting for the rifle to fire.

Rath kept his binoculars focused on the front end of the Iranian truck while Vasquez fired. Rath estimated it wasn't moving more than a couple miles an hour. He saw a puff of dust as the bullet ripped into the tire. It seemed to explode, and the truck lurched to the right and stopped. The driver and another Iranian officer climbed out. Vasquez had timed it perfectly. There wasn't any way the other two trucks could drive around the lead truck, and it would take them at least fifteen minutes to change the tire.

"Captain, this is Lookout One," Rath radioed.

"Go ahead."

"We just bought you ten, fifteen minutes."

"Good work. Come on in. We're leaving in three."

"Roger." Rath nudged Vasquez. "Gather your shit. We're out of here."

"Good. I'm starving."

Naylor's eyes methodically drifted from the HUD to the threat panel every few seconds. The desert floor flashed under his F-16C in a brown blur. He pushed the nose down, making sure he could see the horizon. Experience had indicated that sometimes you could see SAM launches a few seconds before the equipment picked up the missile. And every extra second counted.

The warning tone in Naylor's helmet changed pitch, telling him the nearest SAM site had just locked onto his F-16. Toggling the weapon's ready switch, he locked up the HARM under his left wing. The red square on the threat display was now flashing. Naylor rested his right thumb on the launch button. He wouldn't press until a missile was airborne. If he launched a HARM now, the Iranians could simply shut down their radar, causing his missile to lose lock and fly off-course. However, if they launched, they would have to keep the radar locked up to guide the SAM to the target.

"Come on, kitty . . . come out and play."

On the horizon he saw two lines climbing into the sky—smoke trails from a SAM launch.

WARNING, WARNING, his computer sounded. MISSILE LAUNCH, MISSILE LAUNCH.

"You're dead . . . Magnum," Naylor said, and pressed the launch button on the stick, sending a HARM toward the enemy radar antenna that was guiding the missile.

"Missile launch to the north!" Duke shouted. He twisted around, trying to find the SAM.

"Where's that sixteen?" Newall moaned in frustration. He reached over and hit the backup switches for the ECM. The Pave Low's threat panel was now blinking with six different lights.

"Damn it. I'm showing a systems failure on the secondary ECM," Duke called.

"Get back there and figure out what's going on," Newall said to the copilot. "We need that ECM at a hundred percent."

"Yes, sir." The copilot headed toward the electronics rack located behind the flight deck wall.

"Take her down to fifty feet," Duke advised. "We need to get under their tracking radar."

Newall shoved the cyclic stick forward, pushing the nose of the chopper down. With their forward airspeed at 213 knots, one small screwup would turn them into a hole in the desert.

Naylor watched the smoke trail of the HARM as he pushed upward. He banked the fighter right while looking left. The two SAMs were four miles away and still climbing.

"Come on . . . push over . . . push over," Naylor coaxed. As he did so, the rocket motor of the HARM burned out. The missile was now on the terminal phase of its flight.

WARNING, WARNING. The computer sounded. Naylor looked at the threat panel. A new radar was sweeping to the northwest of his position. Only this one was operating on a different frequency. BAND: H * HEADING: 339 * RANGE: 5.9 MILES * SYSTEM: SA-6 GAINFUL.

His heart crawled up his throat. The equipment showed the SA-6 radar operator was sweeping to the southwest, away from his F-16C. It was trying to lock up on the choppers.

No way, man, no way. Naylor threw the throttle all the way forward, putting the jet into afterburner. As the airspeed on his HUD climbed past 450 knots, he turned northwest and climbed.

Duke watched the radar warning light flicker on, showing that an SA-6 acquisition had just locked onto their Pave Low. "Five miles to the northwest. The son of a bitch. It has us."

"Get ready on the chaff." Newall forced the chopper up. He would need the extra room to maneuver. "Where is it?"

"Two missiles right, two o'clock," Duke called out. "Shit! Four missile right, two o'clock!"

"Coors Leader . . . where the fuck are you?" Newall screamed into the radio.

Duke checked the threat panel. The G-band acquisition light turned off. The first HARM had hit its mark.

Naylor didn't notice the black smoke rising into the sky to his right. The Iranian SA-2 radar antenna was now a burning pile of twisted steel. His attention was focused instead on the four SAMs climbing into the air to his left. Taking the F-16C out of afterburner, he pushed over upside down at 5,300 feet. Popping the air brakes, he did a slow roll, trying to increase his radar signature. The bastards knew he was up there. They just weren't locking up.

It didn't matter. He could target the radar anyway. Banking left, he dropped ten degrees and pointed the nose of the HARM at the radar emitter. He waited for the tone in his helmet to become strong and clear before pressing the button.

The HARM raced away from the right side of the F-16C. Naylor watched it for a few seconds. Just when he started pulling away, the missile went stupid. The HARM nosed over and headed straight for the ground.

"No!" the colonel shouted.

"Altitude, 400 feet. Tell me when to break." Newall's voice was strained.

"Chaff . . . *now*," Duke said, not taking his eyes off the lead SA-6. A trace of silver smoke was streaming out of the rear section of the nineteen-foot-long surface-to-air missile. Duke could see the SAM was going to miss. It impacted the desert floor about two miles west of their position.

The second missile pushed over, arcing toward them several miles away. Duke squinted, trying not to lose sight of the SAM. It appeared to be tracking the Pave Low, but Duke couldn't be sure. "On three . . . break right," he ordered. The second SAM made a course correction and banked back of the east. Suddenly, it broke apart from the stress of the high G turn. The missile exploded, filling the sky with an orange-and-black fireball.

Two down . . . two to go. Duke was nearly out of his seat as he tried to keep track of the two remaining SAMs. He could see the third SA-6 but not the fourth. The third missile turned and headed straight for them.

"Get ready," Duke warned.

"I'm ready . . . I'm ready," Newall answered.

"One . . . two . . . three. *Break right!*"

The big Pave Low jolted to the right at a forty-five-degree angle. Duke slammed into Newall as the pilot worked the controls of the chopper. Duke hit the chaff button rapidly.

Behind and to the right of the Pave Low, the SA-6's seeker head locked onto the chaff cloud. It turned five degrees east and crashed into the ground a quarter mile behind them.

Duke felt the chopper pitch forward from the force of the explosion. "I can't find the last SAM," he shouted.

*   *   *

Naylor leveled his F-16C at 1,000 feet. He could feel his heart pounding in his chest. He weaved the fighter right and left, trying to break up his radar signature. On a hill a mile and a half away, he could see the black outline of an SA-6 engagement radar.

"You're all mine," he said under his breath. Naylor switched his targeting computer from HARM to air-to-ground. The HUD flashed; the cursor in the center changed to a gun sight. His plan was to spray the acquisition radar with 20-mm cannon rounds.

The fighter pitched up and down. To his left, an ZSU-23-4 opened up. Eight or ten tracer rounds streaked past his cockpit window. Naylor reacted by dropping the nose and descending below 500 feet. He was speeding across the desert at 460 knots.

"More chaff . . . break left!" Duke shouted.

"I don't have enough airspeed!" Newall shouted back.

"SAM dead ahead . . . *break left.*" The fourth SAM was above them less than a mile away, coming out of the west. Duke braced himself.

Newall tried to force the chopper back to the left, but the Pave Low didn't respond. He was down to 140 knots forward airspeed and the big helicopter just wasn't designed for maneuvering.

"We're dead meat!" he screamed.

"It's going to be close . . . everyone hang on!" Duke roared.

An eerie silence fell over the cockpit. Duke dropped the visor of his helmet over his eyes and reached over to do the same for Newall. As his hands returned to his side, a white blur flashed past the front window of the Pave Low. The last SA-6 streaked past the chopper, exploding in the nearest chaff cloud fifty feet away.

Naylor estimated he was a half mile away when he opened fire. The left side of the F-16C erupted with black smoke, as the Vulcan 20 MM cannon kicked out 3,000 rounds of armor-piercing bullets a minute. The cockpit vibrated as he watched the orange tracer rounds streak toward the target in rapid succession. Another triple-A gun opened up to the right of him. Naylor ignored it. Every ounce of concentration he could muster was focused on the target.

"*Yeah . . . yeah!*" he shouted. The radar sight disappeared in a cloud of dust and flying sparks. The wire mesh antenna slowly folded over and collapsed.

He yanked the stick back and climbed to the west. The force of 6 Gs pushed hard on his body, but Naylor hardly noticed. Looking over his shoulder, he admired his work one more time before going into afterburner. "Terminator . . . Coors Leader. Heading home."

The force of the exploding warhead shoved Duke forward. The side of his helmet smashed into the top of the cockpit instrumentation, nearly knocking him out.

Duke sat back and opened his eyes. It took a few seconds to figure out what was happening. The Pave Low appeared to be sliding sideways through the air and was slowly banking to turn to the south. He could hear screams and shouts coming from the cargo compartment. Unknown to Duke, the right side of the chopper had been hit with flying debris. Chunks of the warhead had penetrated the fuselage, wounding several of the Rangers.

His eyes swept the cockpit. The protective armor surrounding the chopper's flight system, designed to protect the pilots and crew from ground fire, had prevented any serious damage. And the good news was that the threat warning panel was clear. "Level her out," Duke said.

Newall didn't respond. His eyes were fixed on the ground.

"Newall . . . level this son of a bitch." This time Duke's voice was loud and harsh.

Again, Newall didn't respond.

Duke looked at the radar altimeter. They were only 300 feet above the ground and slicing toward it. He looked at the pilot. There wasn't any blood; he just looked dazed and disorientated.

"Newall . . . damn it . . . wake up." Duke reached over and slapped the man across the face. He then reached down and grabbed the cyclic, leveling the chopper. The altimeter read seventy-three feet.

"Ah, shit . . . what happened?" Newall said, shaking his head.

"Never mind. Just fly this thing."

Newall took a deep breath. Working the controls, he eased the Pave Low into gradual climb.

"Six minutes to the coast," Duke called. He looked over and saw his handprint on Newall's face.

Newall glanced at him, and then back at the desert.

"You all right now?" Duke asked.

"Yes, General. I'm fine. I just want to get the hell out of here."

"Me, too. So let's haul ass," Duke said, and sat back.

Chapter Thirty-five

BAHRAIN AIR BASE

Tom Staffer watched the two giant choppers make a long banking turn out of the north. Behind it, an AC-130U continued south before veering right and lining up for a landing.

Staffer unbuttoned his suit jacket as the first Pave Low came level with the tarmac and touched down a hundred yards away. The flight deck was bustling with maintenance personnel, medical technicians and crew members gathered around the helicopter. Several were completing their tasks, while others were waiting for the men to unload.

Staffer walked to within fifty yards of the chopper, watching the rotors slow, then finally stop turning. He could see torn metal and puncture holes covering the entire right side of the nearest chopper. Some of the punctures were as large as baseballs. The rear ramp came down and a few seconds later a dozen ragged, sweaty Rangers began emerging from the chopper. Staffer approached closer, watching a medical team remove a stretcher carrying a Ranger. A couple of other Rangers walked down the ramp slowly as if in a daze or just stiff from their ordeal.

Staffer stopped in his tracks. He felt strangely responsible as he stood in the middle of the commotion and watched the men and their different reactions. Some remained silent and solemn, while others laughed with each other or conversed with the crew on the ground. He thought back to when he had advocated this extraction mission, and wondered if he'd feel the same way when it came time to make a decision about sending men in for another.

"Be careful with her," Collins said, watching two medics pick up Perijan's lifeless body on the canvas stretcher.

"Yes, sir."

Collins felt numb knowing he was back on friendly soil. He knew he was glad to be home, but so much had happened that all his emotions had been drained. He thought of Perijan and how differently he would feel if she were alive. His thought that he should have let her go to the ramp first only reminded him that he had broken her unspoken trust. He had promised to protect her. He sucked in a deep breath, trying to fight his feelings of failure. Collins just wanted to get home to his wife and little girl.

Duke took off his helmet and unstrapped himself from the center seat of the Pave Low. He studied the damage, noticing for the first time that the front windscreens were shattered in several places. There wasn't any doubt—if the SAM had exploded a few feet closer to the Pave Low, they would all be dead. He caught Newall's eye. The two men sat motionless for a few moments.

"Are you all right?" Duke finally asked.

"Yeah. Maybe we shouldn't have taken that shortcut, huh?" Newall glanced over at the general.

"Nah, you made the right call. We were behind schedule, and it probably would have been worse if we'd taken any more time getting out of there. That's what it's all about—making a decision and doing your best." As Duke spoke, he thought of Hodges. He realized he had finally come to terms with what he did. Duke knew he had made a decision and done his best. That's all he could ever ask of himself.

"Well, special ops pilots are supposed to be different." Newall still wasn't convinced.

"Don't kid yourself. It happens . . . to everyone, sooner or later." Duke smiled. "If you're too hard on yourself, you'll be filled with doubt and won't be ready for the next hit. It might knock you flat on your ass. If you can't trust your own judgment, you won't be able to trust anyone else around you, either." He had the sudden urge to get home to Katie as quickly as he could. He'd pick her up in his arms and tell her just how much he loved and trusted her. She'd forgive him for being such a jerk. Like she always did.

"Thanks, General." Newall nodded and managed an uneasy smile.

"Yeah, any time." Duke climbed out the back of the flight deck and into the cargo bay. The back of the chopper was empty except for Collins. He was sitting alone, staring at the floor.

"Mark," Duke said quietly.

Collins looked up, his weary eyes glossed over.

"Duke, I didn't even get a chance to ask what the hell you were doing in the middle of the desert."

"Well, I heard that someone who gave me a lift out of the middle of another desert needed a ride." Duke smiled, then added, "How about a cold Coke?"

"Yeah, that's about all I could handle right now." Collins laughed as they walked down the ramp together into the bright morning sun. The heat radiating off the tarmac warmed them, recharging their emotions and energies.

"We have to stop meeting like this, though." Collins glanced over at Duke and smiled. "People will talk."

"Who gives a shit what people say? I just think we'd have a better time someplace where there weren't any damn guns or missiles." Duke grinned, then looked up to see Staffer waiting for them. "You been standing there the whole time?"

"Yeah, smart guy. You two just about scared the shit out of me, you know."

"Well, I guess I've got to come clean, Mark. This is who's really responsible for your ride out of there." Duke looked at Collins, then back at Staffer.

"There wasn't anything special about it," Staffer said. "I was just doing my job and making sure you didn't get any more time off than you already had . . . vacationing at the Iranian Inn."

"Well, I'm thankful you take your job so seriously, Tom." Collins couldn't think of anything else to say, and the two men only nodded at each other when he added a somber "Thanks."

"They're waiting to debrief the two of you at headquarters." Staffer walked alongside them on the tarmac.

"Shit, I don't feel like doing a debriefing. Do you, Duke?"

"Hell no," Duke said. "Hey . . . I know this place off base that serves great steak and eggs. You with me?"

"Yeah, I'm with you. How about it, Tom? Want to join us? Duke's buying cold Cokes."

"I'll go with you guys, but only after you shower. I don't want anyone to think I'm hanging around with the wrong crowd," Staffer answered, then shook his head. "Can't believe two grown men are still ditching class."

They all laughed. Then Collins said, "I've got to see if I can make a call first, though."

"Yeah. Me, too." Duke looked at all the activity around them, then slipped on his sunglasses. "Maybe you should join us out in the desert next time, Tom. Could be you haven't been hanging around the right crowd. Don't want to spend your life waiting on tarmacs."

The three men walked on in silence. *A call home, a hot shower and a big breakfast. Then I'll be ready for another day,* Duke thought, as he took a deep breath.